Paradise Postponed

★   ★   ★

Paradise Postponed

★ ★ ★

John Mortimer

★

VIKING

VIKING

Penguin Books Ltd, Harmondsworth, Middlesex, England
Viking Penguin Inc., 40 West 23rd Street, New York, New York 10010, U.S.A.
Penguin Books Australia Ltd, Ringwood, Victoria, Australia
Penguin Books Canada Ltd, 2801 John Street, Markham, Ontario, Canada L3R 1B4
Penguin Books (N.Z.) Ltd, 182–190 Wairau Road, Auckland 10, New Zealand

First published 1985

Filmset in 10/13 Monophoto Plantin by
Northumberland Press Ltd,
Gateshead, Tyne and Wear

Printed in Great Britain by
Richard Clay (The Chaucer Press) Ltd,
Bungay, Suffolk

British Library Cataloguing in Publication Data

Mortimer, John, *1923–*
Paradise postponed.
I. Title
823'.914[F]   PR6025.07552

ISBN 0–670–80094–5

Second printing April 1986

For Penny, Emily and Rosamond

Acknowledgement is gratefully made by the author and publishers to the following:

Faber & Faber for kind permission to reproduce lines from *Look Stranger* XXX in W. H. Auden's *Collected Poems*, edited by Edward Mendelson, copyright 1937, renewed 1965, by W. H. Auden, and for the same extract to Random House, Inc.

The National Trust for Places of Historic Interest and Natural Beauty and Macmillan London Ltd for kind permission to reproduce an extract from *The Gods of the Copybook Headings* in *The Definitive Edition of Rudyard Kipling's Verse*, copyright 1919 by Rudyard Kipling, and for the same extract to the National Trust and Doubleday & Co., Inc.

The Literary Trustees of Walter de la Mare and The Society of Authors as their representative for kind permission to reproduce lines from 'The Listeners' by Walter de la Mare.

Chappell Music Ltd London for kind permission to reproduce lines from 'Twilight Time', lyrics by Buck Ram, music by Morty Nevins and Al Nevins, copyright © 1944 by Campbell Porgie, Inc. and by Duchess Music Corporation. Copyright renewed 1972 and assigned to Devon Music, Inc. N.Y. for U.S.A. Rights in Canada administered by Manitou Music (Canada), a division of M.C.A. Canada Ltd. Used by permission. All rights reserved.

Mills Music, Inc. for kind permission to reproduce lines from 'Ain't Misbehavin'', copyright © 1929 by Mills Music, Inc. and renewed. All rights reserved.

Frank Music Corporation for kind permission to reproduce lines from 'On a Slow Boat to China' by Frank Loesser, copyright © 1948 by Frank Music Corporation. Renewed 1976. All rights reserved.

Belwin Mills Music Ltd for kind permission to reproduce lines from 'St James Infirmary' by Joe Primrose.

1

Contents

7

Part One

In the houses
The little pianos are closed, and a clock strikes.
And all sway forward on the dangerous flood
Of history, that never sleeps or dies,
And, held one moment, burns the hand.

from *Look Stranger*, XXX
W. H. Auden

★ 1 ★
Death of a Saint

'I had a disagreeable dream,' the old man said.

'What?'

'I thought we'd grown out of all that in first-year theology.' He looked bewildered. 'God on a cloud, a sort of pink electric light bulb behind his head. He was actually busying himself,' he clearly found the conduct he had to describe unsympathetic, 'judging people! Parting the sheep from the goats. That sort of thing.'

'Don't worry.'

'He was surrounded with cherubim. Your mother would find them dreadfully vulgar. She wouldn't give them shelf room in porcelain.'

'It's not true,' the younger man said.

'I suppose not. I shan't have to wait very long to find out.'

The old man was wearing striped flannel pyjamas and lying on a bed on which sunlight was falling. He was tall and thin, looks which gave him, in the course of his lifetime, the appearance of a rather bothered eagle. Now, white-haired and thinner than ever at the age of eighty, he was almost beautiful. His name was Simeon Simcox, and he was Rector of the village of Rapstone Fanner.

There was nothing ecclesiastical, however, about the Rectory bedroom. There was no crucifix or prayer-book by the bed. Like the rest of the house it was furnished in austere taste, betraying a nervous embarrassment at the idea of ornament or ostentation, with only a few discreet china objects, a William Morris chest and a Paul Nash landscape by way of decoration. There was about the room rather more comfort than might be bought on the stipend of a Church of England clergyman.

On the dressing-table, beside the Rector's silver-backed hairbrushes, were some framed family photographs: his two boys in long shorts and short haircuts in the Reetory garden; Simeon Simcox and his wife, Dorothy, at the time of their wedding, standing outside Rapstone village church, he in a dog-collar and tweed suit, she in a silk dress that was deliberately unbridal, looking gently amused and vaguely 'artistic'. There was also a yellowing Victorian group showing members of his family and a selection of loyal workers standing outside the Brewery in the local town, over the gate of which, an entrance for dray horses and loads of barrels, the gilded sign read 'Simcox Ales'.

The other occupant of the room was in his late forties, a doctor who was there as a son. Fred Simcox lived alone in a flat above his surgery, played the drums and listened to old jazz records in much of his spare time. Looking at his father he felt a wave of affection for the old man, who seemed to be approaching death, like most of the other events in his long life, with a puzzled good will under which lay a certain dogged persistence. He thought, almost for the first time, that he could understand what his father was saying and it made him smile. But the joke, if it were a joke, came too late, like something shouted from a train window, after the last awkward and prolonged goodbyes have been said and after, to everyone's relief, the guard has blown his whistle. All the same, he sat now, by his father's bed, and showed an interest.

'The ridiculous thing was...' Perhaps it wasn't a joke. Simeon seemed genuinely perturbed. 'He bore a remarkable resemblance to Dr Salter. Salter's an unbeliever, of course, and he hasn't even got a beard. You'd think he'd be nothing whatever like God but the resemblance was quite striking.'

'You say he was parting the sheep and the goats?'

'There was some sort of judgement going on.' Simeon Simcox frowned unhappily.

'You shouldn't worry about that.'

'Shouldn't I?'

'Of course not.'

'Judgement!' The Rector turned his head to look at his younger son and spoke with a fading urgency. 'I should like you to know that it hasn't been so simple.' And then his voice came from further away, as though the train were already drawing out of the station. 'Not half so straightforward as it might have looked.'

The Rapstone Valley is only some two hours' drive to the west of London but its inhabitants have been spared, no doubt for longer than they deserve, the slow but inexorable march of civilization. At the head of the valley the road divides, one way leading south to Rapstone Fanner, the other north to the villages of Skurfield and Picton Principal. Standing by the signpost and looking down at the landscape spread out below you can see beech woods, thick hedgerows and fields of corn, with an occasional tiled roof over a flint and brick building, a group of barns and the distant tower of Rapstone Church. After a deeper acquaintance with the place you may realize that the flint cottages have been converted to house a pop star or a couple in advertising and the roof of what looks like a farm-building now covers an indoor swimming-pool with sauna attached in which guests flop like woozy porpoises after Sunday lunch. Such matters are discreetly arranged. The first sight of the Rapstone Valley is of something unexpectedly isolated and uninterruptedly rural; a solitary jogger is the only outward sign of urban pollution.

As with the countryside the changes in Rapstone village are behind the walls, which have been carefully preserved to placate the planners. It is true that what was once a shop has been turned, skilfully and expensively, into a weekend cottage with a B.M.W. parked in front of the aubretia-covered garden wall. What was once the school, which still has a bell in a little turret on top of it, has been taken over by two ladies with grey hair and booming voices who illustrate children's books. In fact the only institutional buildings left unchanged are the church, with its Norman tower, its ornate seventeenth-century tomb and Victorian additions, and the Rectory, approached through an open gateway, past the dark and dusty laurels of a short driveway and entered, under a pointed, neo-Gothic porch, through a front door which is never locked. There were an unusual number of cars parked in front of the Rectory and round the churchyard, and there was a small clutch of reporters and a couple of press photographers on the day of the Rector's funeral, for Simeon Simcox had, in his lifetime, achieved a fame, some would say a notoriety, which stretched far beyond the boundaries of his parish.

'We brought nothing into this world, and it is certain we can carry nothing out,' said the Reverend Kevin Bulstrode, Vicar of Skurfield, conducting the service in the unavoidable absence of the Rector of Rapstone.

'*Naked* came I out of my mother's womb, and naked *shall* I return thither,' a furious and gravelly whisper came from the congregation. The Vicar of Skurfield, who would shortly take over Rapstone also when the parishes were amalgamated under a new scheme of 'rationalization', did his best to ignore the interruption. 'The Lord gives and the Lord takes away, blessed be the name of the Lord,' he continued bravely.

For a moment the interrupter was quiet. He was a tall, thickening fifty-year-old, whose red hair was now flecked with grey but to whom watery blue eyes and a look of perpetual discontent gave the appearance of an irate, retired sea captain. He wore a thick tweed suit in spite of the late summer weather, with a heavy gold watch-chain, and a bright silk handkerchief lolled from his breast-pocket. When Henry Simcox, the late Rector's eldest son, published his first novel his name had been connected with a group of angry young men; now he was a grumpy, late-middle-aged man. Once his political ideas had been thought as red as his hair; now he gave many warnings on the menace of the Left and wrote articles for the Sunday papers on the moral disintegration of life in Britain today. In these contributions he never failed to denounce the abandonment, by the Church of England, of the King James Bible and the older forms of prayer, although his knowledge of these matters was sometimes unreliable.

'Shush, Henry,' his wife Lonnie, sitting beside him, had whispered nervously when he interrupted the Vicar, but Henry grumbled to himself, 'Why should the Rev. Trendy Kev get away with castrating the prayer-book?'

Lorna (Lonnie) Simcox was not only concerned on account of her husband's liturgical complaints. She looked behind her from time to time during the prayers. She was conscious that she was, as she would say, Mrs Henry Simcox Mark Two, the Numero

Due, and the Numero Uno was seated a couple of rows behind her gazing at her, as she imagined it, with studied contempt.

In fact Agnes Simcox, Henry's first wife, née Salter and the only daughter of that late Dr Salter whom the Rector had, in one of his last dreams, so strangely confused with the Almighty, was not seeing anything but a blur, as she had left her glasses in the car. Short-sightedness added to her habitual expression of ironic contempt, so that she looked as though she were watching a theatrical performance which she had decided not to enjoy. She was huddled into a raincoat with a fur collar, dressed for the damp and draughty inside of the church rather than for the bright sunshine of the day outside. She was in her late forties, but when a shaft of light from a clear window struck her face it was only a moderately unkind blow; her beauty was, on the whole, less ravaged by the passage of time than she had the right to expect. Agnes was thinking a little of her past, her long knowledge of the Simcox family and the days of her childhood, but mainly she was longing for a cigarette. She heard the Vicar say, 'I'm sure that neither death, nor life, nor angels...' and 'I am *persuaded* that neither death...' she heard Henry Simcox, her ex-husband, correct him gloomily.

So the Reverend Simeon Simcox lay enclosed in a long box, surrounded by these people and other local inhabitants. There sat Lady Fanner, with a face dead-white and powdered, a head apparently held up by a choker of pearls and a mouth like a small wound. The Simcox family solicitor, Jackson Cantellow, joined in the prayers which he knew as well as his forms of conveyancing, and the Rural Dean was there to represent the Bishop. Also in the congregation were some of the wives of Rapstone Fanner, comparatively new arrivals whose husbands were busy in London offices, large, healthy women who called their children 'The Young' and drank brandy at coffee mornings because they were bored with being left alone in the country. There were a few, only a few, men and women from those cottages which hadn't yet been turned into commuter houses; among them old Percy Bigwell, known as 'Peasticks' because of his splayed legs and two walking-sticks which had brought him, in a slow crablike motion, across the village green to pay his last tribute to the Rector. Among these

15

people sat strangers to the village with familiar faces, some ageing Labour politicians, journalists, broadcasters and representatives of the various groups and movements connected with peace, political prisoners and racial equality for which Simeon Simcox had been known for many years as a constant campaigner.

Shortly after the service began a large, official Rover, with a lady chauffeur at the wheel, passed the signpost at the head of the valley and descended quickly on Rapstone. Sitting alone in the back was a man of obvious importance, wearing a dark suit and a black tie. In contrast to the 'progressive' politicians already assembled round the late Rector's coffin, the Rt Hon. Leslie Titmuss, M.P., was a power in the Conservative administration. He was a pale man with inquisitive, almost colourless eyes who, in spite of his receding hairline and gaunt features, had preserved, since his childhood in the Rapstone Valley, an expression of simple, boyish cunning. He sat forward on his seat as though late for an appointment and, as the car stopped outside the church, he opened the door and hopped out in the eager way of a man ever anxious to appear energetic to photographers. On his way to the lychgate he was waylaid by a loitering reporter and he switched on an instant smile.

'Minister!' The reporter fluttered a notebook. 'We hardly expected to see you at the funeral of a left-wing cleric.'

'Certain things transcend political differences. Simeon Simcox was a great man. He was an old family friend and a tremendous influence on my life. Thank you, gentlemen.' Having given his quote Leslie Titmuss turned off his smile and hurried into the church.

Fred Simcox and his mother were whispering together as the Reverend Kevin Bulstrode climbed into the pulpit. Dorothy Simcox looked pained. Her hair, which like her elder son's had been copper but had become grey, was gently out of control. The silk scarf she wore round her neck seemed to float away and she was staring with fierce concentration at a particular floral tribute which lay on her husband's coffin. It was a huge and expensive affair, a great circle of dark twisted leaves pierced by the white military trumpets of lilies and spears of gladioli; the sort of thing which some ostentatious Head of State might lay on the tomb of his unknown soldier.

'It's appalling!' Dorothy Simcox complained.

'It's only a wreath, Mother.'

'Your father would have hated it.'

'Perhaps he wouldn't have minded.'

'Where could it possibly have come from?'

Fred didn't answer his mother. His head had turned at the sound of the church door opening and footsteps on the flagstones. The Rt Hon. Leslie Titmuss had joined the congregation.

'For Simeon Simcox,' Bulstrode was saying, 'the Church of England wasn't the Establishment at prayer, it was the force of progress on the march. One of the many obituaries in the national press suggests he may have been a bit of a saint. If so, he was a saint smoking a pipe, dressed in that old tweed jacket with leather patches we came to love and know so well, a very caring sort of saint, be it at the Worsfield Missile Base or leading us in prayer outside the South African High Commission.'

Dorothy was still gazing in incredulous horror at the wreath, hardly hearing the well-meant words from the pulpit above her. 'One of his parishioners, our old friend "Peasticks" Bigwell, must have the last word. "He were a smasher, our old Rector, weren't he?" Peasticks said to me. Well, perhaps it wasn't the description we'd all use.'

'Hardly,' Henry whispered to Lonnie, 'for a dedicated pacifist.'

'But, you know, I think Simeon would have understood. Today we are gathered together to say goodbye to a "smasher".'

After the funeral service many of the congregation, some starting to chatter, others lighting cigarettes, all relieved that the worst was over, crowded into the Rectory to be met by Dorothy with a look of considerable dismay. Henry Simcox, turning away from the crowd for which his mother had clearly made no sort of preparation, went to the cupboard in a corner by the french windows and found it almost bare. 'It'd need a miracle,' he told Lonnie, 'to divide one bottle of strictly non-South African, anti-apartheid sherry among all those thirsty mourners. I don't suppose *he*'d've managed it. My father wasn't much of a man for miracles.' Then he saw another dusty bottle behind a row of glasses, took it and held it up to the light. 'There's a drop of brandy, left over from the Christmas pudding.'

'Agnes shouldn't've come!' Lonnie was looking across the room at the Numero Uno. 'Not after all that's happened.'

'Agnes enjoys anything at all tragic.' Henry poured himself a brandy. 'It was summer holidays she found so terribly harrowing.'

'It's embarrassing for you!' Lonnie was always more concerned for her husband than he was for himself.

'Don't exaggerate, Lonnie.'

'And for your mother.'

'The Simcoxes don't embarrass as easily as that.'

As Henry raised his glass he looked out of the french windows and did not drink. He could see, across the unweeded garden, his younger brother Fred standing, alone and in silence, by his father's grave. The sight seemed to cause Henry Simcox some displeasure.

'I'd say Kevin Bulstrode did us a very fair service.' Jackson Cantellow, the family solicitor, was talking to Agnes. She inhaled a Silk Cut greedily, pushed one clenched fist into her jacket pocket and coughed with deep satisfaction. 'I'm not really an expert on funerals.'

'Have to be in our job,' Cantellow told her. 'A family solicitor has to be. Has its compensations, of course. I think I gained my taste for sacred music at clients' funerals. We don't always get a legacy but we do occasionally get the Parry. They used to do an absolutely super Stanford in G when old Bagstead was at Hartscombe. Now of course it's all this taped stuff. Not the same thing at all, I'm afraid. We had "Going My Way" from a cassette at Bill Backstay's cremation in Worsfield.'

'So long as it wasn't "Smoke Gets in Your Eyes".' Agnes looked round the room, feeling trapped and wondering how long it would be before Henry produced the sherry.

'What did you say?'

'Nothing. I said absolutely nothing.' She was relieved to see Dorothy moving towards her.

'No sort of will surfaced yet.' Cantellow tried to get down to business with the widow. 'I was always pestering Simeon to make one. Well, once we've got over this we'll make our searches.'

'Agnes, I'm glad you came.' Dorothy ignored her lawyer. 'Simeon would have been so glad.'

'Would he?'

'He liked you. You know, he always regarded you as a challenge.'

'I think I'm rather tired of being regarded as a challenge.'

'I know you don't like discussing business' – Cantellow was insistent – 'but some time, Mrs Simcox. Some time soon.'

'Not now,' Dorothy said. Dismissed, Cantellow gave a little bow of resignation and moved away. Dorothy looked round the room and hoped that the crowd assembled wouldn't expect to eat any-- thing. As though in answer to her unspoken thoughts, Lonnie came bustling by on her way to the kitchen.

'I thought I'd just put out some biscuits,' she told them.

'Oh, Lonnie! What a wonderful little brick you are.' Agnes gave one of her weariest smiles and Numero Due almost hissed back at her, 'I do think it's embarrassing of you to come. I know Henry's embarrassed.'

'Why on earth should he be?' Agnes spoke quite loudly. 'It's not *his* funeral, is it?'

'I'll go and put out those biscuits.' Lonnie went on her way with her face set and Dorothy looked as though she hadn't been listening.

The Rural Dean was doing his best, on the minute glass of sherry provided, to make the party go. He said how impressive it was to have the Cabinet represented in the shape of Mr Leslie Titmuss. He recalled how very famous Simeon Simcox had been. 'Not a conventional clergyman, of course. The Bishop had to haul him over the coals when he was getting too deeply into politics. Saints are never the easiest people to get along with. You put that across jolly well, Kevin.'

'Thank you.' Bulstrode was gratified. 'I think we managed to strike just the right note of reverent informality.' Unfortunately he was within earshot of Henry, who came delightedly in on the cue.

'I think you struck a perfectly ghastly note. That castrated edition of the prayer-book may be perfectly suitable to bless the union of a couple of crimpers in a unisex hairdo establishment. It's got no place in the Christian burial of a priest of the Church of England.'

'May I suggest' – Bulstrode was tentative – 'that we've got to make things clear to the common man?'

'However common the man he could understand the old prayer-

book perfectly well. Ask the Right Honourable Leslie Titmuss.'
But then Henry saw his younger brother coming in through the
french windows and moved away.

'Powerful turn of phrase!' Bulstrode told the Dean admiringly.
'No wonder he's always off to America.'

'What were you doing?' Henry asked when he met Fred by the
corner cupboard.

'Saying goodbye.'

'With a certain amount of quiet ostentation?'

'I'm sorry you thought that.' Fred had discovered that the
Christmas brandy bottle was empty. He took the sherry from
Henry and poured himself the last half glass.

'I was away,' Henry said, 'when it happened.'

'Yes.'

'I had to go to the Coast.'

'The coast of what?' Fred asked, although he knew perfectly
well.

'You know. Hollywood. The suburbia of the soul.' Henry made
a habit of abusing what was still a considerable source of his
income. 'You were with him, though. At the end?'

'Yes, I was with him.'

'Did he say anything in particular?' Henry asked the question
as though it had no great importance and Fred finished his sherry.

'Not . . . so far as I remember.'

'I don't suppose he would.'

'What?'

'Say anything in particular to you.'

'He seemed to be frightened.' Fred moved away, wondering
why, on this of all days, meeting his brother was like another round
in a contest which had been going on as long as either of them
could remember.

There was a pervasive smell of face-powder and Chanel Number
Five and Fred found himself looking down into the ravaged face
of Lady Fanner, who had once been beautiful. 'So many funerals!
We've had Elspeth Fairhazel and the "Contessa" and old Uncle
Cecil. I'm quite exhausted.'

'I'm sorry, Grace. My father should have consulted your engagements.'

'Now that's naughty of you, Fred. I was devoted to your father, even though he sometimes looked at me as though he disapproved of my not being black. Well, I get discriminated against too. I told him that so often. That horrible little man in the fish shop in Hartscombe absolutely declines to serve me.'

'My mother's been cornered by Leslie Titmuss.' Fred looked across the room.

'Poor woman. Well, do go and rescue her then.'

When Fred arrived at his mother's side she was telling the Cabinet Minister how strange it was to be at a service in Rapstone Church and not to hear Simeon's voice and he, in turn, was apologizing for having arrived late at the ceremony. 'When the P.M. calls a breakfast meeting you really can't say "no". But nothing would have made me miss the old man's funeral.'

'Why ever not, Leslie?' Dorothy seemed not to understand his having felt the burying of her husband to be such an important occasion.

'I remember how good he was to me, when I was a young lad. How good you all were.'

'Is that what you remember?' Dorothy was still puzzled.

'Sad occasion, of course. But beautifully done.'

'Except for that wreath!' Dorothy told him and went on regardless of Fred, who muttered a warning 'Mother!' 'Whoever could have sent that perfectly appalling object?' She gave out a small, mirthless laugh. 'They must have pinched it off the Cenotaph!'

'Please, Mother!'

'My secretary ordered it actually,' Leslie admitted. 'He's got an uncle in the business.'

'Oh dear!' But Dorothy's disarray was only momentary. After Fred had praised the kindness of the thought, she went on firmly, 'You shouldn't've done it, Leslie! It's the way you used to carry on when you were a little boy. You really mustn't spend your money on such foolish objects.'

It was with relief that the Minister then caught sight of his uniformed lady chauffeur, standing in the garden, waving silently. 'I think I can see my driver making a signal. Respects to all the family. Sorry I've got to rush. Working lunch with the C.B.I.' And then he assured them both, 'I'll always be grateful.'

21

When Leslie Titmuss was on his way out through the french windows, Henry joined his mother and brother and they all three looked at the retreating dark-suited figure of the man who was now one of their rulers.

'I wonder what he'll always be grateful for, exactly?' Dorothy appeared to find the question amusing. 'I remember he used to bring us presents. So embarrassing! Things he'd saved up for.'

'Or things he'd nicked from Woolworths.' Then Henry turned to his brother. 'You said just now that our father was frightened. Of what exactly?'

Fred thought for a moment before he answered, 'Heaven.'

★ 2 ★

Children at the Rectory

'It's Leslie, Simeon. Leslie Titmuss.'

'Welcome, Leslie! Have we no cake or any such thing?'

'I think he's come to do a job,' Dorothy said firmly.

A long war, widely thought to have defeated the forces of tyranny and injustice and ushered in the age of the Common Man, whoever he was, had been over for three years. The British had dismissed Mr Churchill and installed a Labour Government, an event which caused Simeon to choose, as a frequent text, Revelation chapter 21, verse 1, 'And I saw a new heaven and a new earth; for the first heaven and earth had passed away.' His sermons at the time often referred to the New Jerusalem in a way which may have been unclear to his congregation, who were being told by the Government to pull in their belts and who found, despite their undoubted victory, that everything was still on coupons.

After a cold spring and early summer the weather became exceptionally fine and hot, as it was on the day that the twelve-year-old Leslie Titmuss stood in the Rectory garden, wearing long shorts and grey socks which fell like a couple of woollen concertinas over his dusty shoes. In honour of his visit to the Rector and his wife he had slicked his hair down with brilliantine ('Anzora masters the hair') and it was as flat and shiny as patent leather, apart from a little crest which stood up stiffly on the crown of his head, giving him an eager and birdlike appearance. His arrival had interrupted Simeon's dictation of letters of protest to the Bishop on the Church's lack of leadership on the question of apartheid in South Africa, and worried Dorothy, who was afraid that, if left to his own devices, Leslie might dig up her most tender plants.

'Why, Leslie,' Simeon said. 'Whatever's that?' The child had in his hands a small statuette of a lady in a bright red bathing-suit standing on a rock. She was leaning slightly forward, one hand stretched out behind her, the other with a finger laid lightly on her cherry-coloured lips. Her eyes were open very wide, her expression could only be described as 'roguish', and the base of the statue bore, in gilt letters, the legend 'A Present from Cleethorpes'.

'It's for you, Mrs Simcox.' Leslie held out the trophy towards Dorothy, who retreated slightly.

'Dear me. Where *did* you get it?'

'I got it for you,' Leslie said, not quite answering the question.

'Leslie! You must learn not to do things like that.' Dorothy sounded severe but her husband interrupted her. 'Leslie Titmuss comes bearing gifts! How exciting. Do let me see.' To his wife's despair he took the object.

'It's a present, Mr Simcox.'

'It's a beautiful object.' Simeon sounded almost convinced. 'My dear, isn't that a most beautiful object? Wasn't it kind and thoughtful of Leslie?'

'Leslie. As you're here,' Dorothy said firmly, 'I was thinking about the nettles.'

'The nettles by the old croquet lawn?' The boy sounded eager.

'Yes, Leslie. Those nettles.'

'We shall treasure this, Leslie. We shall keep it on our mantel-piece,' said Simeon, who was left holding the gift as young Titmuss marched off to get a hook for the execution of the nettles.

'Shall we have to?' Dorothy said, when he was out of earshot.

'Of course.'

'But the thing's hideous!'

'Hideous things are something we have to put up with,' her husband explained patiently. 'We can't shut our eyes to them. That wouldn't be right.'

'I can shut my eyes to a present from Cleethorpes any day of the week. Simeon! You're not going to put it next to my little bit of Spode?'

'We really can't offend the boy.'

'I don't see why not. He's such a particularly disagreeable child.'

'That's not a very Christian thing to say.' Simeon looked at his wife sadly.

'Why not? Perhaps God made people like Leslie Titmuss so we can find out who's nice. Freddie!' As she said the last word Dorothy looked upwards and sighed. In his bedroom her younger son was accompanying a record on the second-hand drum set they had allowed him to save up for at Christmas. She went upstairs to Fred's room, knowing that her husband had a busy afternoon ahead. She switched off the gramophone and 'My Very Good Friend the Milkman' was cut off in mid-flow. The accompaniment also fell silent. 'Your father's working,' she said. 'He's trying to write letters to the Bishop.'

'What about?'

'About what they're doing to the black men in Africa, if you must know.' Fred was gently swishing on a drum with a wire-brush. 'Fats Waller's black,' he said, 'and you switched him off.'

'Try not to be childish, Freddie,' his mother advised him.

In the end she had her way about the present from Cleethorpes. It didn't disturb the Spode in the living-room. It landed up on the mantelpiece in Simeon's study, along with a number of invitations to lecture, a clock that kept poor time, a wood carving of a pregnant woman he had brought back from a visit to an Anglican bishop in Nigeria and a small bust of Karl Marx.

Although the summer holidays seemed endless the boys were never bored. There was always too much to do at home. Fred played his records and practised from manuals with such titles as *Jazz Drumming for Beginners*, for which he sent away. Henry was writing a long novel in a number of school notebooks which he kept hidden in his sock drawer and was secretly hurt that Fred had never asked to read them. When it was hot they bicycled down to Hartscombe, the local riverside town, and took out a dinghy. They quarrelled about the efficiency of each other's rowing (Henry always steered them out to mid-stream and Fred got their heads scraped by overhanging willows near the bank) and pulled up past the lock where they swam in the river. The water was dark and brackish, filled with rasping reeds, and, if your foot touched the bottom, black mud oozed between your toes. Sometimes they had wished on them the company of Agnes Salter, whose father was their doctor and a family friend. They seemed to quarrel less when Agnes was with them. She dived better and more neatly than they did and showed no terror when Henry deliberately rowed towards the churning, yellowish water of the weir. When she was in her black one-piece Jansen bathing-suit Fred would avoid looking at her, afraid he might find her beautiful. When he was alone he thought mainly about Betty Grable.

Dorothy was busy gardening, preserving, making jam and potting meat, seeking refuge in such occupations from too much contact with her husband's parish. She had been an Oxford professor's daughter, brought up on Boar's Hill in a small house where the garden was filled after lunch on Sundays with high-pitched, excitable voices discussing the reviews in the *New Statesman* and Fabian Socialism. Such an upbringing didn't equip her for running white elephant stalls at local fêtes, or afternoons with the Women's Institute. She believed that, in an ideal world, the working classes would rule the country, but she had no particular desire to ask any of them to tea.

Simeon pursued his political interests more doggedly. He sat for long hours at the desk in his study, among a clutter of pipe-racks, walking-sticks, pamphlets, Left Book Club volumes, Penguins and blue papers, cuttings from *Tribune* and the *News Chronicle*, haphazard shelves supporting the works of Engels and R.H. Tawney, H.G. Wells and Bernard Shaw, the Webbs and Bertrand Russell. He went regularly to meetings, committees, protests and deputations in London. During such absences Henry sat in his father's chair and became quite intolerably bossy.

On the whole they were a closely knit group and, like all parsons' or policemen's families, set apart from their neighbours. When Simeon had an evening away from his correspondence they played bridge. Henry overbid outrageously and quickly lost interest. Fred underbid but played his hand with determination. Dorothy joined in with her mind elsewhere and Simeon had an unexpectedly good memory for the cards and took a great pleasure in winning. Once, when he went to the lavatory during a deal, Henry contrived to present him with all the hearts. When Simeon picked up his hand he was bubbling with triumph and a kind of childish glee, until he realized that he'd been deceived and became disappointed and sad.

Often the boys decided to get up plays, but openings were postponed because they couldn't agree. On one remarkable

26

occasion Simeon offered to accompany them in scenes from Shakespeare given to the single audience of Dorothy. As he had played
Lady Macbeth at school their father undertook the 'Letter Scene'
again, his tall, bony figure fitted into one of the old black evening-
dresses Dorothy was about to send away as jumble, and a sort of
lace mantilla. Inappropriately, considering the climate at Glamis,
he carried a fan. While waiting in the hallway to make an entrance
Simeon heard the front door bell ring and unthinkingly opened it
to a young couple who'd come to be prepared for marriage. Seeing
what they took to be the Rector *en travesti*, they backed away into
the darkness. Much was to be made of this incident in the distant
future, but such extraordinary events were rare. Most of the time
life at the Rectory was quiet, as it was on the summer afternoon
when Leslie Titmuss hacked at the nettles on the edge of the old
croquet lawn, and Henry lay on his stomach in the long grass with
an open exercise book in front of him, chewing a pencil.

'What are you doing?' Leslie paused in his work to ask.

'Just writing a novel.'

'What's a novel?'

'It's a picture of our society, from top to bottom. A human story.'
Henry began to write again, as if to deter conversation.

'Got any bits about girls in it, has it?' Leslie fell upon the nettles
again, slaughtering them wildly.

'Yes. But you wouldn't understand them.'

'Is it difficult? Writing that, I mean.'

'For some people.'

'I bet it's not as hard as getting rid of these old nettles.'

Henry looked up at Leslie, as though at some specimen whose
activities he was about to record in a nature notebook. 'What're
you doing that for?'

'Your mum gives me half a crown.' Leslie didn't stop hacking.

'My parents exploit you! It's the beer money.'

'I don't get any beer money.'

'They do,' Henry explained patiently. 'Out of Simcox Ales. The
Brewery in Hartscombe keeps our family going, so they can exploit
the workers.'

'They're all right. I brought your dad a present, a statue. He was
delighted with it.'

'It's because you live in Skurfield,' Henry told the worker. 'My parents think everyone who lives in Skurfield's there to be exploited. They don't ask *me* to cut down the nettles.'

'Your mum says she's asked you. But you don't ever do it.'

Henry started to write again. 'When the revolution comes,' he said, 'they'll be the first to go.'

'Where?'

Henry was busy and didn't answer.

'*Where* will they be the first to go?'

'Never you mind.'

Leslie stopped hacking and pushed back his sticky hair. 'Where will *you* be, Henry? When the revolution comes?'

'Probably in charge.'

Fred said, 'Leslie Titmuss is going to Hartscombe Grammar.'

'Leslie's done well. He's got his wits about him.'

'I'd like to go to Hartscombe Grammar.'

'I suppose none of us can have everything they want in this world.'

Fred was with his father in the church vestry, with its smell of mice and old prayer-books, among the choir surplices and bleeding hassocks in need of repair. He was pumping away at a harmonium, playing the chorus of 'My Very Good Friend the Milkman', which he could do because he had an ear for music. Simeon was at a table, cutting bread into small cubes for the Communion service. Both the boys had been to a preparatory day school not far away. Now the plan was to send them to a public school, Knuckleberries, on the Norfolk coast. Simeon had himself been to this remote establishment, and his brother, Pym Simcox, who was Chairman of the Brewery (Pym later shot himself in the hop loft for some unfathomable reason), spent his schooldays there. This period of Uncle Pym's life, wretchedly unhappy at the time, later became a source of mysterious and almost mystical pride to him. Pym always, even at the moment of death, wore the O.K. tie, and regularly reported his unchanging circumstances in the *Knuckleberrian*. It seemed to Fred that he and Henry were being mercilessly dispatched to this mysterious institution as some sort of compensation for Uncle Pym Simcox's untimely death.

'Why do I *have* to go to Knuckleberries?' Fred stopped playing and asked, not for the first time that summer. 'I mean, I thought you believed in everyone being equal. Don't you believe in everyone going to Hartscombe Grammar?'

'I suppose things aren't always so simple.'

'Why aren't they?'

'I respect that in you, Frederick,' Simeon assured him. 'I respect you for asking questions.'

'So will you tell me why I have to go to Knuckleberries?'

'Perhaps it's the will of God.' Simeon spoke in a somewhat offhanded manner of the Divine Plan and then pulled a wristwatch with a broken strap out of the pocket of his cassock. 'Good heavens. Parish meeting! Couldn't you do the rest for me?'

Fred got up and went reluctantly to the table and fiddled with the knife. 'Does it turn into flesh, during the service?' he asked, looking at the bread.

'Freddy! You know it doesn't.' Simeon looked as though his son had expressed a literal belief in Santa Claus.

'It might do. One day it might surprise you. I don't suppose you can be certain. Well, if it doesn't do anything interesting, why do you have it in the service?'

'To celebrate the basic things of life, Frederick,' Simeon explained patiently. 'The bread that's made simply. Kneaded and put to rise in the oven.'

'It's a sliced loaf, isn't it? Doesn't it get made in a factory?' Fred looked up at his father surprised, for when he said that Simeon appeared, on his way out of the vestry, to be laughing.

That afternoon Fred went to the village shop with his mother and he asked her, 'Is it the will of God, Henry and me going to Knuckleberries?'

'It may not be the will of God,' Dorothy said. 'It's something that's been arranged.'

'Did Dad arrange it?'

'Well, no. He doesn't always arrange things. You know he's so busy.'

'What's he so busy at, exactly?'

'Good heavens, you know! The Labour Party and the Worsfield

29

Mission and the United Nations and the Peace Pledge Union and South Africa...'

'*You* arranged it!' Fred's voice was accusing.

'It's much better for you and Henry to be away at school. Anyway, you know your Uncle Pym went to Knuckleberries.'

'So you arranged for us to go there too?'

'I suppose I did.'

'So it's the will of God?' Fred took an apple out of the shopping-basket and bit into it. He felt then that he was powerless in the hands of fate. His mother, he knew, was an implacable, unpersuadable force. She looked at him, smiling vaguely, and said, 'Poor Freddie! You do come out with some strange ideas.'

3

Knuckleberries and After

What Fred hated was the dormitory. He longed for his small maid's bedroom in the Rectory with its dormer window, his drums and records and pinned-up pages from the *Picturegoer*. He wanted to be alone, with his milk and biscuits, to read *The History of the Blues* in peace. The dormitory was a long, dark, bare, barrack-like room with iron bedsteads and icy draughts which blew in through the compulsorily opened windows direct from Siberia with no intervening mountain range. It was also the scene of sudden outbreaks of violence, the selection of victims and lightning shifts in popularity from which, it must be said, Henry always emerged unscathed and Fred only occasionally suffered.

One night he was sitting up in bed in his dressing-gown, pyjamas and socks before lights out. Parted from his drums he had a tin chamber-pot inverted on his lap and, with a pair of wire-brushes, he was swishing out the rhythm of 'Slow Boat to China', a recent hit. Around him some boys were on their knees, some were throwing slippers at those praying, others were taking advantage of a last chance to clean their teeth before the water froze. Henry was pacing the deck looking masterful, taking advantage of his privileged position as dorm leader to be wearing a long woollen muffler and a cap with his dressing-gown and pyjamas. That night's victim, a boy called Arthur Nubble, had been satisfactorily reduced to a sobbing, blanket-covered lump in the corner.

Most of the boys in the dormitory thought of the war as a rare treat which they had missed and which would never be on offer again. One tall, red-faced boy with a premature five o'clock shadow, a great masturbator named Maybrick, told them stories of his father's exploits in the Navy. 'Six days in an open boat, my dad was,' he said, not for the first time. 'One of the ratings went raving mad!' 'My father did commando landings in North Africa.' This was Pusey, a minute boy in the corner, lying hopelessly. 'One of the young sailors in the open boat just couldn't take it.' Maybrick ignored the interruption. 'My father cradled him in his arms all night.'

'I saw that film.' Henry looked at Maybrick, who stared back at him red-faced and angry. The dormitory fell silent; only Fred sang quietly to his own wire-brush accompaniment:

'Get you and keep you
In my arms evermore,
Leave all your lovers
Weeping on the faraway shore.'

'That film had Richard Attenborough in it.' Henry was determined to shut Maybrick up. 'I saw it at our local Odeon in Hartscombe.'

'So that was your bloody war service, Simcox Major.' Maybrick was clearly planning to start a slipper-throwing, anti-Henry landslide. 'Watching flicks in your local Odeon.'

'And what did you do for Britain, challenge the German High Command at pocket billiards?' It was an easy laugh, not typical of Henry at his best, Fred thought, and Maybrick came back with a dangerous question, 'What was *your* father in the war anyway?' The answer 'a parson' was too awful for Fred to contemplate, and he waited for the attack on both of them, the flailing towels, hurled bodies and flung slippers, which it was bound to provoke. 'Secret Service,' Henry said with great authority.

'What?'

'He did Secret Service disguised as a parson,' Henry said to end all further argument. 'And now I'm going to see if anyone's unthawed the bogs.'

There was an awed silence after he had left, until Maybrick asked quietly, 'Simcox Mi. Why does your brother tell such amazing lies?' During a sickening pause Fred again felt that public opinion might be about to turn against him. Happily a diversion was caused by Pusey hopping out of bed to pull the blanket off the sobbing heap in the corner.

32

'What's the matter with Nubble, has he got the screaming hab-dabs?' The small boy looked down with clinical interest at the cowering bulk. 'Of course he has,' Fred told them when he was sure no one was listening. 'Haven't you noticed? This dorm's just like being adrift in an open boat. Thirteen weeks among the ice-floes.'

In the afternoons, even if they were not down to play in any particular game, the boys at Knuckleberries were ordered to 'take exercise'. For Fred this meant changing into football clothes and running shoes and hiding in the sour-smelling 'bogs' or sprinting off to a neighbouring spinney where he would crouch in the bushes to read the *Picturegoer* or those novels, which Henry told him were an essential part of his education, by Aldous Huxley, D.H. Lawrence and Norman Mailer. He kept these works stuffed up his football shirt and he was pounding along one afternoon looking vaguely pregnant when he heard a stirring in the undergrowth and stopped to discover Arthur Nubble, also in full running-gear, taking cover. Nubble looked up at Fred with plaintive, soft brown eyes; he had full lips and curling dark brown hair and was not so much fat as inappropriately overweight for a schoolboy, like an Italian tenor who has to squeeze into the costume to play a romantic lead.

'What on earth are you doing?'

'Hiding from your brother.' Nubble spoke in an accent which Fred's mother would have described as 'slightly off'. 'He's meant to be in charge of exercise. I seem to spend most of the time at Knuckleberries hiding from people. Bloody awful place, isn't it?'

'Pretty terrible, yes,' Fred agreed.

'My dad told me it'd be bloody awful. Ghastly grub and I'd be homesick and miss our mum's cooking, but he said it was worth it all because I'd meet useful friends. You look like a nice sort of friend for me to meet, Simcox Minor.'

'I'm not all that useful, really,' Fred assured him.

'Why?' Nubble sounded disappointed. 'What do you do then?'

'I turn on people.'

'You *what*?'

'I lead people on to trust me and then I turn on them. I'm

well known for being treacherous.' Fred thought of his habitual behaviour in the dormitory.

'Couldn't you be a useful friend for me, just until you start being treacherous?'

'We'd better get moving.' Fred started to walk on, deeper into the wood, and Arthur Nubble trotted after him, panting, 'Fond of a bit of brawn, are you?'

'What?' Fred began to run slowly and Arthur lolloped behind him, talking incessantly. 'Ox tongue, peaches in a decent white wine syrup, chicken in aspic, liqueur chocolates off coupons. My dad says it's shocking the rationing we've still got in England. He says for all we won the war, we might as well be bloody Germans. He puts it all down to us having a Labour Government. He says it's ridiculous, us not being able to get a bit of brawn if we've got a fancy for it.' Arthur Nubble stopped then, and looked at Fred appealingly. 'Look, as long as we're friends, let's go down the music huts.'

'Why the music huts?' Fred stopped too. He hadn't, after all, come out in exercise clothes to run.

'Because,' Arthur muttered darkly, 'nobody here learns the double bass.'

Music did not have a great following at Knuckleberries, which specialized in Latin, mathematics and rugby football. The music huts were long, low, prefabricated buildings at the foot of the kitchen gardens from which scales and arpeggios were infrequently heard. The cubicles containing pianos or other instruments became places of hiding for nervous boys or shelters for solitary love affairs inflamed by illicit copies of *Reveille* or *Titbits*. In one such room, furnished with broken chairs and rusty music-stands, Arthur Nubble showed Fred an old double-bass case which opened like a cupboard to reveal various tins of food. The two boys, still in their running clothes, sat on the floor and hungrily consumed sweets and savouries, serving themselves with Nubble's pocket-knife, a weapon usefully equipped with a tin-opener and a corkscrew. Post-war austerity and the indifference of the school cooking left Fred permanently hungry. He tucked into the exotic fare with fierce concentration.

'My dad knows why there's no brawn available,' Arthur Nubble told him in a knowing way. 'It's because of that Attlee and Ernie Bevin and Sir Stifford Crapps. They keep all the brawn and peaches and white wine to themselves. And the same goes for the liqueur chocolates when they can get their sticky fingers on them. Like ox tongue, do you? Better than the muck you get here, eh?' As he watched Fred eat, Arthur Nubble had all the pride of a society hostess laying on an elaborate dinner party. 'Our headmaster ought to get himself in the Cabinet. Bet your father says the same thing about the Labour Government?'

'He doesn't,' Fred told him between mouthfuls.

'Doesn't he?'

'My father's a Socialist.'

'Sorry.' Arthur clapped a hand over his mouth. 'Dropped a brick.'

'That's all right.'

'No, I'm sorry. You must be bloody poor, if you're a Socialist. Come here on a charity place? Well, we can still be friends. You'll probably depend on me for a bite to eat.'

'I thought you said Socialists were rich.' Fred was working on a tin of marrons glacés.

'Not *Socialists*,' Arthur explained. 'Not the rank and file. Just the Cabinet. The Cabinet get all the tinned stuff off points. The rank and file'd be better off as Germans.'

'My father's not especially poor,' Fred admitted.

'He's not?'

'In fact I think he owns most of a brewery. Simcox Ales. You know. All that sort of nonsense.'

'He owns best part of a brewery and he's a *Socialist*?' Arthur Nubble was laughing as he passed the chocolates. 'Have a Tia Maria centre. He must be bloody *crackers*!'

Nubble didn't have long to wait before he had more material on which to judge Simeon Simcox's sanity. As an old boy and a priest who often got his name in the papers, the Rector of Rapstone was invited by the Headmaster to preach at Knuckleberries, and to his sons' horror he accepted. Fred sat, his nails dug into his palms, his fists clenched with embarrassment, and Henry listened stony-faced, giving nothing away in the icy, sham-Gothic school chapel. As soon as he heard the text, Revelation, chapter 21, verse 2, Fred's heart sank, feeling sure that his father was going to preach about the Labour Government. 'And I John saw the Holy City, New Jerusalem, come down from God out of heaven, prepared as a bride adorned for her husband.' A few of the smaller boys giggled at the word 'bride', but Simeon beamed down upon them all. 'What's the great virtue of an English public school?' he asked them. 'What did I, for instance, get out of Knuckleberries? A great deal. I mean, it's no use having a *sensible* education. No. What we all need is something to rebel against. The ridiculous importance attached to football, the absurd rules about which side of Coppers Piece you can walk down after two years with your hands in your pockets, the Armistice Day sermons I've heard from this very pulpit about the Christian virtues of blowing each other up, wonderful stuff; thank God it all made a revolutionary of me! I mean, if Our Lord hadn't heard a lot of rubbish preached by the Pharisees, he'd never have been driven to write the Sermon on the Mount.' There was a sharp intake of breath from the Headmaster, but Simeon continued undeterred. 'Perhaps my belief in a Just City, a New Jerusalem, an equal society, was born out of intense boredom on the playing-fields of Knuckleberries. Really I have only this advice for you all. Be rebels when you're young or what on earth will you have left for your old age?' No one answered his question, and Arthur Nubble, hunched against one of the few radiators at the back of the chapel, bit into a liqueur chocolate.

Sunday evening was always a bad time in the dormitory and Fred went upstairs with dread. He was not surprised to find a hostile crowd round Henry and to be greeted by a low murmur of mistrust.

'Was *that* your father, Simcox?'

'Of course.' Henry was perfectly calm. 'He's keeping up the disguise. The war's not really over, you know. We've still got lots of enemies.'

'What's he need a disguise for?'

'Perhaps for when he goes to Russia.' Henry sighed, as though having to explain himself to idiots. 'He needs *some* sort of cover, doesn't he?'

The boys looked puzzled but they slunk away and later threw

their slippers at a boy called Catchpole, who wore shiny pyjamas.
He made a change from Nubble.

It clouded over after lunch on the day of Simeon's funeral. Fred
and Henry and Henry's second wife were drinking coffee in the
living-room of the Rectory when Lonnie said that she thought it
was coming on to rain. To check his wife's forecast Henry went
over to the barometer on the wall and found that there was nothing
to tap. When Dorothy came into the room with a note in her hand
he looked at her with suspicion.

'It's gone,' he said. 'Father's old barometer's gone.'

'She must have taken it,' Dorothy answered vaguely, and asked,
'Did you see her?'

'Who on earth are you talking about?'

'Francesca. Your Frankie.'

Lonnie winced slightly at the name, as though she had taken a
mouthful of ice-cream and awakened a dormant toothache. She
had tried, she often told herself that no one could have tried harder,
to get on with Francesca, Henry's daughter by his first wife, the
child of Numero Uno. She had been quite prepared to take
Francesca on. It was clearly no life for the girl in a poky flat down
the wrong end of the Fulham Road, having to put up with Agnes's
smoking and great flashes of gloom. But since the age of six
Francesca had, she thought, whenever the child was compelled by
the terms of the divorce settlement to come for the weekend,
consistently disapproved of her. So Lonnie pursed her lips when
she heard who was responsible for the theft, as though she had
suspected it all along.

'Francesca took my father's old barometer?' Henry made it
sound an unnatural crime, like patricide.

'Well, I gave it to her.'

'You *what*?'

'I said she could have it.'

At this Lonnie thought it right to intervene, purely in the
interests of justice and her husband. 'I think Simeon would have
liked Henry to have the barometer. As the eldest son I think he's
entitled to have it.'

'Why?' Fred asked. 'Is Henry starting out on a career as a weatherman?'

'Henry was always to have the barometer and the clock,' Lonnie answered with dignity, 'and as the only writer in the family he has to be entitled to the desk. That was to be Henry's.'

'She left a note when they took the things.' Dorothy put on her glasses and read without expression from the paper she was carrying, ' "Darling Gran. Came this morning for the stuff. Didn't want to disturb you but it was the only day we could get the van." '

'Came this morning when we were *what*?' Henry's voice rose in outrage.

'Well we were in church, weren't we? I think she must have forgotten the date. I mean, she says she didn't realize until she got here and by then, of course, it was too late.'

'Not too late to loot the place. Who did she come with?'

'Oh, I think Peter,' Dorothy told him.

'So my daughter and her boyfriend raided the Rectory during my father's funeral and took away his furniture!'

'Only the desk and the barometer. Oh, and the little kitchen clock.'

'What on earth did they want the little kitchen clock for?'

'How about telling the time?' Fred suggested, it seemed unhelpfully, because his brother glared at him and started his tirade. 'Brutes! Robbers! Barbarians! Francesca the Hun!'

'I'd told her she could,' Dorothy assured him. 'And they're young.'

'Young and with all the tact and delicacy of a crowd of drunken mercenaries.'

'It's appalling,' Lonnie chipped in. 'You'll have to speak to her, Henry.'

'Just a few things' – Dorothy was understanding – 'so she can remember Simeon.'

'A barometer!' Henry was working himself up into a thoroughly enjoyable rage. 'What do they want a barometer for? They don't *have* weather in Tufnell Park.'

'The young have no sort of consideration,' Lonnie agreed.

'Consideration! All Francesca's consideration's reserved for South American guerrillas, under-privileged Eskimos and one-parent lame lesbian families living in Greater Manchester.' Listening to him Fred began to think how remarkably his brother had inherited their father's habit of preaching. 'Oh, I forgot,' Henry went on. 'And whales! Huge bloody whales swimming about in the sea, spouting and suckling their young and never even realizing that all the concern that normal girls lavish on their parents, all the reverence that decent-minded daughters might feel for a death in the family, is entirely concentrated on their bloated, inarticulate, blubbery bodies. We were never like that.' He looked at Fred and added, less certainly, 'Were we?'

Having his brother at school seemed no sort of advantage to Fred. Henry's presence reminded him of home but offered none of its consolations and as Henry moved steadily up the school, driven by an ambition Fred could not understand to be head boy, he chose different friends and became contemptuous of his younger brother's association with Arthur Nubble. 'Do stop hanging around with that fat spiv.' Henry knew nothing of the feasts in the music huts. 'Can't you see you're letting the family down?'

Separated at school the boys remained apart during the holidays. Henry wrote in his notebooks, went to stay with school friends and joined the village cricket team. Fred went on solitary bicycle rides. On one of these he made a discovery and a friend who was to prove, it seemed, as much of a let-down to his family as Arthur Nubble.

He was riding down a path in the woods when he heard a pheasant calling – the sound seemed near to him and close to the ground. He got off his bicycle, dropped it, left it ticking in the leaves and went to investigate. A little away from the path he found a cage in which the calling bird was imprisoned. He knelt down and had some idea of liberating the cock pheasant from the trap when he heard a voice behind him.

'You let him be. He's happy enough in there.'

'What's he doing?'

'Calling out to all the ladies in the neighbourhood. With a bit of luck they'll all be round to see him shortly, they find his voice very attractive.' The man was fat, dressed in an old flannel vest and shapeless trousers; he had a sharp nose, bright eyes and an expression of considerable glee, particularly when he was carrying, as he was at that moment, a shot-gun under his arm. 'Aren't you the Rector's boy?'

Fred admitted it.

'Grown, haven't you?'

Fred admitted that also.

'Tom Nowt. Used to come up and see your father a bit in the old days, used to bring him rabbits. Mother keeping well, is she?'

Fred supposed his mother was well.

'All right then. I'll make you a cup of tea.'

The man set off through the bushes and down a rutted cart-track until they reached a haphazard sort of building that looked as though it had been cobbled together in odd moments out of old planks, bits of hardboard, asbestos and corrugated iron. Inside it was warm, damp and stuffy. There was a paraffin stove and as the man made tea, sweetened with sugar and condensed milk, for both of them, Fred looked round and saw an old brass bed, assorted chairs, a broken sofa leaking horsehair and another shot-gun and a rifle in the corner. Deer skulls hung among the pin-ups on the walls, fleshless heads with dark eye-sockets and proud antlers. It was the first of many visits he was to pay to Tom Nowt's hut.

In time it became the first place he would make for when he came home for the holidays. He came to know more about Tom, that he lived in a cottage at the edge of the wood with his wife, Dora, and a number of children, that his hut was merely his shooting-lodge, and that he was mistrusted in the village since a tree he was felling had dropped wrongly and permanently injured old Percy Bigwell's legs. Although he undertook casual farm labour it was said that his real occupation was the secret shooting of deer that, having escaped from the Fanners' park at Rapstone Manor, bred freely in the woods. He also took pheasants by various means and shot over other people's land. None of this mattered to Fred, who sat, when he had got to know Tom Nowt better, nursing yet another warm mug of tea and condensed milk and said, 'How did all those die, Tom?'

'Some say they was got quietly by cross-bow bolts,' Tom told him solemnly. 'Some say they was dazed in an old car's headlights and a rifle did them. Those particular ones, I am prepared to take my oath, passed over peaceful, in their sleep.'

Fred had been suppressing laughter. Now it erupted. 'Been eating a lot of venison have you lately, Tom?'

'Breakfast, dinner *and* tea.' Tom sat down beside Fred and gulped tea. 'Nothing better than a deer's brains on toast for breakfast. How they been treating you, Fred?'

'Oh. Badly, Tom. Terribly badly.' Fred chose to look pathetic.

'What do they do to you, boy?'

'At school? Half starve us, make us sleep in a dormitory where the bogs freeze, hit us quite often for silly reasons, teach us Latin poetry so slowly you can't ever understand what it's about. And do cross-country runs where you have to break the ice and wade through streams. I cut my legs on the ice this term.'

'You're part of the privileged classes, of course.'

'Is that what we are?' Fred looked at a brace of unplucked birds hanging by the door. 'Been a bad year for pheasants, has it?'

'Has for the Stroves up Picton House. Some says it's due to a nasty outbreak of raisins soaked in brandy put on fish-hooks.'

Fred bubbled with laughter again. 'But you wouldn't know anything about that, Tom, would you?'

Next morning in the Rectory Fred asked, 'Why don't we ever have deer's brains on toast?' He was dipping soldiers into a boiled egg, a childish habit of which he was trying to break himself.

Simeon was reading an article on himself, topped by a Vicky cartoon, in the *New Statesman*. ' "Unbelievers can see the benefit of no beggars, no hungry children, no one out of work. It's harder for Christians. We seem to find starving children rather useful, I mean there has to be someone to receive the collection. I tell you," ' he read his own words with a certain satisfaction, ' "it's easier for a camel to go through the eye of a needle than for a Christian to enter the Kingdom of God." It's rather good,' he told Dorothy and held up the magazine.

'I do wish you'd try and keep out of the *New Statesman*.' His wife looked genuinely distressed. 'It's so embarrassing. What were you talking about, Fred?'

'I believe deer's brains make a smashing breakfast.'

'Could you try and not be quite so disgusting,' Henry said wearily. 'Watching you eat a boiled egg is revolting enough. Try not to put us *completely* off our food.'

41

'Tom Nowt has deer's brains every morning. Of course, he doesn't dazzle them in his headlights and shoot them out of his old banger with a point 22 rifle. Oh no!'

'Simcox Minor!' Henry used his Knuckleberries voice. 'Do shut up!'

'And would he put raisins on fish-hooks to catch all the Strove pheasants round Picton Principal? Raisins soaked in brandy? Tom Nowt wouldn't do that now, would he?'

'Where ever have you been, Fred?' Dorothy refilled his cup.

'Oh, I was down at Tom's old hut, in Hanging Wood.' And then he looked down the table and saw what he had never seen before, his father angry.

'Well, you're not to go there again.'

'What do you mean?'

'I don't think that was a particularly obscure remark. I don't want you to go there again.'

'Why ever shouldn't I?' Fred was trying to keep his end up but Simeon, collecting his letters and *New Statesman*, spoke with unusual severity.

'Because I'm telling you not to. For once in your life.'

'But *why* are you?'

Simeon stood up; he seemed to Fred to look suddenly very tall. 'Don't always be asking questions!' he said and banged the dining-room door behind him as he left.

So, before the holidays ended, Fred went down to say goodbye to Tom Nowt. He didn't go into the hut although invited but stood with his bicycle among the fallen leaves. 'My father doesn't want me to come down here any more.'

'Not when you get back from school?'

'Not ever. Why do you think that is?'

'He's got his reasons, I expect. Wouldn't he tell you?'

'No.'

'Well, then. I don't suppose he would.'

Back at Knuckleberries Fred noticed a change in Henry. His brother actively sought out his company, and that of Nubble. This was a mystery to Fred until he discovered that what Henry wanted to do was to read passages of his novel aloud to someone, and he had more sense than to choose his immediate friends and contemporaries, those who might become his fellow prefects, as a preview audience. After a good many hints and half-promises Henry met Fred and Nubble outside the old games pavilion carrying his notebook. He led them inside and they sat, on a damp Sunday afternoon, on the lockers while he read out the title, '*A Tale Told by an Idiot: A Novel by Henry Simcox*. What on earth's eating you?' for Nubble was having a fit of the giggles. 'Isn't it by you, Simcox?'

'Yes, of course it's by me.'

'Well, are you the . . .' Nubble didn't quite dare to say it.

'God! Are you completely illiterate?'

'Almost completely,' Nubble admitted.

'It's a quotation from Shakespeare. *Macbeth*.' At that stage in his literary career Henry didn't realize that his title wasn't entirely original. ' ". . . a tale told by an idiot, Full of sound and fury".'

'Well. How were we to know?'

'Really there's no point in reading it to you now.' Henry closed his notebook, although Arthur Nubble begged him not to.

'Go on,' Fred urged his brother wearily. 'We've been asking you to read it for ages.'

'Well, it's not finished. It's only a first draft.'

'Read it to us when you've finished it then.' Fred stood up and prepared to leave.

'So you *don't* want to hear it!' Henry sounded almost triumphant.

'I said read it to us when it's finished. I'm going to Ma Price's to get an egg and chips.'

'Apparently everyone wants me to read my novel except my own brother!'

'I didn't say that.'

'We all have to sit for hours while you murder "Slow Boat to China" on those old scratch drums.'

'You mean you want to read it now? All right then.' Fred sat down again and waited patiently.

'Well, apparently Nubble's been looking forward to it.'

'Oh yes, Simcox! I've been looking forward to it immensely.'

'Don't let's disappoint Nubble,' Fred agreed.

' "*Told by an Idiot*",' Henry started again.

'Good title, that,' Arthur said eagerly. 'Isn't it, Simcox?'

'Chapter one,' Henry went on firmly. ' "You'll hardly believe this, Alan," said Lady Cynthia Plumley, wrinkling her small retroussé nose and raising her plucked eyebrows, "but I've never actually made love in a punt before." '

'That's good. The first sentence gets you,' Arthur Nubble told them. Henry had hit on a technique which he would discover was known in the film world as 'coming in on the middle of a scene'. He went on reading. ' "But then, thought Alan Podgson, neither have I." ' Henry was getting into his stride. ' "As the son of a brewery worker Alan had never been able to afford such luxuries. In a way he felt ashamed, he was betraying his class, and his mates at work, by falling so much in love with Lady Cynthia, the owner's daughter. He felt even more ashamed of his heavy boots and his baggy Aertex underpants." '

'Can you say "underpants" in a book?' Arthur wondered.

'Don't be ridiculous, Nubble. You can nowadays.' And Henry read on. ' "Alan started to make love in the expert way he had learnt with the girl workers in the bottling department. Cynthia felt small, delicate kisses land like butterflies on the backs of her knees, the inside of her elbows. Slowly and cunningly she was raised to a purring fever of excitement." '

A master in sports clothes pulled open the door and looked at them with disapproval. 'I thought you fellows were meant to be taking exercise.'

'We've taken it, Sir,' Arthur Nubble chirped up respectfully. 'Simcox was just reading us his history essay. It's jolly interesting.'

'Oh, is it?' The master put out his hand for the exercise book. 'Let's have a look.'

'Oh, you couldn't read it, Sir.' Arthur seemed to have taken charge of the situation.

'Why ever not?'

'Simcox has got such awful handwriting, he's going to copy it out neatly later.'

'Really?'

'It's terribly interesting, Sir. All about the relations between capital and labour in industrial England.'

'Not my subject, that. Hope you all show as much keenness on

44

your geography. All right, you fellows. Carry on with the prep.' The master loped away and was soon lost in the mists of autumn.

'You know what, Nubble?' Henry said. 'You're not quite so terribly unintelligent as you look.'

A week later disaster struck. Arthur Nubble came up to Fred during a break between Latin and yet more Latin. He was in a state of advanced panic and deathly pale, bearing ghastly news about a new chap called Strove.

'I know him,' Fred reassured him. 'He lives near us.'

'Well, I was talking to him and he said he had to go. He was late for his music lesson. Oh, Simcox Mi, what do you think he's learning?'

Fred didn't wait to be told. As of one mind the boys started running towards the music huts. As they did so Fred asked breathlessly, 'Nubble! What did you do with the actual instrument?'

He didn't have to wait long to find out. When they got to the prefabricated huts Nubble pointed to the dark space between the floor and the ground. There in the shadows, hidden from the world like some lurking jungle beast, lay the inert form of a huge double bass. And when they peered for a moment into the usually empty room they saw the music master with his back to them, seated at the piano. They watched with horror as Magnus Strove, a rather pretty, curly-haired boy with an astute financial sense, opened the tall, standing, double-bass container out of which poured, as from some mythical cornucopia, what appeared to be the entire tinned food department of Fortnum and Mason.

'Cheerio, Nubble!' Fred took to his heels then and didn't stop running until he had arrived, five minutes early, for the next Latin lesson.

'Nubble's going to be sacked,' Fred told Henry later in the dormitory. Arthur had been isolated in the sanatorium although suffering from no known disease.

'Has he been jumping rather too low in the leap-frog?' Henry used the usual Knuckleberries euphemism.

'Not that. Running a black-market food stall in the music huts.'

'Quite right then. You can't have spivs at Knuckleberries.'

'You're not serious?'

'Aren't I?'

'I mean, I thought you were all for the revolution, blowing up Knuckleberries or something.'

'Of course I am. But while it's *here*, well, it's far better to keep the spivs out of it.'

Only Fred paid a brief tribute to the departed. 'Poor old Nubble. I don't suppose we'll ever see him again.'

4

A Game of Murder

In the spring of the next year Simeon Simcox got a dose of flu and sat shivering by his study fire wearing a dressing-gown and a muffler, occasionally coughing as he read a large number of pamphlets on global concerns. Dr Salter was shown by Dorothy into his presence. Agnes Salter's father was a short, broad-shouldered man with close-cropped greying hair, strong hands and stubby fingers. Dressed in a check hacking-jacket and still wearing breeches after his morning ride, he looked more like a hard-bitten horse-dealer than Hartscombe's leading G.P.

'He gets this wretched chest,' Dorothy explained. 'And his voice is going.'

'Cut down on the sermons, I'm sure the congregation'll be delighted. And,' the Doctor asked, 'I don't suppose you've got a spot of brandy left over from Christmas?'

Dorothy looked at Simeon, who nodded his permission, and she went off to find it. When she had gone the Doctor pulled up an armchair, stretched his boots to the fire and lit a thin, aromatic cheroot which made Simeon cough. 'Well,' the Rector said plaintively, 'surely you'll take my temperature?'

'I doubt if that's going to do you much good.'

'Dorothy thought we should call you in.'

'Can't imagine why.' The Doctor blew out a perfect smoke-ring which floated up towards Karl Marx. 'Surely a man of your persuasion ought to be grateful for a touch of spring flu. Don't want to hang about in this vale of tears, do you? Fellows like you ought to get in the queue for heaven as quickly as possible. You want me to tinker with divine providence with a couple of aspirins and a bottle of cough mixture?'

'For a doctor you have a remarkably simple-minded view of the Christian religion.' Simeon couldn't see why he should be expected to die of flu just because he was a clergyman.

'Christian religion? I thought it was based on the extreme desirability of death.' Dr Salter leaned back comfortably in his chair. 'It's a lesson I wish my patients would all learn. Duty of the sick, in my opinion, to get out of the way and make room for a few healthy breeders. But you take the Bishop of Worsfield, never knew a fellow so remarkably coy about meeting his Maker!' Dorothy returned to them with a small liqueur glass about half full of brandy. 'Is the Bishop not well?' Simeon was concerned to know.

'That's amazingly generous of you, Dorothy.' Dr Salter took the brandy, squinted at it like someone assessing a microscopic specimen, and finished it at a gulp. 'The good Bishop has never been quite the same since you made him take part in an all-night vigil in his draughty great cathedral to protest about the South African Government.'

'You can't blame me for that.' Simeon was troubled. As though to cheer him up Dr Salter slapped his jacket pockets, produced a pad and pencil and started to scribble a prescription.

'Of course it was remarkably effective! Soon as the dear old Boers heard that you and the Bishop had gone without a night's sleep they decided to elect a Blackamoor as prime minister. Or isn't that what happened?' The Doctor laughed, a short splutter of rapid gun-fire, and handed the prescription to Dorothy. 'Get that made up for him in Hartscombe if you like,' he said. 'It can't do him any particular harm.'

Dorothy, taking it, smiled unexpectedly. 'We've missed you lately,' she said.

'Simeon doesn't have to get sick for me to visit. In fact I avoid ill people as much as possible.'

'One of the great mysteries of life,' Simeon brooded with his head down, 'is why you ever chose to become a doctor.'

'Why did you choose to become a parson? Only one reason. Neither of us could hold down a decent job in a biscuit factory.'

Since his wife had died Agnes's father often took her on his rounds with him during her school holidays. In fact she was outside the Rectory now, sitting in the passenger seat of the Doctor's beautifully polished old Alvis coupé. And from nowhere in particular Fred emerged and stood by the car, scuffling his shoe in the gravel of the drive. He started, tentatively at first, to engage her in conversation, while indoors his mother was confiding her anxieties to Agnes's father. 'I'm worried about Simeon,' she told him. 'He gets so tired, and all these little colds of his. Is there nothing you recommend?'

'Take up hunting.' At which Simeon, a paid-up member of any society against blood sports, was seen to shiver in his chair and murmur, 'Hardly!'

'Not for killing foxes. That's not the point,' the Doctor explained. 'They do you a wonderful death on the hunting-field! One minute you're up there, sun in your face, fresh air in your nostrils, giving a brush hedge a clean pair of heels, and then you'll come smack on the hard ground – break your neck and it's over in a second! To hell with bed-pans and the cottage hospital. I plan to finish up on a long run round Picton Principal.'

There was a silence then. Dorothy wandered to the window. 'Your Agnes home from school, is she? Do let her come in.'

'No. I don't think so. She's like her father. Can't stand the sight of illness.'

But as she sat in the Alvis, Agnes was telling Fred that it was a shame and that she'd like to go in and look after the old people. In fact she wanted to be a nurse but her father wouldn't allow it. 'He says wanting to be a nurse just shows an unhealthy interest in disease. Fathers!'

'Yes. I know.' There was a long silence between them and then Fred went on, 'What're you doing for the holidays?'

'Sitting out in the car. I told you.'

'I thought of going on the river.'

'In a rowing-boat?'

'Yes. A boat on the river.'

Agnes shivered at the idea of the river in March. 'Have you got any better at guiding it?'

'I've always been rather good at navigation.' Fred was nettled.

'I don't know. Just as long as you don't get us suddenly out in the middle of the river and then want to *go* urgently.'

'Oh.' Fred sounded disappointed. 'You remember that.'

'Did you think I wouldn't?'

There was another prolonged silence, and then he asked, 'Are you going to Charlie Fanner's party, at Rapstone Manor?'

'Everyone's going to Charlie Fanner's. They've asked *everybody*,' Agnes said. 'They like doing that, don't they? Inviting the tenants.'

'I know,' Fred agreed. 'It's a sort of national event! They've even asked Leslie Titmuss.'

Rapstone Manor is an old house on a hill a little way out of the village and has been, since Edward IV rewarded a steward with a sense of humour with the gift of a manor and the estates of Rapstone, the home of the Fanner family. The house was begun in the middle ages, added to under the Tudors and extended at the Restoration, when the Fanners received their reward for continued loyalty to the Royalist cause. An eighteenth-century Fanner built a new façade and added a folly in the shape of a Gothic tower in the park, and a Victorian Fanner put on the ostentatious portico which gives the house the disconsolate air of a small city railway station set down in the middle of the countryside, with no trains. It's a house shaded by large trees, approached up a long drive, set in a park where the deer are constantly on the look-out for ways of escape from death at the hands of Tom Nowt.

The countryside was much divided during the Civil War. The Fanners at Rapstone were Royalists, the Stroves of Picton Principal, which then incorporated the entire village of Skurfield, supported Parliament. The Fanners were known as good landlords, usually cheerful and, perhaps because of their origins in the medieval catering business, fond of feasting the tenants on all occasions. The Stroves of Picton House were private people, often of a gloomy and withdrawn disposition, and much given to hanging their tenants from the boughs of the old yew tree by Skurfield Pond. When the young heir, Nicholas Fanner, was celebrating his twenty-first birthday at Rapstone in the usual manner with ox-roasting, bonfires, Morris dancing and a quite exceptional amount of feasting, the then Doughty Strove sent a number of Skurfield villagers to the party secretly carrying crowbars and reaping-hooks. These invaders fell upon the Rapstone tenants, Doughty rode in with a troop of Parliament men and Rapstone Manor was captured for the Puritan cause. Young Sir Nicholas was arrested, certain women of the household were raped, the barns burned and crops commandeered. During the Protectorate Rapstone Manor suffered a further series of violations.

At the Restoration the Stroves were deprived of much of their land, including the village of Skurfield itself, which was added to the Rapstone estate. These events naturally encouraged the gloomy and solitary nature of the Stroves. They became addicted to such private pursuits as spiritualism, social credit and studying the dimensions of the Great Pyramid. The lands they were left with deteriorated. They took to financing impractical schemes for re-claiming parts of Central Australia, or building garden suburbs in Matabeleland. Magnus Strove (died 1917) improved matters a good deal by buying up slum property in Worsfield at a time when the biscuit factories were expanding and inadequate housing was needed there for cheap labour. However, his son Doughty lacked his father's remorseless energy and spent a great deal of time sunk in gloom, when he was not trying to convert his long-isolated valley to growing sunflower seeds for cosmetics or prospecting, without any particular optimism, for various mineral deposits. Doughty's son, Magnus, however, had more of his grandfather's business sense. In his first year at Knuckleberries he cornered the market in horror comics, which he sold at a wide profit-margin, and started an insurance scheme for those likely to be beaten. He had considerable charm and a quick head for figures.

Although rewarded on the restoration of the monarchy, the Fanners, like their neighbours, the Stroves, declined at the end of the eighteenth century. A succession of Sir Nicholas Fanners, although continuing to feast the tenantry, spent most of their nights at the gaming-tables and one Sir Nicholas contrived to lose the villages of Cragmire and Hulton Bathsheba by a single throw at hazard. During his time a wing fell into ruin, the grape house collapsed, dry rot overtook the folly and the squire spent his days, when he could no longer show his face at Boodles, laying wagers with his butler, Garthwaite, about the number of flies which might be caught in the spiders' webs which festooned the dining-room ceiling. (The family fortunes having been founded on a friendship between a royal person and his steward, the Fanners were always most at their ease in the master–servant relationship, particularly now they had become masters.) On his death it was discovered that Garthwaite was owed £1,000 from gambling on spiders, a debt of honour which the next Sir Nicholas paid honourably, enabling the servant to open the grocery and provision shop in Hartscombe (Garthwaites) which survived for many years. In the latter half of the nineteenth century the Fanners sobered up considerably, went into politics and became fairly undistinguished parliamentary secretaries and junior ministers in a number of unmemorable Conservative administrations. They remained popular landlords and great organizers of garden fêtes, firework displays and children's parties. The ruined part of the house was pulled down and tidied up, the greenhouses let out to a market gardener and Rentokil has done its best with the folly.

The presiding Sir Nicholas Fanner, at the time of this eventful birthday party, had just turned fifty. He was a tall, comfortable and amiable man who believed in buying his trousers large and loose enough to admit of their being hoisted on with the braces fixed ready and without the necessity of undoing any of the buttons. He was A.D.C. to a general who translated Horace during the war, and then became Chairman of the local Conservative Party (where he was criticized for a lack of determined hostility to the Attlee Government), and President of the All England Begonia Society. It had come as a surprise to many people, including Nicholas, when he married Grace Oliver. Everyone knew Grace; she was at every party, race-meeting and country-house weekend, although her father Tommy Oliver had decamped and left her mother in a state of penurious confusion. Grace borrowed clothes from her friends, did a succession of odd-jobs 'helping-out' interior decorators, charity organizers and Great Hostesses. She was known to be beautiful and thought to be impossible, but she was an asset at a party. Her tireless activity was felt to be in search of a great and glittering marriage and her final acceptance of the dullish Nicholas Fanner was widely held to be something of a defeat.

Charlotte (Charlie) Fanner was their only child. On her eighth birthday she was a puddingy girl who lacked her mother's startling good looks and Nicholas's comfortable ease of manner. A throwback through history, he thought, who looked most like that Charles Fanner who earned the friendship of Edward IV, she had the same pale face, colourless hair and small eyes, but she was without the jokes which had endeared his old servant to the King.

Late in the afternoon of Charlie's party, Grace, wrapped in a silk kimono and not yet fully made-up, looked out of her bedroom window and saw Leslie Titmuss, stiffly dressed in his best Sunday shorts and jacket, belted mac and Hartscombe Grammar cap, being regarded dubiously by Wyebrow, the Fanners' manservant, a lugubrious fellow who had been Nicholas's batman during the recent war.

When Leslie had been admitted, after some hesitation on the part of Wyebrow, Grace turned discontentedly into her bedroom, which contained a curtained four-poster, many photographs of minor royal persons and of Grace when young and beautiful taken by Cecil Beaton, drawings of her by Cocteau and Augustus John and, less pleasing to her at that moment, her husband Nicholas standing, almost apologetically, in his loose-fitting suit in the centre of a faded, rose-coloured carpet.

'Please come down. Charlie wouldn't like you to miss her party.'

'I look terrible.' Grace flinched at her reflection in the mirror.

'To me you look beautiful.'

'You always *say* that. You'll say it when I'm old and covered with tramlines and my teeth have fallen out.' Grace was displeased by the compliment.

'Charlie would hate it, if you missed her party.'

'It doesn't mean anything to you, telling me I look beautiful. It's something to say, like "How're the crops?" or "Good planting weather." I can't face all those people.'

'They're only children.'

Grace moved away from the mirror and faced her husband with contempt. 'Charlie's party! Our great social event.'

'We've got all the children from the cottages. Rapstone *and* Skurfield.'

'How terrifically exciting! What do you want me to do? Slip into an evening-dress so you and I can play sardines? Look at me. I'll scream if you tell me I'm beautiful!'

53

'Charlie's all tricked out.' Nicholas's words came tiptoeing carefully out, as though crossing a minefield. 'In her party dress and so on.'

'I hope you didn't tell *her* she looked beautiful.' Grace moved to the bed and flopped down on it, her long, chalk-white legs protruding extensively from her kimono. 'It was never so boring during the war. At least there were the Americans. And we even got the odd bomb that missed Worsfield.'

'I'm sorry . . .' Her husband moved to the door.

'What're you sorry about now?'

'I'm sorry we couldn't keep the war going to entertain you a little longer,' Nicholas found the courage to say, before he left her.

'Go on, Miss Charlie. Your mother told you. You're to make an entrance.' Charlotte Fanner, miserably shy and lumpy in her party dress, which stuck out round her like bright orange chicken-wire, was being pushed from the darkness of the bedroom corridor to the top of the stairs by Bridget Bigwell, a small, agitated woman, who had been in service at the Manor for thirty-five of her fifty years.

'Mummy's not here.' Charlie peered down the staircase in the way that someone contemplating a suicidal leap off the top of a building might look from the dark height to the brightly lit and crowded street below. In fact the hall was full of milling children and from under the big chandelier her father called up, a blood-chilling cry of 'Pray silence, everyone, for the birthday Queen!'

With tears blurring her vision Charlie stumbled down to the crowd as they sang 'Happy Birthday' in what seemed to her a tone of menace. She knew hardly any of the children from the cottages and she liked none of the girls from the convent school in Harts-combe where she went daily. She particularly dreaded an encounter with Magnus Strove, who called her 'Apple Charlotte' and pulled her hair. She decided to pretend that it wasn't her at all, that she was still safely up in her bedroom and it was all happening to someone else, someone she didn't like, perhaps to a girl at school called Rachel Bosey whom she hated and had never spoken to at all. 'Happy birthday, dear Rachel' – she clenched her fists and sang savagely to herself – 'happy birthday to you!'

In this state of non-participation Charlotte was swept into the sitting-room and thrust into a game of musical chairs. Wyebrow was operating the wind-up gramophone, playing the family's old records, including the version of 'You're the top!' made specially for her mother (including the lines 'You're the top! You can trump the A – ace, You're the top! You're the Lady Gra – ace'). One by one the children dropped out and sat stuffing themselves with such cakes as sugar rationing would allow. At the end Charlie found herself lolloping round a single remaining chair with a flushed and bright-eyed Leslie Titmuss, who seemed to scent victory. However Wyebrow, with a rare loyalty to the family, stopped the record when Charlie's bottom was hovering nearest and Leslie departed sniffing with disappointment.

'What on earth's the matter with you?' said Henry, who met him on his way out of the room. 'You didn't ever think you were meant to win, did you?' To the company in general he said, 'Come on. We're going to play a decent game of murder.' So, taking instructions from Henry, the children found an old opera hat, property of Nicholas, and drew from it many folded-up bits of paper. 'There's one for the detective,' Henry told them, 'and one for the murderer. All the others are blank, get it?' When Fred opened his message it told him that he was the detective.

Simeon Simcox arrived rather too early to collect the boys, stood by the front door and waited for Wyebrow to open it. He heard the sounds of laughter and stooped to peer through the letter-box. When he had done so he saw the lit hall and a crowd of children picking bits of paper out of a hat. He thought of a way of amusing them and of a dramatic entrance. Accordingly he went down on his hands and knees on the doormat and, swinging one arm as a trunk in front of him and the other as a tail behind, was ready for the front door to open. When at last it did so he entered Rapstone Manor on his knees, trumpeting like an elephant, but the children had vanished in search of a murder and he found himself looking up at the startled faces of Wyebrow, Nicholas and Dr Salter, who had also arrived early, apparently to collect his child. Slowly, and in the circumstances with some dignity, the Rector rose to his feet. This, also, was an incident which would be remembered.

Fred had wandered upstairs and was walking along a corridor, not at all clear what his duties were in detecting a murder which hadn't yet happened. He found the door of a chilly spare bedroom a little open and, looking in, saw Agnes hiding from the party, lying on the quilt reading a pile of old *Vogues* and *Tatlers* which were kept on the bedside table. She didn't look up as he plonked himself on the bed beside her. He thought that she looked pretty in her party dress and she smelt of Wright's coal-tar soap and, more faintly, of strawberries.

'You know who that is?' Agnes showed him the photograph of a beautiful fair-haired young woman enjoying a joke at a party in the Casino at Cannes.

'She's wearing pyjamas.' Fred observed the picture closely.

'Of course.'

'Pyjamas in public!'

'Poor Charlie.'

'Why?'

'To have a mother who was once so beautiful. For heaven's sake, Fred, what on earth are you doing?'

For Fred had suddenly noticed Agnes's sprawling legs and the slender white backs of her knees. Some memory of Henry's book stung him and he leant down and started to plant what he hoped were small, delicate kisses on that part of her body.

'Butterfly kisses,' Fred explained. 'Don't they rouse you to a purring pitch of passion at all?'

'It feels like having insects crawling all over you!'

Leslie Titmuss, whose paper had been blank, was walking down a dark, ill-decorated passage that led from the hall to the kitchens at the back of the Manor. Since being pipped in the finals of musical chairs he hadn't enjoyed the party. Among the crowd he was as lonely as Charlie, his hostess, but they hadn't spoken to each other. He had no clear idea of how this game of murder would turn out but he suspected it would be alarming and that he would be made to look foolish in front of the other children. As he walked he heard footsteps on the stone flags behind him. Leslie didn't turn his head but pulled open the first door he came to and went in.

He found himself in a big, untidy cloakroom, littered with gumboots, shooting-sticks, raincoats, fishing-rods and a shepherd's crook. There was a lavatory in a corner, beside which was a yellowing pile of *Country Lifes*. Leslie sat disconsolately on the large mahogany seat, merely for a place of rest, and looked fearfully about him.

Upstairs Bridget Bigwell walked along the corridor to turn down beds. She was opening the door of Grace's bedroom when Henry, having found the main switch somewhere outside Wyebrow's pantry, pulled it down and extinguished the lights. Bridget stepped into darkness and a mouthful of abuse from her Ladyship for what might, if the room had been illuminated, have been an even more unwelcome interruption.

Sitting on the loo seat Leslie was expecting something horrible to happen. When the lights went out he didn't scream. He sat on breathless, motionless, listening, but he heard nothing until a pair of young hands came out of the darkness and fastened round his neck. Then he screamed fit to blow the roof off, giving out huge echoing yells, remarkable for a boy of his size, with which he further terrified himself.

It couldn't have been very long before the lights came on again. Children came out of doors and clattered downstairs. Wyebrow, Bridget and Nicholas all made for the downstairs passage. When they reached it Dr Salter was already there, as was the Rector. The Doctor opened the door and they found Leslie Titmuss alone, lying huddled on the floor, still screaming.

'Cheer up, young fellow! You're not dead yet,' the Doctor told him. Behind him the children were gathering, looking down with interest at the small, yelling victim on the floor, but it was Simeon who knelt by the boy and put his arms about him and comforted him until the screaming turned to a low sobbing and then died away.

★ 5 ★

The Will

Not long after Charlie's party a tall, doleful-looking man came to call on Simeon at the Rectory. 'Ah, Titmuss.' Simeon rose from behind his desk where he had been drafting a letter of protest to the Bishop on the Church's complacency about sub-standard housing in Worsfield. 'This won't take long, it's about my boy.' Mr Titmuss didn't sit. He was a man who had spent twenty years as a clerk in the Simcox Brewery in Hartscombe and he regarded the Rector, in spite of everything, as part of the management.

'Young Leslie.' Simeon fumbled for a pipe. 'Extremely helpful lad. He lends a hand with our nettles here occasionally.'

'Not any more,' said Mr Titmuss. 'I'm afraid all that must be put an end to. It won't suit, you see.' He spoke in a deliberate and extremely boring voice, which caused his utterances to be dreaded at the meetings of the Parish Council. He was, undoubtedly, a direct descendant of one of those dedicated Skurfield Puritans who attacked Rapstone Manor with crowbars and reaping-hooks during the Civil War.

'It won't suit?' Simeon frowned. 'I'm sorry. I don't understand.'

'I suppose you know what tricks your family has been playing?'

'Tricks?'

'Your boy playing games. Near scared my lad to death. We've had to have Dr Salter to him.'

'Oh, yes. I was there. I'm sorry.'

'It's his mixing with people as he didn't ought to mix with.'

'Surely not?'

'Coming up here puts thoughts in the boy's head which is more than he can contend with.'

The Will

'Leslie's not in any sort of trouble, surely?' The Rector frowned anxiously.

'Not if he keeps to himself. But it's all this play-acting and helping with the nettles, and listening to books being written and stupid games at the Manor. That's not going to be any help to my boy. You ought to know that.'

'Surely you'd like him to widen his horizons?'

'I would not.' Mr Titmuss was quite firm about that.

'No?'

'I would like him to stay at home in Skurfield when he's back from school and mind his own business. Minding your own business is what I set great store by, Rector, as I'm continually trying to point out in Parish Council meetings. Them as chooses to live in South Africa can take care of themselves.'

'Well. Perhaps not entirely . . .'

But Mr Titmuss was looking at the florid lady-bather, the present from Cleethorpes, beside Karl Marx on the Rector's mantelpiece. 'You had that ornament long, have you?' he asked deliberately.

'Not . . . not very long. No.' Simeon hesitated and no doubt sounded guilty.

'May I ask you a personal question, Rector?' Mr Titmuss said, after a long pause.

'Please. Please do.'

'Have you ever, in actual fact, *been* to Cleethorpes?'

'Now you mention it, I can't say I have.' The Rector was doing his best to sound casual.

'Well, I have visited that resort. And I bought a memento, a keepsake to mark the occasion. It was very like this lady-bather here. Unfortunately it has gone missing.'

'I'm sorry to hear that, of course.'

Mr Titmuss took the statuette in his hand and stood looking at it with deep suspicion. 'Rector,' he said, 'can I ask you to explain the presence of this ornament on your mantelpiece?'

At this point Simeon became entirely vague. 'No, I don't think I should. That is to say . . . I don't think I can at all. It's a matter of confidence,' he said, and felt that he had explained nothing.

'Then you would have no objection to my removing this from

59

your possession?' Mr Titmuss, without waiting for further permission, put the statuette into his pocket.

'No objection in the world.' Simeon laughed a little. 'In fact its removal might come as a considerable relief to my wife.'

'Would it indeed?'

'Oh yes. I dare say it would.'

'Then I'll say goodbye to you, Rector. From now on it will be formal communication only on the business of our joint Parish Council.' He went to the door. 'Fine words on the subject of Socialism may come to you very easy, but they hardly excuse the acquisition of the other person's little ornaments.'

Simeon was left looking at the closed door in surprise and bewilderment.

After his father's funeral Fred returned to the practice he carried on in the old house in Hartscombe, which had once belonged to Dr Salter. It was a busy time, for which he was grateful, and he avoided thoughts of the past, failing to return a number of calls he had from Jackson Cantellow, the family solicitor. Driven to desperation by this conduct Cantellow called at the surgery, where Miss Margaret Thorne, Fred's strict, grey-haired receptionist, made him sit for while in a row of sick people, reading back numbers of *Punch* and *Good Housekeeping* or staring into space. 'I'm not ill,' he protested, 'it's a matter of urgent business!', when a staggering four-year-old offered to show him her colouring book. At last Miss Thorne relented and said, 'Doctor will see you now, Mr Cantellow.'

'I've got to talk to one of you, and I can't get a word of sense out of your mother.' Fred looked up at the red face hovering over him above a purple bow-tie and wondered if he should suggest taking the patient's blood pressure. 'A word of sense about what?'

'The position! You realize of course why the Rector could afford to be so independent, why he could cock so many fine liberal snooks at the Bishop and Synod and the Parish Council? The stipend at the Rectory could hardly have kept him in pipe tobacco or bought your mother's little pieces of china. It was his shares in Simcox Ales, that's what Dorothy might have expected to depend on.'

'*Might* have?'

'I've been trying to explain it to her. Of course it pains your mother to talk about money and you can live a pure and unselfish existence writing out chitties for days off work and tending to the slightest whims of your National Health patients.' Jackson Cantellow, a pillar of the Worsfield Choral Society, was accustomed to give way to such arias. 'Oh, it's all very fine and elevated, no doubt, to be perfectly uninterested in money when you've got plenty of it. But you haven't now, Dr Frederick. Your family hasn't.'

'I never expected any.'

'Never?'

'I supposed Simeon would leave it all to Mother.'

'Well, let me tell you what's happened.' Cantellow sat down and went on with the relish of a man who has bad news to impart. 'For years I'd been urging your father to make a will, but he never gave me instructions. Now I hear from a little firm in Worsfield who do police court business, that sort of thing, and it seems . . .' Jackson Cantellow looked deeply shocked. 'It seems that your father went to them entirely without my knowledge and made a will, quite recently. He left none of the Brewery shares, which must be worth about two million nicker, if I know anything about it, to your mother, or to you, or to your brother, Henry.'

'Well, who did he leave them to?' Fred was growing bored, as he sometimes did with a long list of patients' aches and pains.

'He left the whole bloody shooting-match' – Jackson Cantellow came to the point at last – 'to the Right Honourable Leslie Titmuss, M.P., absolutely and forever.'

On the day after this meeting Henry and his second wife, Lonnie, drove down to the Rectory and saw Fred and Dorothy in what the older brother called a 'Council of War'. 'Of course we're going to fight it!' Henry said, pacing the study in considerable anger.

'I don't see why "of course".'

'Oh no, Fred. You wouldn't. You never fought anything. You never even cared about winning when we played games.'

'I always thought that life was rather too short to care about losing to you at ping-pong.'

'Then you'll be a great help in defeating the abominable Titmuss!'

'Such an unattractive child,' Dorothy remembered. 'I always thought that must have been very hard for him to bear. As a boy he always smelled, as I remember it, of lead pencils. I pitied him for it.'

'Well, no need to pity him any longer,' Lonnie said. 'He's got all our money.'

'*Mother's* money,' Fred corrected her, and Henry gave him an unfriendly look. 'Such an extraordinary thing for your father to do!' Lonnie went on undeterred. 'Do you think he meant it as some sort of joke?'

'Did he mean many things as a joke?' Dorothy asked.

'Perhaps only his profession.' Fred smiled, but Henry looked extremely serious. 'Our father, perhaps you need reminding, was a priest of the Church of England.'

'Exactly.'

'I don't know. He never told me he thought being a parson was funny. He never said it in so many words.' Dorothy started to collect their teacups.

'Well, I'm going to fight it if nobody else is,' Henry told them. 'Quite clearly our father was out of his head.'

'He was a saint,' Fred reminded him.

'What?'

'You heard what Kev the Rev. said at the funeral. We have lived in the presence of a saint.'

'Or a complete raving lunatic?' Henry asked, and answered, 'That's what we're going to have to prove.'

After Henry and Lonnie had gone back to London, Fred left his mother and drove into Hartscombe. He saw the sights of his childhood, the bridge and the broad river made for pleasure, the moored punts and canoes and white launches, the willows and pubs by the water. He passed the long, red-brick brewery buildings and the sign of 'Simcox Ales'. He came to the rather shabby Victorian house where he lived and worked and parked his car in the space marked 'Doctor'.

The working day was over. He looked in on Miss Thorne, who was putting away the patients' cards, and went up to the top floor.

His room was untidy, it was a bachelor's living-room with piles of books, records and his old drum set. He found a 78, wiped the dust off it and put it on the record-player. Then he gathered up the plate and cup and saucer which he had used at breakfast and carried them out to the kitchen as Benny Goodman started to play 'Slow Boat to China'. He sat at the drums and began to accompany the record, singing softly also,

> 'Get you and keep you
> In my arms evermore,
> Leave all your lovers
> Weeping on the faraway shore.
> Out on the briny,
> With a moon big and shiny,
> Melting your heart of stone,
> I'd love to get you
> On a slow boat to China,
> All to myself alone . . .'

As he played the years vanished. He thought of nothing very much, except, for some reason, the sound of wire-brushes on an upturned chamber-pot, and wondered, not for the first time, why their father had sent them so far away from home.

Part Two

Let's be frank about it. Most of our people have never had it so good. Go round the country, go to the industrial towns, go to the farms, and you will see a state of prosperity such as we have never had in my lifetime – nor indeed ever in the history of this country.

Harold Macmillan
Bedford, July 1957

★ 6 ★
The Deserter

Fred had seen them again on a yellowing newspaper photograph he found in an old tea-chest of Simeon's belongings which he was going through after his father's death. There was the Rector marching along as proud as a field marshal, swinging the stick he took out on country walks and smiling for the camera beneath a huge black banner which proclaimed 'March from Aldermaston, Easter 1958'. Beside him was Ben Leverett, once the Labour M.P. for Hartscombe, and his wife, Joanie. Behind them young men and women marched with the seriousness and dedication of soldiers in a war they had missed. Many of them held up circular C.N.D. signs or slogans such as 'Ban the Bomb or the Human Race'. Behind the leaders the trailing procession included men with caps and macs, for it was a miserably wet Easter, playing trumpets, trombones and penny whistles. And among them Fred saw, looking absurdly young, the faces of himself and Henry. His elder brother was frowning, clearly taking the matter extremely seriously. It seemed as though Fred had made a joke and Henry hadn't laughed.

'Peaceful demonstrations!' Henry said that Easter as they trudged out of London. 'I mean, what peaceful demonstration ever altered the course of history? Do you honestly imagine that the October Revolution could have been brought about by a few people tootling on penny whistles and a couple of vicar's sons carrying sandwiches?'

'There are more people here today.' They had started off as a few hundred from Trafalgar Square and had lunch by the Albert Memorial. Even then a number of their better-dressed supporters had defected at Turnham Green and taken the tube home. As they marched along the Great West Road there was a flurry of snow and somewhere a man had run out of his house to tell them that Cambridge had won the Boat Race. Somewhere a woman advised them to get back to Moscow, but there were new recruits, men carrying rolls of blankets and sleeping-bags for the nights they were to spend in churches or village halls, and mothers pushing prams. In one section the marchers played and sang protest songs, they were those whom critics of the enterprise would call the 'beards and weirds'. It was the first of such expeditions, the small start of a period which would be marked by an uncontrollable escalation in bombs and demonstrations.

'Do you really think,' Henry asked, 'that Marie Antoinette would have gone scooting out of Versailles at the approach of a few students strumming guitars and a couple of overweight M.P.s? The idea's ridiculous.'

'Why are you here then?'

'Well, I think, in my position, I should stand up and be counted,' Henry said in all modesty.

'I'll count you then.' Fred looked at his brother and said, after some calculation, 'One!'

'Oh, really! At times you are excessively childish.'

But they were children no more. Fred was then twenty-three and had done his National Service, unheroically in the Pay Corps. He was still at Cambridge, Simeon's old university, where he found himself reading politics and economics with a growing lack of interest. Henry was twenty-six, his National Service had taken him to Malaya, so he had a travelled and somewhat world-weary air. He read English at King's, joined the university Labour Party, had three of his plays acted by undergraduates, engaged in several notable love-affairs and was the subject of a profile in *Granta*. When he came down he got a job in a publishing firm where he wrote scathing reports on the novels of middle-aged and established authors.

> 'Will you see your children die?
> Men and women, stand together,
> Do not heed the Men of War!
> Make your mind up – now or never,
> Ban the bomb for ever more ...'

The song, taken up and then let go around them, drifted away over the wet hedgerows and soggy fields. Some sang full-throatedly, and quickly gave up with the effort of marching; others, adopting the more professional nasal whine of the transatlantic protest singer, kept it up longer. The children joined in, guessing at the words or breaking into giggles when a group of adults changed it to 'Ban the bum'.

'What *is* your position, anyway?' Fred asked.

'Well, with the book just coming out,' Henry explained patiently, 'it's obvious that an artist should take a stand.'

Henry's first novel, *The Greasy Pole*, had just been accepted for publication by a rival and more go-ahead firm than his own and he was nervously awaiting disaster or life-long fame. In fact the book was to get some good notices and moderate sales. Although *The Greasy Pole* might have appeared as the latest word in the new style of comic, social and sexual realism introduced some years earlier, it was about the tenth re-write of the work which Henry read to Fred and Arthur Nubble by the playing-fields at Knuckleberries.

'Which artist?' Fred asked, a question so foolish that Henry did not bother to answer it. By the time they had stopped for lunch Fred had decided that, although he was prepared to take all reasonable steps to save mankind from self-immolation, sleeping with his brother on the floor of a church again was an act over and above the call of duty. A plan began to form itself in his mind, but he knew himself well enough to doubt whether he would ever have the courage to put it into operation. They sat outside a pub. Ben Leverett, who made a good thing out of journalism and liked more than an occasional glass of champagne, a tipple which it was his avowed intention to spread evenly among the labouring classes, was panting and wiping his forehead with a red-and-white spotted handkerchief. His wife, Joanie, made of sterner stuff, was still singing, 'Ban, ban, *ban* the bloody H Bomb!' to the tune of 'John Brown's Body' with a group of Worsfield women. Simeon reacted with smiling detachment to a request for prayer from a group of Christian Pacifists. It was when he said, 'I think at the moment I'd rather have a pint of wallop,' and, 'Today we're praying with our feet,' that Fred felt driven to go into the saloon bar and make a telephone call. His hands were hot and smelled of the pennies he had been clutching; he waited as the number rang and had almost decided to go back to the marchers when the ringing stopped and he heard a voice say, 'Yes? Who is it?' As usual she sounded desperate, as though the house had caught fire and she was trapped at the head of a blazing staircase with no possibility of escape.

'Agnes!' He had pressed Button A and now he was committed to at least try for an adventure.

'Where on earth are you?' She asked the question as though she felt no real need to know the answer.

'By a road somewhere. I'm doing something with my father,' he insisted on telling her, 'but I might be able to get away this evening. I mean, would you like to do something? Or something,' he ended lamely.

'I wanted to go to Worsfield tonight.' Agnes was standing in the hall of the Doctor's house in Hartscombe. Down the passage the living-room door was open and she spoke quietly, not wishing to be overheard. 'To go dancing,' she told Fred. 'Is that an extraordinary thing to want to do?'

'I don't suppose so. Where?'

'There's an absolutely horrible club where they have the most repulsive food. I thought that might be a good place to go.'

'Oh. All right then.' It had to be better than the night with Henry in the church and he now felt that if he didn't take her out he would be a failure in Agnes's eyes for ever.

'I can get over in my father's car, but not if you don't want to. How will you get over?'

'Oh, I'll hitch a lift or something. What's it called?'

'What's what called?'

'The awful place.'

'Oh. The Barrel of Biscuits, isn't it ghastly? It's in West Street, so far as I can remember. But honestly don't bother.'

'Yes. I want to. You know I want to. About eight o'clock?'

'Just don't expect anything much.' When Agnes put the telephone down she walked along the passage, past the half-open sitting-room door. She didn't go in as her father was there with a lady. She was Mrs Dorothy Simcox, Fred's mother, for whom he was pouring a second glass of lunchtime sherry.

'Guilt,' Dr Salter was saying, as he often did, 'is a most malignant disease.'

Fred wasn't discouraged by Agnes's description. That afternoon he told Henry he was going to march with the musicians; he was doing so, he hinted, out of professional interest. So he fell behind his father and his brother, and when the guitar players passed him he loitered behind them also. When the whole procession had vanished up the road he thumbed a lift from a passing lorry.

Worsfield, home of the biscuit and an ailing furniture industry, is a place which seems like a grim northern town set down unexpectedly in a south-west riverside landscape. Its cathedral is a barrack-like red-brick 1930s building, its university a series of concrete blocks specializing in engineering and its streets glum and ill-favoured. Fred arrived there about two hours early for his meeting with Agnes. He went into the Railway Hotel lavatory and washed with liquid soap and wondered if he needed a shave. As he saw no way of getting one he brushed his clothes, cleaned his shoes on the machine provided and checked, without any particular optimism, the continued presence of a single french letter in the corner of his wallet. When he thought about it sanely he couldn't imagine that Agnes who, although beautiful, had not a good word to say for all the other pleasures in life, would have much time for sex.

He had no difficulty in finding the Barrel of Biscuits, a converted warehouse in West Street, and no difficulty at all in becoming a life member. As he sat at the bar and waited, drinking slowly to preserve his money, Fred began to tell himself that Agnes wouldn't have wanted to meet him unless ... Well, after all, it had been entirely her suggestion. He'd been dragged away from a most important protest march at her insistence and what else could that mean? When he got out a pound note to pay the barman he felt the circular ridge in the inner pocket of his wallet and thought it might come in useful after a long period of inactivity. And then she was half an hour late and he decided she wasn't coming at all. Well, perhaps it was all for the best. He looked towards the dance floor, at the girls in huge circular skirts, rustling petticoats and ankle socks. They seemed to be totally unaware, he thought, of the coming destruction of mankind.

71

'Aren't you hungry?' He looked round and Agnes was there. She'd changed into a tight-fitting skirt and wore a cardigan improbably buttoned down the back. 'I've kept you waiting.' She sat on a stool at the bar beside him and picked up a menu. She lowered her head and he saw her thin neck and the ridge of her backbone vanishing under the cardigan buttons.

'I didn't mind.' A group of boys in drainpipes and duck's-arse hair-do's, laughing and punching each other's arms, invaded the dance floor. A waitress who looked about fifteen appeared to take their food orders. 'Curry and chips,' Agnes told her. 'And draught bitter. A pint.'

'Yes. All right.' Fred had no other ideas.

'Curry and chips twice. And two pints of Simcox.'

'Is that the best?' Fred asked when the waitress had left them.

'The worst.' Agnes sounded pleased. 'The curry smells of the monkey house.'

'Why do you like that so?' he was bold enough to ask.

'Like what?'

'Things that are really ghastly.' He felt angered by her expression of sad superiority. She looked as though she had been through experiences she was afraid he would never live up to and didn't deserve to share. However she smiled now, almost timidly, and seemed to take him into her confidence.

'I don't know,' she said. 'My mother liked everything nice.'

'You never talk about her.'

'Oh, she was a great beauty. Anyway, you know she snuffed it. When I was ten.' Fred had heard the story from his parents. The beautiful Mrs Salter saved up her coupons and went up to London to buy a dress in the sales and a stray buzz bomb caught her. It was a chance in a million of course but there were people in Hartscombe who still felt it showed a sad streak of flippancy to die for a new frock in Oxford Street.

'Your father had to bring you up?'

'We brought up each other.' The curry came and Agnes pursued it gently round her plate with the back of the fork. 'It was a shock for him.'

'Is that why he doesn't seem ... well ...'

'Well, what?' She took a few mouthfuls and then pushed the plate away with a look of gratified disgust. Fred was eating almost with pleasure. 'Why he doesn't always seem tremendously keen on curing people like my father.'

'That's what he *says*.'

'Doesn't he mean it?'

'Does *your* father mean what he says?'

'Yes. Yes, I quite honestly think so.'

'A new heaven and a new earth? My father says that's what yours is always talking about.'

'He wants things to be better, yes. Not like before the war. Not with unemployment and dole queues and hard-faced business men in charge of everything. Nothing particularly wrong with that, is there?'

She didn't answer, indeed she appeared to have lost all interest, not only in the conversation, but in him. He stumbled on, not caring if he was boring her. 'You don't want an H bomb dropping on Worsfield, do you?'

'Worsfield?' Agnes seemed to be thinking it over. 'Well. Perhaps now if you'd said Hartscombe or Rapstone Fanner ... Anyway, what's he doing to stop it? What *can* he do?'

'He's marching. At least he believes in it enough to march.'

'Shouldn't we dance to the rotten music?' As Agnes said it he thought she was giving him a last chance to stop being a bore. They finished their beer and as he followed her towards the spot-lit floor he thought he was going out for a test but felt confident that he could dance rhythmically and rather well. Agnes did a creditable imitation of the pony-tailed girls twirling round them. It had its own expertise but it was a parody of something she half envied, half thought ridiculous. She raised her eyebrows in mock admiration as Fred went through his repertoire of steps, collected her and sent her gyrating away from him like a yo-yo and then pulled her resolutely back again.

'You're quite good at this,' she shouted at him.

'Surprised?'

The music changed, quietened, began to pour out of the juke-box like treacle. He decided to hold Agnes and dance closely to

73

her. She didn't move away and he felt that her breasts were not at all supercilious and her thighs made no effort to patronize him. Suddenly elated by this discovery, and by the pints of Simcox Special that he had drunk with the curry, he began to sing along with the Platters,

> 'Heavenly shades of night are falling,
> It's twilight time,
> Out of the mist your voice is calling . . .'

'You must be better at dancing than you are at marching.' Agnes's voice was unexpectedly close to his ear.

'I didn't want to march especially.'

'Why?'

'I could think of better things to do.'

She stood still then, looking at him. 'I think I'd like another drink.'

'Are you sorry,' he asked her when they got back to the bar, 'that I'm quite good at dancing? I mean, would you feel better if I fell about and stood on your feet?'

'I don't know. I haven't made up my mind yet.'

The beer, when it came, slopped over the pint mugs, drowning the change. Fred decided that he could cope with Agnes best if he were either drunk or dancing, preferably both.

When they left the Barrel of Biscuits a good many pints later, Fred put out his hand for the Doctor's car keys. 'I'll drive,' he said.

'Are you good at that too? How appalling!' But Agnes got into the passenger seat and he drove her out of Worsfield. They hadn't met often since he went away to Cambridge and she went to a Worsfield university, but they had gone out on a few occasions to pubs or the Hartscombe Odeon. The first time she had kissed him non-committally on parting and, as he went home alone to the Rectory, he had decided that he was in love with her and that his success or failure with Agnes was a test on which the whole of his life would be judged. He put off any decisive attempt however because he wanted to postpone failure. But the night he deserted from the march he had decided was the time for winning or losing everything. Driving her home he knew that he had lost and that he

74

had been unentertaining. Even his small skill at dancing would be held against him.

They drove to Rapstone first, where he would leave her, and parked beside the lychgate which led into the churchyard. He was about to give her the driving seat and to go home and pretend that the evening had been more eventful than it was. He might hint at great happenings and even lie about it to himself. Fred knew that he had a capacity for self-deception which could cushion many disappointments. He kissed her, as he had done after their other meetings, a tentative and token 'good-night', and was astonished at the strength, almost the desperation of her reaction. He felt himself dragged down, below the level of the windows, and was conscious of the taste of her mouth, a vague worry about villagers peering out from behind lace curtains and the inconvenience of a gear-stick in the groin.

After what seemed a long while Agnes surfaced for air. Fred looked at her, with a new sort of assurance.

'What do you think?' he asked her.

'It beats butterfly kisses.'

'So you remember Charlie's party?' He was pleased.

'No,' Agnes said decidedly. 'I don't remember.' Then she kissed him again, it seemed endlessly. When she came up for the second time she said, 'What do you call this then?'

'Heavy petting?' Fred suggested. 'Seventy per cent of fifteen-year-old Americans pet to climax-point two to five times a week.'

'How on earth do you know that?' She was looking at him with disapproval.

'A boy called Arthur Nubble smuggled the Kinsey Report into school.'

'How absolutely disgusting!'

'Yes,' he had to agree with her.

'I hate heavy petting,' Agnes now decided, pushing him away from her. 'It's *Yank*.'

'Is it?' Fred asked, feeling in a confused way that he was being blamed for the embarrassing researches of Dr Kinsey, and that the evening was over.

'Terribly Yank. Let's get out of the car at least.'

Fred looked out of the window. A thin rain was blurring the moonlight. 'Isn't it a bit wet?'

'Oh, for God's sake!' Agnes was losing her patience. 'You didn't mind marching in it!'

The pews in the church had been pushed aside and the marchers slept on the floor. Simeon was stretched out in a sleeping-bag, reading *Human Society in Ethics and Politics* by Bertrand Russell. He remembered that he had not seen Fred for a long time.

'There's a lot of beards and weirds with guitars about the place.' Henry unstrapped his blanket and his sleeping-bag in an efficient and military sort of way. 'Fred must be with them.'

'I suppose so.'

'Trust young Fred to get himself lost. He'll never get himself round to banning anything.'

In the graveyard, where he would come to stand over his dead father, in a dark corner under the wall, Fred lay on Agnes. Her clothes were pulled up, her long white legs were wrapped round him. He felt a great sense of triumph. It was a victory over Henry, although he would never tell him of his undoubted and unlooked-for success.

Later Agnes and Fred, more or less composed, were standing hand in hand by the car. They spoke in whispers. Agnes had to drive back to Hartscombe and, confident now that he could do anything, Fred insisted on turning the car round for her. He reversed in a fine arc and backed into the wall by the lychgate, producing a bang which might have wakened the long buried inhabitants of Rapstone and the sleeping Fanners in the nave of the church. He stood with Agnes and examined the dented bumper.

'What will your father say?'

'Nothing much. I'll drive it now.' She got into the car and left him standing.

'Shall we go dancing again?' he called after her.

'Possibly.' She let in the clutch and drove away from him.

After she'd gone, Fred let himself into the Rectory. The light was still shining under his mother's bedroom door but he went silently, with his shoes off and still feeling triumphant, into his own bedroom. He was delighted with himself the next morning also when he left the Rectory before his mother was awake and walked up the long road to the signpost which pointed to Rapstone in one direction and Skurfield in the other. Then he thumbed a lift from an early morning farmer's van which came rattling out of the mist. Another young man was bicycling up the road from Skurfield to get on to the Hartscombe road; he was wearing a cheap, dark, gent's suiting, bicycle clips, and a row of pens in his breast-pocket. He was Leslie Titmuss and he saw Fred board the van, but Fred didn't see him.

The newspapers had ridiculed the well-known supporters of C.N.D. for not turning out on the march, so a number of journalists and politicians, some of whom would live to attend Simeon's funeral, joined on the last stage as did a lot of less well-known faces, so the numbers were swollen to thousands. Fred found them on the heathland of gorse and pines round Aldermaston and he saw a crowd listening to Simeon, who was making a speech by the high wire fence round the atomic research establishment. 'Peace through fear! God had a similar idea once . . . Goodness through the fear of hell fire . . . Not one of his most brilliant notions.' Fred heard his father's words blow away across the waste-ground, projected towards the anonymous huts behind the wire. 'I can't remember the fear of hell stopping much slaughter . . .'

'I've been looking for you,' Fred told his brother when he found him.

'Where've you been?'

'With a band. We found an old van to sleep in.'

'Dear little Freddie.' Henry looked at him, almost with kindness. 'You're such a hopeless liar!'

★ 7 ★
The Informer

'I've taken counsel's opinion,' Henry said.

'What about?'

'You know what about. Our father's alleged will.'

Some months after their father's death the two brothers, one just on the wrong, the other still on the right side of fifty, were having dinner together in Henry's club. The Sheridan is a meeting-place for lawyers, actors, writers, publishers and the more presentable type of advertising agent. Its premises are somewhat dusty, its carpets worn but its pictures of past novelists, vanished players and dead judges are famous and its brand of nursery food (overdone roasts, mashed potato and jam roly-poly) is very popular with the sort of Englishman who has never totally recovered from an emotional relationship with his nanny. Henry was proposed for membership of the Sheridan by his second publisher, having left the firm who had accepted *The Greasy Pole* because of what he thought were disappointing sales.

' "Alleged"?' Fred asked. He was already regretting the rare visit to London and the meeting which his brother had told him was of such urgent and secret importance.

'Well, it's not his real will, is it?' Henry explained with carefully simulated patience, as though Fred were still in his first term at Knuckleberries and needed instruction on the harsh rules about undoing buttons. 'Simeon couldn't have meant to ignore his entire family in favour of that jumped-up little sod Leslie Titmuss.'

'I always found it difficult to discover what he really meant, quite honestly.'

'The thing's perfectly obvious!' Henry was visibly allowing his patience to wear thin. 'That ridiculous will's either a forgery ...'

'A forgery by a cabinet minister?'

'It's been known. Or Titmuss leaned on our father in some way. Blackmailed him, I mean. Or the old man had simply gone stark-staring mad, which to judge from his behaviour is, in our barrister's opinion, by far the most likely explanation.'

'*Our* barrister's?' Fred had never met this adviser.

'Of course I'm protecting your interests as well, Fred. We're all in the same boat, you know. As a family we sink or swim together.'

'Simcox!' Henry had been hailed by a tall, florid-faced old man with white hair, a dark suit and a Sheridan club tie, who was ambling past the table. He was a judge, Mr Justice Mervyn Haliburton, who sat in the Chancery Division and happened to be expert on the trying of will cases. Knowing this, Henry rose in his seat with exaggerated respect. After having directed him to sit down the Judge said, in that tone of mild self-congratulation which people always use to an author whose work they have endured, 'Saw that old film of yours last night on my telly-box.'

Henry waited for judgement. Instead Haliburton explained to him, in case he might have forgotten, what the work was about. 'It was the one where the lad from the Brewery rogers the girl in the punt.'

'*The Greasy Pole.*'

'Oh, I dare say. I liked the snaps of the countryside. I don't suppose you took the snaps, did you? I suppose they have special fellows for that.' Henry made no comment. Fred was pleased, and a little surprised, that his brother took no credit for the camerawork. The Judge said, 'You haven't introduced me to your guest.'

'I'm sorry. My brother, Frederick. Mr Justice Haliburton.'

Fred didn't rise. He wanted no part of this sudden involvement with the legal profession. The Judge was looking curiously at Henry, as though he not only needed telling his own plots but was inexplicably forgetful of his closest relations.

'We don't hear about your brother, Simcox. Never read about any brother in those thumbnail sketches of you we always get in the Sunday supplements. Perhaps your *brother* doesn't like to get himself into the papers.'

'I'm a country doctor,' Fred explained.

'Oh well. I suppose that might account for it. Do carry on. Don't let me stop you having food.' The Judge wandered off, beaming as though he had trapped an unwary witness, and Henry laughed, Fred thought, a little nervously.

'There's nothing like the Sheridan,' Henry told his brother, who wished he were far away, in the Badger at Skurfield, playing a session with a middle-aged jazz group who were still tolerated at occasional gigs. 'You meet actors, judges as you can see, wonderful old characters, and the occasional bishop.'

'Just a typical cross-section of British society in the eighties?'

'You do agree, don't you?'

'Oh yes. It's fascinating.' Fred only wanted to stop his brother talking. He longed for the company of the ageing trumpet-player from the Imperial Wine stores in Hartscombe with whom he could exchange quotations from old Louis Armstrong records they both knew by heart.

'You do agree that the conduct of our father' – Henry persisted – 'over the years, showed every sign of complete insanity?'

'He was credulous. He believed in causes.'

'That hardly explains his entering other people's houses on his hands and knees, trumpeting like an elephant.'

'There was a reason for that.'

'You'd find a reason for everything! I don't know why you should make excuses for him. He cut you out of his will too.'

'Perhaps he didn't think I needed the money.' Fred stole a glance at his watch. It was still lamentably early.

'Don't be ridiculous!' Henry looked hard at his brother. 'You never quarrelled with him, did you?'

'No,' Fred answered quickly, not giving himself time to wonder if he were telling the truth.

'Never. On any occasion?'

'No. Never.'

'May I come in?' Fred stopped helping out King Oliver on the drums as his father came into his room after they were all back from Aldermaston. 'Is it the noise, are you trying to write a sermon?'

'Are you expecting one?' Simeon moved a pile of records and sat on the end of the bed. 'Odd, this need people seem to feel for sermons. I could never understand it. You know, often on Sundays, I look down at those upturned faces and I feel an irresistible urge to say, "Oh, for heaven's sake go home to lunch. Don't flatter yourselves by feeling that you've sinned." What do you want a sermon about?'

'Nothing.' Fred tapped his drums impatiently. 'I don't want a sermon at all.'

'About the march ...' Simeon began, but his son interrupted him. 'Don't tell me I made the slightest difference to the march. No one could've noticed whether I was there or not.'

'Don't be modest, Fred, don't feel you're grand enough to be modest. I expect you think all that marching is quite futile. Perhaps the good it does is to those who take part in it, it makes them feel they're not simply leading dull, materialistic lives, perhaps ...'

'It all sounds extremely self-indulgent.' Fred was longing to be left alone, to play his drums and think about Agnes.

'I'm sorry we're not pure enough for you,' Simeon smiled.

Fred continued his attack. 'Perhaps you can achieve the same result with Simcox's Best Bitter, and it's not half so hard on the feet, or with any inexpensive pleasures like ...'

'Like what?'

'Oh, never mind. How did you find out I left the march, did Henry tell you?'

'No. No, it wasn't your brother.' The question apparently caused Simeon some embarrassment. He fumbled for a pipe and started to fill it clumsily, dropping shreds of tobacco on the carpet. 'It was Leslie who told me.' He seemed apologetic.

'Leslie?' Fred enjoyed sounding incredulous.

'Young Titmuss.'

'*What* did he tell you?' Fred was now able to feel betrayed and was surprised at how defensive his father had become.

'He saw you getting a lift, early in the morning.'

'Leslie Titmuss! I can't believe it.'

'You know he works at the Brewery now,' the Rector said, as though it explained something. 'Well, he bicycles in early even at weekends. He's studying for a degree in advanced accountancy, his father told me that. I believe he's anxious to take up some sort of public service.'

81

'Like spying on my movements?'

'That's not charitable, Fred. Leslie's had absolutely none of your advantages. He wants to make something of his life.'

'And something of mine too?'

At lunchtime Simeon asked Dorothy if she had been away from the house on the last day of the march and she said that she had been in the garden all day and at home in the evening. She had seen nothing at all of Fred. Her husband held a green apple in one bony hand and, with the other, he peeled it carefully. Not for the first time he felt the simplicity of the great issues, he knew exactly what should be done about South Africa and urban poverty and the bomb. It was the small events, those nearer home, that seemed to him forever shrouded in mystery. He bit into the apple with sudden determination and a small wince of courage, like a swimmer who plunges briskly into the sea on a cold day.

Leslie Titmuss would have stayed in the office at lunchtime, with the sandwiches and Thermos his mother had prepared for him, if he hadn't had some business to attend to. He never liked crossing the Brewery yard; the wide expanse smelled of sour beer and horse shit from the four great stamping Suffolk Punches Simcox's still kept to advertise the Brewery and enter for the County Show. Huge lorries were always backing in and out of the gates and he had an irrational feeling that the barrels which were rolled on to them might bound away out of control, trundle across the yard like huge cannonballs and snap his thin legs like matchsticks. As he picked his way across this danger zone in his dark suit and white detachable collar, older men in aprons, enjoying their free beer in the shadows under shed roofs, would call out at him, asking him questions about his uneventful sex life, which he pretended not to hear.

That day he had got safely to the gates without being shouted at or coming to any harm. He was about to set out on his mission when he heard his name called in a peremptory, not to say hostile manner and turned to see Fred standing in the road outside the Brewery entrance, waiting for him.

'Mr Frederick.' Leslie meant to appear casually surprised. He was conscious that his voice sounded startled and ingratiating.

'Oh, for God's sake, Leslie. Don't bother about the "Mr Frederick". You've been speaking to my father.'

'Yes. He lets me. I'm very grateful.'

'*Why*, for God's sake?'

'Shouldn't one speak to the Rector?' Leslie spoke in a hushed, almost reverent tone which Fred would have found funny if he hadn't been so incensed. 'If one has spiritual problems?'

'Am I one of your spiritual problems?'

'No, "Fred", of course you aren't.' Leslie tried another cautious smile. 'I just happened to mention I saw you up early. I thought your father'd like to know that.'

'When I ought to have been with him, banning the bomb?'

'I don't agree with that, exactly.' Leslie Titmuss was quick to state his position.

'Oh, don't you?'

'We need the bomb.' Leslie looked nervously back at the Brewery yard, as though he were thinking of his personal protection.

'*You* might need it,' Fred told him with some contempt. 'It might come in frightfully handy for you in the accounts department at Simcox Brewery. It may be absolutely vital for your daily cycling to work from Skurfield. But I don't know why anyone else has the slightest need for it.'

'Think of England.' Fred was surprised to find Leslie looking at him with a kind of pitying sincerity.

'What?'

'Think of England, "Fred", and the defence of freedom.' This came out in such a new, carefully modulated and confidential voice, so far removed from the squeaky and complaining tones of the old Leslie Titmuss, that Fred asked, 'What on earth's happened to you?'

'You should learn about that.'

'About what?'

'About the defence of freedom. You going to be at the Swan's Nest on Saturday night, are you?' The question seemed so irrelevant to the cause of freedom that Fred was at a loss for an answer. 'Dinner dance of the Young Conservatives,' Leslie told him. 'Dress is formal.' And as Fred stood looking at him Leslie started to retreat hastily, saying as he went, 'You want to join the Y.C.s, Mr Frederick. You want to make something of yourself.'

Fred might have followed Leslie Titmuss in order to protest further, or to make an appropriate reply to his invitation to join the Young Conservatives, but he was himself summoned to account by an insistent voice calling him from the other side of the road.

'Come here, young Fred!'

Dr Salter had emerged from a terraced house where he had been visiting one of that class of people whom he considered pampered and overprivileged, the sick. He was clearly glad to be out of the bedroom and was gulping in fresh air mixed with smells from the Brewery and standing beside his cherished antique sports car, which Fred couldn't help noticing, as he approached it guiltily, had a buckled bumper and a dented rear-end.

'I positively approve of your battering down Rapstone Church,' Dr Salter said, 'but I would be obliged if your lust for destruction stopped short at the backside of my old Alvis.'

'Oh,' Fred affected surprise, 'is it damaged at all?'

'Get in,' said Dr Salter, and opened the car door.

Faced with the crop-headed, unsmiling, square-shouldered Doctor, Fred felt like those characters in the gangster-movies he most enjoyed who were hustled into cars by mobsters with bulging pockets and taken to a cement overcoat in the East River. 'I'll buy you a couple of pints in the Badger at Skurfield. Dora Nowt's just about to drop her fifth. She's a reasonably cooperative patient, usually manages to pull it off before lunch. Agnes has gone up to London,' the Doctor went on, interrupting Fred, who seemed about to make some excuse, 'so don't pretend you've got anything better to do.' They drove for a while in silence, but when they reached the place where the road divided at the signpost which pointed one way to Rapstone and the other way to Skurfield, Fred, who hadn't stopped thinking about it, asked, 'Where did you say Agnes had gone?'

'To London. She went to stay with her Aunt Molly. Wanted to admire the holes in the latest exhibition of stone carving, some such fascinating occupation.'

'She's gone to the Henry Moores?' Fred felt reassured.

'If that's the fellow's name. At least, that's what she told me,' Dr Salter said, not being reassuring at all.

So they drove on and into Skurfield, an entirely different sort of village from Rapstone Fanner. Although only three miles distant it has a different climate; it's higher, colder, and even when the sun shines on the brick and flint cottages of Rapstone there seems to be a continual dark cloud over its concrete out-buildings and pebble-dash walls. Skurfield is a great place for corrugated-iron sheds, greyish washing flapping in the wind and chickens roosting in the abandoned and rusting bodies of Austin Sevens through which nettles and willow herb are growing. The front gardens of Skurfield cottages are unweeded dumps which accommodate prams, bicycles, motor-bikes under constant repair and defunct paraffin stoves. Flowers are rare and seem to have seeded themselves by accident and in spite of their surroundings. The village exists shortly on either side of a fairly wide road which looks determined to go on to Worsfield as rapidly as possible.

At the end of the last century a simple-minded Nowt, who had hitherto spent most of his life sitting at his cottage's gate on an old kitchen chair paring his nails with a pocket-knife and muttering to himself, considered he was suddenly crossed in love, poured a gallon or two of lamp oil into the vestry cupboards of the old parish church and set fire to the building. What remained of the early English structure was restored by old Magnus Strove, ever a parsimonious landlord, with a strict eye to economy. The result was said by the then Sir Nicholas Fanner to look like a public urinal built for a community lost to God. The outside has yellowish bricks and a slate roof, the interior, echoing like an old fives court, is ornamented only with a stained-glass window in which Magnus Strove, wearing a frock-coat and surrounded by pallid cherubs, is to be seen receiving the freedom of the City of Worsfield, and a white marble plaque on which are written the names of the depressingly large number of local inhabitants who fell in two world wars. 'Sons of Skurfield', reads the inscription above it, 'Not lost but gone before'.

Such cheer as there was at that time in Skurfield was dispensed by Ned Gower, the usually surly landlord of the Badger. However, the Simcox Extra was as good there as it was at Rapstone and in the evening a particularly brutal game of bar billiards was played by the regulars for minimal stakes in the white glare of a hissing kerosene lamp. Licensing hours were elastic in Ned Gower's time and the Hartscombe police avoided the Badger with studied disdain. The village also boasted a small shop with a fly-blown window which displayed a sleeping tom cat, a few tins of corned beef, boxes of biscuits and yellowing knitting patterns. The shop had been run by an elderly couple who entered into a suicide pact and died in a state of desperate confusion because they were unable to cope with the system of sweet rationing during the war. There was, however, one small house in Skurfield which stood out like a gleaming porcelain crown in a mouth full of crumbling and nicotine-stained teeth. It guarded the entrance to the village from the Rapstone crossroads, a neat red and white box, striped like bacon and built by a local jobbing builder in the thirties. 'The Spruces' had a trim, low privet hedge, a tirelessly mown patch of front lawn and never, in any circumstances, displayed washing – articles of great privacy which Mrs Elsie Titmuss, Leslie's mother, dried on a clothes-horse in the kitchen. Net curtains kept all prying eyes away from the windows of 'The Spruces' and such precautions were wise because, with both male Titmusses employed in the accounts department at the Brewery, there was certainly property inside, a refrigerator, a handsome electric clock, a set of china ornaments kept in a glass-fronted cupboard, which would have excited the envy and possibly the greed of the Skurfield inhabitants. There was also a small garage, heavily padlocked, which contained the meticulously polished Titmuss runabout, a Ford Prefect, kept only for Sunday driving and 'days out' during the summer holidays.

Admiring the Skurfield landscape was all Fred had to do as he sat in the passenger seat of the Alvis outside Tom and Dora Nowt's cottage. Agnes's father had forbidden him to go in ('You'll only faint or something unhelpful'), but the punctuality he had predicted was fulfilled. There was a faint cry behind the sealed-up, curtained windows, and when the Doctor emerged, accompanied by a respectful grandmother wiping her hands on her apron, he opened the car door and said, 'All right. Let's go over to the Badger. I don't suppose you're any bloody good at darts.'

'Success?' Fred asked him.

'Who knows? The nipper may turn out to be an unmitigated disaster. Most people are.'

During the same lunchtime, in Hartscombe, the young Magnus Strove, by then a good-looking but still boyish twenty-two, whose curling hair and soft, candid eyes concealed the fact that he was as tough as old boots and had a strongly developed money sense, came out of the bank with a giggling cousin, a not-too-distant neighbour called Jennifer Battley, and five pound notes which he was tucking into his wallet. Magnus was constantly aware of what he called his 'cash-flow situation', which meant that he carried as little money as possible and relied on his Oxford friends and Hartscombe neighbours to pick up the bills for his drinks and dinners. Jennifer, who was very stuck on him, usually agreed to 'go Dutch' anyway, which meant that she paid, because at a vital moment at the end of dinner Magnus would slap his pockets in a fruitless search for his cheque book, which he kept always under lock and key in Picton House with all the counterfoils neatly filled in.

So Magnus and Jennifer, arm in arm, went off down the street and, for not much reason, Magnus stopped at the dusty window of a small local outfitter called Henry Pyecroft – 'Ladies and Gents Bespoke and Ready-made – Evening-Wear for Hire by the Occasion at Reasonable Prices – All Garments Impeccably Clean'. He pulled Jennifer to a stop and they looked in. What they saw was Leslie Titmuss being fitted for a hired dinner-suit. Mr Pyecroft, in his shirt-sleeves with a tape-measure round his neck, looked with irritation at the giggling young couple on the other side of the window. Leslie was too busy admiring the image of the fine, sombre suiting with glistening lapels and a wide trouser stripe in the long, tarnished mirror to notice and, in a moment, Magnus and Jennifer had gone laughing on their way.

'I'm sorry. About the car, I mean.'
'Well, if that's all the damage you've done.' Fred and the Doctor were sitting in the draughty interior of the Badger, demolishing Simcox bitter with bread and cheese and breathing in the smell of wet dog.
'Of course, I expect to pay.'
'With your father's money? It'd be a miracle.'
'If you could take instalments.'

'Getting a bit of ready cash out of a wealthy Socialist in a dog-collar would require the talents of Moses striking the rock in the desert,' Dr Salter said, ignoring his offer. 'Charity, according to your reverend father, begins in other people's homes.'

'I don't think that's very fair.'

'You want to argue with me?' The Doctor looked at Fred, his blue eyes cold and his face set.

'Not really.'

'Pity. It's becoming a damn dull lunch.' Dr Salter sounded disappointed. He stood up, collected a handful of darts and took aim. Saying, 'Middle for diddle,' without the hint of a smile, he threw a dart plumb into the centre of the board. 'Did Agnes tell you?' Fred stood up and collected some darts. He had no confidence in his ability to score against the Doctor.

'Tell me? Tell me what?' The Doctor pulled out his dart and then threw again.

'About the car.'

'Oh, about the car. Of course. She told me all about the car.' He removed his darts and chalked up his substantial score.

Fred started to play, unable to get a double or throw a dart into the centre of the board. 'Everyone seems to tell everyone everything.' He sounded resentful and younger than his years.

'Only secrets. The only things people tell are secrets. Foolish to have them. Your family are rather given to secrecy though.'

'My family?'

'Must be the religion that does it.' Agnes's father threw again, scored satisfactorily and scrawled his figures on the board, as illegibly as though they were on a prescription. 'Secret sort of business religion. All that whispering to God behind other people's backs. Damn funny though! Old Simeon leading the multitude into the promised land of peace and all that sort of nonsense and you playing truant in order to bust up my motor.'

'Do you think he's wrong?' Away from home Fred always felt protective about his father.

'I don't deal in right and wrong. I deal in collywobbles and housemaid's knee.'

'Do you think he was mistaken, though, to go on the march?' Fred threw and started his game modestly. Dr Salter stood watch-

88

ing him, his legs apart, as though sizing up some not particularly promising piece of horse-flesh. 'You can't change people. You know that. You can't make them stop hating each other, or longing to blow up the world, not by walking through the rain and singing to a small guitar. Most you can do for them is pull them out of the womb, thump them on the backside and let them get on with it. Isn't that enough?' He threw a dart and asked, 'You love my daughter, don't you? It's really not my business what else you get up to. It might be healthier, if you didn't fall in love.'

It was Fred's turn. His shot went hopelessly wide, struck a tankard on a shelf and knocked it to the ground with a clang which echoed in the empty bar.

'I knew it!' Dr Salter was laughing. 'I knew you'd turn out to be a bloody awful darts player!'

Before his game with Dr Salter Fred had felt his love-affair with Agnes to be a sort of protection, an insurance of privilege and pleasure which kept him apart from less fortunate beings. Now it became a mysterious complaint which brought the familiar ache of doom into the pit of his stomach. It also made him quite unable to think of anything but why she had gone to London. He looked in *The Times* and found that there was an exhibition of Henry Moore's sculpture. This comforted him for a while, until he realized that she couldn't be spending twenty-four hours a day gazing at faceless and reclining people. He rang her number two or three times but she wasn't back from London and her father answered him shortly, as though afraid Fred might start telling him the symptoms of his disease and expect a visit.

About a week later he was having a lonely lunchtime beer in the Baptist's Head in Rapstone and talking to Ted Lawless, the landlord and former Battle of Britain pilot, who kept his bar hung with photographs of Spitfires, parties in the mess and himself with his thumbs up as he climbed into the cockpit. Ted and his wife, Ivy, were starting to make 'improvements' in the saloon with checked tablecloths, knives and forks wrapped in paper napkins and chicken or scampi in the basket at lunchtime. Fred was listening, not for the first time, to Ted's account of a New Year's Eve party at R.A.F. Worsfield when he and Ivy, then a succulent

W.A.A.F., had been having it away in the back of an old transport plane which suddenly took off on a night flight to Dundee. Then the saloon door opened and Agnes walked in wearing trousers and a military-looking mac.

'Where on earth have you been?' she said. 'I've been looking for you for days.'

Fred bought her a drink and thought he did so too eagerly. He couldn't imagine why he felt guilty, as though he were the one who had disappeared and left her no word. In a little while she said she wanted to go for a walk, a thing he'd never known her to do before, and he was afraid that she might want to use the occasion for a serious talk, to tell him that it had all been a mistake, an ill-considered moment which he must never expect to repeat. They walked across Rapstone Park in silence and he didn't know what to expect when Agnes took his arm and led him towards the folly, a place which, because of its rotting staircase and bramble-covered approach, was always sure to be deserted.

It was a stunted Gothic tower meant to give the casual visitor to Rapstone Park the deluded impression that he could see all the way to Worsfield Cathedral. Now Fred and Agnes heard the scuttle of birds nesting in the rafters and climbed unsteadily towards a patch of daylight, the open door on to the roof.

'You told your father!' She had said nothing about her visit to London and Fred needed to prove himself hard done by so he accused her.

'What did I tell him?'

'About us.'

'What is there to tell?'

'I should have thought, something.'

'Would you?'

'You told him about the car.'

'Oh, about that!' She seemed in no mood to take him seriously.

'Everyone seems to tell about everything,' Fred grumbled.

'I'm not accustomed to lie to my own father.' She had reached the top of the staircase and stepped out on to the roof of the tower. 'Why're we coming up here?'

'Because it's Rapstone folly.' Fred followed her out.

'I suppose so.' She was looking out over the parkland, the trees each surrounded with a protective palisade, the herd of deer dappled in the shadows and the drive curving up to the house. Fred went on asking questions, as though the last week were a constant itch he couldn't help scratching.

'How was Henry Moore?'

'Who?' With Agnes, it seemed, the name rang no bell.

'The sculptor,' he reminded her.

'So far as I know he's perfectly all right. What ridiculous questions you do ask.'

'And how's Aunt Molly?'

'Almost as well as Henry Moore, I suppose.' She was laughing at him now.

'What did you do in London?'

'Oh, London? Hung about, went round the coffee bars in Soho; that sort of thing.'

'Who did you stay with then?' He thought he was mad to ask her the question and hoped she wouldn't answer it.

'Oh, just some people.'

'*People?*'

'People I was at college with, that's all.'

'Where do they live, these people?'

'Well, aren't you quite extraordinarily nosy?' She was frowning now, no longer laughing.

'You told your father you were staying with your Aunt Molly. I thought you never told lies. To your father.'

'Well, honestly! No one could ever accuse you of not telling lies to *your* father.'

'When you were in London ...' Fred started again patiently, but Agnes interrupted him, lifting up her arms and joining her hands behind his neck.

'When I was in London I wasn't here, was I? Now I'm here. Why don't we try and make the best of it?'

When she kissed him her eyes were closed. His were open and he looked past her, over the park to the driveway where he could see the minute figure of his father walking purposefully towards the house on some private errand or visit.

The Pastoral Visit

The manservant Wyebrow opened the front door, gave a quick look to assure himself that the Rector was not on all fours, and crossed the hall to knock on the drawing-room door and so produced a sound which was lost in the mounting crescendo of screams which came from the other side of the door, an outcry which had been audible in the driveway and had sent the rooks clattering out of the trees on the other side of the kitchen garden.

When he went into the drawing-room Simeon found Grace was seated at a small, photograph-laden desk writing letters, apparently unconcerned. She lifted her head from the scrawled handwriting on mauve crested paper and nodded wearily towards the hearthrug where eighteen-year-old Charlie stood, her hair awry, her eyes closed, her face purple with indignation, her clenched fists beating against her tweed-covered thighs, kicking up this extraordinary hullabaloo. The effect might have been weirdly comic, like the sight of a fully grown comedian acting the part of a baby screaming in its pram, if the anger behind the outcry had not been so obvious. The Rector only glanced at the mother and approached the deafening girl. He took her arm and said, 'Now then, Charlie. Isn't it time I took you up?'

There was a moment's silence and then the girl, with another howl, tried to shake Simeon off, but the laying-on of hands had been accompanied by unexpected strength. She found herself gripped firmly by the Rector, who had apparently been sent for to perform a miraculous cure, or at least minister to her spiritual needs, and propelled to the door, through which she went still screaming. She was still doing so when Wyebrow came out of his pantry and, looking up from the well of the stairs, saw the ill-assorted couple disappear into Charlie's bedroom. Bridget Bigwell, sweeping the upstairs corridor, saw it too, paused, clicked her tongue in mild disapproval and then continued her work with renewed determination.

The bedroom door closed; the intervals between the screams increased in length. Then the cries died away, turned to low irregular sobs and finally to silence. Wyebrow returned to his pantry and continued with his letter to an old wartime friend, now an officer in the New York City police. 'Dear Chuck,' he wrote. 'Thrilled to bits to hear about your new leisure-wear and wish I could see you in it. I haven't bought anything exciting in the way of trousers lately owing to the shops in this part of rural England being distinctly below par.' Grace also sent her pen scurrying across the paper, writing to those distant members of her husband's family she suspected might be divorcing, or sick, or even dead, always avid for news to relieve the heavy monotony of life in Rapstone Park.

Charlie lay silent, fully dressed under the warmth of the eider-down. Her sensible shoes had been removed and put side by side in front of the fireplace. Her face was red, her eyes swollen but she was silent now, gently sucking the knuckle of her first left-hand finger as the Rector turned to the bookshelf. From among her childhood favourites including *The Scarlet Pimpernel*, *Little Women* and *Five Go Adventuring* he selected one from which he started to read to soothe her anger. ' "A propeller, set behind two exposed seats, revolved slowly." ' Simeon used the voice he kept for the lessons. ' "Beside it stood a tall, thin man in flying-kit; his leather flying-coat, which was filthy beyond description with oil stains, flapped open, exposing an equally dirty tunic, on the breast of which a device in the form of a small pair of wings could just be seen. Under them was a tiny strip of the violet-and-white ribbon of the Military Cross. 'You one of the fellows on the new course?' he asked shortly. 'Er – er – er yes, sir,' was the startled reply. 'Ever been in the air?' 'No, sir.' 'What's your name?' 'Bigglesworth, sir. I'm afraid it's a bit of a mouthful, but that isn't my fault. Most people call me Biggles for short.' A slow smile spread over the face of the instructor. 'Sensible idea,' he said." '

93

' "All right, Biggles, get in." ' Charlie supplied the words, quite calm now.

'What did you say to her!' Simeon was angry by the time he got downstairs to Charlie's mother.

'Nothing very much. I mean, nothing to cause all that fuss. I think I was saying that at her age all my friends were thinking of parties and dances, being presented at Court. It was just the time when we were all being "brought out". "But with you, Charlie," I told her, "there's nothing at all to bring." '

'How did you *expect* her to react?' He spoke with some contempt.

'Oh, I don't know. When I was Charlie's age we didn't have a brass farthing. Daddy had pushed off and taken most of his miserable army pension with him. I used to fill my handbag with bits I scrounged from cocktail parties. That was my lunch.'

'How the poor live!'

'All the same I managed to not wear the same party frock too often.' Grace was looking in a succession of alabaster and mother-of-pearl boxes for a cigarette. 'I was typing letters for old Lady Naboth's dreadful charities and dancing until three o'clock most mornings. Can you see any of your precious trades union members working hours like that?'

'Their night-shift probably doesn't entail much dancing.'

'You're angry just because I tell Charlie what I think! Don't you want me to be honest with her?'

'It might be better to be kind, or at least take an interest in her?'

'Oh, you think everyone's interesting. That's because you're a Red. I don't. I believe that quite a lot of people were just manufactured when God was thinking of something else.'

'Like the next cocktail party.' Simeon seemed to despair of the woman, and she also looked at him with genuine disapproval. 'Don't be blasphemous, Simeon,' she said piously. 'Please, do try not to be blasphemous!'

That afternoon Nicholas Fanner had also been out visiting. Percy Bigwell had been a skilled and expert woodman and an elegant dancer and so won the love of Bridget Bigwell, then only one of the Fanners' housemaids, when they were both in their teens. In middle age Percy still worked in the woods, felling trees and sawing them into lengths suitable to be taken into the furniture factories in Worsfield. A few months before, Tom Nowt, felling an old elm in a brutal and inexpert manner (all his skills were for shooting), caused the accident in which Percy's legs were broken. After this incident Tom Nowt was rightly blamed, shunned and became more isolated in the village and spent more time in his hut in the woods.

Nicholas, with his comfortable, well-meaning smile and his baggy clothes, wandered into the stuffy back room of Percy's cottage and urged the crippled man not to get up. He was sure that Percy would soon be out again, beating on the next shoot that Nicholas shared with Doughty Strove of Picton Principal. Percy told him that Dr Salter didn't hold out much hope for that and added, 'And Doctor says the worst of it is, I'll probably last like this another thirty years. I'll be a creaking gate, he reckons, and they goes swinging on forever.'

'Dr Salter never has been terribly keen on keeping his patients alive,' Nicholas admitted. 'He's a bit of a gloom merchant, quite honestly, Bigwell. No need for us to listen to all that doom and gloom now we've got rid of the Socialists.' He rose to go on his cheerful way. 'We'll be together again this autumn, you'll see. You putting up the birds with your old ash stick and me and Mr Strove bagging them high on the wing. You get well, old man. We can't do without you.' As he went Nicholas decided to send Bridget home with a box of biscuits for Percy. He didn't know, because they had never told him, that the Bigwells didn't like Worsfield biscuits and had a cupboard full of Mrs Bigwell's employer's presents.

When he got home Nicholas found that the Rector had come to tea and that Charlie was upstairs resting. Grace told him that she had sent for Simeon because of another of the girl's ridiculous tantrums. 'It's the excitement, I expect,' Nicholas said, noticing that Simeon had polished off all the buttered toast. 'She's excited about the Young Conservatives dinner dance. Well, Charlie doesn't have many treats.'

'Take sex, for instance.'
'What do you want me to do with it?'

'Try to be serious for a moment. Take the sex life of our father.'

Dinner at the Sheridan club was over and Fred was hoping that the meeting with his brother, and another indignant and frustrating discussion of the Rector's will, would soon be over also. He thought of the last time he had seen his father, an old, dying man in pyjamas who smelled faintly of the inside of linen cupboards. Even after a couple of brandies he felt extremely reluctant to discuss sex and his father. 'It's something I'd rather not think about,' he said. 'We all come into existence as a result of a momentary embrace by our parents which we find impossible to imagine.'

'You talk exactly like he did.' Henry was impatient.

'We all assume we're the result of our own particular immaculate conception. You mean, I talk like our father?'

'No. I mean like Dr Salter. My dear Frederick, that ludicrous will can't have been an isolated incident of complete irresponsibility. Our barrister wants further examples of eccentric behaviour.'

'Is sex eccentric behaviour?'

'If you happen to be a vicar. I'll have to ask Mother.'

'I don't think you should do that.' Fred became serious.

'I'll have to.'

'I don't believe that those are the sort of questions our mother would care to answer.'

'I'll have to make systematic inquiries.'

'Why? Are you such an expert?' Fred resented his brother adopting the role of detective.

'On sex?'

'No.' Fred looked at his brother. 'On fidelity.'

Henry let the accusation go by, as though it were a sneaky and underhand ball thrown at him which it would be beneath his dignity to touch. He sipped his brandy and said, 'Another thought occurs to me.'

'Does it?'

'Of course you know our father was a Commie.' Henry said it as though he were stating the obvious. 'A raving Red, quite clearly. I mean, suppose he was spying for the Soviets and Leslie Titmuss got wind of it. Suppose it was a simple case of blackmail!'

'My God, Henry!' Fred laughed. 'You mean he was selling the

secrets of the Parish Council to Russia? Brilliant! Good enough for one of your movie scripts.'

'Seriously. What do you think?'

'I think you've got to a dangerous age.' Fred stood up. His brother looked up at him inquiringly, no doubt thinking their conversation was again going to concern itself with sex. 'The age when you sit in the Sheridan club drinking too much brandy and dreaming about spies.'

On his way out Fred passed a telephone in a glass box by the front door. He lifted it and dialled a number. The voice which answered him sounded, as usual, as though it was trapped in a burning building with no possibility of escape.

'Agnes? It's Fred. Freddie Simcox. Well, could I come round and talk to you for a moment?' When she asked him what he wanted to talk about he said, 'Well, of all things, Leslie Titmuss.'

Fred found Agnes in her rent-controlled flat at the far end of the Fulham Road. She had turned herself, since her divorce from Henry, into a one-woman organization called the Flying Kitchen and cooked, alone or with occasional help from unemployed actresses, for dinner parties, directors' lunches and such-like functions, work which she carried out efficiently but without many smiles. As she spent so much of her time cooking she had knocked her kitchen and living-room together, the resulting space being a dark but workmanlike cavern with a lot of shelves, wooden surfaces, cookery books, yellowing recipes pinned to the walls, pots and pans well scoured, bunches of herbs hanging up to dry. Agnes was wearing trousers and canvas shoes, smoking industriously and with a litre bottle of red wine beside the old rocking-chair in which she had been sitting.

'You should have rung earlier. You could've had the remains of an oxtail I had left over from a ghastly dinner party I cooked in Highgate last night.' She shuddered at the memory and poured him a glass of wine. 'Rag trade!'

In the dim light the shape of her face seemed unaltered; for all her cooking she had remained thin. Her smile was, as always, one of rueful courage against enormous odds. Fred thought that what he had loved was her unhappiness, although it was a quality which made him feel uneasily inferior to her. He had thought she knew of great cosmic causes for discontent of which he, in his mundane way, was cheerfully unaware. This unhappiness, which she gave off like a rich and potent smell, had been, for the years, the decades he had known her, the secret of her sexual attraction.

'Are you doing a lot of cooking?' He knew it seemed a trivial question in the face of so much heroically borne grief.

'Henry doesn't like me doing it. He's dead scared of showing up at some film mogul's house with La Lonnie and finding me slaving away in the kitchen.'

'Look. About Leslie...' Fred started when they were sitting beside her small but genuine and smouldering fireplace.

'Leslie Titmuss!' Agnes refilled her glass and, because she was used to living alone, forgot his. 'He's a cabinet minister and his mother was a cook. My father was a doctor and I'm a cook. Perhaps I passed him on the way down, or did he pass me on the way up?'

'About the will.' Fred felt it necessary to explain his visit.

'I never knew your father had such a sense of humour.'

'Well, about the will. I want you to stop Henry.'

'What?'

'Stop him blundering about, trying to unearth secrets, attacking everyone. He's coming out with the most ridiculous ideas about my father.'

'What makes you think I've got the slightest influence on him?'

There was a silence. He wondered how he was going to control his rogue brother. 'Has Lonnie any influence?' he asked.

'Of course not. He married her for her remarkable talent for agreeing with absolutely everything he says.'

'Francesca? Would he take any notice of your daughter?'

'Strangely enough, I think he's afraid of Francesca. She's young, you see. Young people alarm him now.'

'You see her?'

'Sometimes.' She smiled and this made her look unhappier than usual. 'She was coming tonight, actually. I was going to cook her supper.'

'What happened?'

'She chucked me.'

Fred got up, refilled his glass and wandered round the room. He smelled herbs and spices and started to read about how to make a simple, classic *blanquette de veau*. It was like a tone-deaf person reading a musical score. 'Are you comfortable here?'

'Quite.'

'Not lonely?'

'No. Are you?'

'No.' Fred put away the recipe book he'd taken from the shelf. 'Sometimes I wonder why not.'

'You've got all those ill people to keep you company.' She said it seriously, not as a joke, as her father would have said it. Then she asked, 'What are you going to do now?' and gave him no hint as to whether it was a general inquiry about his remaining years or an invitation to stay the night.

'I suppose . . .' Fred found the question difficult. She gave him no help. 'I suppose I shall drive back to Hartscombe.'

'Well. That's that then.' She stood up and threw her cigarette end at the fireplace in a business-like sort of way.

'Yes.' He moved to the door. 'Thanks for the wine.'

'Any time.' But before he went she said thoughtfully, 'Leslie Titmuss! I wonder what on earth your father really liked about him.'

★ 9 ★

A Formal Occasion

Elsie Titmuss was a maid at Picton House, in the employment of Doughty Strove, when George Titmuss, already a clerk in the Brewery, met her at a Skurfield church-outing and they entered into a prolonged engagement and a ferocious programme of saving money. This culminated in marriage and the birth of their only child, the young hopeful, Leslie. Elsie was a surprisingly beautiful young woman with a calm and untroubled expression which survived her long and demanding life as a wife and mother in the Titmuss household. On the evening of the Young Conservatives dinner dance she was fussing round her son with obvious pride, dabbing at him with a clothes-brush and arranging a white handkerchief in his top pocket, as he stood in his hired dinner-jacket in front of the mirror over their sitting-room mantelpiece, his hair neatly combed and slicked down with brilliantine, his face industriously shaved and lightly dusted with his mother's talc.

'You use the handkerchief for display purposes only, Leslie,' his mother instructed him. 'Don't go and blow your nose on it, will you?'

'Mother. I do know.'

'Stop finicking with the boy, Elsie.' George Titmuss sat under a relentless overhead light at the dinner table, his jacket hung on the back of his chair, and he wore sleeve-grips to keep his cuffs high and his bony wrists free. The green velvet cloth was spread with files and papers. He was working late on the Simcox Brewery accounts.

'Or you can have it in your sleeve.' Elsie took the handkerchief from her son's top pocket. 'When I was in service a lot of the gentlemen carried the white dinnertime handkerchief in the cuff.'

'I'll have it in the display pocket.' Leslie, who was always firm with his mother, returned the handkerchief to its previous position.

'I don't know why the boy has to be sent out looking like a tailor's dummy,' George grumbled as he added up a column of figures.

'When I was in service with Mr Doughty Strove at Picton House. Pre-war, when I was in service . . .'

'Yes, Elsie,' George said. 'I think we've all had our fill of when you were in service.' Neither of the men in her life wished to hear about Elsie's past in the Stroves' kitchen.

'It was dress for dinner every night,' Elsie continued happily. 'Except Sundays. Sundays it was casual dress and cold cuts, naturally, with beetroot and a lettuce salad. But any other day of the week it was one gong for dressing and then half an hour later the second gong for dinner.'

'Yes, Elsie. We do know all about it.'

'Can I borrow the Prefect?' Leslie asked his father over his mother's head.

'Oh, go on, George. All the other Young Conservatives'll be there with their own transport.' As always Mrs Titmuss supported her son.

'I suppose it'll stop people talking.' Mr Titmuss gave the matter the careful consideration he bestowed on the agenda at the Parish Council. 'At least you won't be hanging round the bus stop dressed like a waiter.'

'He looks handsome.' Elsie stood back in admiration. 'Doesn't our Leslie look handsome, George?'

'I'd rather see him looking handsome at eight-thirty in the morning when we've got our annual audit at the Brewery,' George grumbled.

Elsie, giving the collar of her son's jacket a final brush, noticed his ready-made bow-tie clipped on to the front of his starched white collar. With the knowledge she had gained in service she was shocked. 'Oh, Leslie. They didn't give you one of them!'

'One of what?'

'Ready made! They ought to have given you a tie-your-own. They always wore tie-your-owns when I was in service.'

'It doesn't matter.' Not for the first time Leslie found his mother irritating. 'No one's going to know, are they?'

'I suppose not.' Elsie was doubtful.

'I bet it cost enough, whatever sort of tie it is.' George was still muttering over his columns of figures.

'Well, you didn't have to pay. I said, you didn't have to pay, did you, George?' Elsie asked as she gave the spotless dinner-jacket its last brush.

'You're always spending out your money on the boy.'

'Well, you ought to be grateful. I put by enough for all his little bits and pieces. You ought to be grateful for what I put by.'

A twisted gilt and china clock on the mantelpiece struck metallically. Leslie escaped from his mother's clothes-brush. 'I'm going to be late. It's seven for seven-thirty.' He went to the present from Cleethorpes and found the car key under it. As he went out into the hall his mother called after him, 'Goodbye, Leslie. It looks so well on you.' But he was gone in silence and his parents heard the front door slam. Elsie looked at her husband and smiled happily. 'Don't you feel proud of him, George, seeing him go off like that?'

Mr Titmuss looked up from his figures. They were clear signs of a steady increase in the consumption of beer, but he wasn't smiling. 'Why should I feel proud?' he asked.

Fred was also on his way to the dinner dance, as part of the band. It was almost a year since he went to a Chris Barber concert in Worsfield and met Joe Sneeping, who worked at the off-licence in Hartscombe market place and devoted his spare time to the trumpet and the work of the New Orleans musicians recorded in Chicago during the prohibition era. Fred also knew Terry Fawcett, who worked at Marmaduke's garage and had played the clarinet since his schooldays, and through Joe he met Den Kitson from the Brewery, who could double on banjo and guitar and even play the bass when one was available. Together they formed the Riverside Stompers and they'd played in pubs up and down the river. They owed their present gig to Fred, who had cashed in on his old acquaintance with Magnus Strove. At least, he had said, they'd be cheaper than the Swinging Romeos from Worsfield. Joe had agreed to sully the purity of the group with dance-hall numbers, Terry had got hold of a saxophone to double on and they had rehearsed 'Always' and fallen about laughing.

The Swan's Nest at Hartscombe is a pleasant, low, brick and weather-boarded building by the river. Its untended garden stretches down to the water, where a few punts and rowing-boats are moored for the pleasure of visitors, and swans glide in a ghostly fashion over the dark water. In the twenties and thirties the name of the Swan's Nest was synonymous with adultery and illicit weekends. It figured in society divorce-cases and it achieved that somewhat raffish reputation which it cannot quite shake off, although the Guards officers and debutantes, the dubious foreign Counts and undependable married ladies no longer trail their fingers in the water from its punts or order champagne in its bedrooms. At the end of the 1950s it was a respectable, rather down-at-heel hotel living, like Grace Fanner, on memories of more eventful days. In the course of time it would be taken over by a motel chain, re-christened Ye Olde Swan's Nest and given piped music, colour T.V.s in every bedroom, Teasmades instead of discreet rustic chambermaids in black bombazine, an enlarged car park and the Old Father Thames Carvery.

When Leslie Titmuss went there for his first formal occasion he caught the hotel between its notorious past and its bleak future. Up to the end of dinner the occasion was uneventful. Prawn cocktail, chicken, ice-cream and pineapple slices had been served. The carafe wine had been supplemented by those Young Conservatives prepared to pay for their own drinks, and the buzz of their voices had risen to a pitch of excitement which had more to do with extra bottles of champagne and brandy than the immediate prospect of a few words from Sir Nicholas Fanner, Bart., in his role as Chairman of the Hartscombe and District Conservative Association.

At the top table the Chairman beamed about him with his usual amiability. He was sitting next to Doughty Strove, then the Hartscombe M.P., who was known as a dependable Party member and had greatly assisted the proceedings in Parliament by rarely opening his mouth. So far as his political opinions went he was known to be in favour of capital punishment, corporal punishment and large subsidies for those landlords who were doing their best to grow sunflower seed in bulk. He was also greatly in favour of severing diplomatic ties with France, a country which he regarded with particular horror and suspicion. At Doughty's right hand sat Grace, who made no secret of the fact that she thought him both unattractive and dull; indeed she was flirting outrageously with the Young Conservative President on her left, a serious-minded junior stockbroker, who was finding the fluttering of Grace's middle-aged eyelashes unnerving, her jewelled hand on his sleeve alarming and her low, gravelly purr inaudible. Charlie was sitting on the other side of her father and was wearing a green dress made of some shiny material which did nothing for her. She was frowning and the fact that she did not scream or burst into tears was of little help to the nervous Young Conservative beside her who had vainly tried to arouse her interest in cricket and the idea of a European Free Trade Association. In time he gave up and concentrated on the toothy girl to his right.

The President beat on the tablecloth with a spoon. Nicholas rose slowly to his feet and began a low-key, somewhat inaudible address which was more like random jottings from the diary of a Conservative gentleman of the old school than a speech.

'I look around this room at you,' he began, 'and I see young, some very young, *Conservatives*. You know, there was a time when to be young meant that you were sure to have one of those sort of red tweed ties. Do you remember what I mean?' The question was clearly rhetorical, and no one answered it. 'If you were young you wore a corduroy jacket and you were,' his voice was shrill in comic and pretended fear – 'a *Red! a revolutionary!*'

Around him the Young Conservatives, most of whom belonged to the organization for the same reason that they joined the Hartscombe Amateur Operatic Society, to meet each other and fall in love, smiled faintly. There were a few more serious faces. Leslie Titmuss looked pale and intent, concentrating fiercely on Nicholas's ramblings as though the way to the future might be revealed in them. He was sitting, by some quirk of the placement, next to Jennifer Battley, who was not delighted to have him as a dinner companion. At a table opposite them young Magnus Strove was sitting with a party of pink-faced young men and braying girls, the junior members of the Hartscombe Hunt who had brought their own drink and cigars. Prominent among the group was one who looked plumper and even more prosperous than the rest. His name was Christopher Kempenflatt, heir to the Kempenflatt family building firm, a young man whose eyes always seemed to be popping with carefully simulated surprise and whose moist lips were now open to admit a large Monte Cristo cigar. He was responsible for the fact that the group around him were mopping up more old brandy than the rest of the Young Conservatives and getting more rapidly out of control.

'Looking round this fine old room' – Nicholas looked around it – 'and after a dinner well up to the Swan's Nest's high standards . . .'

'Kitty Kat and soggy potatoes!' Kempenflatt had unplugged his cigar, and was greeted by a salvo of giggles from the girls around him.

'It wasn't so bad,' Magnus Strove told them. 'I actually found a prawn in my cocktail.'

'Probably got in there to die,' was Kempenflatt's opinion.

'Looking around me,' Nicholas went on, 'I see that to be young is to be Conservative. To be on . . . on the "other side" is, if I may say so, distinctly "old hat".'

'Well, he should know about old hats,' Kempenflatt told the girls.

'You mean that amazing tweed thing he wears with the flies in it?' Magnus increased their helpless laughter.

'There was a moment of aberration' – Nicholas seemed not the least disconcerted by the hunt members – 'some of you may be old enough to remember, when Hartscombe itself went Socialist. That was as unfortunate as the time when Oliver Cromwell's levelling soldiery occupied Rapstone Manor!'

'Some of us may be old enough to remember that!' Kempenflatt raised his glass to the Chairman.

'But now England has come to its senses.' Nicholas beamed at them all in a mildly congratulatory manner.

'Charles the Second's back!' Magnus announced.

'Boffing the girls.' Christopher Kempenflatt filled in the details. Leslie Titmuss looked angrily at the claque opposite him and led a scattered volley of clapping.

'And my old friend Doughty Strove is back where he should be' – Nicholas continued with the good news – 'in the House of Commons. Thanks to your tireless canvassing.'

'Hear! Hear! Give your dad a hand, Magnus.' Kempenflatt was puffing out smoke and clapping with his cigar in his mouth.

'Good old Dad! The silent member for Hartscombe.' Magnus was not applauding. 'I don't know why they don't replace him with a cardboard cut-out.'

'But you've heard enough from me,' Nicholas said and got, from the Kempenflatt table, the warmest applause of the evening. 'Unlike the doom merchants of the Socialist Party we can enjoy ourselves. There will be dancing too . . . Who will there be dancing to?' He stooped to hear the Secretary whisper to him, 'Joe Sneeping and his Riverside Orpheans.' The Secretary whispered again, Nicholas again bowed his head and came up smiling. 'Oh, Riverside Stompers,' he said. 'I stand corrected. And the bar will remain open until midnight.' The Secretary whispered again. 'I understand it's a question of "buy your own" from now on. "Let joy be unconfined; No sleep till morn, when Youth and Pleasure meet".'

'I do wish Nicholas wouldn't do that,' Grace said to the Young Conservative President. 'He does make such a fool of himself when he quotes poetry.' Nicholas sank back into his seat to the apparent relief of everyone including himself. The Stompers began to play the music that the Young Conservatives liked to dance to, selections from *South Pacific*. They were parodying 'Bali Hi, They Call It', grinning at each other over their instruments and raising their eyebrows in despair at each syrupy swoop of the music. Then they did their own jazzed-up version of 'I'm Going to Wash That Man Right Out of My Hair' and felt more at ease. Den Kitson, wearing a tartan dinner-jacket he had borrowed for the occasion, slapped the bass and wondered what the chances were of picking up a bit of Conservative crumpet. Joe and Terry both wore dark suits with black bow-ties and Fred the dinner-jacket he had spent out on in his first term at Cambridge. None of the guests seemed to look at the band, and neither Leslie nor Charlie had shown him a flicker of recognition. Nicholas and Grace were both unaware of his presence. He began to enjoy being overlooked, a pleasure which would grow on him in the years to come.

'You know Doughty Strove, of course?' Leslie Titmuss broke a long silence to ask his neighbour, Jennifer Battley, this unenlivening question. He looked with a certain awe to where the square-faced member for Hartscombe, deserted by his neighbours in favour of the dance floor, sat nodding out of time with the music.

'Oh, yes. He's my uncle.'

'I say. Is he really?'

'His son Magnus is over there. He's my cousin, actually. Do you know Magnus?'

Leslie looked to where Magnus Strove and Christopher Kempenflatt, surrounded by girls, were enjoying a joke.

'Well, *I* don't really know him,' Leslie admitted. 'Of course, my people know the family.'

'Your people?'

'My mother.'

'Oh, really?' Jennifer was laughing at the sympathetic yawns Magnus was performing for her at the table opposite. Leslie, who hadn't seen Magnus's mime, asked her, 'Do you know who puts up the nominations for the Y.C. Committee? Does Mr Doughty Strove have a voice in these decisions, in your view, Miss Battley? Just the General Committee, you understand. I'm not looking as far as the F. and G.P. yet. It's early days, of course, that's understood. Or would Sir Nicholas, the Chairman, be the fellow to contact?'

At which point a crusty bread roll, thrown by Magnus, whizzed past Leslie Titmuss's right ear.

'He's such a fool!'

'Sir Nicholas?' Magnus was puzzled.

'No, Magnus, you idiot! He's my boyfriend, you know. Such a cretin! I say, are you going to eat that roll?' Jennifer seized it without waiting for his answer and, with a strong throw learned on the cricket field at Benenden, hit Christopher Kempenflatt on the forehead.

'Of course,' Leslie said, paying no attention to the fusillade but looking at the guests on the top table, 'that's Sir Nicholas's daughter, Charlotte. You know her? I must say she looks awfully left out.'

'Oh, bull's eye!' Jennifer couldn't help clapping as another bread roll, hurled by Magnus, got Leslie on the cheek. He stood up quickly, looking very pale. 'I say.' Jennifer tried to stop laughing. 'You're not miffed, are you?'

'No. Not at all. Of course not. It's terrifically good fun. Would you mind excusing me a moment?'

'Of course not. Take all the time you want.' Jennifer told him and Leslie was still smiling as he set off towards the top table, and continued to do so when another roll struck him on the back.

Charlie was sitting alone. Her neighbour had gone to dance with the girl on his other side. Nicholas and Doughty Strove had joined a group at the bar, and Grace had suggested a dance to the President of the Young Conservatives, an offer which he had not felt able to refuse. So Charlie was bored to despair, sitting alone and talking to no one. She kept her head down and stared at the pattern she was making with fork lines on the white tablecloth, wanting at all costs to avoid catching a glimpse of her mother steering an apprehensive young man round the floor with relentless charm. She didn't raise her head when Leslie glided up to her and spoke. 'Frightfully jolly party, isn't it?'

'You think so?'

'Rather! You wouldn't care to dance, would you?'

'No, I wouldn't care to.'

'Then shall we?'

She looked up at him and saw a look of extraordinary determination. Astonished and a little alarmed by his pale intensity she put down her fork and stood up, her arms held out in what looked like an attitude of self-defence rather than an embrace. He put a hand on her waist and manoeuvred her towards the floor where they moved awkwardly, self-consciously and without great skill or enthusiasm. Fred tried to embark on an ambitious drum roll, met a warning look from Joe Sneeping and returned obediently to the straightforward rendering of 'Some Enchanted Evening'.

'Good fun, these do's, aren't they?' Although he found that it required great concentration to talk and dance at the same time, Leslie felt that Charlie looked so ill at ease that he was bound to divert her. His hand at her waist felt very warm, as though he were touching a radiator. When she didn't answer he repeated, 'I said these do's are pretty good fun.' And added, 'Of course, there's a serious point behind them. I mean, I don't suppose I'd be here at all if I didn't want to get on in the Party.' He danced on in silence, waiting for a comment that never came. Christopher Kempenflatt hove up behind them, shunting a tall girl backwards. Magnus was in front, dancing with Jennifer.

'I say, Titmuss. I say, old boy,' Kempenflatt shouted as he approached. 'Who's your tailor?'

'Like your tie, old fellow.' Magnus steered alongside. 'Bet it took simply hours to get such a perfect butterfly.'

Leslie looked at them, puzzled. Holding the solid, embarrassed Charlie he came to a slow halt as Magnus's hand snatched the clip-on tie from his collar. He gazed after it and saw it settle, a black bow in Jennifer's hair.

'You old cheater!' Magnus's voice was high-pitched, accusing. Leslie seemed to be surrounded by young men, healthy-faced, loud-voiced, and Charlie had abandoned him as the music stopped.

'Where did you get that suit, Titmuss?' Kempenflatt asked, and Magnus was pulling open Leslie's jacket, searching for the label. 'Savile Row, is it? Huntsmans?'

'Better than that,' Magnus announced. 'Please see this garment is returned to Henry Pyecroft, Gents Outfitter, River Street, Hartscombe.'

'Lovely bit of schmutter, isn't it?' Kempenflatt said in a stage-Jewish accent, feeling the cloth between his finger and thumb, and Magnus went on reading the label to announce, '"All clothing impeccably clean". Ugh!'

'Look here. I know it's just a bit of fun but ...' Leslie smiled round at the strange faces, anxious to enjoy the joke. As he did so he felt a jerk behind him and Kempenflatt was pulling off the jacket. Magnus was saying persuasively, 'Take it off, Titmuss. You don't know where it's been.' Leslie began to panic, wondering where this unsolicited undressing was going to end.

'"Impeccably clean"! Strong smell of mothballs.' When it was off, Kempenflatt sniffed the jacket and chucked it to Magnus, who said, 'As last worn at the Municipal Sewerage Workers Ball,' and did a quick pass to Jennifer, who held it uncertainly in front of her in a dark bundle.

As they stared at him Leslie said, 'Can I have it back, please?' After that the silence seemed endless and then Fred, who had been watching with interest from behind his drum set, started to whistle and tap out the rhythm of 'Always'. The other Stompers joined in. Jennifer looked at Magnus and then handed the jacket back to Leslie. He thanked her and turned away towards the glass doors that opened on to the hotel garden, walking as quickly as he could, but he still heard Kempenflatt boom, 'I say, Magnus. Do you actually *know* that fellow?' And the answer, 'Of course I know him. His mother was our skivvy.'

When they had begun to gather round her partner and attack his clothing, Charlie had gone out into the garden. It was still early in the summer and the night wind soothed her burningly embarrassed skin. She crossed the grass and stood on the old landing-stage, looking down at the moored punts which had been put out during the Easter holidays. The water rattled the boats at their moorings, dangerous-looking swans glided by about their business and she heard Leslie say, 'It was all good fun.' He was still smiling, wearing his jacket now, but not his tie.

'Was it?' She couldn't accept his description of an evening which had come so close to making her scream.

'They're all right really,' he told her. 'Just excited.'

'My mother wouldn't have let them behave like that.'

'No.'

'My mother would've given them one look and they'd all have knelt down and kissed her hand.' She spoke with contempt. 'Like slaves! They all fell in love with her at dances. They'd have obeyed her breathlessly.'

'I expect she was very beautiful.'

'That's what she keeps telling me. You've lost your tie.' She seemed to notice it for the first time.

'Yes.'

'My mother hates me, because I'm not beautiful. I don't suppose she cares very much for you either.'

'But your father?' Leslie, who wasn't in the least interested in Grace, asked anxiously.

'My father's sorry for me. You know what he's president of, apart from the Conservatives? The All England Begonia Society. And you know why he chose begonias?'

'No. I don't know.'

'He says they're such ugly little flowers. He feels sorry for them.'

'Sorry for begonias?' Leslie Titmuss was out of his depth.

'Such ugly and vulgar little things! He says somebody has to look after them.'

There was a silence, and then Leslie tried to cheer his partner up. 'I think you look jolly nice in that dress.' It wasn't a remark calculated to give offence, but Charlie was offended.

'Isn't it horrible? Please. Tell me it's horrible. *She* made me wear it.'

Further down the landing-stage Leslie saw Young Conservatives and their girlfriends climbing into punts, shouting, laughing, pushing away from the bank.

'Look. Would you like to have a go on the river? It might be a bit of fun.'

Charlie didn't say anything, but after the boat containing Leslie's tormentors had got clear, and the splashing and laughter had died away in the darkness, she allowed him to help her into a punt. He stood up stiffly and remembered the lessons in poling the Simcox boys had given him once, long ago, when they all went on the river. He was cautious at first but soon gained confidence and threw up the pole between his hands and steered them away from the willows which overhung the bank. Charlie sat on a cushionless seat, trailing a hand in the welcome chill of the water, wondering what she thought she was doing, but glad to be away from the dance floor and to hear the music of the Stompers fade as they drifted away from the hotel. She would have been quite calm if Leslie hadn't felt the need to pay her compliments.

'You've got nice hair, too. That was the first thing I noticed about you this evening. The niceness of your hair.'

'Don't say that!' She thought his voice had sounded extraordinarily loud, echoing across the water and alarming the swans.

'I never noticed your hair. Not when we were kids.'

'Please. Don't say things like that to me.'

Then they heard the shouting and the laughter again. The punt paddled by Christopher Kempenflatt and a crew of girls had turned and was being driven fast towards them. Magnus Strove was standing in the prow holding the huge pole like a lance at a medieval tilt-yard. He gave a wild cry of triumph as his weapon struck Leslie Titmuss in the chest and sent him and his dinner-jacket, with his arms and legs waving helplessly, into the dark, brackish water of the Thames.

George Titmuss worked on his accounts and Elsie sat up knitting, determined not to go to bed until Leslie was safely home. They had the wireless on, playing late-night dance music, and she thought of her son, so immaculate and debonair, floating round the dance floor with a girl in a white dress who was smiling up at him. Then she heard the car arrive and the garage door shut. She went into the hall to meet him.

She heard his step on the gravel and opened the front door. He was still soaking wet, the starch gone out of his shirt and his brilliantined hair standing up in spikes because he had tried to rub it dry with his handkerchief. He stepped into the hallway, leaving a small puddle on the linoleum, and came very near to his mother to whisper, 'Bastards!'

The Temptation of Henry Simcox

After her visit to London Fred never felt entirely secure with Agnes, but that was nothing compared with the rising panic he felt at the thought of being without her. He had left Cambridge with no clear idea of what he wanted to do: except that he was certain that he wouldn't be a parson. Agnes was finishing her course at Worsfield University and spent her weeks in a hall of residence and her weekends at home. Fred found that he thought about her always and when they weren't together he was spending more and more time with her father.

His habit of joining Dr Salter on his rounds, which had started with the birth of Dora Nowt's fifth, grew as Fred tried to fill his uneventful days, waiting to see Agnes at weekends or on occasional evenings. He took to going into the cottages the Doctor visited and learned to change a dressing or turn an old woman in bed. Dr Salter's methods were a continual source of amazement to him. He could quieten a child with a broken arm or a woman with a crushed finger by producing what he called 'a special pain-killing pill flown in to me from America' which he kept in a small paper in his waistcoat pocket. When Fred asked him what it was he said, 'It's a rare drug known as an Extra-Strong Mint.'

'You're an old fraud,' Fred told him.

'Of course, I'm just like your father. It's faith, that's what we're both after.'

Dr Salter told Fred that when he was a young man he also had joined an old doctor on his rounds. 'Alfie Dawlish. Invented all sorts of imaginary ailments for the family at the Manor so he could rob them and treat the village for nothing. It was his primitive version of the Health Service. Finally old Lady Fanner, Nicholas's mother, sacked him for giving her an uncalled-for enema and charging ten quid. She didn't mind the money but she couldn't look Alfie in the face again. After that infant mortality in Skurfield rose considerably. I was a bit like you in those days. You know what Alfie Dawlish called me? The Sorcerer's Apprentice.'

Simeon, although far too liberal to do anything about it, didn't approve of the hours that Fred spent with Dr Salter and this disapproval did nothing but increase his son's respect for the medical profession. After all, he argued with relief, doctors weren't concerned with the reform of the world, or spiritual values, or protests about some faraway injustice it was impossible to remedy. A doctor's concern was entirely practical and had nothing whatever to do with the patient's soul. When Fred asked Agnes's father if that was why he had wanted to become a doctor he got a short answer. 'Balls! I had no choice. I couldn't pass the bloody exams to be a vet.'

But Fred had chosen his profession. When he told Agnes she looked at him quite nervously and said, 'Not because of me! Don't do it because of me, I couldn't take the responsibility.' He told her that of course it wasn't because of her, but he wasn't altogether telling the truth. The house in which Agnes was the only woman, the fact that she had become, apparently so easily, his lover, and her father who laughed at ideals, wished to die on the hunting-field, approved of backing into church gates and showed so little concern for his patients except when he was treating them, these things acted as an irresistible magnet to a young man brought up in the rarified atmosphere of Rapstone Rectory.

Fred had done classics at school. He needed A-levels in science before he started his medical studies, so he lived at home, drew five pounds a week from his father and set to work on chromosomes and enzymes and the biology of the newt. Agnes got her degree but she showed no signs of leaving Hartscombe. She said she thought her father needed looking after, she didn't want to go anywhere else much, particularly not to France. Doing modern languages at Worsfield had apparently spoiled her for France. So she stayed at home, a state of affairs which suited Fred perfectly.

In his happier, more optimistic moments he thought she would stay until she became the new local doctor's wife and then they would both live there forever. Dr Salter said, 'Someday someone's going to have to come and take her off my hands.'

'You used to tell me not to fall in love with her.'

'It was excellent advice. She was a child who grew up too quickly. It gave her a great deal of character. No one but a fool wants a wife with a great deal of character. I suppose you disagree?'

Fred said yes, he supposed he did.

England entered into the 1960s.

In the great world of politics sixty-nine Africans were shot at Sharpeville and Simeon Simcox wrote far more than sixty-nine letters. *Lady Chatterley's Lover* was adjudged suitable reading for the English people, an event which had no noticeable effect on the love-affair of Fred and Agnes Salter. In the Hartscombe Conservative Association there was a general feeling that Mr Macmillan was in his heaven and all was more or less right with the world. Attendance at the Y.C. evenings began to fall off in this somewhat complacent atmosphere, but Leslie Titmuss never missed a meeting. Christopher Kempenflatt, who became the Secretary, was often in London 'getting to know the ropes' of his father's firm. Leslie Titmuss offered to lend a hand by taking the minutes, which he did industriously and in great detail. When Kempenflatt became totally immersed in his father's business Leslie let it be known that he was prepared to take on the office of Secretary and, one afternoon when the Committee were anxious to get home early, he was nodded through. He was always pleasant, usually quiet and the President of the Young Conservatives began to depend on him to draw up the agenda.

The first year of the decade was also a historic one in the life of Henry Simcox. It was when he first came into contact with that brave new world where he would make his money, achieve success and finally enjoy the pleasure of disillusion. Almost two years after the publication of *The Greasy Pole* he received a letter on heavily embossed writing-paper from Atalanta Film Productions to inform him that Mr Benjamin K. Bugloss, Executive President in Charge of Artistic Enterprises, would be fulfilling a cherished ambition if he were able to meet with Mr Henry Simcox for a working breakfast in the Dorchester Hotel and would 8 for 8.30 a.m. be convenient?

Henry judged it right to present himself at the suite at 8.15 and it was some considerable time before his ring was answered. Finally the door was opened a chink and a gravelly voice said, 'Just leave it outside there, will you?'

'I'm Henry Simcox.'

'You're not room service?' The voice sounded suspicious.

'No. I'm Henry Simcox. I wrote *The Greasy Pole*. You asked me to breakfast.'

'Mr Simcox! This is a very great honour. Come in, why don't you? We were expecting room service.' The door was thrown open to reveal a large, suntanned man of indeterminate age who wore nothing except a white towelling dressing-gown on the breast of which was embroidered the simple inscription 'Hotel George V', and a pair of Gucci slippers. Looking round the suite Henry saw magazines, copies of *Variety* and a number of novels, so new that they appeared unread, including *The Greasy Pole*, which he picked up and admired, not for the first time, the photograph of the young, smiling author Henry Simcox. 'You really like it?'

'I don't like it.' Henry put his book down, disappointed. 'My dear, I love it! Tell me quite frankly. You must have become a lover at a very tender age. At what precise moment was it you first became a lover?' Mr Bugloss wandered to a bureau and discovered a cigar box. 'Don't worry, my dear. Tell me later. Do you care for a cigar?' He opened the box and discovered that it only contained one, which he took out and lit thoughtfully. 'That guy who works in a flower shop. Isn't that a hilarious conception?'

'It's a brewery.'

'What?' Mr Bugloss puffed on his cigar and frowned.

'He works in a brewery.'

'Are you sure?'

'Well, *I* wrote it!' Henry felt he had to remind him.

'So you did, my dear. And if I had my way you'd have sole writing credit. Of course, I have a partner.' Mr Bugloss went to the window and stood looking out over Park Lane. After a considerable silence he spoke, slowly and impressively. 'In our business,' he said, 'our names are written, Mr Simcox, on the sands of time. But there is one project, just one perhaps, by which someone hopes to be remembered. My dream is that your *Greasy Pole* should become a major motion picture.'

'That's marvellous.' Henry welcomed the news.

'I can give you certain things, Mr Simcox. I will fly you to the Coast. I can put a limo at your disposal. There will be a reception given in your honour. Subject to the views of my partner, my thought is that you should participate in profits. I should like to see you with a percentage, Mr Simcox.'

'Well, yes. I mean, so would I.'

'A percentage, after the deduction of my reasonable living expenses. Plus a small contribution to the cost of my boat, used for entertaining and general promotion. What's the title of your property again?' Mr Bugloss slumped into an armchair and sat smoking, thoughtful and anxious.

'*The Greasy Pole,*' Henry explained brightly, trying to cheer Mr Bugloss up. 'It's a game they used to have at regattas. A pole's covered with grease and you have to try and climb it but of course you can't. You keep sliding and falling into the river.'

'In the States they don't.'

'Don't what?'

'Have such things at regattas.' Mr Bugloss was positive. 'And a title like that might give serious offence to an ethnic minority. I have a great idea.' He got up, apparently cheerful. 'And I will present it to you as a gift with no strings attached. How do you like our title, *Indiscretions*?'

'I'm not sure.'

'And another thing, my dear' – Mr Bugloss ignored his doubts – 'how does your storyline end? Remind me.'

'Well, he ᴄould marry the girl, of course, and live in the big house.'

'The big house! I like it. Cute girl too, as I remember.'

'But he decides to stay in his job at the Brewery. Well, I suppose in a way he feels he has to be true to his class.'

'Then he's a schmuck!'

'You don't like the ending?'

Mr Bugloss went to the sofa and sat by his author, putting his arm round him. Henry tried not to look at the expanse of hairy stomach now exposed beneath the dressing-gown.

'I find it moving! I find it very artistic. I find it strikes a deep note of truthfulness, even if that makes him a bit of a schmuck. But who the hell's going to pay two dollars together with what it costs for a simple meal out and parking the car and a babysitter nowadays to see the story of a schmuck? I think my partner would have problems with your present ending. Some people think solely of finance.' Before Henry could reply Mr Bugloss went to the telephone and growled into it, 'Room service.' At which moment the bedroom door opened and a rather beautiful, nervous young woman, dressed like a Hampstead housewife, came out. 'Mr Simcox. This is an old friend of mine. Mrs Wickstead. You read Mr Simcox's great novel?'

'Never.' Mrs Wickstead sat down, sighed and pushed back her hair. She was not only beautiful but appeared to be English.

'I gave it to you. How come you didn't read it?' Henry noticed how strangely Mr Bugloss's accent varied. Most of the time he was American; when, as at that moment, he was irritable he sounded German; when he changed again and smiled with genuine charm he might have grown up in the London suburbs. 'You two will get on, I can see that. I can sense an empathy. We shall arrange a lunch at the Green Giraffe. Are you room service?' He spoke into the telephone he was still holding and then looked up at Henry. 'You don't care for any champagne to celebrate our association?'

'Well . . .' Henry thought he might care for a little.

'No champagne,' Mr Bugloss said firmly and spoke to the telephone. 'We'll just take some of your fresh orange juice. Make it three. And a coffee. And I'll take one of your hot bread rolls, with just a little butter for the sake of energy. Do you have some nice butter?' He put down the phone, blew out smoke and said in a voice now hushed with reverence, 'Peck wants to do a picture with me.'

'Gregory Peck?'

'Who else? Mrs Wickstead knows that, don't you, my dear?'

'*Do* I?'

'She knows. Greg Peck can't wait to do a picture with me. I *see* Greg in *Indiscretions*.'

'*The Greasy Pole.*' Henry remained firm on the point.

'I think this is one Greg Peck will really go for. If we get the script right.'

Henry, suddenly determined, rose to his feet. It was about to become his finest hour. 'Mr Bugloss.'

'Oh, please. Benny.' Mr Bugloss smiled modestly.

'Benny. Have you considered that the leading character in my book is a twenty-three-year-old Englishman who works in a small country town? I don't see how he could be played by a middle-aged American actor.'

'Peck can't help that, don't hold his years against him.'

Henry started to move out of the room. He knew how Michelangelo might have felt when the Pope suggested cutting Adam out of the ceiling in the Sistine Chapel. 'And I'll never agree to change the ending.'

'Middle age will come to you too, my dear, eventually.'

'I don't think I want anything to do with your trade.' Henry had reached the door. 'Nothing but visual tricks. No depth. No feeling. A few superficial snapshots of life and nothing but glamour and emptiness and using the whole wide world as a sort of stage set for inflated fantasies! I don't want any part of it, thank you very much.'

When Henry had gone Mr Bugloss turned to Mrs Wickstead and said thoughtfully, 'There goes a young man who's absolutely hooked on the movies.'

Benny Bugloss rose to power in the film world at a rare moment in history, when life in England was thought to be interesting to the American public, and when American producers found that costs and taxes were lower on the other side of the Atlantic. He was 'close to' the heads of various Hollywood studios, who liked to buy their suits in Savile Row, their pipes at Dunhill, to rent houses in Eaton Square and in general behave like their idea of an Englishman. From this position they could produce films about North Country boys whose old grandads kept racing pigeons.

'Where to now, girl?' Fred said in a Yorkshire accent, coming out of a cinema showing one such film. He and Agnes were on a rare outing to London. Agnes knew how impressionable he was – he had been speaking French when they came out of *Hiroshima*

Mon Amour. They started one of their frequent discussions about where they should go and Fred suggested her coffee bar.

'*My* coffee bar?'

'The one you say you hang about in when you come up to London. I mean, the one where you meet your friends.'

'Arturo's? Why not?' She led the way down the street from the cinema. 'I knew I'd end up by deciding.'

'*I* decided,' Fred protested.

'You decided that I should decide.'

So they sat in a dimly lit jungle of rubber plants, among a lot of people wearing duffel-coats, scarves and beards, listening to the muted music of Cliff Richard and the Shadows, with the photographs of stars on the walls, Tommy Steele, Alma Cogan and Dickie Valentine, and drank 'froffy' coffee out of see-through cups.

'Where shall we go?' Fred held Agnes's hand across the table. 'I mean, from here?'

'Back to Hartscombe on the train.'

'What about the friends in London you're always talking about, hasn't one of them got a room we could borrow?'

'No.' Agnes removed her hand. 'None that would be suitable. You'll go back to the Rectory, and drop me off at the surgery.'

'Not even go to our country place?' He smiled at her. 'Nowt Hall.' When desperate for accommodation they had been known to borrow Tom's hut in the depths of the wood where no one ever came.

'You like all that. It makes you feel grown up.'

'Enormously. I couldn't go back now.'

'Back to what?'

'Back to doing without you.'

'Please.' She sounded distressed. 'Don't say things like that.'

'I think we ought to go now,' Fred told her. 'We'll miss our train.'

'Why do you want to go suddenly?'

The reason was sitting alone, smiling and slightly drunk at the other end of Arturo's coffee bar. They had to pass Henry on their way to the door and he called out, 'The country cousins! My little brother, stumping round London with manure on his wellies. Hullo, Agnes.'

'We've got to go,' Fred told him.

'Or you'll turn back into a pumpkin. I have news for you, young Freddie. I've saved my soul. That's what I'm celebrating, and you've got time for another froffy before you go back to vegetate in rural Rapstone. You don't seem to be very interested in the state of my soul.'

'Did you say you'd saved it or something?' To his disappointment Fred saw that Agnes was sitting at Henry's table. He sat beside her and refused all refreshment.

'I'll tell you.' Henry was looking at Agnes. 'I'll tell you both. Mephistopheles appeared to me in the shape of an overweight monstrosity called Benjamin K. Bugloss. He lured me to the Dorchester. He offered me everything! A trip to Los Angeles, massage by starlets. He promised to deliver me champagne and Gregory Peck, all I had to do was to change my ending. Oh, and he wanted a new title for my book. Can you believe it? He called it a *property*. *The Greasy Pole* a *property*, like a tasteful home in Esher or something. He offered me all that, plus a dinner with a Mrs Wickstead who has beautiful frightened eyes and is clearly looking for ways of escape from Benjamin K. And what did I do?'

'Signed the contract?' Fred looked ostentatiously at the clock surrounded by brass sun-rays on the wall.

'You misjudge me, Frederick. I spurned his offer! I shook the dust of the Dorchester off my feet. I shall never see Los Angeles. I shall never meet Greg Peck. Mrs Wickstead will remain a closed book to me. I have preserved my integrity!'

In the corner of the carriage Agnes slept with her head on Fred's shoulder. The train shuddered to a halt at the small, ill-lit station, there was a sound of doors banging and an elderly guard shouted 'Hartscombe! All change, please!' Agnes opened her eyes. 'What on earth was Henry talking about?'

'His soul. I wonder where he keeps it.'

★ 11 ★
Borrowers and Lenders

After Simeon's death Henry and Lonnie were looking through the big cardboard boxes of family photographs that were kept in a cupboard under the Rectory stairs. There were pictures of the family dressed up for various entertainments, Henry as a pirate, Fred as a girl. 'Pity he never married, make a good wife to someone, old Frederick would,' Henry said. There was even a picture of Leslie Titmuss cutting down nettles. In the photographs it always seemed to be summer. Dorothy appeared rarely but Simeon was a sort of star. He was to be seen digging, greeting the Bishop, holding babies he had recently christened or upstaging the bride after various wedding ceremonies he had performed.

'Your father always looked so serene,' Lonnie said. 'So saintly.'

'It's perfectly easy to look serene if you happen to be completely off your head. Haven't you noticed that dotty people always have that wonderful saintly expression.'

Henry picked up a photograph and examined it closely. It was blurred, yellowed with age, but once in the Rectory garden a man in an old torn jacket was holding up a pair of dead rabbits which hid most of his face. Simeon Simcox was looking at the man, smiling broadly and accepting the rabbits as a gift. Dorothy was smiling in the background of the picture. Now, having taken out the coffee tray, she returned to the living-room.

'Who's that extraordinary man holding up rabbits?' Henry gave the picture to his mother who took it over to the window and examined it closely.

'That's Tom Nowt.'

'Tom Nowt the poacher?'

'A poacher? Well, I suppose he must have been, although we

didn't like to say so. He used to bring us rabbits sometimes, and I used to make pâté with them, although I expect he got them from our bit of woodland.'

'Tom Nowt, who used to have that broken-down hut in Hanging Wood?'

'Did he? I may have heard something ...' Dorothy became vague. 'I can't exactly remember.'

'But he and our father look perfectly friendly.'

'Your father always got on with everyone.'

'Not with Tom Nowt, he didn't!' Henry remembered. 'He disapproved violently of Tom Nowt, for some reason. The only time I saw him angry was when Frederick had been hanging round Nowt's hut.'

Dorothy shook her head. 'With Fred? No, really, I'm sure you must be mistaken.' She put the photograph in her cardigan pocket and when Henry held out his hand, asking for it back, she refused, smiling. 'Whatever do you want it for ? An old photograph.'

'It just might become useful evidence.'

'Of what, on earth?'

'Father's irrational prejudices.'

'You know Henry's starting a court case,' Lonnie explained.

Dorothy stopped smiling. She stood, still firmly holding the photograph in her pocket. 'I think it's disgusting.'

'It's to help you, Mother,' Lonnie went on, 'as much as anyone.'

'I can get on perfectly well without help, thank you.'

'We've got to get at the truth.' Henry did his best to control his rising irritation. At this his mother, who had decided to go out and snip off a few dead heads, turned on him instead. 'The truth! I'm not sure you'd know the truth if you found it. I mean, all those stories and films and things you're always working at. They don't have much to do with the truth, do they?'

'I suppose I could say that there's a deeper sort of truth which can only be reached by fiction.' Henry had said that often on television arts programmes.

'You wouldn't say that, Henry. You wouldn't be so silly!' Dorothy was laughing at him now.

'Henry's been to see a lawyer, Dorothy,' Lonnie was explaining, as though to a child. 'So if Leslie Titmuss goes on claiming Simeon's money . . . Well, there'll have to be a case in court.'

'You mean I'd have to stand up in public and answer questions?'

'It might have to come to that, mother. Yes.'

'We'd hope it wouldn't,' Lonnie assured her.

'You wouldn't be frightened, would you?' Henry tried to sound reassuring.

'Frightened? I'd be humiliated!'

'I don't know why.'

'To stand and talk about our family, about Simeon, in front of a lot of total strangers, to have it all written up in the paper, for Glenys Bigwell to read, and Grace Fanner at the Manor, wouldn't that be humiliating? It's just like you, Henry, to arrange that. Just like those awful film stories you sent us to read, and your father and I were so embarrassed! We didn't know how you could bring yourself to do such things.'

Before Henry could reply his mother had gone off into the kitchen where she opened the Aga and dropped Tom Nowt and his rabbits, in the company of her smiling and departed husband, on to the burning boiler nuts, where they were quickly consumed. Then she forgot about the past, and thought of her immediate future. Now Simeon was dead she would have to leave the Rectory and move into somewhere much smaller.

Fred was lying naked under a damp blanket on the old iron bedstead in Tom Nowt's hut. Agnes, wearing nothing but Fred's shirt, lifted the kettle she had put on the paraffin stove and stooped to light a cigarette from the flame. On the walls the antlered deer skulls and the pin-ups were expressionless. They had bicycled down to the hut an hour earlier, skidding on wet, fallen leaves, and Fred had laughed and shouted. Now he was quiet, it was time to ask the question he dreaded every month.

'No curse?'

'Nothing.'

'It's just late.'

'Nearly three weeks.' She made tea for them both and then came and sat on the bed beside him. 'What would you do, Fred?'

He looked at the shadow where the shirt divided, at her long white legs and avoided her question. 'It's awful having to start from scratch. If only I'd done science at school! Science was considered a bit common compared to Latin.'

'And now you feel a little science might come in handy?'

'If I'm going to be a doctor.'

'Oh, for that. Yes.' She drank her tea.

'You know I shan't make any money for years. I mean, I can't make plans or anything.'

'No. I do understand. It's cold in here.' She stood up, shivering. 'I'm going to get dressed.'

He didn't say anything more then, feeling that he would never say anything right.

Ten days later Fred had persuaded himself that he had nothing to worry about. It was a Friday night when, as usual, the Stompers met for a session at Marmaduke's garage in Hartscombe. They were playing 'Ain't Misbehavin'' on an oil-stained concrete floor, under naked electric light bulbs, among gutted Ford Populars and behind a jacked-up Daimler. Glenys Bigwell, a fair-haired, strong-minded girl, daughter of Bridget and Percy, was sitting on a wooden box looking starry-eyed at Terry Fawcett with whom she had been walking out since her schooldays. Glenys worked in a Hartscombe stationers and did part-time secretarial work for the Rector. Although her typing was enthusiastic, her spelling was weak and Simeon, too much in a hurry to correct it, sometimes signed letters to the Bishop protesting about 'apartaid' or racial 'descremination'.

Terry did his clarinet solo and then gave way to Fred, who went into a great burst of bravura drumming. When he was at the climax of his performance he saw Agnes step into one of the pools of light. His drumming quietened and finally died away, as though the sight of her, standing so quiet and unsmiling, had drained away his talents as a musician. Joe Sneeping, who was also looking at the new arrival, decided to stop the session and ask Glenys to get a brew on. Fred got up and followed Agnes into a quiet space between two cars. She said, 'I've found someone.'

'You mean . . . ?'

'Yes. Someone a friend of mine knows about.'

'Where? In Worsfield?'

'You don't have to worry about where. All you have to worry about is getting hold of a hundred pounds.'

'A *hundred*?'

'Well, that's not the difficult part, is it? In pound notes, apparently, and not too new.'

Joe had lifted his trumpet and was blowing the melody of 'Snake Rag'. Agnes seemed to be crying. Fred put his arms round her and told her that of course he'd get it. Agnes sniffed, wiped her eyes on the sleeve of her duffel-coat and, suddenly saying, 'Goodbye, Fred,' released herself from him and walked away. He would have gone after her but the session was starting again. 'Get on the skins, man!' Joe called in his best New Orleans accent and Fred returned obediently to his drums and beat out the rhythm he had known so long, and which represented musical purity for the Stompers, with no taint of commercialism. A hundred pounds! He couldn't remember ever having seen a hundred pounds, all at one time. He found himself envying his father, who had nothing to worry about except the future of mankind.

Charlie and Leslie did not meet for some time after the disaster of the Young Conservatives dinner dance. She had found herself thinking of him often, as of a strange, intense creature, a foreigner in her small world, who had moved her by his unhappiness and anger. When she thought of how much she disliked the young men her mother had wanted her to go out with she found herself warming to the memory of Leslie Titmuss. One afternoon she had been to the cinema in Hartscombe on her own and sat down to a lonely tea in the Copper Kettle in the High Street, when a voice said, 'No objection to my sitting here at all?' Leslie didn't wait for a reply but made himself comfortable and ordered the set tea. He seemed in a mood of high excitement, and to have quite forgotten the humiliations he had suffered when they last met. 'I've been looking forward to telling you,' he announced at once. 'I've done it.'

'Done what?'

'Got on the Committee.'

'The Committee of what?'

'The Young Conservatives, of course.'

'You mean the people who pushed you in the river?'

'Well, that was all a bit of fun, wasn't it? I'd like to go for Secretary eventually. Do you think your father would put in a word for me?'

'I don't expect so. He's awfully vague about that sort of thing.'

'We can't really talk here, can we?' Leslie seemed prepared to accept the Chairman's vagueness for the moment and was concerned with the grey-haired tea drinkers around them.

'You seem to be managing all right.'

'Those old girls looking at us!'

'Perhaps they know about you being on the Committee. I mean, you must be famous!'

'Don't ever do that,' Leslie warned her.

'What?'

'Take the mickey.'

His rebuke startled her so that she felt in no position to refuse his suggestion that they might go out some time, and their meetings became curious oases in the desert of her life at home with her parents. Leslie seemed anxious to be discreet and suggested dates in unfrequented pubs near to the railway station or back streets behind the Brewery. During such meetings Leslie would tell Charlie about his political plans and ambitions and explain to her that the office of Secretary to the Y.C.s would, in the course of time, help him to a place on the Committee of the more senior branch of the Hartscombe Conservative Association. Whatever happened, he told her, he was determined to make something of himself. When she asked him, as she often did, what he intended to make, Leslie would smile enigmatically as though he were about to enter a new world which she would never be able to understand.

Sometimes he borrowed his father's car to take her for a 'run out into the country'. He always picked her up for these excursions at some neutral spot and explained that his parents didn't know that he was taking Charlotte Fanner out.

'Are you going to tell them?' Charlie asked.

'Of course. Eventually.'

'Why not now?'

'Oh, they're old-fashioned. My mother used to work for the Stroves. She worked in the kitchen. It made her very class-conscious. Me going out with the daughter of Rapstone Manor! She'd find that very shocking. Here, sit on this. You don't want to spoil your skirt.' He had driven her up to Picton Ridge, from where they looked down the valley and had a view of both villages and the factory chimneys around Worsfield on the distant horizon. He had taken a neatly folded tartan rug out of the back of the Prefect and was doing his best to insert it under Charlie.

'What would they do if they found out?' she asked him, raising herself for him to spread the rug beneath her.

'My father'd probably make a respectful call on yours and tell him to put a stop to it. He's quite capable of that.'

'Poor Leslie.'

'Oh no, don't feel sorry for me. In the end I'll bring them all round to my way of thinking. I say, I like your hair. In the sunshine. You're very beautiful.'

She hadn't screamed for a long time, not really since she had seen him, like a long black seal, slither out of the water in evening-dress. Now, however, she felt an awful upsurge of anger. 'Don't say that! You promised never to say that again!'

'But what would *your* father and mother say?'

The anger subsided and she felt a return of happiness. 'Mother'd be as sick as a dog but she'd have to lump it, wouldn't she?'

It was then, kneeling beside her, that Leslie Titmuss, after a slow courtship, took Charlie by the shoulders and kissed her. It was a carefully thought out, long-term move, to which she reacted with unexpected enthusiasm. To his surprise he found her kneeling in front of him, pulling at his belt as though such things were part of her everyday experience and not some long-cherished dream. Whatever fantasy it was it remained unacted. Leslie finally steered her hands to less controversial areas and, though he kissed her for a long time with concentration and zeal, it was clear that further developments still lay among his plans for the distant future.

While Leslie Titmuss and Charlie Fanner were spread out high above the Rapstone Valley, Fred sought an interview in the Rector's study. He went into the room to find his father sleeping, his long legs stretched in front of the fire, the report of a Royal Commission open and face downward on his chest. This retreat from the problems of the world, and in particular those of Frederick Simcox, irritated him. He banged the door shut and said, 'I want to talk to you.'

'Always. Always feel that you can.' Simeon opened his eyes and looked tolerant.

'About money.'

'Ah. Then I don't see that there's very much to discuss. I'm prepared to continue your modest allowance during the lengthy period it seems to take you to learn how to cut up frogs and . . .' he searched for a suitably dismissive phrase, 'pill-popping, bone-setting, and so on.' He stifled a small, remaining yawn. 'I know nothing of these mysteries.'

'They're not mysteries really.' Fred felt called upon to defend his chosen profession.

'To me, they are mysteries.'

'They're perfectly sensible, useful bits of information.'

'What a chameleon you are, my boy. You spend your days with the Salters and bring home all the Doctor's "sensible" expressions. It's like an infection.'

'I want to be sensible for a moment.' Fred sat down at the fireside also, opposite his father. 'Look, I'd be glad if you didn't tell Mother this.'

'Not tell her what?'

'You know what she is. She worries.' Fred fell silent and, when he thought it could be put off no longer, said, 'I need a hundred pounds.'

'And you shall have it!' Simeon leaned forward and put his hand on his son's knee, a gesture which Fred was too relieved to find embarrassing.

'Well, thank you very much.'

'Over the next five months, at the rate of five pounds a week.' Simeon got up, selected a pipe from the mantelpiece and began to fill it. Fred suspected that his father only smoked a pipe in order to irritate him at these interviews.

'No. No, that won't do. You see, I do need it now. In cash. You'll have it back. We've got a few gigs.'

'Gigs?' Simeon looked puzzled. 'You're talking about a kind of conveyance?'

'Jobs. With the band. Dances and . . . Well . . .'

'Oh, I wouldn't want you to neglect your medical studies and take to full-time on the kettle drum, for the sake of paying a debt to me.'

'I'll pay you back when I qualify, but I need it now. In one-pound notes.'

'You think you need it.' Simeon was exhausting his usual quota of matches. Fred knew, with a sinking of the heart, that they were about to drift away on a tide of moral philosophy.

'I know I do.'

'I'm not asking you what you think you need this money for. I shan't ever ask you that, Fred.' Tolerance was always one of Simeon's most effective weapons.

'Good.'

'It's your own life, and you must lead it as you feel it is most fitting. If you feel that it's in any way seemly to come and ask me for a hundred pounds . . .'

'*Used* notes. They don't have to be new at all.' Fred sounded as though he hoped that would make it easier.

'I'm not asking what you *think* you need it for and I don't want to know. But I will tell you one thing, Fred, it's not the answer.' He began to pace the room, as though in the early stages of composing a sermon. 'Money is never the answer! *They* think it is, don't they? Our new masters! Oh, they think money's the answer to everything. "You've never had it so good". Put a refrigerator in every cottage in Rapstone and a family runabout at every door.'

'I'm not asking for a refrigerator.' Fred felt the argument slipping away from him. 'Or even a family runabout.'

'And there'll still be a great longing, a great emptiness at the heart of the people.' Simeon was standing, looking at his son with quizzical sincerity. 'Because they do, they really do long for what money can't buy. Justice, equality, *caring* for those who aren't born with our advantages. I don't suppose you want this sum of money for any charitable purpose?'

'Not exactly charitable,' Fred had to admit. 'No.'

Simeon sat at his desk then, knocked his pipe out in the waste-paper basket and gave some hardly welcome advice. 'Neither a borrower nor a lender be, Fred, that's a pretty good rule for life. I think you'll find a greater peace of mind, just living within your allowance. *Used* one-pound notes, did you say?'

'Yes.' Fred felt a small stirring of hope but his father was, unbelievably, chuckling. 'You'll find they're just as hard to get hold of as the nice, crisp, crackling new ones.' He ended on a serious note, 'I'm glad we had this talk, Frederick. I'm sure you'll come to agree with me when you think hard about it.'

After Fred had gone Simeon put out his hand to one of the small wooden columns that separated the little drawers and cubby-holes on the top of his writing-desk. At the touch of a spring the pillar slid forward revealing a narrow, hidden compartment from which the Rector took a long, brown envelope. He didn't open it, or read its contents, but he made a short note with his fountain pen on the back of the envelope, initialled and dated it, and after a short pause when he might have been praying, or simply doing mental arithmetic, he returned it to its hiding-place.

Fred decided against telephoning his brother; instead he took an early train to London and prepared to take him by surprise. Henry, always lucky, had been able to find three rooms at the top of his publisher's house in Islington at a minimum rent. The publisher's wife looked after him, fed him whenever he looked plaintive and put his washing into her machine. His rooms, the servants' quarters of the tall Victorian house, were small, basically furnished by his landlord, but full of Henry's books, his old Russian political posters, stills from silent movies and the general clutter of his bachelor existence. He was pleased to have the hard task of writing interrupted by a visit from his younger brother and was amused by Fred's blurted-out request.

'A hundred pounds! Dear little Freddie. Did I hear you say a *hundred* pounds?'

'It's not a terrifically complicated sum.'

'I don't know whether you were listening that night in the coffee bar, young Fred, but I've saved my soul.'

'Oh, *that*.' Fred couldn't honestly see what his brother's soul had to do with it.

'Yes. "*That*", as you so lightly dismiss it, means that I am absolutely skint. Broke. Down to the bare bottom of my overdraft. I have rejected the appalling Bugloss and his thirty pieces of silver.'

'I don't want thirty pieces of silver,' Fred tried to explain. 'Just a hundred pounds.'

'Poor Fred, how little you understand the life of an artist.'

'I don't suppose I do.'

'Look. Let me put it to you in words of one syllable. I have given up money for Lent, or at least until I finish my next novel. I have taken money off my diet sheet. I live almost entirely on cold ham and tomatoes and Algerian cow's piss which I get in litre bottles from the off-licence.'

'It doesn't sound too bad.'

'I don't go out, Frederick. I simply never go out; have people *round*, of course.' He got up and went to inspect the view from his window. 'It's Agnes, isn't it? Agnes with what we used to call a bun in the oven. You must feel tremendously proud of yourself.'

'I'm not really.'

'I think you should have the little one. I think you owe it to the world to see what a small Frederick would be like, your one tiny hold on posterity.'

'Well, it's true I haven't written a novel.'

'No, you haven't, Fred, have you?' Henry turned away from the window and asked, quite casually, 'Do you think of what Agnes must be feeling?'

'I don't think she wants it, particularly.' Fred found the question unexpected and, coming from his brother, unfair. 'Obviously she doesn't. She asked me to find the money.'

'And you?'

'Can't you see? It's impossible now I'm going in for medicine.'

'Well, I always thought that was remarkably selfish of you.'

'I mean, our father . . .'

'Who art in Rapstone?'

'Father allows me five pounds a week, that's about all I'm going to earn for years. I mean, how could we possibly . . .'

'Dear old Fred. I always knew you were the ruthless one of the family.' Henry came and put a hand on Fred's shoulder, behaving more like an elderly uncle than a brother. 'It's impossible!' Fred was conscious that he was sounding plaintive and hated himself for it. 'I'll pay you back. I mean, you can't be short of a hundred pounds. You've only got to write a film script.'

'Write a film script?' Henry dropped his hand in mock horror, as though any contact with his brother might prove fatal. 'Are you trying to corrupt me? Get thee behind me, Frederick!'

In the days to come Fred scraped the bottom of the barrel. He found his mother rolling out pastry on the kitchen table and when he asked her if she had any money she wiped her hands on her apron, got her handbag off the dresser and said she had two pounds twelve and six. Asked if she could possibly lend him a hundred pounds, Dorothy smiled tolerantly. 'What silly things you come out with sometimes,' she told him.

As a last resort Fred walked the three miles to Picton House where he found Magnus circling a nearby wood with a gun and a spaniel. He remembered the young Strove's talent for making money at Knuckleberries and that Magnus had come into something under his grandfather's will. As they tramped through the brambles together the latest Strove told Fred of his plan to buy up Garthwaite's, the old family grocer's in Hartscombe, and start what he hoped would become a chain of Easy-Bite Dining-Parlours. 'Do an all-in evening meal, steak or scampi and French fries, cheese-board and half a bottle of Mateus Rosé for three quid all in. Of course, my partner and I are having a bit of trouble with the Council. They keep going on about "preserving the Georgian character of the High Street" and all that type of balderdash. I expect we'll win in the end.'

'So you'll make a lot of money.'

'Bob or two, I hope.'

'So you could afford to lend me a hundred pounds. I mean, I'd pay you back.'

A rabbit came scuttling out of the bushes, death blew it into the air for a second until it fell and the dog panted off to retrieve it. Magnus smiled charmingly. 'Sorry, old boy, not with all this going on. We're fully stretched, you know what I mean, absolutely fully stretched.'

When Fred telephoned Agnes she was busy, washing her hair, or going over to Worsfield to see a girl she had known at university, or having to entertain some cousins from Canada. However, she agreed to meet him at Tom Nowt's hut the next Saturday afternoon. They could do all their talking then, she told him.

In spite of his failure to solve their problem, to come up with the money in used notes, or any sort of notes, Fred bicycled down through the woods with excitement. At least he was going to see Agnes again and he could lie down with her and share her secrets. Perhaps, after all, the situation wasn't so desperate. Perhaps it was all a false alarm, or, he imagined in some way that would still need working out, they could have a child and marry and live together without dry-mouthed telephone calls and having to borrow Tom Nowt's to go to bed together. He arrived five minutes before the appointed time, but when she was not already there he knew that she was not coming.

All the same he waited for an hour and a half and then bicycled into Hartscombe and found Dr Salter alone and having tea. The Doctor looked at Fred with pity and asked if he really didn't know that Agnes had gone to London.

'Where in London?' Fred suddenly realized how little he knew of her friends there, or where he could telephone to find her.

'I believe she said, the usual places. It seems that she doesn't tell either of us very much.'

So Fred caught a train from Hartscombe and that evening found himself sitting alone in Arturo's coffee bar with no very clear idea of what he was going to do next. At last he tried asking the waitress who brought him his third espresso if she happened to have seen a girl with long hair who answered to the name of Agnes and smoked a lot.

'Sounds like everyone. I'll ask Arturo. Arturo! Do you know anyone called Agnes?'

The proprietor approached them and Fred looked up and saw him for the first time. His hair was slicked down, he had a small moustache and a sort of pallor as though he rarely saw the light. Arturo was wearing an Italian silk suit, a gold bracelet and pointed, patent leather shoes. He said, 'Hullo, Simcox Mi. Haven't seen you since the good old days at Knuckleberries.'

'Arthur Nubble! What on earth are you doing, posing as an Italian?'

'Nothing to it, old boy.' Arthur sat down with a sigh of relief, as though his shoes were killing him. 'It's all they want nowadays. An Italian name. A few rubber plants. Take enough black coffee to cover a postage stamp and blow a cloud of steam up its arse, add a bit of froth and charge ninepence. I'm just providing a service.'

'The last time you did that you got the sack.'

'I resigned. I'd had far too much education. Did you say you were looking for a girl? There's one working the steam pump I'm anxious to dispose of.' Fred looked at a plump girl pulling the handle of the hissing espresso machine. 'Your waitress?'

'No,' Arthur told him gloomily. 'My wife. You look as though you need a drink. Abandon that ink and candy floss. Let's go to a party!'

'You haven't seen Agnes?'

'Who's Agnes?'

'The girl I'm looking for.'

'You want one in particular?'

'Yes.'

'You were always a difficult customer to please, Simcox. Probably comes of you being Labour.' He stood up, wincing at the tightness of his shoes. 'Come to the party! There's bound to be some of Arturo's regulars around there. They may have seen your Agatha.'

'Agnes.' Fred also stood up, but without much hope. 'Her name's Agnes.'

'I'm sure you know best.'

They went out of the back entrance to where Arthur Nubble's dented, second-hand Jaguar was parked on the pavement. Fred got into the car which smelt strongly of coffee and Arthur drove very fast, coming to rest in front of a tall house in a square. The top-floor windows were open and modern jazz drifted down to them.

'This is where my brother lives.'

'Well, anyway we'll get a drink.'

'Don't be too sure,' Fred warned him as they got out of the car. 'Anyway, nothing but Algerian cow's piss.'

Fred was wrong about that. When they got up to the party a large, suntanned man wearing a silk scarf and a hugely checked tweed jacket poured him a glass of champagne. There were a lot of girls in the shadows, sitting on the sofa, whispering in corners, even dancing together to the calculated murmurs of Dave Brubeck. Some of them called out 'Arturo!' and Arthur hobbled off to join them. Fred thought that he saw some new bits and pieces, some black-shaded lamps and a new silky rug on the floor. Henry, who had clearly been buying furniture, was nowhere to be seen.

'Are you a friend of the genius?' the man who had been pouring Fred's champagne asked him.

'Which genius is that?' Fred was puzzled.

'Mr Henry Simcox.'

'Oh, *that* genius. I'm his brother.'

'Henry never told me he had a brother.'

'No? So far as Henry's concerned it's a closely guarded secret.' Fred suddenly felt a large arm round his shoulder. The man had come unacceptably close to him. 'Honoured to meet you, my dear. I'm Benny Bugloss. And I'm overjoyed to be translating your brother's great work into a major motion picture. We shall try, Mr Simcox, my dear, and we shall overcome.'

'*The Greasy Pole?*' Fred asked, extricating himself from Mr Bugloss's embrace.

'Isn't that a great title? And I'll tell you something, we're keeping it *exactly as it is*!'

'You're Mephistopheles?' Fred looked at Mr Bugloss.

'No. Bugloss. Benjamin K. Bugloss. Has someone else got an interest in the film rights?'

'Oh, I don't think so.'

'I have told your brother. I want to be absolutely true to his conception.' Mr Bugloss was deeply serious. 'You see, in the end this guy decides to give up the Ladyship and go back to his job in the Brewery. He's true to his class, you understand. Some would say he's a schmuck, but I say, "No. He's a hero."'

'What about Gregory Peck?' Fred remembered what Henry had told him.

'No.' Mr Bugloss was thinking deeply. 'Somehow I don't see Peck in this. I more likely see someone along the lines of Albert Finney, someone British. Shall I tell you something? Britain is bankable right now, Britain could be good news at the box office.'

'So you took Henry up on to a high mountain?'

'Our first meeting didn't go too well. But he called me and I met with him again. In the Dorchester, my suite, we worked something out. A *modus*.'

'A what?'

'A *modus vivendi*.'

'You showed him all the kingdoms of the world in a moment of time.'

'I told him I'd fly him to the Coast.'

'"And said unto him, all this power will I give thee."'

'Hey, what're you talking about?'

'How much did you pay him?' Fred, on his third glass of champagne, made so bold as to ask.

'Thirty thousand dollars, plus a piece of the action. It may not be all the kingdoms of the world, my dear, but it certainly ain't peanuts.'

A young woman emerged from the shadows and Mr Bugloss introduced her. 'This is a friend of mine. Mrs Wickstead. This is Mr Simcox.'

'Hullo.'

'Absolutely *loved* your book,' Mrs Wickstead told him.

'That wasn't me. It was my brother.' Fred allowed his glass to be refilled and looked towards the bedroom door which had suddenly opened. The lights were on inside and the party was beginning to spill into it. When Henry came out of the door he had a bottle of champagne in one hand and his other arm round Agnes's waist. They both looked at Fred, he thought, with a smile of faint amusement.

'Hullo, young Fred.' Henry seemed not at all surprised to see him. 'Welcome to our farewell party. I'm off to the Coast. Of course, Agnes is coming with me.'

When he thought about it, and he thought about it always, it seemed to Fred like some sickening accident, the prolonged moment when a car slithers out of control and you wait, helplessly, for the inevitable crash, the tearing of metal, injury or death. He remembered Agnes smiling patiently as, humiliated, he held her arm, tried to drag her away from the party and back to Hartscombe. She didn't move, or try to shake him off, but waited, still smiling, until he released her and then she walked away into the kitchen where three or four girls were getting food ready for the party. He remembered Henry, also smiling, speaking as though his younger brother had left him with a heavy responsibility which he had, selflessly, agreed to discharge.

'You abandoned her, Fred.' Henry was holding a short sausage on a stick and taking small, eager bites as he spoke. 'You let her down, you didn't give her what she needed most.'

'You know what that is?' The room had become misty and Fred had an appalling suspicion that he might burst into tears.

'Of course. Money was required and I provided it. As a matter of fact I made a considerable sacrifice. Just because of you, Fred, I'm writing a film for Benjamin K. Bugloss. If you hadn't let Agnes down so badly my soul might have remained a virgin. I say. You're not going to blub, are you? I haven't seen you blub since we were at Knuckleberries.'

Fred didn't blub. Instead he drank everything he could lay his hands on until Arthur Nubble told him he looked ghastly and should be taken away. As they left, they passed Mr Bugloss in the doorway.

'Did I have a problem persuading your brother to write this screenplay? Well, artists are not easy people or they wouldn't be artists, would they?'

'I fixed it for you.' Fred assured him.

'You son of a bitch! How did you manage that?'

'Well, you see, my brother's hang-up was his soul. I can reliably inform you that he hasn't got a soul any more. There's absolutely nothing to stop him working for the movies.'

They left with several girls from the party and, organized by Nubble, went to a dark, reverberating club somewhere high over Leicester Square. In the gents, Nubble found that he had a packet of purple hearts about him and offered them to Fred.

'No thanks, really.'

'What's the matter with you, Simcox? You never want to take what anyone has to give. It was the same at school. You never really wanted the bit of pâté de foie I got hold of. People don't like it, you know, if you don't take what's offered.'

So Fred chewed purple hearts for the sake of not offending

Nubble and returned to stumble round the dance area guided by a girl called Denise whom he had last seen cutting up sandwiches at Henry's flat. She appeared to him as a mildly attractive blur and he heard himself talking to her as though his was the voice of a distant stranger.

'I think you're beautiful,' the voice said.

'You're pissed.'

'You mean I think you're beautiful therefore I must be pissed? That's an a priori argument. But I'm pissed therefore I think you're beautiful. A posteriori.'

'Try not to be vulgar.'

'God's in his heaven. All's right with the world. Does that mean God's there so the world's all right, or does it mean the world's so sodding marvellous that there has to be a God?' The stranger who was talking seemed to Fred to be a pretentious and patronizing idiot.

'You're tense. That's what your trouble is.' The girl's face was almost entirely out of focus. 'You've got inner tension.'

Later he thought he was in bed with Agnes who was wearing nothing but one of his shirts, a silent, almost inert Agnes who said nothing and kept changing her shape. When he woke in the morning feeling terribly ill he looked for the deer skulls on the walls of Tom Nowt's hut and found that he was in a put-u-up bed in Arthur Nubble's Pimlico maisonette, and that his shirt was on the otherwise naked Denise, who was sitting up beside him repairing her make-up.

'Just remind me,' she said. 'Did we knock it off last night?'

In the kitchen, to which Fred had staggered for a glass of water, Arthur Nubble was wearing the sort of camelhair dressing-gown and flannel pyjamas that were uniform in the dormitory at Knuckleberries. He was grilling some lambs' kidneys he had been lucky enough to put his hands on for breakfast.

'I say, Simcox. You know that girl you were looking for at the party?'

'Yes.'

'I remember now,' Nubble told him. 'She was a bit stuck for a name and address. Well, I was able to fix her up with someone, of course, but she couldn't come up with the hundred pounds.'

When he got home, Fred went for a walk in the woods to Tom Nowt's hut. He heard his voice, hoarse, strained and despairing, calling 'Agnes!' through the trees. Overcome with exhaustion, alcohol, purple hearts and the indulgence of grief, he sank to his knees in the fallen leaves, and there he was when Dr Salter, hacking his old grey, found him. The Doctor took Fred to his house and treated all his complaints with the medicine he trusted most, the passage of time.

But when he found him, kneeling in the wood, he said, 'For God's sake, young Fred. Don't tell me you've taken to prayer!'

Part Three

Life must be lived forwards, but it can only be understood backwards.

Sören Kierkegaard

★ 12 ★
Chez Titmuss

On a Saturday morning, not long after Fred's visit to London, George Titmuss was washing and cleaning the Ford Prefect in front of 'The Spruces', according to his established practice. He hosed, shampooed, washed off and polished the car's maroon exterior, Windowlened the glass and hoovered the inside. Then he opened the glove compartment in order to give it a good dust and made an unwelcome discovery. A lipstick, a headscarf and a small crumpled handkerchief, still faintly redolent of perfume borrowed from Grace, were there found lurking. George removed these objects and took them into the house, where his son was finishing his breakfast, three rashers and two eggs on a fried slice prepared by his mother, and reading the *Financial Times*.

'You've taken to wearing lippie-stick, have you, boy?' George asked with an unwonted but not good-humoured smile. Before his son could answer, George Titmuss had gone into the kitchen, found a carrier-bag for the three exhibits, and was setting out for Rapstone Manor.

Nicholas received him in the conservatory, and there, among the begonias, George Titmuss laid out the damning relics saying, in the manner of a police sergeant giving painful evidence at a particularly repulsive murder trial, 'Traces of your daughter, Sir, have been found in my vehicle. The handkerchief displays her name-tape.' He produced Exhibit A: 'C. Fanner. No doubt she'll have had it marked for going away to boarding-school. My son, Leslie, never went away to boarding-school,' he added, as though to clinch the prosecution case.

'Of course, there's a great deal to be said for keeping the family together.' Nicholas was conciliatory.

'There's a great deal to be said for only doing what you can afford.'

'And of course, we have a magnificent state education. We must take the credit for that, you remember Rab Butler's splendid Act? It's done a great deal for the youngsters.' Nicholas avoided looking at the traces of Charlie on the table, taking refuge in wider political issues.

'We don't complain.' George was clearly speaking for the youngsters also.

'I'm sure you don't. And your young man, if I may say, is making something of himself. He chipped in at a meeting the other day. I'm not saying we'll see him on the Executive Committee for a year or two yet. But he's making his mark.'

Leslie had, Nicholas remembered, been particularly passionate at one recent gathering, when local issues had been discussed. He wanted the Hartscombe Party to get behind a plan to pull down Garthwaite's, the old grocer's shop, and allow some appalling chain restaurant to be built in its place. The Conservative majority on the Town Council, young Titmuss had told them all, must move with the times, although Nicholas didn't see the need for it himself. Now he wondered uneasily if George Titmuss had also come in pursuance of the scheme to pull down the old family grocer's shop, founded by a long-dead butler of a long-dead Nicholas Fanner. A silence fell on the two fathers in the conservatory, and Nicholas looked round at the stunted plants, too brightly coloured for their own good, which moved him to pity.

'You don't care for begonias, Titmuss?'

'Our only child will do perfectly nicely in his niche at the Brewery, just as I did before him.' George failed to answer the question. 'We don't want our Leslie disturbed by any undesirable friendships. I am referring, Sir Nicholas' – George shaped slowly up to the object of his call – 'to your daughter, Charlotte.'

'You call her undesirable? Well, I suppose that's reasonable.'

'Imagine if it went too far,' George went on gloomily. 'If it led to marriage, for instance.'

'Marriage? Is that what you have in mind?' Nicholas smiled with a tolerance which appeared to irritate Leslie's father.

'I do not have it in mind, Sir Nicholas. I certainly do not. Mrs

144

Titmuss and I have something of a reputation around Skurfield.
We are well known for keeping ourselves to ourselves.'

'Yes. I've heard that, of course.'

'Do you think we want to be invited here all the time for dinner
parties, cocktails and the like? Do you think my Elsie wants to sit
down to dinner with Mr Doughty Strove?'

'Well, poor old Doughty does rather bore for England, of course.
But she could probably talk to whoever's on her *other* side,'
Nicholas suggested helpfully.

'It's got to be put a stop to,' George said firmly, no doubt feeling
that the discussion was about to drift into backwaters of irrelevance.
'Our Leslie and Miss Charlotte, they've got to be told it won't do.
They mustn't see each other again, that's for the best.'

'It may be for the *best*,' Nicholas admitted, 'but we live in the
world of practical politics. What can we do, even if it's not for the
best?'

'It's simple, isn't it? Your daughter's not twenty-one, you've
just got to put your foot down!' George looked at Nicholas who
was shifting uncomfortably, as though prepared to put his foot
anywhere but down. 'Or, if you can't manage that, no doubt her
Ladyship can.'

Charlie had no idea whether or not she loved Leslie, but she
thought about him incessantly and these thoughts puzzled her.
Sometimes he looked so unnaturally pale and fragile that she felt
sorry for him and afraid he wouldn't last the winter, then his almost
grotesquely grown-up behaviour and serious ambition made him
even more vulnerable and pathetic. At other meetings he seemed
indestructible and the possessor of unnatural energy. He made
Charlie, who often felt like a decent night's rest almost as soon as
she had got up in the morning, tired to look at him. He was neat
and precise where she was slapdash and untidy. When they were
together, she would be laughing at one moment, sullen and silent
the next. He was always practical and business-like, particularly
when he was kissing her. Then she knew that, when his arms were
round her neck, he was looking at the time through the forest of
her hair. His mother was always waiting up for him.

For Charlie, Leslie's great attraction was that he was undoubtedly one of the young men her mother would approve of least. She knew she had been a perpetual disappointment to Grace. She was never beautiful. She never wanted to spend a day in London buying hats and having tea in Fortnum's. She never discussed boyfriends with her mother, so that Grace could become, once again, a vicarious débutante. The fact that her mother disliked her had for years been a misery to Charlie, but now she revelled in it. She only wanted to feed the flames of her mother's hatred, and for that Leslie Titmuss would come in very handy. She had also, and rightly, come to the conclusion that her mother was a snob, and such a person, in Charlie's view, thoroughly deserved all the social embarrassments that Leslie was so well-fitted to provide.

But Leslie was not only a marvellous irritant for her mother; Charlie saw him as a way of escape. Rapstone Manor, the old rambling house with its draughts, its tweed hats, gumboots and shepherds' crooks in the downstairs loo, its guns and family portraits, its domineering servants and the endless emptiness of its long afternoons, was literally, from time to time, making her scream. The dinner parties for the few inhabitants of the local big houses, or the Committee Members of the Hartscombe Conservative Association, or withered ladies who wore jewellery and cardigans and who had 'come out' with Grace, were worse than loneliness. Once settled with Leslie Titmuss, Charlie thought she might fly to a wonderful world of sauce bottles and meat teas, of gossip in saloon bars and holidays on the Costa Brava, of days out in the car and of Leslie's fiercely concentrated copulation on the hearth-rug in front of the electric fire, among scattered pages of the *News of the World* on Sunday afternoons. It was a romantic dream of working-class delights which showed how little Charlie knew of the world at that time.

Her longing to escape was frustrated by Leslie's initial determination to keep their love-affair a secret from George. But then a change came and he invited her to meet him, not among the dark scrub on Picton Ridge, but in the full glow of the cocktail bar at the Swan's Nest Hotel. Whether he had gone there to exorcize the memory of his great humiliation, or merely to mark a change in his plans, Leslie was even more pallid and intense when they met. His father, it seemed, had found certain personal possessions of

Charlie's in the glove compartment of the Prefect, and their great secret was a secret no longer. Even Nicholas had been told. They could either retreat in confusion, or go into the attack, and Leslie had no doubt which course they should take. One way would lead to a lifetime's separation, the other might take them to the altar of Rapstone Church. As Charlie burrowed into the chaos of her handbag to pay for their gin and tonics, Leslie outlined his master-plan.

'Tell her,' he ended, 'this evening.' And he added, as though in an attempt to temper the blow, 'After they've had their evening meal.'

So Charlie was able to save up the revelation, as a child leaves the largest strawberry or the cherry on top of the cake, until the end of dinner. She sat, for the most part, in silence, hardly answering Nicholas's well-meant inquiries or Grace's criticism of her dress and the tedious nature of her company. She knew that she had the power, once the long meal was over, to produce a most satisfactory explosion. She waited patiently until Bridget had brought the coffee tray into the drawing-room and then lit the blue touch-paper and announced that she planned to marry Leslie.

'Marry Leslie Titmuss!' Grace showed that her lungs, when called upon, were quite as strong as her daughter's. 'You're bloody well not going to marry Leslie Titmuss!'

'Why not? Tell me one reason why not.'

'Why not? The idea's obviously ridiculous. You're not even going out with Leslie Titmuss again and that's absolutely all I've got to say on the matter. Your father will tell you exactly the same thing.'

In fact Nicholas said nothing. He was sitting in a chair at the fireside, his knees pulled up, his long legs folded in the attitude of an aeroplane passenger anticipating a crash. He had noticed that Charlie had been looking unusually contented at dinner and had rightly interpreted the fact as a danger signal.

'Why do you have to care who I marry?' Charlie's question was triumphant. 'You can forget me! When I'm married to Leslie you can absolutely forget me. Don't even come to visit us!'

'Where do you think I'd come to visit? In some little semi-detached on a council estate in Worsfield?' Grace had picked up *Vogue* and was turning the glossy pages as though the subject was no longer worth discussing, when her husband told them that George Titmuss had paid a call on him, a fact which he had, up until then, decided not to mention in the interests of family peace.

'And I suppose he's tickled pink with the idea of his son marrying into the Fanners.' Grace sniffed. 'Probably put the boy up to it.' She pretended to make a close study of a photograph of a model wearing a fur coat and sitting in a dustbin.

'Not at all, he's violently opposed to it. I'm afraid Father Titmuss is a terrible old snob.'

'Thank God there are a few of us left!' Grace murmured piously.

'Tell her she's wrong! Tell her to mind her own bloody business. Tell her it's my own life. Go on, tell her!' Charlie had moved to sit on the arm of her father's chair.

'So far as I'm concerned, you may marry exactly whom you want.'

'Tell her then!'

Nicholas seemed to be apologizing for his beliefs as though they were begonias, a rather ridiculous sort of hobby. 'But I believe, well, I *do* believe it's up to us not to cause embarrassment, unhappiness even, to people who're not quite so lucky as ourselves.'

'Lucky? You think I've been *lucky*?'

'You're born into a certain family, Charlie. We have certain responsibilities, you might say.'

'To *her*?' Charlie looked with loathing towards the screening cover of *Vogue*.

'I was thinking more of the Titmuss family. It's going to be jolly awkward for them, Charlie, you do see that don't you? Now I'm sure young Leslie Titmuss is a perfectly decent . . .'

'Decent?' The description was too much for Charlie's mother. '*Decent!* Have you seen him? Hair oil and a row of pens in his breast-pocket. I couldn't believe it when I saw you dancing with him, Charlie, at the Y.C.s' ball. Poor child, I thought, she must be pushed for a partner.'

'You see,' Nicholas went on courageously, 'it really would rock the boat in the Titmuss household. He's an only child, just as you are, Charlie, and his mother won't want to visit here. I know that for a fact. You're going to cause a frightful lot of embarrassment, old thing.'

'Embarrassment!'

'You can't change people, Charlie. They've been going on too long.'

'All this quarrelling!' Grace slapped her magazine shut, a sure sign of bedtime. 'It's making my head ache and it's quite unnecessary. I'm going up now. You can forget all about it, Charlie, forget all about marrying Leslie Titmuss.'

'I can't forget it,' Charlie told her. 'Neither can you. I'll have to marry Leslie.'

'What *do* you mean?' her mother asked and Charlie's answer was as Leslie had planned it, although not in his exact words.

'Surely you know, don't you, mother? Isn't it the sort of thing you and your dried-up old girlfriends meet to giggle about in Fortnum's?'

After Henry had decided to contest his father's last will, he called on his daughter, Francesca, at the flat which she shared with her boyfriend, Peter. He had rarely visited that address, taking the view that anyone setting out for Tufnell Park would need a map and a compass, together with native bearers who could speak the local dialect. When he got there, after a taxi ride of no particular difficulty, he was surprised and a little shocked to find Francesca's living-room so warm and cheerful. A coal fire glowed in the grate and the place was decorated with Victorian relics, pictures and jugs depicting the Queen and Prince Albert, and Imperial battle scenes hanging on the walls. Although he sniffed cautiously, he could not detect that pungent odour of burning carpets which he always associated with the young. Henry had also come to denounce the loud and cacophonous music Francesca must surely like and he was put out to hear only a little gentle Telemann tinkling from the record-player.

'Is this *really* the sort of music you like?'

'Yes, Father. Don't you?'

Francesca was then twenty-one, only a couple of years younger than Lonnie had been when Henry had married her, a pretty, serious girl whose look of anxiety in no way reflected her firmness of purpose.

'I'm sorry Peter's not here.'

'I'm not,' Henry assured her.

'He's going into a new business.'

'Furniture removal?'

'No, of course not. Computer programming.' Francesca felt a pang of guilt, remembering the morning when she had found the Rectory empty, and only noticed the group of mourners in the churchyard after she and Peter had loaded up the van. She was prepared for an attack from her father but he was looking at the real object of his visit, Simeon's old desk which had been stripped to a naked buff colour and used as a stand for potted plants.

Henry sat down in front of it and went through the drawers methodically, telling his daughter that he was looking for anything that would spike the guns of that abominable little creep, Leslie Titmuss. At first he found nothing. The drawers had been cleared out, it seemed, and all their contents left at the Rectory. He had almost given up the search when he felt the wooden columns that supported a shelf at the back of the desk and a spring opened a secret and hidden drawer. From it he rescued a long folded paper on the back of which the words 'Last Will and Testament' were printed in archaic script.

At first Henry was enormously excited, for the newly found document in fact benefited Dorothy and the Rector's two sons. But when he took it to Jackson Cantellow it was clear that the homemade will, dated before the war, was revoked by the later, Henry thought insane, testament, made as late as 1983 in the office of a small Worsfield firm, whom, it seemed, his father had never used before.

'At least this shows what his true intentions were,' Henry said, when he called at Cantellow's office, interrupting his lawyer in a little solitary practice for a performance of Mendelssohn's *Elijah* in the Worsfield Free Trade Hall.

'What his intentions were in 1939.'

'Before he went mad,' Henry said firmly, 'and decided to benefit the appalling Titmuss.'

'I agree, it's a little strange that he should have left his money to

Mr Titmuss as late as 1983, when the Minister was presumably quite comfortably off. But if that will had been made earlier, when the beneficiary was starting out in life, when he got married for instance ... Now when was that exactly?' But Henry thought he had been away on the Coast, so the marriage of Leslie Titmuss passed without him noticing it at the time. He also refused Jackson Cantellow's offer of tickets for the oratorio *Elijah*, so their meeting was, on the whole, satisfactory to neither party.

After the initial battle between Charlie and her mother over the marriage question, there was a period of uneasy truce at Rapstone Manor. Nicholas spent as much time as he could walking round the home farm, smiling in a good-natured manner at the pigs, or he took a gun out to distant woodlands. Charlie stayed in her room a good deal and, at mealtimes, preserved a sort of triumphant silence which her mother found especially irritating. Grace's mind fluttered desperately between a number of plans which included a trip to Switzerland where Charlie might learn French and visit a discreet clinic, an accouchement in some remote nursing-home followed by immediate adoption and the wild hope that, when her immediate problems were solved, her daughter might undergo a religious conversion and become a nun. She put all these plans to her husband whenever she caught sight of him.

Grace also managed to capture the Rector after church on Sunday and, having rounded up Nicholas, imprisoned them both in the library and announced that she was seeking the help of her spiritual adviser because 'Charlie was in pod by the appalling Leslie Titmuss'. To her dismay, Simeon seemed to find the news less catastrophic than she had expected.

'I suppose people are always telling you the most ghastly things, but there can't be anything much more horrible than this! Where could we send her, somewhere quiet in the country?'

'This is somewhere quiet in the country,' Simeon told them, it seemed unhelpfully, and added, 'Young Leslie Titmuss is going to make something of himself.'

'I don't care what he makes of himself.' Grace was positive. 'I don't want him making little bastards with Charlie.'

'It might just be that Leslie Titmuss is the future.'

'If he is I'm not waiting for it. I never want to think of Leslie Titmuss again, so long as I live.'

'But there is someone you'll have to think about.'

'Who?'

'Your grandchild.' And Simeon asked her seriously, 'Have you considered a really desperate remedy?'

'Of course.' She was glad to have the Church's approval.

'I mean marriage.'

'Over my dead body! I'm not having a grandchild, and Charlie's not having a wedding. I thought I'd made that perfectly clear.' And that appeared to be Grace's last word on the subject.

Simeon came away from his meeting with the Fanners curiously cast down. He became more cheerful when Leslie Titmuss called at the Rectory and requested a private audience in the study. It turned out that he wanted to book the church and, of course, the Rector's services, for a wedding. He couldn't yet name the date but it was bound to be quite shortly after the Worsfield Show. The bride's name was Charlotte Grace Fanner and, although she was under age, he had no doubt that her parents would finally give their consent.

Perhaps Leslie had hoped for a greater reaction from the Rector, a more considerable surprise or a burst of congratulations. Instead Simeon looked as though things were turning out much as he expected. He found a pencil, made a note in his diary and asked an entirely practical question.

'Where are you going to live? When you get married, I mean.'

'Sir Nicholas'll give us one of his cottages.'

'Do you think so?'

'He'll have to, won't he?'

Simeon looked up at the young man sitting opposite him and wondered, not for the first time, what it must be like to have been born without a sense of doubt. Would that be a blessing or a curse or a mere physical deprivation, like being born without a sense of smell? He failed, for the moment, to make up his mind on the question.

Putting Up a Tent

The Worsfield Show is one of the more pleasant occasions connected with that unattractive city. It takes place on Worsfield Heath, not far from the by-pass. (It can be said in favour of Worsfield that it is surrounded, and to some extent immunized, by the countryside.) It is true that the factory chimneys, now almost hiding the Cathedral tower, are visible from the site, but once a year they are fronted by sideshows, showing-rings, horseboxes and sheep pens. The beer tents are open all day, and there farmers mix with commuters. Girls from Tesco's and the biscuit factory mingle with pigmen, stockmen, bingo-callers, fortune-tellers and dedicated showjumpers. Huge quantities of Simcox ale are drunk and great rivers of bubbling urine course down the troughs in the flapping lavatory tents and manure the common. Children in jodhpurs and hacking-jackets are mounted on midget ponies and forced over jumps by relentless parents greedy for rosettes. Worsfield Show is a place where you can still bowl for a pig, buy a horse or a pound of homemade marmalade, and watch a calm girl in a fringed cowboy suit being picked out by quivering knives hurled by her nervous and chain-smoking husband.

The show in the year of the Titmuss wedding was held in golden summer weather. The air was full of lowing, grunting, shunting, barking and the starting of reluctant horseboxes. Leslie was walking with his mother and father towards the Women's Institute bring and buy stall, when he saw his old adversaries, Magnus Strove and Christopher Kempenflatt, both dressed in precociously aged tweed suits, both with pinched trilby hats set on their foreheads, enjoying taking potshots at a number of ping-pong balls, which were dancing elusively on jets of water. Far from turning their guns on Leslie they hailed him with considerable goodwill and thanked him for the moving speech he had made at the local Party's meeting, supporting, in the name of go-ahead political thinking, their plan to tear down the old High Street grocer's and substitute a new Easy-Bite eatery.

'It was my duty,' Leslie said in answer to their thanks. 'I feel it's up to us in the Party to encourage business initiative among young people.' Both being a few years older than young Titmuss, they looked at him in some surprise, and Kempenflatt, still genial, offered to send him round a dozen bottles of the best bubbles. Leslie chose another reward, a loan of the blue and gold cardboard shield – the passport to the Steward's enclosure – which dangled from Magnus Strove's lapel.

'I'll bring it back in half an hour,' he promised, when his wish was granted. 'By the way, if you're acquiring the Garthwaites' site, have you thought about buying through a Bahamian partnership, with shares at a no-par value?'

Leslie had been reading the *Financial Times*, and taken advanced accountancy at evening classes. Kempenflatt thought he wanted to borrow the Steward's enclosure badge so that he could put on side to the other clerks in the beer tent.

In fact Leslie did as he had always planned, and went straight to the Steward's enclosure. If he hadn't been able to gain a badge he was prepared to resort to any extreme, even to forcing an entry into the back of the reserved lavatory tent and emerging, zipping up his flies and appearing nonchalant, on the hallowed ground of the 'Steward's'. As it was he walked unchallenged past the show of hunters in the ring and, crossing the grass where elderly men in bowler hats and riding macs sat perched on their shooting-sticks, he strolled into the Steward's tent. He saw the group he was looking for immediately, laughing together over champagne and sandwiches, by the banked hydrangeas at the far end of the marquee. He walked steadily towards them and, once in earshot, said like some Shakespearian messenger bringing glad tidings from the battlefield, 'I've fixed things up with the Rector.'

The faces which turned towards him at this news were variously surprised, uninterested, outraged or amused. The outrage came from Grace, who clutched her champagne glass as though for support and clenched her teeth to stop herself shouting. The group around her consisted of Nicholas, who went on looking benign, Doughty Strove, M.P., who looked his usual sullen self, and a number of tweeded friends, none of whom were as young as they liked to remember. Leslie knew exactly who they were. There stood Bridget Naboth, wife of Lord Naboth of Worsfield, one of the major local contributors to Party funds. With her was a thin, pink-faced man known to them all as the 'Contessa', who lived in a small Queen Anne house on the outskirts of Hartscombe with his aged mother and a magnificent collection of snuff-boxes (articles which a Royal aunt, on her occasional visits to Hartscombe, used to carry off as an expected tribute in her handbag after tea with the 'Contessa's' mother). There were two middle-aged sisters, enthusiastic gardeners, who were known as the Erskine girls, Uncle Cecil Fanner and Mrs Fairhazel, who, because she was the spare woman at every dinner party, carried gossip about the neighbourhood like a jungle telegraph.

'You know young Titmuss?' Nicholas smiled vaguely round the assembled company when no one seemed inclined to ask what had been fixed up with the Rector.

'Aren't you Elsie's boy?' Doughty Strove's memory went back to the days when Leslie's mother grew up in the kitchen at Picton House. 'Never get treacle tart nowadays like Elsie used to give us.'

'Titmuss is very active with the Young Conservatives now, Doughty. He speaks up at meetings.'

'Not for too long, I hope,' said Doughty, whose political philosophy had always been to avoid speaking up whenever possible. Try as he would Nicholas could think of no more small talk. He bit into a sandwich and steeled himself for his wife's inevitable question.

'What exactly have you fixed up?' She forced her teeth apart to inquire.

'Oh, the date of the wedding.' Leslie was matter of fact. 'Simeon Simcox has pencilled in the twenty-first of next month.'

'Getting married are you?' Doughty felt he should show an interest in their old cook's boy. 'Who's the lucky lady?'

'Who?' Leslie seemed amazed at the man's ignorance. 'Charlotte Fanner, of course.'

Bridget Naboth stood frozen in mid-sandwich. The Erskine girls gaped. Mrs Fairhazel's eyes shone with eager anticipation of a dozen dinner parties. Nicholas pulled a gold watch out of his waistcoat pocket and wished he had a train to catch. Grace stood motionless and closed her eyes; the thinly veined eyelids could be seen to tremble as Leslie returned to the attack.

'You know she doesn't want to be kept waiting,' he said. 'Very impatient girl, your Charlotte. Well, I can't be kept waiting either, can I, mother-in-law to be?'

Grace pulled herself together with an enormous effort. She opened her eyes cautiously and said, 'I rather think it's time we got back to the horses.' She was on the move and her group was preparing to trail obediently after her. Leslie almost had to shout after them.

'Sorry I can't join you. Got to find my people. My mother'll have all sorts of preparations to make.' And he added, for the particular benefit of Doughty Strove, M.P., 'Treacle tart and so on.'

'What do you imagine they all thought?'

'That we'd agreed to it, I suppose.'

'Of course they did. And furthermore, they must have got the strong impression that we were holding a shot-gun to the repulsive head of the pimply Titmuss. I wish to God we were.'

'Well, I'm sorry. It took me completely by surprise.'

'I dare say it did, almost everything takes you completely by surprise, Nicholas. Well, it's put paid to the chances of Charlie slipping off somewhere under the cover of French lessons.'

'Couldn't we explain . . . ?'

'Explain to that ghastly old Doughty Strove, and Bridget Naboth, who can't keep her mouth shut on any occasion, and your Uncle Cecil Fanner, who'll tell the entire family, and the "Contessa" and the Erskine girls, and that absolutely poisonous Fairhazel woman? Explain that Charlie's expecting by some village oik, and we have no intention of letting her marry? No. You'll have to *talk* to him.'

They were the words Nicholas dreaded. He was fully dressed, perched on the edge of his wife's bed, while she sat at the looking-glass, scrubbing at her face with fingerfuls of cottonwool and staring at herself with barely controlled despair. He had absolutely no desire to talk to Leslie Titmuss and no idea what to say to him.

'He's clearly only in it for the money.' Grace arched her eyebrows and sucked in her cheeks. Thank God, she thought, momentarily cheering herself up, I've still got my bones. Her bones, which in the past had seemed a sort of luxury, were fast becoming the sole comfort of her advancing age. 'See what he'll take to tell them it was some kind of ghastly practical joke. He can explain he was squiffy on the Steward's champagne or something. The little bugger simply has to be paid off even if it means selling woodland.' She did herself the kindness of switching off the light over her mirror and moved towards her bed. 'You'll be sleeping in your dressing-room, of course.'

'Of course.' Nicholas, getting the order for release, moved gratefully towards the door. 'I don't think you'll find he's got them, you know.'

'Got what?'

'Pimples.'

In fact the boy's skin, Nicholas thought when inevitably and at last they met, was remarkably pale but clear of all blemish. He had invited Leslie to tea on what he hoped was neutral ground, the lawn of the Hellespont Club, founded by Victorian rowing-men in a house which commands a fine view of the river. At Regatta time, white-haired ex-oarsmen, wearing the bright green socks and schoolboy caps of the Hellespont, together with yellowing flannels and blazers which no longer button across their stomachs, sit on the lawn drinking Pimms and lamenting the decline in rowing. Leslie, in his dark suit, burnished black shoes and remark-able pallor, seemed out of place in this setting. He was also, to Nicholas's amazement, extremely angry, and went into the attack with his eyes blazing before the waitress, who had brought them scones, was out of earshot.

'It's pretty hard on me. It really is.'

'Milk and sugar?' Nicholas was being 'mother'.

'Just two lumps. I'm just starting out, you see. I was going to make something of myself. I was going to leave the Brewery and go for my accountant's qualifications. Your daughter's put paid to all that. Now I'll have a family to see after.'

'Really, Titmuss!' Nicholas protested mildly as he handed the cup. 'What did she do? Ravish you or something?'

'Let's just say, she was very determined.'

Determination, Nicholas thought, was a characteristic of the women in his life. His Uncle Cecil had described Grace as a 'butterfly with a will of iron'. And the butterfly had made a dead set at him, a fact which he had never been able to explain. She didn't actually ravish him, of course, not as far as he could remember, but Grace's implacable persistence, when it came to the matter of marriage, made him able to understand Leslie's concern. He said, 'You pose us a bit of a problem, Titmuss. What on earth are we going to do about you?'

'What does Lady Fanner suggest?'

'I see you go straight to the heart of a matter. The family would be prepared to do something for you, of course. If we could regard the unfortunate incident as a bit of a joke.'

'What unfortunate incident?' Leslie was carefully balancing a spoonful of strawberry jam on his buttered scone.

'Your extraordinary behaviour at the Worsfield Show.'

'What would you be prepared to do?' Leslie bit into a scone and chewed steadily.

'I hardly know. What're your immediate needs?'

There was strawberry jam on Leslie's chin, bright and shiny as a drop of blood. Nicholas longed to lean forward and wipe it off with his paper napkin.

'Somewhere to live.' Leslie clearly had a list prepared. 'I can't stay with the old people for ever. And I've been taking the minutes when Kempenflatt's away, which he is the best half of the time. I'd like you to put in a word for me as Secretary of the Y.C.s with a place on the Local Executive. Oh, and I want to get a qualification and perhaps start my own business.'

Leslie wiped his own chin and Nicholas felt unreasonably relieved.

'And you'd agree to Charlie going away quietly?'

'Charlotte's never going to go away quietly.' Leslie smiled for the first time, and took a gulp of tea. 'You must know your daughter better than that. She's going to stay here and scream her head off, and she'll tell everyone what's happened. But I'm quite prepared to marry her, *if* you can see your way clear to helping us. Only thing is, one of you'll have to talk my old folks round, you know what they're like.'

'What?' Nicholas was frowning, feeling that he had lost his tenuous grasp of events.

'Oh.' Leslie's smile was wider and really quite charming. 'They're dead against me marrying Charlotte.'

Nicholas had not been looking forward to reporting the result of his interview with Leslie Titmuss to his wife. Accordingly he loitered on his way home, made a couple of calls in Hartscombe, visited the farm office, and when he reached Rapstone Manor at last, made straight for the conservatory. From there, he was surprised to see his wife and the Rector sitting out on the terrace, where Wyebrow was opening a bottle of champagne. It seemed that Simeon had been actively campaigning on behalf of the young couple. A long talk with Charlie had persuaded him that she would never abandon the idea of marrying Leslie. He had repeated his opinion of Leslie's bright future, based on legitimate ambition and tireless work, but his trump card had been the absence of other suitors for Charlie. Did Grace really want her daughter sharing their house for ever, permanently pining for Leslie Titmuss? For a while Charlie's mother sat in silence, considering this bleak prospect. Then she cautiously allowed that there might be two sides to every question. By the time her husband finally emerged to announce that he had no success in deflecting the determined Titmuss, she was persuaded to make the best of what might not be such a bad job after all. There would be no further need to explain away the extraordinary scene at Worsfield Show, and she might never have to listen to Charlie screaming again.

'Titmuss very nobly said he'd go through with it and marry Charlie,' Nicholas reported.

'Yes. That's what we've decided.'

'You've decided?' He felt like a man who has been sent out on a desperate mission to no man's land, only to return, bloodstained and exhausted, to be told that the peace was declared some time ago.

'Oh, for heaven's sake, have a glass of champagne. You can't discuss weddings without a glass of champagne. It's like having an operation without an anaesthetic. Get Wyebrow to bring out another glass.'

'I don't think you'll regret it,' Simeon smiled at them both. 'I'm sure Leslie Titmuss is going to make something of himself.'

'But what exactly?' Nicholas wondered.

'Something.' Grace was impatient. 'Does it really matter what? It's quite a relief to have it all settled.'

'Well, not quite settled.' Nicholas was still doubtful. 'It seems that someone's got to sell the idea to the Titmusses.'

Grace Fanner changed her mind frequently and each change was signalled by a burst of frenzied activity. Once she had decided on Charlie's wedding she wanted no delay and she certainly wanted no opposition. Accordingly she rang the musical chime on the front door of 'The Spruces' one morning, and was admitted by a somewhat flustered Elsie Titmuss who, in an overall and rubber gloves, was in the middle of washing up.

'I know exactly what it's like,' said Grace, to whom the home life of the Titmuss family was a mercifully closed book. 'Nothing but chores. All the time. Men do leave such a mess about the place, don't they? Come on, why don't we muck in together? You finish washing and I'll dry.' She was, to Elsie's considerable dismay, heading for the kitchen. 'And I do promise not to break anything.'

'Won't you take a seat, your Ladyship? I'll put the kettle on for a cup of tea.'

'Later. When we've earned it. Don't they do such amusing teacloths nowadays?' Grace had taken up one decorated with pictures of the Tower of London and was dabbing at a cup with it. 'Now do get on with the washing up, Mrs Titmuss, and we'll talk.'

'What exactly did you want to talk about?' Elsie, dazed and obedient, returned to the sink and plunged her rubber gloves into the Fairy Liquid. 'I do think the war made a tremendous difference to our lives, don't you?' Grace answered unexpectedly. Elsie, unaware of any profound change since V.E. day, felt vaguely guilty.

'It was terrible, of course. Absolutely terrible! But people did learn to muck in in the most marvellous way. Count on me, Mrs Titmuss, all hands to the pumps.'

So Elsie washed up the small number of breakfast dishes and laid them out on the draining-board, and Grace forgot to use the teatowel, releasing a flood of wartime reminiscences.

'Of course, I could've been an air-raid warden in Hartscombe, but who'd bother to bomb a few grocers' shops and the Brewery?' She remembered. 'My husband was away fighting for his country and I said, "Give me Worsfield!" Of course they were after the railways there, and they got the Cathedral. Worsfield was the place where you could get your tin hat blown off if you weren't too careful! I remember, one day in Corporation Street, it was really lovely sunshine, spring weather, and I was trudging along in my old tin hat and my boiler-suit and a truck, an American truck, passed and some doughboy leaned out and whistled at me! You know the way they did, terribly cheeky, of course, but quite appealing? And suddenly there was a terrific blast. It absolutely knocked me back into a shop doorway. Timothy Whites? I think it was Timothy Whites. And when I looked up the road, well, the truck had been hit. Smashed to pieces. Everyone in it dead. They looked so pale! He whistled at me and I was his last view of England. Well, that's where I learned to dry up. In the A.R.P. And help make sandwiches. I don't think we should ever forget what we learned in the war.' The reminiscence over, Grace stood, teatowel in hand, motionless and smiling. After a suitable and respectful pause Elsie asked almost fearfully, 'Have you come about Leslie and Miss Charlotte?'

'My husband and I have absolutely no doubt about it, Mrs Titmuss.' Grace woke from her reverie. 'We should see them married.'

'I don't know . . .' Elsie was still doubtful.

'And the Rector.'

'The Rector?' Elsie seemed startled at the mention of Simeon's name.

'Mr Simcox has gone into the whole thing most carefully and he's all for a wedding.'

'That's what Mr Simcox wants, is it?' Elsie asked, a little breathlessly.

'I told you, all for it.'

'Well, I suppose, if that's what the Rector wants . . .' It was as though, in Elsie Titmuss's opinion, God had spoken and there was no more to be said on the subject.

Charlie and Leslie went out for a picnic on the river. It was a sunny Saturday afternoon, but with a sharp smell of autumn and there were few other boats about. Charlie rowed the craft and Leslie steered expertly, past the Hellespont Club, where the tea tables were now deserted and the swans cruised malignantly, searching in vain for scraps of generously thrown scones or Dundee cake.

'Register office at Worsfield. No family. Couple of witnesses off the street. Then go for fish and chips. Afternoon in the Odeon. Don't let's do a single thing she wants.' Charlie spoke in short bursts, in time to the dipping of her oars. 'No Uncle Cecil Fanner. No Naboths. No horrible old "Contessa". No bridesmaids. No tent on the lawn.'

'We'll stop here,' Leslie told her, 'by the island.' The island was the site of a couple of bungalows, let to summer visitors, but now empty. In a few months the river would rise, flooding their gardens and loosening their kitchen linoleum. From their mooring the couple could see the Swan's Nest Hotel, the rocking punts and the landing-stage; the scene, as Leslie didn't fail to remind Charlie, of his great humiliation, a moment which he now appeared to treasure.

'You know what they thought,' he told her, when he had gone once again through the occasion which ended with him being sent home to his mother like a drowned rat. 'They thought that's the end of Elsie Titmuss's son, the boy who used to cut down nettles and hang around our kitchen.' Charlie wondered if he had ever cut Magnus Strove's nettles, but thought it better not to interrupt him. 'They're going to have to take that back, Charlie. They're going to have to take it all back.'

'Why bother about them at all? You shouldn't, you know.'

'I'm going to bother, I really am.' He looked at her and, as was rare with him, he was smiling. 'Let's make them put up a tent.'

'Perhaps marriage is the greatest test we are put to. That's what I tell my young couples. It's a case of facing up to your responsibility for the consequences of a single headstrong moment, when you may be drunk with the smell of orange blossom. How many of us think of the appalling consequences that may flow from a brief conversation in front of the altar?' Among the many wedding formalities which Leslie had insisted on was the preliminary chat with the Rector. They were gathered together in Simeon's study and Leslie listened intently as Charlie stared thoughtfully out of the window to where Dorothy was bent like an elegant and elderly croquet hoop in the border, making an early planting of winter pansies.

'That's what I say to all the young Jacks and Jills, the Harrys and the Doreens, the Leslies and the Charlottes,' Simeon assured them, although he seemed to be speaking mainly for the benefit of himself. 'The consequences may be quite unforeseen. You throw a pebble into a still pond and who knows where the ripples will end? They will end up far away, generations later, when you and your little stone will be quite forgotten. I know what you're going to ask, you're going to ask, where does God come in all this? Is God the ripples? Is God the pebble? Is God, as our Eastern friends would have us believe, simply the surface of the pond? Or are you God? Leslie and Charlotte. Are you creating a future which you have chosen not to control? Difficult, isn't it? Terribly difficult. We can only hope to do justice. Hope to . . .' Simeon's voice died away, apparently discouraged. He looked at Charlie and had to admit that no one could have called her beautiful; he turned back to Leslie Titmuss, and the task in hand. 'Of course, it's easy for you now Leslie, easy when Charlotte is in the bloom of youth. But when she's older, when she's tired of life, when she starts to be afraid of death, when her looks are vanishing it'll be difficult for you then, terribly difficult! That'll be the test.'

There was a prolonged and not particularly cheerful silence. Then Simeon knocked out his pipe with relief.

'Well now, at this stage, I usually offer my young couple a bottle of Simcox's light ale, or would you rather we strolled across to the pub for a pint of wallop?'

Nothing in the subsequent ceremony was to be as painful to Leslie and Charlotte as this act of preparation. In fact the day, when it came, appeared for both of them, and in their separate ways, to be a moment of triumph. Having made her mind up, Grace behaved as though her daughter's marriage came as the fulfilment of some long-held ambition. Nicholas greeted the guests with unfailing cheerfulness, and the 'friends of the bride', who filled most of the church, were delighted by the source of so much future speculation. Fred, who was spending long, penniless days and nights in his old room at the Rectory studying anatomy and human biology, had received a surprise visit from Leslie Titmuss, who was without a best man. 'Say you'll do it,' Leslie had begged him. 'For the sake of old times. Remember how we used to play together.' Fred couldn't recall many games with the infant Titmuss, but he had agreed to stand beside Leslie and hand him the ring. Apart from anything else, it was the only party he seemed likely to be asked to for the rest of that year.

So Leslie had everything he had stipulated, including a tent. During the course of the celebrations, Nicholas, looking across at the bride and hoping as always for the best, said he thought Charlie looked really quite handsome in his grandmother's lace.

'Do you, Nicholas?' Grace asked him with exaggerated patience. 'I'll tell you one thing she doesn't look.'

'What's that?'

'Pregnant.'

★ 14 ★
The Coast

Henry took Agnes to the Coast not once but on several occasions before and after the making of *The Greasy Pole*. They travelled first class at the expense of the various production companies with which Mr Bugloss was connected, and were met at Los Angeles airport by a limousine long enough and black enough to accommodate, Agnes thought, a lengthy coffin and any number of mourners. They were put up at the Beverly Hills Hotel, where the telephone operators instantly knew their names and the staff constantly told Agnes to have a nice day, an instruction she received with an ironic smile. Henry lay in the sun, bought 'leisure-wear' in the hotel man's shop and looked to Agnes as if he were always dressed for a cruise. He telephoned his agent a good deal from the side of the pool, and, from time to time, looked anxiously at Agnes, wondering if she found the place awful enough to be enjoyable.

'It's the wonderful thing about writing,' he told her defensively, 'you can write a little novel about Simcox's Brewery, and it'll transport you to the other side of the world.'

'I know it's a miracle.' And Agnes gave him the smile which seemed to him to say, I'm awfully sorry that you can't see the joke.

On one of their visits, Mr Bugloss took them to lunch at a then fashionable restaurant on the Strip. All around them producers and agents rose from their tables like surfacing sealions to greet each other with loud honks of recognition, embraced each other with their flippers, and then sank back, gurgling towards their lunch.

'Jack Polefax, I don't believe it!' Mr Bugloss stood and grabbed a very small, grey-haired man who was about to join a similar man waving to him from another table. 'I just want you guys to meet

Jack, who *is* Galaxy International.' Mr Bugloss's American accent, hardly noticeable in Shepperton Studios or the Dorchester Hotel, flowered and darkened in the sun. 'Henry Simcox wrote *The Greasy Pole*. My last picture.'

'You a writer?' Polefax spoke, with a sort of pity, a line which caused Mr Bugloss intense amusement. 'Don't let him kid you! Don't kid him, Jack. Everyone knows Henry Simcox, or they will after the next one. He's just come up with this terrific idea.'

'My God! Can you believe who's here? Julie. Julie Salario. Isn't that incredible?' Mr Polefax had spied a corpulent and balding man semaphoring desperately from a distant table, and Agnes wondered why the sight of their old friends, whom they had presumably known for years, should fill Hollywood producers with such amazement. 'I just have to go over to greet Julie. Great to meet you, Mr Simcox.' He nodded towards Agnes. 'Like to have you both come up to the house for Sunday brunch. Laurel Canyon. Get Benny to bring you.' And he was off, hallooing, 'Julie! Long time no see you at all.'

The waiter hung with chains and silver tasting-cups was hovering now, and Mr Bugloss greeted him as warmly as though he were a film producer. 'And right now, Charles,' he said, 'we could use one of your great vodka martinis.'

'I'd like some wine.' Agnes knew that if she didn't get a word in early she'd be condemned to a cocktail and iced water.

'A couple of vodka martinis, Charles.' Benny Bugloss knew that Henry had taken on the customs of the Coast. 'And bring us some nice wine.' As the waiter retreated, he went on, without drawing breath. 'You know, I've always been pretty close to Jack. When I visit the Galaxy lot, when I'm in the Commissary there, Jack will invariably come up and take me by the arm.'

'What's that a sign of?' Agnes asked.

'It's a sign that if we play our cards correctly we may get Galaxy International to distribute Henry's next movie.'

'I hadn't heard about his next movie.' Agnes looked at Henry, who wasn't giving away the fact that he hadn't heard about it either.

'Why do you think I brought you two over here again? Henry and I, my dear, are about to cook the perfect hamburger.'

'You're going in for catering?' Agnes sounded innocent, and Henry frowned.

'I speak in metaphor of the American dish that all the world loves to eat. *Pole* was fine. Good business in Britain. O.K. critical reception here. But what did it do in Tokyo? And in South America we couldn't give it away. What we need is the hamburger. We cook it right here in town and they pay to eat it in Japan and Rio and Iowa and Hong Kong – all those territories. I tell you, my dear, I have the title of the perfect hamburger. And I have had the foresight to bring it with me.'

At which Mr Bugloss put his hand in his pocket and proudly brought out a paperback edition of *The Canterbury Tales*.

'That's the perfect hamburger?' Agnes was surprised.

'I want it updated,' Mr Bugloss told Henry. 'I want you to bring out the erotic aspect. And I want these pilgrims to come from all over: Rome, Paris, New York, Tokyo. You see, each territory has its own story. That way we get the international appeal.'

'And they all end up in Canterbury?' Agnes asked.

'That is not necessary. Henry should feel free. There are people in this town who have no idea where the hell Canterbury is.'

'You mean they're all engaged in some sort of quest?' Agnes's tone of serious inquiry brought Henry no comfort.

'You've got it! A quest!' Benny Bugloss looked triumphantly at Henry. 'You see, Agnes likes the idea.'

'Well, they've always been good stories,' Henry said, and Agnes turned on him, still asking as though for information, 'You mean, you think it's a good idea, Henry?'

'Nothing wrong with them as stories,' Henry repeated as Mr Bugloss gave the idea the final accolade.

'And it's in public domain! *Canterbury Tales* is our hamburger!'

'What's Henry have to do? Put on the ketchup? Will you excuse me a moment?' Agnes stood up and smiled down on the producer.

'Go ahead, my dear. You want to powder your nose?'

Before she went through the door marked 'Señoritas' Agnes had no fixed plan of campaign but when she was safely locked in the hispanically tiled cubicle, breathing in carbolic and air freshener, she decided that she must at all costs avoid returning to Mr Bugloss's table. She couldn't bear to see Henry mutely accepting some great storyline for Chaucer's hamburger and she was afraid of the pieces of her mind that she might be tempted to throw at Mr Bugloss. She couldn't go back and yet her only way of escape lay through the restaurant. Suddenly, in need of air, she pushed open the window of her cubicle and saw, only a few feet down, the lot used for Valet Parking. Without a moment's thought she climbed on to the seat and was out of the window and walking to freedom.

Walking was, of course, an unknown folly on the Sunset Boulevard of the early sixties. As she passed the Body Shop and the Cock and Bull, as she walked under the huge signs advertising the latest movies and the most lavish burial grounds, people stared at her from car windows, and cops regarded her with deep suspicion. Agnes walked unconcerned, as though she were in the woods round Rapstone, unconscious of the office towers and the palm trees with the rustle of rats among their high, grey leaves. A vista of hills, as beautiful as the background of an Italian painting, could be seen hovering above the smog, and Agnes's eyes were stinging and her feet aching as she set out for the pink and green palace which had become her improbable home.

While she was walking her desperation evaporated. Alone she felt safe, as she had once felt with Henry when he took over her and her problems, told her, with comforting certainty, exactly what she was going to do and arranged for her to do it. Henry had found the softly spoken German doctor in Belsize Park who had ended her pregnancy like a common cold. When she was then afflicted by an extraordinary loneliness, as if, single-handed, she had unpeopled the world, Henry had suggested journeys, aeroplane tickets and flights to the sunshine at the expense of Benjamin K. Bugloss. She had been pleased to be with him, and glad to put the greatest possible distance between herself and her old home, the surgery, the woods, Tom Nowt's hut and even Arturo's coffee bar, which seemed to her now to belong to a world of disappointment and death.

What surprised her was the amount of time that passed before Henry made love to her. She had assumed that she wasn't going to be taken abroad merely for the sake of friendship, but for a long while Henry booked separate bedrooms, kissed her good-night at her door and talked to her about everything but themselves. It was as though her progress through so many airport lounges and hotel lobbies was a sort of process of churching and he was waiting for her to recover and be purged from the ministrations of not only the doctor in Belsize Park but his brother Frederick also.

As time and distance separated her increasingly from home Agnes became more confident, less dependent on Henry for the organization of her life and, strangely, fonder of him. He wasn't, she noticed, half so self-confident as he liked to let on. He would arrive unnecessarily early at airports (Agnes had a distinct taste for catching everything by the skin of her teeth) and as he checked in she often noticed that his hands were sweating. He had an initial lack of confidence about his writing, and would only feel secure when it had been enjoyed by someone. It didn't seem to matter who praised it and Agnes, who at first enjoyed voicing her views, found that the good opinions of a secretary who re-typed the first draft were equally consoling to Henry . When she told him, as she thought, that *The Greasy Pole* was much better as a book than it ever became as a movie, he flew into a defensive rage and shouted at her in a way which she found almost touchingly helpless and quite unalarming. It seemed that Henry had pinned all his faith on Mr Bugloss as the first principle and guiding spirit of their new way of life and all his anti-Bugloss stories, of which he had many, were like jokes made by devout Catholics about the Virgin Birth. In his favour it should be said that Mr Bugloss had finally produced a sensible and well-received adaptation of *The Greasy Pole* which greatly enhanced Henry's reputation throughout the world.

Henry's second novel, which came out four or five months after their first visit to Los Angeles, was, inevitably, less well-regarded and, after a scene which left him almost speechless with despair, Mr Bugloss announced that he didn't see it as a movie property. It was then that Agnes and Henry began to make love, and if she knew she was, perhaps, only second best to a rave review, she felt pleased to repay the debt she was sure she owed him. Everything about going to bed with Henry surprised her, his gentleness, his curious lack of invention, something she hadn't expected in a writer, and his obvious need of her. It was a need she found touching but it left her, at times, remote. When she thought of

Fred, which she did as little as possible, she remembered their love-making as a silent voyage of self-discovery. In bed with his elder brother she was discovering almost all there was to be known about Henry, for he was rarely silent before, during or after the act of coition. Listening to him and sensing the insecurity beneath his most extravagant boasting she fell into a trap which she thought afterwards that she of all people should have avoided. She wanted to improve Henry.

So she began to resent his trips to the Coast, his adaptations for Mr Bugloss which earned money but rarely got made into films, and Henry felt himself subject to her judgement which became the more intolerable as he came secretly to agree with it. So their quarrels started, because she couldn't resist saying what she thought and he couldn't forgive her for it. They were tempestuous quarrels, for which Henry showed a dramatic talent, and sometimes she thought they brought them closer to each other. She couldn't remember a time when she had seriously quarrelled with Fred.

As she walked she remembered the awful evening at the Barrel of Biscuits in Worsfield which she had enjoyed in Fred's company, and wondered why the awfulness of the Hollywood restaurant gave her no pleasure. She wanted to be alone, to sleep, not to have to make conversation or pass judgement any more that day.

'Having a nice day?' the hotel doorman asked when she arrived and she told him, 'No, not particularly.'

In the restaurant, Benny Bugloss said, 'She's missing her wine.' Henry looked towards the 'Señoritas' with a kind of desperation, fearing that Agnes's failure to emerge was not due to illness or any natural cause but merely to contempt.

'I walked.'

'Don't be silly. No one walks here.'

'Somebody does.'

'You were a great help! You left me looking ridiculous.'

'You were looking ridiculous before I left. Agreeing with all that rubbish.'

Henry had found Agnes lying on a chair by the pool with her eyes closed. He thought she was pretending to be asleep. Around them on the towelling-covered day-beds, or under the yellow canopies of their private tents, lay men in bathing-trunks and women in flowered bathing-caps who were pursuing the great poolside sport of making telephone calls. One old fellow shouted greetings into the phone cupped in his shoulder, while his hands kneaded suntan oil into a woman's back. The tannoy announced names wanted for other telephone calls: 'Mr Irving Lazar, Mr Richard Zanuck, Mr Ed Pringle, Miss Gwenda Grammercy ... to the telephone, please.'

Henry had told Agnes that some actors paid their agents substantial retainers to make these calls so that their names might be heard regularly around the pool at the Beverly Hills Hotel and Agnes thought of them going on remorselessly long after the actor had given up and left the profession, perhaps after he was dead.

'It's very easy for you, isn't it?' Henry told her. However angry he was he still kept his voice down so as not to disturb the half-naked telephoners around them. 'Oh yes. You can be so prim and superior and despise Benny Bugloss from a great height! You don't have to pay the bills.'

'You don't have to pay them like that.'

'I have to pay them.'

Agnes swung her legs off the side of the day-bed and sat up. As she spoke the twittering of telephone calls subsided, the sunbathers had begun to listen.

'Pay them by creeping and crawling to old Benny, my dear, by turning Chaucer into a hamburger, by having your arm squeezed by Jack Baby? You know what? I'd rather die than go to lunch in Laurel Canyon with a lot of old men in necklaces and women with heads covered in rubber flowers.'

'Why do you have to be so difficult?' Henry sounded genuinely puzzled.

'I don't know, I don't know why I have to be.' She stood up, snatched at her towelling dressing-gown and put it on. 'What did you honestly think when you took me on, that I was going to be easy?'

She ran away from him, past the now silent telephoners, past the puzzled Swede who was carefully folding yellow towels, past the dusty, luxuriant flowerbeds and past the great banana leaves on the wallpaper of their bedroom corridor. And Henry came after her with what dignity he could muster, moving as quickly as he could without looking as though he were chasing a woman from the pool. Once in the shadows of the hotel he made up speed and was able to put his weight against their bedroom door just as Agnes was trying to push it shut.

'You've got a short memory,' he said, when they were in the bedroom together. The calm way he spoke was calculated to drive her to distraction.

'What are you talking about?'

'The time when working for Ben Bugloss paid for what you wanted.'

'What I wanted?'

'Got you out of trouble. My little brother's trouble. You were desperate!'

'You think I'm not desperate now?'

'Agnes!' By now he was smiling at her. 'You're so self-indulgent!'

'*Me?*'

'Enjoying the luxury of feeling desperate in the Beverly Hills Hotel.'

It was a false, even a monstrous accusation; she had only wanted to save Henry from himself or at least from Mr Bugloss and his absurd pilgrimage

She had no answer but to attack him, hitting him, scratching his neck, her fists pummelling him uselessly. He held her and they stumbled among the pink table-lamps, between the sofa and the bamboo tables, in front of pictures of fishing boats at sunset, until they fell, almost by accident, across the kingsized bed, and so their daughter Francesca was eventually conceived.

While his elder brother was away on the Coast, Fred was working towards the end of the long process of turning himself into a doctor, which seemed at times hopeless, exciting, unbearably tedious, rewarding, futile and all he had ever wanted to do. He lived in the lecture halls and dissecting rooms of his London hospital, slept, mostly alone, in a room he found in Battersea, and went back to Rapstone whenever he could to get his clothes mended, his stomach filled and to be exasperated by his mother and father. Although he felt it was perfectly normal that he should find it dull to visit

Simeon and Dorothy, he expected them to be more enthusiastic about having him to stay. When he was in the country he went riding with Agnes's father, or joined the Doctor on his rounds to discover how different the theories he had learnt at St Thomas's were from the practice of medicine in the sick rooms of Hartscombe and the Rapstone Valley.

'It seems Agnes has deserted both of us,' Dr Salter said.

Fred often sat in the Doctor's living-room, a place which looked shabby by day but comfortable at night when the fire was lit, the stains on the wallpaper hidden, and the light fell softly on paintings of shot game and long-dead horses. They drank brandy and listened to gramophone records, Elgar and Brahms, and the scratchy voices of music-hall performers, Will Hay, Robb Wilton and Max Miller, at whom the Doctor would laugh until his eyes filled with tears and he had to dab at them with a huge silk handkerchief.

'Have you any idea why she should desert us?' Fred to whom any talk of Agnes was like tearing at an open wound, didn't answer. 'You prefer not to say?' Dr Salter looked at him with his diagnostic expression. 'I'm not sure I approve of that. Our secrets have an awful sort of immortality, they return to haunt us. They went off to America did you say?'

'That's what Henry said.'

'Of course you'll miss her now, just as I missed my Annie. She didn't fall in love with my brother, not that I ever had a brother. She was unfaithful to me with a flying bomb. I thought I'd never get over it, but in time, you know, there can be compensations.'

'Compensations?'

'The silence all over the house, stretching your legs across an empty bed, an end to all the responsibility of being loved.'

'Is that a responsibility?'

'Oh yes, the greatest responsibility of all. It was really too much for you, wasn't it?'

One summer holiday Fred was with Dr Salter in a widow's house in Sunday Street, a small row of Victorian cottages that ran behind the Brewery and down to the river. Mrs Amulet was dying with quiet determination, and they had been discussing how much she should be told of her condition. Then Dr Salter had gone upstairs alone and Fred stood in the sunlit patch of garden. Among the hollyhocks and geraniums he saw, against the wall of the house, a small tombstone, of the sort that is erected for a child. Fred read the inscription on it:

IN MEMORY OF TEDDY
A TINY MARMOSET
BELOVED OF COLIN AND KATE AMULET
DEPARTED THIS LIFE THE 23RD OF MARCH 1948
WE SHALL MEET BUT WE SHALL MISS YOU

'An evilly disposed ape,' Dr Salter said when he came out of the house. 'Not house-trained, of course, and with an appalling liver condition. Spent more time and trouble trying to keep Teddy alive than Kate Amulet would want me to waste on her.'

'Does she know?'

'Oh yes.'

'You told her?'

'No. No, I didn't tell her.' They walked towards the gate. 'I shall have to tell you though.'

'Tell me. What?'

'It's difficult to know when to give out the bad news about death or marriage. It's often best to let the patient draw his own conclusions.'

'Marriage?' In the small, sunlit garden, among the hollyhocks, Fred felt as cold and helpless as the old woman upstairs.

'A lady Baptist minister married them, in a place called San Bernardino. The cable was full of unnecessary detail. Must have cost a fortune.'

'Did she want you to tell me?' Fred asked.

'She didn't say.'

The next day Simeon and Dorothy had a similar cable from Henry. His mother put a hand on Fred's arm and said, 'Poor boy. Poor old Fred.' She was smiling as she said it, but it seemed to him that her eyes were full with tears, something he didn't remember ever having seen before.

★ 15 ★

Living in the Past

That year the papers were full of extraordinary news; more and more scandals were unearthed, and the serious face of the nation cracked into an incredulous smile of second-hand delight, before prim looks returned and there was much talk of the need to preserve standards in public life. The Secretary of State for War was found to be sharing a mistress with a Soviet naval attaché but this was only the aperitif before a banquet of revelations which culminated in the search for a mysterious masked figure, some person of great political distinction who, naked but for his mask, was said to act as butler and enjoy other humiliations at the dinner parties of the rich and influential figures of the time. The masked man serving the potatoes was never identified but the golden age of Conservative Government, the period when the Prime Minister had told the British people that they had never had it so good and they had believed him, seemed about to disintegrate into a widespread chorus of unseemly giggles.

Charlie Titmuss read all this news with delight each morning before she went off to pursue her social welfare course at Worsfield Polytechnic. But her husband was unsmiling and refrained from comment, as though he felt it was too early, even at their breakfast table, for him to commit himself on a great national issue, and one which, he felt, might have a considerable influence on the future of Leslie Titmuss.

In the evenings he would get home from work as soon as possible and listen to the news in the cottage Nicholas had given them, plainly furnished with Charlie's childhood books and photographs of ponies, and with few signs of Leslie's occupancy. He studied advanced accountancy while his wife drank beer in the Worsfield pubs with a group from the Poly and gossiped about problem families and their favourite delinquents.

'We can all understand your wife taking up welfare,' Elsie said when she brought a basket of her son's clean shirts round one evening. 'Even if she's never going to take up ironing. She's got to have something to look after. Ever since it turned out to be a false alarm about the baby.'

'It's not a bad thing for a politician's wife to be in the welfare service. It does no harm at all.'

'I never heard of Mrs Strove being interested in anyone's welfare when she was alive. I never heard of that at all.' Elsie had brought some homemade rock cakes for Leslie's tea and she was putting them out on a plate.

'You must have known old Doughty Strove pretty well?' Leslie asked his mother casually.

'Since I was eighteen and in service.' Leslie looked pained at the word 'service', but cheered up when his mother added, 'Quite a lad was Doughty, in his younger years.'

'What's that mean?' Leslie took a rock cake and buttered it. 'One for the girls?'

'Well, he'd come down to the kitchen for a slice of pie, something to take out shooting, and he'd try and put an arm round you, all that sort of nonsense. You wouldn't believe it, would you? Not looking at him now.' Elsie had made tea for Leslie, something she understood him not doing for himself before his wife came home, and now she poured him a cup.

'Was there anyone in particular?'

'Well, they did say Bridget Bigwell. It was all just talk.'

'Go on!' Leslie smiled, sugaring his tea.

'Bridget worked at Picton House, you know. Then she left to go to the Fanners and married Percy and had Glenys, well all on top of each other! I don't suppose there was anything in it.'

'Glenys Bigwell! She does typing for the Rector.'

'Glenys was a bright girl. Always seemed bright above her station, as you might say.'

'The Rector said she can't spell. Perhaps she inherited that from Doughty Strove!'

'No.' Elsie sat beside her son, delightedly shocked at the suggestion. 'It's talk, most likely. They were all the same, though. The young men in those days. Not enough to do and too much money to do it with.'

'*All* the young men?'

'All the same, all tarnished with the same brush. Of course, I mean the gentry.'

Leslie was munching rock cakes and looking at his mother. 'What about the Rector?'

'Mr Simcox was different.' Elsie smiled distantly. 'He was always different from all the rest.'

'In the old days. When they never got about much. Well, before the invention of the bicycle, Skurfield stayed Skurfield, and Rapstone never left its frontiers and their inhabitants simply bred with each other!' Another authority on the past of the district, Dr Salter was instructing Fred as they rode together up Picton Ridge. 'Cousins with cousins. Closer than that sometimes. Well, rabbits don't stop to ask, "Excuse me, but are you my sister by any chance?" and yet they're perfectly lively little creatures.'

Fred rode a little behind him, mounted on a small stolid hack from the riding-stable, a great deal slower than the big, black, nervous hunter, a new acquisition from the Worsfield Show, on which the Doctor was turning in the saddle, shouting back against the wind. 'Can't see all that in-breeding did much harm. They cut down their own trees, managed to turn very decent chair legs in the huts they put up in the beech woods. Look at the dates on the tombstones in your old father's churchyard, they lived far beyond any reasonable time for living. Of course the bicycle changed all that. Then they got over to the next village and rogered girls they weren't even related to. In the old days there were Nowts in Skurfield and Bigwells in Rapstone, and that was about the size of it.'

'I was thinking about Tom Nowt.'

'Oh, were you?'

'I just wondered why my father's always so against him. I remember, when I was a child, the fuss he made when I went to his old hut.'

'His hut?' Dr Salter sounded puzzled.

'His hut in the woods, you must know it?'

'I don't think so.'

'But I was there! When I got back from London and Agnes had gone off with Henry to that Coast of theirs. It was where you found me. By Tom's hut!'

'A hut in the woods?'

They had come to the top of the ridge. Their walking mounts snorted and rolled their yellow eyes, quivering neurotically.

'I didn't notice.' Dr Salter kicked his hunter and galloped away, a stocky figure sitting stolidly in the saddle. Fred followed as best he could. He was never entirely at his ease with horses.

After another ride, and before another Sunday lunch, the bell rang and Fred opened the Doctor's front door to discover Agnes standing on the step and smiling. She had come without her key and apologized to him, and he, looking down at her swollen stomach, managed to congratulate her.

'I'm sorry. I so wanted you to be there,' Fred heard her say, and was about to hug her gratefully when he realized that she had not said it to him but to her father, who had come more slowly down the stairs behind him.

'I was there in spirit,' Dr Salter said.

'In San Bernardino, with this female minister telling us to take God into the bedroom with us? I don't think you were there at all.' Then she kissed her father and they began to walk up the stairs together. 'Henry's in London, writing very hard, so I just came down to collect a few things. I will stay for lunch of course, if you ask me. Is it Mrs Beasley's mince? I thought of that so much in California, we used to get jumbo-sized prawns and jumbo-sized tomatoes. It all tasted of cottonwool and I used to think of Mrs Beasley's grey mince which tasted of good, honest dishwater.'

All through lunch Agnes was cheerful and unusually talkative. 'I haven't talked for so long,' she told them. 'You can't talk to American film producers, they just talk to themselves and expect you to listen.' She told them about lunch with Mr Bugloss and climbing out of the window of the 'Señoritas'. 'The last three years, we seem to have gone to the Coast so often and sucked up to Mr Bugloss. It isn't writing for Henry, really it isn't, it's more like interior decorating. But Henry's running away from Mr Bugloss too now, he's writing another novel.' Fred thought of Henry's soul, and the way it was always being saved for him. Then Agnes said, 'It's going to be extremely good. Don't say you're sorry to hear that.'

'I didn't.' Fred denied it.

'You did nearly. You'd've hated yourself if you had, wouldn't you?'

Later, in her old bedroom, Fred helped Agnes pack the clothes and books she needed. He was sorry that there were so few of them, and that their little time together would so soon be over. She was silent for a long while, and then she said, 'Why have you moved in here?'

'I haven't.'

'Not yet, but why do you spend so much time with him? Why are you always helping him, why?'

'I suppose because he's teaching me.'

'Teaching you what?'

'All I want to know.'

'All?'

'Almost all.'

'It's not because of me? I couldn't bear that.'

'It's not because of you.'

'I mean that'd be like living in the past, wouldn't it?' She crammed the remaining things into her suitcase. 'Condemning yourself to stay still all the time. You wouldn't do that, would you?'

She was struggling, unusually agitated, with the suitcase and he closed it for her. As he carried it downstairs he asked her if Henry was pleased, looking again at the distended stomach which she had told him made her feel ridiculously helpless.

'Would you be pleased? I mean if you were Henry?'

'If I were Henry I have no idea what I'd feel.'

When she had gone, Fred did his best to forget Agnes and Henry and their expected child. This left him short of an obsession and he began to concern himself irrationally with the question of Tom Nowt. Why had Dr Salter pleaded ignorance when reminded of old Tom's hut and why, he wondered after so many years, had the place been forbidden to him as a child? He found Simeon, one day, sleeping in his study, or at least stretched out in his chair with his eyes closed in an attitude which he always called 'thinking up a sermon'. As the door closed, his father woke with a start.

'What do you still find to tell them in sermons?' Fred asked. 'When I was a child I can't remember you giving me any advice at all. Or only once.'

'Once?'

'When you told me not to go to Tom Nowt's hut.'

'Nowt's hut? I really can't recall.'

'I'm sure you can. Whatever was wrong with going there?'

'When do you expect to qualify?' Simeon climbed out of his chair and felt in his pocket for a pipe.

'In about three years with any luck.'

'I can't see how it can take all that time to learn Salter's trade. All he does is tell me not to cling on to life and then gives me a couple of aspirins. Oh, and he tipples my brandy.'

'But about Tom Nowt's hut . . .'

'Some people, I'm sure you'll find this out, bring bad luck.' Fred realized that any answer that might be coming his way would be lost in the mists of a sermon. 'That's the point of my sermon. God put such a lot of luck in the universe. Sometimes He seems to have thought He was creating an immense casino. I'm not suggesting that there's anything essentially evil about Tom Nowt, it's just that people like that provoke accidents.'

It wasn't until a weekend visit much later that Fred met the provoker of accidents in the public bar of the Baptist's Head. It was a crowded Saturday night with the pints of Simcox's Best slopping as the drinkers pushed their way from the bar and Fred found himself squashed into a corner inappropriately shouting the question that concerned him.

'The old hut?' Tom answered, grinning over his beer. 'Picked up a bit of something new, have you?'

'No. It's just that Dr Salter . . .'

'Keep out of the man's way. They reckon he'll see you off quicker than a shot-gun in the chest.'

'Ever been to your hut, has he? I mean, has he ever taken anyone there?'

'No questions, boy, then you won't get no lies.'

Fred considered the matter and decided on another line of inquiry. 'What've they all got against you, Tom?'

'Who?'

'My father, I remember how angry he was when I told him I'd been there. And Dr Salter says he's never heard of the place . . .'

'Don't forget her bloody Ladyshit.'

'Grace?'

'Wanted me in the nick. Well, of course, she had her reasons.'

'What reasons?'

'You want to know?'

'Yes.'

'And you're really not meeting up with a young lady?'

'I promise you. No young lady.'

'Then we'd better show you, hadn't we?' Tom held out his empty mug for a refill and said, as though it was part of his request for another drink, 'It's time you got blooded.'

Before Fred could ask for any further explanation, he saw Terry Fawcett, clarinet player of the Stompers, pushing his way towards them. It seemed they were all going on together in Terry's muddy and battered old Zephyr Zodiac. They called at a big and rather melancholy pub by Hartscombe station to collect Den Kitson, and had a surprising number of shorts for which Fred found himself paying. No one seemed prepared to tell him if the evening was to be devoted to drink or music; there was no further mention of blood, and as they came out of their final pub, the Badger at Skurfield, he had ceased to care. Den and Fred sat in the back of the Zephyr. Tom Nowt was in the front with Terry, who drove down the narrow lanes with the dark hedgerows whipping the sides of his old banger with untrimmed branches. Terry began to sing softly; Den joined in and Fred beat out a rhythm, slapping the worn plastic on the seat beside him: 'I don't stay out late. Don't want to go. I'm home about eight. Just me and my radio.' The dark shapes of trees, the straightening of a bend in the road, told Fred, who had known this landscape all his life, that they were going to Mandragola. This was a ruined farmhouse at the head of a hidden, isolated valley, a long stretch of woodland, fields and patches of grassland which had never been cultivated by the Stroves, who owned the land, so that it was rich in butterflies, shells, wild flowers and small strawberries, as well as scrub, brambles, rabbit warrens and hawthorn bushes. Soon Fred saw the shape of the farmhouse walls, and a few cottages with broken windows and fallen-in roofs which Doughty had never found the money to repair, and then the car turned and bumped down a rutted woodland track. They heard owls hoot and saw squirrels scuttle across the road.

Then, at the edge of a wood at the corner of an abandoned field, Terry stopped the car and switched off the lights. Tom put a stop to the singing. They sat for a long while in a silence which was incomprehensible to Fred, and then he heard a faraway rustling sound. Tom nodded and got out with Den. When they came back from a quiet visit to the car boot they were both carrying rifles. They sat with their barrels pointing out of the windows, so that the car looked like an old man-of-war, as Terry started the engine and it creaked slowly forward along the track. The lights were still off and the darkness of the wood seemed to press against them like fog. 'Stop,' Tom whispered, as though he had heard something else, and, after a long silence, 'Now!'

When Terry snapped on the full beam of the headlights, the woodland ride in front of them was lit up like a pantomime transformation scene and dazzled, staring motionless into the glare of the lights, was a tall deer crowned with antlers. It seemed to Fred to stand wide-eyed for a long time before the rifles cracked and it sank gently, reverently, to its knees in front of the car. He felt Den take his arm and pull him out and saw Tom take out his knife and go for the animal's throat. Then a bloody thumb was on his forehead, and he was initiated as brutally as a child who sees its first kill on the hunting-field.

After Simeon Simcox died, Kevin Bulstrode (Kev the Rev. to Henry Simcox) moved into the old Rectory from which he could direct religious operations at Rapstone, Skurfield and Picton Principal. The Bulstrode children fought and screamed and slept in the rooms Fred and Henry had once occupied, and Mrs Bulstrode held her meetings: 'Women for the Priesthood', 'Women against Discrimination' and 'Women against Rape' ('Are there any women *for* rape, I wonder?' Dorothy had murmured when she heard of the last organization) in the big drawing-room. Kevin Bulstrode took over the old Rector's study. He felt a little in awe of the place at first, calling it the Holy of Holies, and then complained, only half joking, of the fact that no journalists came to ask *his* opinion on every subject from punk hairdo's to the Resurrection. He was, he often said, only a simple parish priest, and not in the Top Ten of popular parsons.

Kevin Bulstrode was not entirely easy with what was left of Simeon's possessions; in particular the bust of Karl Marx appeared, at times, to regard him with a sort of lofty disdain and he was afraid that the Rural Dean, or even the Bishop, might call and find it inappropriate. Accordingly, he packed the bearded head and a large number of Simeon's books, pamphlets and assorted papers into tea-chests and lodged them in the attic, telling Dorothy that perhaps she would send someone to fetch them whenever it was convenient.

'Oh you can keep Karl Marx if you care for him,' she said. 'I have so little room now in my minute house in Hartscombe.'

'I'm so glad you've settled in comfortably.' Kevin did, in fact, look considerably relieved. There was a long period when he feared that Simeon's widow was going to be as much a fixture at the Rectory as the joint author of the Communist Manifesto. 'Of course we were worried about how you'd manage, particularly when we heard that Simeon has left everything to Mr Titmuss.'

'Don't worry, Mr Bulstrode. I had a little something of my own.' They were talking in the church where Dorothy still came regularly to do the flowers. The air was heavy with pollen and the dust from old hassocks.

'To leave everything to a Conservative cabinet minister!' Kevin Bulstrode pursed his lips in enjoyable speculation. 'It seems so unlike the Simeon we knew and loved.'

'I suppose he thought he should be fair, even to Conservative cabinet ministers.'

Dorothy's house was indeed small, a flint cottage in a side street. She settled in quickly, Dora Nowt came and did for her, and she thought that the house might have some advantages over the old Rectory. It was going to be impossible for her to have Henry and Lonnie to stay, for instance, and she'd hardly be able to squeeze any number of old parishioners in for tea. In fact, with any luck, she'd be left alone with her patch of front garden.

'I thought a real cottage garden,' she told Fred. 'Cabbages and roses together, and sweet peas all mixed up with the runner beans. I could never do that at the Rectory. Your father had an unusually tidy mind for a Christian Socialist.'

'It's a bit of luck you have the house.'

'And a few investments Simeon's Aunt Pauline left me.'

'Did Simeon's Aunt Pauline leave you the house? I can't remember.'

As always at the mention of financial transactions Dorothy looked vague and withdrawn, as though the conversation had suddenly taken an improper turn. She took the head of a hollyhock between her fingers and looked down on it with mild disapproval. 'Oh yes,' she said. 'I think so, don't you?'

It was only then that Fred saw something which made him remember standing with Dr Salter in the same small garden so many years before. There was the white headstone, almost covered with ivy, against the wall of the house. Half the inscription was hidden, but he could still read ... MORY OF TEDDY ... INY MARMOSET. Then he realized that they were in the house in Sunday Street, where Mrs Amulet and her monkey had both departed this life.

'Are you going to cut back the ivy?' he asked his mother. 'Make a feature of it?'

'Poor monkey's grave!' Dorothy shook her head. 'I think we should let it hide itself in decent obscurity.'

It was some time later, when Dr Fred was examining Jackson Cantellow as an insurance risk, taking his blood pressure and listening to the cavernous chest of the solicitor, that the question of Simeon's will was mentioned again. 'I don't believe we'll ever explain your father's will. The old Rector moved in a mysterious way, his wonders to perform. Of course it was lucky your mother had a few investments, and the house in Sunday Street.'

And Fred, who had just asked Jackson Cantellow to pull up his trousers and hop on the scales, said, 'Didn't Great Aunt Pauline leave Mother Sunday Street?'

'Oh no. Your predecessor left it to her, he got the freehold from a grateful patient. Dr Salter and your mother were old friends of course.'

'Of course.' Fred was adjusting the scales to measure Cantellow's increasing bulk. 'You need to lose a couple of stone.'

'I need the weight, for the low notes in the *Creation*. Oh yes, your mother's house came from Dr Salter.'

★ 16 ★

Getting Out the Voters

In the great world, far from Mandragola and the Rapstone Valley, the revelations of scandal in high places continued to add zest and flavour to the breakfast tables of the nation. Dr Stephen Ward, who, it was suggested, had procured mistresses for the rich and powerful, was to be tried as a concession to one of the British public's periodical bouts of morality, and to commit suicide by way of a pathetically exaggerated apology. Mr Macmillan fell ill and the leadership of the Party, which numbered young Leslie Titmuss among its adherents, had been assumed by Sir Alec Douglas-Home, who had resigned his peerage and was said, for all his apparent amiability, not to show up well on television. All these doings were reported by Hartscombe's representative at Westminster, Doughty Strove, M.P., to a committee of his local Party Association meeting in Hartscombe Town Hall. After the whole sad story had been recounted and a decent silence had been allowed for those who had fallen in the great scandal, Nicholas said, with his usual fairness, 'One feels sorry for the Minister. It was the lying, of course. I don't suppose anyone cares who the fellow jumped into bed with.'

To which there was a rumbling of general assent and one small, sharp voice, 'I don't agree.'

'Titmuss?' Nicholas was displeased by the interruption.

'It's not only the lying, is it? I mean, a member's private life does have to be above suspicion. If we choose a fellow to represent us, we have to make sure he has absolutely no skeletons in his cupboard.' At which those present were surprised to see the young Titmuss fixing Doughty Strove with what looked very much like a glare of accusation.

'Well, there've been all sorts of stupid rumours, of course. Bloody tittle-tattle!' Doughty Strove was obviously nettled. 'But I've made it perfectly clear that if anyone wants to suggest that there's any connection between me and that fellow in the iron mask – they've apparently got photos of him dishing out vegetables to a party of decadents – well, I wouldn't even know where to buy an iron mask.'

An embarrassed silence met this refutation, after which Nicholas was again the conciliator. 'No Doughty. My dear fellow! Of course you wouldn't.'

'It would be quite wrong of me to suggest that there is anything in Mr Strove's past life that could cause us the slightest concern.' Leslie Titmuss went on in a voice which sounded like a prosecution and continued to give offence. 'But in my opinion our Party has attracted far too many rumours lately and they're quite likely to lose us the next election!'

'We shall weather this little difficulty and be returned next time, whenever it may be, with a handsome majority,' Doughty assured them all.

'I really don't agree.' By now his son-in-law's voice was affecting Nicholas like a rusty nail on a slate. 'We've always stood as the Party of public morality,' Leslie grated on. 'It seems to me that if we lose that reputation we might as well all go off and join the Socialists.' There was a merciful gap in Leslie's speech, into which the Chairman hurried to pour oil.

'Yes, well, I'm sure we're all extremely grateful to our member for his clear report from Westminster and for the quiet, dependable way he's represented Hartscombe. Many of you will have noticed the helpful question he asked about oil-seed rape was it, Doughty? I'm sure no one could possibly suggest that he's a man who could be connected with any sort of scandal.' Nicholas smiled vaguely around him. 'With or without an iron mask. So I propose a vote of thanks to Doughty Strove, long may he represent Harts-combe and Worsfield South.'

'I should like to second that, Chairman.' It was Leslie Titmuss, smiling and quick off the mark. His father-in-law looked at him with the nearest he could come to real anger and, when Leslie emerged after the motion had been carried, was waiting for him by the notice-board in the cold and marmoreal Town Hall entrance.

'Father-in-law!' Leslie smiled. 'Whenever are you going to pay us a call?' Since his marriage to Charlie, Leslie had seen very little of her parents, a fact for which she was profoundly grateful but which he resented. Grace and Nicholas hadn't yet included them in their dinner parties at Rapstone Manor.

'I must say that was a bit strong!' Nicholas was clearly not in a social mood.

'Really? I thought it was a jolly good meeting.'

'People who live in glasshouses, Titmuss' – the Chairman looked round to make sure there was not a Conservative within earshot – 'should keep their mouths shut at meetings. What about your own marriage? Didn't you rather jump the gun?'

'You're not suggesting that Charlotte was pregnant when I married her?' Leslie looked pained.

'If she wasn't I don't know what all the fuss was about.'

'I really think you ought to know that the first night I slept with your daughter was on the honeymoon in Torquay you so generously paid for. I'm sure we've got too much respect for the institution of marriage. Of course we both hope to present you with a grandchild once I get settled in the new business. Best wishes to mother-in-law.'

So Leslie Titmuss went out into the Hartscombe night, and left Nicholas feeling that an act of flagrant immorality had occurred, particularily if, by some strange chance, his son-in-law were telling the truth.

There was certainly a new feeling of morality abroad: the top place on the charts was gained by a Belgian nun who sang to a guitar. The daily excitement of scandalous revelations had been forgotten. There was talk of a coming election when the New Jerusalem might again be on offer, not this time as the austere and serviceable city of Major Attlee and Sir Stafford Cripps, but as a gleaming steel and concrete Shangri-La, humming with the Mersey Sound and the mass production of mini-cars evolved by some new and mysterious technology the secret of which had, apparently, only just been discovered. The 'new business' which Leslie Titmuss had mentioned to his father-in-law was Hartscombe Enterprises, a company recently formed by Christopher Kempenflatt and Magnus Strove. They had asked Leslie to join them as an accountant, partly as a reward for his support and advice in the matter of the Easy-Bite restaurant and other property deals in and around Hartscombe, but mainly because he was prepared to work with relentless energy at all hours and leave the business lunches and 'customer relations' to them. From time to time Kempenflatt and Magnus grew fearful at the threat of another Labour Government; then Leslie, the accountant, gave them a small smile and told them that Hartscombe Enterprises had nothing very much to fear from Mr Wilson, the new technology, or government spending on buildings and public works.

'I'm coming down to Rapstone for the election.' Henry had paid an unprecedented call on his brother and been invited to lunch in his hospital canteen. 'We've both got to work, Fred. We've got to do something for this country.'

'You mean England needs you?'

'England's dying on its feet.' Henry spoke with the experience of someone who'd come back from a long time abroad. 'It hasn't even the horrible vitality of Benny K. Bugloss, or Jack Polefax of Galaxy International. My God, Frederick. What've you got? A fourteenth Earl of a prime minister who does sums with matchsticks, members of the Government chasing call-girls and waiting at table in iron masks!'

'You've become very puritanical.' Fred pushed away his cold stew and embarked on the jam roll and custard, food which always seemed to taste faintly of antiseptic.

'About the only thing you've been able to organize decently is a train robbery.'

'I didn't organize it personally.'

'You're going to help us get rid of this lot, aren't you? I mean, I don't agree with everything our father says, as you know.'

'But you'd like to build Jerusalem in England's green and pleasant land?' Fred noticed that his brother's new taste for austerity stopped short of the jam roll.

'I don't see anything particularly wrong with that.'

They had lunch together and neither of them mentioned Agnes.

Fred was tired of the taste of hospital food, the smell of the hospital corridors and the bad jokes that were essential to keep the students' thoughts away from the hopeless reality of death. He didn't know if Henry had come to make peace between them or as some act of contrition; whatever it was he found it hard to understand why he should be beaten about the head with his father's politics during the short half hour he had before his turn to take blood in the children's ward. He wondered why Henry made everything, from an election to a love-affair, sound like some football match at Knuckleberries in which his younger brother was sure to let down the side.

'The trouble with our father's paradise is that it keeps getting put off, doesn't it?' Fred didn't mind trying to irritate Henry, who was now carefully stubbing out a cigarette by the side of his abandoned pudding. 'The promised land's always just round the corner.'

'At least let's give the people a chance and pull together.' Fred thought Henry might have added 'For the sake of the house'.

'You mean "the workers"?'

'Well, if you want to use an old-fashioned expression.'

'I went out with the workers the other night,' Fred decided to tell him. 'The workers I play all that jazz with: Terry Fawcett, who works in Marmaduke's garage in Hartscombe, Den Kitson from the Brewery and Tom Nowt. You remember Tom Nowt, don't you?'

'Vaguely.' Henry seemed to lose interest once specific workers were brought into question.

'Well, Tom Nowt. We all had a few drinks, of course, and then we went on a spree.'

'What sort of spree?'

'We drove down by the Mandragola Valley, bumped across a field, got into a wood and dazzled a deer in an old Zephyr's headlamps. Then they shot it and cut its throat. Nobody said anything about it when I met Terry and Den the week after and we did a trad night at the Badger in Skurfield. They never mentioned it at all. Tom Nowt smeared blood on me.'

'Does that mean you're against us?' Henry was frowning, trying to do his brother the credit of assuming that this anecdote, although apparently pointless, had some sort of relevance to the topic under discussion. But Fred assured him that it didn't mean that at all, in fact it meant that he was on his side.

After the encounter with his father-in-law in Hartscombe Town Hall, Leslie was daily expecting a summons from Grace. For a long time she left him and Charlie in peace. But one day, when he was walking from his old office in the Brewery, where he still helped his father at the time of the annual return, to the new office of Hartscombe Enterprises, the large black Daimler slowed up beside him, the back door opened, and his mother-in-law invited him in with all the cordiality of a hitman of the prohibition era inviting a rival mobster to take a ride. Leslie obeyed politely and looked at Grace with deep sympathy.

'I know you must have been worried, mother-in-law. Of course, Charlotte and I are enormously keen on starting a family as soon as possible.'

'You lied to us, you both lied!'

'Yes.' Leslie's answer so startled Grace that she was silent for at least ten seconds, and then he began a long, confidential explanation, carried on in a hushed tone of voice that at first angered, then embarrassed her. Before he had altogether finished she was finding the pale and by no means apologetic Titmuss strangely appealing. Did she want to know why they lied, he asked her. Because he knew it was the only way she would agree to his marriage. And because he wasn't going to spend the rest of his life working in the Brewery, coming up to the Manor once a year for tea in the garden and the tombola at the Conservative fête. It was because he wasn't going to settle for the life his father had worked out for him, nine to five in the accounts department until he was old enough to draw his pension. He was not only going to make something of himself, and of Charlotte also. He was going to become someone his parents-in-law would be proud of. In fact he was going to represent the constituency one day when Doughty Strove retired, which event might not be so long delayed as everyone might think. He, Leslie Titmuss, was embarking on a long-term programme for the development of his career and he had to start somewhere, didn't he?

'So you started with us?' Grace noticed that the window which separated them from Brooks, the chauffeur, had been left open, and slid it to, sharply, and much too late. 'Well, at least you're honest, I suppose.' She looked at him and recognized, in a surprising moment, something almost like a fellow spirit. 'What you're telling me is, you would have said anything in the world to get into our family?'

'Said or done anything. Of course there's no reason to hide the facts from you now. The point is, if I'm going to do any of the things I'm planning for me and Charlotte, I've got to begin with the people I'll meet in your dining-room. I mean, where else is there?'

It was the language that Grace understood and she invited Leslie to dinner for the following Thursday night. It was an invitation Charlie heard about with horror. If she'd wanted to eat meals with her mother, why on earth, she said, had she gone to all the trouble of leaving home? Finally she yielded to her husband's persuasion but only on the condition that he wouldn't leave her to be dragged upstairs by her mother while he stayed to drink port and tell dirty stories in the dining-room. To this condition Leslie, who could see no possible political advantage in telling a dirty story to Nicholas, readily agreed.

It was, she remembered afterwards, the first of his broken promises. When Grace threw down her dinner napkin and called on Bridget Naboth, Honor Kempenflatt, Jennifer Battley and Mrs Fairhazel to follow her upstairs, Charlie first looked pleadingly at her husband, then uttered the words 'You promised' in a resounding whisper. It was a cry from the heart which Leslie ignored, being busy telling Magnus that it would have been interesting to have had his father's views on an autumn election.

'Come along, Charlie. Let's leave the boys to their politics.' All the boys, Leslie and Magnus, Christopher Kempenflatt, Lord Naboth, the 'Contessa' and her father, had their heads turned away from her and their eyes averted, as Charlie went off as though to half an hour on the rack.

'I'm afraid Doughty had something on in London.' Nicholas apologized for his old friend.

'I expect you think he's got nothing on in London, don't you, Leslie?' Magnus was laughing. 'I mean nothing but an iron mask?'

'I'm only sorry,' Leslie replied with dignity, 'that your father has so little time for constituency matters.'

'Are you?'

'I'm sure that Doughty would tell us we're going to win the next election, whenever it is.'

'And are we all absolutely sure that would be in the best interests of the Party?'

Faces were turned to Leslie, showing more embarrassment and shock than if he'd told the dirtiest joke Charlie had ever managed to collect from the brightest of her juvenile delinquents.

'What on earth is that supposed to mean?' Lord Naboth was looking profoundly disturbed.

'I'm not sure we don't need a time to re-think.' Leslie smiled in the pleasantest way. 'I don't think we can afford to go on being amateurs.'

'You mean being gentlemen?' Nicholas's mind turned to cricket. 'You want us to be players?'

'I'd like us to be serious. If we lost in the autumn, it might give us time to sharpen up our image.'

'Sharpen up what, Titmuss?'

'Our image, sir.'

'Is that a phrase that has some meaning for you, Archie?' Nicholas turned to Lord Naboth for guidance.

'I'm not sure. I'll tell you one thing though. I bet Alec Douglas-Home isn't in the least worried about the result of the election.'

'I bet Harold Wilson is, perhaps that's the difference between them. Don't worry, Magnus, will you?' Leslie was now positively affable. 'Of course we're all going to work twenty-four hours a day to get your father re-elected.'

Upstairs, in the drawing-room, Grace knew that Mrs Fairhazel was longing to be gently poisonous on the subject of Leslie Titmuss and got her oar in first. 'I think Charlie's really found something in her Mr Titmuss. He knows exactly where he's going and, give him full marks, I honestly believe he's going to get there. At least he pays us the compliment of wanting to join us.' Unfortunately Charlie didn't hear this generous tribute. She was seated in blissful solitude in the downstairs loo, a refuge where her husband had, many years before, been found screaming. She was reading the

193

back numbers of *Country Life* with which the dusty table beside the seat was supplied, and when she came across a photograph of her mother enjoying a joke at some long-past hunt ball, she tore it out carefully, and then, even more carefully, ripped it into even smaller pieces and flushed it down the pan.

The election was held in October. Fred drove his father's elderly Austin and Henry came down the lanes too fast, brushing the hedgerows against the sides of his second-hand Jaguar. They were both there to 'get out' Labour voters, so they found cottages on remote commons, or went down rutted tracks to unknown farms, or ransacked blocks of flats and Old People's Homes. Some of the voters came willingly, having been ready since dawn and regarding the whole occasion as a day out; many thought the election an unwarranted intrusion into their private lives and most couldn't be home until the evening. So, while the Simcox brothers were driving cars plastered with pictures of Harold Wilson, Leslie Titmuss knocked on doors, called on the residents of caravans and barges on the river and drove Conservative voters in the spruce black Rover Christopher Kempenflatt had lent him for the occasion.

Simeon and Dorothy crossed from the Rectory to the school-house, wearing red rosettes, to register their votes. Dr Salter, riding by, called from the saddle to ask them if they were about to start another revolution. 'He's only teasing us,' Dorothy explained, but Simeon waved the hand with his pipe in it and called back, 'A revolution. Of course! Guillotine all the aristocrats and their doctor.' It was a threat which was clearly heard by Grace and her chauffeur, Brooks, who had come down in the Daimler to cast their votes. By the early evening Fred had seen more village halls and schools than he knew existed, had found Hartscombe housing estates he had never visited and had helped old ladies out of bedrooms and transported babies their mothers couldn't leave. He met Ben Leverett, the Labour candidate, his grey hair blowing in the wind and his rosette flapping, as he drew up with a small catch of Labour voters outside the Town Hall.

'Hartscombe's pretty solid Tory and a lot of the villages,' Ben Leverett said. 'But we've got South Worsfield and the housing

194

estates. If we can get all our voters out we might just be in with a chance.'

So, in the faint hope of securing the Rapstone Valley for the People's Party, Fred drove to Worsfield with another crumpled list and inadequate information. He stopped at a traffic light on the edge of the city and looked out at sodium-lit windows on the chance of spotting Mr Wilson's photograph peering back at him. Then he heard a bleep on the horn of the black Rover parked next to him and saw the window being rolled down. In a moment he was in communication with Leslie Titmuss.

'There's a few of your voters up in Attlee Crescent. They haven't been picked up yet.'

'You're telling *me* that?'

'I thought it would be fair.' He glided off in the Rover, an unexpectedly parfit and gentil Knight of a Leslie Titmuss, and when Fred at last found Attlee Crescent he discovered that it wasn't even a hoax.

The result, when the Mayor as the Returning Officer announced it in Hartscombe Town Hall at around one o'clock in the morning, was greeted by cheers and boos and came out as follows: Leverett, Benjamin Arnold (Labour), fifteen thousand and six; Prusford, Michael Charles (Liberal), four thousand six hundred and twenty-four; Ramsden, Michael Matabele (Anti-Vivisection and Free Toilet facilities), sixteen; Strove, Doughty Picton Percival (Conservative), fourteen thousand nine hundred and sixty-seven. And so the said Benjamin Arnold Leverett was duly elected to serve as the member for the Hartscombe and South Worsfield constituency. They had, Fred calculated rapidly, a majority of thirty-nine and he wondered just how many Labour voters he had got out of Attlee Crescent, thanks to the unexpected chivalry of Leslie Titmuss.

Mr Harold Wilson went to Buckingham Palace with his wife, his two sons and his father, to become prime minister at the age of forty-eight. Doughty Strove went back to full-time farming and Leslie Titmuss worked hard for Hartscombe Enterprises. Agnes gave birth to Francesca and became mysteriously happy with the baby. Henry felt he was the only normally discontented person in the household. Fred went on learning more about the human body than he thought it safe for anyone to know, and Simeon became concerned about the military government in Bolivia.

One morning, by the woods in the Mandragola Valley, Doughty Strove's gamekeeper found Tom Nowt lying beside his shot-gun. Tom had bled copiously from a jagged wound in his chest. He was quite dead.

★ 17 ★
The Wrongs of Man

'Let her go. Let her go. God bless her, Wherever she may be,' sang Joe Sneeping, trumpet in hand, fronting the rehearsal session in Marmaduke's garage, and Fred, on drums, heard murmurs from the other musicians. 'Accident?' 'Course, Doctor, she said it was an accident!' and 'Some it suits quite well, Tom going like that.' Those speaking were Den Kitson on banjo and Terry Fawcett on clarinet, who was resting with his instrument on his knee.

'She can look this wide world over, She'll never find a sweet man like me ....' Joe stopped singing and looked rebukingly at Terry Fawcett who raised his clarinet to his lips, and Fred was able to overhear no more about the death of Tom Nowt. All he knew was the finding of the coroner who had heard the evidence of Dr Salter. Death was due to an accident which probably occurred when the deceased stumbled while out shooting at night. He might well have tripped over some low branch or bramble and his shot-gun, with the safety-catch off, discharged accidentally.

The cause of Tom Nowt's death brought less speculation than the future of his cottage on the Strove estate. His children had all left home and his wife, Dora, went to live with a married daughter in Hartscombe. There appeared to be available a rare commodity, an empty cottage in the Rapstone Valley, and no one, they were sure, deserved it more than Terry Fawcett and Glenys Bigwell who had been walking out for six years with nowhere to lie down together but the woods or a bed and breakfast on rare summer holidays.

Glenys could entertain Terry at her parents' and Terry could have her to tea at his mother's, but neither home afforded them permission of a bed or a space to marry. When they discussed the prospect, Bridget said Tom Nowt's place had been kept like a monkey house, and her husband was doubtful about his daughter taking over the home of a man who had crippled him by his habit of letting the sodding trees fall anywhere. Tom Nowt's cottage seemed to Percy Bigwell to be the sort of place which could bring no one any luck. However, Glenys's mind was made up. The cottage would suit them perfectly, and Terry could use the old hut in the woods for repairing his motor-bikes. She mentioned all this to the Rector one morning when she went up to type for him, and between congratulations to members of the new Government, stern warnings to the Bishop of Worsfield, drafts of letters to *The Times* on the subjects of integrated schools in the southern states of America and the situation in the Dominican Republic, Simeon composed a strong note to Doughty Strove on the justice of Terry and Glenys's claim to Tom Nowt's old cottage. He was sure that a wise and fair landlord would immediately grant them a lease. As Glenys saw the words take shape under her fingers and bite blackly into the paper, she believed that the matter had been decided by the Rector and it would only be a matter of time before she and Terry moved in together. On the same morning as she typed the letter, she booked a date for her marriage.

Both Glenys and Simeon had reckoned without a new force in the Rapstone Valley, Hartscombe Enterprises, which body, through its representatives, Magnus Strove and Leslie Titmuss, was taking a close look at Tom's old cottage in the company of Doughty Strove. Leslie had the figures Hartscombe Enterprises would pay the Strove estate – £10,000 for the property including the bit of woodland leased to the late Mr Nowt with the cottage. The cash would be immediately available and the purchasers would be responsible for all repairs and renovations.

'There's only one difficulty.' Doughty looked troubled.

'What's that, Father?'

'Had a note from the Rector, the Bigwell girl is marrying young Fawcett. As they've been walking out together for years, he seems to think they've got some sort of natural right to the place.'

'With all due respect to the Rector' – Leslie was almost apologetic – 'I wonder if he's really thought this one through. Of course Glenys Bigwell is an extremely attractive girl.'

'What's that supposed to mean?' Doughty's eyes, set like dark currants in a wide expanse of bun, became somewhat beady.

'Well, if you did that sort of favour for one particular local girl, mightn't it start old stories again?'

'Old stories?' Doughty looked round furtively, as though there might be whisperers in Tom Nowt's dilapidated cottage. 'I think all Leslie's trying to say, Father,' Magnus came in with the voice of reason, 'is that it would be much better to offer it to someone outside the neighbourhood. That's all you were trying to say, wasn't it, Leslie?'

'That's all, Magnus. That is absolutely all.'

Although she got no formal confirmation from the Strove estate Glenys assumed that the Rector's letter had done the trick. Accordingly she hung a basket full of scourers, scrubbing brushes, floor cloths, rags, Mansion polish and Gumption on to the handlebars of her bike and rode over to Skurfield one afternoon when Simeon and Dorothy had gone off to a concert in Worsfield Cathedral, and the world was let off, for the afternoon, a single letter of protest.

When Glenys arrived at the cottage she leant her bike against the hedge, found the spare key where she knew Tom and Dora had always kept it under a loose brick, went in and, after clicking her tongue a little at the state of the floors, put on an overall and rubber gloves and started to work. An hour later she was gumptioning the sink with such concentrated intensity that she didn't hear a car stop in the lane outside, nor did she hear the woman who came in at the back door.

'The door was open.' Glenys turned to see a well preserved forty-year-old, wearing trousers and a sweater, with a bulging handbag slung across her shoulder, glasses on the end of her nose and a look of amused desperation at all the problems with which life presented her. 'You must have seen the advertisement.'

'What advertisement?' Glenys went on scrubbing.

'We put a card up in that funny little sell-everything shop. You know, paraffin lamps all mixed up with bacon and butter and old fly-papers. But,' and the woman peered at Glenys, pushing her glasses up, 'if you didn't see the advertisement how on earth did you get here?'

'Everyone knows about it now Tom's passed over.'

'Of course!' The woman sounded relieved. 'News travels fast in this little community. Well, we're delighted to see you however you got here.'

'Oh, the Rector fixed it up.' The sink was gleaming white now and Glenys looked at it, contented.

'The Red Rector of Rapstone! We haven't touched base with him yet but we hear he's perfectly charming, in spite of the funny politics. So *he* suggested you came along?'

'He wrote a letter to Mr Strove and I think that'll do the trick.'

'Well, I must say, it's extremely thoughtful of them all.'

It was then that Glenys looked out into the little patch of back garden where Tom grew a few vegetables and a good many nettles, the proliferation of which was due to the burial there of the inedible parts of much slaughtered game. A balding man had spread a rug on the unmown grass and was setting out a picnic for the benefit of two fair-haired and carsick children.

'That's my husband, by the way,' the woman explained. 'Everybody calls him Malley. I hope you will too.'

'Why?'

'His name's Mallard-Greene but everybody at the B.B.C. calls him Malley. We're having our picnic in the garden.'

'I suppose that's all right.'

'Well, thank you!' Mrs Mallard-Greene assumed that Glenys was making some kind of a joke.

'I mean, I shouldn't really be here myself. It's not all signed and sealed yet but I couldn't resist coming in and making a bit of a start.' Glenys looked hungrily round at the cleaning she still had to do; she wanted to get on.

'It's most tremendously keen of you and I'm sure we'll get on like a house on fire!' Mrs Mallard-Greene encouraged her. 'We noticed that you'd brought your bicycle. How many hours are you going to be able to get up here?'

'But I'm going to be here all the time.'

'All the time? We weren't thinking of anyone living-in.'

'Living-in? Of course we'll be living-in, me and my Terry. It's going to be our cottage, isn't it?'

It was then that Mrs Mallard-Greene went to the window,

pushed it open and shouted with surprising volume, 'Come here, Malley. I think there's been a tiny bit of a balls-up!'

'Tom Nowt's dead.' Fred gave his brother the news in a Hartscombe bookshop, where Henry was signing copies of his new novel *The Wrong Side of Sunset Boulevard*. ('A brilliant and savage satire on Hollywood by Britain's brightest and angriest young writer' – *Guardian*.) Fred had been walking down the High Street, wondering whether he'd end his life married to some plump nurse or eager female medical student he had met walking the wards, and then repeating the mnemonic, 'On Old Manhattan's Peaked Tops A Finn And German Picked Some Hops,' a strange, unforgettable vision which never managed to remind him of the names of the cranial nerves. Then his thoughts had turned to Stan Kenton, whose big band arrangements were polluting the purity of jazz, not that Fred thought that music should ever remain as played by a blind negro pianist in Preservation Hall. His steps were arrested by the sight of his brother's face repeated on the jackets of a pile of books. Through the shop window he was appalled to see Henry standing beside Mrs Niggs, the bookseller, drinking white wine which he didn't offer to the customers, who seemed unreasonably anxious to acquire the latest Simcox. Fred pushed open the door and joined the queue.

'Would you mind not signing this one? I plan to read it in odd moments, when Mrs Niggs isn't looking. Anyway, aren't you knocking on a bit for an angry young writer?'

'I might have known you'd be in Hartscombe, Freddie. You never seem to be anywhere else.'

'You will come over to the Rectory for dinner, won't you?'

'Why?'

'They'll expect it. Now they know you're home. Anyway, there's something I want to talk to you about.'

'What's that?'

It was then that Fred told him, 'Tom Nowt's dead.'

At dinner at the Rectory, curried lamb – the positively last appearance of the Sunday joint – washed down with a limited amount of Simcox's bottled ale, Dorothy received the presentation copy of Henry's latest work: 'To Mother and Father, without whom I shouldn't have seen Hollywood, or indeed anything at all', and looked with embarrassed amusement at the photograph on the cover.

'It's not at all like him, is it, Simeon?' She held it up for her husband to peer at from the other end of the table. 'It's not at all like Henry.'

'Not really, but then I've always found it quite difficult to remember what either of you look like,' Simeon told his sons. 'When you're not here of course.'

'Well, we're here now,' Henry pointed out reasonably.

'I do wish you'd write a "whodunit",' Dorothy sighed, as though expressing the longing of a lifetime. 'They do so awfully well in the library. Nowadays the library comes round in a van, such a strange idea, like milk.'

'Who done what?' Henry asked. 'I don't suppose anyone cares.'

'Don't you? People seem to.'

'Henry's written a satirical comedy,' Fred explained, as his brother continued to smile bravely, 'about how much he hates America.'

'Hate it, do you?' Simeon asked as though genuinely seeking information. 'Why are you always going there then?'

'Henry's not always going there,' Fred told him. 'He's always coming back.'

'Anyway, those ghastly film people.' Henry decided to shut his brother up with an anecdote. 'Agnes and I were being bored by one at lunch. You know the sort of lunches they have there – three-storey sandwiches and lethal cocktails and iced water.'

'Iced water!' Dorothy laughed. 'It'd make my teeth ache!'

'Agnes and I looked at each other in the middle of lunch and hit on this scheme, by sort of telepathy. We both went to the loo and climbed out of the window to freedom.'

'Both?' Fred raised his eyebrows.

'We walked back to the hotel,' Henry went on, ignoring his brother. 'Laughing all the way. You know, you don't walk in Hollywood, no one walks in Hollywood, it's a sort of blasphemy.'

At the end of this story Henry laughed a little on his own and Fred felt a moment of sympathy for him. Whether or not he was telling the truth he was doing his best to entertain their parents, who could be hard to please, particularly their mother. She turned big, mournful eyes on Henry, as though he had recounted a tragedy.

'Poor man!'

'Who?'

'The poor man who was buying you lunch.'

'He's not poor at all. He draws the most enormous expenses.'

'All the same, you probably hurt his feelings.'

'Impossible! I put a literal, word-for-word portrait of Benjamin K. Bugloss in my book. I made him the complete comic, dotty Hollywood producer. I thought he'd sue me for libel, or at least never speak to me again. Do you know what? He thinks it's a "great piece of material" and he's bought an option on it for a movie.'

'Your Mr Bugloss,' Dorothy told him, 'sounds something of a saint.'

After dinner, when Dorothy and Simeon had retired to the double bed they still shared, Henry brought in a bottle of whisky from the car and the brothers sat in Simeon's study. 'Do you think Our Father and the Reverend Mother were getting at me slightly?' Henry swirled his drink round the tumbler and looked, with a wounded expression, at the bust of Karl Marx.

'They get at me a lot more,' Fred told him.

'Why's that?'

'Probably because I'm here a lot more.'

'Our father's an extraordinary being. Do you ever get the feeling he's not connected with us at all?'

There was a silence and then Fred told him again, 'Tom Nowt shot himself by accident apparently. I can't imagine Tom shooting anything by accident.'

'Wasn't he some kind of poacher?'

'The point is, no one wants to admit knowing him very well, or his hut in the woods. You remember how angry our father was when I went there, years ago?'

'No one wants to admit knowing him?' Henry frowned.

'Dr Salter doesn't. Or Mother. I had an idea.'

'Try not to, you're not used to it.' What Henry said wasn't really an insult, only an echo of their schooldays.

'I had a strange thought that she and Dr Salter might have gone there together once, years ago perhaps.'

'God, Frederick!' Henry embarked on an outraged aria. 'They accuse me of inventing! You think *Sunset*'s an invention? I tell you. It was all exactly like that only more so. Writers are the only reliable witnesses. We know about the world, young Fred. We've got our feet firmly on the ground but people like you, the middle-class professional men like you're going to be, doctors, lawyers, bank managers, you're all lost in a world of fantasy! Or is your life so dull that you have to invent mysterious secrets about our family?'

'You're middle class too, aren't you?'

'That's hardly the point.'

'And professional.' Fred gave himself another drink out of Henry's bottle. 'Anyway, I don't suppose we'll ever know now.'

'Now?'

'Now Tom Nowt's dead.'

Disappointed of the cottage which he believed to be destined for himself and Glenys, Terry Fawcett called at the Citizen's Advice Bureau. Present during his interview were a Miss Carew, in charge, and Charlie Titmuss, née Fanner, who was there as part of her training in social welfare. Miss Carew, who was caring for the row of potted plants, ferns and succulents, which stood on her window ledge, snipping off dead leaves and applying water from a long spouted can, interviewed Terry. She told him that Doughty Strove was entitled to do what he liked with his own property, that the old cottage no doubt needed more money spent on it than he and Glenys could afford, and that they could put their names down for one of the new council flats being planned for Worsfield in a couple of years' time, although priority would naturally be given to married couples with families. At which point Terry, who had been smoking with fierce concentration, deliberately applied a lighted match to the pile of case notes, pamphlets on Help for the Aged, Baby Care, Rent Tribunals and How to Register a Death, which lay on the table in front of him. Miss Carew swung round from her plants to see her small world alight and burning furiously.

Unexpectedly she cried, 'What the shit, Mr Fawcett?' and doused the flames with her watering-can.

Charlie caught up with Terry as he left the counselling service and persuaded him to come for a pint or two of Simcox's. She commiserated, condoled and joined him in reviling the name of Doughty Strove. She was late getting home to her husband, and bought fish and chips for their supper.

'Not again!' Leslie in his shirt-sleeves rose from another file of accounts and looked at the warm, damp sheets of the Hartscombe *Advertiser* unfolding to reveal the cooling, yellow fish and limp chips. 'I must set them out properly.'

'On a poncey little dish?' Charlie, without removing her mac, had sprinkled vinegar and was eating with eager, well-licked fingers.

'I can't imagine what your mother would say if she could see us.'

'Oh, I can. Mummy would think we'd got dreadfully common. Screw her!'

'It's not something I'd personally undertake.' Leslie picked up a chip, stared at it with distaste and took a determined bite.

'What's the matter with you?' Charlie looked up from her portion of rock salmon. 'You've started to make jokes.'

Leslie ignored this and gave her the news. It was time, he had decided, that they moved on. Hartscombe Enterprises needed a national centre, and London might suit Charlotte very well. It was, after all, absolutely teeming with social problems. Charlie was doubtful and reluctant.

'I don't see how I can leave Terry Fawcett and Glenys. They haven't got anywhere to live.'

'There's a plan for new flats in Worsfield.'

'They don't want Worsfield. They want Rapstone. They were both kids in the village. Why should they have to move to Worsfield?'

'Upward mobility.' As Charlie showed no signs of making coffee, Leslie plugged in the kettle.

'Up a bloody tower block, you mean! In about ten years' time.'

She lit a cigarette, dropping the spent match into the paper which had contained their supper. Leslie made the coffee carefully, filtering it and setting out small after-dinner cups with a milk jug and sugar bowl on a tray. Looking at Charlie he thought that what she was was a snob. She'd been brought up deprived of fish and chips and strong tea and bottles of sauce. He remembered his daily routine at 'The Spruces'. His father always came home at exactly the same time and always said, 'Is tea ready, dear?' When he had eaten he would push his plate away with the usual words 'very tasty, dear. That was very tasty.' If anyone in the family became ill, it was a point of honour not to bother the Doctor, and all deaths were known as 'a blessed release'. At half past nine every evening George Titmuss dropped asleep in the leatherette chair on the right side of the fireplace, his mouth fell open, his breathing became soft and regular and his wife and son would have to sew and read in silence. At ten-thirty exactly Leslie's father would wake up with a start, say, 'Time for Bedfordshire!' and lock up. All hope for a different sort of life was known as 'living with your head in the clouds', all ambition had to be confined to keeping the Prefect in running order, 'The Spruces' front garden the tidiest in Skurfield and the payments to the Prudential regular. Whatever his wife might feel about the glamour of the sauce bottles on the table at tea-time, Leslie knew exactly what the world he came from was like and he was not going back there ever, not as long as he lived.

'There's not a lot I can do about Terry Fawcett's problems yet.' Leslie carried the tray to the coffee table in front of their sitting-room fireplace.

'What do you mean, *yet?*' Charlie was not following him.

'Well,' Leslie told her modestly. 'For that sort of problem, he'd have to go to his local M.P.'

So the Mallard-Greenes took possession of Tom Nowt's cottage, and the young Titmusses moved up to London, at first to a company flat in St John's Wood, and later, when Leslie was made a director, to a small company house off the Cromwell Road. Before they left, Charlie told her father to transfer the lease of their Rapstone cottage to Terry Fawcett, but he was surprised to discover that she didn't know that the cottage had already been sold to Hartscombe Enterprises, a deal he'd agreed to because Leslie had told him that having the place owned by the company would mean 'a bit of security' for Charlotte and himself. 'Really, Charlie,' Nicholas asked, 'doesn't your husband tell you anything?' Tackled by his wife on the subject, Leslie said that Magnus and Christopher Kempenflatt had insisted on the purchase, and they wanted to resell to a young chap from Hambros, who needed somewhere to pop down to for occasional weekends. He had managed to get a bit of commission on the deal which would help them in their move to London. Leslie explained all these things very reasonably and Charlie said little at the time. She felt she had failed, however, and was anxious to get away to London, where she could take a course at the L.S.E. and help such other Terry Fawcetts as she might find, without having to seek favours from her father or permission from her husband.

Some time later Mr Mallard-Greene, wearing corduroy trousers and an anorak, carrying a large tin of paraffin, walked down into the depths of the beech woods which he now owned, with his two children, Simon and Sarah. The young Mallard-Greenes followed him, somewhat reluctantly, not having been anxious to turn out on a chilly afternoon and resenting being wrapped up in gloves and mufflers by their mother. When Simon asked his father about their mission he was told, 'We're getting rid of an eyesore. It's not only because it's ugly to look at, it's because it's not what this woodland's meant for. It's meant for wild life. It's meant to be a home for the badgers and all sorts of birds and butterflies and for squirrels, of course.'

'And for worms,' Sarah suggested.

'Well, of course, for worms.'

'And for woodlice.'

'And for bluebells,' Mr Mallard-Greene summed up firmly. 'There's nothing spoils a natural bluebell wood more than having a sort of rural slum dumped down in it.' They reached Tom Nowt's hut, a scene of considerable activity. Two woodmen with a tractor and trailer, rented for the day, had loaded up all such non-inflammable objects as the cooker, lamps, pots and pans and the big, creaking, brass-knobbed iron bedstead. A couple of walls had already been knocked down and reduced to a pile of timber in the middle of the wooden floor, but the front of the hut had been left standing, with broken windows and a door which opened inwards into the silence of an ancient beech wood. Mr Mallard-Greene, known as Malley in the B.B.C. and a closet pyromaniac, told his children to stand well back and sloshed paraffin in through the front door. Then he struck a match, threw it in and retreated with the fearful delight of a child who has just lit the blue touch-paper of an enormous banger on Guy Fawkes night.

There was a wonderful whoosh, a wind of flame and then a slower crackling as what was left of the hut burned down. The damp afternoon became sultry, lit by showers of sparks and the steady burning of wooden planks and battens. So, as Malley beamed with pride, the workmen looked on without expression, and the children danced with delight and, greatly daring, darted up to throw sticks and fallen branches on to the blaze, Tom Nowt's hut, hunting-lodge and meeting-place for secret lovers vanished as his deer skulls, crowned with antlers, fell from the wall of fire and blackened on the burning floor.

Many years later, and a year after Simeon's death, Henry sat in a room in Lincoln's Inn and tried to explain his case for upsetting his father's will to a couple of barristers and his solicitor, Jackson Cantellow.

'There was an old hut in the woods,' he said. 'My brother, Frederick, once had a strange idea that our mother used to meet the local Doctor there. I really don't know what he was driving at. Perhaps that there was some sort of mystery about his birth, or mine?'

'I don't think we need be in the least concerned, Mr Henry Simcox, at what your brother, Frederick, was driving at.' Crispin Drayton, Q.C., Henry's leading counsel, was a tall, nobbly and abstemious man, married to a lady magistrate. In court he was renowned for his high moral tone and the brutality of his cross-examination. 'Let others speculate, if they feel so inclined. You do understand, I'm sure, that if you or your brother were not the "lawful children" of the deceased Rector, we might get the one thing we *don't* want in this case.'

'What's that exactly?'

'A rational explanation for the will of Simeon Simcox.'

★ 18 ★

The Partnership

In the middle of the swinging sixties people in England were apparently under some sort of obligation to have a good time and most of them didn't. A Russian and an American walked about in space to no one's particular advantage. The Beatles received their British Empire medals and, so it was said, smoked cannabis in the lavatories at Buckingham Palace. American aeroplanes were bombing North Vietnam, but no one seemed to talk about the nuclear holocaust anymore. Even Simeon's letters to *The Times* became rarer and more benign. At such a time Fred became a doctor. He had only a nodding acquaintance with the Hippocratic oath, but was somehow aware that he was committed to Apollo the Healer to look upon his teacher in the art of medicine as one of his parents, not to give any deadly drug to anyone, even if it was asked of him, and especially not to aid any woman to procure an abortion. He knew well enough to enter a house only for the benefit of the sick and to refrain from all wrong-doing and corruption and the seduction of male or female, bond or free.

He got through his final exams without brilliance or disgrace. He was not especially proud of his results, although Dr Salter assured him that success as a healer of the sick had very little to do with being able to remember the names of the cranial nerves. He had, over the years, many of Agnes's father's definitions by heart, such as *Bedrest*: a slow and tedious introduction to death. Tell your patients to keep upright. And when they want to die, get it over quickly. In silence. Best of all is to die standing, like a horse; *Check-ups*: a process by which the customer is subjected to a minute medical examination at frequent intervals, in the faint hope of finding a fatal disease. Naturally the victim feels embarrassed

unless he can produce some sort of interesting complaint to entertain the Doctor; *Dieting*: the only excuse for dieting is poverty.
Voluntary self-deprivation invariably leads to a considerable increase in the original weight once the starvation period is over. By
keeping this lore out of his examination papers, Fred achieved a
celebration party in his room in Battersea and got moderately
drunk in the company of a number of other medical novices, a few
nurses, some of his guests' girlfriends and Dr Salter, who had come
up from Hartscombe for the occasion, and who, after attacking
Fred's more serious friends on the subject of smoking ('Why not?
Saves thousands of people from going potty. Anyway, who wants
to live an extra ten years in a geriatric hospital in Weston-super-
Mare? There's no pleasure in the world worth giving up for that!'),
issued the invitation, which Fred had half expected and half feared.
'Let us raise our glasses,' he said, having banged a beer bottle on
the table for silence, 'and drink to good health, coupled with the
name of Dr Frederick Simcox, soon to be best part of Salter and
Simcox, witchdoctors and medicine men of Hartscombe in the
County of . . . ' Dr Salter looked down into his glass. 'Look here,
old cock!' he said, 'the tide's gone down.''

'Did you say "partners"?' Fred filled him up and got him going
again.

'For God's sake, cocky, what do you think I've been waiting for
all these long years? I thought you'd never qualify.'

So Fred saw his life spread out in front of him, like the Rapstone
Valley seen from the Ridge, familiar and unsurprising, a life which
he might never have undertaken but for Agnes and her father,
which he might have shared with her and now would have to live
without her. He had no idea that only a few years later he would
become solely responsible for running the Hartscombe practice.

The invitation to the partnership was not the only one that Dr
Salter had issued. Fred had thought for a long time about inviting
Henry and Agnes to his party, doubtful how tolerant either of them
would be in the company of young medics whooping it up on
bottled beer. Now there was a ring at the front door and Fred went
down to find not only Mr and Mrs Henry Simcox, but also their
friend Mr Bugloss, holding a magnum of champagne, and his

friend Mrs Wickstead, wrapped in fur and looking as pale and perfect as a rare china object.

'Is this where you live?' Henry asked, amused. 'Wonderfully handy for the Battersea Dogs' Home.'

'Of course I asked her. Didn't you want her here in your moment of triumph?' Dr Salter said, when the party had gone upstairs. Fred offered Agnes champagne from Mr Bugloss's huge bottle but, as he expected, she preferred warm light ale taken with soggy crisps. 'Salter and Simcox,' she said. 'You're really merged into him now, aren't you? What does your father say about married people. One flesh?'

'That's absolute rubbish.'

'Oh, no it's not. You'll both do the same things, know the same things and be absolutely out of bounds, as far as I'm concerned.'

Then she turned to speak with considerable animation to the most boring young doctor at the party. Mr Bugloss approached Fred softly murmuring, 'Dr Simcox.'

'Oh yes.' Fred sounded hesitant, unused to his title.

'Do me a favour will you? Get your brother off my back.'

'He writes about you?'

'Not about me, no. He writes about some Hollywood producer, some schmuck. He blames me for the Vietnam War. It's entirely my fault, it seems, that there are now bombing targets in the North. Did I give the orders?'

'It's a bit thick.' Mrs Wickstead inserted a potato crisp between her small white teeth. She looked surprisingly young and defenceless, Fred thought, still snuggled into her coat as though likely to be on the move shortly. 'Poor Benny's not even American.' And when Fred looked surprised, she explained quietly, almost as though she didn't want Mr Bugloss to overhear, 'You know he was born in Brixton.'

'Not Brixton. Mrs Wickstead has been misinformed. Whitechapel. You know the area?'

'Not intimately,' Fred had to admit.

'It has changed, it was once a deeply caring community. My father owned property there, of course.'

'But you speak fluent American!'

'Have to, dear boy, in our business. However else am I going to get close to the Vice-President in Charge of Product at Galaxy International?'

The party ebbed and flowed. Music was playing and the doctors started to dance as amorous nurses dragged them to their feet. Henry told his brother that sometimes he couldn't understand Agnes.

'Sometimes?'

'She's picked out the most tedious of your fellow medics and won't speak to anyone else.'

'Aren't you used to her doing that?'

'I suppose so. Why is it?'

'Don't you know her? She chooses the worst bar, the most horrible meal, the most tedious man in the party. Then she knows she won't be disappointed. Do you think you can manage it?'

'Manage what?'

'Living up to her expectations.'

In a corner, Dr Salter had started to sing, an ancient and obscene ballad remembered from his distant past as a medical student. Someone put on a Charlie Parker record and Fred was called to do his act of accompaniment. He sat at his drums in a corner of the room and joined the rhythm section behind the Great Birds soaring alto saxophone. He saw that Agnes was dancing and that her father and Henry had discovered one of the few bottles of whisky left under the table.

'You do that rather well.' Fred looked round. Mrs Wickstead was sitting beside him, judging his performance.

'Yes.' Well, he'd practised long enough.

'I've never tried a doctor.' This was what he thought she said but she spoke very quietly. He reduced his playing to the swish of wire-brushes and a diminished thud. Mrs Wickstead seemed to be telling him about the people she *had* tried.

'Film people, producers and all that, you're something they want to have sitting next to them to impress the Executive Vice President. You're meant to smile and say, "Great idea, Jack," and that's all you're meant to say. Of course you get trips. But it's having to smile all the time, the muscles of your face begin to ache.'

'You think I could treat that, medically?'

'Ring me some time, if you want to. I'm not in the directory.'

Then Mr Bugloss called from across the room. Fred stopped drumming and tried to hear the whispered figures.

'Two four six, eight oh two six. Did you get that?'

'No.' He couldn't be sure. But all she said was, 'It seems we're going now,' and wandered away, leaving Fred lonely at the drums.

> 'Drain the Worthington out of my kidneys
> Get the whisky fumes out of my brain,
> Get the night nurses out of my bed boys
> And start up the motor again . . .'

So sang Dr Salter as Fred took him down the stairs to his car. He made his senior partner move over and announced that he was going to drive him back to Hartscombe.

'Why?'

'Because you are pissed out of your mind.'

'So early in your career, Doctor,' the patient murmured obediently. 'And you have come to a completely accurate diagnosis.'

As he drove home, the numbers were arranging and rearranging their series in Fred's mind: eight oh two, two four two six. No. Two four oh, eight six two? Or was it two oh six? The more he thought about it the more endless the possible combinations became. But the next morning he began to dial hopefully.

'Eight oh six two,' said the voice on the telephone. 'Excelsior Meat Importers.' After six or seven calls like that he decided to file his conversation with Mrs Wickstead away in his archive of missed opportunities.

So the partnership began and Fred, whose own life was in some disarray, became clothed with the magic of his profession and, calling on his patients with his black bag, made them feel alarmed or instantly better and turn to him for guidance although most of them were wiser and a great deal more experienced than he was. Giving coherent advice, trying to fathom the complexities of other people's lives, saved him the trouble of understanding his own or laying down any particular treatment for himself. When he started he was excited by being a doctor. On the whole, his customers liked him, and although he had by no means discovered how to live, he became, in time, able to reconcile those he treated and their families to death.

The partnership prospered and in time took on another young doctor, Geoffrey Hardison, who was extremely serious and satisfyingly shocked by everything that Dr Salter had to say on the subject of bedrest, check-ups, diets and smoking.

While Fred lived unnoticed by the world in Hartscombe and Simeon spent more time in the garden and less dictating manifestos to Glenys Bigwell, Henry took on the task of public pronouncement. He signed letters to *The Times*, he sat on the platforms, he read poems and went to rallies, protesting about the Greek Colonels and the continued war in Vietnam, mourning the blacks killed in Detroit riots and the death of Che Guevara. Simeon, listening to his portable wireless while Dorothy weeded, frequently heard his elder son sounding off on *Any Questions* and wondered why people who once took the advice of statesmen and priests now seemed so anxious to be guided by writers of fiction.

Henry, Agnes and their child, Francesca, moved to a flat just off the King's Road, an area where Arthur Nubble had opened a boutique called Sam and Samantha, which did well for a time. Henry was often to be found having lunch in nearby Italian restaurants, meeting-places for models and agents and film directors, where he would sit among the gleaming white lavatory tiles, the low-slung lights and tall dark wooden chairs, wearing a white polo-neck sweater, drinking Verdicchio and holding forth on the injustices of the world.

Charlie was taking a new course in Social Administration at the London School of Economics, an institution made the more exciting for her by the large number of strikes, sit-ins and student protests. In the evenings, when Leslie was dining with clients in the Caprice or the Mirabelle, his wife would meet student activists, for whom she bought many drinks, and would sit on the edge of the group, listening and saying little. On some nights she would go out with young men whose hard cases formed part of her practical training. She found herself in big, noisy pubs, round King's Cross or in the East End. She went drinking in Soho clubs which were open all the afternoon, and, on certain occasions, she

was made love to in the students' rooms or in the backs of borrowed
cars.

At such times she believed herself to be happy in a world far
away from Rapstone and the small, neat London house, forever
humming with the carefully controlled chatter of property devel-
opers, which was Leslie's home in London. When she came in, her
husband didn't ask her where she'd been, nor was he interested in
her explanations about late seminars or committee meetings. He
went to sleep quickly, tired out by his business dealings. He didn't
seem to care that their worlds had divided and, to her great relief,
never expected her to join him and Christopher Kempenflatt in
their working dinners in Mayfair.

In time Mrs Mallard-Greene became discontented in Tom
Nowt's old cottage. Her children were away at boarding school
and Malley left at six o'clock each morning for his job in the B.B.C.
She never quite knew what he was doing there although she
suspected that he was taking his secretary out to long lunches
where they gloated over the sweet trolley together and then what?
He always came home exhausted and never hungry, and obliged
her by going to sleep in front of the telly at half past nine. Left in
the country Mrs Mallard-Greene attacked the earth over the buried
deer bones, bought a lot of plants from the Hartscombe Garden
Centre but finally surrendered to the weeds. She made the acquaintance of a few similarly abandoned wives and had coffee and
nips of brandy with them in the mornings, quarrelled with them
and had difficulty keeping a cleaning lady. In the afternoon she
often sat watching the rain on the hedgerows, the mounting willow
herb and the blossoming cow parsley. She felt a tightness in her
chest and sent for Dr Simcox.

'What's the trouble?'

'Look out there, that's the trouble! It's so green and quiet and
it's always bloody raining.'

'That's England, Mrs Mallard-Greene. I'm afraid there's no
known cure for it.'

In the last months of her pregnancy, Glenys and Terry Fawcett
were at last moved into a two-roomed flat at the top of a Worsfield
tower block. Glenys thought they could make it quite cosy once
they got the curtains up, and they would be able to put the pram

out on the narrow walk-way overhanging the precipice on which they were perched. Far below was a small patch of green where dogs were not allowed and, on a section specially railed off, their child might be allowed to play. As Glenys outlined her plans for the future, Terry assembled his clarinet and began to play 'Ain't Misbehavin' ', even before he had laid the carpet.

About six months after he qualified Fred stopped for a beer in a pub on Picton Ridge and made a final attempt at dialling Mrs Wickstead's number. Up, like a row of cherries on a fruit machine, came her voice apparently not in the least surprised. If he ever came to London she would certainly have lunch with him, dinner wasn't so simple, nor was it sensible to ring her in the evenings, she was usually out. Fred named his next day off and a restaurant in Jermyn Street that Henry had often talked to him about.

He arrived almost twenty minutes early for their first lunch together and Mrs Wickstead was exactly a quarter of an hour late. He was in a state of near despair when he finally saw a waiter, a man who had been studiously avoiding his eye, escort her proudly over to him. He had bought a new shirt and tie, and taken what had seemed an immense sum out of the bank and realized in a panic that fifteen pounds was only just going to cover their lunch.

When she was sitting beside him, Fred forgot about the money; he staked everything on Mediterranean prawns, grilled sole and a bottle of Chablis. Mrs Wickstead ate exactly what he had ordered and she listened to him talking about his patients, and the extraordinary views of Dr Salter, wide-eyed and enthralled. When it was over she said, 'You know, you shouldn't have spent out on all those Mediterranean prawns. Quite honestly, I'd rather have had the money.' She was smiling and he was sure it was a joke. 'The trouble with lunch is thinking where to go afterwards.'

'Where do you live exactly?' He had put his hand on hers as they sat side by side on the plush bench, under the red satin walls and shaded electric candles which imparted a pink glow to Mrs Wickstead. 'Couldn't we go there?'

'Oh I don't think you'd like that. I don't think you'd find that at all suitable.' Then she was laughing at his look of disappointment. 'I do have a girlfriend though, with a sort of a flat. It's in

Notting Hill Gate. For God's sake, next time, don't spend so much on lunch. We could bring sandwiches.'

'Are we going to have a next time?' Fred continued to hold on to Mrs Wickstead, conscious that his hand was hotter and probably damper than it should be for the accomplished luncher-out and boulevardier.

'Oh, I think so, don't you?'

'I was wondering.'

'What?'

'About Mr Wickstead.'

Only then did she remove her hand. 'Mr Wickstead ,' she said, 'is entirely my business!'

Fred took the train back to Hartscombe, feeling that fate, which hadn't been very generous to him since he parted from Agnes, had handed him a huge slice of luck on a plate. He began to 'see' or 'go out' (which really means staying in) with Mrs Wickstead. Three weeks later they met in a small Italian restaurant in Notting Hill Gate, lunched hurriedly and walked to the flat for which she had a key. Making love to Mrs Wickstead was a far simpler, even more innocent experience than Fred had expected. She was laughing as they undressed, then enthusiastic, and finally sleepy. As she closed her eyes, Fred who had become domesticated during his bachelor life, put on one of the two towelling dressing gowns that hung on the bathroom door and made tea. He wondered a little about Mrs Wickstead's girlfriend who seemed to have left few traces of her personality on her home. He could see no pictures or books, no photographs, and only half a bottle of milk and a bottle of champagne in the fridge. He wondered if the fitted cupboards in the bedroom were full of her clothes but before he had a chance to investigate, Mrs Wickstead opened her eyes, sat up and put out her hand for a cup of tea.

'This girlfriend of yours seem extremely tidy.'

'She works. She's frightfully well organized.'

Mrs Wickstead, sitting up naked in bed, put down her tea and stretched her arms towards him. Fred asked no more questions about the girlfriend.

Sometimes he didn't see his new-found friend for weeks, even months at a time. After their long partings she would turn up suntanned and murmuring about Nassau or Gstaad or the Greek Islands, but she never showed him snaps or recounted her adventures on these holidays, apparently preferring to hear him talk. Sometimes, when he had tried to telephone her for weeks without reply, she would call the surgery and leave a message. On his next day off he would wait for her in a big, gloomy pub by Notting Hill Gate tube station and she would arrive smiling, always in a rush to get there a quarter of an hour late. They had given up restaurants now, bought rolls, pâté and cheese in a delicatessen, together with bottles of champagne, which Mrs Wickstead insisted on paying for. When they got to the flat they would make love at once, she apparently as eager as he was after weeks of separation. Then they had a high tea, always washing up and leaving the flat as tidy as they found it. She had, of course, he discovered, other names but he always thought of her as Mrs Wickstead, because that was how she had been introduced to him, and because his use of her Christian name, Virginia, didn't make him feel that he knew any more about her.

So on and off, punctuated by long intervals and enthusiastic revivals, secret, simple and satisfying, Fred's friendship with Mrs Wickstead continued. The surgery receptionist got used to leaving notes with her name on them and Dr Salter asked no questions. One Christmas in the flat they opened their presents to each other. Her gifts to him had been lavish: cufflinks, a shirt from Harrods, a pair of shoes which fitted, because he never bought shoes for himself, and LPs, old recordings of Louis Armstrong and the Hot Five with the original crackle.

'There you go. Have you got everything you want?'

'Except for one thing.'

'What's that?' It was the most anxious he had ever seen her look.

'I'd like to show you where I live. I mean I want you to see Rapstone and all my country.'

'Well.' She looked relieved, as though she had been expecting an impossible claim. 'I don't see why not.'

'Mrs Shelley's in the clear.' The lab tests had arrived and were on Dr Salter's desk in the surgery. Fred had come in to his senior partner's room to learn the secret constituents of his patients' blood, and was considerably relieved about a young mother in a sudden panic about the cause of her exhaustion.

'That's very good.' Dr Salter was slitting open an envelope. He glanced at the report it contained and, as his partner was searching for the names of his other patients, slid it under the blotter on his desk.

'This weekend...' Dr Salter began, but Fred, who had been waiting for a chance to mention it, interrupted him. 'Oh, I was going to ask you about this weekend.'

'Were you?'

'I've got... Well, a friend of mine's coming down from London.'

It was a weekend when Fred would normally be on duty, and the only one when Mrs Wickstead could make an expedition to the English countryside.

'I think, I rather think I shall have to go hunting.' Dr Salter lit a cheroot and blew out smoke. Fred felt a great wave of disappointment, like a child who had been suddenly deprived of a long-promised treat.

'Oh, well. In that case...'

'Yes. I feel the time has come for a brisk ride to hounds. Don't worry though, old cock. Young Hardison can look after the shop.'

After Fred had gone, Dr Salter took the report out from under his blotter. He read it again carefully, although he knew quite well that there had been no mistake. Then he tore it into strips and set fire to them in his ashtray.

The hunt met at Rapstone Manor on a Saturday morning when the trees were till black lines across a grey sky and spring was a faint hope for the future. Nicholas came out to chat, Dr Salter took a stirrup cup from Wyebrow, and Grace shivered as she viewed the proceedings from her bedroom window. Fred, standing on Hartscombe station, telling himself not to expect too much, was amazed when a train arrived, a door opened and the single passenger not going on to Worsfield was Mrs Wickstead. She stepped out, looking puzzled, as though she had arrived in a strange country and didn't expect to hear English spoken.

'I'm glad you came.'

'I do think it was quite brave of me.'

He put his arm round her, trying to keep her as warm as possible on their way to the car park.

The hunt was moving off down the lanes and across the fields away from Rapstone as Fred drove up to the ridge and showed Mrs Wickstead the view down the valley. He felt he was letting her into his childhood. 'It hasn't changed,' he told her. 'Not really very much, ever since I can remember it. Some of the cottages have been converted, of course. And the summers don't seem so hot now. That's Skurfield over there. We think of it as full of rather glum, short people who keep chickens in clapped-out Austin Sevens. You know the sort of thing?'

'Not really.'

'What do you think of it?'

'Cold.'

The hunt was fanning out now, across a stretch of open country. Dr Salter was up with the leaders riding the big hunter he had first seen at Worsfield Show on the day that Leslie Titmuss announced his engagement. He was smiling, taking jumps easily, as though enjoying the best day out in his life.

Fred had no intention of taking Mrs Wickstead to visit his parents at the Rectory. He wanted to spare her Simeon's Olympian curiosity and Dorothy's amused unconcern. However he risked a visit to the church. 'It's Norman basically,' he told her. 'Of course it's been added to a lot. There's some Victorian bits.' He opened the door of the vestry, breathing in the familiar smell of mice and hassocks. 'When I was a child, I used to sit in here with my father. Cutting up bread for Communion. What's so funny?'

'Englishmen.'

'Why?'

'Once they start going to bed with you, they always want to take you into churches.'

The hunt had walked round a square of ploughed field and was now moving again, the hounds following a straight line towards a copse on a hillside, the riders spreading out, the leaders galloping with mud flying, others struggling to keep up. By a hedge the protesters shouted, blew whistles and waved their banners, angered by the bright coats, the beauty of the horses and the concentrated and elaborate pursuit of death. Fred and Mrs Wickstead lay

· together, warm at last, in his bedroom above the butcher's shop in the Worsfield Road. Later they planned to eat the food he had bought and drink a celebration bottle of champagne.

Those in the lead at the hunt remembered Dr Salter moving away from them. He left the line and galloped diagonally across a stretch of pasture, pounding the thin grass so that black earth was thrown up by his horse's hooves. He was riding at a high, an impossibly high hedge with a gate leading to a road. But he swerved from the gate and went straight for the huge hedge, faster and faster for a jump which his horse took bravely, hopelessly, into a tangle of dark wood, and below the dim light of the sky.

'Don't answer it, please!' Mrs Wickstead said when the telephone rang, but Fred got out of bed and stood naked in his living-room while Hardison told him the news. And then he was dressed and walking down a rubber-smelling corridor in the Worsfield General with a white-coated houseman. The walk seemed endless, but at last they swung open a pair of doors and were in a room where Dr Salter lay flat on his back with his eyes open.

'Sorry,' he muttered when Fred looked down at him. 'I seem to have made the most almighty cock-up!'

Some months later Simeon called on Dr Salter, whom he found in a room above the surgery, somehow diminished in size, and seated in a wheel-chair in which, from then on, he would spend his waking hours. Simeon entered the room with an expression of serious concern and was a little taken aback to be greeted by a burst of laughter, nothing like the sound made by the old Dr Salter, but all the same, the patient seemed to be enjoying a joke.

'You can laugh?'

'About all I can do. I'm still alive but unfortunately not kicking. He's got quite a sense of humour, your old practical joker.'

'Mine?' Simeon declined to be identified with whatever power had prescribed the Doctor a broken back.

'The old gentleman you claim as such a close acquaintance. The one with the beard and the irritable expression. A great prankster, apparently. No doubt time hangs heavy on his hands, waiting for you to lecture Him on the joys of the Welfare State every Sunday from Rapstone pulpit. Probably longs to get hold of a bit of fire and brimstone and smite a few backsliders for idolatry.'

Simeon waited for the Doctor's speech, which he clearly relished and had, possibly, rehearsed, to be over. It took a little longer.

'When you're next on your knees tell Him it was very funny but hardly worth His while. I mean, hasn't He got enough on His hands with wars and earthquakes and famines without spotting one ageing G.P. on the hunting-field, a fellow out with the sole purpose of getting his neck broken, and turning him into a useless sort of lump that can't even *walk* to hounds?'

Silence fell between the two men, and then Dr Salter thought to ask, 'I say. Do you think the Almighty's a member of it?'

'Of what?'

'The League Against Cruel Sports?'

'Of course not. Why should He be?'

'Well, according to you, He's a paid-up member of the Labour Party.'

Simeon smiled patiently, and asked the Doctor a question. 'Did you say you went out with the sole purpose of getting your neck broken?'

'Of course. I always told you they did you a decent death on the hunting-field.' But then the joke was over and he said seriously, 'Tom Nowt did it far more efficiently.'

'What did Tom Nowt do?'

'We get these little verdicts you know.' Dr Salter gave what he seemed to feel was the obvious explanation. 'Decisions. Lab tests. Quite simple. They either condemn you to death or let you off provided you promise to be of good behaviour and not get ill. Tom Nowt and I were found guilty of the serious crime of carcinoma for which there can only be one penalty. He mitigated the sentence with a shot-gun; on the hunting-field I simply added a few minor disabilities to the final judgement.'

'Tom Nowt shot himself?'

'I was never a shooting man.'

'You told the Coroner that Nowt's death was an accident.'

'Didn't want any rubbish talked about unsound mind. Box of cheroots on that table by the gramophone, mind passing them? Might as well assault the lungs as well as everything else.'

Simeon stood up and moved across the room. He felt guilty, a tall, walking man in his sixties, looking down at the helpless Doctor who had been forced to surrender to illness, his life-long enemy.

'Would you like me to come and sit with you? I've plenty of time now.'

'No.' Dr Salter selected a cheroot from the box Simeon held for him. 'I don't think I should like that at all.'

So Fred took over the running of the Hartscombe practice, with the help of young Hardison and occasional advice from the wheel-chair in the room upstairs. When Agnes called to see her father, Dr Salter said he didn't want visits to the sick, then he told her to go back to London and look after her child. It was as though he were ashamed of his condition and didn't want his daughter exposed to such an obscenity. Mrs Beasley cooked for him and did the housekeeping, otherwise Dr Salter was looked after by the District Nurse. Smoking, drinking brandy, listening to his records and disliking the District Nurse were now his occupations.

Part Four

'Who breaks his birth's invidious bar,
And grasps the skirts of happy chance,
And breasts the blows of circumstance,
And grapples with his evil star;'

from *In Memoriam*
Alfred, Lord Tennyson

★ 19 ★
Leslie's Long Weekend

Leslie Titmuss came down for breakfast at Rapstone Manor and almost fell headlong over Bridget Bigwell, who was frantically polishing the brass stair-rods.

'Oh, do mind yourself, Leslie!' Then she remembered that he was a guest. 'I'm sorry, Mr Titmuss. Once a week we have to get all our stair-rods up.'

'You were always thorough, Bridget, I always heard that, when you were at Picton House.'

'Twelve bedroom fireplaces to be done when the visitors were down for their breakfast and coal scuttles to be polished so you could see your face in them.'

'My mother told me a lot about when you were in service with Doughty Strove.'

'Mr Doughty! He was more or less a young lad then.'

'Well, yes. Exactly.'

And Leslie was off to join his host and hostess at breakfast. Nicholas was hidden behind *The Times* and Grace was opening envelopes, reading the scrawled handwriting of friends she had 'come out' with, bringing her news of death, disease and divorce. Leslie, having helped himself to a full plate of eggs, sausages and bacon, was determined to chat.

'Mother-in-law . . .'

'Do try not to call me that.' Grace didn't look up from her correspondence.

'What would you like me to call you?'

'Call me Grace. Call me Lady Fanner. For heaven's sake call me Mother Teresa if you want to.'

'But not mother-in-law?' Leslie was anxious to get it right.

'It's the sort of expression that might be used by Mr Harold Wilson.'

There was a pause while Grace opened more letters and Leslie got stuck into his breakfast. Then he said, apparently seriously, 'If I say anything like that again, Grace, anything that irritates you in any way, I'd be very glad if you'd let me know.'

'Don't you worry.'

'We're sorry Charlie couldn't come with you.' Nicholas peered round the edge of his newspaper.

'Charlie's studying.' Grace knew.

'Yes. They're keeping her pretty busy at the L.S.E.' Leslie was now at work on the toast and marmalade. 'So I thought someone should come down to give the parents all the latest news from the big city.'

'To give your parents?'

'Well, no. I meant the Fanner family. You, Grace and Nicholas, of course.'

'In my day a young wife wouldn't think of studying.' Grace harked back to an earlier deception. 'She'd think of babies. And real ones, this time, *if* you please.'

'Well, not yet, Grace, not until the business really gets established. Magnus Strove and I are hoping to pull off the big one. The Tasker Street development.'

'What on earth's Tasker Street?'

'It's a row of little shops at the moment, not far from Liverpool Street station. We're hoping to develop it.'

'You make it sound like a photograph.' Grace went back to her post.

'Offices for people to sit in while they plan to build more offices.' Nicholas was not convinced. Nor, when Leslie suggested it, did he want to come in with them. He remembered Magnus Strove as a small boy: 'Every time I saw him he seemed to be able to make me part with ten bob! Some story about collecting for disabled seamen, or poor children in the East End. He could be very convincing.'

'Well, he's managed to persuade the bank. It's our first, our only, real gamble. If we can pull this one off we can have everything, babies, anything you like.'

'I didn't say I liked them exactly.' Grace was gathering up her letters, resigning from the task of keeping her son-in-law entertained until Monday morning. 'I suppose you can amuse yourself this weekend?'

'I was wondering, Nicholas,' Leslie asked as though for the realization of a childhood dream, 'if there would be any chance of having a look round the farmyard this morning?'

'My dear boy, of course. We'll go now. Finish up your coffee.' The world was surprisingly short of people who actually asked to see Nicholas's pigs.

'How absolutely super!'

It was in the farmyard, picking his way through the cowshed in a pair of borrowed wellies and admiring the new milking-machine, that Leslie delicately approached a subject which lay considerably nearer to his heart than a conducted tour of the home farm. He didn't, of course, come at it head on, but in a circuitous fashion, by way of the lack of support the politicians of the day were giving to the Great British Breakfast. Speaking for himself, Leslie didn't remember Doughty Strove asking a single question in the House about bacon.

'You may be right. More of an oil-seed rape man is Doughty.'

'Of course the old fellow's done yeoman service for the Hartscombe constituency.'

'I seem to remember some suggestions you made about the purple past of Doughty Strove.' Nicholas saw no reason why one of his contemporaries should be called 'old'.

'Rumours! I was only reporting on some rather damaging tittle-tattle. Personally I don't believe there was a word of truth in it. I'm sure we all want to see Doughty reap his just reward.'

'Glad to hear you say so.' They had arrived at the sties and Nicholas was mollified, not only by Leslie's retraction, but by the sight of the well-fattened animals with small intelligent eyes snorting with contentment. Those with red crosses on their rumps were destined for an early visit to the abattoir. 'But what sort of reward are you talking about exactly?'

'His elevation.'

'The elevation of Doughty.' Nicholas laughed, having a sudden

229

vision of his stout neighbour levitating mysteriously, and in a bad temper.

'To another place,' Leslie explained patiently. 'The Upper House. Well, they're bound to offer Doughty the Lords, aren't they? He's been the member here for so many years, off and on.'

'You mean they'd give Doughty a peerage?' Nicholas raised his eyes reluctantly from his pigs. 'I never heard any talk of that.'

'But it's possible, isn't it?' Leslie was pushing gently. 'Quite likely in fact.'

'I suppose' – Nicholas felt it would be disloyal to dismiss the suggestion out of hand – 'it is reasonably likely.'

'Well, we'll have to start looking round, won't we?'

'Looking round? Whatever for?'

'A new Conservative candidate. For the Hartscombe and Worsfield South constituency.'

Grace didn't have to entertain Leslie much that weekend. Magnus Strove had invited him to dinner at Picton House, partly to discuss Tasker Street and partly to persuade his father to try and make some money out of his gloomy and underpopulated house and the large park that surrounded it. For instance, a pop festival in the grounds might be profitable and Hartscombe Enterprises would undertake the organization. 'Popular music?' Doughty had a momentarily comforting vision of a band playing selections from Gilbert and Sullivan, but he knew that was not what the young men had in mind. 'Look at it this way,' Leslie suggested. 'At the moment Picton represents locked-up capital with a minus income factor. Let it pay its way occasionally.'

'I wouldn't have to have lions, would I?'

'No, Father. Not lions. Just a lot of frightfully nice people wearing beads.'

'Of course.' Leslie refused port, keeping a clear head for this delicate stage of the conversation. 'Picton'll become even more famous after you've gone up.'

'Gone up where?' For an appalled moment Doughty thought that young Leslie was planning his death.

'Oh, haven't you heard anything?'

'Anything about what?'

'It's just that Nicholas was saying this morning that it's more than likely, in fact it's pretty well certain. Of course they don't tell people, do they?'

'What don't they tell people?' Pale old Doughty had an edge of panic in his voice.

'It's all meant to be a tremendous secret, I suppose that's why Nicholas won't talk to you about it. Well, I promise you I won't say a word.'

'Won't say a word about what? For heaven's sake, Titmuss. I've absolutely no idea what you're talking about.'

'Such a pity it's only life peerages with the Socialists in power. Still, I suppose he'll be the Honourable Magnus.'

'Honourable Magnus?' Doughty savoured the future which he understood at last. 'I've always wanted the House of Lords. I think it would be right for the family.'

'No one deserves it more, according to my father-in-law.'

'Vague sort of chap in many ways, but Nicholas is pretty near the heart of the Conservative Party.'

'I'd rather you didn't mention it to him. It was told me in confidence and one simply doesn't gossip about these things.'

'What would the style be, I wonder?' Doughty sounded dreamy. 'Lord Strove of Picton Principal? Lord Picton?'

'Not Lord Skurfield, Daddy.' Magnus laughed at the inelegant title and Leslie paused, like a snooker champion planning a long pot into a distant pocket. Then he played the shot. 'Of course, you'd have to give up the idea of fighting Hartscombe in the next election.'

'Give up the parliamentary candidacy?'

'They'd want you to make that clear before any final decision. I mean if you get in they wouldn't want to move you to the Lords, couldn't risk a by-election.'

'I see.' Doughty thought that he did.

'It'll be a bit of a relief to you, won't it?' Leslie was understanding. 'To be out of the dust of the arena? Leave the hard slog to a younger man, won't that be a relief?' Doughty Strove seemed to think that perhaps it would.

★

On Sunday morning, Leslie went to church. In the evening he sat by the fire in Rapstone Manor watching Grace playing patience while Nicholas read dutifully through the proceedings of the Begonia Society.

'So Charlie's studying to love the poor?'

'Something like that, yes. You could put up your Red Queen.' Grace's refusal to wear glasses when they had visitors, even such visitors as Leslie Titmuss, made her miss many tricks in her solitary card games. 'I suppose she's got to love someone. She can't love me.'

'And the Black Jack.' Leslie moved it for her.

'I don't think it's at all necessary to love a person, just because they happen to be your mother or your daughter. There's no need for anyone to feel guilty about such things.'

'The Ace can go up.'

'I may not be the most practical person in the world, but I *can* manage my own patience.'

'I'm sorry, moth ... I mean, I'm frightfully sorry, Grace.'

'And don't feel sorry about things! There's far too much of that about, if you want my opinion. Anyway, stop watching me like a hawk. I fully intend to cheat a little.'

So Leslie moved away obediently and told Nicholas that old Doughty Strove seemed to be slowing down a bit. 'He complained to me that he gets tired very easily. Politics are beginning to take it out of the old chap.'

'Lifting a heavy brandy glass in the Members Bar must be absolutely exhausting!' Grace dug into the pack and extricated the Red Seven she had been hoping for.

'In fact he's extremely doubtful whether he's going to stand at the next election,' Leslie was able to tell them. 'No sort of final decision on that as yet of course.'

Although he left early on Monday morning, Leslie didn't go directly back to London. He spent the day doing some business with local estate agents and had a drink at lunchtime with the editor of the Hartscombe *Advertiser*. George had just got home from the Brewery when Leslie called at 'The Spruces'. The table was set with lettuce and tinned salmon, slices of bread and butter, cake and biscuits. 'There's more than enough for three,' Elsie said, and started to lay another place.

'Thank you, Mother, but I'm having dinner in London. Magnus and I are meeting a couple of fellows from the bank.'

'Feed up, boy.' George was thumping the bottom of the salad cream bottle, which then emitted a hefty white dollop. 'You've got a journey to go.'

'He'll be having his later, Father, in the form of dinner.'

'And I can't go out with the fellows from the bank and not be hungry. It wouldn't be polite.'

'So it's more polite to come here and not be hungry, is it? I mean it's all right not to be hungry in your own home.' George took a large mouthful and chewed steadily, as though it were now his duty to eat for his son as well.

Then Leslie told them that he might, he might just possibly be offered something rather important. Elsie guessed that it was a position, but he said he couldn't tell them any more about it because it wouldn't be fair to 'someone who isn't in the very best of health'. However, he wanted them to know that he'd always be proud of them, proud of having been brought up in Skurfield and proud of having been taught not to be above going out to cut nettles to earn a bob or two when it was needed. After this speech Elsie sat looking at her son in silent admiration, and George, pushing away his emptied plate, said, 'Very tasty dear. That was very tasty.' At which moment there was an unexpected chime at the door and Leslie hurried to admit a Mr Narroway, a photographer from the *Advertiser*, who had, it seemed, called to take a family group of the Titmusses. At last a somewhat bemused George was persuaded to stand on the left of his son in front of the fireplace, while Elsie was on Leslie's right. Prominent in the background was the statuette of the bather from Cleethorpes which, as a boy, Leslie had once rashly given to the Rector. 'Will all this be something to do with your new position?' his mother asked, and Leslie murmured, 'Let's hope so,' as Mr Narroway caught them all three, startled and wide-eyed in the flash.

Although Elsie searched the *Advertiser* with excitement during the next months the photograph was delayed until the Tasker Street development was securely launched and Leslie started to acquire the fortune which would allow him to devote his life to the work to which he had apparently become dedicated. '*Politics*: the thankless task of bossing around a lot of people who don't want to be bossed and don't care who's trying to do it. The work is extremely dull and its only reward is a temporary illusion of power' (Dr Salter's definition). Such was the mysterious 'position' which he had hinted at, and which his mother had hoped to be something moderately high up in a bank.

On the day the demolition gangs moved into Tasker Street, Elsie was rewarded by the sight of her family, her own front room and the bather from Cleethorpes featured in the *Advertiser*. 'City Developer at Home in Skurfield', was the headline, and the readers were told that it was Mr Leslie Titmuss, a partner in Hartscombe Enterprises, now involved in an important development scheme in the City of London, pictured at home with his parents. 'Mr Titmuss Senior has just completed forty years' service in the accounts department at Simcox's Brewery.'

Elsie posted a copy of the paper to her son but he was more interested in the scarcely prominent paragraph in the *Daily Telegraph* which appeared later. He read it aloud over breakfast, while his wife was standing, gulping coffee and chewing toast, on her way to what was to be a rare working-day at the London School of Economics: 'Doughty Strove, the former Conservative Member for Hartscombe and Worsfield South, has announced that he will not be contesting the seat at the next election. "I hope I shall be able to be of service to my country," Mr Strove said, "in another capacity." Hartscombe is a Labour marginal where Ben Leverett, M.P., had a majority at the last election of only thirty-nine.'

'Is that the big news in the paper?' Charlie asked on her way out. 'Of course,' Leslie told her. 'It's the big news for me.'

★ 20 ★

The Lost Leader

'Henry Simcox. May I ask you what you're writing now?'

'Something we started on a few years ago, but couldn't get off the ground. You know about movies? They die and get resurrected time and again before they appear in public. This is an idea I had about characters who come from all over the world to go on this – well, this pilgrimage.'

'But it's not religious?'

'No. I promise you. I'm more interested in live sinners than dead saints.'

'Are you a contemplater?'

'Am I what?'

'Have you got a god-sized hole in you? I mean one takes the point about Christianity, but the religions of the East . . .'

'Eastern complacency's even more repulsive than English complacency. I've got no time for blokes who sit in Kathmandu contemplating their navels and putting up with poverty and starvation, and the worst class system outside Bournemouth. I'd like to see all those gurus get off their backsides and start demonstrating . . .'

'Camera reloading,' a voice called from the shadows stopping him in mid-flow. The interview was being filmed in his flat. He sat in a pool of white light and chatted until the camera was ready to receive the image of Henry Simcox once more.

'You know we've got a cottage in your neck of the woods.' The interviewer was Mr Mallard-Greene of the BBC Arts Programme. 'My wife absolutely adores it.'

'That was terrific stuff! Going very well,' the director called from the darkness. 'Pick it up from "get off their backsides and start demonstrating".'

'Bit of a dry mouth,' Henry discovered.

'Lonnie! You've got Mr Simcox's coffee?'

'Yes. Yes of course.' An enthusiastic girl appeared in the pool of light carrying a mug of Instant. Although not especially pretty she was remarkable for her soft voice and expression of deep concern. 'I can easily heat it up again if that's what you'd like.'

'It's fine thank you. I only wanted a swig.'

'When you're finished I'm going to pluck up courage and ask you to sign one of your books for me.'

'Of course.'

'Please. Don't forget.'

They were ready for another take and Henry gave his mug back to the girl, who retreated with it reverently, as though she had just been handed the Holy Grail.

'So you are in favour of demonstrating?'

'Certainly. What are we supposed to do about Vietnam? Well, at least we still have the right to shout!'

As though taking her cue from this, the four-year-old Francesca, who had just fallen over in the bedroom, let out a series of piercing shrieks. 'All right, cut.' The director sounded weary. 'Lonnie, see if you can do something about that child.' So Agnes, comforting her daughter, was surprised by a plumpish girl whose eyes seemed to be rather too close together and who looked at her with a kind of tolerant despair. 'Please. Could you try and keep the child quiet. After all we *are* shooting.'

Agnes went to Grosvenor Square because she believed in the protest and thought that Henry believed in it too. Although there were many women there with toddlers, and even babies, she left her child at home with a babysitter, thinking that Francesca was not yet able to make decisions in matters of world politics. She and Henry were together at first, marching in the detachment from Oxford Street. In front of them she could see the helmets of policemen trying to stop the column but the helmets retreated. Agnes was marching solemnly, like a new recruit, still anxious to do her best. Henry walked excited beside her. He was shouting and seemed to be protesting for everyone he could think of: Czech students, as well as children in Asian villages, American blacks and even the inhabitants of Rapstone who found themselves short of cottages. His anger came out in great whoops of delight and he smiled frequently at the marchers around them. Although he was a well-known writer he seemed to pass unrecognized and, like his wife, he was merely a private in this army. Round them the placards waved like banners and there was a great deal of shouting of 'Hey, hey, L.B.J., how many kids have you killed today?' It was when Henry joined in this cry that Agnes noticed that he did so with an American accent.

It was far removed from the gentle walk across the English countryside which Fred had escaped from to meet Agnes when the threat of war had seemed less important than love in a churchyard. The reality of fighting on the other side of the world, the burning villages and the laid-out bodies of dead children, received the tribute of a pale, imitation war in the West End of London. When Agnes got into the square she saw that the garden in the centre was already occupied and a column was wheeling round to advance on the front of the American Embassy. She saw people running, throwing stones, clods of earth from the garden, and over the crowd she saw the mounted police and the heads of the horses. Smoke bombs and fire crackers went off in front of her and she began to run with the rest of the demonstrators.

Even as she ran, Agnes thought of the absurdity of the situation. What would a stone thrown, a policeman's helmet knocked off in Grosvenor Square, do to stop mass killing on the other side of the world? The shouting, the waving placards, seemed as ridiculous as the solemn cavalry, brought out as if to fight some ancient battle, forgotten in the history books. Yet as she realized the day's pointlessness, she became excited. She began to get nearer the horses, she wanted to see the charge. It was then that she looked round and saw that Henry was no longer with her.

It wasn't until she was on the pavement opposite the Embassy that she saw him again. She was standing against some railings looking towards South Audley Street, as a crowd of reinforcements tried to force a police barrier. She saw a large, silver-coloured motor car parked, and beside it stood Henry talking to, of all people in the world, Mr Bugloss. Had Benjamin K. suddenly become a peace demonstrator, was he about to risk his valuable connection with Jack Polefax and Galaxy International for the sake of one glorious shout in front of the Embassy? Agnes tried to wave at him and to call out words of encouragement. Then she saw both men get into the car and Henry was driven away from the battlefield. Agnes left the railings as the police horses began to trot in the face of the crowd. She stood still, amazed by the sudden beauty of the sight.

'Judging me! You're always sitting there judging me!'

Agnes didn't say anything. She was giving Francesca her tea, egg and toast soldiers, after she had arrived home from the engagement in Grosvenor Square. 'I suppose' – Henry was walking up and down the room in increasing anger – 'you think I haven't lived up to your extraordinary standards.'

'Just one more bite, Francesca.' Agnes offered a yellow-dipped soldier.

'One more bite! To end the Vietnam War.'

'You were the one who was keen on the demonstration.'

'Look! Ben Bugloss heard about my interview on television. He's just on the point of doing a deal for *Pilgrims* with Galaxy. Naturally he didn't want his writer arrested for storming the American Embassy!'

'Very reasonable, I'd say.' Agnes was eating the soldiers for Francesca.

'Well, I was there, wasn't I?'

'Oh, yes. You were there, Henry. You stood up and were counted.'

'Why do you have to say it like that?'

'Say it like what?'

'Looking down from a great height! Passing judgement.' He turned away from her and opened the stripped pine cupboard where the bottles were kept. 'I'm having a drink. Do you want a drink?'

'No, thanks. I've just had Francesca's tea.'

'My little brother Fred ran out on a demonstration.' Henry returned to the attack. 'He sneaked off to see you, as I remember.

238

You snogged in a churchyard. You didn't blame little Fred for that!'

'No. That wasn't what I blamed him for.'

'So it's just *me*, is it? You only want to condemn *me*! That's what really makes you feel good.' He was into one of his speeches now, Agnes knew, spreading the ointment of words on the pain he felt. 'That's what gives you your great, warm, comforting assurance of feminine superiority. "I married Henry Simcox, but he turned out to have feet of clay. Just like everybody else. Did you hear how he ran out of the Battle of Grosvenor Square? Of course, I stayed on. So I wouldn't be ashamed when Francesca asked me, 'What did you do in the Great Demo, Mummy?'"'

'That's quite funny.'

'Well, not for me, it isn't! For me it's like going to bed with an amateur Joan of Arc.'

'I'm sorry.'

'Where's the whisky?' Henry returned to the cupboard.

'I'm sorry it's like that for you.' Agnes was serious.

'Somebody's drunk all the bloody whisky!' He held up the empty bottle as though it were part of the conspiracy against him.

'I think you gave it to that film crew. You were being very generous.'

'All right. I'm going to the pub.' He moved away from her. 'I'll be back later, for a night of penance. Why don't you start ironing the hair-shirt?'

Henry went to a number of pubs that evening. He rang Lonnie, whose telephone number he had secured when he signed his book for her, from the Cross Keys. He bought a bottle of whisky and took it round to her bedsit near the World's End and there they went to bed together for the first time. It was an act which Lonnie took as a compliment and Henry felt no sort of judgement was being passed on him. She was particularly understanding when he told her he had to get home and helped find one of his socks under her bed. 'Of course,' she said. 'Of course, you must get back.'

'To all that disapproval.'

'I don't know what Agnes wants.' Lonnie gave him a puzzled smile. 'She must have everything anyone could wish for, you and Francesca.'

'Even the child looks as though it's condemning me for something. I think she teaches it.' Henry was sitting on the edge of the narrow bed, putting on his sock. 'Agnes thinks I should do more demonstrating.'

'That's silly. Your work's your demonstration, isn't it?'

'I suppose it is.' He stood up and kissed her, it was so much what he wanted to hear. 'I'm glad you were in when I called.'

'Oh, don't worry. I'll always be in.'

That was the great thing to be said for Lonnie, she always was.

★ 21 ★

The Candidate

One evening that summer, Leslie Titmuss, neat in his dark blue suit, sat with Doughty Strove in the study at Picton House, discussing some business of mutual interest to Hartscombe Enterprises and the Strove estate. Lifting his eyes from the drink his host had poured him, Leslie saw a girl with pale hair loom out of the dusk and, waving her arms and legs rhythmically, appear to swim past the window. From where he sat he couldn't be sure if she were dressed in some light-fitting garment or if the colours in whirls and scrolls, flower and heart shapes, were painted on her body. He looked down into his glass and when he looked up again she was gone. Outside the still uncurtained windows, from the lakeside and the park, there was a sound like a distant storm and the flashing of lights. The other guests had gone out to join in the festivities and the two men, young and old, sat huddled together in the study as though for safety, discussing business. Doughty rose and drew the curtains, feeling that what they couldn't see wouldn't harm them.

'Magnus tells me I'm going to make money out of this.'

'I'm sure he's right.'

'Is he? I wish to God it were all over.'

So did Terry Fawcett. He stood under the trees with Glenys, far away by the side of the lake, where the group of the moment pranced and strutted like marionettes on the small, lit stage. The music came to them doubled and redoubled, crackling and echoing from amplifiers in the trees. Terry looked at the crowd, strangers from London, perhaps some from Worsfield. Like the music they were alien to him, and seemed to come from another age.

If the crowd in Grosvenor Square had been a pale imitation of an army at war, the mass of young people at the Picton House Pop Festival seemed to parody the idea of peace. The badges they wore like campaign medals not only said 'Make Love Not War' but 'If It Moves, Fondle It', 'Down with Pants' and 'Position Wanted'. The boys' hair was not yet shoulder-length – many of them looked like chunky young van drivers, storemen or roadworkers wearing cowbells, beads and an occasional flower behind the ear. The girls had long, straight hair and short dresses. They sat or lay in the grass, speechless beneath the blare of the music. Most of them stared or frowned at more ornate figures, wealthier students in embroidered Nehru jackets, who strutted among them like officers walking aloof through a dispirited encampment. The strong smell of pot which came to Terry on the summer breeze produced isolated giggles but little laughter. Now and again, a girl stood up to dance and some, closer to the lake, threw off their shirts or peeled off their jeans and attracted little attention. Now and again fights broke out under the trees.

'It's not music,' Terry told his wife. 'Not in any understood sense of the term.'

'You mean it's not the Riverside Stompers.'

'We shouldn't have put your mother to the trouble of babysitting, not to have our eardrums blasted off.'

'Terry!' He looked round and at first didn't recognize Charlie. She had added to the short, cotton, Indian-patterned dress she had worn at dinner with Doughty Strove, and had put on more beads, bells and a button which said 'I'm a Hippie'. A flower was painted on her forehead, her legs and feet were bare, and she looked lonely and pleased to see him. 'Look, Terry,' she said, in an accent which she had carefully flattened and sent down-market since her husband had begun to imitate the clenched-teeth delivery of Magnus Strove. 'Bloody awful about Tom's old cottage. And ours.' She apologized. 'I did try, really.'

'We're quite comfortable, thank you.' Glenys sounded brisk. 'The Council fixed us up with one of the new flats in Worsfield. There wasn't no need for all them drinks you took Terry for, round the Citizens' Advice.'

'It's a great evening.' Charlie looked towards the crowd. 'Don't you think it's great? Everyone's so relaxed.'

'Terry isn't relaxed, he's going to request, "Ain't Misbehavin'"'.
Come along, Terry, we might as well go and look at them dancing.'
As Glenys removed her husband, Charlie said, 'Enjoy!' and raised
her hand in a gesture of peace which looked dispirited. She stood
alone for some while before taking a deep breath and walking down
to the crowd by the lake, like a nervous bather steeling herself to
plunge into a cold and possibly dangerous sea.

Leslie looked at his watch and decided that it was time to take
his wife home. He left Doughty and set out for the terrace, where
he saw three hippies passing round a joint which hovered between
their fingers like a glow-worm. They were Magnus Strove, wearing
a long, silk, high-necked jacket and a headband with a feather in
it, Jennifer Battley with carnations and tinsel in her hair, and
Christopher Kempenflatt complete with an embroidered Afghan
waistcoat and ornate boots.

'Charlie's gone to the ball,' Magnus told him. 'She's already lost
both of her slippers.'

'At midnight she'll probably turn into a hash cookie,' Jennifer
thought.

'Or Mrs Leslie Titmuss.' Kempenflatt made it sound a grimmer
fate. 'Come and sit down, old boy. Join the party. Now we really
have got something to celebrate.' Buyers had been found for the
Tasker Street offices, and both the bank and Kempenflatt's family
construction firm had breathed huge sighs of relief. Leslie accepted
the invitation, and sat for a while on the terrace wall beside them.
When Jennifer held the rather sodden joint towards him he shook
his head.

'You're a puritan!' Kempenflatt took it instead.

'I suppose I am.'

'Not a bad thing having a puritan in charge of the accounts.'

'Not so much of a puritan, our Leslie,' Magnus told Jennifer.
'He's not above a bit of mini-skirt accounting.'

'What's that?'

'Shows off all the figures except the vital parts!' They laughed
loudly above the sound of distant music. Then Kempenflatt announced that, as their trickiest bit of business was settled, and now
Doughty was no longer in the contest, he was going to do what he
had always wanted and become the parliamentary candidate for

Hartscombe and Worsfield South. 'I can count on your support, Leslie,' he supposed, 'in the constituency Party?'

'I'm sorry.' Leslie spoke quietly out of the darkness. 'Can't be done.'

'Why?'

'I mean to be adopted for Hartscombe.'

'A *Titmuss*, representing Hartscombe?' Kempenflatt was incredulous.

'You find that more outlandish than a Kempenflatt?'

'Well, there is a slight difference, isn't there?' There was light from the windows in the house and Kempenflatt could be seen smiling.

'Oh, I agree.'

'It really comes down to a background, doesn't it?' Christopher Kempenflatt was at his most kindly. 'No one can say it's the least little bit your fault. No doubt it's due to circumstances entirely beyond your control. And I must say the way you've pulled yourself up by your boot-straps does you enormous credit.'

'Pulled himself up by what?' Jennifer was puzzled.

'His boot-straps, apparently,' Magnus told her.

'But able as you may be, Leslie, confoundedly able, as a matter of fact, where's your background, eh?' Kempenflatt demanded. 'Tell me that now.'

Leslie got off the wall then and moved into the light. 'No. I think I'll save that to tell the Selection Committee.' And then he started down to the lake to fetch his wife.

Charlie had been dancing around a young man with bare feet and no shirt. The flowers, leaves, lips and crosses painted on his chest and arms, scrawled across his cheeks and nose, looked like wounds. He had large hands with a cigarette between his stubby fingers, short hair crowned with a plaited hairband and he danced on flat feet with heavy, unsmiling concentration. For a long while he seemed not to notice her but then he changed direction, plodded towards Charlie in time to the music and they were dancing nearer to each other, she smiling and clapping, he stamping as he stared at her. Then Leslie grabbed his wife's arm and pulled her out of the crowd. She resisted only a little, but laughed at him. 'Look at you,' she said. 'Can't you relax ever? Just for once couldn't you climb out of that tired old business suit?'

'We're going home now. When we get to the car I'll have something to say to you and you'd better listen!'

'Something to say? That'll be a turn up for the book.'

When he got her into the car, he didn't speak immediately. He drove out of the Picton gates, through Skurfield and stopped on a quiet stretch of the road to Rapstone. Then the words poured out of him. 'I've put up with you,' he started. 'I've put up with you without complaint. That's because I promised someone I respect that I'd look after you, no matter how difficult it was. No matter how you resented it. Well, I've done it!'

She sat silent, whether or not she was listening to him. He had twisted himself towards her and she thought how pale he looked in the reflected light of the dipped headlamps.

'I've put up with you taking courses in social services, where you learn nothing because you're always on strike. I've put up with your "caring" activities which are designed to make you feel good and help no one else at all. I've accepted the fact that you find any gormless slob in a t-shirt morally superior to me in my tired old business suit, as you call it. You owe me for all that, Charlotte. And now I'm calling in the debt.'

'I don't know what you mean.' She was listening to him now.

'I'm sorry. I should have remembered, the subject of money is something far beneath you, isn't it?' He moved closer to her; she could smell his breath faintly tinged with Doughty Strove's whisky. 'Let me put it in terms even you can understand. I can win the Hartscombe seat. That's not the problem. The problem is, I've got to be selected and nowadays they look at wives. God knows why but they do. And if they took one look at you at the moment I'd be out on my ear. Scrubbed! Ruled out! Not chosen! Understand what I mean? Do you?' He grabbed her wrist, pulling her up sharply when she tried to lean back and away from him. 'So listen to me, Charlotte. Scrub that bloody chrysanthemum off your forehead. Get yourself a dress you can't see through. Get your hair done at Chez Giorgio in Hartscombe. Get yourself a hat. And stop fawning on all those drug-headed, overpaid, screaming teenagers who think you're a joke anyway. Just till I'm elected you'll bloody well practise your caring skills on your husband. You get behind me, you see – what do they teach you to say – in a supportive situation?'

He let her go. She looked down at the red mark on her wrist and gave a small smile. She remembered then why she had liked him in the first place. He was rough trade.

Nicholas was in the garden, seated on a low stool and cutting dead heads off the begonias, when Christopher Kempenflatt, uninvited, approached him across the lawn. 'I'm down here with my people for the weekend. I thought I might drop in for a word.'

'What word is that?' Although what he was doing wasn't in the least interesting, Nicholas didn't like being interrupted.

'Of course you'll be chairing the Selection Committee for the new candidate, when the time comes. There *is* something. I couldn't really say it on the day, as it were, more of a word of warning in your shell-like, about Titmuss.'

'About my son-in-law? You don't think he'd make a suitable member?'

'So far as I can see he's hard-working, clever and extremely ambitious.'

'Not the sort of fellow we're used to in the Conservative Party?' Nicholas smiled faintly in the direction of the flowerbed.

'Not that. Actually, the word of warning is about his wife, your daughter.'

'About Charlie?'

'I don't suppose you know this, but she's been getting into some rather unusual company.' Nicholas didn't react so Kempenflatt tried to explain tactfully. 'You know what comes of helping lame dogs over stiles ...'

'Can't say I do, Kempenflatt. It just doesn't seem to have arisen. I mean, I've never seen a lame dog that *wanted* to get over a stile.'

'No doubt she gets friendly with that sort of person from the best of motives.' If there had been a joke, Kempenflatt ignored it. 'But you can get a little too close to them, if you know what I mean. People are bound to talk. Not the sort of talk that's particularly healthy, when it's about a candidate's lady.'

There was a silence then, and Nicholas looked to the begonias for help. 'Such a lot of them to water. Hideous plants, aren't they? And they get uncommonly thirsty.'

'Just thought it was worth mentioning.'

'And they have a tremendous appetite for bone meal. Your people will be expecting you, won't they? Do get Wyebrow to show you out.' Nicholas was suddenly very angry so he spoke with unusual gentleness.

The Selection Committee was due to meet in November. In October, Dorothy, arranging flowers in Rapstone Church, saw Leslie kneeling in solitary and silent prayer, a proceeding which Simeon of course permitted, but never did much to encourage. She knew enough of the local gossip to be quite sure what he was praying for. It must be the first time, she thought to herself, that God had been asked to select the Conservative candidate for Hartscombe and South Worsfield.

'I think they want to see you now.' Christopher Kempenflatt emerged from the Committee Meeting and called in on the little room where Leslie Titmuss was still waiting. His rival's pallor had that day, he noticed with some pleasure, taken on a positively greenish tinge. He thought he had done pretty well. He had assured the selectors that his wife, Honor, was behind him every inch of the way. He had gently reminded them of the Kempenflatt background and the Kempenflatt family money, ever a productive source of Party funds. He had assured them of his soundness on the question of the death penalty and his intention to live permanently in the constituency. There had been perhaps a slight coolness in the Chairman's manner but he put this down to Nicholas's determination not to show his preference too openly.

'Off you go then, Leslie. May the best man win.'

'Oh yes.' Leslie got slowly, almost reluctantly, to his feet. 'I think he probably will.'

Once faced with the Selectors, sitting on an upright chair in front of a long table, stared at by men and women, most of whom were as old as his parents, and none of whom were his age, Leslie embarked on his carefully prepared speech in answer to the inevitable question 'Why do you think you're particularly suitable to represent this constituency?' which Nicholas was deputed to ask him.

'Background!' he started. 'I expect you've been hearing something about background. Let me tell you mine. My father was a clerk all his life in the Brewery. My mother worked in the kitchen for Doughty Strove. What you call your "living-room", they call the "lounge". What you call "dinner", they call "tea". Perhaps you think they talk a different language from you?'

Leslie had begun by speaking very quietly, so that his hearers had to strain their ears and pay attention. He also looked ill and so gained some puzzled and embarrassed sympathy. As he got into his stride, his voice became louder and a hint of colour returned to his cheeks.

'I went to the village school,' he told them. 'Then I got a scholarship to Hartscombe Grammar. Weekends I used to go out on my bike and help people with their gardens. I grew up to understand the value of money because it took my father five years to save up for our first second-hand Ford Prefect. Every night he finishes his tea and says to my mother, "Very tasty, dear. That was very tasty." He always says the same thing. He falls asleep in front of the fire at exactly half past nine and at ten-thirty he wakes up with a start and says, "I'll lock up, dear. Time for Bedfordshire!" Always the same. Every night. Just as he got to work at exactly the same time every morning for forty years. He's loyal to his job and my mother was loyal to the Stroves. You know what my parents are? They're the true Conservatives! And I can tell you this. They're tired of being represented by people from the City or folks from up at the Manor. They want one of themselves! You can forget the county families and the city gents and the riverside commuters. They'll vote for you anyway. What you need to win is my people. The people who know the value of money because they've never had it. The people who say the same thing every night because it makes them feel safe. The people who've worked hard and don't want to see scroungers rewarded or laziness paying off. Put it this way, ladies and gentlemen. You need the voters I can bring you! They are the backbone of our country. They aren't Conservative because of privilege or money, but because of their simple faith in the way we've always managed things in England!'

A small man in a tweed suit and rimless glasses seemed disposed to clap but he restrained himself and there was a silence. Leslie sat back in his chair smiling. Some of the Committee smiled back. Lord Naboth seemed interested, and leant forward to speak. Leslie prepared himself to give his views on a balanced budget. Instead he heard, 'Mr Titmuss, we haven't had the pleasure of meeting your wife.'

'Really? She's your chairman's daughter.' Lord Naboth smiled and papered over what might have been seen as an appeal to nepotism.

'I mean, we haven't all had the opportunity of asking her how she feels about taking on the rather onerous constituency duties.'

The Association Secretary, who had been called out of the room during Leslie's speech, came back quietly and whispered a message to Nicholas.

'Well, Charlotte is a hundred per cent behind me, naturally.' Leslie was showing as much conviction as possible.

'It seems she's here,' Nicholas announced, as surprised as anyone. 'Charlie is here apparently.'

'Very well' – to Lord Naboth it appeared perfectly simple – 'why don't we have her in?'

Nicholas whispered to the Secretary who went out. The Committee Members doodled, coughed or whispered together. Nicholas stared up at the ceiling as Leslie looked anxiously at the door. He saw the Secretary usher in his wife, set a chair for her and leave. He saw Charlie, but a Charlie transformed. She had had her hair done in Hartscombe. She was wearing a tweed jacket and skirt, sensible shoes and a hat. Had she been out of doors, she gave the impression she would have been wearing a headscarf.

Nicholas nodded to Lord Naboth who asked the question, 'Mrs Titmuss, would you be prepared to appear on your husband's platforms and undertake social engagements, fêtes, coffee mornings and so on? We do depend a good deal on our coffee mornings.'

'Of course,' Charlie started to say, 'I'm a hundred per cent behind Leslie and . . .'

'Oh, I don't suppose Charlotte'll be able to do too much of that,' her husband interrupted her.

'Why ever not?' Lord Naboth frowned.

'Well, you see, we're doing what every other young couple with faith in Britain longs to do. We're starting a family.'

There was a murmur of approval. Leslie looked pleased, proud and relaxed. There were certain people in the world, he thought to himself, whose prayers deserved to be answered.

★ 22 ★

That Christmas

'I thought we might have a word about the case.' Henry had called on his mother at her house in Sunday Street, about a year after his father's death, and not long before the Probate Action about the validity of Simeon's will was to come to court. 'Our barrister wants the answers to certain questions. You see the other side, that is the toad Titmuss and his gang, will try and find some logical reason for father turning against his family. It's most important that we shouldn't give them the slightest encouragement.'

'What an extraordinary device!' It was just before Christmas again – Dorothy thought that Christmases seemed to come round far more often these days, and Henry had brought her a present wrapped in bright paper. 'I'll open it now,' Dorothy had said. 'I can't have it standing about here for days with me wondering if I'm going to like it.' To her surprise it seemed to be some sort of a machine. 'What can it be, a bomb?'

'It's a Teasmade, Mother. Lonnie thought of it. It'll wake you up and give you a cup of tea.'

'But I can give myself a cup of tea when I wake up.'

'This will wake you up at a certain time, Mother.'

'But nowadays I don't have to wake up at a certain time. What can Lonnie have been thinking of?'

'What I was trying to say' – Henry returned to the real object of his visit – 'is that we don't want to hand evidence to Titmuss on a plate. Obviously every family has misunderstandings, but there are certain incidents it would be better not to mention. Speaking of Christmas . . .'

'It's not yet you know, not for another week. Lonnie's got her dates mixed up.'

251

'There's really no need,' he told her firmly, 'to mention that Christmas when we all came to stay, Mr Bugloss and everybody.'

'Oh.' Dorothy appeared to be re-wrapping her Christmas present. 'You mean *that* Christmas.'

That Christmas, the Christmas of 1969, the year after Leslie Titmuss was selected as Hartscombe's Conservative candidate, was certainly the most disastrous that Fred ever spent at the Rectory. It was one of those occasions in which a malign fate seemed to take a special interest. It began for Fred, shortly before the festivities, on the day he visited old Mrs Fawcett in her cottage in Rapstone. 'I always took the work easy. Slow and steady, not like Bridget at the Manor. Bridget goes at her stair-rods like a hurricane, always has done. Yet it's me that gets the heart, isn't it?' Maggie Fawcett complained.

'We're going to move you somewhere where you'll be more comfortable.'

'The Worsfield General?'

'Well, yes.'

Maggie Fawcett lay, beached in bed, a huge and alarmed woman, who, ever since Fred could remember, had helped out at the Rectory. 'We'll get you a bit of treatment, and hope to have you back here.'

'Before Christmas?'

'Let's say, before the spring.'

'I don't like to leave the old cottage. My Tina's got her plans. She and her Gary. They've got their arrangements.'

Tina Fawcett was an overweight, broody and determined young woman. Fred found her and her boyfriend Gary Kitson, the younger brother of Den, the banjo and double bass of the Stompers, sitting at the table in the downstairs room drinking tea and smoking. Fred told them that he was going over to the pub to call an ambulance and they said they'd reckoned he'd be taking her away.

'Gary's going to do this old place up,' Tina told him, 'when we get married.'

'Well. That'll be something for your mother to look forward to, won't it? When she gets back from hospital.' It was not a thought that seemed to please either of them particularly, so Fred left to make his telephone call.

Ted Lawless was sticking holly up over the photographs of old aeroplanes in the Baptist's Head. As he stood at the pay phone on the wall, Fred looked at the cold and dripping churchyard and was surprised to see his brother and Mr Bugloss appear from the west door and walk briskly towards the lychgate. By the time he had finished his call they were in the bar.

'Quite typical!' Henry greeted him. 'While Ben and I are in church, you're sozzling in the pub.'

'I'm waiting for an ambulance.'

'Feeling seedy? Three pints, Ted. Simcox Best Bitter.'

'Your village church is going to make a great location for *Pilgrims*.' To the film producer, Fred thought, it seemed as though Rapstone Church had found its destiny at last.

'This is our country, Benny,' Henry told him. 'We were born here, among these hills. You need to get back to your roots occasionally.'

'I guess so. I never felt all that longing to get back to Whitechapel, I must say,' Mr Bugloss told Fred. 'Your father has been very gracious. We have a Midnight Mass scene in *Pilgrims*, so the Rector has generously invited us to stay over on Christmas Eve to get the feel of the occasion.'

'Invited us?' Fred looked at him doubtfully. 'You mean you and Henry?'

'I mean me and a friend of mine.' Mr Bugloss sounded modest. 'Hey. Didn't you once meet Mrs Wickstead?'

'I'm putting her in the parrot room, and Mr Bugloss in Henry's old room.' Dorothy was trying to work the sleeping arrangements out on the back of an old envelope while Fred and Simeon decorated the Christmas tree. 'There's nothing of any sort *between* them is there?'

'Oh I don't think so,' Fred told his mother. 'Mrs Wickstead's extremely respectable, she lives in Hampstead.'

'Hampstead, eh?' Simeon was threading coloured bells on to the branches. 'Do the sins of the flesh stop short at Hampstead?'

'I just don't want to dread going to the lavatory for fear of meeting them creeping about the corridor. However, she is called *Mrs* Wickstead, that sounds reassuring. Henry and Agnes can have the pink room. I'd put Mrs Wickstead there but she's not used to the boiler.' Dorothy consulted her envelope. 'Francesca can go in the pink room too, on the camp bed.'

'On the camp bed!' Simeon approved. 'She'll be excited about that.'

There were four bedrooms on the first floor of the Rectory, two on each side of the corridor. At the front, looking out on the cemetery, were Simeon and Dorothy's matrimonial bedroom and a room with wallpaper covered with parrots (known as the parrot room), in which Dorothy had planned that Mrs Wickstead should sleep. At the back there was a double bedroom with pink wallpaper (known as the pink room), in which Francesca's camp bed had been set up and in which Henry and Agnes were to have the large bed. Also at the back was a small room where Henry used to sleep. This was to be awarded to Mr Bugloss. Fred's old room, in which he was to stay over Christmas, was up a narrow staircase and once formed part of the servants' quarters. He had been put there as a child so that Simeon could be removed as far as possible from the sound of his drums.

These carefully worked-out arrangements were challenged, when the guests arrived on Christmas Eve, by Francesca who immediately announced that she wanted to sleep with the parrots, that she loved the parrots on the wall, and that anyway she always had the parrot room at her granny's house. Agnes was left upstairs trying to persuade her child of the many superior advantages of the pink room, while the other members of the party, except for Simeon who was writing his sermon, assembled in the sitting-room.

'Mrs Wickstead' – Dorothy came up to her smiling – 'may I hang up your coat?'

'Oh, please can't I keep it on?' Fred had been prepared for her coming, but not entirely for his suddenly urgent need of her as she stood clutching her coat about her, standing as near to the sullen fire as possible. It had been a bad year for their meetings. Mrs Wickstead had been away a lot, the practice had been extra busy and now the only present he wanted was to be with her in the anonymous flat in Notting Hill Gate. What he didn't want was to be tormented by the sight of her unattainable across a stretch of cold carpet, surrounded by Henry, his mother and Mr Bugloss.

'You find the Rectory a little fresh?' Dorothy looked at the gently shivering object of Fred's desire. 'Simeon used to say that the only talent you need for a career in the Church is an ability to survive draughts. You've never dined with the Bishop of Worsfield?'

'Can't say I have.'

'The water has been known to freeze in the fingerbowls. I've put you in the parrot room, it looks over the churchyard. I do hope you'll be comfortable.'

In the end, Francesca was reconciled to the pink room and was looking at a book and waiting to be settled down for the night, her stocking on the end of her bed and a glass of sherry and a mince pie ready in the fireplace, when the door swung slowly open, and, not to her surprise, for she had seen such manifestations before, Simeon entered on his knees, one arm swinging like a trunk in front and the other like a tail behind him, trumpeting like an elephant. She laughed politely, and when he came to sit on her camp bed, he told her she should go straight to sleep, and, when she woke, she might find that a miracle had taken place.

After dinner the party were to walk through the churchyard to Midnight Mass. Tina Fawcett was bringing her boyfriend Gary Kitson in to babysit, although Dorothy said that if she were a child and had to choose between waking up alone next door to a churchyard or having Tina Fawcett looming over her she knew which she'd choose.

They were all assembled in the hall, wrapped up against the cold night and the colder church, except for Simeon who had already gone over. Dorothy pulled open the front door. Fred saw Mrs Wickstead shiver and Mr Bugloss take her arm. Then Henry said, 'I'll catch you up.'

'Why?' Agnes wanted to know.

'Last chance of a pee before the sermon.' When Henry was left alone he went to the telephone on the hall table, dialled a number and said, 'Lonnie. Thank God you're there!' Although really it came as no surprise. 'What are you doing? Tell me everything you're doing!' She sounded breathless, as though she had been waiting for the call for a long time, and then when he told her, she asked incredulously, 'Not going to *church?*'

Halfway across the churchyard, Dorothy noticed that she had left her handbag containing her spectacles and money for the collection in the sitting-room. Agnes volunteered to go for it and turned, scrunching back along the gravel path. She opened the Rectory front door and saw her husband standing with the telephone to his ear.

'It's just that I probably won't get a chance to ring you on Christmas Day, my darling. Well, family. Yes. Can't get a moment to myself. I'll be thinking of you at midnight. Thank you for being there.'

'I'm always here,' Agnes said, as Henry put the phone down and saw her. He said nothing. She went into the sitting-room, got Dorothy's handbag and they walked in silence across to the church together. They prayed together and stood together to join in the final carol, 'O Come All Ye Faithful'.

At about half past twelve they got back from church. Gary and Tina were interrupted in the middle of a snog, paid and departed. Dorothy went into the kitchen and returned with a tea-trolley on which she had set out coffee and sandwiches. Fred opened the bottle of whisky he had brought with him. He poured drinks and they wished each other a happy Christmas. Agnes was silent. Mrs Wickstead took her whisky neat, and kept her coat on. The telephone rang and Agnes went to answer it.

'Who can it be at this time of night?' Dorothy asked, handing round sandwiches. 'It can't be good news.' Agnes came back from the hall to announce that Mr Bugloss was wanted. At the same time, Simeon came in in his belted cassock, having said Happy Christmas to the last of his congregation, and asked Mrs Wickstead if she'd enjoyed the service.

'I've been a lot more bored in movies.'

'I'll take that as a compliment.' The Rector accepted a whisky and soda from Fred.

'At Midnight Mass' – Henry was frowning – 'to celebrate the mysterious birth of Christ, do we really want a lecture about low-rent accommodation in the Rapstone Valley?'

'I thought Christmas was a story about low-rent accommodation,' Simeon smiled.

'Oh, Henry's very keen on mysteries nowadays.' Agnes bit into a sandwich. 'Mysterious trips, mysterious phone calls, he finds it terribly inconvenient to explain anything.'

Simeon sat beside Mrs Wickstead on the sofa. 'I suppose it might have saved an awful lot of trouble if it had never happened,' he suggested to her.

'If what had never happened?' Henry felt that he was being attacked from all sides.

'Christmas!' Simeon was still speaking confidentially to Mrs Wickstead. 'I mean, before that, absolutely no one had to feel sorry for slaves. You could watch gladiators being killed as part of an afternoon's entertainment. Wars were glorious and probably rather enjoyable. Nobody minded a bit about infant mortality or starving tribes in Asia Minor or the housing shortage south of the Tiber and all that sort of thing. If Christmas had never happened, it would have saved all those petitions, and appeals and letters to the Bishop and marches. Well, it would have saved a fortune in stamps, wouldn't it?'

Fred was put out to see that Mrs Wickstead listened to his father with the same flattering attention she gave him. In the silence that followed Simeon's views on Christmas, Mr Bugloss returned to them and announced that Jack Polefax had just flown in from the Coast and checked in to Claridges. He wanted a breakfast meeting on *Pilgrims*. Much as he regretted it, Benny would have to drive back to London, so that he could set out some figures to 'lay on Jack' in the morning.

'Surely your Mr Polecat can have breakfast on his own?' Dorothy was puzzled.

'I'm afraid he's not used to that. Anyway it's all to the good of Henry's project. Shall I drive you back, Mrs Wickstead?'

'Oh, but surely you'll stay?' Dorothy turned to Mrs Wickstead who had greeted Mr Bugloss's suggestion with a prodigious yawn.

'It's very kind of you. So sleepy.'

So Mr Bugloss wished them all a Happy Christmas and left. In a short while Simeon and Dorothy went up to bed and Mrs Wickstead, after a last drink, braved it up to the parrot room. Fred, who could feel that Agnes's stormy silence was about to explode in thunder, pushed the trolley helpfully out into the kitchen, where he gave himself a final drink. He shut the door carefully behind him, cutting himself off from the scene which then took place.

'It's that girl, isn't it?' As she said it, Agnes was sickeningly conscious of all the wives, at all times, who had started a quarrel with the same form of words.

'It's what girl?'

'I could tell when you poured the last of the whisky out for her. I could tell by the awful way she came oiling up to you and asked you to sign your book. "Oh, thanks ever so, Mr Simcox, I shall treasure that. Always."'

'She didn't say that!'

'She didn't say what?'

'"Thanks ever so". Lonnie doesn't say things like "thanks ever so".'

'"Lonnie",' Agnes said with deep contempt, 'that's who she is. "Lonnie!"'

The door opened to admit Mr Bugloss in his overcoat, carrying his case. 'I'm sorry about this. It's been a most moving occasion. A great experience . . .' And when no one answered him he ended with a heartfelt 'Happy Yuletide!' and left. There was a short, unhappy silence before Agnes burst out again.

'You know what Lonnie is? She's your easy option. You won't have anything difficult in your life now, will you? No demonstrations. No fights. No *me*! You can sit forever in a warm bath, soaping yourself with mysticism and little Lonnie's adoration, until you get old and pink and your skin begins to pucker. How comfortable for you. How horribly comfortable!'

Henry went to the door, opened it and stood looking at her. 'Bugloss has gone.'

'What on earth's that got to do with it?'

'I can sleep in my own bed.'

'How wonderful! Henry can go to sleep in his own little bed again. Henry Simcox who was going to change the world and ended up with Lonnie!'

He was gone and the door banged after him. She lit a cigarette and blew out smoke, then she heard Francesca crying.

Woken by the banging door, Francesca had discovered that she was not in her favourite parrot room and staggered out on to the landing to protest loudly. Mrs Wickstead, who had not undressed, came out of the bathroom to see a child seated at the top of the stairs with Agnes trying to comfort her. At the same time Fred was coming up from the kitchen.

'What's the tragedy? I know so little about children.'

'It's nothing really. Just that she wants to sleep in the room with parrots on the wall.'

'The one I'm in?'

'That's what I told her.'

'Then we'll swop. Not a problem. I've been far too cold to unpack.'

'It's incredibly kind of you.' Agnes looked up, genuinely grateful, and when Fred reached them, and asked if they were all going to spend the night on the stairs, the situation was explained to him. So Agnes and Francesca climbed together into the big bed in the parrot room and, to some extent, comforted each other. Mrs Wickstead went into the pink room and Fred retired up the stairs to the old servants' quarters. Henry lay on his back in his small bedroom, staring at the photograph in which he appeared as head boy at Knuckleberries.

When he tapped on Mrs Wickstead's door and pushed it open, after what he judged to be a discreet interval, Fred found her with the fur coat still fastened on like a life-jacket, sitting by a small and ineffectual electric heater, looking nervously at the white bed which stood like a glacier in the middle of the pink room. She looked up regretfully. 'I daren't go to bed with you.'

'Because of my parents?'

'Because it's freezing.'

He held her, warmed her. At last they dived between the sheets like crazy swimmers who break the ice on Christmas Day. They were stung by the first frosty moments into frenzied activity, zealous, enthusiastic and hungry after a long separation. Then, as their movements became slower, as they searched for, and finally found, a corner of warmth in the draughty house, Fred saw Mrs Wickstead looking over his shoulder, her eyes wide, her expression startled, as though she had just seen a ghost enter the room. He turned his head and saw, by the dim light of the pink-shaded bedside lamp, not a ghost but his father, the Reverend Simeon Simcox, Rector of Rapstone Fanner, white-bearded and fully tricked out as Father Christmas, advancing stealthily towards them with a stocking full of Francesca's presents.

Early on Christmas morning, Fred went into the kitchen to make tea before driving Mrs Wickstead to Worsfield Junction so she could catch one of the few trains back to London. He found Simeon seated at the table, warming his hands on a mug of coffee, all ready, in his cassock, for the day's business. It was the first chance they had had to speak since his father backed hastily out of the pink room. Fred thought it best to dive in at the deep end.

'Did you manage to deliver Francesca's stocking?'

'Oh yes. I guessed she must have got her way about the parrot room. It's the one she always wanted.' There was a silence, then he said, 'Mrs Wickstead seems to be a very pleasant person.'

'Yes.'

'Do you know *Mr* Wickstead at all?'

'Not at all. No.'

'Not know Mr Wickstead at all!'

Fred sat at the table with his father, who was carefully considering the matter. 'It's a case of acting up to your responsibilities,' he said at last. 'You throw a pebble into a still pond, and who knows where the ripples will end?'

'They will end up far away, generations later. When you and your little stone will be quite forgotten.' Fred supplied the words for him.

'You knew what I was going to say?'

'It's what you said to all those married couples.'

'I never told you.'

'We used to listen at the door.'

'You wanted to find out what we used to call "the facts of life"?' Simeon was almost laughing.

'We wanted to find out if you knew them,' Fred told him. 'I was just thinking about the beard and the Father Christmas uniform. Francesca would have been asleep. She'd never see it. Was it honestly worth it?'

'I don't see that it matters in the least whether she saw it or not.' Simeon finished his coffee and spoke with some pride, 'Even if she saw absolutely nothing, I have played my part.'

'Patients and nurses. That's how you can divide the world,' Dr Salter said when Fred called on him on the afternoon of Christmas Day. 'I was a nurse who got conscripted into the Patients' Brigade. Your father's definitely one of the patients. We always had to look after him.'

'We?'

'Your mother and I. Can't say I noticed you or your brother putting in much time at the bedside.'

'*You* looked after my father?' Fred was puzzled.

'I helped your mother, it was a bit too much for one nurse however devoted. What's that you've brought me?'

'I know you've got it.' Fred handed over the wrapped gramophone record, the *Enigma Variations*.

'I'm glad I've got it. I don't want to embark on new music.' He was in his wheel-chair, a small grey shadow of himself, exhausted by the effort of tearing at the wrapping paper.

'Yours had got a bit scratchy.'

'I rather enjoy playing the scratches.'

Then the door opened and Agnes joined them. Her father looked at her, unsmiling. 'You've come over from Rapstone?'

'Yes.'

'Alone?'

'Yes. Alone.'

Dr Salter looked from one to the other of his visitors, judging them.

'And you two are both nurses. That's true.'

'What about my husband?'

'Yes. What about Henry?'

'Oh, I'd say one of the world's natural patients, wouldn't you?' Then he smiled and asked Fred to put on his new, unscratched record.

'Are you going to throw me out again?' Agnes asked.

'Don't be ridiculous.'

261

That Christmas

Then she knelt beside him, putting her arms round her father, as the musical variations, whose basic theme is never stated, played and Fred stood watching.

And a Happy New Year
to You, Too

Grace had invited the in-laws, George, Elsie and Leslie Titmuss, to lunch that Christmas Day at the Manor. It was a small party – the cook had gone off to her family and Bridget managed the turkey and plum pudding. They sat now, with the food eaten and the crackers pulled, round the table. Grace, Elsie and Leslie were crowned with paper hats, Nicholas, Charlie and George were bareheaded. The talk didn't flow freely and, after George had told them that he planned to spend his retirement digging a small lily pond in the garden of 'The Spruces', silence fell. Then Grace asked what on earth there was to do on the afternoon of Christmas Day.

'The Queen,' George told her. 'We usually watch the Queen.'

But Grace was away, on a flood of reminiscence about Christmas afternoons in various country houses in the golden days pre-war. 'Of course we used to do all sorts of things. Charades. Treasure hunts. Or we'd roll up the rugs and have dancing. Private, private dancing from tea-time to breakfast. Come on!' She looked at their somnolent faces. 'Why don't we have a bit of fun, why don't we roll up the carpet in the sitting-room? I've still got my records.'

Only Leslie smiled politely. Charlie sighed and said, 'Oh, please, Mother. For heaven's sake!'

'What's wrong, Charlie? You're always the same, when you were a child you were a most terrific spoilsport!'

They moved into the sitting-room and Grace put Leslie to work on the carpet, while she opened a cupboard and took out her old pile of 78s. She found what she was looking for at last, and smiled round the room with delight, not noticing that Nicholas had slipped off unobtrusively to the conservatory.

'I've found Pinky's record! The one he gave me. "You're the Top!"'

'Pinky?' Leslie was on his knees, rolling up a long strip of Turkey carpet revealing the naked floor. 'That'll have to be polished again when you've done standing on it,' Bridget warned when she came in with the coffee tray. And Elsie, enthroned by the fireplace, said, 'First-class meal you put on, Bridget. You did really well.' 'Very tasty,' George added, from the edge of sleep.

'Pinky Pinkerton,' Grace explained. 'A simply enormous spade in full evening-dress, killingly funny! Sang at the old Café de Paris, before the bomb got it. Voice like black treacle poured out terribly slowly. Surely *you* remember Pinky, George?'

'Don't think we ever visited the old Café de Paris, did we, Mother?' George Titmuss was enjoying a joke.

'Leslie' – Grace handed him the record – 'we simply have to dance to this.'

'Please don't!' Charlie was on the edge of despair but Leslie told her that it was Christmas and surely if her mother wanted it . . .

'"You're the Top!", and Pinky put in some words for me.' Grace sang them in a surprisingly high, girlish voice:

> 'You're the top!
> You can trump the A–ace.
> You're the top!
> You're the Lady Gra–ace . . .'

'I remember dances too.' Elsie was still wearing her paper hat. 'When Mr Doughty was a young man there was always a dance at Picton House, New Year's Eve. Of course they've stopped all that since the war.' Grace wasn't listening, she was looking ecstatically at the strip of dance floor. 'Oh, well done, Leslie, awfully well done! All that shining parquet for us to glide about on, just like the old Café de Paris before the Jerries got it.'

'I'm not going to be able to stand this.' Charlie was convinced.

'Of course you will, Charlotte,' Elsie reassured her. 'Your mother's only having her bit of fun.'

And then the music started. The dark velvety voice of Pinky Pinkerton emerged above the scratch and hiss of the old record to pay its tribute and Charlie was faced with the awful spectacle of her husband dancing with her mother. She heard Grace carrying on a long, staccato monologue directed at Leslie's right ear. 'Nicholas was away at the beginning of the war. Where was it? Bognor? Some such nowhere. Doing something tremendously heroic in Army Intelligence. And I used to go up to London by train. In the black-out, to the Café de Paris! The bombs didn't worry me at all. Not at all. There was something so exciting about the sound of broken glass. And in the mornings, after the all-clear, the streets were so wonderfully quiet. Such times! Now it hardly seems worth the trouble of going up to London.'

It was then that Charlie clenched her fists, stood up and screamed, filling Rapstone Manor with a sound not heard since her marriage. Eventually she let her husband take her upstairs and she lay on her bed sobbing, while he read her the chapter of 'Biggles' with which Simeon used to calm her nerves before Leslie Titmuss came into her life.

In the dead days between Christmas and New Year's Eve events happened to Nicholas which he didn't entirely understand. He received a visit from Tina and Gary, who told him that they had been to see Maggie Fawcett in hospital, where she was likely to remain for some time. It seemed she was very worried about losing her cottage during her long absence, and it would take a great weight off the old girl's mind if the rent book could be put in Tina's name. Of course Nicholas agreed to this reasonable request, and sent them off to his estate office for the change to be made. Later he was able to tell Simeon that he had put his Midnight Mass sermon into practice and secured low-rent accommodation for the villagers of Rapstone.

During that week also Nicholas went on a shoot, and had a conversation with Doughty Strove, during which he wasn't sure that he quite followed the old boy's drift. They had stopped for lunch, which was laid out on trestle tables in the farmhouse at Mandragola. As they munched cold steak and kidney pie and drank cherry brandy, Doughty admitted that he was looking forward to New Year's Eve.

'Paper hats? Singing "Auld Lang Syne"? I've never cared for it personally. You having a party, Doughty?'

'Not *a* party. Service to *the* Party, you might say. I mean it should be published by then, shouldn't it? Our little secret.'

'*Ours?*'

'When it's announced, perhaps you'll join me for a dinner. In another place.'

'What other place?'

'Do I really have to spell it out for you, old fellow?' Doughty's voice sank to a confidential whisper and he looked round nervously in case the beaters should overhear. 'The House of Lords.'

'Oh, I'm not expecting anything like that,' Nicholas said modestly. 'Not for a local chairman of the Party. We don't get a leg up to the Lords. Besides, it's a terribly dangerous place, Bob Naboth was telling me.'

'Dangerous?'

'You can't get into your seat without tripping over fellows' crutches. Bob Naboth tells me that in the corridors you're likely as not to be run over by a peeress in her own right, driving a self-propelled invalid chair. The House of Lords! Believe me, it's a place to be avoided.'

'But it's not *you* that's going there, is it?'

'I suppose it's not.' Nicholas looked at Doughty and chewed thoughtfully. 'What are we talking about?'

'My dear old Nicholas.' Doughty Strove was laughing as he cut himself another slice of pie. 'You do play your cards remarkably close to your chest.'

Fred was also looking forward to New Year's Eve. The Riverside Stompers had been asked to provide the entertainment at the Badger which had become bigger and brassier under new management. They rehearsed their favourite standards in Marmaduke's garage and decided to give the inhabitants of Skurfield a whiff, as genuine as they could make it, of the brothers of New Orleans in the great days. 'What do we do if they request "White Christmas"?' Den asked.

'Ignore it!' said Joe Sneeping. The Christmas rush had made him sick to the teeth of paper streamers, Santa Claus wrapping-paper and 'Jingle Bells' or 'Once upon a Winter Time' which his employers wanted to emerge from a record-player in the off-licence to stimulate the sale of cut-price spirits. 'The only concession we make is "Auld Lang Syne" at midnight. Otherwise we stick to the stuff we've always wanted to play. Who knows? They may even like it.'

Both Joe Sneeping and Doughty Strove were due for a disappointment. Unable to contain himself any longer, Doughty rang the *Daily Telegraph* on the night before the Honours List was due to be published. He sat in his study and asked for the news desk. He told a reporter who had just come back from the pub that he was the ex-Conservative member for Hartscombe and, although apparently unimpressed, the young man was full enough of the spirit of goodwill to read out the list of peerages announced in the next day's paper. 'Is that all? You're sure that's all? No mention of Strove? That is s, t, r, o . . . No? Well, it's extremely decent of you to let me know. Yes. And a happy New Year to you too, of course.' When he had put down the receiver, Doughty sat for quite a long while, staring at nothing very much.

On New Year's Eve, Gary Kitson, Tina and a group of their friends called at the Mallard-Greenes' cottage and collected young Simon, who, though under age, was tall enough to be accepted in pubs and had enough money to pay for a good many rounds of drinks. Malley was up in London, doing a B.B.C. Arts *Review of the Year*, and his mother was prepared to let Simon go on the promise, which she knew wouldn't be kept, that he be home before midnight.

The big, gloomy Badger had been redecorated in the age of affluence, but not improved. It now had fake beams, plaster bas-reliefs of porridge-coloured horses and pictures of tearful clowns and pool-eyed children. The bar was full. There were still a few jazz fans, now growing middle-aged, and wearing duffelcoats, who had travelled to hear the Stompers, but most of the clientele were buying drinks, chattering or trying to dance to unfamiliar rhythms. Simon, free with his Christmas present money, was buying a good many rum and Cokes, snowballs or vodka and blacks. His party agreed that the music was depressing, got you down, made the place sound like a bleeding funeral parlour and needed livening up.

'Ssh!' Glenys had come to hear Terry play and wasn't going to have his evening spoiled by Gary and Tina, even though she sometimes felt her husband should move with the times.

'Council flat all right, is it, Glenys?' Tina challenged her.

'Course it is. We were lucky to get it,' Glenys whispered back against the din of the bar.

'My Gary wouldn't consider no council flat in Worsfield.'

'Well, your Gary may have to.'

'I don't reckon he will. He's going in for window-cleaning. Setting up his own business. If he wants something he gets it. Not like your Terry. My big brother don't think about nothing but tootling his little clarinet.'

Terry was tootling, apparently happily. Fred was behind the drums, contented with the music if not the venue. Joe Sneeping lowered his trumpet to sing a verse of 'St James Infirmary':

> 'When I die I want you to dress me in straight lace shoes,
> Box back coat and a stetson hat,
> Put a twenty dollar gold piece on my watch chain,
> So the boys'll know that I died standing pat.'

And then, young Simon Mallard-Greene shouted from the bar, 'Cheer up, sounds like you're going to a funeral!' Joe stopped singing and looked pained as the barracking came at them like rifle fire from Simon, Gary, Tina and their friends. 'Don't you know no groovy sounds?' 'Nothing we can dance to!' 'How about "Honky Tonk Woman"?' ' "A Boy Named Sue".' 'Listen, Grandad, we've got a request here. "Honky Tonk Woman".' 'He can't hear you, Simon!' 'Get your hearing aid in!' 'Wash your ears out!' And then an empty Coke tin came tumbling through the air and thudded against the front of the drum. The band was silent and Joe stooped to pick it up.

'Who chucked that?'

'My sodding little brother,' Den Kitson, with his banjo on his knee, called out. 'Isn't it past your bedtime, Gary?'

'We came here for a bit of entertainment,' Gary shouted. 'Not to hear you moaning away up there.'

'What are we going to do?' Joe asked the Stompers in a kind of desperation.

Fred looked at his watch. It was ten minutes to midnight but he had no doubt of the solution. 'Play "Auld Lang Syne". Bloody loudly!' They did, and, in an instant, the crowd in the Badger was linking arms, singing, kissing, hugging and making breakable resolutions. So the year 1969 slid into history, was forgotten or only occasionally brought to mind.

★ 24 ★

The Myth of Happiness

A few days before he died, Dr Salter, lying in his own bed, with a full-time nurse now in attendance, spoke to Fred, who sat by him whenever he could get away from the practice.

'Never jump your fences too soon. I jumped mine years too soon. Bloody silly thing to do. Look after her, won't you?'

'Agnes?'

'Your mother.' Dr Salter's voice was fading with his life. 'She may suffer from his sense of justice. Nothing more unfair, you know, than a sense of justice.' After a silence he said, 'What's happening in the world outside?'

'Nothing very much. There's a new Conservative Government. Leslie Titmuss won Hartscombe.'

'Leslie Titmuss? Sounds a good time to go. Look after her, won't you?' He put an almost weightless hand on Fred's arm. 'I should've liked to have stayed on till Friday. Mrs Beasley does fish pie on Friday.'

Fred, Henry and Agnes had Mrs Beasley's fish pie on Friday after the funeral. Henry wanted to know if it was really what Dr Salter wanted – Worsfield Crematorium, in all its ugliness, no music, no flowers, no prayers, nothing. Agnes asked, 'Why? Do you think your father feels done out of a funeral?' and Fred told him, 'Nothing. That's what he wanted.'

There was little left to arrange. Everything belonged to Agnes, but Fred was going to buy the house from her. He and the remaining partners would take out a mortgage, so that the practice could continue there. She wanted him to have the gramophone records and some of her father's pictures. Henry thought that final details should be left to the lawyers. So Dr Salter was divided up,

270

passed on and his ashes scattered. When Agnes and Henry had gone Fred went back to work. He could think of nothing else to do.

Later Henry felt excluded by his wife's grief as he had felt obscurely jealous of Francesca when she claimed so much of Agnes's attention. Some weeks had gone by when he said with a hint of impatience in his seriously sympathetic voice, 'It was bound to happen some time.'

'Some time. Yes.'

'He was an extraordinary man.'

'He told the truth.'

Henry, wrongly, took that as a reference to himself. He didn't answer it, however, but went to his desk and picked one off a pile of newspaper-cuttings. 'We've got away with it. My new book, remember? Bloody great piece in *The New York Review of Books*. Socking great caricature of the author.'

'I'm glad.'

'Do you want to read it?' He held the cutting out to her. She shook her head. 'I said I was very glad.'

Henry had changed since the retreat from Grosvenor Square. His new enthusiasms were for tweed suits, the Church of England, English watercolours and Victorian animal paintings. His latest book, *The Myth of Happiness*, was a collection of essays in praise of these articles and denouncing the modern fallacy that the human race is born with some sort of divine right to work, financial security and personal satisfaction. Its publication coincided with the defeat of Harold Wilson's Government, but Henry claimed no credit for this. Indeed he found Mr Heath's Conservatives just as crassly materialistic and blind to the virtues of human suffering as their Labour alternative. He restored the press-cutting to its pile. 'I'm glad that the new book's got away with it. Just as well. I don't think Benny's having much joy raising the money for *Pilgrims*.' He poured them both a drink; Agnes took hers without speaking. 'You're still thinking about your father?'

'His illness came between us like another woman. He was ashamed of it so he didn't want to see me. When I was young,' she remembered, 'when I was living with him over the surgery, I felt so safe. I could really enjoy anything awful.' She gave him a small, regretful smile. 'Nowadays I'm so grateful for anything a bit pleasant. It's pathetic!'

'For God's sake! I've tried to make you happy. I have.'

'I know.'

'I've given up ...' He claimed the credit. 'Given up having anything to do with anyone else.'

'I never thought I'd develop into a person someone had to give things up for.' She took a gulp of her drink and looked at him with regret.

Fred and Mrs Wickstead never talked much about the eruption of Father Christmas into the pink bedroom. When his father had withdrawn Fred had gone back to his own room, and when he drove her to the station she seemed to have forgotten the incident. Afterwards they continued to meet, only a little less often than before, and such meetings were rare oases of pleasure in the dry months of his practice. He talked to her about all sorts of things but never about Christmas. Strangely enough the absurd incident made him feel fonder of Simeon; the old man hadn't preached him a sermon, nor did he seem anxious that his son should feel ashamed. So Fred began to see more of his father and, on his afternoons off, they would go for walks together, exploring the countryside in a way which took the place of his rides with Dr Salter.

Maggie Fawcett came out of Worsfield General after a long spell and discovered that her daughter had become the tenant of her cottage. She spent most of her time upstairs in her room, avoiding the company of Tina and Gary. 'I can't sit down there, Doctor,' she said when Fred called to see her. 'Not with them fish goggling at me. "However much does it cost," I said, "to keep them awful little animals in tropical waters?" "Don't you worry your head," he says. "We can afford it." So they can afford the electric organ and all the other stuff they got. He's given up the building, you know, and gone into cleaning windows. Perhaps he *has* got a good business.'

'You say you signed something in hospital?'

'Letter they brought round from Sir Nicholas. Said it made sure the family kept the cottage. If I was away a long time, like. It meant *they* kept it.' The sound of Pink Floyd percolated up through the floorboards. 'It's the record-player too, all hours of the day and night. It was always so peaceful in the General.'

'I'll have a word with them.'

'Don't upset them, Dr Fred. My Tina can be ever so spiteful when she's upset.'

Downstairs, Fred found that Gary had come home for lunch and was sharing a cardboard box of chicken and chips with Tina. They were sitting on the plastic leather sofa, their feet on the mock leopardskin rug, backed by the knotty pine wallpaper. Round the room the huge telly, the record-player and the small electric organ gleamed metallically. In a large bubbling tank mournful but brightly coloured fish threaded their way through imitation mother-of-pearl obstacles such as underwater pagodas. 'Your mother's not been well.'

''Course not. Been in hospital, ain't she? Better now though.'

'I want you to keep her comfortable.'

'She's comfortable all right.' Gary was sure. 'In her bedroom all the time. Can't trouble herself to come down here and be a bit sociable.'

'I don't think she likes the fish.' Fred looked at the tank and decided he didn't like them either.

'What's she got against Gary's Oriental Hot Lips?'

'And she says the music keeps her awake.'

'Did you put her up to that? I could tell you had no love for music, Doctor' – Gary smiled at him over a grey and hairy chicken drumstick – 'that night down the Badger.'

On Christmas Day, after having been surprised at the telephone, Henry promised that he would never see Lonnie again. After the death of Agnes's father he seemed almost anxious that she should discover evidence of his broken undertaking. He left stubs of air tickets to Manchester on his desk on which Lonnie's name was still legible. He often put the phone down when Agnes came into the room, or got up early to collect the post, sometimes leaving an envelope with what she suspected was Lonnie's handwriting, postmarked SW10, crumpled in the kitchen tidy-bin. In a way, Agnes started to feel sorry for Lonnie. Other girls got trips to the South of France or Venice from their married lovers, poor old

Lonnie got a literary lunch in a room full of ladies in hats in Manchester. All that would be on offer, Agnes knew, would be grapefruit segments, chicken and frozen peas, and Henry making a speech about himself. And then Lonnie had to man her phone twenty-four hours a day. It was no doubt a tough assignment, being the other woman in Henry's life.

Jack Polefax of Galaxy International had, so Mr Bugloss explained, 'gone cold' on *Pilgrims*, so the movie was once more postponed. Henry was working on a new novel and taking part in a series of television documentaries called *Writers' England*, in which various authors could reveal the parts of the country which had most inspired them. For his number Henry was 'going back to his roots' in the Rapstone Valley. One day he said to Agnes, 'Look, I want you to be very sensible about this.'

'What've I got to be sensible about?' she asked nervously.

'Lonnie Hope'll be working on the project.'

'Lonnie Hope's been working on the project for some time, hasn't she?'

'I honestly don't know what you mean. She'll just be doing her job. You won't object to that, will you?' He was clearly not prepared to believe that any woman could be so unreasonable.

Agnes thought about it and finally said, 'No, I suppose I wouldn't object to that.'

'I'm glad' – Henry looked relieved – 'we understand each other.'

When Henry had first told her that he was making a film about his roots, Agnes said that it sounded like *Gardeners' Question Time* and he hadn't laughed. Lonnie at least took him seriously as he stood in front of the camera with the Rectory behind him and said things like: 'I could see the whole of village life from that window. The children brought for christening and the old people brought for burial. Perhaps that's why I was never entirely convinced by facile optimism and all the claptrap about the right to health and wealth in the pursuit of happiness. The only undisputed right anyone had was to six foot of earth under the cedar trees in *that* churchyard.'

One night he arrived back at the flat with Lonnie who was carrying a briefcase and a long-legged doll dressed as a clown. 'I brought Lonnie back for a drink,' Henry explained. 'She's just going to type out a bit of script for tomorrow.'

'I hope you don't mind me turning your front room into an office? We met the last time we filmed with Henry. I'm Lonnie Hope.'

'Yes. I know.'

'Campari and soda, Lonnie?' Henry was pouring drinks.

'Henry knows what I like.'

'Apparently.'

'And how's little Francesca?' Lonnie asked as she sipped her drink. 'I brought her a present.'

'Lonnie brought that marvellous clown for Francesca.'

'Really? How amusing. Perhaps I'll give it to her in the morning.'

'Oh, I say. I do like the way you've done your front room.' Lonnie walked round it admiringly. 'What gorgeous cushion covers! Are they antiques?'

'Henry's mother gave them to us. They come from the Rectory.'

'Oh, we're filming there. Henry's promised to introduce me to his father. The old Rector sounds an absolute sweetie! Your father was a doctor, wasn't he? Henry told me that your two fathers were always arguing – in the nicest possible way, of course.'

'I don't know if I'd describe my father as "nice".'

'Oh, I'm sure he was if you're anything to go by.'

'You think I'm nice, do you?' Agnes spoke in a voice of doom, apparently unnoticed by Lonnie. Henry thought they had better get on with typing the scene.

'Your husband's so marvellous on screen, you know,' Lonnie said, as she settled down to work. 'He does it so naturally.'

'Well, it's something he's used to, isn't it?' Agnes was leaving for the kitchen. 'Talking about himself.'

Shortly after that evening, Agnes looked for a flat in Fulham. When she had found one she left, taking Francesca and all their possessions except the clown doll. As she told Henry, she couldn't really enjoy anything awful any more.

★ 25 ★
The Party

After only two years on the back benches, Leslie Titmuss got a job in the Government and became a parliamentary private secretary at Advanced Technology. This news was welcomed particularly by Christopher Kempenflatt and Magnus Strove, who saw that Leslie would have to resign his directorship and leave them in control of the now extremely profitable Hartscombe Enterprises. 'Do you think we could bear life without Titmuss?' Magnus asked, and Kempenflatt thought that they might be very brave about it. When Leslie was approached he surprised them by saying that he wouldn't only resign his directorship, but sell all his shares. He expected to get a pretty good price for them.

'Don't worry, old man,' Kempenflatt said. 'We're prepared to buy you out at a substantial profit. More than you ever dreamed of getting your hot little hands on when you were working at the Brewery.'

'Of course it would have to be deferred.' Magnus took it for granted. 'Well, you wouldn't expect readies, would you?'

'Haven't you got a future interest you could raise a bit on, if you're short of cash, Magnus? I mean the Strove estate? By the way how *is* old Doughty?'

'Daddy doesn't get out much nowadays. Fred Simcox says it's depression. He's given him a handful of pills for it.'

'I'm terribly sorry to hear that.' Leslie looked concerned. 'You will give him my best wishes, won't you? After all he kept the seat warm for me, all those years.'

In fact Doughty Strove had fallen into strange habits. The staff at Picton House were dismayed to find him wandering, tieless and unshaven, about the upstairs corridors, muttering, 'Strove,

Doughty Picton Percival, Lord Strove of Skurfield in the County of . . . First Baron. Doughty Picton Percival Strove, first Baron of Skurfield in the Peerage of England . . .' So Doughty was in no condition to join the drinks party that Nicholas and Grace felt they should give to celebrate their son-in-law's promotion.

Grace said that, in the old days, they didn't have to wait for someone to become Secretary to the Water Works or whatever it was before they had an excuse for a party. However she climbed into a cocktail dress, took a few pieces of jewellery out of the bank and the hall at Rapstone Manor was filled with familiar faces and some unfamiliar ones, eager, youngish men with dark suits and businesslike expressions who were Leslie's new colleagues. Fred, who had called in after a day's work, found himself talking to someone who was quite unknown to him, a man who had smooth, dark hair like a seal, a suit, shirt, tie and breast-pocket handkerchief in various shades of blue, a heavy gold wristwatch and Gucci shoes. He spoke in a controlled and persuasive voice, as though he were forever selling some product.

'Never seen Leslie in the ancestral surroundings before.' The man was looking across at the Fanner family. 'Doesn't go with his image, really.'

'What's his image?' Fred wondered.

'My firm does P.R. for Hartscombe Enterprises,' the man explained. 'We've taken on Leslie's political profile as well. You know, gritty man of the people, all that sort of rubbish. Good thing there's no press about. He ought to be at the Young Business Man of the Year do at the new Worsfield Motorway Inn, not swigging champagne up at the Manor. Known Leslie a long time, have you?'

'Oh, since we were children.'

'I imagine he's changed a lot since then.'

'Oh no,' Fred told him. 'Hardly at all.'

On the other side of the party, Mrs Mallard-Greene had introduced herself to Simeon. 'Sorry we haven't got round to coming to church yet.' 'That's all right,' Simeon assured her. 'As a matter of fact, I hadn't noticed.'

'Of course, *we'd* like to go. But our *young* aren't in the least interested. Such a difficult time for young people, isn't it?'

'It usually is.'

'We always hoped our Simon would follow Malley into the B.B.C., but now it's come to the crunch they've got nothing to offer him. All the same, I've got to hand it to Simon. Rather than hang about round the house he's going into window-cleaning with Gary Kitson. I think they're doing rather well but it wasn't what we had in mind when we sent him to Bedales.'

Simeon smiled and wandered away from her then. He wanted to speak to Bridget whom he had seen taking out a tray of empty glasses. He followed her into the kitchen corridor and called after her, 'Bridget! It's been so long since we've seen anything of Glenys. I do miss her typing so.' She stopped with her back towards him. 'Is she well? And the baby, not a baby now, I suppose.'

Bridget turned slowly to face him and stared silently over her tray. 'I've got my fires to do,' she said.

'You're not working too hard, Bridget, I hope?'

'Fireplaces need blacking. You've got to get up early for that. I can't stand here gossiping.' She turned away from him, leaving him for a moment alone and staring after her. Then he went back to the party where he was immediately engaged in conversation by the 'Contessa', who wanted to know why Grace kept telling everyone that Leslie had joined the Water Board.

'Wonderful types you get in country houses, like a lot of antiques. That cleric talking to the old queen in the corner, for instance. Terrific face!'

'You think so?'

'Get a face like that to endorse a product and you could sell cannabis to nuns. Good old Church of England parson, is he? The Tory Party at prayer.'

'As a matter of fact,' Fred told him, 'my father's a Socialist.'

'Your father?' The man looked at him, apparently amazed. 'What did you say your name was?'

'I didn't. But it's Simcox, Fred Simcox.'

'Not *Doctor* Simcox.' Fred nodded and it was then that the man started to laugh. 'Good God, that perfectly wonderful story! So it was you who got the Christmas stocking. What a life you must lead, down at the Rectory. I say, we never got properly introduced. I'm Wickstead. Kenneth Wickstead. I believe you know my wife.'

Fred looked at him and could think of nothing whatever to say. Luckily there was a diversion – Leslie appeared on the staircase carrying the baby he had just insisted that Charlie should allow downstairs. 'Great bit of P.R.,' said Mr Wickstead and wandered off towards his client.

'My Lord, Lady Naboth, Sir Nicholas and Lady Fanner, ladies and gentlemen,' Leslie called out to them all. 'Will you please welcome a future prime minister, Nicholas George Titmuss!'

'Well!' Grace murmured. 'I must say we had to wait long enough for him.'

But Dorothy moved to the bottom of the stairs, put out her hand and touched the baby's head. 'He really *is* rather handsome, isn't he?' she said.

'He knew! Your husband knew all about Christmas. And everything.'

Fred had met Mrs Wickstead, not in their usual pub in Notting Hill Gate but in the bar of the Great Western Hotel at Paddington station. 'Yes.'

'But how did he know? That's the point.'

'I told him, of course.'

'You what?'

'We're very honest with each other. We don't have secrets.' Fred had come up from Hartscombe in the afternoon, deliberately missing lunchtime. Now it was six o'clock: the bar was full of businessmen with briefcases and large ladies with Harrods bags all having a stiffener before facing the long train journey back to the country. Mrs Wickstead looked into her vodka and tonic. 'You rather like secrets, don't you, Fred?'

'Some secrets. I mean, some things *are* private.'

'Priests have secrets, doctors and lawyers, all those sort of people. Well, Kenneth's just an ad-man. We find it works to tell each other the truth.'

'What about Mr Bugloss?'

'What?'

'What about Mr Benjamin K. Bugloss? Did you tell Kenneth about him too?'

'Of course, not that there was much to tell. Benny's so in love with the movie business that he hasn't got much energy for anything else. He really kept me on for the sake of appearances.'

'And does Mr Wickstead keep you on for the sake of appearances?'

'Not entirely. But he doesn't mind. Can't you get that into your thick head? He really doesn't mind at all.' She looked at Fred and smiled. 'That shocks you, doesn't it?'

'Yes.'

She finished her drink and spoke quietly. 'I've been stupid.'

'I didn't say that.'

'I should have pretended that it was all a great mystery and we were deceiving Mr Wickstead. You'd've liked that better, wouldn't you?'

Instead of answering her, he asked, 'The flat in Notting Hill Gate, was it for both of you?'

'I suppose so. From time to time.'

There were shouts and chuckles from the other end of the bar. One of the businessmen was telling his friends and the barman a joke.

'Did Mr Wickstead laugh a lot when you told him about Christmas?' What Fred couldn't put up with was the thought of them both laughing at his father.

'I knew he'd think it was funny. That's why I told him. Oh, come on, Fred. It *was* funny, wasn't it?' When he didn't answer, she said, 'I've blown it, haven't I?'

'It's probably my fault.'

'Why miss something enjoyable, just because Mr Wickstead knows about it?'

'I know it sounds unreasonable.' He took out his wallet and left a note on the table to pay for the drinks.

'But you've got a train to catch?'

'Yes.'

'And I'm not coming with you?'

'Not tonight.'

'Or any night. I'm sorry you had to find out about Mr Wickstead.'

Fred's anger soon died. It gave way to a dull ache and a long period of emptiness during which he only just resisted the temptation to telephone Mrs Wickstead. He thought about her perpetually at first, then less often, and finally only with a stab of regret when anyone mentioned Notting Hill Gate, or he saw a young woman immerse herself in a fur coat.

Leslie had less than two years in his government job before the miners went on strike. There were power cuts and fuel shortages and the great British public, reduced to working a three-day week, was expected to make an important decision. The young P.P.S. at Advanced Technology took his family down to Rapstone for the weekend so that he could put the Chairman of his local Party in the picture. 'Ted Heath's going to call an election.'

'Your Mr Heath's making a mistake,' Nicholas thought.

'Why? Do people really want the country run by the miners?'

'I don't think people want to be asked. They put Ted Heath there to get on and deal with things like miners' strikes. They want to get on with watching their telly boxes, and filling in their pools and . . .'

'Watering their begonias?' They were in the sitting-room after lunch, and Charlie spoke from behind the shelter of *New Society*.

'Well, exactly! They don't want Ted Heath asking them questions all the time. I think they may teach him a lesson.'

'I expect to double my majority in Hartscombe.' Leslie was confident. 'Meanwhile, it's up to all of us to save the country.'

'Are we having a war again?' Grace was cheered by this call to arms. 'I must confess I did rather enjoy the last one.'

'We've got to take the situation seriously,' Leslie told her. 'I mean, we've got bricks in all the toilet cisterns. Speaking for myself, I do clean my teeth in the dark.'

'Well, I hope your Mr Heath doesn't expect Nicholas and me to "take a shower" together! That's all I hope. I'm going up to my room. It's not exactly entertaining down here. Discussing bricks in the lavatory.'

'I had a good letter today, from Nicholas George's headmaster,' Leslie told Charlie when her mother had gone.

'Nick's only three. He hasn't got a headmaster.'

'The Headmaster of Knuckleberries,' he explained to Nicholas. 'Your grandson's been down since birth, of course. I've been

281

writing regularly, keeping the Headmaster in the picture. Simeon put in a word for me.'

'He did that, did he?'

'Oh yes. The Rector's taken a considerable interest in him. So in due course we'll be packing young Nicholas George off to Knuckleberries.'

'Don't you be too sure,' Charlie warned him.

'Of course I'm sure. You know who really governs the country? Not Ted Heath *or* the miners. It's the fellows who went to Knuckleberries, so that's why Nick is going to be one of them.'

Up in her bedroom Grace wasn't resting. She was playing Pinky Pinkerton's old record of 'You're the Top!' and dancing to herself. She thought no one saw her, and, in her elaborate turns, didn't notice the window-cleaners. Gary Kitson, up his ladder, could see her and he called down to his partner, Simon Mallard-Greene, to join him. Watching the old woman pirouette on her own they laughed so much that Simon nearly fell off the ladder.

★ 26 ★

Collecting the Evidence

SIMEON HENRY SIMCOX
BORN 1ST JANUARY 1903
DIED 21ST MAY 1985
FOR FIFTY YEARS RECTOR OF THIS PARISH
BELOVED HUSBAND AND FATHER
' "I KEPT MY WORD," HE SAID.'

Such was the inscription on Simeon's tombstone. Dorothy was busy with her trowel and secateurs, cutting the dead heads off the standard rose she had planted at the head of the grave, and then clearing the weeds that had grown up around it. As she knelt she saw that a pair of uncleaned black shoes and unpressed grey flannel trousers had come to join her. The Rev. Kevin Bulstrode told her that he did like to see a family caring for the grave.

'I suppose most families have got better things to do.'

'Your son was here the other day. I saw him from the Rectory window.'

'You saw Fred?'

'No. Your eldest son.'

Dorothy stood up and thought that it was rather disgusting how well roses did on graves – she could never get a Mrs Sam Macready to flower like that at home.

'Henry? What on earth was he doing here? Never weeding!'

'So far as I could see he was taking photographs.'

'Whatever of?'

'Of the headstone so far as I could tell, and of the inscription.'

When Dorothy got home, unloaded her small car and struggled up to the front door with her handbag, shopping bag and tray full of gardening tools she found Jackson Cantellow, the solicitor, smiling and anxious to help.

'Are you very busy?'

'Extremely, the Bishop's coming to tea.' Dorothy didn't want to be bothered with Mr Cantellow.

'Is that true?' Cantellow was carrying her possessions into the sitting-room. 'No,' Dorothy told him. 'It's a thundering lie. What on earth can you want with me?'

'Don't you know, Mrs Simcox? Didn't you get my letters?' She had seen the envelopes neatly typed and marked Cantellow and Machin. She told him that she burnt them unopened. 'You couldn't have anything of the slightest interest to say to me.'

Cantellow smiled, prepared to take his time. 'Aren't we going to have a cup of tea?'

'I am.'

'That's very thoughtful.' But when he followed her into the kitchen she used only one cup, one tea-bag and a little milk. She drank on her own.

'Mrs Simcox' – Cantellow ignored the lack of hospitality and perched himself on a high stool – 'if you had read my letters you'd've been aware that your son, Henry, is attacking his father's last will on the grounds that the late Rector was of unsound mind, memory and understanding. We shall need your views on that.'

'Well, of course Simeon was mad.'

'Really?' The solicitor was gratified.

'Aren't we all? Aren't you, Mr Jackson Cantellow?'

'Me?'

'I would say, mad as a hatter.' Dorothy was sitting at the kitchen table, sipping her tea. 'Writing me letters which I have no desire to read. Asking a lot of questions I have no desire to answer. Singing in those awful concerts.'

'I really don't see what the Worsfield Choral has to do with it.' For the first time Cantellow looked hurt.

'Ha! Ha! Ha! Ha! Ha! Ha ... le ... lu ... Hallelujah! Taking forever just to sing one word! On and on and on until everyone dies of boredom. Why couldn't you just say "Hallelujah" and get it over with, like a normal person?'

'The evidence we already have shows signs of unfortunate

mental instability growing in the late Rector since the end of the last war.' Cantellow decided to ignore Dorothy's attack. He opened his briefcase in a businesslike manner and took out a typewritten statement. 'We give instances,' he went on. 'An occasion when he appeared on the doorstep of Rapstone Manor on his hands and knees, apparently trumpeting like an elephant. A time when he opened the front door to a couple seeking guidance on the Christian approach to marriage and was seen to be clad in female attire. An incident during an election when he wished that the guillotine might be reintroduced, for aristocrats and their doctors.'

'This is total madness! What's that you're reading from?'

Cantellow handed her the document. 'A draft, Mrs Simcox, of your proof of evidence. I thought we might go through it together and I can include any further little nuggets that you might wish to add.'

As soon as she had it Dorothy tore the 'proof' into small strips and dropped them into the tidy-bin. Cantellow seemed not at all perturbed as he told her he had a copy, of course, back at the office. 'Some time you'll have to tell us about these matters, Mrs Simcox, painful as they may be. Steps can always be taken to compel a reluctant witness to come to court, in the interests of justice.'

'In the interests of justice I have to be visited by the awful little slimy hymn-singer! I have to be besieged in my own living-room! I have to be asked the most ridiculous questions about your father! Naturally Simeon went down on his hands and knees and trumpeted like an elephant. It was something he thought amusing.' Dorothy had burst furiously into Fred's consulting room, surprising the local bank manager who had come to chat about his piles.

'Please, Mr Grimsdale. Could I ask you to wait outside? Just for a moment.' When his patient had gone, Fred protested mildly, 'This is a doctor's consulting room, Mother. I don't know if you remember?'

'Well I wish you'd prescribe something for Mr Singing Cantellow, preferably rat poison. And you must stop Henry bringing this wretched case. You must know how to do that,' she ended somewhat illogically. 'You're a doctor.'

Fred told her that it would take more than a doctor to stop

Henry, a feat which could hardly be performed by a battleship armed with Exocet missiles. So far as he could tell the only thing which would prevent Henry going on to contest the will in court was something he could see no sign of, a logical explanation.

'A what?'

'A sane reason for our father leaving his money to Leslie Titmuss.'

'It was his money, wasn't it? I suppose he could do exactly as he liked with it.' Dorothy was still trembling with rage after the solicitor's visit. 'That Mr Jackson Cantellow thought I was going to make him a cup of tea. But I didn't, you know!'

When Dorothy had left him, Fred telephoned his brother. He said he was coming up to London that evening and might he call in for half an hour? As he drove out of Hartscombe, across the bridge, up the hill and towards the motorway, Fred began to feel that he had a new purpose in life, that of protecting Simeon's memory. He saw no reason why any court should find his father guilty but insane because of his will, or his jokes, or his political beliefs, and the fact that the Rector was no longer in a position to explain himself made Fred even more determined to discover the truth. If he had been entirely honest he would have had to admit that not allowing Henry to get his own way had its place somewhere in his list of aims and ambitions.

When he arrived at the flat off the King's Road he found Lonnie laying the table for a dinner party in the big room. While Henry poured drinks, Fred looked idly down at his brother's desk and saw, to his considerable surprise, a photograph of their father's tombstone.

'Rather an important part of the evidence, don't you think?' Henry handed him a glass. Lonnie was muttering to herself as she laid out forks, 'Is Fred staying for dinner? If he is it's going to play silly buggers with my placement.'

'You remember the inscription?' Henry said it as though putting his brother through some kind of basic intelligence test.

'Do you think I'm likely to forget? " 'I kept my word,' he said." From the Bible, I always thought.'

'You always thought! The trouble with you, young Frederick,

is that you hardly ever think at all. As for the money wasted on your so-called education at Knuckleberries ...'

'It would mean sitting Fred next to another man – I could put him beside Ronnie Archpole.' Lonnie was worrying round her dinner table.

' "Is anyone there?" said the Traveller, Knocking on the moonlit door." ' Henry took a drink to his second wife and handed it to her as he spoke to Fred. 'Does that ring a faint bell?'

' "Tell them I came, and no one answered, That I kept my word," he said.' Lonnie recited it as she moved the place-mats around. 'Walter de la Mare.'

'The brilliance of a well-stocked mind!' Henry applauded her.

'Of course Ronnie Archpole is tremendously gay. Fred won't mind that, will he?' Lonnie wanted to know but her husband was asking his brother the next difficult question.

'Have you considered the significance of our father choosing that quotation for his final resting-place?'

'Have you?'

'The climax of megalomania! Simeon clearly regarded his passage through the world as a sort of Second Coming. He called on the great, inert masses to answer his call and accept the Kingdom of Equality, Christian Socialism and the Welfare State! Poor old Father. Nobody answered. That's how he saw himself. The Great Prophet rejected. The misunderstood Messiah! Our psychiatrist says his hospital's full of them.'

'Our psychiatrist?'

'The one we're calling to give evidence.'

'Anyway.' Fred was thinking about the inscription. 'Our father didn't quote the lines about no one answering. He quoted the bit about keeping his word.' He had picked up a dish of nuts and was eating thoughtfully. Lonnie removed them from him.

'I was just going to set those out on the coffee table.'

'Perhaps he gave his word to someone,' Fred suggested.

'You mean to Leslie Titmuss?' Henry was contemptuous. 'If he tries to say *that* ...'

'It might be true.'

'It can't be! Simeon had no possible reason to promise Titmuss anything.'

287

'But if he *had* a reason your case would collapse, wouldn't it?'

'What reason can you suggest?'

'Perhaps I can find one.'

'Why would you want to try?'

'Your solicitor . . .'

'*Our* solicitor.'

'Cantellow's been pestering Mother. She'll never give evidence.'

'She may have to.'

'Would you force her?'

'It isn't because you're so concerned about Mother, is it?' Henry, much pinker than he used to be, flushed to a deeper shade. 'She stands to gain as much as any of us. It's because you can't bear a fight. One thing you can say for the terrible Titmuss, he's a fighter! You've always been the same, Frederick. You couldn't even fight me all those years ago. You had to cave in, over Agnes.'

Lonnie, reacting to the mention of the Numero Uno, dropped a spoon, picked it up, flustered, and wiped it with a table napkin. 'Well, is Fred staying to dinner or isn't he?'

'He isn't,' Fred told her. 'I'm leaving now.'

'Going to sample my ex-wife's experiments with herbs, down the wrong end of the Fulham Road?' Henry asked him.

'You know about that?'

'You'd better take it I know most things about you.'

After this visit to his brother Fred was more anxious than ever to discover the true reason for their father's will. He thought how little he really knew about Leslie. What secret did this politician, whom Fred had always found faintly ridiculous, have which made him deserve Simeon's sudden and secret generosity at the Simcox family's expense? Intent on discovering some clue to the Titmuss mystery, Fred thought of Leslie's long-time friend and business associate. He invited Magnus Strove and his wife, Jennifer (née Battley), to lunch at the Swan's Nest Hotel. They accepted eagerly and arrived dead on time.

Their table was in the new Old Father Thames Carvery, where they were attended by a malign-looking Portuguese waiter wearing a soup-stained purple dinner-jacket. Piped music tinkled and gurgled incessantly and Fred noticed that the platform, where he had once played for a dinner dance with the Riverside Stompers, had been abolished. Magnus's boyish good looks had faded, he was now a balding, disappointed, middle-aged man, wearing a blazer and an old Knuckleberries tie. His wife, Fred thought, had worn rather better. She had become a determined and rather tough woman, the organizer of a family which had fallen on harder times than they ever expected to encounter. Both the Stroves looked down at their plates with approval. 'It's a while since we had smoked salmon, isn't it, Magnus?' 'Rather a while. Of course, you quacks must be making a fortune out of the National Health. And when you and Henry win the battle for the Simcox shares ...'

'That's what I wanted to ask you about. I want your help.'

'Well, absolutely anything we can do to scupper the toad, Titmuss. Isn't that right, Jennifer?'

'Absolutely anything to scupper the toad.'

'You know my father left his whole estate to Leslie?'

'Then he must have been off his chump, quite definitely. What do you say, Jennifer?'

'I'm awfully afraid to say that the late Rector must have been entirely off his chump. Not hereditary, of course,' Jennifer added hastily.

'Tell me a bit more about him, Magnus. After all you were in business together for a long time.'

'Hartscombe Enterprises. Its name's engraved on my heart.' Magnus looked pained.

'Was he ever in need of money?'

'Leslie in need of money?' He gave a small and mirthless laugh. 'That's pretty rich, isn't it, Jennifer?'

'Yes, it is. Pretty rich.' These Stroves, Fred thought, clearly supported each other.

'Look. You remember when Leslie first got into the Government? Under-Secretary for Public Urinals. Some damn thing or other ...'

'Advanced Technology.'

'Jennifer knows all about it. Anyway, he had to get out of Hartscombe Enterprises just at the top of the property boom. We couldn't go wrong at the time. Offices, hotels, blocks of flats were going up like mushrooms. And we were coining the stuff. So

Christopher Kempenflatt and I were delighted to buy the toad out, even though we had to pay through the nose for it, in readies.'

'Cash down!' Jennifer told Fred.

'That was it. We didn't want to deplete the company so I borrowed a load on my expectation of the Picton estate.'

'The house?'

'Of course, and the cottages and woodlands, couple of farms in hand – the whole bloody boiling. Well, Daddy was going into a state of depression about the peerage he never got and I knew it'd all be mine in pretty short order. I thought I'd pay off the mortgage out of the company profits. That's what I thought!'

'That was when Hartscombe Enterprises went broke?'

'Worse than that. When he was our accountant, do you know what the toad made Christopher and me do? Only give our personal guarantee to the bank. Of course we needed a loan to expand in those days.'

'And Leslie didn't give a guarantee?'

'Toad Titmuss? He wouldn't guarantee his own child the price of a Mars bar.'

'So when Doughty died Magnus had to let the whole estate go back to the mortgage company.' Jennifer carried on with the story as Magnus seemed to momentarily weaken with disgust. 'And you know who was the principal shareholder of *that* little enterprise?'

'He can guess, Jennifer. Fred can guess.'

'Yes, I suppose I can.'

'The Honourable Member for Hartscombe and Worsfield South, otherwise known as the Toad. Now we're left with nothing. Of course, Jennifer's got her physiotherapy and I fill in as part-time secretary at the Golf Club. That's the poor, starving little brewery clerk your father decided to leave his money to.' Magnus looked out of the restaurant window at the river and the line of punts which still bumped gently against the landing-stage. 'We made a big mistake that night at the dinner dance,' he said. 'We ought to have drowned the little bugger.'

The events which Magnus Strove had described took place in the years after 1974, when Mr Heath fell prey to the miners and Leslie in opposition was able to devote his time to his new business interests. The quick upward climb of 'fringe' banks and property companies, such as Hartscombe Enterprises, was over and they began to slide towards disaster. Leslie had jumped for safety just in time. So, in due course, the changes in the market and the death of Doughty delivered him Picton House and the Strove estate. When he first took possession of Magnus's old house Leslie stood for a while on the terrace, surveying his domain. Then he walked through the rooms, huge, empty and dusty with marks on the walls where the Strove ancestors had once hung. Standing in the hall he heard a strange sound in that house, the sound of laughter. He went down a number of draughty corridors to the kitchen and there found his mother in rubber gloves and an overall preparing for a good clean-up. She was laughing her head off.

After he had entertained Magnus and Jennifer at the Swan's Nest, Fred had a further opportunity to research into the character of Leslie Titmuss. He came back from a call and Miss Thorne, the receptionist, told him, with a certain amount of pride, that the Minister had been on the phone asking for Dr Hardison to visit; the great man had lost his voice.

'I might go over to Picton myself.'

'He did especially ask for Dr Hardison.'

'But Hardison's not back yet, is he? I mean we can't leave a politician without a voice.'

Leslie was not delighted to see Dr Simcox. Owing to the pending case, he whispered, he felt it was quite improper for Fred to treat him. 'You mean it might be contempt of court to look at your larynx? Don't be ridiculous!' Fred got out his torch and spatula. 'Now if you'd just sit down and open your mouth.' Such are the magical properties of the doctor's black bag that the Minister obeyed him.

The Picton living-room was now furnished according to Leslie Titmuss's specification and looked as though everything had been ordered in one lot from Harrods. On the gold striped wallpaper there were oil paintings of watermills and cardinals drinking wine. On the copy antique console table stood signed photographs of the Queen visiting Leslie's department, President Reagan, Mrs Thatcher, Lee Kwan Yew and the Pope. For all the money spent on it the room gave no more sign of individual taste than the

Residents' Lounge of a chain hotel; it was warmer but not less grim than it had been in Doughty's day. In the midst of this splendour the Cabinet Minister sat with his chest bared, his mouth open and his tongue depressed by Fred's spatula.

'Really you and I don't have to quarrel about anything.'

'Oo-shoo-arr . . . ber . . . hat.'

'What did you say?'

'You should ask your brother that,' Leslie croaked when Fred removed the spatula.

'Henry thinks my father was mad to leave his money to you.'

'Do you agree with him?'

'My difficulty is finding any sort of logical explanation.'

'It's obvious, isn't it? Your father was . . .'

'Open again, will you? I'll just take another look at those remarkably overworked tonsils.'

'En . . . essly . . . sappointed . . .'

'What?'

'Endlessly disappointed.' The spatula was removed and the croak returned. 'Your brother left his wife for some sort of typist, didn't he? I don't imagine that went down very well at the Rectory. Besides which he used to be a Socialist, now he's criticizing Margaret for being soft on the unions. Did you read his article on Sunday?'

'I thought you might approve of that.'

'The Rector wouldn't have.'

'He might have been disappointed in Henry but that doesn't begin to explain why he should have left everything to you.' Fred took out his stethoscope in as authoritative a way as possible. 'I mean, you're somebody who's led a totally wasted life.'

'Wasted! My life wasted?' Outrage and laryngitis silenced Leslie.

'You *have* got a nasty cold.' Fred was listening attentively to the Titmuss chest.

'What do you mean wasted?' A still, small voice returned. 'Ever since I was a kid, ever since I cut your nettles, I've been determined to make something of myself.'

'What went wrong? Just cough again for me, will you?'

Leslie coughed and was about to protest when Fred went on. 'I mean you were set for life, you might have done a very decent job as head of the accounts department at the Brewery, getting the beer circulating efficiently. You might have done a lot of good in the world.'

'Look.' Titmuss spoke in a furious whisper. 'I told you I'd asked for Hardison.'

'But you couldn't stick to it. You had to go into property, turning corner shops into offices and doing no possible good to anyone. And getting into the Cabinet! Where's that got us all? Back to where we were before the war: wasted lives, no jobs, back to the years before Simeon made his well-meaning offer of Paradise. Why on earth would our father have left everything to a person like you? You can do your shirt up now.'

Leslie stood and did so. Anger gave him back some of his voice.

'God! You're arrogant,' he rasped. 'I always thought Henry was the bloody superior one. Always on television, always writing about himself, knowing everything, laying down the law. Henry's got nothing at all on you! You're the one for arrogance, aren't you? You don't do anything, don't commit yourself to anything. It's all far beneath you, isn't it? Politics! Business! Property! Writing books! Even getting married and giving birth to another human being. All that's far beneath your dignity!'

'I wouldn't say that.' Fred was writing out a prescription.

'You're so pure, aren't you, Doctor Frederick? So uncorrupted. Doing your rounds in your tweed jacket and old flannel trousers. The decent, quiet country doctor and we all know why Simeon cut *you* out of his will!'

Fred packed up his medical bag, the consultation almost over. 'Do we? I'll leave this here.' He crossed to put the prescription on the mantelpiece. 'You'll probably get better just as quickly without it.'

'*That* Christmas in the Rectory,' Leslie muttered.

'*That* Christmas?'

'The respectable country doctor was found tucked up in bed with someone else's wife when the simple-minded Rector was delivering a Christmas stocking.'

'Who told you that?'

'Someone I can call to give evidence in court.' Leslie, triumphant, suddenly spoke clearly.

'Mr Wickstead, I suppose. Isn't he in charge of your image? At least I've done one thing for which you ought to be extremely grateful: you seem to have completely recovered the power of speech.'

As Fred left the room he heard the front door bell ring, and in the hall, Janet Nowt, one of old Tom's daughters and now part of the Titmuss household, was letting in a portly figure who announced himself in an ingratiating manner.

'The name's Nubble. I was told that the Minister was working at home this morning.' And then, with a grin, 'Hullo there, Simcox Mi.'

'What on earth are *you* doing here?' Fred asked.

'The "Creevy" column.' Nubble sounded inexplicably proud of himself.

'The what?'

'You know what the name of the game is nowadays?'

'Coffee bars? Boutiques? Flower power accessories?'

'Gossip! People love it. All the truth about everyone you'll never meet. I'm interviewing Titmuss. What've you been doing?'

'Much the same thing.'

The living-room door opened and Leslie came out to find Nubble and Fred renewing their acquaintance.

'Minister!' Nubble was obsequious. 'So awfully decent of you to see me.'

'Do you two know each other?' Leslie was whispering again now and puzzled.

'Of course,' Arthur Nubble told him. 'We were at Knuckleberries together.' The old school fellows stood silent and Leslie looked at them both with deep suspicion, as though he suspected them of forming some sort of alliance against him.

Part Five

As it will be in the future, it was at the birth of man –
There are only four things certain since Social Progress began:
That the Dog returns to his Vomit and the Sow returns to her
Mire
And the burnt Fool's bandaged finger goes wobbling back to the
Fire;

And that after this is accomplished, and the brave new world
begins
When all men are paid for existing and no man must pay for his
sins,
As surely as Water will wet us, as surely as Fire will burn,
The Gods of the Copybook Headings with fever and slaughter
return!

from 'The Gods of the Copybook Headings'
Rudyard Kipling

★ 27 ★
The Best for Nicky

'Rough shooting's better since Tom Nowt left us. Fellow had a talent for luring away my pheasants. Never saw a hare either, not when Nowt was alive.'

'He had his ways, Sir, did old Tom Nowt.'

'Of course my wife could never stand him, wanted me to prosecute if I remember rightly.'

'Tom was a red rag to her Ladyship.'

'For goodness sake, we've got enough rabbits to go round. I mean if you own a decent bit of rough shooting, you're under an obligation to have your game pinched occasionally. My wife can't see that. Do you remember when she summoned in the Constabulary?'

Since the death of his friend Doughty, Nicholas went round with a gun, a dog and Wyebrow who had become, after years of secret practice, an excellent shot. They walked along the edge of the woodlands, and through the sifting rain, two old men, master and servant, indistinguishable in their tweed caps and jackets. A lurcher and a spaniel sniffed and dived under bushes, causing an occasional drum roll of wings or the streak of a rabbit.

'Of course the officers of the law never found Tom's old hut and I didn't give them directions.' Nicholas sneezed. He was coming up for a cold on a bleak day in the 'winter of discontent', a time when hospital porters and gravediggers went on strike, and those hostile to Mr Callaghan's Labour Government could ask what sort of a Britain was this in which the luxuries of falling ill and being buried in the ground were apparently denied to the citizens. Nicholas, being in a privileged position, fell ill privately and at home. His cold developed into pneumonia. Fred called, dosed him

297

with penicillin, and Simeon, smiling and ruffled like a cheerful bird of ill omen, came to sit by the patient. 'Haven't come to administer the last rites, have you?' Nicholas asked. 'If you want to hear my confession, I must say you're in for a damn dull evening.'

Simeon felt for his pipe, changed his mind about smoking in the sick room, and settled down to listen. 'It's a terrible thing, you know, to look back over a long life and have no sins worth confessing. Not that I've had many opportunities to sin. Married Grace when I was a young man and before that I was living with Mother.' Nicholas looked back, dismayed by a blameless life. 'Of course, I might have had a sin or two when I was parted from Grace during the war. But I never took advantage of that. More fool I! I suppose some people would say.'

'No. I'm sure they wouldn't say that.'

'I might have done a bit of sinning when I was stationed at Bognor,' Nicholas calculated. 'Grace was always dashing up to London for evenings out. She enjoyed the air raids, you know. All I did was go for walks along the sea-front or over the Downs. I stayed away from home – not that I stayed away *with* anyone, you understand.'

'I understand.'

From along the bedroom corridor they heard the strains of another Pinky Pinkerton special, 'Smoke Gets in Your Eyes'. Grace, determined that her husband should not be the only one to spend a comfortable day in bed, was listening to her gramophone, propped up on her pillows and sorting through the contents of a mother-of-pearl box which she usually kept on her dressing-table. She reminded herself of old bits of jewellery buried in it and in its depths she found a brooch in the shape of a Maltese Cross, set with garnets which flashed in the glow of her bedside light. It was nothing very grand or expensive, of course, nothing like his mother's pieces which Nicholas had given her and which were always kept in the bank, but she was glad to see it because it reminded her of something that happened during the war. Under the jumble of rings and necklaces, ear-rings and bracelets, was a letter on pale blue notepaper together with a few other scraps of correspondence that she kept for the same reason.

'You never liked Grace, did you?' Nicholas asked Simeon over the distant sound of music.

'You want me to tell you the truth?'

'Isn't that what we're here for? A truth-telling occasion.'

'No. I never liked her.' Simeon smiled. 'In fact, I think I disapprove of everything about her!'

'Spoilt, overprivileged, selfish and intolerant?' Nicholas suggested.

'Yes.'

'I thought that's what you'd say. But there's always something I shall remember about Grace. She was so beautiful and I was rather dull, but she married me, you know. Do you do much of this nowadays?'

'Much of what?'

'Hearing confessions.'

'Hardly any at all.'

'People don't believe in it, eh? I'm not sure I do. Good heavens! What's the point of remembering things that never happened so long ago?'

From Rapstone, Simeon drove to Picton House. He was admitted by Janet Nowt, and found the curtains drawn in the hall and the standard lamps at the foot of the stairs illuminating a theatrical scene. The Rector was delighted to see a small figure, wearing a beret of Janet's with a pheasant's tail feather stuck in it, a black, curly moustache painted on his face, clad mainly in a tartan car rug, climbing the stairs with a bread knife at the ready, undoubtedly intent on murder. Half-way up, the nine-year-old Nicholas George Titmuss struck the old dinner gong, a relic of the Stroves, and recited the only lines he could remember:

> '. . . the bell invites me.
> Hear it not, Duncan; for it is a knell
> That summons thee to heaven or to hell.'

So, with a bloodcurdling laugh, Nick vanished into the shadows, and Simeon, standing at the back of an audience consisting of Charlie, Elsie Titmuss and Janet Nowt, clapped loudly.

'We did it when I was at school,' he said. 'I had the other part. And my boys did it with me, one Christmas at the Rectory.'

'They were taken to see it at Stratford, and they've been doing scenes,' Charlie explained. 'Such a good school! I can't imagine why Leslie wants to move him.'

Elsie shivered. 'I don't think it's right to teach children things like that.' At which moment Nicky ran delightedly back down the stairs. 'I've done it now. I've stabbed the old King! Ring the bell and pretend it was the servants.'

'Oh that's not fair!' Elsie protested but Nicholas, his face, hands and the bread knife liberally smeared with crimson water colour, hit the gong again.

'Ssh,' said Charlie to the mother-in-law. 'It's the sort of thing Thanes do.' But the show was suddenly over; Nicky bowed to prolonged applause, then Elsie took him away to clean him up and Janet Nowt went off to get tea. 'I've been summoned by your father,' Simeon told Charlie when they were alone. 'He wanted to make a confession.'

'He's not seriously ill?'

'Fred hasn't said so.'

'Poor Father.' Charlie smiled. 'He finds it hard to do anything seriously.'

'Yes. Well, what I wanted to say to you, is' – Simeon was positive – 'he has absolutely nothing to tell you.'

'To tell me?'

'Has he tried to say anything to you?'

'No. Nothing serious.'

'Well, that's the point, isn't it ? So, well, if he summons you to tell you something, it'll really be nothing very much. Nothing for you to be concerned about in any case.'

'I'll try to remember that.' Charlie was laughing, then she went back to the question that concerned her most. 'Why does Leslie want to send Nicky away from me? Would you send a child of yours away?'

'It's something we've all done,' Simeon admitted.

'Doesn't he understand?' He saw Charlie's fists clench, her back stiffen and he remembered how she used to be just before she started to scream. 'For God's sake! Who else is there for me to talk to?' Simeon wondered if he'd have to resort, as he had before, to a reading of *Biggles of the Royal Flying Corps*. Then the door opened to admit Nicky, still in his costume, Elsie Titmuss and Janet with a tray. 'We've washed the blood off our hands,' Elsie told them. 'But we've decided to keep our nice moustache.'

When Charlie said that Nicky was the only person she had to talk to, she was scarcely exaggerating. Her longing to have someone helpless to look after, which had disposed her towards Leslie when he was thrown into the river, and had been distributed among a random selection of hard cases and students she thought badly done by, had concentrated itself powerfully on her child. She forgave Nicky everything, including not being homeless or under-privileged or living below the poverty line or in constant trouble with the police. Deprived of these disadvantages, she thought her son had compensating problems. He had a father who had managed to become extremely rich and too busy to see much of him. Nicky was an only child, as she had been, and therefore must be lonely. In fact he grew up to be a pale, contained but self-reliant small boy, who wore glasses, read a lot of books and never minded being left alone. He found little to say to his father and thought of his mother as someone who needed a great deal of looking after.

When her son was growing, Charlie decided he should be brought up in the country. Leslie agreed. It was no bad thing that his family should live in the constituency although he spent most of the week in London. He thought it politic for Nicky to start his education at the village school, although he was later sent to a small fee-paying day school in Hartscombe. So Charlie gave up her social studies, her case work and her clientele of lame dogs. She spent no more time in afternoon drinking clubs in Soho, students' bedrooms or the backs of vans. She enjoyed her days in the country and looked forward to Nicky coming home at tea-time far more keenly than she did to her husband's return at weekends. A shadow hung, however, over the peaceful landscape of Nicky's childhood. As doom-laden as the pronouncements of the witches in *Macbeth* came Leslie's constant references to the day when their son would have to go away to Knuckleberries.

When Charlie tried to argue about Nicky's education, Leslie merely smiled tolerantly and changed the subject. The date was fixed, it seemed to Charlie, like that of an execution. Pleas for clemency were met only with a polite smile and a quick glance at the calendar. It's fair to say that Nicky, reading on his stomach in the long grass all the summer, seemed unaware of the condemned cell in which he was waiting.

'Leslie never went away to school. You kept him at home. Did you want to get rid of him?' Charlie did her best to get her mother-in-law to sign the petition for a reprieve.

'Get rid of him?' Elsie smiled at the absurdity of the idea. 'Of course not. He was always his mother's boy. I never thought George really understood his ways. Besides which Leslie was always one for my cooking.'

'Then will you tell him not to send Nicky away?'

'He wants him to have all the advantages.'

'The advantages of being buggered and beaten and brought up by a lot of bloody snobs?' Charlie sometimes reverted, at moments of emotion, to the language of the London School of Economics.

'There now.' Elsie was making rock cakes for tea. 'I'm sure Leslie only wants the best for Nicky.'

It was still two years before the date of his son's banishment, when Leslie Titmuss found himself fighting his third election. It was the end of the sad seventies, a decade whose contributions to history, the Watergate scandal, President Carter, hot pants and the skate-board, vanished from the memory more quickly than a Chinese dinner. The country, it seemed, was prepared to atone for the greatly exaggerated sins of its past. The dreams which Simeon had were dying at last, and a new age was coming to birth. Young people in black leather, loaded with chains, with white faces and pink, green and purple hedgehog hairdo's hung round the market square in Hartscombe, some wearing swastikas and iron crosses, nostalgic for an old horror. Leslie stood on an empty beer crate at the Brewery entrance and addressed his former workmates through a loudhailer. Stuck on his campaign van were posters, showing Mrs Thatcher looking prepared to face a grim future for a lot of other people with considerable fortitude. 'You're worried about your jobs?' Leslie's magnified voice bounced round the vats, the barrels and piles of hops to be disregarded by a group of drivers enjoying their mid-morning pints; although someone in the accounts department stuck his head out of a window to listen. 'Of course you're worried with a Labour Government giving you one and a quarter million unemployed! Thank your lucky stars Simcox Ales hasn't been nationalized. It hasn't been taken over by the Socialist bureaucracy. This is just the sort of small business we want to see prosper. Your jobs are going to be safe after the election.'

And after the election Leslie found himself a job as a Minister. His rise, as always, was rapid, and, in an early reshuffle, he entered the Cabinet.

Hartscombe is in the more fortunate half of England and was not as desolated by the abandonment of old industries, or the complete hopelessness of unemployment, as the remote and foreign North. All that happened in the riverside towns was a little 'slimming down', a bit of 'rationalization' and 'cutting down on overmanning'. There were also a large number of bankruptcies. Fred went away on a holiday and came back to find a change had come over Marmaduke's garage. The pumps were now self-service, and the only attendant was a lumpy girl sitting in a burglar-proof booth who handed out, through a tiny grille and with the change, green plastic men. Collecting about five hundred 'greenies' could mean the infliction of garden tools, Pyrex dishes or a cuddly toy. Marmaduke's had given up repairs, and had also given up Terry Fawcett, who sat in his tower block, thinking of his dwindling two thousand pounds redundancy money, and wondering why it was proving so unexpectedly difficult to find another job.

'Glenys is back typing for your father,' he told Fred when he visited. 'I do the shopping and fetch the kid from school. I'd make a lovely wife.'

'I tell him he ought to go into window-cleaning. Look at all Tina's got round her, it's through Gary's window-cleaning. That's what she's always telling us.' Glenys had just got home from work.

'Gary doesn't want me in his business. Well, who needs to live with a lot of tropical fish, anyway?'

'Do you ever get the feeling the whole world's going backwards? It's as if we got tired of chugging on slowly and put the whole engine into reverse. Back to the dole queues and poverty being thought of as a shameful little secret, something respectable people don't get involved in. Nicholas wouldn't have approved however much he called himself a Conservative.' Simeon and Fred were on one of their walks together, threading their way down a long, overgrown bridle-path, walking in single file so that the Rector's random thoughts were shouted back over his shoulder. 'Poor old Nicholas! At the end he seemed to let go of life. Not that he ever had hold of it very firmly.'

'Not like you!' Fred smiled at his father, who was striding along as though on a Fabian Society walking tour of the Lake District. 'You're remarkably tenacious.'

'Your predecessor, Dr Salter, used to tease me about that. He said Christians ought to give death a warmer welcome. Well, Salter was an unbeliever but he went first.'

'So he did.'

'And he was always so strong.' Simeon was hitting at brambles with his walking-stick, clearing the path for both of them, with as much relish as if he were using a machete in a jungle. 'Of course, I've always known you were the tough one of our family.'

'Am I?' Fred was surprised.

'Henry's not as strong as you. But he can look after himself, don't you think?'

'Does he have to? Now he's got Lonnie to look after him.'

'Lorna! Your mother doesn't hit it off with Lorna at all.' They were slithering down the steep end of the path. The wood stretched out around them, coloured by pools of bluebells. 'There *is* something rather unsettling about her, though. About Lorna, I don't mean about your mother.'

'What's that?'

'Lorna would appear to be deeply religious,' Simeon said as though it were much to be regretted.

'Oh dear!' Fred laughed.

'Of course, Henry goes to church whenever they come down for the weekend. He's become such an old English country gent, it makes me feel quite young sometimes. You don't go to church, do you?'

'Not at all.'

'Can't say I blame you. But I look across at Lorna during prayers. Most people – Well, there aren't many of them now – adopt the usual sort of Church of England crouch: bottoms on the edge of the pew, head stuck forward, you know the sort of procedure? Not Lorna! She's down on her knees, hands together, eyes tightly shut, lips moving. Sometimes I want to leave the altar and go over to her and say, "For heaven's sake, my dear girl, give it a rest! Don't try so hard." I don't think God likes to be pestered, do you?'

'I suppose not.'

'So you admit the existence of a God who doesn't like to be pestered?' Simeon asked quickly.

'I didn't say that.'

'No.' There was a gate at the end of the path. The Rector climbed it and sat for a moment, perched on the top bar. 'But you're all right, Fred. You'll always be all right. Are you happy?'

'Not particularly.'

'Of course not, foolish question.' Simeon dropped from the gate. Fred followed him and they came out on the edge of a cornfield. They walked for a little and Fred saw a track going back into the wood behind them. He suddenly realized where they were, in that part of the Mandragola Valley in which, one long past night, he had seen Tom Nowt shoot a deer.

'You know we all think, I certainly thought,' Simeon told him, 'that our lives are so different from our parents'. We think differently, feel differently, all that sort of thing. But it's not true, is it? We all find out the same things, and when we've found them out, well, then it's time to go.'

'Not for a long while yet.' They were walking side by side along the muddy edge of the field and Fred took his father's arm.

'Why? Do you think I'm about to make some great new discovery?'

As the date crept slowly towards Nicky's first term at his big school (Leslie's description) or his imprisonment, his execution, his being sent off to the front (as Charlie called it), the process seemed to his mother to have a sickening inevitability. Leslie was quite set on it. Elsie was not going to help. Grace, Charlie knew without asking her, would be worse than useless. Faced with what she regarded as a huge disaster, Charlie could only exercise the right that Henry had once claimed in the face of the Vietnam War. She did not, it's true, organize a march with banners or attract the attention of the mounted police; she demonstrated in the sitting-room at Picton House after dinner and shouted at her husband.

'You hated them once, didn't you? You really hated them when they threw you in the river! That was when I thought I could love you. You were some sort of a person, I thought, a real, live, fighting, kicking, human person.' She turned away from him and started a journey up the carpet. 'Now you've stopped hating. Now you feel so safe and smug and sure of youself. What are you now? Nothing.'

'Nothing?' Leslie sat in front of the coffee tray. He was nibbling at an after-dinner mint, always having had a sweet tooth. 'Only a member of Her Majesty's Government. Only in the Cabinet.'

'Exactly what I said. Nothing!' The last word rose in volume to just under a scream. Leslie put the rest of the mint into his mouth, wiped his fingers delicately on his handkerchief and urged his wife not to shout. '*They'll* hear.'

'Who'll hear?' Charlie pounced on his fear. 'The servants? My God, let them hear, if it interests them in the least.' She went to the door, wrenched it open and yelled down the kitchen corridor. 'Listen to this, Janet Nowt. Listen, Cook. The Right Honourable Leslie Titmuss is *nothing*!' There was no reply from the brightly lit kitchen where the radio and the washing-up machine were both playing loudly. Charlie banged the door shut. 'Pity the gardener's gone home. He might have been interested.'

'For God's sake, Charlotte. I've tried to make you happy.'

'Happy? Does that include separating me from my child?'

'You're being ridiculous. It happens to everybody.'

'Everybody? Who's everybody? Magnus Strove and that horrible Christopher Kempenflatt and all those braying imbeciles who threw bread rolls and laughed at your dinner-jacket. Have you forgotten? Have you quite honestly forgotten?'

'It's a long time ago.' Leslie finished another mint and this time he licked his fingers quite delicately.

'And now you want Nicky to join them?'

'Your father went away to school.'

'My father! Poor man.'

'His main problem in life was being married to your mother. I must say' – Leslie couldn't help smiling – 'you get more like her every day.'

'Don't say that! Don't ever say that!'

'Now I suppose you're going to scream?'

'No.' Although Charlie was controlling herself with difficulty. 'I'm not going to have to scream any more. I'm going to leave you, Leslie. I'm going to live in London. We'll find a flat somewhere.'

'We?'

'Nicky and I. He can go to school on the state. Just like you did. He'll be like you, a mother's boy. But I'll tell you one thing. I'm not staying here, living with a nothing who can't hate any more.'

'Breakfast meeting with the Americans.' Leslie stood up and stretched. There was a little chocolate stain on his top lip; his tongue emerged and licked it away. He had behaved, he knew, with perfect manners and considerable restraint. 'Isn't it time we both went to bed?'

When Charlie went into Nicky's room, she found his light on and that he was fast asleep wearing his glasses and holding *Vanity Fair*. She took his glasses off gently and put his book away, being careful not to lose his place. She switched off his light and closed the door, full of hope for the future.

During those long summer holidays, both Grace and her daughter came in contact with the law. A detective sergeant and constable were summoned to the Manor. 'No one in Rapstone ever locked their doors. Ever!' Grace stood in the hall in her dressing-gown and lectured the two bewildered young officers on the decline of civilization as she knew it. 'And all we had was one bobby, Harry Jimpson. He had an old push-bike, of course, not some luxurious motor with flashing lights like you've parked out there. But nothing ever got stolen when Harry Jimpson was our bobby!'

'You say it was a box with some pieces of jewellery?' The sergeant looked at such notes as he had been able to take, and wondered why the old bag wanted to get him back on a bicycle. 'And there's no signs of a break-in?'

'Well, there wouldn't be, would there? They must have been far too clever for you. Yes, a mother-of-pearl inlaid box. Locked. With some jewellery and other personal things.'

'No very costly pieces you say? Sentimental value only.'

'And that's exactly why I want them back.'

307

'We'll do our best, your Ladyship.'

'Your best may not be good enough!' Grace squared her small jaw. 'My son-in-law's in the Cabinet you know. He sees the Prime Minister every day. Law and order's very much her thing, isn't it? I don't suppose she'd like to discover she's being let down badly by the police in the Rapstone Valley.'

Charlie met the law in the shape of a Mr Rattling, a tall, grey-haired and dignified man, the sort of solicitor who acts for Cabinet Ministers. Rattling had walked through the garden at Picton and she first saw him as he stood, a dark and alien figure, beside the croquet lawn, where she was being ruthlessly defeated by her son.

'Mrs Titmuss? I'm Ted Rattling, by way of being your husband's solicitor.'

'I don't need a lawyer,' she told him, squinting in the sun.

'If we could just have a word in private? Before anyone takes a step they're going to regret.'

'You play, Nicky.' Charlie crossed the lawn and stood looking up at the strange man who seemed to have grown in height as she approached him.

'You'll take independent advice, I'm sure. This is just to get the position quite clear.'

'Mr Rattle...'

'Rattling. Ted Rattling.'

'Mr Rattling.' She paid no attention to the 'Ted'. 'I've no idea what you're talking about.'

'Have you not? It seems that in conversation with your husband, you suggested a parting of the ways. Look, shouldn't we discuss this indoors?'

'Where are you going, Mum?' Nicky called after her as she allowed the man to lead her across the terrace and in by the french windows. 'Won't be long,' she told him. Indeed, it was not to be a lengthy interview, just a preliminary sniff round the problem as Ted Rattling described it, just so Mrs Titmuss could know what her husband's present 'thinking' was, just so she could 'take on board' his probable reaction.

'I don't really care *what* he thinks. I'm going to London and taking my son with me. Has my husband got any objection to that?' From the living-room window, Charlie could see Nicky working out several devastating shots with mathematical precision. 'If you embark on that course,' she heard Rattling tell her, 'your husband's instructed me to take divorce proceedings, based on your intolerable conduct.'

'That'll suit me down to the ground.'

'And immediate proceedings for the custody of the child of the marriage. Nicholas George, is it?'

'That's ridiculous.' Charlie turned towards him, full of contempt.

'In the normal case, of course, one would expect an order of custody to the mother. However, it seems that you, Mrs Titmuss, were a student and later active in the social services.'

'Is that some sort of crime?'

'Not in itself. No.' Rattling could sound very judicial, indeed many judges behaved more like common or garden solicitors than he did. He prided himself on being able to see at least two sides to every question. 'But what your husband has instructed me to allege, in any proceedings, would be "intimacy" on quite a sizeable scale, as I understand it, with the young males who happened to be in need of the social welfare services. Your husband used the words "rough trade", Mrs Titmuss. Of course, all custody cases are distressing, but when it comes to an incident, which the child himself might be asked to recollect...'

'What incident is that?'

'I'm sure you remember, Mrs Titmuss. When your husband was up in London and a young person "on probation" came to spend the night here. When the child was in the house?'

It was then that Charlie remembered Percy Denham from Wandsworth. He had been one of her special cases and he still telephoned her occasionally. Percy had been after a job in Worsfield and seeing friends, he explained, 'in the area'. She asked him to visit Picton and gave him a meal, and, to Janet's silent disapproval, a bed for the night. Some time during that night, Charlie, long ignored by her husband, had visited Percy in one of the spare bedrooms. She had felt healthy for about two weeks afterwards, and yet it seemed to her that one night had lost her the battle. Now, she thought, it was all inevitable, the endless sewing on of name-tapes, the sorting-out of clothes' lists, shirts blue, shirts white and shorts running, the bleak farewell at the railway station, the tea out at Half-Term, when they would neither of them know what to say. She had come to the centre of a maze of loneliness and there was no escape except by the way she had come in.

'I'm sorry to disappoint you, Mr Rattling,' she said, 'but there isn't going to be a case.'

Leslie was able to get away from his Ministry in time to join Charlie and Nicholas at Liverpool Street station. Father and son said goodbye to each other with distant politeness, although Nicky treated his mother with unusual consideration. When the train had gone, the Minister said he hoped Charlie would be responsible for writing the letters. He had, after all, so little time. They parted then, and she went back to Picton.

She couldn't stay in the house that night, and, after a lonely dinner, she took the car and drove down to the Baptist's Head, planning to buy cigarettes. She was sitting alone at the bar, when someone spoke to her.

'Hear you had a friend of mine down to visit you. Percy, wasn't it? He said you were very hospitable.' She looked round at Gary Kitson.

'Yes.' Charlie saw a well-nourished young man with black ringlets and brown eyes, dressed in jeans, cowboy boots and a leather jacket. 'I expect you'd like a drink.'

'Large rum and black, please, Ted.' Gary held up his empty glass. 'And the lady's paying.'

★ 28 ★
Just Like Old Times

'Sovereignty is not negotiable. We've made that perfectly clear. What we have is ours, and nobody else's.'

'There may only be a few of them, but they're our sort of people, aren't they?'

'Are you a sheep farmer, Contessa?'

'No, my dear. But I am Scottish, somewhere in the dim and distant past.'

'Are *they* Scottish then?'

'Bound to be. Nobody but the Scots would think of going to live in a place like that.'

'I wish someone would make it clear to me exactly where the Falkland Islands are.'

'It's going to be quite a problem with combined ops. It's going to be quite a party.'

'Not a *garden* party?' Charlie had been drinking a good deal and the dinner-table conversation stopped for a moment around her.

'I mean more like a D-Day party, Mrs Titmuss. On a far smaller scale of course. But it'll be quite like old times.'

Leslie was entertaining the neighbours, regulars like the Naboths and the 'Contessa', Mrs Fairhazel and the Kempenflatts, the Erskine girls and a few members of the Committee of the local Conservative Association and their good ladies. As they ate their Black Forest gâteau, the British Navy was steaming off to the South Atlantic, to take part in a war which brought back irresistible memories of the Empire, maps on classroom walls, largely coloured pink, and newspapers full of distant campaigns which didn't put them in the slightest danger. A dozen miles away Worsfield Heath had become an American Air Force base in preparation for a different sort of war entirely. It was left to Lady Naboth to draw the parallel. 'When I think of our fellows steaming out there. To the Arctic? It *is* the Arctic, really. And those ghastly women in bobble hats and smelly anoraks camped round the Heath. Deserting their husbands and talking about peace as though they'd only just invented it. Peace! I'd like to see them doing it in Russia.'

'Doing what?' Charlie wanted to know.

'Camping in their horrible bobble hats. I really don't know what they're thinking about.'

'Perhaps they're thinking about Nicky.'

'I say. Your lady isn't one of the disarmers is she, Leslie?' Mrs Fairhazel was alarmed.

'I am.' Leslie spoke with the sort of quiet conviction that Charlie had discovered he adopted when he didn't altogether mean what he said. 'I've got a certain amount of respect for the women of Worsfield Heath, but I'd go a lot further! I want the whole world to disarm at the same time. That's all. Not just us. Not just the Americans. Not just the Russians. All of us. Until then, of course, we must keep up our defence capability. I'm sure that's what Charlie has in mind.'

'Oh well.' Mrs Fairhazel looked relieved. 'I suppose that's all right then.'

His wife might have said more but Leslie looked at the clock above the large painting of dead game on the dining-room wall. 'Perhaps it's about time, Charlotte.'

'About time for what?'

'Wouldn't you like to take the ladies upstairs?'

'Take them upstairs?' Charlie pretended ignorance of a ceremony she detested.

'People usually do it,' Leslie explained patiently, 'after dinner.'

'Do they?' Charlie didn't move. 'I thought people usually had a nice cup of tea and went to sleep in front of the telly after dinner.'

'Well, shall *I* lead the way?' Mrs Fairhazel took command of the situation.

'Lead the way? Where?'

'Upstairs, of course. The ladies want to go upstairs.'

'Well, of course. Up you go.' Charlie gave her permission. 'If you're absolutely bursting for a pee.'

In the weeks that followed Leslie had no chance of coming home to Picton. He sat, with his Cabinet colleagues, in remote control of a distant war which came flickering on to the television screen in the saloon bar of the Baptist's Head. There was news of Marine casualties at a beachhead and of Argentine Sea Hawks shot down. Ted Lawless stood behind the beer handles, backed by photographs of Spitfires, of himself with a silk scarf, sheepskin jacket and Brylcreemed hair, and of Ivy, his wife, as a W.A.A.F., and felt young again.

'A drink for the lady, Ted. They can get on and capture Goose Green without you.' Gary Kitson shouted for the landlord's attention; Charlie had just come into the Head to join him for the evening.

'An estimated forty aircraft took part in the attack, and some got through the missile defences to drop their bombs on the ships below. The Argentine planes were finally driven off by the Navy's Sea Harriers, flying almost continuous combat patrols.' The television set in the Rectory described the victory at Goose Green. 'Shall I turn the machine off?' Dorothy wondered.

'If you like.' Simeon was looking depressed.

'If I'd known it was going to have that sort of thing on it I'd never have let it in. Now what exactly do we do to quieten it?' She could never remember so Simeon got up and found the switch. 'I told Fred we were going backwards. That's not exactly right. What we're doing is going round in circles. I mean, is this where we came in?'

'What do you mean?'

'We used to go to the pictures at the Hartscombe Odeon.'

'Did we do that?' Dorothy went back to her mending.

'Of course, even before we had the children. And we were always late.'

'*You* were always late.' She remembered that.

'Yes. So we'd sit on and watch until we said, "This is where we came in." Films used to go round and round in those days. First attraction. Second attraction. Then start all over again.'

'In the last war at least we only had wireless.' To Dorothy that seemed to have been a mercy.

313

'And we sat glued to it for the latest news of people killing each other,' Simeon reminded her. 'So much enthusiasm. So much hope. Where do you think it all went to?'

'I was never all that concerned about the New Jerusalem.' Dorothy attacked another sock. 'I suppose I've always had far too much to do in the garden.'

'It's going to go round and round, like at the old Hartscombe Odeon.' His pipe had gone out and he started to strike matches to little effect. 'Is that all that's ever going to happen?'

'Probably.' Dorothy sounded reasonably cheerful about it.

'What can we do?'

'Only what we have to.' She looked at her husband and repeated more positively, 'Do what we have to, that's all. And hope for the best.'

On the night when Goose Green was captured Charlie and Gary Kitson entered the Rapstone Cricket Pavilion by forcing a window. After a long evening's drinking at the Baptist's Head they made love on a bed of towels in the middle of the floor. When it was over, Gary zipped up his jeans, buckled his belt, did up a few shirt buttons and combed his hair carefully before putting on his leather jacket.

'You don't really like me, do you?' he asked Charlie, who was sitting naked in a patch of moonlight, ransacking her handbag for a cigarette. 'I don't suppose I like you,' she told him. 'No.'

'What is it then?' Her nakedness irritated him. 'You lonely?'

'That must be it.'

'Where's your husband?'

'Up in London. Winning the war.'

'He's done pretty good for himself then, hasn't he?'

'I suppose so.'

Charlie was sitting under a plaque on the wall which announced that the Pavilion had been donated to the village by the Rt. Hon. Leslie Titmuss, M.P., in memory of Sir Nicholas Fanner, Bart.

'What about your kid?'

'He's away too.'

'So you've just got your mum?'

'Oh, no. I haven't got her.'

Gary finished work with the comb, cleaned it with his fingers and stowed it in his back pocket.

'I know a bit about your mum. It might surprise you.'

'What?'

'Oh, just things. Things I heard about her, I mean.'

'I can't believe you heard anything interesting.'

'I'd say it was pretty interesting, yes. I mean, perhaps it's something you really ought to know.'

'Tell me.'

'All right. But for God's sake, get your clothes on.'

She looked at him for a moment, then she obeyed him. Later, he told her something which she kept as a secret, entirely to herself.

To understand his father's will, Fred told himself, he had to understand Leslie Titmuss, but nothing that he had learnt from Magnus Strove, nor while examining the larynx of the Minister himself, seemed to throw much light on the problem. Simeon was beyond questioning. To whom should he turn next? He had been to visit a patient on the ridge, and was driving back along a narrow road through a wood near Rapstone, when he saw a familiar grey - haired figure, wearing an old mac, stooping to fill a plastic sack with kindling wood. He stopped his car and went to help his mother, although she said, 'Really, shouldn't you be caring for the sick or something? I'm perfectly capable of getting my own kindling.' All the same, he picked up dead and fallen sticks for her, snapped them and loaded up her bag in silence until he felt able to raise her least favourite subject.

'All this business, about father's will.'

'For heaven's sake, doesn't anyone remember anything about Simeon except his wretched will?' She whacked a branch against a tree to break it. 'Firelighters are so expensive nowadays.'

'I know what you want is to stop the case coming to court.'

'It takes no time to get a bag of kindling.'

'I can stop it. I think I can stop it if I can tell Henry the truth.'

'Anyway, it's a treat coming out to Rapstone Woods, much better than a trip round Tesco's.'

'Tell me what you know about Leslie Titmuss.' Fred tried to

make it clear that he hadn't stopped to discuss firewood. 'I mean, who *is* Leslie Titmuss?'

'Isn't he the Minister of something or other? I thought everyone knew that.' Dorothy moved further into the wood but her son followed her.

'Is he ... I mean, it would make father's will understandable at least.' Fred tried to put the suggestion as tactfully as possible. 'Is he related to us?'

'Related?' She had turned away from him, filling her sack. All he saw was the stooped back and the old, flapping mackintosh. 'Perhaps.'

For a moment Fred thought his mother was going to explain everything in a way that even Henry would have to accept but, when she straightened up and turned towards him, she was laughing. 'Perhaps in the Middle Ages, there was some romance between an old Lady Simcox and a medieval Titmuss! What a perfectly killing idea. I can't really imagine a medieval Titmuss, can you? A Titmuss in shining armour!'

'You know, if we can't explain it, they're going to say father was a lunatic.' Fred tried to persuade his mother of the seriousness of the situation but she was unimpressed. 'It won't be the first time,' she told him.

'No?'

'When he was a young curate in Worsfield I'm sure the Bishop called him a lunatic. Simeon got his revenge, of course. He never stopped writing the poor fellow letters.'

'But about Leslie Titmuss?'

'There.' Dorothy tugged her sack to his feet and left it there. 'I think that's about filled up now. As you don't seem to have anything better to do, Fred, could you put it into my motor? Try and be careful not to drop any out.' And after that she was answering no more questions.

The sitting-room at 'The Spruces' had seen a few changes since Leslie made his fortune: wall-to-wall carpeting, a giant colour telly, a velvet-covered three-piece suite and central heating were some of the new amenities. 'He wanted us to move into the big house, you know,' Elsie explained to Fred when he came to call.

'But George didn't think it right, me going back to live where I used to be in service. George gets funny ideas sometimes. He sits out there all weathers now, by that old bit of pond he put in when he retired.' Mr Titmuss the elder was visible, through the sitting-room window, with a rug over his knee like a traveller on a transatlantic liner. He seemed to be asleep. 'Of course, his memory's not what it was. He forgets they've retired him sometimes and worries about getting along to the Brewery. As though the accounts department couldn't do without him! What've you called in for, Doctor? We're not ill, surely?'

'No of course you're not.'

'Anyway, we usually have Dr Hardison.' Elsie looked at him with suspicion. 'Are you collecting for something?'

'I suppose you might say so. I'm trying to get hold of a few facts.'

'Oh yes.' Elsie had suddenly lost interest in the Doctor's visit.

'You know about my father's will?'

'The Rector was always so kind to our boy.' Elsie smiled. 'Isn't there going to be a court case? Between you and Leslie?'

'Between my brother and Leslie,' he corrected her. 'I don't want any court case. I just want to explain the will. Look, you knew my father when you were young.'

'Of course, everyone knew the Rector.' Elsie was non-committal.

'You probably got on well with him?'

'George had a quarrel with him once. It was about a statuette. Leslie gave the Rector one of our ornaments, and his father was quite angry about it. He thought the rector shouldn't have held on to it, you see.'

'Was that the only time?' Fred asked the question gently as though he were trying to diagnose a disease. 'That George was angry about my father?'

Elsie moved to the mantelpiece and touched the plaster figure of the lady from Cleethorpes. From this contact she seemed to derive the strength to conclude the interview.

'I shouldn't be answering your questions.'

'Shouldn't you?'

'Not with the court case coming on. You shouldn't be asking

them either. Anyway, if Leslie's had a bit of good luck over the will, he deserves it, doesn't he?'

'Does he?'

'After all he's gone through. After all *she* put him through, more likely. I must ask you to go now, Doctor. I've got George to see to.' She went out then to straighten the old man's rug. Fred left 'The Spruces' with none of his questions answered.

★ 29 ★

Worsfield Heath

One autumn evening, after the glory of Goose Green had been almost forgotten, and as the women of Worsfield Heath bedded down in their sleeping-bags, Charlie went to meet Gary Kitson in the Badger at Skurfield. She waited a long time in the almost empty bar, sitting on a stool, drinking whisky and refusing to notice the stares of the two boys in the corner. They had Youth Opportunity Programme jobs, short-term employment, sweeping floors in a Worsfield biscuit factory and had come to Skurfield where the only entertainment they found was in watching Charlie and whispering about her. At last, at very long last, the door was pushed open to admit Gary Kitson, his wife, Tina, and their friend Simon Mallard-Greene. This trio advanced to the bar, apparently for the sole purpose of buying cigarettes and announcing that the place was dead, had no one in it, and that they would try the bar of the Station Hotel, Hartscombe, in search of a bit of life. As Simon paid for the Rothmans King Size, and Tina just popped into the toilet, Gary apologized to Charlie. 'Sorry about tonight. Tina insisted on coming with. Know what I mean?' Yes, Charlie knew what he meant. Gary left with Tina and Simon in a bad mood. He was angry with his wife for coming out with them and angrier at her for having foolishly set out wearing a garnet brooch in the shape of a Maltese Cross, a glowing piece of sentimental value only. Gary had made Tina take it off before they got into the Badger.

When she was left alone again, Charlie went over to the YOPs and, in order to wipe the silly grins off their faces, bought them both a drink.

She was late getting back to Picton. She and the YOPs had gone to a pub up on the ridge without a bar, where Simcox bitter was poured out of barrels in a front room with a stained carpet, and a sofa leaking stuffing, a place where the licensing laws, if ever known, had been long forgotten. It was past midnight when she arrived home, her lipstick smeared and her step unsteady. She had some difficulty unlocking the front door. When she did so she was surprised to see a light on in Leslie's study and its door open. She couldn't get to the staircase without being seen by him as he sat at his desk, a red dispatch box open in front of him. He called out to her, and, as she couldn't escape him, she went into the room.

'I thought you were in London.'

'I'm sure you did.'

'What happened, no war this week?'

Leslie kept some decanters on a side table for visitors who came on constituency business, and she poured herself a drink. 'I had dinner alone,' he told her. 'Where've you been?'

'Out.'

'That's obvious.'

'I needed some air. I was driving. I walked a little.'

'Where did you have dinner?'

'Nowhere. I had dinner nowhere.'

'You do lie awfully badly, Charlotte.' He smiled at her in a way calculated, she thought, to unhinge her. She gripped her glass tightly. 'Of course, you're speaking as an expert,' she told him. 'Have you heard yourself on telly?'

'Your dinner consisted of too many whiskies and a packet of onion-flavoured crisps in some pub or other.' He was still smiling. 'With a lot of undesirables.'

'Who's undesirable?' She was angry and the words came flooding out of her. 'You mean with one or two *desirables*? Anyway, what's wrong with onion-flavoured crisps? I thought you got where you are on onion-flavoured crisps. And bottles of sauce. And meat teas. And money in the Prudential. Aren't you the good old working-class lad with his pint of Simcox Best and his heartfelt ambition to buy his own council house? That's who you taught me to admire. What did you call yourself? The backbone of England!'

'I wasn't talking about a handful of spivs.'

'Spivs? What a charming old-fashioned word! They wouldn't know what it meant.'

'They'd know what it is, though. Scrounging on the welfare. Everything on the never-never. Or dropped off the back of a lorry, more likely. Taking advantage of the rest of us. Taking advantage of you.'

'You've never been taken advantage of, have you, Leslie? You should try it some time. It's really quite enjoyable.'

'You're letting me down, Charlotte.' He got to his feet and stood over her. 'You're letting yourself down and Nicky.'

'Don't talk to me about Nicky!' She stared up at him. It was a look of contempt such as her mother might manage.

'I don't expect you to stay here, all by yourself. I know it's lonely.' He had put on the reasonable and disarming voice he employed at Question Time in the House of Commons.

'Do you?'

'Of course it is. But couldn't you get some sort of decent interests?'

'What a good idea! You mean the Women's Institute? Fruit-bottling? Flower-arranging? Evening classes in basket-weaving?'

'Something more serious,' he suggested. 'History, perhaps. Or politics.'

'Politics?' She looked at him, took a gulp from her glass and managed a slow smile. 'Is that what you'd really like me to do?'

On Worsfield Heath, once the site of the Annual Show, where stockmen paraded heifers and children in jodhpurs gritted their teeth and kicked their ponies towards the jumps, it was rumoured that the cruise missiles would come out at night to take exercise. The women hung their washing, their scarves and brightly coloured anoraks, even their plastic buckets and frying-pans, on the tall, wire fence, guarded the gates and waited in the hope of seeing and deriding these expeditions. They slept in tents until such shelters were removed by the police. Then they hung plastic sheets across the branches of trees and slept under their flapping cover.

They moved seriously, importantly, about their tasks, although occasionally cheerfulness or anger would break out and they would shout at the police on the other side of the wire; young men who would react with embarrassed silence or occasional obscene suggestions. Some of the younger guards said they would come out from behind the wire and ravish the women, converting them, by the joy of sex with an energetic military policeman, to a true appreciation of the value of nuclear missiles. It was a plan they had no intention whatsoever of putting into practice. The women asked the military police if they were on the side of death or life, a question the young men seemed to find difficult to answer.

Debates about the missiles, arguments destined to have no influence whatever on the course of events, continued. Leslie gamely agreed to attend one such discussion at Worsfield University. His ministerial Rover forced a slow passage through a crowd of angry students outside the Convocation Hall, and policemen reclined backwards on struggling bodies. He was met with a hailstorm of eggs, ink bombs and abuse through which he smiled as though with real enjoyment, perhaps feeling that being thrown into the river by Young Conservatives marked an important stage in his political development.

After he had been hustled into the hall, where his speech was to be made inaudible by boos and cat-calls, the demonstrating crowd drifted away, leaving one older than the rest, Charlie, who had come to join in the chorus of abuse. She stood quietly for a moment, pleased to have taken part in the event. Then she went back to Rapstone to call on her mother, whom she found in the conservatory, watering pots of begonias.

'You're keeping them on?'

'Well, they're here so I might as well water them. Is Leslie with you?'

'Leslie's never with me nowadays. That's the difference.'

'What do you mean, the "difference"?'

'Father was always here, always in Rapstone. You saw him all the time.'

'He was away in the war.'

'Yes. In the war. Of course he was.'

'Doing what he felt to be his duty. I expect Leslie's doing the same, isn't he?'

'Oh yes. Leslie and his friends who arranged to put a lot of wonderful new things for blowing up the world on Worsfield Heath. They're meant to make us feel safer.'

'Leslie understands, Charlie.' Grace watered on like a woman who had never felt any particular hostility to bombs. 'He's got all the information.'

'Oh yes. Leslie understands. It seems these things have to be exercised like dogs. They have to go out walkies.'

'Are you quite well?' Her mother put down her watering-can and looked closely at Charlie, as though she suspected her of being about to get some tedious childhood complaint like measles. 'What've you come here for? You never come here.'

'I just thought I ought to warn you, Mother, if you ever meet one on your way home from Bridge at the Hellespont Club. Don't try and pat it, that's all.'

'Do stop talking nonsense, Charlie! Leslie knows these things are necessary. For our protection.'

'Yes, of course. Leslie always knows best.' And, after a silence, she said, 'I'm sorry for you, Mother.'

'Sorry for me! Whatever for?' Charlie, quite unexpectedly, put out a hand and touched her mother's arm. 'Having to have a child you couldn't love.' She moved to the door, on her way out. 'Oh. By the way. That burglary you had, did you ever hear any more about it?'

'Nothing.' Grace was outraged. 'I asked your husband to mention it to the Prime Minister.'

'Terrible, isn't it?' – Charlie was going – 'how many old crimes go undetected.'

On Worsfield Heath, a small boy, about three years old, wandered away from his mother, who was washing up plates in a plastic bucket, and ran across a patch of ground, a small, bright figure in scarlet gumboots and a mac. Charlie, standing alone and lost, saw him trip and fall. She picked him up to comfort him. The child stiffened and cried in her arms and wouldn't be consoled. In a little while the mother came to claim him, looking at Charlie with what she felt was hostility.

Although she knew no one there and felt lonely and ridiculous, Charlie stood about near the fence, shouted when the others shouted, and later simply sat on the grass until daylight ended. Then the fires were lit, kettles started to boil, and Charlie finally found a group who appeared not to resent her. She offered round her cigarettes, and sat warming her hands on a mug of tea they gave her. Later on, a fat, grey-haired grandmother, bundled into layers of clothing, began to sing, and the others joined her.

> 'Early one morning before the bombs were falling
> I heard a woman singing in the valley below
> Politicians hate us
> They'd obliterate us
> Don't let them treat a poor world so.
>
> I will be gone and gone will be my true love
> Gone will be the trees in the valley below
> If we don't stop them
> Now let them drop them
> Don't let them treat a poor world so.'

The small children joined in enthusiastically, as though it were a nursery rhyme, and Charlie sang, also, with gratitude. She clapped in time to the music, and when a tall, thin-haired woman sat beside her and began to talk about her social security, Charlie was able to give her a few tips she remembered from her days in the Welfare. Then others began to talk to her, about the things they had shouted over the wire, and about the way they had run round the Heath keeping their tents out of the way of the police. They seemed excited and cheerful, as though they had got away from unwanted husbands to go on some illicit holiday. Only occasionally did they sit silent and brooding, staring into the ashes of the fire until someone threw on another branch and then they started to sing again. None of them seemed to have the slightest doubt of the usefulness of their mission.

It was almost midnight before they saw the police cars coming. The blue lights revolved and flashed and delivered reinforcements to line the road that led from the gates of the encampment. The women started to run away from the fires and out of the shadows. Some clung to the wire and tried to climb it, until they were pulled down. Others formed up on a length of road the police had left unoccupied. Charlie ran with them, not sure of what was going on, unaware of the rain which had begun as a few heavy drops sizzled in the camp fire and now ran down her cheeks and flattened her hair. The women she was with burst through a clump of bushes and came out on a tree-lined stretch of road. There they linked arms and formed a close, warm, wet barricade. They waited a long time, but remained in possession of the road. The police guard was still between them and the gates of the Air Force station.

At last they saw a high and distant light moving through the tops of the trees, illuminating the driving rain. It came on to shouts of derison from the unseen women and the hum of an engine. Her arms held on each side of her, Charlie peered into the darkness. Then there were two other points of light far down the road.

> 'And if one cruise missile
> Should accidentally fall . . .
> There'd be you and I my darling
> Left hanging on the wall . . .'

The women were still singing and she heard shouts of 'Walking the dog, darling?' and 'Daddy wouldn't buy me a bow-wow-wow!' Then the lights got bigger and seemed to rush towards them, becoming clear as the headlamps of police outriders. Charlie felt released by the women on either side of her as they scampered to the side of the road. She was alone on the wet, black surface, under the dripping trees, and, as the lights came towards her, she started to scream. It wasn't desperate or unconsolable, nor the sort of cry that needed a chapter of *Biggles* to calm it. It was louder, stronger, more like a battle call or a yell of triumph.

The policeman on the first bike, helmeted and oil-skinned, saw Charlie and swerved to avoid her. His heavy machine skidded on the wet surface, slithered helplessly out of control and crashed into her sideways, silencing her and blacking out her world which had become strangely and unaccountably happy.

'My wife was always interested in social work and the caring professions. One of her projects was to visit the women of Worsfield Heath. Many of them were experiencing marriage problems, and the strains and stresses of bringing up children in one-parent families. My wife's death occurred during one of such visits and was purely accidental.'

Leslie stood on the terrace of Picton House and read out a prepared statement to the news cameras, microphones and note-books of a group of reporters. The wind fluttered the sheet of paper in his hand and slightly dislodged his hair, exposing his bald patch. 'No blame of any sort can be attached to the officer whose motor bicycle skidded, and I wish him a speedy recovery. He was doing his duty and playing a vital part in the defence of our democratic way of life. My wife died carrying out duties which she also believed to be important.' He folded the paper and put it into his jacket pocket. 'Thank you. That's all.' Of course, it wasn't. Questions were hurled at him, and Leslie, an old hand by now, fielded them expertly.

'Minister. Did you approve of your wife going to Worsfield Heath?'

'Of course, I had the greatest admiration for her social work.'

'Are you saying she took no part in the demonstrations against cruise missiles?'

'My wife wasn't interested in politics. She was simply dealing with the women's social problems.'

'Minister. Was your wife a member of C.N.D.?'

'I can categorically assure you that she was never a member of that organization.'

'Minister.' Someone was holding a microphone up to Leslie's face. 'Can you explain why your wife was doing social work after midnight?'

'I'm afraid there isn't any "knocking off time" for the caring professions,' he explained with charm. 'Both of us were accustomed to work all the hours that God gave us.'

'So far as we can discover, your wife wasn't attached to any of the regular social services.'

'Charlotte wasn't a great joiner, she was impatient of bureau-cracy. Aren't we all? She was very much her own person.'

'The women at Worsfield Heath don't seem to have known her.'

'I don't suppose those women like to talk to you about their personal problems.' Leslie smiled at them all. 'I can't say I enjoy it much myself.'

'Minister. You don't *approve* of the Worsfield women?'

'I respect their sincerity,' he answered carefully. 'I think they're terribly misguided. But we're all after the same thing, aren't we? Peace in our time. Now, ladies and gentlemen. If that's all . . .' He was about to move back into the house when he was asked: 'What are your future plans?'

'To go on doing my job as long as the Prime Minister wants me.' A modest smile. 'And she hasn't said she doesn't.'

'Apart from that?'

'My life' – he was serious now and it was the last thing he said before he vanished into the house – 'will be devoted to the care and upbringing of our son.'

Some time after Charlie died, Simeon did what he didn't recommend to his parishioners. He went into Rapstone Church alone and knelt for a considerable time in prayer. Meanwhile, Leslie and his son Nicky faced each other from opposite ends of the dining-table at Picton House. Their meal seemed endless and they found little to say to each other. Nicky didn't want to talk about his school, and his mother's death was a subject both of them avoided.

★ 30 ★
Visiting

'I was expecting you to call,' Jackson Cantellow said. 'I've left countless messages at your surgery. Where on earth have you been?'

'Trying to find out the truth.' Fred had called as part of his own investigations. 'Not the sort of thing you would encourage, I suppose, as a lawyer.'

'We put our case. The truth remains a matter for the trial judge to decide.'

'You must know it though.' Fred looked at the large, complacent face opposite him and wondered if he did.

'*I* must?'

'You must know why he made that will.'

'How should I know that, Dr Simcox?'

'You were my father's solicitor for years.'

Cantellow got up and went to a filing-cabinet from which he took a tin of throat pastilles. He selected one with care and popped it into his mouth.

'Alas, we know so little of our clients. In any event, the Rector chose a Worsfield firm for his last, his extraordinary last, will.'

'There must have been a reason! You don't want to find it though, because you're arguing my brother's case.' There was something about the singing solicitor that made Fred understand Dorothy's rage. 'That's what he's paid you to do.'

'We have to live, don't we, Dr Simcox? I suppose some might say we both thrive on the sickness of mankind. That, I feel, would be an uncharitable view.'

'My father must have told you *something*.'

'Very little. I don't think he had a great deal of respect for lawyers.' Cantellow was starting to shuffle the papers on his desk. 'Wyebrow's statement,' he muttered and put it away. 'Ah, yes.' He found his place in the notes he'd been making. 'Perhaps you could throw some light on the Tom Nowt incident. We have these rather over-simplified headings.' He apologized. 'Your brother has seen photographs of Nowt and the Rector looking entirely friendly, but didn't your father suddenly forbid you to visit the man's cottage?'

'Not his cottage, his hut in the woods.' Fred thought about it.

'Wasn't *that* rather extraordinary?' Cantellow looked up. 'Your father was supposed to be so liberal, such a democrat, the friend of all the world. Did he object to you visiting any of the other cottages?'

'No. No, I don't think so.'

'A sudden irrational phobia, you see. That's the view of the psychiatrist we shall be calling. He turned against people for no reason.' Cantellow was delighted. 'I really would like to take a witness statement from you, Frederick. Couldn't you just help me by remembering all about the Tom Nowt incident?'

'Why should I want to help you?' Fred, having decided that he was only going to be asked questions and given no answers, got up and started to leave. 'Who do you want to help? Not Leslie Titmuss, surely?' Cantellow asked, pained, but Fred was gone.

After visiting the solicitor Fred had to call at Tom's old cottage. Mrs Mallard-Greene, in a state of high anxiety and rattling with tranquillizers prescribed by a London doctor, had rung up for a visit, although her trouble, as it turned out, was hardly of a medical nature. The problem was her son, Simon. His car had been stopped after midnight and in the boot the police had found a certain amount of hi-fi equipment, reported missing by a Hartscombe dentist. 'Thank God you've come.' There was a brandy bottle on the kitchen table, and an ashtray overflowing with stubs. 'I just couldn't sit in the queue of National Health patients with everyone looking at me, hearing them whispering about Simon. You know he's due up before the Magistrates?'

'Mrs Mallard-Greene, I'm a doctor. If you need a lawyer ...'

'Receiving stolen property! He was just selling a few bits and pieces he'd bought off some fellow in the Badger.'

'If that's true, no doubt he'll be triumphantly acquitted.'

'But if it isn't true?' Mrs Mallard-Greene had obviously considered the possibility.

'Well then ...'

'You've known Simon since he was a schoolboy. He was highly strung as a child and he's always been extremely nervous.'

'A nervous window-cleaner?' Fred was doubtful.

'I don't think Malley ever understood Simon. And there was the sibling rivalry with Sarah, of course. Simon was always trying to *prove* himself against a powerful father with a job in the B.B.C. All that achievement! I'm sure you could tell the Magistrates that it's a well-known psychiatric condition.'

'Receiving stolen property?' It wasn't a disease that Fred had learned about at St Thomas's.

'He needs help, Dr Simcox.'

'Don't we all?' Fred went to the window and looked out. 'I've told you, I think, that I remember this when it was old Tom Nowt's cottage.'

'I wish to God it was still Tom Nowt's cottage!' The words came from the bottom of Mrs Mallard-Greene's heart. 'It's supposed to be so restful in the country, so secure, so peaceful. You know what it's really like? Extremely dangerous! Simon's arrested, not for drugs, not for something like everyone seems to do when they're young, but for being mixed up in stealing! We'd all have been so much better off in Highgate.'

'Would you mind if I took a look at your woods? There used to be an old hut ...'

'Oh, that's gone. I think it went years ago. Malley was clearing up there when he was terribly rustic. You will tell them, won't you?'

'Tell them?'

'Tell the Magistrates about Simey. It's no use them trying to blame him really.'

'He'd better come and see me.'

'I knew you'd help us!' Mrs Mallard-Greene was enormously

relieved. 'Underneath that cold professional manner, I knew you'd understand.'

At the place where Tom Nowt's hut once stood Fred picked up part of a deer's antler, blackened by fire. He looked across to a patch of sunlight at the edge of the wood and heard children's voices. Still holding the antler, he walked towards them and found Dora Nowt, Tom's widow, Janet, his daughter, and three of his grandchildren, Janet's nephew and nieces. The children seemed to be searching in a patch of rough, chalky grass, a meadow isolated between two patches of woodland that had never been ploughed. Dora Nowt, an old woman now, saw Fred first.

'Dr Simcox. You don't remember me, do you?'

'Of course.' In fact he had hardly recognized her, and said, 'Dora Nowt,' hoping for the best.

'No one used to take much notice of me, nor of the wife. Tom was the one who had all the posh friends, wasn't he? Now, did you ever call on *me* when you was a little boy, did you? No, you come straight down to see Tom in his old hut.'

'It's gone.' Fred dropped the burnt and broken antler into a patch of brambles.

'Oh yes. They had it burnt down, them townees got our cottage now. Your mother must've been upset about that.'

'My mother?' Fred was surprised, but before he could pursue the matter, a small boy brought the spike of a picked wild flower and gave it to Dora. 'Is this it?'

'Yes, Tom. But you mustn't pick it. You mustn't ever pick those. I bring the children down here for the flowers,' she told Fred, and took the flower from her grandson to give it to him. 'There's the spider orchid. Hope it brings you luck. You don't see many of the late ones. You know where to find them, of course.'

'No, I never knew.' Fred had to admit it.

'The late one's rarer, very rare, Mrs Simcox told us.' Fred had no idea that Dorothy had played such a large part in the life of the Nowts. 'She used to visit Tom and me, and the children. She showed us the orchid places. Always very good to Tom and the family, was your mother.'

Janet had moved away with the children, who were finding snail shells and butterflies. Dora seemed talkative and anxious to make up for having been so much ignored by Tom's friends in the past. 'When Tom couldn't get work anywhere, just after the war when Lady Grace put the police on to him, no one would give him anything, not beating, not wooding, nothing! Well, your mother helped us out when Tom wanted to build his hut in the woods. We've always been grateful to her for it.'

'What about my father?' Fred looked at her and waited for an answer which might have been important to him.

'Tom used to see a lot of the Rector in the old days. He used to take up rabbits to him. After it all happened, well, he never used to see so much of your father, then.'

'After *what* all happened?'

'After Tom fell foul of her Ladyship. Well, Tom was never a churchgoer, was he? And your father was that busy putting the world to rights.'

Then the old woman was called by the children about the find of a bird's skull. Fred remembered that it was Thursday, his mother's afternoon for doing the flowers in Rapstone Church. He found her in the vestry, surrounded by vases, attacking long grasses and delphiniums and sprays of leaves with her secateurs. He held out his hand on which lay the warm and wilting spider orchid found by young Tom Nowt.

'You know what this is, Mother?'

'You don't surely?' Dorothy looked amused by him.

'A late spider orchid. Rather rare. You know where they grow?'

'I think so,' she admitted.

'By Tom Nowt's old hut. Why did you never tell us?'

'Tell you what?' She bashed the end of the long stem of a rose.

'When we were young. Why didn't you tell us where the wild orchids grew? Isn't that the sort of knowledge parents usually pass on to their children?'

'I didn't tell you' – Dorothy sounded reasonable enough – 'because you weren't in the least interested in that sort of thing. Henry was always writing the most unsuitable stories, from all I ever heard of them! And you were stuck up in your room drumming. I didn't think either of you cared tuppence for wild flowers.'

'I suppose the Nowts did?' Fred asked her. 'Brian and Annie

and young Janet Nowt and the grandchildren as they came along. You helped them find the orchids in their own wood?'

'We used to go for walks and find flowers. Before Simeon, well, before . . .'

'Before *what*, exactly?'

'Before he got so occupied.'

'You helped Tom Nowt' – Fred tried not to make it sound like an accusation – 'when he was down on his luck!'

'That was the sort of thing Simeon approved of.'

'But he didn't approve of Tom.' Fred was far from understanding. 'He was angry when I talked about the old hut. What sane reason did he have for that?'

'What *sane* reason?' His mother looked at him with mistrust.

'You'll have to tell me some time. And when I've found out I'll tell Henry he hasn't got a case.'

'Will you enjoy doing that?' She looked towards the open vestry door and seemed to welcome the sound of someone moving about in the church.

'For heaven's sake, Mother, help me to do what you want.'

'What I want? What I want is for everyone to stop asking me questions.' She went to the door and called, 'Mr Bulstrode!' Kev the Rev. trotted in, obediently, having been pinning up children's drawings in the Sunday School area.

'So good of your mother to go on helping with the flowers,' he told Fred. 'Of course, my wife should take it over if it ever got too much.'

'It's not too much, thank you.' Dorothy suddenly lowered her voice as though repeating a scandal. 'Do you know Dr Simcox was never confirmed?'

Fred was surprised that his mother should raise such a subject. The Rev. Kevin Bulstrode looked at him with sympathy.

'Simeon said the boys could wait to be done until they'd made up their minds. Freddie, it seems, never has.'

'Mother!'

'Couldn't you oblige him with some sort of ceremony for those of riper years? Why don't you have a nice long talk with Mr Bulstrode, Freddie?'

'I say, I'd love to have a go.' The new Rector was enthusiastic.

'I'm not your father, of course, so I haven't got all the answers. What's troubling you exactly?'

'A few unanswered questions.' Fred was looking at his mother.

'Oh, I do know.' Bulstrode was beginning to enjoy himself. 'Why the good, the omnipotent God allows wars and concentration camps, and children with leukaemia . . .'

'And that awful music in the Hartscombe supermarket!' Dorothy nodded, refilling her vases.

'I'm as much in the dark as you are,' Bulstrode admitted to Fred, 'I rather suspect. But if you could spare half an hour in my den, well, your dear old father's den, in the Rectory, we might sort of feel our way into the darkness together.'

'I'm afraid . . .' Fred started to retreat.

'Aren't we all? But talking does help sometimes. It really does.'

'I'm afraid I've got a lot more calls. Illness you know. There's a lot of it about.' When Fred walked past her out of the vestry, his mother whispered, 'Coward!'

So he left the church, passing the marble tablet which commemorated certain dead Fanners whose names were written under the scrolled bas-relief of a lady in Regency costume, weeping over an urn. The latest words to be carved were:

CHARLOTTE GRACE
23 MARCH 1940 TO 19 APRIL 1984
BELOVED WIFE OF THE RT HON. LESLIE TITMUSS, M.P.

and under the inscription stood a small, newly arranged vase of flowers.

Rapstone Manor was next on the list of visits, there was a problem, Miss Thorne had said with awe, 'about her Ladyship's leg'. Wyebrow led him upstairs and Fred let him know that he had heard that the butler was to be a witness in the coming Probate Action.

'I think that's a matter we probably shouldn't discuss, isn't it, Doctor?' Wyebrow smirked proudly, knowing that he had it in him to give a devastating account from the witness box of the late Rector on all fours, trumpeting like an elephant. 'But I'll be doing my best to help Mr Henry Simcox.'

'I'm not sure that's what my mother wants.'

'I shall be sworn to tell the truth, shan't I? On my Bible oath.' Wyebrow gave a pious sniff. 'I shall tell it all, exactly as I saw it happen.'

Grace had fallen while dancing. She lay on her bed in her lace nightdress and padded dressing-gown, showing more of her white, matchstick legs than was essential for the examination of a sprained ankle. 'Not bad, are they?' She squinted critically downwards. 'And they used to be absolute stunners!'

'Does that hurt?'

'Absolute agony! But better a little pain than no one ever coming to visit. You won't believe this, my dear, but during the war years, all through the Blitz, the Allied Forces would have queued up to touch that ankle.'

Fred started to bandage. 'I'm afraid you'll have to stop dancing for a while.'

'Dancing alone, ridiculous isn't it? I do everything alone now. I can't even have my grandchild to tea. Have you ever heard of such a thing? Nicky,' she told him, 'used to come bicycling over from Picton.' It seemed he enjoyed having tea up in Grace's bedroom, looking at the old photograph albums, the holiday snaps of St Moritz and Cannes and the Bahamas, and of the fancy dress parties at Rapstone when Simeon came dressed as Rudolph Valentino and Doughty Strove, not a pretty spectacle this, as Mae West. Nicky also showed an interest in Grace's old dresses, her Teddie Molyneux evening-jacket which was like a shower of gold coins and her Chanel sewn with pearls. Nicky said that in the Molyneux she looked like Danaë, a legendary figure who, it seemed, was someone he learned about at school. And then, just when they were enjoying themselves, Leslie had driven over, pushed his way past Wyebrow in the most loutish manner and sent his son home, with orders never to return again. He had also said things to her that could never be forgotten, told her, for instance, that Nicky had better things to do than spend his afternoons stuck in a bedroom going through Grace's moth-eaten wardrobe. According to Leslie the Fanner family had brought him nothing but ill luck – even Charlie would never have gone off on her dotty causes and died if she'd really cared for Nicky. He said other things which Grace didn't

335

repeat to Fred, among them that she was a lonely old drunk with no one but a child to bore with her stupid stories about useless people and the scratchy records she had once danced to. But she did tell him that she and Nicholas had made his career by putting up with his spotty presence when a young man at their dinner parties and trying to ignore the appalling noise he made when eating soup.

'I also remember him as a ghastly child screaming when the lights went out in our downstairs loo. He was scared out of his senses, perhaps that's what he's got against us. Anyway he told me that I was unsuitable company for young Nicky. Perhaps I was unsuitable company for old Nicholas too.'

Fred had finished strapping the old and fragile ankle: 'Rest and keep it up as much as possible.'

'You look extraordinarily like your father sometimes,' Grace told him.

'I'll give you some pain killers.' He scribbled a prescription. 'You mean I look mad?'

'Why should I mean that?'

'My brother wants to prove my father was insane. Your Mr Wyebrow's going to provide evidence in support of the proposition.'

'I shall give him the day off to go to court.'

'Because you believe it's true?'

'Because we all want to do in Titmuss, don't we?'

'Do we?'

'Of course. He wanted to join the family circle, we let him in and he kicked us in the teeth. He's got my grandson, in fact he's got it all. And your father's money!'

'How did he manage that, do you suppose, without any legitimate claim?'

'I'll tell you one thing, *Doctor* Simcox. That four letter Titmuss hasn't got a legitimate claim to more than a charge of shot up the backside of his awful little city gent's off-the-peg suiting!'

'I don't think he gets them off-the-peg any more.'

'Get that into your head, absolutely no legitimate claim of any sort. Is the operation over?'

'Quite over.' Fred was packing up his bag.

'Then it's time for the anaesthetic. You'll find it in the bathroom. We'll use toothmugs – Wyebrow looks disapproving when I ask him to bring up a drink. It's what I hate most about growing old, you're so at the mercy of the servants.'

'Most of my patients don't have that problem.'

'I shock you, don't I, Dr Simcox?' Grace was looking more cheerful. Fred went into the bathroom and came back with the bottle of champagne he found nestling in the washbasin. As he filled their toothmugs he happened to mention, 'What did you have against Tom Nowt?'

'Nowt?' Grace took a swig of tepid Moët. 'He was a poacher.'

'Is *that* what you had against him?' Fred was unconvinced.

'He got above himself. He tried to interfere with other people. He was the first symptom of the national disease that spread alarmingly and became Leslie Titmuss.'

'My mother got on well with him.'

'Your mother got on well with the most extraordinary people. Before you go, would you mind putting on a record?'

Coming downstairs, Fred saw Wyebrow waiting for him in the hall. The muted music reminded him of a children's party, years ago, with nervous Charlie, the birthday girl, being pushed down the stairs, and musical chairs, two children anxiously circling an empty seat and the manservant switching off 'You're the Top!' to decide the contest. When Wyebrow opened the front door, Fred paused to ask him a question, with no particular hope of an answer. 'You don't know why Lady Fanner quarrelled with Tom Nowt, do you? I mean, it can't have just been the poaching?'

'That's all, as far as I know. Bridget was in the house when he came up and they had their disagreement. She never talked much about it.'

'And Bridget's in "The Meadows",' Fred remembered.

'Oh yes. It's my opinion Bridget always took her work far too serious.'

'The Meadows' was Hartscombe's one small hospital, a modern glass and concrete square built in the expansive seventies, along the Worsfield Road, as an alternative to a theatre or an arts centre. It housed a few geriatrics and a labour ward. The Out Patients department came in useful for those who got kicked by their horses or maimed by chain-saws. Bridget, whose journey back to the hard days when she was first in service was now complete, had been there for almost a year. She was quite sure that the bleak and modern building was Picton House, where she worked as a young girl.

'You come for the weekend, Dr Simcox?' She smiled at Fred as they sat in the Day Room, among the potted plants, the repro-duction Van Goghs and the old people inert in front of *Play School* or tottering round on their Zimmers. 'I got up early to see to a nice bright fire in your bedroom.'

'You like it here, do you, Bridget?'

'Lovely old house, of course, but so inconvenient. The job I have finding the fireplaces! They've got to be done, you know. Mrs Smurthwaite's that keen on her fireplaces and her stair-rods. Well, I've always been particular about my stair-rods. But it's not too bad, I help with the silver in the butler's pantry. We get a few laughs sometimes, when Smurthwaite's up in her sitting-room.' Bridget giggled like a young girl. 'Having her little nap or is it her "nip", we wonders. There's rules though, and regulations. Everyone in by ten o'clock and no followers.' A nurse came with cups of tea for both of them. Bridget whispered, 'Old Smurthwaite doesn't half keep her running.' She sat smiling around her, her cup held closely under her chin.

'I was going to ask you. You remember Tom Nowt, I'm sure. Old chap who had a hut in the woods.'

'He doesn't come here no more.' Bridget sipped tea with great delicacy. 'Ladyship sent him away. Well, he had no right to do that.'

'Do what, Bridget?'

'No right to come round asking her for money.'

'You heard that?'

'I was on the stairs polishing up. I couldn't help hearing.'

'Of course not. Of course you couldn't help it. What did he want money for, do you remember?'

'Something he'd noticed in the park.' Bridget nodded.

'The park?'

'Tom Nowt'd seen something there and he wanted money for

it.' Course, Ladyship sent him about his business! Said she'd ruin him in the district. But it's my belief he was ruined already. He never came to any good, did he?'

'He died,' Fred admitted.

'There now! I knew he came to no good.' She drank her tea with satisfaction. 'Whatever made you think of Tom Nowt?'

'You've got everything you want, Bridget?' Fred didn't answer her question.

'It's just not easy to find the fireplaces.' Bridget shook her head. 'And that Percy Bigwell! I just don't want him to come here at all odd hours. Smurthwaite won't tolerate followers.'

Fred was shown out by the Matron. 'She seems to have trouble finding the fireplaces,' he told her. He breathed the air in the car park, free from the smell of old people.

'Well, of course she does.' The Matron was young, and kept resolutely cheerful. 'Seeing we're all central heating. Sometimes I think we ought to send her home but when I suggest it to her she cries and thinks I'm giving her the sack. How did you find her, Doctor?'

'Nothing wrong with Bridget's memory.'

'So far as it goes.'

'Yes.' Fred was thoughtful. 'I just wonder how far that is, exactly.'

A few days later, just as he thought he had finished his surgery, Miss Thorne told Fred of one last patient, and Simon Mallard-Greene came in, flopped into the patient's chair and spoke as though he were in a position to put a bit of welcome work in the Doctor's way. 'You're going to be my expert witness, aren't you? You'll be able to tell them about my childhood and all that.'

Fred had been given the Mallard-Greene notes. 'You come from a comfortably off, middle-class family and you got a good education. Isn't that your background?'

'I never got on with my father, know what I mean?'

'It's not a particularly obscure remark.' It was what Fred's father used to say.

'He was totally orientated to his career at the B.B.C. He was unsupportive to my mother and to us as a nuclear family.' Fred

looked at the pale, unsmiling Simon, whose fair lashes and eyebrows gave his face a curious look of nakedness; he seemed perfectly
qualified to act as his own social worker. 'I suppose, looking back
on it, I was doing it all as a challenge to my father.'

'Buying bits and pieces of stolen hi-fi equipment in a pub in
Worsfield?' Fred was trying to understand. 'To rival his telly
programme on *The Arts in Our Time*?'

'Basically, I did it that way because I wanted to get into
trouble.'

'Well, at least you've had one resounding success.'

'It wasn't really a crime at all, you see. It was more of a ...' He
looked suspiciously at Fred, who didn't seem to be paying him
serious attention. 'What's the matter?'

'I thought for a moment you were going to say a "cry for
help".'

'We're not having you on the National Health, you know.' Simon
frowned. 'We're doing this private. I don't think my father cares
what you charge within reason.'

'I'm sorry. I'm not a psychiatrist.' Fred stood up to terminate
the interview.

'All the same, I do reckon you'd better help me, Doctor.' Simon
smiled in a chilly and unattractive manner. 'I don't think it'd do
your family any good if you didn't.'

'My family?'

'Gary knows all about your family.'

Fred went back to his seat, and looked at the young receiver of
stolen property. 'Gary Kitson? What does he know?'

But Simon wasn't giving anything away. 'Things I don't suppose
you might like to have said around, that's all. He didn't tell me the
whole story. He would though. He's a good friend is Gary.' The
young Mallard-Greene was no longer giving instructions to his
medical man – what he said came out as a threat. 'I think you ought
to take Gary Kitson seriously, Dr Simcox. And you'd better be
there to help me, on my day in court.'

Fred finished the interview by promising to think about it and
then he drove over to Rapstone. He stopped at Gary Kitson's
cottage and saw the For Sale notice in the front garden. Then he
went over to the Baptist's Head, where Ted Lawless told him that

the Kitsons had cleared out suddenly and no one knew their address. 'Did he owe you money too, Doctor?'

'No.' Fred took a gulp of Simcox bitter. 'Information.'

★ 31 ★
Neverest

The Probate Action 'In the Estate of Simeon Simcox deceased, Simcox *v*. Titmuss' was fixed for a date in the spring and estimated to last two weeks. Leslie told his lawyers that there could be no question of a compromise – winning outright and getting possession of the Brewery shares was something he felt he owed his son. Henry was also prepared for a fight to the finish. Whatever the Brewery shares might be worth, and they had not yet had a final valuation, he was determined to see they remained in the Simcox family. Their attitude was extremely welcome to the lawyers on both sides, who saw a profitable piece of litigation ahead. Roderick Rose, Henry's junior counsel, was so sure of the number of refresher or daily fees that the case would provide that he organized a little dinner party in his Kensington house to which he invited his leader, Crispin Drayton, Q.C., their instructing solicitor, Jackson Cantellow, and, almost as an afterthought, their client, Henry Simcox. 'An informal get-together for your legal team,' Rose told Henry. 'Just so we can have the picture quite clear and get our "act together" as no doubt you show-folk would say.' The only ladies present were Roderick Rose's wife, Pamela, and Lonnie, who became enthusiastic about the food provided.

'Super sort of herby taste! Provençal?' she suggested. 'Well, I don't know. I can't help you about that actually.' Mrs Rose was vague on the subject, and offered no further information when Lonnie guessed, 'Oregano! You must have relied heavily on oregano.'

'And not a bad drop of Beaujolais either.' Henry sniffed at it. He had lately taken up the study of wine and could be quite boring on the subject.

'I thought something light' – Rose refilled his glass – 'if we're going to go over our plan of attack.'

'We have to face up to the fact' – Crispin Drayton as the Q.C. in charge of the case put an end to the gourmet chatter – 'that the burden will be on us to prove your father's insanity.'

'Did he *honestly* dress up in drag to give marriage guidance?' Pamela Rose was giggling with delight. 'Of course, I suppose that might be considered quite trendy nowadays.'

'I'm sure we all understand' – Drayton looked at his junior's wife with disapproval – 'that the late Rector's extraordinary behaviour must have been deeply distressing to his family.'

'Or is it a touch of tarragon I'm detecting?' Lonnie stared thoughtfully upwards as she masticated her *coq au vin*.

'Of course it was extremely embarrassing for all of us. My mother always tried to cover up for him,' Henry told his leading counsel. 'I think that's why she's refusing to get involved.'

There was a short, almost reverent pause of understanding, and then Rose struck a cheerful note. 'I think our medical evidence is pretty clear. Monomania, or an insane aversion to members of his family.'

'Or an insane affection for Leslie Titmuss?' Lonnie suggested.

'It went deeper than that,' Henry told them. 'What he suffered from was an insane optimism about the future of mankind.'

'With respect, we want to avoid generalizations.' Drayton struck a note of caution, but Henry launched yet another attack on the myth of happiness. 'He suffered from the great insanity of our times. The pathetic fallacy that we'll all get better and better, nicer, kinder, more concerned about each other, more disinterested, more enthusiastically against fox hunting, capital punishment and nuclear war. These idiotic beliefs took hold of him like a disease. They haunted him like strange hallucinations. In the end they corrupted his judgement and addled his brain. He became terrified of his own wealth and decided to unload it on the most undeserving object he could find.'

'You mean, he wished to leave you the gift of poverty?' Drayton was afraid they might be finding a motive.

'It sounds appropriately idiotic.'

'I'm not sure that I like that.' Drayton shook his head. 'It might have some sort of sound religious basis.'

'You're thinking of the eye of the needle?' Rose suggested.

'We're safer with psychotic monomania, and the specific acts of insanity we've pleaded in our defence,' Cantellow said firmly, and Drayton, who had formed the view that Henry would have to be kept on a tight rein in the witness box, found himself in complete agreement with his instructing solicitor.

'Can anyone manage a tiny bit more?' Pamela Rose invited them all, and Lonnie asked whether it would be frightfully piggy of her. Piggy or not, Mrs Rose took Mrs Simcox's plate to the service hatch, slid it open and said to whoever was on the other side, 'Just seconds for one, could we? If that's at all possible.'

Agnes knew that it would have to happen some time. She had been cooking for years in houses which Henry and Lonnie might have visited, doing dinner parties for publishers and actors, television producers and literary agents. She hadn't expected any such accident to occur when she was rung up and asked to cook by a barrister's wife, who insisted, much against Agnes's better judgement, on avocado with prawns and *coq au vin*, the whole to be topped up with chocolate mousse. She stood by herself in the kitchen full of knotty pine and blunt knives, a place which seemed to have been used merely for providing scrambled eggs to be eaten in front of the television, and tried not to listen to her ex-husband's voice which came booming through the open hatch as she spooned out another plateful for Lonnie.

'My brother Fred is either a natural traitor, or he's inherited our father's insanity. I can't really figure out his game. Apparently he's going round asking questions, behaving like some ridiculous kind of amateur sleuth.'

'Thank you so much.' Pamela Rose took the plate, the hatch door was shut, and Agnes could hear no more. In the dining-room, Lonnie tucked in gratefully. 'I really must ask you for the recipe.'

'To be brutally honest,' Pamela confessed, 'the recipe is the Flying Kitchen.'

'Oh really.' Lonnie seemed to have gone off her food.

'The person out there does rather look as though she despised our fitted cupboards, but she leaves it all surprisingly tidy. I can give you the telephone number, if you want it.'

'That's very kind, but I don't think we need it, do we, darling?' Her husband, in a voice of doom, agreed, 'We don't need it.'

When they were saying their goodbyes Henry asked to be pointed in the direction of the loo, went down a passage and, hearing the whirl of a washing-up machine, pushed open the kitchen door. Agnes was sitting at the wiped-over table, smoking a cigarette and finishing the Beaujolais.

'Did Fred send you here to spy on me?'

'You didn't *like* the wine, did you?' Agnes didn't seem to think his question worth answering. 'I mean talk about thin . . .'

'Fred's taken to playing detectives. How else did you get here?'

'I was rung up by Mrs Rose. She found me in the Yellow Pages. I didn't know they were part of your legal Mafia.'

'How much did you hear?'

'Not a lot. I was busy doshing out Lonnie's seconds.' Henry came and sat on the edge of the table then, swinging his legs, took a swig from her glass and tried to sound friendly. 'You ought to be on our side.'

'Ought I?'

'For Francesca. She'll benefit eventually if we end up with the Simcox shares.'

'You mean if you end up with them.'

'Money never did much harm to anyone, even Francesca.'

'How much should she take for having her grandfather found insane?'

Henry got up from the table. Before he left her he looked round the kitchen and sniffed. 'All those herbs!' he said. 'They smell of our old quarrels.'

The next day, Fred decided what to do about young Mallard-Greene. He drove to Tom Nowt's old cottage, outside which a window-cleaning van, with a ladder fastened to the top, was parked. Simon was at home resting between windows, drinking a cup of coffee and listening to Radio One. He switched off Wham and looked reassured when Fred told him that he was prepared to give evidence before the Magistrates at Simon's trial.

'You'll tell them I'm sick?'

'Oh yes, of course. You're suffering from a fairly well-known condition.'

'What's that, Doctor?'

'Greed. You were injected by a strong desire to make a quick wadge of folding money for some bits and pieces of hi-fi equipment you and your precious friend, Gary, nicked when you went cleaning windows. It's a condition which may lead to a term of close confinement, in serious cases.' For a moment Simon thought he was getting helpful medical advice. When he understood that he wasn't his colourless face set in a look of hatred.

'You want me to go in there and say what Gary knows about you Simcoxes?'

'What does he know?'

'I'll have to ask him, won't I?'

'You may find that hard. Mr Kitson seems to have deprived Rapstone of his company. Perhaps he didn't want to share the limelight with you in the Magistrates' Court.'

'His friends know where to find him.' Simon smiled in a way that wasn't in the least engaging. 'So why don't you go and get your act together? Court's in two weeks' time, Dr Simcox.'

About fifteen minutes after Fred had left the cottage, Simon Mallard-Greene went out to his van and looked up and down the road. He saw no one so he got in the driver's seat and started towards Hartscombe. Waiting in a side road, Fred saw the ladders moving above a hedge and set off to follow at a discreet distance. When he got to the town he took a route away from the main street and emerged to see the window-cleaner's van crossing the bridge to the London road. He waited for a couple of cars and a lorry to get between him and Simon and then went after him.

Up the long hill through the wood, past soggy autumn fields and in and out of villages, Fred followed the van to the motorway entrance. Simon, bucketing along in the fast lane, looked in his mirror and saw only the lorry behind which Fred was concealed. So they travelled towards London and at last Fred saw the van dive away down the Paddington exit. He followed, and, for a long minute, was stuck at a traffic light, which Simon had driven through. He was lost in Bayswater, and then he looked down a side road and saw the van turning into a mews. He went after it, parked in the main road, and saw Simon walking into the office of O'Leary's Mini Cabs, '24-hour service'. Fred waited and after ten minutes, Simon came out and drove out of the other end of the mews.

A pair of legs was sticking out from under a wounded Consul. A face peered out as Fred asked the man if Gary Kitson worked there.

'There isn't no Kitson, my friend.'

'Who owns this place?'

'O'Leary. Desmond O'Leary.'

'Where's he?'

'Ask her in the office.'

The office was small and dark, littered with spare parts; a plump girl sat clattering on an upright typewriter with her back towards the door. Above her a brown and naked calendar beauty stood on some faraway beach, sand on her buttocks, advertising brakelinings.

'Mr O'Leary's not here today. I'm sick of telling everybody.' Then Tina Kitson turned round. 'Dr Simcox!'

'Everybody? You mean Simon Mallard-Greene or the police?'

'I mean everybody.' Her eyes were red and puffy. 'He doesn't tell me anything.'

'I'm sure he doesn't.'

'I'll let him know you want him. *If* he happens to call.'

'I think he's got something I might be interested in.'

'They all say that. I'm sick and tired of it. Honestly I am.'

Fred moved to a cluttered mantelpiece over a broken gas fire. He saw a business card, clean and white, among the crumpled bills and notes for drivers. He picked it up and read the name of the Neverest Detective Agency and an address in Fetter Lane.

'You're trying to have him traced?' He showed Tina the card.

''Course not! I'm not as worried as all that. That's a guy who called. Gary was here then.'

'What happened?'

'I don't know, do I? How could I know?'

'Try and remember.'

Tina looked at him, and decided to do her best. 'I think Gary

347

sold the man something. Did some sort of a deal anyway. He seemed pleased. Anyway I haven't seen much of Gary since then.'

'Sold him what?'

'I don't know do I?' Tina was becoming angry and near to tears again. 'Could have been an old banger for all I know. Could have been anything.'

'Yes.' Fred put the card carefully back on the dusty mantelpiece. 'Yes. I suppose it could.'

As he left, Tina went back to pounding the old typewriter, writing letters for a business her husband had apparently deserted.

Fred couldn't find a parking meter, so he squeezed his car into a space between two vans in Fetter Lane. He pushed his way into a dim hallway, went up three floors in a groaning lift, and found himself in the outer office of the Neverest Detective Agency: 'All Inquiries Undertaken. Complete Confidentiality Guaranteed'. 'I'm after a detective,' Fred explained to the depressed secretary who was knitting at her desk, clearly short of work. 'I think a client's gone in.' 'Yes,' Fred told her, 'me.' He opened the door into the inner office. 'Of course,' he said when he got inside. 'I should have guessed.'

It was a small room. On the wall a group photograph of the boys at Knuckleberries, taken in the Summer Term of 1948, hung beside a certificate of affiliation to the Private Inquiry Agents Association. Arthur Nubble was sitting behind the desk, eating a sandwich, drinking a packet of milk through a straw and reading the *Tatler*.

'Oh, hullo Simcox Minor. I thought you might be turning up.'

'The last time I saw you, you were a journalist.'

'Bit of a cover that, actually.' Nubble smiled modestly. 'Of course, I do manage to pick up a little gossip from time to time. Some of it finds its way into the papers.'

'And some of it you keep for your clients?'

'Well, that's the name of the game nowadays, isn't it?'

'What is?'

'Information.'

Fred sat on a rickety office chair and wondered how many games Arthur Nubble had known the name of since he ran a delicatessen in an old double bass case at school. Now, he supposed, it was divorce cases, the following of errant husbands, industrial secrets and, perhaps, wills.

'Who's your client in the estate of the late Simeon Simcox?'

'Titmuss *v.* Simcox and Others?' Nubble seemed to enjoy the formality of the title.

'Words to that effect. I suppose you're acting for Leslie Titmuss. Didn't we meet at his home?'

'I say, steady on.' Nubble looked hurt. 'You're doing me an injustice. Anyway, I understand Titmuss is a bit of a shit.'

'They speak of him as a future prime minister.'

'That's probably why. No, I wouldn't act for Titmuss. One has a certain loyalty. After all, we were all at Knuckleberries together.'

'All three of us.'

'You and I. And your brother, of course.'

'Henry!' Fred stood up. 'He hired you to check up on Leslie Titmuss?'

'And to collect evidence for his case. Yes.'

'And to stop me collecting evidence which might make his case impossible. Is that what Henry asked you to do?'

'I really don't know what you're suggesting, Simcox Mi.'

'There is a bit of evidence. I'm not at all sure what it is, except that it throws a good deal of light on our family circumstances. An appalling youth called Gary Kitson got hold of it by some means or other, probably theft, and you've just bought it from Gary. I don't imagine it's anything that my big brother thinks I ought to know about.'

'Your brother hasn't said anything about it.' The Neverest detective appeared to be enjoy a joke.

'Hasn't he?'

'In fact, we haven't had time to discuss it.'

'Have you not? So it's a piece of virgin evidence untouched by the interested parties.'

'If it exists.'

'And if it exists I'd like to see it.' He held out his hand. 'Please.'

Nubble didn't answer at once. Then he said, 'You never got on with Simcox Major, did you?'

'Not especially.'

'I took to you at school, you know. I wanted you to be my friend. None of the others had much time for me.'

'I remember.'

'You told me you were treacherous. Was that true?'

'Possibly,' Fred admitted. 'Treacherous to Henry.'

'Why?'

'My father may have had his failings, plenty of them. But he wasn't insane. I'm never going to let that be said. Never!'

Nubble looked at him and then stood up. Panting slightly he went to a battered safe in a dark corner. After searching for his keys he unlocked it and modestly produced a couple of sheets of blue notepaper, a letter that Grace kept at the bottom of her box of cheaper jewellery among other objects of sentimental value only.

'What are you offering me for this?' He held it to show the address printed on the first sheet.

'Money?' Fred supposed. 'Isn't that the name of the game nowadays?'

★ 32 ★

Faith Unfaithful

The Miners' Strike, the prolonged war over dying pits and dying towns and villages, struck only a small echo in Hartscombe. There was a little posse of pickets outside Simcox's Brewery and placards which read 'Hands Off Our Beer', 'Save 300 Jobs', 'We Demand the Right to Work', and even 'Drink to the Workers!' From time to time a number of police and pickets enjoyed a brief push as some anxious secretary tried to get in or out. It had been Christopher Kempenflatt's scheme: unlike Magnus Strove he had recovered his fortunes since Leslie dropped a dying Hartscombe Enterprises on them and his eye finally lighted on the large Brewery site by the river in Hartscombe. What a waste of space it was, and how much more profitable might the area be if it were turned into a shopping precinct. Kempenflatt saw a pedestrian walk-way, a fine selection of shoe shops, music centres, and boutiques, all paying high rents and employing far fewer people than were needed to brew a beer which, in any event, was losing ground to cans of imported lager in the self-service winery.

Trafford Simcox, a thin, anxious and good-natured cousin to Fred and Henry, had been brought up to be Chairman of the Brewery. He sat in the office which had seen generations of Simcoxes, men who no doubt thought that their ales would last as long as the river which flowed past the windows, and worried a great deal. He worried about the loss of jobs, the destruction of the old buildings and the departure from the world of Simcox Best Bitter. Yet the offer was one his shareholders could hardly refuse, and, in the absence of Best Bitter, it might keep him and his family in champagne for the rest of their natural lives.

'There's only one slight complication,' he finally had to admit

351

to Christopher Kempenflatt. 'The law-suit going on about the old Rector's shares.'

'Who do we have to buy them from?'

'I suppose that will depend on the result of the case.'

'I may have to deal with Leslie Titmuss,' Kempenflatt supposed gloomily. He was looking down into the yard, where a disturbance of a minor sort was going on. Leslie's father had arrived at the gate, apparently suffering from the delusion he still worked there. 'You've got to let me in,' he told the pickets. 'There's things I've got to do in Accounts.' Some of the younger men told him to get lost, and one, who had no idea who George was, called him a scab. Den Kitson, bored on the picket line, was relieved to see Elsie arrive in her car and take the retired pillar of Accounts home to tea. 'He's been retired,' Den explained to the others. 'For donkeys' years.' 'Yes,' Elsie said, as she shepherded her husband away, 'and sometimes he forgets all about it.' 'All right, Dad,' they shouted as he left, 'call again, when the dispute's over.'

When they had finished tea and George had called it tasty, he went to the mantelpiece in 'The Spruces' and picked up that lady from Cleethorpes his boy had once given to the Rector. 'It's a while since we went on that holiday.' Elsie was clearing away.

'Leslie shouldn't have done it. He was all take was the old Rector.'

'The boy meant no harm. Leslie was always made welcome up at the Rectory.'

'I had to go and speak to the Rector about it.'

'You did, George. We all remember it clearly. It was the only time in his life Leslie took anything to which he wasn't strictly entitled. We all remember when you went up to speak your mind to Mr Simcox.' Elsie took the ornament from George and put it carefully back on the mantelpiece. 'You came home with our ornament in your pocket and there it's been, safe and sound, ever since.'

'The Rector always got that much more than what he was entitled to.' The old man yawned, thinking that it was time for Bedfordshire. 'It's been a worry to me.'

*

352

Faith Unfaithful

'If you win this wretched case, I'm going to have to buy the old Rector's shares from you.'

'And if I lose, you'll do a better deal with Henry Simcox?'

'At least he's a human being. He doesn't live entirely for money.'

'If I win, I shall charge you top price. It's the least I can do for Nicky.' Leslie looked at his watch. He saw no point in continuing the interview with Kempenflatt, who had called, without warning, one weekend at Picton House.

'Which leads me to wonder . . .' Kempenflatt showed no sign of leaving.

'To wonder what?'

'If you should be fighting this case at all, a sordid sort of legal scrap about the will of a well-known constituent. There are those in the local Party who think . . .'

'That it doesn't look good?' Leslie smiled at the simplicity of the Kempenflatt approach.

'Exactly!'

'Like rented dinner-jackets' – Leslie's smile turned to anger – 'and made up bow-ties and meat teas and string vests on summer holidays. I don't give a damn how it looks.'

'Perhaps I ought to warn you, you're a little more vulnerable these days.'

'You mean since I became a Minister?'

'I mean since you married one of the Worsfield peace women.'

'Charlotte was never one of them,' Leslie answered quickly. 'You read my statement to the Press.'

'Oh, everyone read that.' Kempenflatt got up to leave. 'The trouble is not everyone believed it. Underneath their sensible hats and blue rinses, some of our dear Conservative ladies have got remarkably suspicious minds.'

When Fred left the Neverest Agency, he experienced a feeling of great elation. It was the end of a quest, a task he had set himself. Something had been achieved, finished with, done. The past was no longer a mystery and its solution was far from the warring contentions of Henry and Leslie Titmuss. When he walked out into Fetter Lane, his face was hit by rain. Peeling the wet parking ticket off his windscreen, he was prey to a sudden temptation. He

353

might crumple it and the letter he had bought, throw them into the gutter and keep the secret he had discovered to be shared only by himself and the other two who must surely know it. Henry and Leslie could keep on battering each other in blind ignorance, and he would go quietly about his practice, knowing what they would never learn, and might, in any event, never clearly understand.

He drove into Fleet Street, crawled with the traffic down the Strand, peering out between his windscreen wipers, and, when he reached the park, found, almost to his surprise, that instead of turning north towards Paddington, the motorway and Harts-combe, he went on towards the Fulham Road. When he got to Agnes's flat, he sat for a long while in the car before he decided to ring the bell. Even then he decided she wasn't in, and was turning away when the buzzer went and her disembodied voice invited him up.

'I knew I couldn't escape cooking Lonnie's dinner for ever.' He had come to tell her of a revelation, but she had immediately started on her own story, half in outrage, half in amusement. It seemed she owed him an explanation for waiting on Henry. 'Do you think it's funny?'

'I suppose it is.'

'Your brother wasn't at all amused. He came into the kitchen to accuse me of spying on him.'

'Spying? Whatever for?'

'For you.' He felt unexpectedly flattered by Henry's accusation, and by the fact that Agnes accepted his visit as part of her day, with no particular motive behind it. She was making a steak and kidney pie to drive off to that night's dinner party, cutting out a pastry flower to decorate the top. 'What've you been doing anyway?' she asked him.

'More or less what your father did. Oh, and I've started to play again with the Stompers.'

'Aren't they getting a bit old by now?'

'All jazz players are getting a bit old. We've got another gig at the Badger in Skurfield. We might be a bit less pure this time. Perhaps they'll only throw tin cans during "St James' Infirmary".' She had finished decorating and was wrapping the pie in silver foil, ready for the journey. 'Why don't you come?'

'To hear you play the drums?'

'You haven't for a long time.'

'Aren't you any better at it?'

'Come and see.'

'Would you like coffee?' She put the pie into a cardboard box with other silver-wrapped courses. 'Or a drink or something?'

'A drink or something.'

There was a bottle of white Rioja open in the refrigerator. She splashed some into tumblers and they drank. 'Why did Henry think I might want you to spy for me?' asked Fred.

'He said you were playing at being a detective. Is that true?'

'It was. I've finished now.'

'Good.'

'I've got the truth.' He tried not to sound triumphant.

'What are you going to do with it?' She was sitting at the kitchen table, in front of her drink, her lighter and packet of cigarettes, prepared for a chat. He sat opposite her and thought clearly for the first time in his life about his father and felt a surge of affection for the man who had often seemed remote and too involved in the simple solution of world problems to notice his immediate family. And, as he understood Simeon, he knew he couldn't let his brother go on publishing his misunderstandings to the world. 'I'm going to stop Henry making out our father was an idiot,' he told Agnes. 'At last I can shut him up.'

'Is that what you really care about?'

'What?'

'Shutting up your brother.'

'No. Of course it isn't. But he needs to be given a little truth, after all these years.'

'What sort of truth exactly?'

Fred took out his wallet, extracted the folded blue letter and handed it to her. Agnes took it reluctantly and, for a while, didn't care to look.

'Please. I want you to see.'

She started to read and he was glad that she was the first person to whom he had shown the letter. After a while she looked up at him. 'Careful,' she warned him, 'how you go about it.'

*

When Dorothy had moved out of the Rectory she had left a lot of bits and pieces from the study, books and papers, articles of no particular value, and promised to pick them up sometime. She had never done so and Kev the Rev. had often telephoned Fred to say he had a tea-chest full of Simcox memorabilia in his attic, and what would be a convenient time to call for it. Fred, wondering if he really had room for dozens of Left Book Club volumes and Fabian tracts, had put off this transfer of property but now he decided that it was a convenient moment.

The Reverend Kevin was on his way out when Fred arrived at the Rectory. 'Twenty-four-hour vigil in Worsfield Cathedral for better industrial relations.' He impishly displayed a paperback of *The Dogs of War*. 'Jolly naughty of me, I know, but these occasions can get deadly boring. Have you come for a good old bash at the problem of evil?'

'No, I told you, for my father's bits and pieces.'

'Oh, right. I'm sure Monica'll show you. It's Dr Simcox, darling!' Kevin Bulstrode shouted back through the front door. 'Can you let him have the stuff in the attic?'

Fred went past his old bedroom. Through an open door he saw a pile of clothes on the floor and a child's unmade bed. He went up a ladder to push open a trap-door, and climb into the dark, flyblown cavern above the rafters. He switched on a naked, dangling light bulb and recognized some of his and Henry's old toys, a tailless rocking-horse, toy guns, an old cricket bat and a box of dusty Christmas decorations. And there was his first, childhood drum set. He worked the pedal and produced a sagging, hollow thud. Then he saw the tea-chest with the bust of Karl Marx in a nest of pamphlets. When he got it home he found even more treasures, pipes, tobacco jars, faded posters, petitions for forgotten causes together with African carvings and Indian gods which had been presents from politicians, peace groups and bishops in distant lands. At the bottom he found an old 78 record; he looked at the label and was not particularly surprised. He took it out of its envelope and blew off the dust, then he adjusted his record-player and put the old disc almost reverently on the turntable. Karl Marx's bust was lying on its back, staring at the ceiling with sightless eyes, as Pinky Pinkerton's piano tinkled and his soft voice began to caress the old Cole Porter number 'You're the Top!'

Once more Mr Bugloss had bought champagne. After so many years, after so many hopes and disappointments, a city consortium had put together a deal with a Canadian, an Italian and several Germans, and the first day of principal photography, the day when everyone hoped to get paid for *Pilgrims*, was fixed. 'I shall be there,' Henry told him, 'provided it doesn't clash with my giving evidence in court.' 'My dears' – Mr Bugloss raised his glass in Henry's flat – 'good luck to our dear movie, and all who sail in her! She has a great script. May she receive twenty Oscar nominations, and make us all rich and famous. Jack Polefax must be kicking himself he never took up his option. Remember when we first had the idea? In that restaurant on the Coast, and you' – he looked at Lonnie more in sorrow than in anger – 'you disappeared into the john, and never came out again.'

'That was his other wife.' Lonnie was displeased.

'Of course.' Mr Bugloss smiled, not at all put out. 'And she walked home. I mean, his other wife walked.'

'Agnes wasn't dull, was she? You couldn't say that about her.' The phone began to ring on Henry's desk at the other end of the room, and he went to answer it. 'Not dull!' Lonnie muttered when he had gone. 'He says that to me!'

'She *walked*!' Mr Bugloss was still amazed, after so many years. 'About thirty blocks along Sunset. I can bear witness to that ... er, Mrs Simcox.' Mr Bugloss played for safety. 'You've been right behind your husband through eight re-writes of *Pilgrims*. It's paid off, you see? We've got the end money guaranteed.'

'And what do *I* get for always supporting Henry?' Lonnie asked him. 'For always being on his side against everyone? He tells you, "There was one thing to be said for Agnes, she was never dull"!'

'That was Fred. He wants us to come down to Hartscombe and see our mother.' Henry returned from the telephone with other things to talk about.

'See Dorothy?'

'He thinks she might be ready to make a statement.'

'Is Fred on our side now?' Lonnie wondered.

'I honestly don't know what he's up to now. I've got to find out. Do you want to come?'

'Oh, yes, I'll come.' Lonnie included Mr Bugloss in her sigh. 'I'll be there supporting you, naturally I will.'

On the day that Henry and Lonnie were to come down to Hartscombe, George Titmuss, temporarily eluding his wife, presented himself once more at the Brewery gates and talked to Den Kitson, who was again on picket duty. He still wanted access to the accounts department. 'Mistake to retire,' he said, 'Mother doesn't want me at home, get under her feet all the time, nothing to do but sit out in the garden. 'Course, we always paid the old Rector his wages.' He went on talking at random. 'Not that he did a stroke of work for it, other than marches and pinching other people's ornaments. It's the pre-war balance sheets, that's what needs to be looked at.'

'You mean you want a look round your office for old times' sake?' On that basis, and although it was an official dispute, the pickets were persuaded to let George in as a tourist for a trip down Memory Lane. Later that afternoon, Trafford Simcox, working on the final details of the Brewery sale, was disturbed by sounds from the deserted accounts department. He went along the corridor to find old Titmuss surrounded by dusty ledgers, annual statements and balance sheets which hadn't been looked at for years. 'I'm not blaming you, Mr Trafford.' George spoke calmly, as though he had been expecting the interruption. 'It was done in your father's time. It was done in Mr Pym's day. I think it was kindly meant at first, and then it got written up wrong. I shouldn't have passed it, not when it was written up like that. It's got to be put right some time.'

'What's got to be put right, George?' Trafford Simcox, forever anxious, sat down beside George Titmuss and had it explained to him, at considerable length.

'Young Dr Fred's still out on his rounds,' Mrs Beasley, Dr Salter's old housekeeper, and now Fred's, told Henry and Lonnie when they arrived at the surgery. 'He wants you to go on up.' In the living-room Henry wondered what you had to do to be called 'young' in middle-age. 'Never move on,' he suggested to Lonnie. 'Stay where you're planted, and like Fred, you can be called "young" till the day you die.'

'He hasn't put much of himself in here, has he?' Lonnie looked round at Dr Salter's old furniture. 'Except the drums.'

'It's the room of a man totally unaware of his surroundings,' Henry agreed. 'Or of a man pretending to be totally unaware of his surroundings,' he added. 'That's the impression Fred wants to give; he's very devious.' He helped himself and Lonnie to drinks from the sideboard. 'There's absolutely no limit to the deviousness of little Freddie. For instance, he'd like us to believe that he's quite uninfluenced by the thought of money. It's dishonest. People who say they don't care about cash are usually lying, or they're after something far more unpleasant.'

'Such as?'

'Moral superiority,' Henry decided. 'The principal vice of our father.'

'I thought your father was meant to be mad.' Lonnie had learned to answer back a little, over the years.

'That too, of course.' Henry defended his position. 'Madness was his other vice.'

Fred came in then and apologized for being late. One of the Hunt boys, up near Mandragola, had got his hand caught in a tractor belt; it had given the Doctor a chance to do a bit of stitching.

'Jolly considerate of the Hunt boy to get his hand caught then. Is Mother coming here?'

'No. But I thought we should meet here first. At Sunday Street the drink flows like cement.'

Lonnie wondered where in the evening's events dinner would be fitted in. Her heart sank when they arrived at Dorothy's house and her mother-in-law greeted them with 'I really don't know why you should want to come all this way. I'm not putting on a dinner party you know.' As they went in and disposed themselves round the living-room, a place which in its own small way preserved the Rectory's reputation for howling draughts, Dorothy expanded on the subject of her not providing food. 'Simeon and I always avoided dinner parties. I started to notice the way people eat. I never listened to what they were saying then, I just watched them chewing or trying to slip food into their mouths when they thought you weren't looking, or, worse still, picking their teeth furtively with a little finger-nail. Once you notice people eating it's an end to dinner parties.' She looked round at her visitors with amusement. 'All the family!'

'I suppose I'm a bit of an outsider.' Lonnie was hungry.

'Yes.' Dorothy looked at her thoughtfully. 'Still, you go with Henry, don't you? You always go with Henry.'

'Perhaps a cup of coffee?' Henry suggested. He looked at Dorothy who didn't move, so Lonnie got up and went out to the kitchen.

'Mrs Nowt ... You know old Dora Nowt lives in Hartscombe now? Anyway, she brought me some elderflower wine. I do wish she wouldn't,' Dorothy whispered confidentially. 'It's particularly revolting.'

'Fred told us' – Henry called the meeting to order – 'that you felt ready to make a statement.'

'A statement? Good heavens, what about?'

'About our father.'

'I think what Henry's looking for,' Fred told her, 'is some sort of explanation.'

'Oh, dear. I do hope an explanation won't be necessary.'

'It wouldn't be if Henry decided to give up the case.'

It was, Fred knew, an impossible request. The truth would have to be shared and he supposed it was better done in the sitting-room in Sunday Street than in a law court, with a judge writing it all down and barristers to ask questions and throw doubt and newspapers to report it and old men in macs, wandering in off the street for the sake of the central heating and the free entertainment, to hear all about it. All the same he avoided looking at his mother, and came to the matter obliquely, by way of the tea-chest in the attic.

'Perhaps I should tell you what I did this afternoon,' he said. 'I got a box of our father's bits and pieces out of the attic in the Rectory. You know what I found?'

'Not another will?' Henry had little hope of it, all Simeon's papers had been searched by the solicitors before they were stored away.

360

'More important than that. I found a gramophone record.' Fred looked at Henry, still turning away from his mother. 'Down at the bottom of the box was Pinky Pinkerton's rendering of "You're the Top!" If you remember, it contains the immortal line "You're the Top! You're the Lady Gra – ace!" It's something Grace Fanner plays to everyone. It even got played at children's parties. She gave a copy of it to our father.'

'What on earth's the point of bringing us here to tell us someone gave Simeon a gramophone record?' Henry acted superhuman patience.

'There would be no point at all if only you hadn't said our father was insane.'

'Go on then, what do you want to have said about him?'

'He wasn't in the least mad. He wasn't a saint either, not a saint at all. He was a man, like anyone else, who falls in love and can't possibly explain it.'

'Of course, his behaviour was completely irrational.' Henry was triumphant, and then he said, more quietly, 'Who are you suggesting he fell in love with?'

'Do you want to tell them?' Fred looked at Dorothy, but she offered him no help, only murmuring, 'I don't see why any of these things have to be said.'

'Some things have to be.' Fred stood up. Now the time had come he felt tired, as at the end of a long day's work with the most difficult patients still to treat. 'I suppose it was about the beginning of the war, before the bomb hit the old Café de Paris, when the late lamented Sir Nicholas was doing his bit in Bognor. I suppose it was the time Charlie was conceived.'

'Charlotte!' Henry was genuinely puzzled.

'Oh yes,' Fred told him, 'she's one of us. She *was*. She was really the problem, wasn't she, Mother? She wasn't beautiful. She wasn't interested in clothes. She wasn't even a snob. So Grace hated our father's child.'

'It can't possibly be true!' Henry looked at Dorothy, angrily, accusingly, as if whatever had happened must have been her fault. She started to speak then, as though released by his disbelief, and the words, held in so long, came flowing out of her. 'That's why he always felt so guilty. Poor Simeon. He was guilty about

361

practically everything, living off shares in Simcox's Brewery.' She smiled. 'Just like any other capitalist, not having sufficient faith in Socialism. Not believing enough in God, and then, of course, having a child he couldn't acknowledge, who got no love from her mother.'

Lonnie chose that moment to come back from the kitchen with a tray of coffee and biscuits, cheerfully announcing, 'It's only Instant.' The others seemed not to notice her, and Dorothy didn't stop talking. 'And having a secret from me, I suppose. Of course, it couldn't stay a secret forever, because of Tom Nowt. I'm afraid Tom saw Simeon and Grace, oh, I don't know exactly where. He wasn't bad you know, Tom was never bad. He probably wouldn't have said anything if that stupid woman hadn't gone after him about his poaching. She complained to Nicholas so that any stories Tom spread about her could be called malicious slander. In the end, Tom never told Nicholas. The only person he told was me. Perhaps he thought I should know about it. Anyway, we were friends. We both knew about the woods. I used to show his children where to find the spider orchid. He told me about Simeon, and I persuaded Tom not to tell anyone else. I gave him a bit of help for his hut for instance, things like that. I really don't think I could have managed it on my own but I did have a friend.' Lonnie bit audibly into a biscuit. Dorothy noticed her but went on telling them. 'A friend to advise me. He was a sensible man. Much more sensible than Simeon, of course. And he was kind to me. He knew that Simeon might want to pay for his ... his adventures in the end. So Dr Salter left me this little house.' She looked round the room, smiling. 'I must say, it's a good deal easier to dust than the Rectory.'

There was a long silence. Henry was not prepared to give up without a struggle. 'None of that explains why Simeon could possibly have wanted to benefit Leslie Titmuss.'

'Poor Leslie!' Dorothy was still smiling. 'He was never a really happy child. Of course your father must have been delighted when Leslie married Charlotte, and there was someone to look after her. It was a load of guilt off his mind. But then Charlie became unhappy, and of course she died. Simeon thought perhaps she'd killed herself and it was all his fault again. He had to pay a debt to her and to her child. So he left his money to Leslie Titmuss.' She looked round at them all, at Henry silent and Lonnie, apparently frozen, holding up her half-eaten biscuit. 'It wasn't entirely his idea,' Dorothy explained. 'I thought that if he left the money to Leslie, Nicky would benefit. I'm sure he will.'

'*You* thought . . .' Henry couldn't believe it.

'It made Simeon feel better, about all the wrong he imagined he'd done to Charlie. It was such a little thing, after all. He knew you'd be all right. "Henry'll be all right," he said. Only that character you put on, I suppose it's some sort of reaction against your father, pretending to be a crusty old English blimp; Simeon was afraid that'd grow on you and you'd be trapped in it forever – if the wind changed or something. But he always said, "Henry's got the gift of the gab. He'll be all right." And you . . .' She looked at Fred. ' "Fred's indestructible," he said. He thought Leslie was the one who needed help. Poor Leslie. He loves money and power and all that sort of thing so much, he's bound to lose them in the end. These things only stay with those who have a certain contempt for them. Simeon was afraid for Leslie's future. He was afraid for the future of poor dead Charlie's child.' Suddenly she had had enough of talking, the explanations were over and she hoped they'd all go away. 'It's such a long story,' she said, 'and it was all so long ago.'

'I really don't see what it's got to do with our case.' Henry was still determined to look on the bright side. 'After all there's absolutely no proof that any of it ever happened.'

'Only the letter our father sent Grace when Charlie was born. It was something she kept with old gramophone records, bits and pieces of jewellery, scraps of her past. I don't suppose she really cared if Nicholas found it or not.' Fred took the blue sheets out of his wallet, looked at them, but didn't unfold the letter.

'Where did you get that?' Henry stood up and crossed the room in a purposeful way.

'It was being offered for sale, more or less on the open market.'

Henry put his hand out for the letter, but Fred returned it to his wallet. 'The case is over. Leslie Titmuss knows just why our father left him the money. At least, he can prove it wasn't insanity.'

'Prove it?' Henry was contemptuous. 'What can he possibly prove?'

'Oh, most of it.' And then Fred told him. 'You see, I sent him a copy of the letter too.'

There was a cry of agony from Lonnie. 'You've lost our case!'

Henry, of course, told them that it wasn't over at all, not by a long chalk. He was going to see the lawyers, he wasn't going to let Fred's treachery do any of them out of their legal rights and he doubted whether the precious letter was evidence of anything. And yet, as he and Lonnie left, Fred knew that it was over, and that Henry knew it also. After a while they would meet again, in a world where their father was not demonstrably insane, and they were the two half-brothers of Charlie Titmuss.

When Henry had gone Fred tried to explain himself to Dorothy. 'It was the only way, Mother. I had to stop him somehow.'

'Oh, yes.' She withdrew her interest from him. 'I suppose you did.' She stood up then and went to lock the back door, ready for bed. 'Just don't expect anyone to love you for it.'

★ 33 ★

The Simcox Inheritance

When they had all gone, and the story had been told, Dorothy took the cold, untouched Instant coffee Lonnie had made and poured it away down the sink. As she washed the cups she thought of the big Rectory kitchen on a day at the end of the summer, early in the war. She had evacuees, she remembered, three small boys who had come to escape the bombs on Stepney. They were copious bed-wetters who looked at a field of cows with more terror than they had ever felt for the Luftwaffe. Simeon had put himself out for them, taking them on long country walks which they disliked, or playing 'Beggar My Neighbour', at which they cheated, with them in the evenings. Dorothy found little to say to them but they followed her about the house with extraordinary devotion. She remembered the events which came on them as suddenly as the black-out curtains, the sound of bombers droning through the sky towards Worsfield, or the three prematurely aged children with their luggage labels pinned to their jackets 'I don't think anyone else knows,' she told Simeon as they stood in the Rectory kitchen. 'Only Tom Nowt.'

'I can't explain it.' He seemed genuinely puzzled.

'No.'

'I can't explain it at all. I've always, really always, tried to believe in fairness and equality, all the things she finds completely ridiculous!'

'I don't think it's about politics this time.' Dorothy was looking for something in the larder.

'And she's selfish and spiteful and trivial as well,' he admitted. 'Quite funny, I suppose. A woman who paints her finger-nails purple and wears pyjamas in the day-time and enjoys the Blitz,

365

God help her. She's everything I most despise and I found her irresistible.' He seemed to be faced with a mystery darker than any he'd met in his profession. 'How can that happen?'

'It's over now.' She found the big basket in a dark, cluttered corner of the larder floor and pulled it out of its hiding-place.

'I suppose I'm back to some sort of sanity.'

'I hope you don't regret it.'

'The affair with Grace?'

'No. Getting back to sanity. Come on, let's pick the crab apples.' It was something they always did at this time of the year, so they went down to the trees together.

'He let me marry his little by-blow, his wrong side of the blanket. He let me have one of the Simcoxes, and I didn't know a damn thing about it!'

A copy of Simeon's letter had arrived on Leslie's breakfast table at Picton House. Before embarking on the long day ahead (opening a Worsfield Job Opportunities Centre, a flight to a speech at the Euro-Computer Exhibition in Birmingham, a five o'clock meeting at the Ministry and dinner at the Worshipful Company of Breeches Makers) he stopped his ministerial Rover outside Rapstone Manor, and found Grace in her dressing-gown, submitting her face to the filtered sun in the conservatory.

'I can't imagine how Charlie ever came to marry you,' was her answer to his opening volley.

'I must seem very disagreeable to you. I don't know anything about lying and cheating and saving up traces of old adulteries as though they were something to be proud of! That's not the way people carried on where I was brought up.'

'Your family had extraordinarily dull lives, I've always thought so.'

'Just let me tell you this. I've got my lawyer coming out to meet me and if Henry Simcox goes on fighting this case I'll drag you to court on a subpoena and make you spit out the truth, the whole truth and nothing but the truth.'

'The truth? We had nothing in common, Simeon and I. Absolutely nothing. I suppose, when all's said and done, it was some

The Simcox Inheritance

sort of challenge.' She gave a small and satisfied smile. 'I made him
fall for me, you know.'

'God help him.' Leslie looked at his watch because he was
working to a tight schedule. 'Who else knew about this? Did his
wife know?'

'The long-suffering Dorothy? Of course she knew everything.'

When Leslie had gone Grace felt nothing but hatred for him,
and yet his visit had been an event at a time when life produced
few surprises. It brought back memories of a past which had once
excited her. Perhaps she would call on Dorothy. They would have
something to talk about now, even if it were only Simeon's guilt
about Charlie, and its expiation in showering favours on the
appalling Titmuss. She told Brooks to get the car ready.

'I'm going out, Dora.' Dorothy in a mac and headscarf found
Mrs Nowt washing the kitchen floor in Sunday Street. 'I'm going
up to the Manor.'

'To her Ladyship?' Dorothy had told Grace's story. She had
spoken of something she had thought never to have to speak of
again, although it hadn't been her intention to give away Grace's
secret. Surely she should explain that to the woman? Well, perhaps,
after all, not. She sat down on a kitchen chair. 'I don't think' – she
undid her scarf – 'that there's any more to be said.'

'You're not going out?'

'No, Dora. I'm not going out at all.'

Grace, walking a little unsteadily, reached the car door which
Brooks held open. She also had second thoughts. She looked up at
a sky which threatened rain and gave further instructions. 'Put the
motor away, Brooks. Really, I have nothing at all to say to Dorothy
Simcox.'

As soon as he got Fred's letter, and even before his visit to Grace,
Leslie Titmuss, puzzled but triumphant, had telephoned his lawyer with the good news and ordered an immediate meeting. The
problem was finding a free half hour of the Minister's valuable
time, so he suggested a car to bring Rattling to Worsfield's minute
airfield where they could discuss the new evidence before the

367

helicopter took off for the Birmingham Exhibition Centre. So, in the airport building, which was little more than a collection of huts, with his secretary and a man from his Ministry hovering in the background, Leslie gave his solicitor the copy of an old love letter. 'That wraps it up surely? A perfectly clear, rational explanation for wanting to benefit my family. They won't go on with it now, will they?'

'No, I don't suppose they will,' Rattling agreed.

'So we've won!' Leslie was a little irritated by the lawyer's look of embarrassed gloom. He hadn't expected the man to cheer loudly but there was surely cause for a good deal of quiet satisfaction.

'The question is' – Rattling wore the expression he kept for the funerals of important clients – '*what* have you won exactly?'

'The Simcox estate. We know what that is don't we?'

'Let's say,' Rattling sounded a note of caution, 'we thought we knew.' And then he took a deep breath and explained. 'When the Simcox family business was reconstituted, back in the early twenties, in a certain Pym Simcox's time, the Reverend Simeon was given a large number of B shares. They carried no voting rights whatsoever. They should have produced no income.'

The windows rattled at the sound of the helicopter landing. Leslie looked confused by the noise and the information.

'But he was always paid, every year.'

'Indeed.' Rattling looked as grave as if he were describing some hitherto undetected murder. 'It seems at the time the family realized the Rector had no means of support other than a pretty miserable stipend. So they doled him out a comfortable voluntary income. As he was paid regularly, it came to be assumed in the accounts department that he had A shares, producing regular lolly. So – Rattling coughed nervously – 'a bit of a mistake crept into the annual returns.'

Outside on the landing strip, the helicopter fell silent. The building was quiet and airless, the only sound that of a distant telephone ringing unanswered. Leslie looked at his feet and seemed to find them, for some time, objects of interest. When he raised his head his habitual air of jaunty self-confidence had left him. He looked his age.

'Worthless? The shares worthless?'

'An old fellow who used to work in the Brewery Accounts spotted it. It'd been on his mind. The Brewery rang Jackson Cantellow this morning, and Cantellow got on to me before I left London.'

'I think I know who the old fellow is.' And then Leslie asked again, 'Worth absolutely nothing?'

The telephone had stopped ringing. There was the squawk of an announcement on the tannoy, and the two men with briefcases told the Minister that the chopper was at his disposal. They were puzzled when he looked at them and repeated, 'Nothing!' Then he walked out of the building, the wind ruffling what remained of his hair, to go about his business with no benefit whatever from the Simcox estate.

In Cantellow's office the same news was given to Fred. 'Shares with no voting rights. Paying no dividends. Producing no income.' Jackson Cantellow rolled the words round his tongue like a lament from an oratorio. 'Of course they'd been wrongly entered for years. A gross piece of negligence.'

'All you lawyers and Q.C.s from London have only just discovered that?'

Cantellow asked, 'What on earth's the matter, are you quite well?' for Fred, sitting back in the client's chair, seemed to be overcome with laughter.

There was no laughter, however, in 'The Spruces' when Leslie called on his parents. George sat in his armchair after tea, feeling, for the first time in his life, frightened of his son although, to be fair, Leslie hadn't blamed him for anything and agreed that the truth would have had to come out in the end. Elsie also looked nervously at the silent figure who stood in front of the fire, suppressing his anger. She didn't know why he had come except to blame them and she wished he'd do that and go back to Picton House where she felt he belonged. 'Your father's right,' she said. 'The truth had to come out.'

'He had nothing to give us.' Leslie picked up the lady in the red bathing-dress, who had been for years in the act of diving off a rock. 'I wanted to give him that,' he said. 'It was all I could think of. And he gave us nothing.'

369

'Our ornament!' Elsie cried out as her son sent the object crashing against the opposite wall. And then she was down on her hands and knees, carefully picking up the pieces.

None of these events were completed. All had life left in them and continued to stir and trouble their participants, although, with time, strength was spent. Like the pebble in Simeon's well-used pond, they produced diminishing effects. Simon Mallard-Greene, defended by an expensive barrister, was fined by the Magistrates, and his mother told Fred that they had decided to sell up and move to London. 'We're getting rid of what you call Tom Nowt's old cottage,' she told him. 'I've always known that there was something evil about the place.'

Christopher Kempenflatt, without any particular difficulty, got hold of a list of members of the Worsfield branch of the C.N.D. and sprung a surprise under Any Other Business at a Conservative Association committee meeting to which Leslie was invited. He startled the members by charging the Minister with lying to the Press, having categorically denied that his wife was ever a member of the organization when her name was clearly listed in a document which had conveniently fallen into Kempenflatt's hands. Of course there was nothing illegal about C.N.D., but a Member for Hartscombe must have an unimpaired reputation for veracity. Did they not all remember, in the distant days, a certain Minister for War . . . ?

'Of course I lied,' Leslie interrupted sharply, cutting off what seemed to him Kempenflatt's pathetic attempt to be revenged after the collapse of Hartscombe Enterprises.

'You admit it?' The accuser was disappointed. He had wanted to see his old partner wriggling on the hook.

'Did you want me to give a boost to the pacifists? Think of the publicity they'd've got out of that: "Minister's Wife One of the Worsfield Women". Did you honestly want that sort of headline?'

'The point seems to be . . .' Lord Naboth looked at the photostats of the old press-cuttings Kempenflatt had unexpectedly tabled. 'There does seem to have been a lack of frankness . . .'

'You've told us you lied.' Kempenflatt would allow no euphemism. But Leslie, with his look of patient sincerity, smiled round at their worried faces. 'And wouldn't you lie, Mr Kempenflatt, wouldn't every man in this room lie to protect the honour of the dead wife he had loved above all things?' It was not much of a tight spot, but Leslie had got out of it, as he would get out of many in the years to come. 'Never apologize for winning,' he told Nicky, when his son came home for the holidays. 'Never apologize and never explain. And when you win, you're entitled to feel triumphant.' But the boy seemed uninterested in this advice. He left the dinner table because, he said, he wanted to get on with his book.

'Our father was deceiving us all those years,' Henry told Francesca. 'He let us think he was well off.' Peter, Francesca's boyfriend, had been converted to high-tech and the flat in Tufnell Park was now filled with black metal shelves, chromium lights, canvas deckchairs and banks of stereo equipment. She was wearing a white boiler-suit, and Simeon's old desk, empty of all wills, had been painted black and, with its top drawers removed, was fitted with chrome handles. 'It's you I'm thinking about, Francesca,' her father told her. 'I was planning to do something for you.'

'Do what? Give me money?'

'Don't you undervalue it. I've had to work for every penny.'

'Down the film studio, every morning. Hacking scripts out of the coalface.'

'Sometimes you look exactly like your mother,' Henry noticed. 'Sometimes you sound exactly like Agnes.'

'You never got to know much about me, did you?' Henry didn't answer. 'You might have quite got to like me. I ought to have told you that I hate loud music, I've never taken drugs and, here's another thing, I absolutely don't give a damn about whales.'

Pilgrims was being filmed at last, and vans were parked outside Rapstone Church, together with camera cars, a catering wagon for the incessant procession of sausage butties, cakes and tea, and a generator from which a complicated system of cables snaked across the churchyard and in at the west door. None of this activity was visible to Dorothy as she walked across the fields to do her flowers.

371

She had been cutting willow and beech sprays to go with the flowers she had brought. Inside the vestry, she put her basket on the table, unconscious of the activity in the church, where silence had just been called for. She filled a bucket from a tap outside, plunged her flowers in the water, and then opened the door which led into the church to collect the vases.

Light, white and almost blinding, struck at her. Perhaps, in the shadows, there were a good many people. All she could see was the back of a stooping figure in an old tweed jacket, who turned towards her. He was smoking a pipe, wearing a dog-collar and had the look of a rather bothered eagle. In a moment of extraordinary, unreasonable hope, she called out, 'Simeon. Oh, my dear!'

From the darkness, the director shouted, 'Cut.' The actor sighed, knowing that he would have to start the scene all over again.

Whether it was because the audience at the Badger had grown more tolerant, or because the Stompers were less relentlessly traditional and gave their own jazz versions of such popular numbers as 'Hello Dolly' and 'As Time Goes By', the gig was an unexpected success. Joe smiled in a superior manner during the rendering of these tunes, as though he had chosen them as a sort of private joke against himself. Den, who had been delighted to discover no sign of his young brother in the bar, slapped the double bass he had available for the night with the enthusiasm of a man enjoying an evening of dubious delight. Terry Fawcett played his clarinet with new invention, having had long and empty days to think about it. Only Fred, with a nervousness which he despised in himself, was drumming with moist hands and a dry mouth, waiting for something to happen as though he were a young doctor again setting out for his first lunch with Mrs Wickstead. They played 'St James Infirmary' for the sake of auld lang syne, and no one threw a Coca-Cola tin. So, as a reward to the audience, Joe Sneeping nodded to signal that he was going to permit the piece of commercialism which Fred had played since childhood. 'One, two, three, four. We know what we're waiting for,' Joe murmured in his deep South Hartscombe accent, in order to give it some sort of style, and then he went into the first bars of 'Slow Boat to China'. The Stompers played a chorus together, and Joe sang.

'Get you and keep you
In my arms ever more
Leave all your lovers
Weeping on the faraway shore . . .'

Terry Fawcett was allowed a perfect eight bars on the clarinet,
and then Joe, raising the bell of his trumpet to the sky, went into
the solo Fred had heard so often that it was as familiar to him as
the common cold, Mrs Beasley's arthritis, or the road to the
surgery. When Joe had exhausted his repertoire of clichés, during
which Den Kitson leant on his double bass and softly chatted up
a youngish girl, while Terry drank most of a pint, Joe grudgingly
waved his trumpet at Den for his solo. Then they all took up the
tune.

'Out on the briny
With a moon big and shiny
Melting your heart of stone,
I'd love to get you
On a slow . . . slow boat to China,
All to myself alone.'

It was Fred's moment for the final outburst. He started quietly,
being careful not to become too busy to lose the beat, and it was
when he was doing a little complex work on the side drum that he
saw her. She was moving out of the shadows beside the bar, as she
had once stepped into the light in Marmaduke's garage at the
moment he had failed her. That was over too now, even, perhaps,
forgiven. She had come a long way to meet him, and he started on
a triumphant drum roll to welcome her.

Some time later they were walking through the beech woods
together over a spot which no longer showed signs of fire and there
were no charred antlers.
'So that's it,' Agnes said. 'No one got anything from your father.'
'We got what we are, Henry and I, in our different ways.'
'Leslie got nothing.'
'I think he created Leslie more than any of us. Poor old Dad,
God help him!'

They were walking side by side, but with a yard separating them, between the grey-green trunks of trees. He thought how old it would be now, the child they had never had. And he thought of his father's child, of Charlie, whom the old man had loved.

'That's a bit sad!' Agnes gave him a look of mock despair. 'You think we're just what our fathers and mothers made us. Haven't we got any choice?'

'We had a choice once. You and I, I mean. I made the wrong one.'

'It's a bit late to think of that now.'

He walked in silence and then kicked up a small cloud of dead leaves as he had when he was a child. 'I don't think it's late.'

He looked at her trudging beside him, her fists pushed down into her pockets, smiling as though at a joke so awful that no one else could see it, as he had always known her.

'It's never really too late,' he said. 'To begin.'

Library of Congress Cataloging-in-Publication Data

Harvey, Karen D.
   How to teach about American Indians : a guide for the
school library media specialist / by Karen D. Harvey with Lisa D.
Harjo and Lynda Welborn.
      p.   cm. — (Greenwood professional guides in school
librarianship, ISSN 1074–150X)
   Includes bibliographical references and index.
   ISBN 0-313-29227-2 (alk. paper)
      1. Indians of North America—Study and teaching.   2. Indians of
North America—Library resources.   3. Instructional material
centers—United States.   4. School librarians—United States.
I. Harjo, Lisa D.   II. Welborn, Lynda.   III. Title.   IV. Series.
E76.6.H364   1995
970.004'97—dc20   95-9305

British Library Cataloguing in Publication Data is available.

Library of Congress Catalog Card Number: 95-9305
ISBN: 0-313-29227-2
ISSN: 1074-150X

First published in 1995

Greenwood Press, 88 Post Road West, Westport, CT 06881
An imprint of Greenwood Publishing Group, Inc.

Printed in the United States of America

∞™

The paper used in this book complies with the
Permanent Paper Standard issued by the National
Information Standards Organization (Z39.48-1984).

10 9 8 7 6 5 4 3 2 1

Copyright Acknowledgments

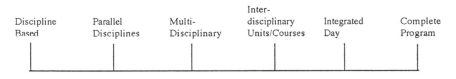

Figure 10.1
Families and Characters in *Love Medicine*

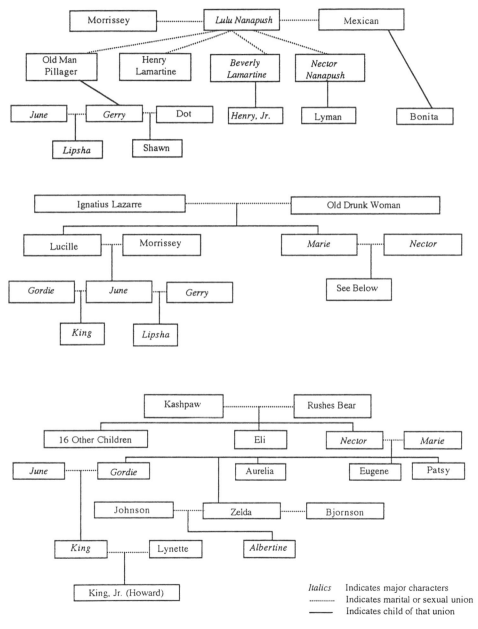

Italics   Indicates major characters
....   Indicates marital or sexual union
————   Indicates child of that union

Index

How to Teach about
American Indians

Greenwood Professional Guides in School Librarianship

School Library Media Centers in the 21st Century: Changes and Challenges
Kathleen W. Craver

Developing a Vision: Strategic Planning and the Library Media Specialist
John D. Crowley

Serving Special Needs Students in the School Library Media Center
Caren L. Wesson and Margaret J. Keefe, editors

Collaborations for Literacy: Creating an Integrated Language Arts Program
for Middle Schools
Rochelle B. Senator

How to Teach about American Indians

A Guide for the School Library Media Specialist

KAREN D. HARVEY
with LISA D. HARJO
and LYNDA WELBORN

Greenwood Professional Guides in School Librarianship
Harriet Selverstone, Series Adviser

GREENWOOD PRESS
Westport, Connecticut • London

Library of Congress Cataloging-in-Publication Data

Harvey, Karen D.
    How to teach about American Indians : a guide for the
school library media specialist / by Karen D. Harvey with Lisa D.
Harjo and Lynda Welborn.
      p. cm. — (Greenwood professional guides in school
librarianship, ISSN 1074–150X)
    Includes bibliographical references and index.
    ISBN 0-313-29227-2 (alk. paper)
    1. Indians of North America—Study and teaching.   2. Indians of
North America—Library resources.   3. Instructional material
centers—United States.   4. School librarians—United States.
I. Harjo, Lisa D.   II. Welborn, Lynda.   III. Title.   IV. Series.
E76.6.H364   1995
970.004'97—dc20   95-9305

British Library Cataloguing in Publication Data is available.

Library of Congress Catalog Card Number: 95-9305
ISBN: 0-313-29227-2
ISSN: 1074-150X

First published in 1995

Greenwood Press, 88 Post Road West, Westport, CT 06881
An imprint of Greenwood Publishing Group, Inc.

Printed in the United States of America

Contents

Introduction

The feathered and blanketed figure of the American Indian has come to symbolize the American continent. He is the man who through centuries has been moulded and sculpted by the same hand that shaped its mountains, forests, and plains, and marked the course of its rivers.

The American Indian is of the soil, whether it be the region of forests, plains, pueblos, or mesas. He fits into the landscape, for the hand that fashioned the continent also fashioned the man for his surroundings. He once grew as naturally as the wild sunflowers; he belongs just as the buffalo belonged. (Standing Bear, 1978, p. 247)

Teachers throughout the country, from kindergarten to high school, teach about American Indians. Although the study of Indians has been common in our schools, only recently have teachers and the general public become aware that the standard curriculum and knowledge about American Indian people have been a collection of isolated and often meaningless facts that are generally biased or distorted, frequently inaccurate, and certainly incomplete.

Recognizing that the school library media specialist is the *key* figure in every school in encouraging and facilitating change and fostering a new vision about Native Americans, past, present, and future, we hope this reference book will be of immediate and practical assistance—to them and to all educators who believe that the American Indian people belong in our study of American history, our literature and arts, our classrooms, and our contemporary lives. Throughout this book we are mindful that the library media specialist has multiple roles that extend far beyond checking out books, teaching isolated and discrete library skills, and monitoring library

behavior. In the rapidly changing schools of today, the library media specialist still manages the collection(s) within the school but also (1) works collaboratively with teachers and students in accessing, evaluating, and using new sources of information, (2) instructs both students and teachers in the selection of appropriate and useful materials, and (3) helps to bring the best of instruction and instructional materials to a dynamic curriculum. Each chapter ends with a brief summary and checklist directed to the unique responsibilities of the school library media specialist.

This guide provides a framework for selecting appropriate information for teaching and learning about American Indians; promotes an interdisciplinary approach to teaching; and offers guidance in teaching about holidays, culture, literature, religion and spiritual practices, history, government and Indian policy, and contemporary Indian life. Two chapters supply guidelines for the selection of instructional materials and activities. The book also suggests ways of using community resources that may have been previously ignored. Finally, in most chapters there are sample lesson plans or activities that demonstrate how the concepts and ideas presented in the chapter may be implemented in the classroom or library media center. *Creative educators will expand on these idea-starters.*

Elementary and secondary school library media specialists will find the guide's information practical. Moreover, sample resources are given for all ages and grade levels. However, recommended materials and resources have not been designated for a particular level. With the exception of recommendations for very young children, the distinction between materials that are strictly elementary or strictly secondary was often difficult to make. For example, we have found that some books for children are so beautifully written and illustrated that they can be enjoyed by all readers; and many video materials are suitable for nearly all students, intermediate through high school. Teachers learn by reading materials at all levels.

Although the book is written for educators at all grade levels, some chapters may have more direct relevance to particular levels. For example, the issues related to sovereignty of Indian nations could be considered conceptually difficult and suitable for secondary students only. Nonetheless, we encourage school library media specialists to expand their thinking and consider several issues as they use this volume. First, the most common problem to be addressed—and the one most easily resolved—is the general lack of credible knowledge about American Indian cultures and history. Library media specialists and teachers need multiple ways of informing their own practice. The material in all chapters (and at all reading levels) will increase educators' knowledge about indigenous cultures and the place of American Indians in America.

Second, just as in any other content area, a sound curriculum about American Indians must build on previous knowledge; a firm foundation must be established in order for students to continue to develop more so-

phisticated, in-depth knowledge. A coordinated and cohesive curriculum, one without gaps or unnecessary overlap, will depend on library media specialists and teachers understanding what knowledge has been developed previously and what will be introduced, extended, and/or developed as students mature and proceed through the grades.

The library is the center of the school. The contemporary library media specialist embodies (1) a model for teachers and students of an inquisitive and open mind, (2) an ability to change both attitudes and behaviors, (3) a willingness to master innovative teaching strategies as well as ways to acquire new information, and (4) a persistence that doesn't settle for biased, inaccurate, or incomplete knowledge.

[L]et the white brother face about and cast his mental eye upon a new angle of vision. Let him look upon the Indian world as a human world; then let him see to it that human rights be accorded to the Indians. And this for the purpose of retaining for his own order of society a measure of humanity. (Standing Bear, 1978, p. 251)

REFERENCES AND RESOURCES

Standing Bear, L. (1978). *Land of the spotted eagle* (reprint). Lincoln: University of Nebraska.

How to Teach about
American Indians

The Roles of the School Library Media Specialist

1

Your first impression when entering this beautiful new elementary school building is that many things never change. In a kaleidoscope of color and with a good-natured attempt at orderliness, children still tumble off school buses and through the front door. Teachers still welcome them with warm smiles, gentle reminders of school protocol, and pleasant comments about new hairstyles and backpacks. Children still giggle with their friends, run when they should walk, and generally approach their day with the exuberance of youth. But in this school, many things are very different, too.

Notice that the library media center (LMC) is located in the center of the school. Being in a hub position, it buzzes with activity. Engaged in reading, writing, viewing, performing active research, and publishing activities, students and adults are learning. Learning is the focus of the center. In the library media center, the concept of storage has been replaced by service—service to students, teachers, administrators, and other school personnel as well as community members. This library is the heart of the school.

If you look closely at this particular school and most other elementary and secondary schools, you can't help but notice that learning takes place in different ways today. Knowledge is no longer *dispensed* through teachers and books, and learning is most likely concerned with helping students *construct* meaning through diverse and rich experiences. And the person who directs the library—the library media specialist—is the person who, through many roles, really creates and directs the heart of the school.

The book *Information Power: Guidelines for School Library Media Programs* (1988), which was prepared by the American Association for School Li-

brarians and the Association for Educational Communications and Technology, lists the following objectives for the school library media program:

1. to provide intellectual access to information,
2. to provide physical access to information,
3. to provide learning experiences that encourage users to become discriminating consumers and skilled creators of information,
4. to provide leadership, instruction, and consulting assistance in the use of instructional and information technology,
5. to provide resources and activities that contribute to lifelong learning,
6. to provide a facility that functions as the information center of the school, and
7. to provide resources and learning activities that represent a diversity of experiences, opinions, and social and cultural perspectives, supporting the concept that intellectual freedom and access to information are prerequisite to effective and responsible citizenship in a democracy.

The dour librarian and the hushed and stuffy school library have gone the way of the steam engine. We live in the age of information—and more information—and more information. Furthermore, the school library media specialist bears the major responsibility for ensuring that students and faculty learn how to access, evaluate, and use it.

The multiple roles of library media specialists must be considered in relationship to goals for student development and achievement. Therefore, before discussing the multiple roles of the school library media specialist as applied to teaching and learning about American Indians, it is important to briefly mention the standards for information literacy for students that commonly guide the primary tasks of the school library media specialist. Information literacy guidelines provide all students with a process for learning that is transferable among content areas and from the academic environment to real life (Colorado Department of Education, 1994). This learning process is critical to their ability to become lifelong learners in a world that is changing rapidly. Even though the study of American Indians is both interesting and important, the skills and processes used in the mastery of content are critical to building information literacy.

With the mission that students and staff will become effective users of ideas and information (*Information Power*, 1988), the majority of states and communities are in the process of developing, refining, and implementing information literacy guidelines or standards that are integrated with content standards. Guidelines developed by the Colorado Department of Education in cooperation with Colorado Education Media Association are congruent with the following statement, which describes students who are information-literate:

Information-literate students are competent, independent learners. They know their information needs and actively engage in the world of ideas. They display confidence in their ability to solve problems and know what is relevant information. They manage technology tools to access information and to communicate. They operate comfortably in situations where there are multiple answers, as well as those with no answers. They hold high standards for their work and create quality products. Information-literate students are flexible, can adapt to change and are able to function independently and in groups. (Colorado Department of Education, 1994, p. 1)

The purpose of this book is to indicate specific ways in which school library media specialists can further the information literacy of students (and colleagues) as they explore rich and complex American Indian cultures, historical perspectives, and contemporary issues. Figure 1.1 at the end of this chapter illustrates the multiple roles played by library media specialists in terms of the seven objectives, or responsibilities, identified in *Information Power*.

THE SCHOOL LIBRARY MEDIA SPECIALIST AS RESOURCE TO TEACHERS AND STUDENTS

School library media specialists are consultants to teachers as they employ a wide range of resources and teaching methodologies to meet the intellectual and developmental needs of students. (*Information Power*, 1988, p. 34)

The school library media specialist is "supposed to know" where to find the information that answers teachers' questions and forms the intellectual foundations of their curriculum. Because teachers frequently build curriculum on available instructional resources and appropriate information, as consultants, school library media specialists must be able to meet requests as well as extend teachers' thinking about what is *available*, what is *possible*, and what is *preferable*.

In teaching about American Indians the school library media specialist faces additional challenges, for libraries are filled with materials that are inaccurate and probably should no longer be used in classrooms. Many older collections and—far too frequently—new additions are not appropriate for instruction. The commemoration of Columbian Quincentennial—the 500th anniversary of Columbus' arrival in the Western Hemisphere—sparked a renewed interest in American Indians from a more sophisticated and informed perspective. In response to this interest in Indian cultures and their place in American history, books, films, videos, and instructional materials have proliferated. Many are of excellent quality. However, other new materials retain uncritical perspectives and biases rooted in an uninformed past or a romantic illusion. New is not always better.

Nonetheless, educators have become increasingly aware of the historical bias that has resulted in inaccuracies and denigrating stereotypes perpetuated in books and instructional materials for both younger and older students. With specialized knowledge and informed awareness, the school library media specialist has the professional responsibility to ensure that all instructional materials are accurate and authentic. In later chapters, guidelines for the selection of instructional materials will be discussed; however, it is important to note that in addition to being accurate and authentic, instructional materials must encourage critical thinking, decision making, problem solving, and personal and social responsibility (i.e., good citizenship).

For those who have the responsibility of being a major resource to teachers and students, the importance of specialized resources related to American Indians cannot be emphasized enough. Because so much of the curriculum related to American Indian people and cultures places them in a time frame frozen in the past and analyzes them from a Euro-American perspective, it is incumbent on the school library media specialist to acquire specialized knowledge of contemporary Indian newspapers, journals, publishers, producers, authors, organizations and agencies, film distributors, and community resources. This requires academic detective work and persistence.

THE SCHOOL LIBRARY MEDIA SPECIALIST AS CURRICULUM DEVELOPER AND COORDINATOR

Membership on curriculum committees provides library media personnel with opportunities to advise the educational staff on the selection, acquisition, use, and evaluation of specific media and media services as they pertain to meeting learning objectives. (*Information Power*, 1988, p. 35)

The school library media specialist holds an overall view of the district and school curricula and in this role must assist both the development and coordination of curricula. There are predictable places in the curriculum where American Indians are addressed and where the special knowledge and expertise of the library media specialist is sorely needed. These areas include:

- the study of national holidays such as Columbus Day and Thanksgiving,
- children's literature in elementary classes utilizing a whole language approach to reading and language arts instruction,
- the study of state histories,
- the study of geographic regions of the world—frequently in the study of the Arctic, Great Plains, and Desert at the third or fourth grade levels,

- the study of American history—usually in fifth, eighth, and eleventh grades,
- middle and high school language arts classes or literature courses (occasionally),
- secondary-level arts classes—clay, fiber, and jewelry (occasionally), and
- secondary-level contemporary issues and American government classes (infrequently).

As professional educators who assist in the development of district and school curricula, school library media specialists have an ancillary responsibility to help teachers and administrators discern that which is worth teaching. In terms of the study of American Indians, they must be (1) familiar with the guidelines and materials of the major professional organizations as they relate to this topic (e.g., National Council for the Social Studies, National Council for Teachers of English, National History Standards Project) and reports and documents such as those from the Bradley Commission on History in the Schools, the California History–Social Science Framework, and guidelines provided by the National Geographic Society, and (2) knowledgeable about existing and emerging research related to teaching and learning, including such efforts as the teaching of thinking skills (Marzano, 1988; Jones & Idol, 1990), cooperative learning strategies, whole language instruction, alternative methods of assessment, and ways to meet the needs of exceptional students. This additional knowledge allows school library media specialists to make reasonable decisions regarding the most appropriate media and media services.

In addition, those who serve American Indian students must learn about the ways of learning that are common to American Indian children and youth (appropriate resources are available). Generally, the academic achievement and school retention rate of American Indian students is dismal, the lowest of any ethnic minority in the nation. Indian parents, educators, and elders attribute a significant part of this failure to the non-Indian educator's lack of knowledge of Indian ways of learning and insensitivity to the culturally based needs (and strengths) of Indian students. With regard to this special population, the uninformed library media specialist must extend his/her knowledge about providing a rich and encouraging curriculum, including media and instructional materials, for Indian students.

In recognition of this need, the American Library Association has formed a special group, the American Indian Library Association, that works to improve Indian library, cultural, and information services. Luther Standing Bear (1978) eloquently states the case for Indian students:

But Indian youth! They, too, have fine pages in their past history; they, too, have patriots and heroes. And it is not fair to rob Indian youth of their history, the stories of their patriots, which, if impartially written would fill them with pride

and dignity. Therefore, give back to Indian youth all, everything in their heritage that belongs to them and augment it with the best in the modern schools. (p. 254)

As school reform movements gain momentum, a noticeable trend is to encourage individual schools to develop their own curricula, usually in accordance with identified standards or outcomes. In many classrooms and schools, strict adherence to district curricula or teachers' guides to textbooks is increasingly rare. Coordination of the curriculum and materials used in instruction is imperative for two major reasons. Both reasons resonate with common sense.

First, the curriculum and instruction must be developmental. Concepts, generalizations, and content must be intellectually accessible to students and must appropriately increase in complexity as students mature physically, emotionally, socially, and cognitively. A balance should be maintained so that the content is difficult enough to be intriguing and challenging and easy enough to seem possible to master. Accordingly, instructional media and the materials must be developmentally appropriate. After all, significant knowledge is developed in a spiral fashion. For example, students may study the tradition and change in Indian cultures in both the first grade and as high school seniors, utilizing different and developmentally appropriate content, activities, and instructional materials. The cumulative effect is a deep understanding not only of Indian cultures but of major social science concepts and principles that can help students understand other world cultures and how they both change and remain the same.

Second, without a coordinated curriculum, students (and their parents) can become bored and critical with needless repetition—same books, same videos, same stories, same projects. Elementary curriculum frequently relies too heavily on tipis, buffalo, kachinas, and rain dances; secondary curriculum (when Indian people and cultures are included) on Indian wars, famous chiefs, and a few well-known pieces of literature written by established Indian authors. Teachers who have limited knowledge of traditional and contemporary Indian lifeways, history, and current activities and issues are especially vulnerable to repetitious curriculum, relying heavily on romantic stereotypes and inaccurate history.

Beyond boredom, a curriculum that lacks coordination and coherence and is mindlessly repetitive at beginning levels impedes the development of more sophisticated understanding. Many ideas are introduced but are rarely elaborated and deepened. When this superficial "coverage" is encouraged, as opposed to in-depth study, students are denied the richness of Indian histories, spiritual practices, arts, and peoples. What is omitted from the curriculum is impoverishing.

THE SCHOOL LIBRARY MEDIA SPECIALIST
AS COLLECTION MANAGER

Students must have access to a wide range of information resources. Both students and teachers are entitled to collections that provide access to current, representative, and appropriate resources and information that will satisfy their educational needs and interests and match their individual learning styles. Resources that cover all appropriate topics and represent a diversity of points of view are essential. (*Information Power*, 1988, p. 70)

In all areas of the curriculum, students must have information resources that are intellectually accessible. This statement acknowledges and accommodates a diversity in physical and cognitive abilities, social skills, reading levels, personal interests, and learning styles. *Learning style* is defined as a person's preferred patterns of perceiving and processing information; it includes the physiological, developmental, and cultural factors that affect how people—children and young adults—learn most efficiently.

Although researchers have proposed a number of learning style models and assessment instruments, perhaps the common principle to keep in mind is that students should be able to learn in ways that are comfortable for them while being encouraged to be flexible and to increase their repertoire of learning strategies Therefore, the advice for school library media specialists is straightforward: to adequately serve students with differing talents, skills, abilities, interests, and needs, it is imperative to develop collections that provide a wide range of information resources. The importance of providing *current, representative*, and *appropriate* resources and information that incorporate a diversity of experiences, opinions, and social and cultural perspectives cannot be emphasized enough. One of the most grievous errors in the selection of instructional materials and media is the assumption that all Indian people, cultures, beliefs, traditions, and lifeways are the same. Although there are similarities, the differences between individual Indian people and tribal nations are striking throughout time and place.

In the selection of print and nonprint resources, consider the following variables in various combinations: (1) urban life in contrast to reservation life, (2) "traditional" ways in contrast to and combined with contemporary ways, (3) geographic location or cultural area (e.g., Arctic vs. desert peoples), (4) unique tribal histories, beliefs, traditions, and ways of life, (5) historical periods and the impact of American Indian policies, (6) degrees of assimilation into the dominant culture that have resulted from education and/or experience (e.g., Indian warriors who served in recent war efforts had unique experiences that have markedly affected their lives), (7) the effects of intermarriage between members of different tribes as well as with non-Indians, (8) the effects of Christian missionary efforts, and (9) the idiosyncratic personalities and characteristics of individual human beings.

THE SCHOOL LIBRARY MEDIA SPECIALIST AS TEACHER

Library media specialists help students build positive attitudes toward the use and communication of information and ideas. Students are encouraged to realize their potential as informed citizens who think critically and solve problems. (*Information Power*, 1988, pp. 332–34)

We acknowledge that school library media specialists teach students, teachers, administrators, and community members how to access, evaluate, and use information, and that they have a particular responsibility to be aware of emerging technologies as well as new and effective teaching strategies. This role is central. However, in the study of American Indian peoples, cultures, histories, and issues that impact their survival as members of sovereign nations, there is a responsibility of the library media specialist that is both fundamental and imperative. In a tumultuous time when our previous knowledge and treatment of American Indians is being challenged and modified, school library media specialists will need to teach by example. They are likely to be the professional educators who lead school efforts to reformulate how we teach about Indians. In this role they must be intellectually open, inquisitive, persistent, reasonable, informed, and sensitive. They should model the ability to (1) seek multiple perspectives on any given event or issue, (2) withhold judgment until a variety of information has been gathered, (3) modify previously held ideas when presented with new and perhaps contradictory information, (4) relinquish both positive and negative stereotypes, and (5) respect ways of living, knowing, and believing that are markedly different from their own.

Finally, we cannot discuss the multiple roles of the school library media specialist without noting the importance of these roles in academic achievement of content (as opposed to skills). Generally, the effectiveness of any school program is embodied in test scores that substantiate curriculum-related achievement and that can be compared to regional, state, and national results. Although we want school libraries and media centers to be engaging places in which students develop the skills that enable them to become discriminating consumers and skilled creators of information and lifelong learners, adept in the use of instructional and information technology, educators and the general public look for that knowledge and those particular skills to be demonstrated in academic achievement. This knowledge and these particular skills and attitudes are used in the context of the school curriculum.

Recent evidence suggests that:

- students whose library media specialists participate in the instructional process are higher academic achievers,

- better funding for LMCs fosters academic achievement by providing students access to more library media staff and larger and more varied collections,
- where LMCs are better funded, academic achievement is higher, whether the schools and communities are rich or poor and whether adults in the community are well or poorly educated, and

Figure 1.1
Roles of the School Library Media Specialist: Teaching about American Indians

Roles and Responsibilities	Resource to Teachers & Students	Curriculum Developer & Coordinator	Collection Manager	Teacher
to provide intellectual access to information	++	++	+++	++
to provide physical access to information	+	+	+	+
to provide learning experiences that encourage users to become discriminating consumers and skilled creators of information	+++	+++	++	+++
to provide leadership and instruction in the use of instructional and information technology	+++	+++	+++	+++
to provide resources and activities that contribute to lifelong learning	+++	+++	+++	+++
to provide a facility that functions as the information center of the school	+++	+	+	+
to provide resources and learning activities that represent a diversity of experiences, opinions, and social and cultural perspectives, supporting the concept that intellectual freedom and access to information are prerequisite to effective and responsible citizenship in a democracy	+++	+++	+++	+++

Note: Symbols indicate the degree of importance or relevance.

- among predictors of academic achievement, the size of the LMC staff and collection is second only to the absence of at-risk conditions, particularly poverty and low educational attainment among adults (Lance, Welborn, & Hamilton-Pennell, 1993).

A professional library media specialist and an efficient, comprehensive library media center will result in higher academic achievement, better thinkers, and more informed citizens of the future. One could reasonably argue that students can learn to read, write, compute, and be effective consumers and creators of information without learning about American Indians. However, these skills are developed through *academic content*; knowledge and skills, or process and product, are of equal importance. This book presents ways in which the study of American Indians not only supports basic academic and information literacy goals but helps students become informed individuals and ethical citizens who are prepared to function comfortably in a multicultural, global society.

REFERENCES AND RESOURCES

Bradley Commission on History in the Schools. (1988). *Building a history curriculum: Guidelines for teaching history in schools*. Washington, DC: Educational Excellence Network.

California State Board of Education. (1988). *History–social science framework*. Sacramento: California State Department of Education.

Colorado Department of Education. (1994, May). *Model information literacy guidelines* (final draft.) Denver: Author.

Dunn, R., J. Beaudry, & A. Klavas. (1989, March). Survey of research on learning styles. *Educational Leadership* 46 (6), pp. 50–58.

Geography for life. (1994). Washington, DC: Geographic Education Standards Project.

Guidelines for geographic education: Elementary and secondary schools. (1984). Washington, DC: Association of American Geographers and National Council for Geographic Education.

Information power: Guidelines for school library media programs. (1988). Chicago, IL: American Library Association; Washington, DC: Association for Educational Communications and Technology.

In search of a scope and sequence for social studies. (1989, October). *Social Education* 53 (6), pp. 376–85.

Jones, B. F., & L. Idol. (1990). *Dimensions of thinking and cognitive instruction*. Hillsdale, NJ: Erlbaum.

K–6 geography: Themes, key ideas, and learning opportunities. (1987). Washington, DC: Geographic Education National Implementation Project, in cooperation with Rand McNally.

Lance, K. C., L. Welborn, & C. Hamilton-Pennell. (1993). *The impact of school library media centers on academic achievement.* Castle Rock, CO: Hi Willow Research and Publishing.

Marzano, R. J. (1988). *Dimensions of thinking: A framework for curriculum and instruction.* Alexandria, VA: Association for Supervision and Curriculum Development.

National Commission on Social Studies in the Schools. (1989). *Charting a course: Social studies for the 21st century.* Washington, DC: Author.

National Council for the Social Studies. (1994). *Curriculum standards for social studies: Expectations of excellence.* Washington, DC: Author.

Reyhner, J. (1992). *Teaching American Indian students.* Norman: University of Oklahoma.

Standing Bear, L. (1978). *Land of the Spotted Eagle* (reprint). Lincoln: University of Nebraska.

A Model for Instruction: What Is Worth Teaching?

2

Today's educators are challenged with continuing public and professional controversy regarding what should be taught and how it should be taught. Test scores are dropping; violence in schools is escalating; employers must train high school graduates to read, write, communicate, and think. Scarcely a day goes by without another expert, politician, parent, or activist presenting yet another solution to the inadequacies of public education.

Every teacher knows that problems exist. Troubled family relationships; insecure economic conditions; social and political unrest; diverse racial, ethnic, and linguistic populations; increased demands on schools and teachers; and diminishing educational resources are not statistics to teachers—they are personal and professional realities. However, every teacher also knows that tomorrow's lesson plans must be completed and that every day, every minute, every period of the school day they must decide what is worth teaching and how to teach it. While controversy swirls around them, school life goes on and teachers teach.

All the questions that plague education are present in teaching about American Indians. But an additional problem exists. There is finally a heightened awareness that most traditional content was *not* accurate, *not* authentic, and probably *not* worth teaching. Too frequently, the study of American Indian people and their cultures has followed the personal knowledge, experience, and interests of the teacher, outdated curriculum guides or textbooks, or available community resources such as museums. School librarians are all too familiar with curriculum and instruction developed from and adhering to the available instructional materials, both good and bad. In addition, instruction is frequently limited to "factlets" or "info-bits" that do not further an understanding of powerful organizing

concepts such as environment, resources, culture, diversity, tradition, change, government, power, discrimination, and conflict.

The elementary curriculum is typically full of tipis (usually spelled *teepees*), Indian princesses, war bonnets, rain dances, kachinas (made from round ice cream containers), and tomahawks, but not *significant* content. Furthermore, there is a tendency to focus only on stereotypes of the past, leading young children to believe that most Indians are relics of museums. Secondary schools usually deal with traditional American history, well-known American Indian literature, or, on occasion, contemporary Indian problems. When the history of Indian people in America and their traditional and contemporary cultures have not been taught with accuracy, authenticity, and sensitivity, the efforts seem to multiply the damage. For example, evidence suggests that (1) teachers of literature have precious little knowledge of historical and cultural context, and (2) students have miserably deficient information on which to make sense of Indian voice of any period or genre, or of contemporary Indian issues. As recently as 1988, a high school teacher who has made an effort to become knowledgeable and to teach about the literature of American Indians commented:

I would not be perfectly honest about the experience of teaching Native American literature if I did not state that my students begin the course with negative stereotypes about "Indians" and extremely limited historical knowledge about the actual treatment of Native Americans in this country. Their attitudes and perceptions have been shaped by John Wayne movies, television programs, and a popular culture that has depicted the "Indians" as bloodthirsty savages who specialized in slaughtering innocent women and children. (Hoeveler, 1988, p. 20)

If the status quo is inadequate or incomplete, what is a preferable and defensible alternative? What is worth teaching? Educational research indicates that a comprehensive curriculum should be focused on concepts and principles that are important to learn, and structured so that students develop a strong foundation of knowledge and understanding. This kind of structured curriculum, which is rich in intriguing content, increases in complexity and sophistication and is preferable to a curriculum that presents isolated facts. Further, educators will discover that a curriculum that builds an increasingly powerful conceptual foundation and that is enriched by stimulating interdisciplinary content makes it easier to plan for instruction, select instructional materials, and evaluate student achievement.

With a conceptually based curriculum, the role of the library media specialist becomes more focused; there is a framework for the selection of instructional materials. The ways in which teachers can coordinate content between grade levels and subject areas to further understanding of significant content become more apparent. Most important, students learn what

is worthwhile, valuable, and enduring. They have a sound foundation for lifelong learning.

WHAT IS WORTH TEACHING?

The proposed model, although developed originally for the social studies, has demonstrated its usefulness in all areas of the curriculum, including literature. Based on five powerful concept clusters, the model organizes instruction in a way that allows students to *construct* understanding, not merely memorize interesting facts (see Figure 2.1). The concepts are primarily interdisciplinary, allowing teachers to choose from a wide variety of content.

Controversy continues regarding the teaching of facts; therefore it needs to be stated clearly that a valid purpose of schooling is the acquisition of a common knowledge base—students need to learn factual content. But if the teacher has a concept or generalization as a goal when teaching factual knowledge, students will develop a way of *understanding* deeper meanings, relationships, and patterns in their existing knowledge base. More important, when the concept or generalization forms a framework or structure (see Figure 2.2), they can bring this understanding to new facts and situations. Indeed, the ability to use knowledge in an uncertain and unpredictable future is critical for those who will be adults in the twenty-first century. For example, if students learn how the traditional Pueblo cultures are in many ways adaptations to the physical environment and natural resources of the Southwest, they will understand that all Indian cultures are not alike and that the Iroquois of the Northeast, the Cherokee of the Southeast, and the Sioux of the Great Plains have cultural ways that differ from those of the Pueblos and from each other. Students will be able to predict how each tribe built their homes, what types of food they ate, the kind of clothing they wore, and the level of sophistication of their traditional social systems.

Each of the concept clusters—Environment/Resources, Culture/Diversity, Tradition/Change, Government/Power, and Discrimination/Conflict—can be developed at varying levels of complexity. Based on the generalization or principle that *the physical environment and natural resources of a region affect how people meet their basic needs of food, clothing, and shelter*, very young children might make traditional foods as a part of their unit of study on Navajos. Middle school students might study the effect of the Navajo stock reduction plan on the economics and culture of the Navajo. High school seniors might study the controversy regarding the mining of coal and valuable minerals on sacred Navajo lands. Literature classes might read the poetry of the contemporary Navajo poet Luci Tapahonso. Art classes might learn about the Churro sheep of the Navajo, and Navajo weaving.

Figure 2.1
Learning about American Indians: Using Concepts to Build
a K–12 Spiral Curriculum

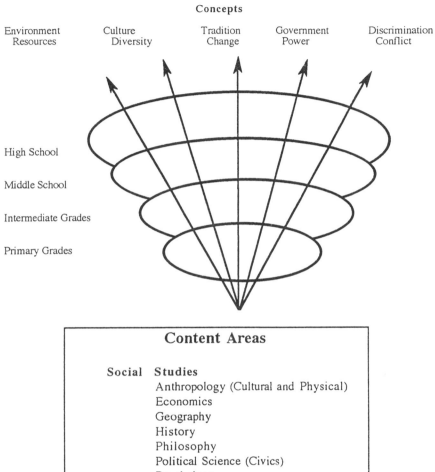

Concepts

| Environment Resources | Culture Diversity | Tradition Change | Government Power | Discrimination Conflict |

High School

Middle School

Intermediate Grades

Primary Grades

Content Areas

Social Studies
Anthropology (Cultural and Physical)
Economics
Geography
History
Philosophy
Political Science (Civics)
Psychology
Sociology
Language Arts and Literature
Written and oral literature (traditional and contemporary)
Science and Mathematics

Adapted from: Harvey, K. D., L. D. Harjo, & J. K. Jackson. (1990). *Teaching about Native Americans*. Washington, DC: National Council for the Social Studies.

- Seek the views and opinions of Native American elders, historians, artists, and tribal members.
- Enjoy cultural events such as powwows, rodeos, and art shows in your community, whenever possible. (Harvey & Harjo, 1994b)

VALUES, ETHICS, AND MORAL BEHAVIOR

Factual and conceptual knowledge without ethical understanding is insufficient for developing citizens of the future. A sound curriculum addresses moral, ethical, and values issues taught in a *responsible* manner. Because the teaching of values has long been controversial and undoubtedly will continue to be so, we first describe what is meant by responsible teaching.

Responsible teaching does not inculcate a predetermined set of values or behaviors; nor does it ignore the human democratic values that undergird our society and the ideals to which American citizens aspire. In our classrooms, responsible teaching of values supports a set of generally accepted democratic values, encourages challenging thought and debate regarding the rights and duties of life in a democratic society, and fosters social responsibility. Serious study of the lives of American Indians—as they have been experienced since 1492 and as the American Indian people adapt to modern technology, endeavor to maintain traditions and beliefs, and plan to enter the twenty-first century as sovereign nations—requires thoughtful attention to the democratic values we hold dear. As citizens of the United States, our obligation is to shape our policies to these values; our historical shortcomings should not be perpetuated.

The following values have been identified as forming the core of generally accepted democratic values:

Authority: a value concerning what rules or people should be obeyed and the consequences for disobedience

Equality: a value concerning whether people should be treated in the same way

Liberty: a value concerning what freedoms people should have and the limits that may justifiably be placed on them

Life: a value concerning when, if ever, it is justifiable to threaten or take a life

Loyalty: a value concerning obligations to the people, traditions, ideas, and organizations of importance in one's life

Promise-Keeping: a value concerning the nature of duties that arise when promises are made

Property: a value concerning what people should be allowed to own and how they should be allowed to use it

Truth: a value concerning the expression, distortion, or withholding of accurate information. (Lockwood & Harris, 1985a, p. 4)

democracy, diversity, honesty, and scholarship. Throughout this book, accurate and authentic materials will be suggested; however, the field changes daily and it is the library media specialist who has the responsibility not only to evaluate instructional materials but to educate others about what is and is not appropriate. Chapter 3 is devoted to guidelines for the selection of instructional materials.

There are some general principles to follow to ensure authentic and accurate content in teaching about American Indians. *First, use the date when the material was first written or produced as a guideline.* In general, older material is written from a Euro-American perspective and is replete with stereotypes and historical and cultural bias. Of course, older materials that *are* authentic (if not accurate)—such as autobiographies, first-person accounts, and historical documents—are excellent.

Second, whenever possible, seek Indian authors, artists, and community resources. A non-Indian person can write honestly and eloquently about Indian topics and issues; their research can be impeccable and their writings useful. However, a non-Indian cannot present an Indian perspective, cannot see in an Indian way, and cannot express Indian spirituality. Be exceptionally cautious about those who profess to have "become" Indian. Although it is possible to respect Indian ways and traditions, it is impossible to "become" an American Indian.

Third, seek diversity of thought and perspective. It is important to recognize that Indian people have many voices: young and old, conservative and militant, traditional and assimilated, honest and dishonest. Like all people, they are individuals with multiple perspectives, diverse lifestyles, and varying values. When you seek these multiple perspectives, you will discover the core values that represent "Indianness," those values and beliefs that transcend differences.

Finally, continue to question, to learn, and most important, to experience.

- Examine your own way of perceiving, analyzing, judging, and understanding the world—your own "cultural lens" that shapes who you are and how you see and interpret your own experiences and the experiences of others. Culture has been called, in computer language, our "software." How has your culture programmed your beliefs and behavior? How does your culture influence your understanding of the cultures of others?

- Develop authoritative information about Native people by taking classes offered by colleges, universities, museums, and historical societies.

- Obtain a variety of perspectives on any given tribe, incident, policy, or period of time. Read works by Native authors, including novels, in order to hear Indian voice and "walk in Indian moccasins." Native newspapers are appropriate resources on contemporary culture and issues.

Figure 2.2 *continued*

ORGANIZING CONCEPTS	ORGANIZING GENERALIZATIONS
	Rules and laws reflect the basic values within a society or institution.
	Different types of political systems are used in various societies to determine public policy and to regulate behavior.
	Organized interest groups attempt to influence public policy when they believe that such policy will affect their goals.
	Conflict arises within a political system when individuals or groups have competing goals and/or interpret the meaning of laws differently.
CONFLICT/DISCRIMINATION	Conflict sometimes leads to social change.
	Conflict frequently results when people from different cultures and subcultures interact.
	Groups are often the victims of discrimination and prejudice because of age; gender; and/or racial, religious, or cultural differences.

Adapted from: Harvey, K. D., L. D. Harjo, & J. K. Jackson. (1990). *Teaching about Native Americans*. Washington, DC: National Council for the Social Studies.

Concepts and generalizations are the point at which teachers usually begin planning for instruction; they organize the content, select the materials, develop the learning activities, and designate the methods of evaluation with this focus. Students, in their experience, reverse the process and begin with the learning activities, developing or constructing an understanding of the concept or generalization as a result of many experiences and activities.

AUTHENTIC AND ACCURATE CONTENT

For the library media specialist, the challenge of identifying authentic and accurate content is formidable. However, it is not quite as daunting as it was before basic information and commonly used materials were challenged and before both Indian and non-Indian people began to produce books and other instructional materials for the classroom. Instruction based on inaccurate information, stereotypes, and bias teaches harmful attitudes, reinforces negative beliefs, and is inconsistent with respect for

Figure 2.2
Learning about American Indians: Organizing Concepts and Generalizations

ORGANIZING CONCEPTS	ORGANIZING GENERALIZATIONS
ENVIRONMENT/RESOURCES	The physical environment and natural resources of a region affect how people meet their basic needs of food, clothing, and shelter.
	Culture is related to geographic location and to the particular time in which people live.
CULTURE/DIVERSITY	Culture is composed of a human-made system of artifacts, beliefs, and patterns of behavior that enable people to meet their needs in their physical and social environment.
	Making and using symbols is an important part of every culture.
	Cultures use a diversity of means to attain similar goals and to satisfy human needs.
	Individuals become human by learning the culture of their group. There are many ways of being human.
	An individual's culture strongly influences his or her behavior and values.
TRADITION/CHANGE	Cultural traditions help to maintain group solidarity and identity.
	Traditional ceremonies and rituals mark important status changes in a person's life (rites of passage).
	Traditional religious practices influence human behavior toward others and toward the physical environment.
	Cultures change when diverse cultures come in contact with each other.
	Cultures consist of elements borrowed from other cultures.
	Culture is an integrated whole. Changes in one part are reflected in all its components.
GOVERNMENT/POWER	Every society and institution develops rules and laws to govern the behavior of individuals.

continued

However, identifying democratic values is not sufficient. History is replete with events that involved complex ethical issues; frequently the issues were not clear, complete information was absent, and values were in conflict. Students can be guided to examine historical and contemporary events, increasing their ability to identify ethical issues and analyze situations that involve conflicts in values. Ultimately, we hope they will become socially responsible, recognizing and respecting the rights of others and acting responsibly in an increasingly complex and multicultural world.

Allan Lockwood and David Harris have developed the following strategy for the social studies classroom; it can be adapted for both historical and contemporary situations or events and can be used in the discussion of literature as well. (Several excellent secondary examples can be found in Lockwood & Harris [1985c].)

1. *Understanding the situation or event:* helping students understand the broader context from which a situation or event has evolved.

2. *Reviewing the facts:* helping students identify the pertinent facts in the situation or event.

3. *Analyzing ethical issues:* helping students distinguish facts from ethical issues, recognize the democratic values embedded in the situation, explore the meaning of those values, and identify possible conflicts among the values.

4. *Expressing one's reasoning:* asking students to make judgments about right and wrong as they struggle with the ethical issues raised in the episode.

> We must fight against those forces
> which will take our humanity from us.
> We must ensure that life continues.
> We must be responsible to that life.
> With that humanity and the strength
> which comes from our shared responsibility
> for this life, the People shall continue.
>
> (Ortiz, 1988, p. 23)

A WORD ABOUT ASSESSMENT AND EVALUATION OF ACHIEVEMENT

It is important to briefly address the assessment of student achievement, for assessment increasingly drives instruction. It is not an overstatement to assert that teachers focus on that which is tested and students increase their efforts if the content is "going to be on the test." This sort of thinking (and behaving) can be antithetical to achieving the goal of responsible, lifelong

learners (students who pursue learning throughout their lives and who demonstrate reasoned judgment, sound habits of mind, and ethical behavior) if it focuses on easy-to-grade tests that require only memorization.

To develop in students the characteristics and skills required of a lifelong learner, assessment of the simple acquisition of facts or skills is inadequate. Consequently, teachers are now learning to focus their efforts on alternative forms of assessment; they are looking to *performance*, not standardized and "pencil and paper" classroom tests, as evidence of achievement. Grant Wiggins points out:

> Our ability to perform with knowledge can therefore be assessed only as we produce some work of our own, using a repertoire of knowledge and skills and being responsive to the particular tasks and contexts at hand. . . .
> Understanding is not cued knowledge; performance is never the sum of drills; problems are not exercises; mastery is not achieved by the unthinking applications of algorithms. In other words, we cannot be said to understand something unless we can employ our knowledge wisely, fluently, flexibly, and aptly in particular and diverse contexts. (1993, p. 200)

What does this mean in terms of the study of American Indian history and cultures? How can assessment tasks replicate authentic challenges and situations, giving meaning to history, geography, social studies, language, literature, and art? What is there to learn about Native Americans that has enduring significance, beauty, and meaning? Most important, what is worth learning?

In acknowledgment of how assessment influences the curriculum, different assessment strategies are suggested throughout this book. It is important that strategies require students to use knowledge, restating, inventing, analyzing, synthesizing, predicting, probing, hypothesizing, comparing, applying, evaluating, justifying, making decisions, identifying values issues, and extending their knowledge to new situations and contexts. Several examples demonstrate (1) how to engage students in using established criteria to assess their progress, working in meaningful, real-life or simulated contexts, and evaluating their own achievement; and most important, (2) how to involve them in acquiring knowledge that enables them to understand and appreciate the world, not isolated, soon-to-be-forgotten names, dates, poems, and cultural trivia.

REFERENCES AND RESOURCES

Harvey, K. D., & L. D. Harjo. (1994a). *Indian country: A history of Native people in America.* Golden, CO: North American Press.

Harvey, K. D., & L. D. Harjo. (1994b). *Teachers' guide. Indian country: A history of Native people in America.* Golden, CO: North American Press.

Roles of the School Library Media Specialist

Resource to Teachers and Students

Help teachers identify major concepts, generalization, principles, themes and values as they teach and learn about American Indians. For example, on Columbus Day, the focus of study could be on the concept of change - how the encounter **changed** the lives of Europeans and America's indigenous people.

Assist teachers in identifying books and instructional materials that teach identified concepts. This identification is important for existing and new materials.

Assist teachers in the development of authentic assessments which require students to refine and extend their knowledge to new situations and contexts.

Curriculum Developer and Coordinator

Encourage teachers and curriculum specialists to review their existing curriculum to ensure that students have the opportunity to explore major concepts, generalizations, and principles in ever increasing depth and complexity.

Begin the development of curriculum units by discussing and identifying concepts, generalizations, principles, and values.

Integrate the study of democratic values into the curriculum, encouraging reasoned and informed thought on historical and contemporary issues that affect American Indians.

Actively discourage curriculum units that are developed around "fun" activities (sugar cube igloos) or disconnected and trivial information.

Collection Manager

Locate supplementary instructional materials that teach identified concepts.

Insist upon instructional materials that are culturally accurate.

Seek American Indian authors, artists, and community resources.

Teacher

Model respect for American Indian people, history, and cultures.

Model an active and inquisitive mind by seeking new information and modifying personal beliefs or attitudes when new information demands change.

Extend your own knowledge of the local American Indian community and its leaders and resources.

Harvey, K. D., L. D. Harjo, & J. K. Jackson. (1990). *Teaching about Native Americans.* Washington, DC: National Council for the Social Studies.

Herman, J. L., P. R. Aschbacher, & L. Winters. (1992). *A practical guide to alternative assessment.* Alexandria, VA: Association for Supervision and Curriculum Development.

Hoeveler, D. D. (1988, September). Text and context: Teaching Native American literature. *English Journal* 77 (5), pp. 20–24.

Lockwood, A. L., & D. E. Harris. (1985a). *Reasoning with democratic values: Ethical problems in United States history.* New York: Teachers College, Columbia University.

Lockwood, A. L., & D. E. Harris. (1985b). *Reasoning with democratic values: Ethical problems in United States history,* Vol 1: 1607–1876. New York: Teachers College, Columbia University.

Lockwood, A. L., & D. E. Harris. (1985c). *Reasoning with democratic values: Ethical problems in United States history,* Vol 2: 1887–the present. New York: Teachers College, Columbia University.

Marzano, R., et al. (1993). *Authentic assessment.* Aurora, CO: McRel Institute.

Newmann, F., & D. Archibald. (1988). *Beyond standardized testing: Assessing authentic academic achievement in the secondary school.* Reston, VA: National Association for Secondary School Principals.

Ortiz, S. (1988). *The people shall continue.* San Francisco: Children's Book Press.

Perrone, V. (Ed.). (1991). *Expanding student assessment.* Alexandria, VA: Association for Supervision and Curriculum Development.

Wiggins, G. (1993, November). Assessment: Authenticity, context, and validity. *Phi Delta Kappan* 75 (3), pp. 200–214.

Guidelines for Selection of Instructional Materials

3

As long as citizens of the U.S. are conditioned not to see Native people as human beings with human aspirations, national interests, and cultural integrity, with a long history of struggle to maintain their treaty rights guaranteed by the U.S. constitution and by international law—just so long will the citizenry of today like the citizenry of 100 years ago and 200 years ago—passively condone or actively support continued aggression by the U.S against Native peoples. (Moore & Hirschfelder, 1982, p. 73)

The school library media specialist can play an invaluable role in selecting appropriate instructional materials about Native Americans. Although a wealth of material is available, much of it is not acceptable because of bias, stereotyping, inaccuracy, and racism. A dedicated professional library media specialist can do the difficult work of locating obscure sources and ensuring that materials about Native Americans in the library media center are the finest available. Unfortunately, the usual collection development principles are inadequate. For example, authentic materials by and about Native Americans often are published by small presses and are not reviewed in the traditional selection resources. Digging deeper and going further will result in a rich collection that gives a truer picture of the diversity of Native American cultures, both past and present.

What are the key points to recognize when choosing materials about Native Americans? Most important, the materials must not contain any misinformation that could harm Native students or perpetuate stereotypes about Native Americans.

PRINT RESOURCES

Characterization

Some of the most loved and used books about American Indians that are used in the classroom do indeed perpetuate stereotypes. Do the books in your collection present the stereotypes identified in Figure 3.1?

In instructional materials, Native Americans have often been the victims of stereotypes, dehumanization, and tokenism. When one considers the treatment of other ethnic groups, it is incomprehensible that "J" should stand for Jew or "M" for Mexican. Yet many alphabet and counting books have thoughtlessly used "I" for Indian and "E" for Eskimo along with the "A" for apple and "Z" for zebra. If you can answer "yes" to any of the following questions, the materials are probably not appropriate.

1. Do Indians wear feathers, whoop, and jump?
2. Are children depicted "playing" Indian?
3. Are Indians portrayed as savages maliciously attacking white settlers?
4. Are Native characters depicted as fully human as white characters?

Figure 3.1
Stereotypes in Literature about American Indians

Male Stereotypes	Female Stereotypes	Other Stereotypes
savage, bloodthirsty	heavyset, workhorse	vanishing culture
stoic, loyal follower	"squaw"	must be rescued
drunken, mean thief	"Indian princess"	all tribes are alike
hunter, tracker	European features	generic artwork
noble child of nature	subservient to men	ecological unrealism
wise old chief		unnamed characters
evil medicine man		demeaning names
brave boy - special "Indian" qualities		limited language

Adapted from: (1) Council on Interracial Books for Children. (1980). *Guidelines for selecting bias-free textbooks and storybooks*. New York: Author. (2) Slapin, B., D. Seale, & R. Gonzales. (1992). *How to tell the difference: A checklist for evaluating children's books for anti-Indian bias*. Philadelphia: New Society. (3) Kuipers, B. (1991). *American Indian reference books for children and young adults*. Englewood, CO: Libraries Unlimited.

5. Are animals dressed as "Indians?"
6. Do Indians have ridiculous names such as "Indian Two Feet" or "Little Chief"?
7. Are American Indians relegated to the toys, games, and costumes of small children?
8. Must Indians prove themselves by performing extraordinary deeds?
9. Is the artwork a mishmash of "generic Indian designs"?
10. Is there a lack of features in drawings of Indian people? Is an unnatural red color used?

Language

1. Does the text contain loaded words such as *savage, brutal, stealthy, stoic, roaming, massacre, heathen,* or *primitive*?
2. Is there a preoccupation with scalping?
3. Is the full name of each Indian given, or are they labeled "the Indian" or "Injun Joe"?
4. Is the speech filled with unnatural "hows" or "many moons ago"? Are Indians portrayed with no language of their own?
5. Are derogatory words such as *buck, squaw,* or *papoose* used instead of *man, woman,* and *baby*?
6. Are American Indians compared to animals in phrases such as *untamed as a wolf*?
7. Are American Indian men portrayed as frightening creatures? Are the Indian people labeled as either friendly or unfriendly?

Cultural Authenticity

1. Does the text present Native cultures from a Euro-American perspective, or is the culture presented respectfully in terms of its own values and belief systems?
2. Are totally different Native cultures jumbled into one "Indian" stereotype?
3. Are Native peoples discussed only in the past tense? Is there a connection of the past and the present?
4. Are pipes, eagle feathers, dances, and ceremonies given the proper religious or cultural significance?
5. Are the contributions of American Indians to Western civilization recognized?

6. Are Indians portrayed in the fullness of their lives, or only given the qualities of great heroes or weak victims?
7. Is diversity among tribes accurately depicted?
8. Are Indians seen as individuals, not just as groups?
9. Are Indian languages and dialects respectfully portrayed?
10. Is the representation of Indian life, both past and present, accurate?

Authority and Authorship

The discussion about whether only American Indians should write or illustrate material about their cultures is ongoing. This chapter does not take a definitive stand but stresses issues of authority regardless of the ethnicity of the author or illustrator. When the author is not American Indian, it is important to (1) analyze the qualifications of the author or illustrator to write about Native peoples, and (2) determine whether the author or illustrator possesses the personal qualities that enable him/her to represent Native peoples in an accurate, respectful manner.

If possible, consult a person who is knowledgeable about American Indians or, preferably, an American Indian person. It is very difficult for a non-Indian to know whether material is flawed by stereotypes or bias. Search for materials that are recommended by an American Indian organization or publication. When purchasing materials reviewed in standard sources, carefully examine the materials and analyze the biographical information on the cover. If the author or illustrator is not American Indian, what recommends him/her as creator of the work?

Historical Accuracy

1. Is one race portrayed as inferior and the other superior?
2. Is the Native perspective of history included? For instance, the study of the Westward Expansion could just as easily be called the Eastern Invasion.
3. Are heroes only those who have been friendly or helpful to whites? Are protestors also included? Are the inclusions limited to those considered "great" or those who made contributions to white society?
4. Are contemporary Native people shown wearing feathers, braids, and beads? Or are they depicted as they actually dress in today's society?
5. Are the achievements of American Indians presented in a context that is beneficial to their society rather than only as a benefit to whites?
6. Are Indians viewed only as figures of the past?

7. Is the clothing depicted suitable for the occasion, or as a prop to establish racial identity?

Examine Your Existing Collections

1. Identify copyright date. Most books published more than 25 years ago present a non-Indian perspective. Copyright dates indicate that the book may be racist or contain inaccuracies or stereotypes. Unfortunately, a recent copyright date is no guarantee that material is acceptable.

2. Determine accuracy and authenticity. If material perpetuates distortions and can hurt Native students, it is better not to have anything on the topic of American Indians.

3. Examine alphabet and counting books. "I is for Indian" or "E is for Eskimo" are not acceptable. Do illustrations present animals dressed as Indians or children "playing Indian"?

4. Reject materials that do not recognize the great diversity of the many tribes. Don't make assumptions that a Navajo from the Southwest represents the voice of a Sioux from the Plains.

5. Build your collection around materials that present Indian cultures as living cultures and speak about the past and the present.

6. Beware of purchasing an entire series. Books in a series are usually written by different authors with varying qualifications for writing about American Indians. If the same author is used for the series, is that person equally knowledgeable about all the subjects in the series?

7. Scrutinize the catalogs claiming to meet all the multicultural needs of your library media center. Multiculturalism has become a major focus in curriculum, and many authors and publishers are producing materials that are not supported by adequate research or are replete with the usual flaws.

8. Adhere to the professional principle that all students have the right to books that develop pride in their cultural heritage and help them build feelings of self-worth.

Responsibilities of the School Library Media Specialist

1. Develop expertise and skill in the selection of appropriate materials.

2. Select from recommended lists produced by American Indian organizations.

3. Ask American Indians who live in or near your community to examine materials and make recommendations.

4. Search for documentation about the author and illustrator or producer of material.

5. Beware of lists created with no criteria other than "being about Indians."

6. Return unacceptable materials to the publisher with a letter clearly explaining the reasons for rejecting them.

7. Eliminate poor materials from your own collection, applying criteria listed above.

8. Attend American Indian events in your community.

Suggested Bibliographies and Other Selection Guides

Caldwell-Wood, N., and L. Mitten. (1991). *I is not for Indian: The portrayal of Native Americans in books for young people.* Chicago, IL: American Library Association. Selective bibliography that includes recommended books, guidelines about books to be avoided, information on selection tools and evaluation.

Cooperative Children's Book Center. (Annual). *CCBC choices.* Madison, WI: Author. Annual listing of the year's best books for children and young adults. Recommended books by and about American Indians are included.

Friends of the CCBC
Box 5288
Madison, WI 53705

Council on Interracial Books for Children. (1980). *Guidelines for selecting bias-free textbooks and storybooks.* New York: Author. Analyzes stereotypes and misconceptions and provides checklists for evaluation.

Council on Interracial Books for Children
250 W. 57th Street
Suite 1527
New York, NY 10107
(212) 662–7871; Fax (212) 662–8138

Hirschfelder, A. (1982). *American Indian stereotypes in the world of children: A reader and bibliography.* Metuchen, NJ: Scarecrow Press (out of print). Presents articles discussing such topics as toys, nicknames, and mascots with Indian imagery; myths about American Indians; bibliography of recommended materials.

Kruse, G., and K. Horning. (1991). *Multicultural literature for children and young adults.* Madison: Cooperative Children's Book Center. Includes annotations for recommended books about American Indians.

Department of Public Instruction
Publication Sales, Box 7841
Madison, WI 53707–7841
1–800–243–8782

Kuipers, B. (1991). *American Indian reference books for children and young adults.* Englewood, CO: Libraries Unlimited. Provides a selective bibliography annotating 200 nonfiction books and information on evaluation of materials.

MultiCultural Review. (Quarterly). Westport, CT: Greenwood Publishing Group. Provides reviews of multicultural materials and information on the subject of multiculturalism. Includes reviews of books, audiocassettes, videocassettes, and periodicals for adults and children.

Slapin, B., and D. Seale. (1992). *Through Indian eyes: The Native experience in books for children.* Philadelphia: New Society. Presents evaluation guidelines, informational essays, and reviews for recommended and nonrecommended materials.

Slapin, B., D. Seale, & R. Gonzales. (1992). *How to tell the difference: A checklist for evaluating Native American children's books.* Philadelphia: New Society. A checklist with examples of criteria to evaluate American Indian materials.

Wisconsin Department of Public Instruction. (1992). *American Indian studies: A resource and planning guide.* Madison: Author. Curriculum guide including a selected bibliography of recommended materials for grades K–12.

Department of Public Instruction
Publication Sales, Box 7841
Madison, WI 53707–7841
1–800–243–8782

ELECTRONIC RESOURCES

Selection Criteria

Because there is a lack of nonprint materials (e.g., computer software, CD-ROMs, online information sources) about American Indians, it would be easy to buy anything just to have some materials on the subject. But the same collection development principles apply to nonprint materials as to print materials. Additional criteria may be used as well (Miller-Lachmann, 1994):

1. Is the American Indian culture an integral part of the program's content, or is it merely a ploy to make drill and practice more palatable?

2. Do Native Americans receive as much attention as people of European descent? Is the Native perspective presented equally?

3. How accurate is the presentation in terms of a culture's diversity and complexity? Do all Native Americans speak the same language and live in the same way?

4. Are the language and terms appropriate? Are Native American names dignified and appropriate? (In one software package, an American Indian villain is named "Tipi Canoe").

5. Do the illustrations or sounds distort or ridicule members of other cultures? Is the language the stereotypical "How," "I help," "I go, make fire"?

6. From whose perspective is the story presented? Does a simulation allow students to play more than one role, rather than experiencing history from a single viewpoint? Does playing only one role reinforce biases? More important, should some simulations be played at all? Does the player have to take actions of dubious morality to win?

7. Does the documentation allow instructors to go beyond the program itself? Do guides offer additional information and activities for the teacher? Are the creators knowledgeable about American Indians? Does the documentation help the student better understand the material?

The potential of CD-ROM, laser disc, and other software is great. They offer appealing text, sound, and graphics. But to be useful instructional tools, their content must be equally strong and substantive. Students must be offered accurate, respectful, and sensitive materials regardless of the format.

CD-ROMs

One of the most significant contributions in the area of CD-ROM about American Indians is *The American Indian: A Multimedia Encyclopedia*, produced by Facts on File. The texts of four highly respected books by Carl Waldman are included: *Voices of the Winds, Encyclopedia of Native American Tribes, Atlas of the North American Indian*, and *Who Was Who in Native American History*. Using the main menu, students are able to access tribes, legends, history, biography, photographs, maps, drawings, sound, documents, and museums or societies. Students can view rare maps, treaties, photographs from the National Archives, and recordings of American Indian music (Wood, 1993).

In Mahnomen, Minnesota, the schools have a rich resource for integrating Ojibwa studies into all curricular areas with CD-ROM. Prior to producing the CD-ROM, two years were spent interviewing tribal elders, searching historical records, digitizing Ojibwa speech, and scanning photographs. The disc includes lesson plans for teachers, self-guided lessons for students, and resources such as Ojibwa vocabulary and history. Prior to this endeavor there were few instructional resources of any kind on Ojibwa culture. The project demonstrates how technology can fulfill a dream by providing students and teachers with authentic information previously not available. Further information may be obtained by contacting the Cultural Education Committee, Mahnomen Schools, Mahnomen, MN 56557; (218) 935–2211 (Stearns, 1993).

Online Resources

The Educational Native American Network (ENAN) is a nationwide telecommunications network sponsored by the Bureau of Indian Affairs

(BIA) and the Office of Indian Education Programs (OIEP). ENAN serves teachers, students, and administrators in BIA and OIEP schools and professionals in Native American education. Participants throughout the country can send electronic mail; participate in online conferences; download data from ENAN libraries; and share ideas, lesson plans, and instructional materials with other teachers. Students are given the opportunity to communicate with peers in other schools, participate in interactive projects, and learn telecommunications skills.

"Only the Best" is an online database guide to the most highly rated educational software and multimedia products. "The Native Monthly Reader," written for Indian students, is available online and may be downloaded. The system was created for use in BIA and OIEP programs, but non-affiliated persons and organizations may be approved for access to the system. Prior approval is necessary, and changes in the program may occur. There are plans to provide Internet e-mail and telnet access. For information, contact the University of New Mexico, Center for Technology and Education, Student Services Center, Room B–87, Albuquerque, NM 87131–1231; (505) 277–7310.

Internet

The Internet is uncharted territory for many educators, and tentative steps are being taken to use this massive and intricate resource. The growth of resources available on the Internet is phenomenal and the potential for the education community is limitless. Rapid expansion of the Internet makes it possible to offer only very general information here.

Educational newsgroups on the Internet enable students to talk with others throughout the world. Messages can be posted online and responses accumulate over time. Currently, Kidsnet is one listserv available to foster national and international networking for students and educators.

The Oneida Indian Nation's "World Wide Web" provides historical and cultural information about the "Onyoto'a:ka"—"The People of the Standing Stone"—through a World Wide Web site, an electronic database project sponsored by NativeNet. Documents are organized according to subject, geography, and culture. There are plans to add Native literatures, Native languages, Native newsletters and journals, Native organizations and bibliographies to the database. Pointers to other Native information sites are also provided.

New information will continually be added to the Internet. Access will become easier, and student and teacher exploration of the Internet will be as common as using the online catalog to find a book.

SELECTING INSTRUCTIONAL MATERIALS: A WORKSHOP FOR TEACHERS

Most teachers rely on materials they have developed and used through the years. They have built personal classroom collections of books, used particular stories and instructional activities, and decorated the classroom with materials accumulated over time. School library media specialists can play a pivotal role in helping teachers select and use only appropriate, accurate, and authentic materials about American Indians. By working with them to increase their sophistication and sensitivity in the selection of materials, you can dramatically improve the quality of their instructional materials. The following ideas can be adapted to brief after-school workshops, teacher study teams, curriculum committees, or even brown-bag lunches.

Time

Teachers' time is precious; use any time available: brown-bag lunches, inservice days, study groups meeting over a period of time. Library media specialists must be adaptable!

Materials

Hirschfelder, A. B. (1993, Winter). Native American literature for children and young adults. *Library Trends* 41 (3), pp. 414–36. (*Make copies for participants.*)

Slapin, B., & D. Seale. (1992). *Through Indian eyes: The Native experience in books for children*. Philadelphia: New Society.

Slapin, B., D. Seale, & R. Gonzales. (1992). *How to tell the difference: A checklist for evaluating children's books for anti-Indian bias*. Philadelphia: New Society. (*These books should be available for teachers.*)

Display a collection of books that includes positive and negative examples of inaccurate or stereotypical portrayal of American Indians.

Negative examples (some favorites of many teachers):

Banks, L. R. (1980). *The Indian in the cupboard*. Garden City, NY: Doubleday.

Hudson, J. (1984). *Sweetgrass*. New York: Philomel.

Martin, B., & J. Archambault. (1987). *Knots on a counting rope*. New York: Holt.

Miles, M. (1971). *Annie and the old one*. Boston: Little, Brown.

Positive Examples:

Big Crow, M. N. (1987). *A legend from Crazy Horse clan*. Chamberlain, SD: Tipi Press.

Blood, C., & M. Link. (1976). *The goat in the rug*. New York: Four Winds.

Goble, P. (1984). *Buffalo woman*. Scarsdale, NY: Bradbury (*or other books by Goble*).

Ortiz, S. J. (1977). *The people shall continue*. San Francisco: Children's Book Press.

Steptoe, J. (1984). *The story of Jumping Mouse*. New York: Lothrop.

Include other materials such as greeting cards, toys, Halloween costumes, worksheets or activity sheets, and classroom decorations.

Objectives

1. To raise teachers' awareness of criteria for evaluating instructional materials about American Indians and to provide them with suitable resources.
2. To stimulate teachers' interest in increasing their own knowledge about Indian cultures and people.
3. To provide a reasonable approach for teachers to become better informed.

Suggested Activities

1. Provide teachers with the handout, "Native American Literature for Children and Young Adults" (Hirschfelder, 1993) before the workshop.
2. Introduce and discuss the checklist presented in Slapin, Seale, & Gonzales (1992). Overheads of the criteria would be helpful.
3. Using the background provided, examine the books listed above. Should they be used in the classroom? Why or why not? Can books that are not perfect be used effectively? Are there other criteria for evaluation that should be noted? Be prepared for a lively discussion; some of these books are perennial favorites!
4. Ask teachers, preferably in groups, to evaluate new books according to the criteria that have been presented.
5. Discuss textbooks, worksheets, classroom decorations, and other aspects of school life that relate to American Indians. Are there reasons to modify or eliminate some of the representations of Indian people?
6. Ask teachers to explore with you how the school could offer only suitable material regarding American Indians. What is needed? How can you help?
7. Make an action plan with goals, timelines, budget, and individual responsibilities listed. Include the building administrator in this discussion.
8. An American Indian person who could speak to this topic would be a powerful addition to any workshop.

Follow-Up Activities

The criteria for evaluating multicultural literature raise an immediate concern. Figure 3.2 lists questions that are of value in evaluating literature about American Indians. The questions in boldface require accurate and authentic information to make a suitable judgment. Unless the evaluator has sufficient knowledge, he/she will be unable to evaluate materials. This raises a serious question. Are the teachers with whom you work adequately informed to make those decisions? If not, how can they become better informed? Teachers should discuss this issue.

The following plan is practical and could be adapted in numerous ways as a follow-up to an introductory workshop. Either as individuals or in groups, teachers may use the following structure to extend their own

Figure 3.2
Multicultural Literature: Evaluation Criteria

1. **Is the traditional setting authentic?**
2. **Is the traditional culture accurately portrayed?**
3. **Is the diversity of American Indian cultures accurately presented?**
4. **Are the factual and historical details accurate?**
5. **Does the book rectify historical distortions or omissions?**
6. **Does the book transcend common stereotypes of American Indians?**
7. Are the American Indian characters portrayed as individuals instead of representatives of a group?
8. Does the author avoid glamorizing, glorifying, or stereotyping American Indian characters?
9. Does dialect have a legitimate purpose, and does it avoid the stereotypical "Indian" stilted language?
10. Will children be able to relate to the characters in the text and illustrations?
11. **Does the author accurately describe contemporary reservation and urban settings?**
12. **Are social issues and problems depicted frankly, accurately, and without oversimplification?**
13. Do American Indian characters solve their problems without intervention by non-Indian people? Are they shown as capable and competent in their own cultural ways as well as in the ways of the non-Indian world?
14. **Does the author avoid offensive or degrading vocabulary?**
15. **Are the illustrations authentic and non-stereotypical?**
16. Does the book reflect a respect for American Indian people and their cultures?

Source: Adapted from D. E. Norton & S. E. Norton. (1995). *Through the eyes of a child* (4th ed.). Englewood Cliffs, NJ: Merrill/Prentice-Hall.

learning about Indian people. First select a particular tribe or cultural region, then follow the recommended sequence, beginning with Native American folklore, in reading either children's books or books for adults—both types increase teachers' knowledge. Teachers should share their knowledge with others in following sessions. How did the literature help them learn about a specific American Indian culture? What did they learn? How could they verify and extend their knowledge?

Examples (Navajo)

Native American Folklore

1. Bierhorst, J. (Ed). (1976). *The red swan.* New York: Farrar, Straus, & Giroux. (*for adults*)
2. Monroe, J. G., & R. A. Williamson. (1987). *They dance in the sky: Native American star myths.* Boston: Houghton Mifflin. (*for children*)

Folklore from Specific Peoples

1. Callaway, S. M., G. Witherspoon, et al. (1986). *Grandfather stories of the Navajos.* Rough Rock, AZ: Rough Rock School. (*for children*)
2. Oughton, J. (1992). *How the stars fell into the sky: A Navajo legend.* Boston: Houghton Mifflin. (*for children*)

Historical Nonfiction

1. Locke, R. F. (1992). *The book of the Navajo.* Los Angeles: Mankind. (*for adults*)
2. Iverson, P. *The Navajos.* (1990). New York: Chelsea. (*for children*)

Historical Fiction

1. Historical fiction is more difficult to find; consider instead biography, oratory, poetry, or books such as: Evers, L. (1986). *Between sacred mountains.* Tucson: University of Arizona. (*for adults*)
2. O'Dell, S. (1970). *Sing down the moon.* New York: Dell. (*for children*)

Contemporary Literature

1. Tapahonso, L. (1993). *Saanii Dahataal: The women are singing.* Tucson: University of Arizona. (*for adults*)
2. Garaway, M. K. (1986). *The old hogan.* Cortez, CO: Mesa Verde Press. (*for children*)

REFERENCES AND RESOURCES

Caldwell-Wood, N. (1992, May). Native American images in children's books. *School Library Journal* 38 (5), pp. 47–48.

Clyde, A. (1994, November/December). Online deals for schools. *Emergency Librarian* 22 (2), pp. 52–54.

Roles of the School Library Media Specialist

Resource to Teachers and Students

Bring new and existing resources, particularly emerging and unfamiliar electronic resources, to the attention of students and teachers.

Curriculum Developer and Coordinator

Connect information resources with classroom curriculum through collaborative planning, teaching, and evaluation.

Make connections with the larger community through collaboration with local agencies and national organizations.

Be knowledgeable about the curriculum and seek ways to integrate Indian history and culture into interdisciplinary studies.

Collection Manager

Discover resources other than standard lists in publishers' catalogs.

Consult selection aids that specifically recommend materials about American Indians.

Develop an awareness and knowledge of available selection aids, particularly those who utilize American Indians people as reviewers or those that are written or published by American Indians.

Seek resources beyond the school through contacts with human resources, electronic information, and resource sharing.

Remove materials which are not acceptable from the collection through continual monitoring and evaluation.

Provide resources in a variety of formats so that information will be accessible to students with diverse abilities, interests, and learning styles.

Teacher

Provide intellectual access to resources, not just physical access.

Help students learn and practice information skills which will enable them to find, evaluate, and use information in many formats.

Provide learning opportunities which address a variety of learning styles and interests of students.

Council on Interracial Books for Children. (1980). *Guidelines for selecting bias-free textbooks and storybooks*. New York: Author.

Dowd, F. (1992, Summer). Evaluating children's books portraying Native American and Asian cultures. *Childhood Education* 68 (3), pp. 219–24.

Gilster, P. (1993). *The Internet navigator*. New York: John Wiley.

Hirschfelder, A. (Ed.). (1982). *American Indian stereotypes in the world of children: A reader and bibliography*. Metuchen, NJ: Scarecrow Press.

Hirschfelder, A. B. (1993, Winter). Native American literature for children and young adults. *Library Trends* 41 (3), pp. 414–36.

Krol, E. (1992). *The whole Internet: User's guide and catalog*. Sebastopol, CA: O'Reilly.

Kruse, G., and K. Horning. (1991). *Multicultural literature for children and young adults*. Madison, WI: Cooperative Children's Book Center.

Kuipers, B. (1991). *American Indian reference books for children and young adults*. Englewood, CO: Libraries Unlimited.

Miller-Lachmann, L. (1994, November). Bytes and bias: Eliminating cultural stereotypes from educational software. *School Library Journal* 40 (11), pp. 26–30.

Moore, R. B., & A. B. Hirschfelder. (1982). Feathers, tomahawks and tipis: A study of stereotyped "Indian" imagery in children's picture books. In A. Hirschfelder (ed.), *American Indian stereotypes in the world of children*, pp. 46–79 (Metuchen, NJ: Scarecrow Press).

Norton, D. E., & S. E. Norton. (1995). *Through the eyes of a child* (4th ed.). Englewood Cliffs, NJ: Merrill/Prentice-Hall.

Scarborough, K. (1990). *Developing library collections for California's emerging majority: A manual of resources for ethnic collection development*. Berkeley: University of California.

Slapin, B., & D. Seale (Eds.). (1992). *Through Indian eyes: The Native experience in books for children*. Philadelphia: New Society.

Slapin, B., D. Seale, & R. Gonzales. (1992). *How to tell the difference: A checklist for evaluating children's books for anti-Indian bias*. Philadelphia: New Society.

Stearns, P. H. (1993). History comes alive. *Electronic Learning* 13 (2), pp. 8–9.

Usabel, F., & J. Roeber. (1992). *American Indian resource manual for public libraries*. Madison: Wisconsin Department of Public Instruction.

Weiss, S. (1994, May/June). New places to go online. *Technology and Learning* 14 (8), pp. 109–16.

Wisconsin Department of Public Instruction. (1992). *American Indian studies: A resource and planning guide*. Madison: Author.

Wood, V. (1993, October). Reflections on history. *Electronic Learning* 13 (2), pp. 34–35.

Guidelines for
Instructional Activities

4

Many people still remember the days when Indian children were forced to go to schools where their hair was cut upon entering and they were punished for speaking their native language. Armed with a better understanding of Indian children and their unique cultures, and working with enhanced pedagogical skills, teachers can help Indian students to overcome any alienation or apprehension that they may feel about our present-day educational system.

In recent years, better communication has helped to bridge the gap between Indian and non-Indian cultures. Educators, and society in general, have given up the notion that everyone must look alike and learn alike. I believe we have made great strides in respecting the differences of people and cultures, but in many respects we still have a long way to go. . . . Without a doubt, teaching is one of the most important and worthwhile professions, and I commend you for taking on the challenge of teaching our Indian youth. (Ben Nighthorse Campbell, quoted in Reyhner, 1992, pp. vii–ix)

Senator Campbell, aware of the impact of painful school experiences and disproportional school failure for Indian students, speaks of the challenge of educating Indian youth, the need for better understanding of Indian children and their unique cultures, the development of enhanced pedagogical skills, and the importance of teachers. That Indian students have not been successful in schools controlled by the dominant group is well documented. However, school failure is common for too many students of all cultural heritages. In today's America, we must continue to respect the differences of peoples and cultures by utilizing a wide variety of instructional strategies that engage students in learning about themselves and

others, promote individual self-confidence and self-esteem, and empower students to be independent learners. Schools should provide a healthy, stimulating learning environment for all students, Indian and non-Indian.

Imagine all young people developing an understanding of Indian people and cultures; learning in exciting ways about individual differences; and acquiring the knowledge, skills, and dispositions that will allow them to continue as learners throughout their lives. It can be done! Although they are proposed in the context of teaching about American Indians, we suggest the following guidelines for selecting instructional activities that are suitable for all students, all subject areas, all grade levels, the classroom, and the library / media center.

"I" IS FOR INSTRUCTIONAL ACTIVITIES

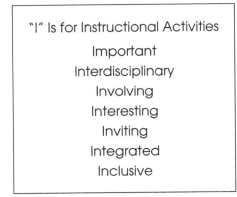

"I" Is for Instructional Activities

Important

Interdisciplinary

Involving

Interesting

Inviting

Integrated

Inclusive

"I" Is for Important

Instructional activities should be *important,* avoiding the trivial and inconsequential facts that so often constitute the study of American Indians. Again, the essential questions are: What is worth knowing? What is worth teaching? What is worth doing? Making tipis of rolls of brown paper, or weaving strips of paper in "Indian" designs, or planting Indian corn is meaningless unless these activities assist students in gaining interest in continued learning; developing the concepts, principles, and skills that help them learn new content in a rapidly changing world; and acquiring greater respect for people of many cultures.

Well-chosen instructional activities support the continual development and refinement of significant content about American Indians but also help students make connections between what they learn about Indians, the many other peoples of the world, and themselves.

"I" Is for Interdisciplinary

Instructional activities should be *interdisciplinary*. "All things are interrelated. It is therefore possible to understand something only if we can understand how it is connected to everything else" (Bopp, Bopp, Brown, & Lane, 1985, p. 26). Not only is it instructionally sound, but it is culturally relevant to approach learning activities in an interdisciplinary manner. Religion and spiritual beliefs cannot be taught appropriately out of the context of daily life. Daily life cannot be taught out of the context of geography and history. Literature cannot be taught as separate from culture and history. Wholeness is important. Everything is related.

"I" Is for Involving

Instructional activities should be *involving*, intriguing, and engaging. Thus, classroom activities should be created to involve students cognitively, emotionally, and when appropriate, physically. Students learn best when they are active, not passive, learners. Learning theory supports the idea that students should be actively engaged in constructing their knowledge—a product of both experience (doing) and reflection (thinking). Teaching is not talking but facilitating the active involvement of students. Teachers should not be quick to correct "errors," and they should ask probing questions and provide activities that require exploration or reflection.

"I" Is for Interesting

Instructional activities should be *interesting*, exciting, and enticing. The study of people is, by nature, interesting. How do people think and behave? What do they believe in? What do they care about? How are they similar? What are their problems, joys, sorrows? Who are their heroes and heroines? Fundamental knowledge of the physical, cognitive, and social developmental stages of students will help school library media specialists plan instructional activities that students find interesting.

Almost any given content—tipis, for example—can be taught in a myriad of ways that are interesting to students of different ages, developmental stages, and talents or abilities. Teachers could focus on gender-related roles; technology of making, erecting, and moving a tipi; artistic expression in the decoration of tipis; tipi etiquette; social structure and the tipi villages; scientific principles involved in heating and cooling; the relationship of shelter to the environment; and so on.

Students of all ages are usually interested in issues of fairness or justice. Controversial issues of or topics that are value-laden should not be avoided. For example, many issues that Indian people face today are in-

deed controversial; they are interesting because they reflect a search for the "right" answer or best solution. The answers are not known; as citizens, we are making history as we search for the right thing to do. History in the making is interesting, as is active involvement in issues that matter.

"I" Is for Inviting

Instructional activities should be *inviting,* proposing challenge and success. The word *inviting* is used to suggest that students must believe that although the learning task appears challenging, they have the knowledge and skills to be successful. In effect, the instructional activity invites success. Learning activities that are too easy appear boring; those that are too difficult are intimidating and evoke students' anger, lethargy, or rejection. Instructional activities that are difficult enough to be challenging, yet not so challenging as to be impossible, are ones in which students are likely to be interested and involved.

"I" Is for Integrated

Instructional activities should be *integrated* in that they use new knowledge, introduce or reinforce skills (including information skills), and examine values in an integrated manner. Recent emphasis has been on the creation of "authentic" learning tasks/assessments for students that require integration of knowledge and "real life" skills. In the sample lesson at the end of this chapter, "The Black Hills of South Dakota," which was originally developed by Indian teachers, students are involved in authentic and integrated activities: they read, write, research, produce a product, and examine personal and social values in addressing an unresolved and real issue.

"I" Is for Inclusive

Instructional activities should be *inclusive,* engaging students as a community of learners and utilizing the community as a resource for learning. The concept of inclusion can be applied to the creation of heterogeneous, cooperative learning groups of students who work together on projects or instructional tasks. It can and should include the use of many local and state resources, Indian people, and Indian organizations in the classroom as guest teachers. It can even be stretched to mean the inclusion of a variety of teaching/learning technologies beyond traditional texts to the latest in electronic media.

The final "I" is not presented in the model but is central to the multiple roles of the school library media specialist. *"I" is for an inquisitive mind* that

seeks new information and new perspectives and provides a model for teachers and students to press beyond what has been previously taught and learned.

"I" IS *NOT* FOR INDIAN AND INSENSITIVITY

Michael Dorris, a prominent scholar and author, has written, " `I' is not for Indian . . . it is often for Ignorance." He speaks out against the stereotypes and caricatures that ignore the rich histories, cultures, and contemporary complexities of the indigenous, diverse peoples of the Western Hemisphere. He deplores the whooping, silly, one-dimensional cartoons; the marauding, blood-thirsty savages, bogeys from the nightmares of pioneers; the mindlessly ecological, brave and true, Indian people who seem to be the cute, special property of children (Dorris, 1982, pp. vii–ix).

In a recent newspaper photograph of kindergarten children preparing to celebrate the Thanksgiving holiday, the children who were "Indians" were dressed in inverted brown grocery bags (with armholes cut out) splashed with a riot of poster paints, and they wore headbands decorated with construction-paper feathers. Were there any Indian children in this class? How did they feel about the celebration? How did their parents feel? What about the Indian people who saw this Thanksgiving photo—how did the picture affect them? How does this cute scene form or reinforce the stereotypes that Dorris deplores?

Classrooms are not the only place where "I" is for Indian is taught and reinforced, but they are major forces in perpetuating some of the silly and damaging stereotypes that are too frequently a part of our culture. Schools don't have to continue an insensitive curriculum. Through thoughtful attention to the following topics, much can be done to improve instructional activities about American Indians in the elementary grades.

Playing "Indian"

Many Indian people believe that having students wear feathered headbands and pretend to be Indian is offensive and mocks the Indian person. Would you have students pretend to be Catholic, Jewish, Hispanic, African American, or Protestant (Hirschfelder, 1982, p. 206)? This admonition serves as a good test. Indeed, if you can comfortably substitute another ethnic, cultural, or religious name, food, ceremonial or religious object, or dance for the corresponding Indian topic in the activity you are planning, you can probably feel secure in using the activity. If it seems inappropriate, stereotypical, or foolish, you can be certain it is a questionable activity. Being Indian is not a role like being a cowboy; roles can be assumed by anyone. Being an Indian is who you are! *It is not a role.*

Taking "Indian" Names

What would be the purpose of asking children to invent and assume an "Indian" name? In terms of authenticity, it is entirely inappropriate. After all, what is an Indian name? In the Southwest, Indian surnames are likely to be Spanish; in areas where the French explored, they are likely to be French. In many missionary schools, when the clergy could not or would not spell or speak Indian names, Christian names were usually assigned. Therefore, Indian names are often representative of other European countries and cultures. The surnames *Yazzie* and *Begay* are as common to Navajo people as *Smith* or *Anderson* are to many non-Indian people, but they are not commonly thought of as Indian names.

Names changed when Indian people intermarried with Indians of other tribes or non-Indians. For example, during the early years of European invasion and later when the Cherokee of the Southeast endeavored to become acceptable to the U.S. government to avoid extinction, there was much intermarriage—particularly with the English and the Scots. Note that the Cherokee leaders during the time of the infamous Trail of Tears were *John Ross, Major Ridge*, and *Elias Boudinot*. The names of Indian people will continue to change as they move, marry, and change their lives. Although the names *Crazy Horse* and *Sitting Bull* have an aura of romance, teachers should recognize that these are names of Indian leaders and that they represent bravery, courage, and wisdom. It isn't right to trivialize the names of such renowned men. Nor is it appropriate or authentic to have children choose Indian names (or, for example, Jewish, Chinese, or Muslim names).

Teaching about Religion

Teaching *about religion* is reasonable and appropriate, because religion has played a major role in the development of civilizations and cultures. However, in recognition of the constitutional principle of separation of church and state, teaching *religion itself* is not appropriate in public school classrooms. The celebration of Christmas in public school classrooms is a case in point. In fact, many classroom teachers have modified their holiday activities, acknowledging that some activities have overly emphasized Christian beliefs and practices.

In teaching about American Indians, the line between *teaching about religion* and *teaching religion itself* can become confusing (see Chapter 8). In other instances, the distinction is clear. For example, in one popular book the following activity is offered for children age 8 and above.

When you are becoming an adult, you can go out to an isolated place to ask for a vision. This is called a vision quest.

This search for a vision means that you are in need of direction in your life. The Creation will show you the way. It can come from many places in nature or even from a dream.

Take a bedroll, your sage offerings pouch, strips of cloth in the colors of the four directions, and water. Place the colors of the directions about 15 steps apart. Place yourself in the center. Stay until you are satisfied within yourself that your answer has come.

Take an adult with you so that there is always someone nearby to attend to any of your needs and to conduct each sunrise ceremony. (McLain, 1990, p. 97)

This activity teaches religion and encourages students to participate (incorrectly) in what many Indian people believe is a sacred rite; it is not appropriate for the classroom. Other similar activities would include burning sage for "smudging," using a pipe, and enacting sacred ceremonies.

All Indians Are Alike

If you examine how Indians and their ways of life are portrayed on greeting cards, in Halloween costumes, in toys, and in many texts and trade books, you will notice that almost all Indians are depicted as Plains Indians. The children mentioned earlier who were dressed for a Thanksgiving celebration were, it appears, meant to look like Plains Indians—quite absurd for those indigenous people of the Northeast who supposedly interacted with the Pilgrims on the "first Thanksgiving." Such lack of acknowledgment of the diversity among tribes perpetuates stereotypes. It also ignores the unique ways in which indigenous people adapted to and survived in environments including abundant woodlands, frozen tundra, vast plains, and arid deserts. Their clothing, homes, foods, and spiritual practices were unique to their tribe and the region in which they lived. Teachers must avoid the stereotypes and search for authenticity.

Checking for Authenticity. How do you check for authenticity? Here are some suggestions:

- Educate yourself to be an informed consumer of educational materials and resources.
- Seek assistance from Indian people, including authors, community members, Indian centers, tribal officials, community colleges, and Native people who are associated with professional and nonprofit agencies.
- Seek assistance from historical societies, museums, and universities.

Using Sacred Objects

There are no firm guidelines regarding the use of sacred objects of American Indian people in the classroom, but common sense and sensitivity can

guide educators. Just as the crucifix and the rosary have deep religious significance to most Christians and baptism and communion are sacramental
religious ceremonies, so kachinas, face masks, sand paintings, and the
calumet (sacred pipe) have sacred significance to many Indian people. Admittedly, some of these objects are made and sold commercially by both Indian and non-Indian people. In many instances what is made and sold
commercially is altered significantly from the authentic object so that it no
longer represents the sacred. However, many traditional Indian people maintain that harm is done to the preservation of Indian cultures by those who are
so ill informed or more interested in the commercial than the sacred.

Educators can explain how all religious groups have sacred objects,
icons, and ceremonies and that these are used in special, spiritual ways.
The appropriate way to approach these objects is with respect for those
who believe in their spiritual and sacred nature. Therefore, it is not respectful or appropriate to make cardboard kachinas, totem poles, or Iroquois
face masks. Nor should students play with the sacred pipe or use it to pray
to the four directions. These activities do not demonstrate respect for the
beliefs and practices of others. In reality, they constitute "playing" Indian.

The making of Navajo sand paintings raises some of the same issues.
However, the use of sand to make designs or decorative items that are not
to be used in ceremonies can be tolerated IF teachers take care to explain
the importance of sand paintings in Navajo ceremonies and clearly differentiate between what students (and artists) create and the actual sacred
paintings of Navajo medicine men or singers.

In summary, the selection of instructional activities follows sound educational practice with the added imperative of presenting accurate, authentic information about Indian people and cultures that demonstrates
respect for the indigenous peoples of America. Teachers must increase
their own knowledge in order to made good judgments about instructional activities.

THE BLACK HILLS OF SOUTH DAKOTA: A LESSON PLAN

The following lesson can be adapted for middle or high school. Give the
following worksheet to students.

At present there is a debate about returning the Black Hills of South
Dakota to the Lakota—the American Indians who lived there before the
United States claimed it. In this lesson your class should analyze the history of the Black Hills, focusing on the treaties that transferred the ownership and changed the use of the land. To what extent did the treaties reflect
varying value systems and the use or abuse of power?

Use at least three different sources for your research (e.g., books, personal interviews, articles and videotapes). Based on what you learn about
the treaties and subsequent use of the land, construct an argument for or

against returning the land to the Lakota. Prepare to present your arguments in a video documentary, a debate, a pamphlet written and produced for the public, a slide show, or an oral/visual presentation to be given at a meeting of public policy makers who are studying the issue.

You will be assessed on and provided with rubrics for the following (Adapted from: Marzano, R. J., et al. [1993]. *Authentic assessment*. Aurora, CO: McRel Institute.):

Knowledgeable Person: Social Studies

- Your understanding of how varying values and power in social, political, and economic spheres influence the ownership and use of resources.

- Your understanding of how land and resources are acquired and the role that power plays in the making and enforcement of treaties.

Complex Thinker: Constructing Support

- Your ability to provide sufficient and appropriate evidence for a claim.

Effective Communicator/Producer

- Your ability to effectively communicate through a specific medium.

The Black Hills of South Dakota: Rubrics for Assessment

4 = exemplary performance, 3 = mastery,
2 = less than adequate, 1 = serious deficiency

KNOWLEDGEABLE PERSON. Does the student demonstrate understanding of how values and power in social, political, and economic spheres influence the ownership and use of resources?

4   The student demonstrates a thorough understanding of how values and power influenced the treaties that gave the Black Hills to the United States; goes beyond a description; interprets and analyzes information to provide some insights into how these forces interacted to influence the treaties.

*3   The student demonstrates a complete and accurate understanding of how values and power influenced the treaties that gave the Black Hills to the United States; describes how specific aspects of the treaties were influenced by these forces.

2   The student displays incomplete understanding of how values and power influenced the treaties that gave the Black Hills to the United States; describes the treaties but does not explain the influence of these forces, or has some major misunderstanding or lack of knowledge related to these issues.

1   The student demonstrates severe misconceptions or lack of knowledge related to the influence of values and power in the Black Hills treaties.

CONSTRUCTING SUPPORT. Was the student's claim supported by a sufficient amount and appropriate types of information?

4   The student presents a clear and accurate treatment of all available evidence that addresses the argument for or against returning the land to the Lakota. In addition, the student considers what evidence is missing and how it affects his/her argument.

*3 The student, with no major errors, treats all relevant evidence that should be used to support the argument for or against returning the land to the Lakota.

2   The student's argument provides evidence for the argument for or against returning the land to the Lakota but may not incorporate all necessary aspects of a convincing argument.

1   The student fails to provide convincing evidence for the argument for or against returning the land to the Lakota.

EFFECTIVE COMMUNICATOR. Does the student effectively communicate through a specific medium?

4   The student uses the conventions and rules of the medium in a highly creative and imaginative way.

*3 The student uses the conventions and rules of the medium to communicate.

2   The student makes significant errors in use of the conventions and rules of the medium.

1   The student demonstrates a lack of awareness or understanding of the conventions and rules of the medium.

REFERENCES AND RESOURCES

* Generally recommended for appropriate elementary instructional activities—be selective, however.
**Highly recommended for appropriate elementary instructional activities.

Bernstein, B., & L. Blair. (1982). *Native American crafts workshop*. Belmont, CA: Pitman.*
Bopp, J., M. Bopp, L. Brown, & P. Lane. (1985). *The sacred tree* (2nd ed.). Lethridge, Canada: Four Worlds Development Press.
Caduto, M., & J. Bruchac. (1988). *Keepers of the earth*. Golden, CO: Fulcrum.**
Caduto, M., & J. Bruchac. (1991). *Keepers of the animals*. Golden, CO: Fulcrum.**
Caduto, M., & J. Bruchac. (1994). *Keepers of life*. Golden, CO: Fulcrum.**
Caduto, M., & J. Bruchac. (1994). *Keepers of the night*. Golden, CO: Fulcrum.**
Carlson, L. (1994). *More than moccasins: A kid's activity guide to traditional North American Indian life*. Chicago: Chicago Review.*

Roles of the School Library Media Specialist

Resource to Teachers and Students

Be cognizant of students' physical, cognitive, and social developmental levels in order to provide materials and activities that meet their interests and engage them in inquiry.

Help teachers and student use the community, including the Indian community, to enrich the curriculum.

Make certain that teachers are informed about Indian religions and spiritual practices so that instructional activities are respectful of sacred objects and ceremonies.

Be aware of how the flexible scheduling of the library media center can enhance interdisciplinary instructional activities.

Curriculum Developer and Coordinator

Ensure that the K-12 curriculum is rich in important, interdisciplinary, involving, interesting, inviting, integrated, and inclusive instructional activities.

Review the curriculum for activities that perpetuate stereotypes of American Indian people.

Discourage instructional activities that focus on recall and rote memory in favor of those who engage students in inquiry.

Advocate active, authentic learning tasks which integrate the development of knowledge, skills, and values.

Collection Manager

Provide a rich variety of print and non-print materials at varying levels of complexity.

Exhibit materials in enticing thematic or interdisciplinary groups or displays.

Review the existing collection for materials that perpetuate stereotypes of American Indian people.

Teacher

Create a learning/resource center that encourages academic research, active inquiry, and real-life experiences.

Model an inquiring mind.

Dorris, M. (1982). "Foreword." In A. B. Hirschfelder (Ed.), *American Indian stereotypes in the world of children* (pp. vii–ix). Metuchen, NJ: Scarecrow.

Hirschfelder, A. B. (Ed.). (1982). *American Indian stereotypes in the world of children.* Metuchen, NJ: Scarecrow.

Lazarus, E. (1991). *Black Hills/white justice.* New York: HarperCollins.

Marzano, R. J., et al. (1993). *Authentic assessment.* Aurora, CO: McRel Institute.

McLain, G. (1990). *The Indian way.* Santa Fe, NM: John Muir.

Reyhner, J. (Ed.). (1992). *Teaching American Indian students.* Norman: University of Oklahoma.

An Interdisciplinary Approach to Teaching about American Indians

5

> One of the important concepts Native American tribal people share with respect to the sacred is that all things in the universe are dependent on each other. This concept is first introduced to a child through the stories and songs of the origin histories. Behind the ceremonials and rituals each tribe carries out throughout the year is the notion of balance and imbalance. (Beck, Walters, & Francisco, 1992, p. 102)

The Lakota people conclude their prayers with the words *Mitakuye oyasin*, which mean, "We are all related." Indeed, everything in the universe is related. The concept of interdependence or interconnectedness forms the foundation of Indian thought and belief. Similarly, the discipline-based knowledge, skills, and values of the curriculum are interdependent. It is only for the sake of efficiency and—we hope—learning effectiveness that they have been divided into individual segments for study.

For most teachers, particularly elementary and middle school teachers, an interdisciplinary approach to teaching makes sense. It reflects the real world. Everything is related! In fact, teachers often find that creating and teaching an interdisciplinary lesson or unit is both creative and challenging, and their students usually become involved and motivated. Other teachers believe that the traditional discipline-based instruction is more efficient and critical to a sound education.

However, educators are beginning to discover that there are compelling reasons for students to have *both* discipline-based and interdisciplinary instruction. The discipline-based approach presents a systematic and sequential way to master concepts, principles, and ways of knowing that are both different and similar. Disciplines are knowledge systems with distinct

characteristics. We acknowledge the importance of the disciplines; and although this chapter will focus on interdisciplinary instruction, we accept the concepts of harmony and balance and support the use of both approaches in all content areas, including learning about American Indians.

DISCIPLINE FIELD: A specific body of teachable knowledge with its own background of education, training, procedures, methods, and content areas (Piaget, cited in Jacobs, 1989, p. 7).

INTERDISCIPLINARY: A knowledge view and curriculum approach that consciously applies methodology and language from more than one discipline to examine a central theme, issue, problem, topic, or experience (Jacobs, 1989, p.8).

Heidi Jacobs (1989) presents the following continuum of options for curriculum design:

Discipline Based	Parallel Disciplines	Multi- Disciplinary	Inter- disciplinary Units/Courses	Integrated Day	Complete Program

For most contemporary schools, four of the options are reasonable and practical. (1) The *discipline-based* option is more traditional and should be used. (2) Balance is provided by the *parallel discipline* option, which is straightforward, convenient, and not disruptive of traditional ways of teaching. (3) The *multidisciplinary* option brings several disciplines together to investigate a theme or issue but requires cooperation and reorganization. (4) The *interdisciplinary units or courses* option engages the full range of disciplines in the schools but requires substantial planning and restructuring. The integrated day and complete program options are dramatic and radical approaches that require the involvement of families and the redesign of traditional schooling structures and practices.

When should an interdisciplinary approach be used? Common sense directs that decision. An interdisciplinary approach should be used (1) when it is important for students' understanding to study or investigate a problem, issue, or event with the tools and structure of more than one discipline; and (2) when students need to discover relevance, make connections, and learn by experiencing and feeling as well as by hearing or reading.

Interdisciplinary curriculum sounds easier to create and implement than it is. Some of the problems that teachers have encountered are vexing and challenging, and students and parents have become legitimately concerned and confused. Some of the problems have been defined in the following ways:

1. *Potpourri problem*: a hodgepodge of contrived activities, from a variety of disciplines, that are clustered around a particular topic or theme and that lack focus and clear, important learning objectives.
2. *Polarity problem*: a conflict that manifests itself in an either/or position between those who advocate a discipline-based approach and those who advocate an interdisciplinary approach.
3. *Practicality problem*: a real-world concern that arises because interdisciplinary approaches require considerable planning, flexibility in scheduling, a variety of materials, administrative support, and parental understanding.
4. *Process/content problems*: difficult decisions that must be made regarding the integration and teaching of thinking and learning skills into content. (Jacobs, 1989)

We will address these problems and suggest ways in which interdisciplinary study of American Indians can be relevant, intriguing, and meaningful. We will provide concrete examples as guides. In these examples, the roles of the school library media specialist become evident.

In the study of American Indians, there are areas in which an interdisciplinary approach can be used easily and effectively. First, and probably most important, social studies is interdisciplinary by definition. The Curriculum Standards for Social Studies (National Council for the Social Studies, 1994) present ten themes that are based on the integration of the social science disciplines and that form the recommended content for the social studies:

1. Culture (Anthropology)
2. Time, continuity, and change (History)
3. People, places, and environments (Geography)
4. Individual development and identity (Psychology)
5. Individuals, groups, and institutions (Sociology)
6. Power, authority, and governance (Political Science)
7. Production, distribution, and consumption (Economics)
8. Science, technology, and society (Interdisciplinary)
9. Global connections (Interdisciplinary)

10. Civic ideals and practices (Political Science and democratic values)

In addition, history itself is interdisciplinary—it is the study of people and institutions as they were in the past. Each of the social science disciplines (anthropology, sociology, political science, geography, economics, psychology, and philosophy) is brought to bear in the study of history.

Culture, the major concept of anthropology, is also interdisciplinary. Culture is defined as the behavior patterns, belief systems, artifacts, and other human-made components of a society. It explores the way in which people have solved the problems of survival. It encompasses the foods they eat; the tools they use; their clothing, myths, religion, art, music, literature, and language; the ways they court, form families, raise their children, provide for their needs, and care for each other. The study of cultures should include games and dance (physical education), music, art, language arts, literature, history, geography, and even science, technology, and math.

How does the interdisciplinary curriculum look in practice? First, let's look at a negative example, one that reflects the problem of potpourri previously described.

EXAMPLE: UNFOCUSED DESIGN

This is a collection of contrived activities without clear learning objectives related to the study of American Indians. The unfocused unit might be entitled "Corn—The Gift of the Indians."

Language Arts:
  Read: Aliki. (1976). *Corn is maize*. New York: HarperCollins.
  Make charts with "corn" words.
  Label samples of corn with color words—white, yellow, red, blue, etc.
  Write recipe for corn soup.
  Read American Indian myths about origin of corn.

Mathematics:
  Make corn soup—buying ingredients, measuring, fractions, temperature, and time.
  Estimate numbers of rows on corn, number of kernels on cob.
  Categorize corn by color, size, etc.

Science:
  Plant corn.
  Identify and label parts of corn.

Chart the cycle of corn growth.

Make popcorn—Why does corn pop?

Social Studies:

Read about Indians—the Hopi of the Southwest, and the Iroquois of the Northeast.

Art:

Make corn husk dolls.

Make a mosaic with corn kernels of different colors.

Music:

Sing "Indian" songs (a popular but inappropriate activity, particularly if it is "Ten Little Indians").

Make Indian drums.

Physical Education:

Have children jump like popping corn.

Play corn cob dart game.

This collection of activities is not bad, just unfocused. Because the teacher is a primary teacher, she is legitimately concerned with skill development and has integrated some basic skills into the content or theme. The knowledgeable teacher should thoughtfully plan sound learning objectives and then use some of the proposed activities to help students achieve the objectives. For example, the following are good knowledge objectives for young children:

1. Many (not all) American Indian people grew corn to eat; they lived in places where corn could grow.
2. Tribes planted corn in different ways.
3. Many varieties of corn were grown.
4. Corn was cooked in many ways.
5. Indian people learned how to give corn the things it needed to grow—fertilizer (fish) and water (irrigation).
6. Special tools were made to plant corn and to make it easy to cook.
7. Because corn was so important to the people, they had (1) special festivals for planting and harvest, and (2) ceremonies or dances to help them have a healthy crop (e.g., Corn dances, Green Corn Dance, Rain Dance).
8. By growing corn, tribes were able to stay in one place. They were not dependent on hunting and gathering for food.

9. Indian people have many beliefs and stories about how corn was given to them by the Great Spirit.

10. Corn is used in many ways today.

With these knowledge objectives, many of the unfocused activities can become more than a cluster of related activities and can create an interdisciplinary approach to the study of Indian people.

EXAMPLE: PARALLEL DISCIPLINE DESIGN

In this design, two teachers arrange their schedules so the combined disciplines strengthen and deepen students' knowledge of a particular topic. In the elementary school, one teacher can use the perspectives of two disciplines to add richness and understanding to a topic or issue. Because the curriculum doesn't need to be modified, only coordinated, this approach is also easily used in high schools and middle schools where scheduling can frequently accommodate cooperation between two teachers.

For example, in the middle school, two teachers (English/Language Arts and Social Studies) might choose to (1) teach the notable novel for young adults *Thunder Rolling in the Mountains* by Scott O'Dell and Elizabeth Hall (1992), in conjunction with a biography of Chief Joseph (English), and (2) study the Nez Perce War of 1877 (Social Studies). The use of literature in social studies instruction is urged by the professional organizations and individuals who are interested in the improvement of social studies education. Literature provides a human dimension that brings life to historical names, dates, places, and events and, thus, strengthens students' learning.

It is said that the surrender of the Nez Perce in 1877 almost completed the military conquest of the American Indian. What remained was pacification rather than conquest (Josephy, 1989, p. 341). The interaction of the whites and the Nez Perce, culminating with the death of Chief Joseph in 1904, is fascinating and reasonably typical of the conquest and subsequent treatment of the American Indian. Chief Joseph was a man of dignity and honor whose story provides a strong balance for the image of the Indian as "murderous savage" that is often portrayed in the study of the Indian wars. Further, the well-known speeches of Chief Joseph are (1) appropriate content for the oral tradition of the Indian people, as well as (2) powerful statements regarding Indian values and the tragedy of the "winning" of the American West.

The young adult novel *Thunder Rolling in the Mountains* helps this period of history to come poignantly alive. The English teacher can also integrate the study of Chief Joseph's autobiography and numerous biographies about him. The following objectives and resources would be an appropri-

ate beginning for a middle school interdisciplinary unit that utilizes a parallel discipline approach.

Disciplines

Social Studies and English/Language Arts

Social Studies Concepts

Conflict, conquest, technology, power, leadership

Social Studies Generalizations

1. Conflict usually results when people have competing needs.
2. This conflict frequently escalates when the people involved represent different cultures and have different values and ways of dealing with conflict.
3. Superior technology usually provides power, including military power, to those who have access to it.
4. Every culture has leaders who demonstrate admirable qualities and who provide models for others.

Objectives

Content
The student will:
1. describe the life of the Nez Perce in the time of Chief Joseph.
2. discuss the impact of the missionaries on the Nez Perce.
3. list the major provisions of the treaties of 1855 and 1863.
4. identify the reasons why the U.S. government wanted to force Chief Joseph onto a reservation and why he and his people did not want to go.
5. list the major events of the last stand of the Nez Perce.
6. describe Chief Joseph's character and roles that he played during this time.
7. determine what factors influenced the defeat of the Nez Perce.

Skills
The student will:
1. organize the major events of the Last Stand of Chief Joseph in chronological order.
2. analyze why Chief Joseph chose to "fight no more forever."
3. compare the events in the novel with the historical event.
4. compare the different perspectives provided by the historian, the fiction writer, the autobiographer, and the biographer.

Values (organic)
The student will:
1. appreciate the bravery, courage, and leadership of Chief Joseph.
2. empathize with the pain and hardships endured by the Nez Perce people.

Suggested Resources

The following list is eclectic—for intermediate and mature readers, students and teachers, and including print and nonprint sources. From this beginning, school library media specialists can work directly with teachers to find resources appropriate to their needs. They will need to pursue biographies of Chief Joseph, trade books on the Nez Perce, and film and video resources to develop instructional materials; textbooks will not contain enough appropriate information. The original *Chief Joseph's Own Story* and stories of his life written nearly 100 years ago are available as reference for teachers or adaptation for students.

Armstrong, V. I. (Comp.). (1989). *I have spoken* (6th printing). Athens, OH: Swallow Press.

Chief Joseph. (1925). *Chief Joseph's own story*. St. Paul, MN: Great Northern Railway. This original resource is still available in large libraries.

Fox, M. V. (1992). *Chief Joseph of the Nez Perce Indians*. Chicago: Children's Press.

Josephy, A. M., Jr. (1989). *The patriot chiefs* (reprint). New York: Penguin. An excellent summary of the last stand of Chief Joseph will provide teachers with a brief background. An extensive bibliography is included.

McWhorter, L. V. (1952). *Hear me, my chiefs!* Caldwell, ID: Caxton Printers.

McWhorter, L. V. (1991). *Yellow wolf* (rev. ed.). Caldwell, ID: Caxton Printers.

Nader, A. J. (Producer). (1994). *America's great Indian leaders* (Video). Chicago: Questar Video.

O'Dell, S., & E. Hall. (1992). *Thunder rolling in the mountains*. New York: Dell.

Taylor, M. (1993). *Chief Joseph: Nez Perce leader*. New York: Chelsea.

Volper, D. (Producer). (1990). *I will fight no more forever* (Video). Chicago: Questar Video.

Yates, D. (1992). *Chief Joseph: Thunder rolling down from the mountains*. Staten Island, NY: Ward Hill Press.

EXAMPLE: MULTIDISCIPLINARY DESIGN

The multidisciplinary design brings one or more disciplines together to investigate a theme or issue. For example, this can be accomplished through the study of tradition, change, and the environment.

High school social studies, science, and English teachers can help students acquire important multidisciplinary knowledge and refine their thinking and communication skills through the study of one of the most important issues that American Indians face today: economic development and stability versus the preservation of traditional, sacred lands.

Objectives for a multidisciplinary unit entitled "What Is Sacred? Making Difficult Choices" might include:

Social Studies:
The student will:

1. discuss the historical background of the reservation system.

2. describe the importance of land and sacred land to American Indian people.

3. analyze the economic conditions of American Indian nations.

4. describe the unique sovereign status of American Indian nations.

5. determine the process whereby Indian nations will decide whether or not nuclear waste will be stored on their lands.

6. develop proposals for the economic self-sufficiency of Indian people living on reservations.

Science:
The student will:

1. describe how nuclear waste is currently discarded or eliminated.

2. determine the long- and short-range effects of the storage of nuclear waste on tribal land.

3. propose viable alternatives to underground storage of nuclear waste.

English (writing, speech, journalism, and/or debate):
The student will:

1. use actual or published interviews with Indian people as part of his/her research.

2. prepare for and participate in a rigorous and reasoned debate on whether or not the San Carlos Apache (or another tribal group) should allow storage of nuclear waste on their lands.

3. present and argue his/her individual position in a position paper, newspaper article, or video or multimedia presentation, using the knowledge gained in social studies and science investigations and the skills developed in the English class. *This activity constitutes the assessment of student achievement. Each teacher should prepare scoring rubrics for the knowledge and skills assessed in the unit* (see the attributes of authentic benchmark assessments listed in Figure 5.1).

Figure 5.1
Attributes of Authentic Benchmark Assessments

---

1. Tasks go to the heart of essential learnings, requiring exhibitions of understanding and abilities that matter.

2. Tasks resemble *interdisciplinary* real-life challenges, not busywork that is artificially neat, fragmented, and easy to grade.

3. Tasks are standard-setting; they point students toward higher, richer levels of knowing.

4. Tasks are worth striving toward and practicing for.

5. Tasks are known to students well in advance.

6. Tasks are few in number; hence, they are representative.

7. Tasks strike teachers as worth the trouble.

8. Tasks generally involve a challenge for which students have to go beyond the routine use of previously learned information.

9. All tasks are attempted by all students.

Source: W. C. Parker, (1991). *Renewing the social studies curriculum* (p. 88). Alexandria, VA: Association for Supervision and Curriculum Development.

EXAMPLE: INTERDISCIPLINARY DESIGN

The interdisciplinary design is effective when the entire school can be involved in a particular topic or issue; admittedly this is more practical in elementary and middle schools. The size and organization of the school and its social culture help to determine whether or not interdisciplinary designs are practical. Creative teachers have developed many ways in which the entire school can become involved in a thematic or interdisciplinary study. The following example models the essence of strong interdisciplinary design and is the result of two schools working together to achieve their mutual and diverse goals.

One elementary school in Colorado developed a relationship with an elementary school deep in the center of the Navajo Nation in Arizona. Like all relationships, genuine friendships and trust built slowly and the curriculum has gained in strength as experiences accumulated and the knowledge of the teachers increased.

After several years, the two schools have developed student exchanges and teacher exchanges. The students, in small groups each year and accompanied by teachers and parents, visit the partner school and live with host families in each location. On the reservation and in the metropolitan suburb, parents and school communities plan exciting events and experiences for their guests. For example, suburban students sleep in a hogan,

attend a rodeo, and explore ancient sites with their Navajo friends. Navajo students attend a major league basketball game, eat pizza and Chinese food, tour a jet (courtesy of a pilot father), and explore museums. Attending the school day with their friends is an unforgettable learning experience.

When the teachers exchange, they bring the special skills and expertise of each individual to the host families, children, and school community. In the suburban school, through an interdisciplinary approach the teachers devote approximately two weeks to teaching about Indian cultures (particularly the Navajo), and the library media center is the hub of varied activities—as is the gym, the playground, and the cafeteria. The school is immersed in Indian history and culture. You will find a traditional Navajo loom and weaver (carding, spinning, dyeing, and weaving), a jeweler, a language teacher, Navajo music and dance, storytellers, and others throughout the school.

From origin stories to contemporary problems faced by those on the reservation, the school "lives" an interdisciplinary study of the Navajo people. The suburban children, as a result of their interdisciplinary experiences and genuine friendships with Navajo children and adults, develop in-depth knowledge of and appreciation for the Navajo people. This knowledge is meaningful and will be a valued part of their lives as they become adults.

ASSESSMENT AND INTERDISCIPLINARY CURRICULUM

It is well to remember that authentic assessment, which is rapidly becoming a part of curriculum development and implementation, not only is *meaningful* but usually is *interdisciplinary*. Authentic assessment relates to "real life" and therefore is particularly appropriate when students must synthesize knowledge gained from different perspectives and experiences and utilize skills in relevant contexts. Walter Parker, a prominent social studies educator, has summarized the attributes of authentic benchmark assessments. These are listed in Figure 5.1.

Is an interdisciplinary approach worth the trouble? We think so. The study of American Indian cultures is complex and intriguing; and only a multifaceted and interconnected approach can begin to reveal the beauty, knowledge, and values that American Indians can bring to all Americans. Perhaps it is through the interdisciplinary study of Indian people that we can truly understand how we are related.

Wholeness. All things are interrelated. Everything in the universe is part of a single whole. Everything is connected in some way to everything else. It is therefore possible to understand something only if we can understand how it is connected to everything else. (Bopp, Bopp, Brown, & Lane, 1989, p. 26)

Roles of the School Library Media Specialist

Resource to Teachers and Students

Be cognizant of what goals teachers have set for a given period of time so that you can help them make connections between disciplines.

Develop a community resource directory that enables teachers to utilize local Indian people and areas institutions to enrich the curriculum.

Make certain that teachers are informed about new fiction, journals, biographies, and non-print, instructional materials that are not in their identified area of expertise (e.g. social studies teachers should be aware of new anthologies of American Indian literature).

Be aware of how the flexible scheduling of the library media center can enhance interdisciplinary efforts.

Curriculum Developer and Coordinator

Be knowledgeable about the scope and sequence of the entire curriculum related to American Indians - particularly the Language Arts/English, social studies, art, and music curriculum.

Encourage cooperation between teachers in various subjects.

Advocate in-depth, interdisciplinary study of Indian history and cultures, instead of fragmented efforts.

Collection Manager

Provide a rich variety of biographies, novels, poetry, and non-print materials at varying levels of complexity.

Develop a collection that presents Indian history in poems, pictures, stories, visual art, and other non-written forms.

Exhibit materials in enticing thematic or interdisciplinary groups or displays.

Provide contemporary source material which provides current information regarding Indian people and issues including newspapers, government documents, atlases, and reference materials. Make these sources known to all teachers - not just social studies teachers.

Teacher

Create a learning/resource center for exhibitions, demonstrations, presentations, and activities that enhance the interdisciplinary efforts of teachers and the entire school.

REFERENCES AND RESOURCES

Aliki. (1976). *Corn is maize.* New York: HarperCollins.

Armstrong, V. I. (Comp.). (1989). *I have spoken* (6th printing). Athens, OH: Swallow Press.

Beck, P. V., A. L. Walters, & N. Francisco. (1992). *The sacred: Ways of knowledge, sources of life* (reprint). Tsaile, AZ: Navajo Community College Press.

Bopp, J., M. Bopp, L. Brown, & P. Lane. (1989). *The sacred tree* (3rd ed.). Wilmot, WI: Lotus Light.

Chief Joseph. (1925). *Chief Joseph's own story.* St. Paul, MN: Great Northern Railway.

Fox, M. V. (1992). *Chief Joseph of the Nez Perce Indians.* Chicago: Children's Press.

Jacobs, H. H. (Ed.). (1989). *Interdisciplinary curriculum: Design and implementation.* Alexandria, VA: Association for Supervision and Curriculum Development.

Josephy, A. M., Jr. (1989). *The patriot chiefs* (reprint). New York: Penguin.

McWhorter, L. V. (1952). *Hear me, my chiefs!* Caldwell, ID: Caxton Printers.

McWhorter, L. V. (1991). *Yellow Wolf* (rev. ed.). Caldwell, ID: Caxton Printers.

Nader, A. J. (Producer). (1994). *America's great Indian leaders* (Video). Chicago: Questar Video.

National Council for the Social Studies. (1994). *Curriculum standards for social studies: Expectations of excellence.* Washington, DC: Author.

O'Dell, S., & E. Hall. (1992). *Thunder rolling in the mountains.* New York: Dell.

Parker, W. C. (1991). *Renewing the social studies curriculum.* Alexandria, VA: Association for Supervision and Curriculum Development.

Taylor, M. (1993). *Chief Joseph: Nez Perce leader.* New York: Chelsea.

Volper, D. (Producer). (1990). *I will fight no more forever* (Video). Chicago: Questar Video.

Yates, D. (1992). *Chief Joseph: Thunder rolling down from the mountains.* Staten Island, NY: Ward Hill Press.

The Land, the Environment, and the People

6

> Every part of this soil is sacred in the estimation of my people. Every hillside, every valley, every plain and grove, has been hallowed by some sad or happy event in days long vanished. The very dust upon which you now stand responds more lovingly to their footsteps than to yours, because it is rich with the blood of our ancestors and our bare feet are conscious of the sympathetic touch. (Chief Seattle, quoted in Armstrong, 1989, p. 79)

American Indians have lived in North America for thousands of years in harmony with and respect for the other living creatures and plants that inhabit the earth. Although the many tribes vary greatly in beliefs and traditions, one belief held in common is that everything in the world is interconnected. That is, all people and things are related to one another, and each depends on the other for life itself. This fundamental belief enabled Indian nations to live for thousands of years without depleting the natural resources or destroying any species of animal or plant. The interdependence of all things of the earth means that survival of each plant, animal, or person is dependent on the survival of all. Moreover, the natural environment, in all its diversity, provides for the well-being of the people who live on the earth; their lives are dependent on it and their cultures are shaped by it. The foods, dwellings, clothing, lifeways, traditions, and spiritual beliefs of any particular American Indian tribe are inextricably related to the geographic region in which they live.

Scholars have identified twelve geographic regions in North and Central America, each with unique physical environments and natural resources. These regions are also known as culture areas because of the

influence of geography on culture. Although the many tribes within a region share numerous cultural characteristics, primarily because of the natural and physical resources available to them, other aspects of their
cultures may vary greatly.

The culture areas described in this chapter are commonly incorporated
in teaching. Supporting material can be found in many sources that will
enhance basic knowledge of any particular region. The regions, ten of
which are illustrated on the map in Figure 6.1, are as follows:

1. Northeast Region
2. Southeast Region
3. Great Plains Region
4. Southwest Region
5. Great Basin Region
6. Plateau Region
7. Northwest Coast Region
8. California Region
9. Subarctic Region
10. Arctic Region
11. Mesoamerica Region
12. Circum Caribbean Region

Two regions not located within the United States, the Mesoamerica Region
and the Circum Caribbean Region, are also important in the study of ancient civilizations and the first significant encounter with the Europeans in
1492.

Culture has been defined as people's solution to the problem of survival; it can be described as the behavior patterns, belief systems, artifacts,
foods, tools, shelter, and languages that a group of people use to shape
their lives. In looking into the past, we will find that the traditional lives of
American Indians were closely linked to available natural resources because their livelihood and well-being depended on what was available.
Practices seen as idiosyncratic and strange can be understood as admirable and creative when viewed as an adaptation to the natural environment.

However, culture is more than the use of natural resources in a particular place. It is a unique worldview that, according to Alfonso Ortiz, "provides people with a distinctive set of values, an identity, a feeling of
'rootedness,' of belonging to a time and a place, and a felt sense of continuity with a tradition that transcends the experience of a single lifetime, a
tradition that may be said to transcend even time" (1983). Thus, two tribes
in the same natural environment, even a few hundred miles apart, devel-

Figure 6.1
Ten Culture Areas in North and Central America

oped differing cultures even though they may have used the same resources in similar ecosystems.

The following discussion will highlight ten regions, summarizing the natural and physical resources and the traditional lifeways of the Native people who inhabited each one. In this brief overview of the lives and cultures of the Native people of North America, the vital link between the land, the environment, and the people will become evident. As traditional lifeways are explored, it is important to remember that contemporary American Indians live with both the ancient traditions of the past and the changes initiated by developing technologies and interaction with cultures of today's world. The contemporary Indian world is an extension of the past combined with the experience of the present. The descriptions in this chapter refer to Native Americans before contact with the Western world. And although many changes have occurred, modern American Indians are still remarkably similar and very diverse.

NORTHEAST REGION

Natural and Physical Resources

The climate of the Northeast Region is dramatic, with harsh winters and cool summers in the north and mild winters and hot summers in the south. This expanse of territory includes mountains, coastal areas, valleys, lakes, and rivers and yields abundant resources. Forests furnished fuel, building materials, tools, and homes for the animals that provided food and clothing. The rivers and lakes provided water, fish, and a means of transportation.

Native People

This cultural area was the home of some of the most well known of the ancient prehistoric cultures, the Adena and Hopewell cultures. The area is rich in archaeological sites. One of the most awesome and mysterious mounds, the Great Serpent Mound, is located in Ohio. The material and spiritual cultures of these Native people reflected the abundant resources, the cold climate, and the need for allies. People (and their animals) lived in permanent shelters such as wigwams and longhouses; these served them well, providing safe storage for food and protection from the harsh weather.

The Micmac, Abenaki, Narragansett, and Delaware tribes lived in the coastal areas. These people lived in wigwams, which are dome-like houses built with frames of saplings covered with slabs of bark and deerskin. Separated from the coast by the Appalachians, the Mohawk, Oneida, Onondaga, Cayuga, Seneca, Huron, Neutral, and Erie lived in longhouses

built with logs and bark. These people developed large, fortified villages. In the regions around the Great Lakes and parts of Ohio, Kentucky, and West Virginia, the Erie, Shawnee, Kickapoo, Miami, Winnebago, and Fox lived in villages, venturing out to hunt, fish, gather, and farm.

The Native people of this region were not only hunters and gatherers but also fishermen and farmers. They wore practical clothing made of the skins of animals hunted for food, including caribou, beaver, otter, moose, and bear. Their clothing was adorned with shells, beads, and quills that often depicted flowers, butterflies, and other aspects of the natural environment. Their moccasins, as well as pouches to carry their belongings, were made of hides. Cooking utensils, both pots and spoons, were made of clay and bark.

SOUTHEAST REGION

Natural and Physical Resources

Both the tropical coastlines and the continental interiors of the Southeast Region are very humid. The temperature is generally mild to hot in the summer, with cold winters in the north and rainy ones in the south. The land includes coastal plains, saltwater marshes, grasses, and strands of cypress along with the mountain highlands in the north. The mountains and valleys are home to vast forests. Lakes and rivers are located throughout the region, yielding fish and water fowl.

The Southeast Region is very different today from its aboriginal condition. At that time, cane brakes stood in the swamps alongside the cypress. The silt washing down through the swamps and waterways created fields that were easily nurtured and productive. The available resources of hundreds of years ago included both saltwater and freshwater fish, berries, nuts, and fruits. Because of dramatic changes in the environment since those early days, many of these resources have been lost.

Native People

The ancient culture of the Southeast area, the Mississippian, surpassed the earlier cultures of the Eastern woodlands. The Mississippian culture began in the lower Mississippi valley around the year A.D. 700. Unlike the earlier mound builders, the Mississippians distinguished themselves as agriculturalists; this enabled them to live in larger settlements and build more impressive ceremonial centers. Some of the tribes we know today, such as the Natchez, are direct descendants of the Mississippians. Other major tribes of the Southeast include the Creek, Choctaw, Chickasaw, Cherokee, Seminole, Caddo, Catawba, and Alabama.

The people of this region enjoyed abundant wildlife, moderate temperatures, and fertile land; and they were able to live in settled communities. They wore clothing made from reeds and grasses as well as hides from small animals. They raised crops such as corn and squash, which came from the early cultures of the Southwest.

The spiritual life of the people was linked to daily life. Corn was central to the annual celebration that marked the new year, the Green Corn Ceremony. Prayers were said on behalf of all the abundant resources that provided for life.

The people of this region lived in two types of shelters: the chickee, and the wattle and daub home. The chickee was a stilt house, open on all four sides, that was built on four poles with a roof of thatched palmetto leaves and a floor of split logs. Unique to the Seminoles, the chickee was connected to the environment and available resources. The other people of the Southeast lived in wattle and daub homes, which were shelters constructed with a pole framework, woven with branches and vines, and covered with mud plaster.

GREAT PLAINS REGION

Natural and Physical Resources

This region encompasses nearly one million square miles of rolling hills and grasslands, valleys, and buttes. The climate in the west is semi-arid; in the east there is a greater amount of rainfall from storms originating in the Gulf of Mexico. The grass that grows abundantly has adapted to hundreds of years of drought and has supported buffalo, elk, deer, goats, sheep, wolves, bear, and birds.

Native People

The Native people of the Plains primarily lived a nomadic life before the coming of the Europeans. The further west on the Plains, the more the people depended on the buffalo and other small and large animals for subsistence. Here they followed the herds, living in temporary shelters and using the animals to meet many of their basic needs. In the eastern part of the Plains the rainfall was greater and the people were farmers, living in villages along the river valleys.

The people of the Plains depended on buffalo, antelope, and other animals for food, shelter, and clothing. Their diet consisted of wild meat and wild vegetables. The meat of the buffalo and other game was consumed at the time of kill or dried for the times when the herds were not so easily accessible.

People dressed for the severity of winter and the heat of summer. Garments were constructed of hides after laborious preparation. The animals' bones were used as needles and their intestines as thread. Clothing was decorated with beads made from shells acquired through trading, porcupine quills, and the hooves and teeth of deer and elk.

The nomadic tribes' lifestyle required that shelters be quickly set up and easily transported. The typical shelter was the tipi, which was made of hides sewn together to make a large, conical room with a single entrance and a smoke hole at the top. The structure was supported by several poles that were carried from camp to camp. Settled tribes, such as the Mandans, Hidatsa, and Caddo, lived along the rivers and dug permanent earthen lodges in the ground.

The coming of the Europeans brought horses and dramatic change to North America. Life for the nomadic people became easier because they now had horses on which to travel and carry their belongings. Hunting became easier also, and food became more abundant. Consequently, the Sioux, Pawnee, Ponca, Iowa, Cheyenne, and others fleeing droughts and invading Europeans emigrated to find food and shelter on the Plains.

Spiritual practices were directly linked to the resources and environment of the Plains. For example, the buffalo was the focus of many rituals and ceremonies held to ensure successful hunts, abundant food, and well-being.

SOUTHWEST REGION

Natural and Physical Resources

In the Southwest Region the summers are hot and dry, and winters are moderate. The people, animals, and plants of the desert have evolved to meet the challenges of this environment.

Native People

People have inhabited the Southwest Region for over 10,000 years. The Clovis, Folsom, and Plano cultures were the earliest in the area. Later cultures, the Anasazi, Hohokam, and Mogollon, lived in the area beginning around 300 B.C. These people were hunters and gatherers who later became agriculturalists. Some domesticated corn, beans, and squash and built irrigation systems to carry water for their crops. Their descendants are the Pueblos, Yumans, Pimas, and Papagos. Newcomers to the region in approximately A.D. 1000, the Navajo and Apache, were nomadic people who learned from others to survive in the desert.

Inhabitants of this region had a healthy diet of corn, beans, and squash as well as deer, rabbit, and other small animals. Villages had safe places to

store the crops for times when the people were unable to harvest enough food.

Homes of the Southwestern tribes included wickiups, brush lean-tos, hogans, earth lodges, and pueblos. A wickiup is a conical hut with a pole frame covered with reed mats, grass, or brush. The walls of pueblos and hogans are made of dirt or clay, which insulates against the heat of summer and the cold of winter. The Pueblos built strong, walled fortresses for protection.

The people of this region began weaving fiber and cotton into cloth hundreds of years ago (they were also expert basket makers). Their clothing, light in weight and color, was made of skins, cotton cloth, and fiber to protect them from the hot, burning sun.

The religious and ceremonial life of the people of the Southwest Region was infused into every part of their lives. Many ceremonies and religious figures were related to corn, beans, and squash, which supported their way of life. The Pueblo and other tribes practiced religious ceremonies that related to soil fertility and the scarcity of rain and water.

GREAT BASIN REGION

Natural and Physical Resources

In the Great Basin the land varies from open, rolling hills with grasslands and rivers to the dramatically layered canyons of the Colorado River. The region is marked by numerous saline lakes, including the Great Salt Lake. Extreme heat and cold characterize the region; the hottest extreme is found in Death Valley, where summer temperatures reach as high as 130 degrees Fahrenheit.

Native People

The major tribes inhabiting this region were the Paiute, Shoshoni, and Ute. Because of the harsh environment and limited availability of food, they foraged for roots, wild vegetables, berries, pine nuts, snakes, lizards, insects, and rodents. They also hunted small game The relative lack of water and firewood influenced the meager size of the population and determined their nomadic lifestyle. Their homes, which were simple to construct and could easily be left behind, were made of twigs and wood woven into wickiups and covered with sod or hides. The women wove baskets for cradleboards, shoes, burden baskets, hats, spoons, and even clothing.

Because resources were scarce, the Native people of the Great Basin had high esteem for all creations. When gathering plants, for instance, they prayed or left an offering to the plant for what was taken. They named the

constellations in the heavens after the animals that roamed the earth, and they looked to the sky for signs of the seasons and the right way to live.

The coming of the horse dramatically changed their way of life. With greater mobility, it was possible to hunt larger animals and to carry more possessions each time they moved. Eventually the Utes and Shoshonis adapted to the Plains lifestyle and began to live in tipis and hunt buffalo.

PLATEAU REGION

Natural and Physical Resources

The land of the Plateau, which covers 200,000 square miles, teems with beautiful forests, valleys, and mountains; clear rushing streams; and open meadowlands. The rivers carry salmon, sturgeon, eel, whitefish, and trout. Beyond the rivers are treeless plains without the water and resources needed to sustain life.

Native People

Some of the tribes that inhabited this area include the Klamath, Modoc, Nez Perce, Yakima, Coeur d'Alene, Flathead, Kalispel, and Spokane. The people of this region relied on the rivers to supply their food, travel, and trade with other Indians. They ate berries, nuts, and salmon or other fish, which they speared. The eastern part of this region was not as densely populated as the Northwest Coast region just to the west, because of the diminished resources.

Homes were similar to the tipis of the Plains. Seven to nine poles were stacked around a tripod in a conical fashion, and a covering of mats woven from cattail or tule was added. In winter the lodges were sunk about two feet into the ground and were covered with three or four layers of mats. In some areas, large lodges housed several families.

Clothing was made of hides. Before the horse, the hides came from antelope, rabbit, beaver, and other small animals. However, once the horse entered the Plateau Region the people could hunt deer, buffalo, and other animals of the plains; this caused a change in their diet and way of life.

NORTHWEST COAST REGION

Natural and Physical Resources

The Northwest Coast is temperate and moist, with abundant rain and lush forests. Water was plentiful throughout the region, and the natural resources enabled the people and the animal and plant kingdoms to flourish.

Native People

The abundance of resources and the subsequent leisure time enabled the Native people of this region to develop complex societies. Their life revolved around group ceremonies such as the potlatch, during which an individual is honored by how much he can give away. Most of the tribes based their lives on the cedar and the salmon, which they honored and respected through ceremonies.

Salmon provided the people much of their diet along with the clams, mussels, and oysters that were available throughout the year. Mountain mammals added variety to the diet and also provided materials for clothing and other necessary items. These animals' horns were fashioned into spoons, needles, and other tools; their wool was spun into yarn to be woven for ceremonial clothing. Berries and other plant foods were harvested in the spring and fall.

The tribes of this region were the Tlingit, Haida, Puyallup, Chinook, Lummi, Klamath, Salish, and Makah. The richness of resources allowed them to develop sedentary lifestyles and live in permanent structures. The typical home was the longhouse. Constructed from cedar and other wood from the forests, these lodges were large and often housed more than one family. They were also used for ceremonial purposes. The Native people of this area were skilled artisans, weaving baskets, carving wooden tools and ceremonial pieces, and working stone.

CALIFORNIA REGION

Natural and Physical Resources

In the northern part of the California Region the climate is cool with abundant annual rainfall, and the forests are thick. Toward the south the forests include more diverse trees and plants, including the great redwoods of central California. The southern reaches of the region are desert, with typical desert climate and vegetation. This region is known for its mild climate with hot summers and cool winters.

Native People

The Native people of the California Region found an abundance of plants and animals, which shaped their unique way of life. Even without agriculture, they were able to sustain life. People ate fish and game such as deer, rabbit, buffalo, and wild turkey and many varieties of berries and roots. Tribes living in this area were the Hoopa, Karok, Yurok, Tule River, Chumash, and various Mission Indians.

Villages were usually permanent, and the mild climate required little or no shelter. In the south the weather was warm and people wore only what

was needed. Clothing was made from grass and small hides, often decorated with shells and bones. Baskets and hats, as well as shoes, were woven. The further north the people lived, the more clothing they wore; it was usually made of hides.

SUBARCTIC REGION

Natural and Physical Resources

The Subarctic is the largest region, and it includes a great diversity in the environment. However, it is characterized by long, harsh winters that are only briefly broken by short, mild summers.

The vast majority of the region is covered by taiga, or forest, consisting of pine, spruce, and fir with some aspen, willow, and birch. The area is covered with bodies of water because of the permafrost, which keeps the water on the surface. The most abundant resources were caribou, moose, bear, beaver, small rodents, and fish; these provided staples of the diet and were the source of materials for tools, shelter, and clothing.

Native People

The Native people of this area were the Cree, Metis, Montagnais, Ojibwa, Naskapi, Carrier, Chipewyan, and Kutchin. There were few inhabitants in this region; the people hunted and fished for survival, often following their prey over long distances. Few complex social, economic, or political systems developed here because of the expanse and nature of the environment. People lived independently from each other yet were very dependent on the animal life.

Tanning of hides for clothing and shelter, and preparation of tools from bones and teeth, were common. Sleds, snowshoes, and other items were made from hides. Because the people were nomadic, wigwams (which were made from poles and hides and were easy to disassemble and reassemble during the hunt) were common.

A diet of fatty meats was required to sustain the people through the cold winter months. Their primary source of food was the caribou, along with other small animals and fish. Birch trees provided many items for daily living such as baskets and cooking vessels.

ARCTIC REGION

Natural and Physical Resources

The climate of the north is extremely cold, with ice and snow covering the land for most of the year. Blizzards blow the snow into enormous drifts. The winters are long with little daylight, and the summers warm

with endless days. The land stays frozen for most of the year, and the permafrost prevents most plants with deep roots from flourishing.

Native People

The first substantial evidence of human occupation confirms that Native people inhabited the area from approximately 9000 B.C. These inhabitants are known historically as the Eskimos and the Aleuts. They generally have a short, broad stature, with light skin and the fold in the eyelid that is characteristic of Asian people. The modern-day Eskimo prefer to be called the Inuit, meaning "the People," rather than Eskimo, an Algonkian word meaning "raw meat eaters."

The Inuits of the farthest north country lived in igloos or, when possible, in wooden lodges built above the ground. They traveled in kayaks and sleds in search of food and shelter. They were partners with their dogs in searching for seals and transporting them to waiting families. Other Inuits lived inland and hunted caribou and musk oxen. The Aleuts, who lived in the Aleutian Islands off the coast of Alaska, dwelled in pit houses and depended on the same resources for their survival.

Certainly, there is a relationship between the type of environment that a people live in and the type of culture that develops. For the early Native peoples of North and Central America, the development of complex and sophisticated political, social, and economic systems was related to abundance and surplus of resources to sustain life. The level of differentiation in social class was also linked to abundance and material wealth. However, beyond these characteristics the tribes were unique, multifaceted, and persevering. They shared a respect for the giver of life—the natural world—and they nurtured their relationship with it on a daily basis. Religion, ceremony, and spirituality were not separate from daily life, but *were* daily life.

Our beliefs are rooted deep in our earth, no matter what you have done to it and how much of it you have paved over. And if you leave all that concrete unwatched for a year or two, our plants, the native Indian plants, will pierce that concrete and push up through it. (John Lame Deer, 1972, p. 153)

REFERENCES AND RESOURCES

Armstrong, V. I. (1989). *I have spoken*. Athens, OH: Swallow Press.

Geography for life. (1994). Washington, DC: Geographic Education Standards Project.

Harvey, K. D., L. D. Harjo, and J. K. Jackson. (1990). *Teaching about Native Americans*. Washington, DC: National Council for the Social Studies.

Roles of the School Library Media Specialist

Resource to Teachers and Students

Help teachers and students become aware of television programs and emerging news stories that focus on the special relationship of Indian people to the lands, including return of tribal lands, fishing, hunting, and gathering rights, and protection of sacred areas.

Create databases, lists, or other convenient means for teachers and students to select a variety of instructional materials for particular culture area(s) enabling them to provide geographical context for art, music, and literature instruction about American Indians.

Provide, as part of the professional library, guidelines for curriculum and instruction from the American Geographical Society, Association of American Geographers, National Council for Geographic Education, and National Geographical Society. The most important document is the publication, Geography for Life: National Geography Standards - 1994.

Curriculum Developer and Coordinator

Advocate the integration of geographical concepts into curriculum areas that address American Indian people and cultures - including music, art, literature, and social studies.

Encourage the development of curriculum that compares tribal groups and their unique adaptations to their physical environments and available resources.

Link current emphasis on respect for and protection on the environment as well as constitutional protection for freedom on religion to the traditional and enduring relationship between American Indian people and cultures and the land.

Collection Manager

Display maps and globes (physical, resource, population, temperature, rainfall, location, political etc.) along with print and non-print materials about American Indians.

Provide access to computer programs that enhance geographical skills.

Locate print and non-print materials that illustrate the relationship between the physical environment, natural resources, and the development of culture.

Teacher

Create displays that encourage students to compare homes, foods, shelters, games, stories, social structures, ceremonies, and daily lives of traditional and contemporary American Indian people in differing cultural areas and highlight the relationship of geography and culture.

Source: National Geographic Standards Project. (1994). *Geography for life: National geography standards—1994.* Washington, DC: National Geographic Research and Exploration.

Kopper, P. (Ed.). (1986). *The Smithsonian book of North American Indians before the coming of the Europeans*. Washington, DC: Smithsonian Books.

Lame Deer, J. (Fire). (1972). *Lame Deer, seeker of visions*. New York: Pocket.

Ortiz, A. V. (1983). "Introduction: Cultural Values and Leadership Development." In J. Morris, *Ohoyo training manual—Leadership: Self-help, American Indian–Alaska Native women*. Wichita Falls, TX: Ohoyo Resource Center.

Taylor, C. F. (Ed.). (1991). *The Native Americans*. New York: Salamander Books.

Waldman, C. (1985). *Atlas of the North American Indian*. New York: Facts on File.

Woodhead, H. (Ed.). (1992). *The First Americans*. Alexandria, VA: Time-Life Books.

Teaching about Culture

7

> The music of the original inhabitants of North America stretches back beyond memory. Most importantly, it also reaches to the present and into the future with great vitality and spirit, rooted firmly in tradition but thriving, growing, evolving to reflect the dynamic cultures found across the continent today. These voices have not been stilled by a difficult history. These dances have not been forgotten. The music of Native American Indians was not frozen at a point in time only the old ones remember. Young musicians are absorbing the lessons of the past as well as the present, of the ceremonies as well as the conservatories, blending, melding, working with the raw materials to present sights and sounds distinctively marked with their culture as it exists in the present. (Burton, 1993, cover)

The introduction to B. Burton's book about American Indian music is a good reminder of the living, evolving, and enduring aspects of Indian cultures. They live today with renewed vibrancy and meaning for Indian and non-Indian people. Because America's indigenous peoples are such a vital, contributing, and enduring part of our past, present, and future, it is important that their cultures be understood and respected. There are those who believe that American Indian cultures also have much to teach us as we search for a sustainable and peaceful future. These cultures should be taught as the roots of our democracy, as integral to our history, and as part of the contemporary multicultural fabric of the United States.

If American Indian literature is used in the classroom, if American history and government are taught, if state history is explored, if students consider how people have used and adapted to the physical and natural environment, if they learn about a range of musical and artistic expression,

if they study American holidays, if they learn about America's diverse peoples, then teachers are directly or indirectly teaching about Indian cultures. How can the school library media specialist support this study?

In this chapter we present a workable definition of culture and a practical model for teaching about American Indian cultures. We also suggest resources that explain certain cultural components and are good examples that can begin to form a reference and resource library for educators who teach about Native cultures.

A MODEL FOR TEACHING CULTURE

Culture has been defined as the elements humans use to adjust to their physical and social environment, their solution to the problem of survival. It is the social heritage of a given group of people. Culture consists of the behavior patterns, belief systems, artifacts, foods, tools, shelter, and language that a group of people use in their lives (see Figure 7.1). Nearly all the important differences among lifeways of all people are not biological differences but differences in *learned patterns* of social behavior—the human-made components of every society.

American Indian lifeways, stories and literature, forms of religious practice, art, music, food, traditional homes, technologies, and family and political structures have significant meaning only when they are placed in historical, geographical, and cultural context. Indian cultures must be taught in terms of the intersection between time, place, and people (see Figure 7.2)—how Native people have chosen to live during a particular time and in a particular place. We have adapted this understanding to create a teaching model by adding two important concepts. The first, authenticity, is related to content; the second, respect, is related to pedagogy. Time, place, authenticity, and respect should be present in teaching about American Indian cultures (see Figure 7.3). Only when we acknowledge that people are products of the time and natural environment in which they live can we begin to understand their diversity and creativity. When teachers present authentic (not romantic or stereotypical) American Indian cultures with respect, students will develop knowledge and understanding of the concept of culture and an appreciation for the unique indigenous cultures of America.

For each of the major components of culture, we offer a list of practical, annotated resources that will ensure historical and geographical context, authenticity, and respect. Needless to say, these recommendations are just a beginning. There is no scarcity of materials about Indian people and cultures. The books and materials listed here are general; we assume that most teachers and students need to build a fundamental knowledge base, and that they will search further as they require more complex, specific, or detailed information. In this listing we have avoided highly specialized materials or scholarly works that require in-depth study. Whenever possi-

Figure 7.1
Components of Traditional and Contemporary American Indian Cultures

Basic Needs
  Shelter
  Food
  Clothing

Spirituality and Religious Practices
  Sacred Sites
  Sacred Ceremonies

Family Structures
  Roles and relationships
  Child-rearing practices
  Rites of passage (naming of children, puberty, marriage, death/burial)

Political Structures
  Governance

Language

Literature
  Oral traditions
  Contemporary literatures

Recreation/Games

Technology

Art

Music and Dance

Figure 7.2
Culture: Time, Place, and People

Figure 7.3
Teaching about Culture

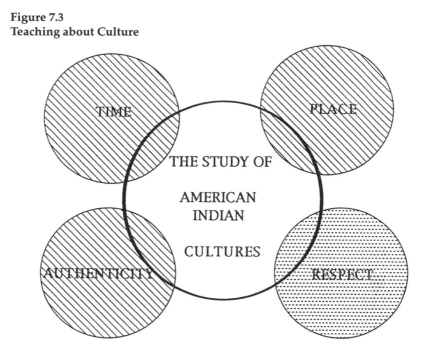

Note: The "respect" circle is shaded differently to show that it is modeled and nurtured and
  not taught directly.

ble, Indian authors are identfied; Indian voice is authentic and, thus, more
useful. The books listed here may not be considered the "best" by others,
but they are our favorites and will lead you to other resources. Only materials that are generally available (not obscure publications or out-of-print
materials) are included.

In the following sections, each source listed is followed by one or more
capital letters in parentheses. These designations indicate general reading
level:

P   Primary
I   Intermediate
H   High school
A   Adult

Of course, the designations are approximate: adults can gain a great deal
from reading books for children, and young readers can "stretch" to more
difficult levels.

MAJOR COMPONENTS OF INDIAN CULTURE: SUGGESTED RESOURCES

Basic Needs

Shelter

First Man said that the young man and woman were to be the source of all life and that they would never be seen on earth again. He then concealed them in his medicine bundle with the coverings of dawn, twilight, sunlight, and darkness and set about creating the first house, the prototype of the homes where human lives would be centered in the future. (McAllester & McAllester, 1980, p. 20)

Laubin, R., & G. Laubin. (1984). *The Indian tipi: Its history, construction, and use* (rev. ed.). Norman: University of Oklahoma. (H/A)

Monroe, J. G., & R. A. Williamson. (1993). *First houses: Native American homes and sacred structures*. Boston: Houghton Mifflin. A unique book of information and legends. (I/H)

Shemie, B. (1989). *Houses of snow, skin and bones: Native dwellings of the Far North*. Montreal: Tundra. These are wonderful, informative books for children. (P/I)

Shemie, B. (1991). *Houses of hide and earth: Native dwellings of the Plains Indians*. Montreal: Tundra. (P/I)

Shemie, B. (1992). *Houses of bark: Native dwellings of the Woodland Indians*. Montreal: Tundra. (P/I)

Shemie, B. (1992). *Houses of wood: Native dwellings of the Northwest coast*. Montreal: Tundra. (P/I)

Shemie, B. (1993). *Houses of earth and shell: Native sites: The Southeast*. Montreal: Tundra. (P/I)

Waldman, C. (1985). *Atlas of the North American Indian*. New York: Facts on File. (H/A)

Yue, C., & D. Yue. (1988). *The igloo*. Boston: Houghton Mifflin. (I)

Yue, D., & C. Yue. (1984). *The tipi*. New York: Alfred A. Knopf. (I)

Food

As is traditional, foods are acquired with reverence and attention to its [*sic*] importance in the balance of nature. Each animal, fish, or plant has unique qualities and powers, and are [*sic*] considered a relative to all life. When any are eaten, used, or worn, these qualities become part of the person utilizing them. Even utensils, weapons, and tools are channels of spirit energy, positive or negative, which can be passed to foods and material goods. (Williamson & Railsback, 1987, Introduction)

Cox, B., & M. Jacobs. (1991). *Spirit of the harvest*. New York: Stewart, Tabori & Chang. (H/A)

Henry, E. (Blue Star Woman). (1983). *Native American cookbook*. New York: Julian Messner. (I)

Penner, L. R. (1994). *A Native American feast*. New York: Macmillan. (P/I)

Williamson, D., & L. Railsback. (1987). *Cooking with spirit: North American Indian food and fact*. Bend, OR: Maverick. (H/A)

Clothing

While men [of the Northeast] engaged in their endless rounds of hunting, the women made clothing for all. Hide wardrobes included shirts, dresses and parkas with and without hoods. The Naskapi dehaired caribou skins and decorated them with painted designs. Athapaskans and Algonquians alike used beaver pelts for robes and fur hats. Athapaskans of the Shield made leather leggings with moccasins attached. Moccasins served well with snowshoes, which often enabled hunters to chase down big prey in winter's heavy snowdrifts. Made with frames of spruce wood, they were laced with *babiche*—rawhide thongs. (Kopper, 1986, p. 117)

Descriptions and illustrations of traditional clothing are most easily found in general and specific tribal books, as well as other resources.

Gabor, R. (1988). *Costume of the Iroquois* (reprint). Ontario, Canada: Iroqrafts Ltd. (I/H)

Horse Capture, G. P. (1989). *Powwow*. Cody, WY: Buffalo Bill Museum. (I/H)

Koch, R. P. (1977). *Dress clothing of the Plains Indians*. Norman: University of Oklahoma. (H/A)

Spirituality and Religious Practices

Sacred Sites

Sacred sites are places of communication with the spirits, portals where people enter the sacred. Thus, they are a link between the world of humans and the sacred, where spiritual power can be attained. Sacred sites are also natural maps that provide direction to life and shape to the world. They give order to both geographic and social space, and by ordering space they order all that exists within it. (Vecsey, 1991, p. 11)

Hirschfelder, A., & P. Molin. (1992). *The encyclopedia of Native American religions*. New York: Facts on File. (I/H/A)

Vecsey, C. (Ed.). (1991). *Handbook of American Indian religious freedom*. New York: Crossroad. (H/A)

Sacred Ceremonies

The Sun Dance is . . . not a celebration by humans for humans; it is an honoring of all life and the source of all life that life may continue, that the circle be a cycle, that

all the world and humankind may continue on the path of the cycle of giving, receiving, bearing, being born in suffering, growing, becoming, returning to the earth that which has been given, and finally being born again. . . . It is only through suffering in sacrifice that freedom is finally known and laughter in joy returns to the world. (Brown, 1992, p. 105)

Beck, P. V., A. L. Walters, & N. Francisco. (1992). *The sacred* (2nd printing). Tucson: University of Arizona/Sun Tracks. (H/A)

Black Elk, W., & W. W. Lyon. (1990). *Black Elk: The sacred ways of a Lakota*. San Francisco: Harper. (H/A)

Brown, J. E. (1992). *The spiritual legacy of the American Indian*. New York: Crossroad. (H/A)

Bruchac, J. (1993). *The Native American sweatlodge: History and legends*. Freedom, CA: Crossing Press. (H/A)

Hirschfelder, A., & P. Molin. (1992). *The encyclopedia of Native American religions*. New York: Facts on File. (I/H/A)

Lame Deer, J. (Fire), & R. Erdoes. (1976). *Lame Deer, seeker of visions* (9th printing). New York: Pocket.

Neihardt, J. G. (1988). *Black Elk speaks* (7th printing). New York: Pocket.

Underhill, R. M. (1965). *Red man's religion*. Chicago: University of Chicago.

Wall, S., & H. Arden. (1990). *Wisdom keepers*. Hillsboro, OR: Beyond Words.

Waters, F. (1984). *The book of the Hopi* (reprint). New York: Penguin.

Family Structures

The resources listed below are fairly general and could easily fit into more than one category.

Roles and Relationships

As a motherless child, I always regarded my good grandmother as the wisest of guides and the best of protectors. . . . Aside from her native talent and ingenuity, she was endowed with a truly wonderful memory. No other midwife in her day and tribes could compete with her in skill and judgment. Her observations in practice were all preserved in her mind for reference, as systematically as if they had been written on the pages of a note-book. . . . In bravery she equaled any of the men. (Eastman, 1971, pp. 17–19)

Bataille, G. M., & K. M. Sands. (1984). *American Indian women: Telling their lives*. Lincoln: University of Nebraska. (H/A)

Farley, R. (1993). *Women of the Native struggle: Portraits and testimony of Native American women*. New York: Orion. (H/A)

Green, R. (1992). *Women in American Indian society*. New York: Chelsea House. (I/H)

Standing Bear, L. (1975). *My people the Sioux* (reprint). Lincoln: University of Nebraska. (H/I)

Standing Bear, L. (1978). *Land of the Spotted Eagle* (reprint). Lincoln: University of Nebraska. (H/I)

Several children's books are excellent resources on how Indian children and families live in contemporary America. The following are good examples; others are certain to be written soon. These books also tell about childrearing practices, homes, and ways of life today—how the culture has changed and endured.

Hoyt-Goldsmith, D. (1990). *Totem pole.* New York: Holiday House. (P)

Hoyt-Goldsmith, D. (1991). *Pueblo storyteller.* New York: Holiday House. (P)

Hoyt-Goldsmith, D. (1992). *Arctic hunter.* New York: Holiday House. (P)

Hoyt-Goldsmith, D. (1993). *Cherokee summer.* New York: Holiday House. (P)

Keegan, M. (1991). *Pueblo boy: Growing up in two worlds.* New York: Cobblehill/Dutton. (P)

King, S. (1993). *Shannon: An Oijbway dancer.* Minneapolis, MN: Lerner. (P)

Maher, R. (1977). *Alice Yazzie's year.* New York: Coward, McCann & Geohegan. (P/I)

Peters, R. H. (1992). *Clambake: A Wampanoag tradition.* Minneapolis, MN: Lerner. (P)

Regguiniti, G. (1992). *The sacred harvest: Oijbway wild rice gathering.* Minneapolis, MN: Lerner. (P)

Swentzell, R. (1992). *Children of clay.* Minneapolis, MN: Lerner. (P)

Wood, T., with W. N. Afraid of Hawk. (1992). *A boy becomes a man at Wounded Knee.* New York: Walker. (P)

Child-rearing Practices (traditional)

I got to know the spring branch, following it up the hollow; the dip swallows that hung sack nests in the willows and fussed at me until they got to know me—then they would stick out their heads and talk; the frogs that sung all along the banks, but would hush when I moved close, until Granpa told me that frogs can feel the ground shake when you walk. He showed me how the Cherokee walks, not heel down, but toe down, slipping the moccasins on the ground. Then I could come right up, and set down beside a frog and he would keep singing. (Carter, 1989, p. 58)

Carter, F. (1989). *The education of Little Tree* (7th printing). Albuquerque: University of New Mexico. (I/H/A)

Eastman, C. A. (1971). *Indian boyhood* (reprint). New York: Dover. (H/A)

Riley, P. (Ed.). (1993). *Growing up Native American.* New York: William Morrow. (H/A)

Standing Bear, L. (1988). *My Indian boyhood* (reprint). Lincoln: University of Nebraska. (H/A)

Rites of Passage (naming of children, puberty, marriage, death/burial)

A man in the back of the hogan stands up slowly, takes off his cowboy hat and says, "Remember, a wedding is like a prayer. The Holy People have blessed you. There is beauty above you, beauty beneath you. Look around, there is beauty all around you as you start your life together." (Roessel, 1993, p. 45)

General books are best for the topic of rites of passage, and contemporary magazines such as *Native Peoples* can provide rich information about these rites today. The following resources, including children's books, are indicative of how Native authors are beginning to enrich our knowledge of this topic.

Bruchac, J. (1993). *Flying with the eagle, racing the great bear*. Mahwah, NJ: Troll. (I)

Bruchac, J., & G. Ross. (1994). *The girl who married the moon*. Mahwah, NJ: Troll. (I)

Goseyun, A. E. (1991, Summer). Carla's sunrise. *Native Peoples* 4 (4), pp. 8–16. (I/H/A)

Mimelfarb, B. (1991, Fall). The Cheyenne way. *Native Peoples* 5 (1), pp. 8–13. (I/H/A)

Roessel, M. (1993). *Kinaalda*. Minneapolis, MN: Lerner. (I)

Roessel, M. (1993, June). A Navajo couple unites with tradition. *New Mexico* 71 (6), pp. 38–45. (I/H/A)

Seymour, T.V.N. (1993). *The gift of Changing Woman*. New York: Holt. (I)

Political Structures

Governance

Among us we have no prisons, we have no pompous parade of courts; we have no written laws, and yet judges are as highly revered among us as they are among you, and their decisions are as highly regarded.

Property, to say the least, is well-guarded, and crimes are as impartially punished. We have among us no splendid villains above the control of our laws. Daring wickedness is never suffered to triumph over helpless innocence. The estates of widows and orphans are never devoured by enterprising sharpers. In a word, we have no robbery under color of the law. (Joseph Brant, Mohawk, 1807; see Armstrong, 1989, p. 42)

Barreiro, J. (Ed.). (1988). *Indian roots of American democracy*. Ithaca, NY: Northeast Indian Quarterly. (H/A)

O'Brien, S. (1989). *American Indian tribal governments*. Norman: University of Oklahoma. This book lists many tribal resources. (H/A)

Pevar, S. L. (1992). *The rights of Indians and tribes*. Carbondale: Southern Illinois University. (H/A)

Language

[W]ords in their sounds are born in the breath of the being from whom they proceed, and since breath in these traditions is universally identified with the life principle, words are thus sacred and must be used with care and responsibility. Such quality of the spoken word is further enhanced by the understood close proximity of the source of breath, the lungs, with the heart, which is associated with the being's spiritual center. (Brown, 1992, p. 3)

Ballantine, B., & I. Ballantine. (Eds.). (1993). *The Native Americans*. Atlanta, GA: Turner. (H/A)

Fronval, G., & D. Dubois. (1985). *Indian signals and sign language*. New York: Bonanza. (I)

Waldman, C. (1994). *Word dance: The language of Native American culture*. New York: Facts on File. (I/H/A)

Literature

Oral Traditions

Legends are not told merely for enjoyment, or for education, or for amusement; they are believed. They are emblems of a living religion, giving concrete form to a set of beliefs and traditions that link people living today to ancestors from centuries and millennia past. (Erdoes & Ortiz, 1984, p. xv)

Bierhorst, J. (Ed.). (1976). *The red swan: Myths and tales of the American Indians*. New York: Farrar, Straus & Giroux. (H/A)

Caduto, M. J., & J. Bruchac. (1991). *Native American stories*. Golden, CO: Fulcrum. (P/I)

Erdoes, R., & A. Ortiz. (1984). *American Indian myths and legends*. New York: Pantheon. (H/A)

Contemporary Literatures

There have always been the songs, the prayers, the stories. There have always been the voices. There have always been the people. There have always been those words which evoked meaning and the meaning's magical wonder. There has always been the spirit which inspired the desire for life to go on. And it has been through the worlds of the songs, the prayers, the stories, that the people have found a way to continue, for life to go on. (Ortiz, 1983, p. vii).

Allen, P. G. (Ed.). (1994). *Voice of the turtle*. New York: Ballantine. (H/A)

Coltelli, L. (1990). *Winged words: American Indian writers speak*. Lincoln: University of Nebraska. (H/A)

Hirschfelder, A. B., & B. Singer. (1992). *Rising voices: Writings of young Native Americans*. New York: Charles Scribner's Sons. (I/H)

Hobson, G. (Ed.). (1981). *The remembered earth*. Albuquerque: University of New Mexico. (H/A)

Ortiz, S. J. (1983). *Earth power coming*. Tsaile, AZ: Navajo Community College. (H/A)

Velie, A. R. (1991). *American Indian literature: An anthology*. Norman: University of Oklahoma. (H/A)

Velie, A. R. (1991). *The lightning within*. Lincoln: University of Nebraska. (H/A)

Recreation/Games

When a crust froze on the snow, we did lots of sledding. Our sleds were made from the ribs of the buffalo. Six or seven of the large ribs, which are curved like the staves of a boat, were lashed together. The ends of the ribs were held the right distance apart with a split cherry stick laced together with strong strips of rawhide. In this there must be much skill, and when a nice job of lacing was done a fine sled was the result. (Standing Bear, 1988, p. 140)

Culin, S. (1975). *Games of the North American Indians*. New York: Dover. (A)

Gryski, C. (1983). *Cat's cradle, owl's eyes: A book of string games*. New York: William Morrow. (P/I)

Macfarlan, A., & P. Macfarlan. (1985). *Handbook of American Indian games* (reprint). New York: Dover. (I/H/A)

Technology

With regard to water travel, Native North Americans were master boat builders with a variety of techniques and designs. There were five types of craft construction: (1) dugouts, (2) canoes, (3) kayaks, umiaks, bullboats, (4) rafts, and (5) plankboats. [They] had numerous boating accessories, including wood paddles, stone anchors, shell bailers, and plant-fiber and hide painters for mooring. . . . [S]hortly after Contact both Arctic and Northwest coast peoples sailed regularly with sails made from animal skins. (Waldman, 1985, pp. 54–55)

Most general books and nonprint materials discuss the technologies developed by each culture, including tools for planting and harvesting; methods of travel; techniques and tools for preserving, storing, and cooking food; tools used in hunting, fishing, and sewing; methods of recording events; crafts; and communicating over long distances. An extremely useful overview is given in the following book:

Waldman, C. (1985). *Atlas of the North American Indian.* New York: Facts on File. (H/A)

Art

Beauty, rather, means balance, the proper order of things. Its affirmation or its restoration implies that society, the natural and supernatural environment, and the individual are in the normal state of health and harmony. . . . Native American art is a system of public communication, a means of sharing symbols and meaning, of confirming and reinforcing the traditional system and its values and, by adding the visible dimension of beauty and spirit to even the most mundane of objects, of affirming their animate nature and the bond of reciprocity among human beings, their works, and the natural and supernatural environment. (Furst & Furst, 1982, pp. 13, 20)

Dockstader, F. J. (1974). *Indian art in America.* New York: Promontory Press. (H/A)

Furst, P. T., & J. L. Furst. (1982). *North American Indian art.* New York: Rizzoli. (H/A)

Hirschfelder, A. (1994). *Artists and craftspeople.* New York: Facts on File. (I/H)

Music and Dance

When the world was new and the first people had been formed out of clay, a great serpent came up from the ocean. The people made a circle of brushwood and the serpent coiled his body inside it. Then the people set the brushwood on fire. When the fire got hot, the serpent exploded and scattered. Inside his body were all the languages, all customs, and all songs. As a result of the fire these were strewn across the land. That is why people today speak different languages and sing different kinds of songs. (Bierhorst, 1992, p. 13)

Bierhorst, J. (1992). *A cry from the earth* (reprint). Santa Fe, NM: Ancient City Press. (I/H/A)

Burton, B. (1993). *Moving within the circle.* Danbury, CT: World Music Press. (I/H/A) A cassette tape is included.

Heth, C. (Ed.). (1993). *Native American dance: Ceremonies and social traditions* (2nd printing). Washington, DC: National Museum of the American Indian, Smithsonian Institution/Starwood. (H/A)

Laubin, R., & G. Laubin. (1989). *Indian dances of North America.* Norman: University of Oklahoma. (H/A)

Rhodes, W. (Ed.). (1987). *Music of the American Indian: Indian songs of today* (reissue). Washington, DC: Library of Congress, Motion Picture, Broadcasting and Recorded Sound Division. (H/A)

In general, it is always best to use multiple resources to learn about one or more Indian cultures; no one resource is adequate. For example, a

teacher who is planning an interdisciplinary unit about the Navajo might consult the following resources:

Amsden, C. A. (1991). *Navaho weaving: Its technic and history* (reprint). New York: Dover. (H/A)

Evers, L. (Ed.). (1986). *Between sacred mountains* (2nd printing). Tucson: University of Arizona/Sun Tracks. (H/A)

Gilpin, L. (1968). *The enduring Navajo.* Austin: University of Texas. (H/A)

Grimes, J. (1992). *Navajo: Portrait of a nation.* Englewood, CO: Westcliffe. (H/A)

Kluckhohn, C., & D. Leighton. (1979). *The Navajo* (3rd printing). Cambridge, MA: Harvard University. (H/A)

Locke, R. F. (1992). *The book of the Navajo* (5th ed.). Los Angeles: Mankind. (H/A)

Navajo (Video). (1982). Flagstaff: Museum of Northern Arizona. (I/H/A)

Tapahonso, L. (1993). *Saanii Dahataal: The women are singing.* Tucson: University of Arizona. (H/A)

Underhill, R. (1956). *The Navajos* (2nd printing). Norman: University of Oklahoma. (H/A)

GENERAL REFERENCES FOR TEACHING ABOUT INDIAN CULTURES

Books

Ballantine, B. & I. Ballantine. (Eds.). (1993). *The Native Americans: An illustrated history.* Atlanta, GA: Turner.

Billard, J. G. (Ed.). (1989). *The world of the American Indian.* Washington, DC: National Geographic.

Hirschfelder, A., & M. K. deMontano. (1993). *The Native American almanac.* New York: Prentice-Hall.

Hirschfelder, A., & P. Molin. (1992). *The encyclopedia of Native American religions.* New York: Facts on File.

Josephy, A. M., Jr. (1988). *The American heritage book of Indians.* New York: American Heritage/Bonanza.

Josephy, A. M., Jr. (1994). *Five hundred nations.* New York: Knopf.

Kopper, P. (Ed.). (1986). *The Smithsonian book of North American Indians.* Washington, DC: Smithsonian.

Maxwell, J. A. (1986). *America's fascinating Indian heritage* (3rd printing). Pleasantville, NY: Reader's Digest Association.

Viola, H. J. (1990). *After Columbus: The Smithsonian chronicle of the North American Indians.* New York: Smithsonian/Orion.

Waldman, C. (1985). *Atlas of the North American Indian.* New York: Facts on File.

Waldman, C. (1988). *Encyclopedia of Native American tribes.* New York: Facts on File.

Magazines/Journals

American Indian Culture and Research Journal
3220 Campbell Hall
American Indian Studies Center
University of California, Los Angeles
405 Hilgard Avenue
Los Angeles, CA 90024–1548
(310) 825–7315

Native Peoples
Media Concepts Group, Inc.
5333 North Seventh Street
Suite C–224
Phoenix, AZ 85014
(602) 252–2236

Videos

Native American Public Broadcasting Consortium
P.O. Box 83111
Lincoln, NE 68501
(402) 472–3522

Recordings (Cassettes and CDs)

Canyon Records and Indian Arts
4143 North 16th Street
Phoenix, AZ 85016
(602) 266–4823

Indian House Recordings
P.O. Box 472
Taos, NM 87571

Indian Sounds Records
P.O. Box 6038
Moore, OK 73153

Smithsonian/Folkways
Office of Folklife Programs
955 L'Enfant Plaza, Suite 2600
Smithsonian Institution
Washington, DC 20560

THE KINAALDA CAKE: AN INSTRUCTIONAL ACTIVITY

There are some activities that are difficult for the classroom teacher to manage, yet are appropriate all-school (or all one grade level) activity. The school library media specialist can indeed coordinate a large-scale activity that engages more than one classroom or group of students and provides multiple opportunities for learning. The following activity would be an exciting and interesting culmination unit on tradition and change in American Indian lifeways. We recommend that the library media center sponsor this activity and include a range of grades or groups of students and teachers.

GRADE LEVEL: Grades 4–8

BASIC CONCEPTS: Tradition and change

ORGANIZING GENERALIZATION: All cultures have unique ways of marking transitions from one life stage to another. These "rites of passage" change over time but retain the essential characteristics that help a people to maintain their unique cultural identity.

CULTURE AREA: Southwest

TIME PERIOD: From the past to the present

BACKGROUND: The Kinaalda ceremony is the Navajo puberty ceremony for girls. Similar to many cultural traditions, the Kinaalda is part of traditional Navajo religion and spiritual practices, yet it has changed in some ways to accommodate contemporary lives. Whether the ceremony given for a particular girl by her family is very traditional or has been adapted in some ways, it nonetheless is vital to the maintenance of Navajo beliefs and cultural identity.

This instructional activity should be done as a culminating activity for a unit of study related to ceremony, rites of passage, Navajo lifeways, or tradition and change. A classroom teaching unit on the Navajo puberty ceremony for girls—especially when the focus is on cultural ceremony—is appropriate for students who are caught up in the wonder of their changing bodies. The activity can provide a context that helps pre-adolescents understand that *all* people—both male and female—undergo the change from childhood to adulthood, and that all cultures mark this important passage. The ceremony also demonstrates the importance the Navajo place on the role of women.

The library media specialist will provide a variety of materials for teachers and students that develop the background for the cooking activity. Two Kinaalda cakes will be baked: one in the traditional manner (see recipe for Ground Cake) and one in a contemporary manner (see recipe for Navajo Cake). The Kinaalda cake for Navajo ceremony is still baked in the traditional way today. This should be a learning experience, not an activity without context or purpose.

OBJECTIVES:

Knowledge (Content)

Students will:

1. recognize that traditions that help to define cultural identity change over time yet remain timeless and important,
2. demonstrate an understanding of how technology has influenced traditions, and
3. make connections to their own lives by discussing how their families and cultures note the passages from one stage of life to another.

Skills

Students will:

1. practice cooperative skills,
2. follow directions, and
3. compare Apache and Navajo puberty ceremonies.

Values (Organic)

Students will:

1. respect the importance of traditions, and
2. appreciate the ancient ways of cooking and celebrating.

ACTIVITIES: Throughout all aspects of this activity, the library media specialist must collaborate with the classroom teacher(s).

Bulletin Board: Prepare a bulletin board featuring both recipes. A quote from *Kinaalda* (Roessel, 1993) could be featured.

Planning: Because the traditional cake will require a hole to be dug and the nontraditional cake will require an oven, make arrangements with school administrators before beginning. Parents should be involved as well.

Students should be engaged in and responsible for the planning process. You will want to form two groups or committees (traditional and nontraditional) and work directly with both groups to plan what to buy and prepare for mixing and cooking the cakes. A third committee should plan how the cakes will be served in a manner that is appropriate.

If at all possible, a Navajo person should be involved in (1) teaching the students about the Kinaalda, (2) preparing the traditional cake, and (3) serving the cakes. Navajo Community College in Tsaile, Arizona, is a resource that could be used via fax, mail, or computer.

The traditional cake should be prepared with the appropriate technology; this may require reducing the recipe to make a smaller cake, estimat-

ing, using stirring sticks, and so on. More than one nontraditional cake should be baked. How will students determine the number of servings in each cake? increase the ingredients for the nontraditional cake? compare the quality and cost? evaluate the effort required for the nontraditional

---

GROUND CAKE

This authentic Navajo recipe, made in two ways, is similar to the corncake of the Kinaalda.

Ingredients:

50 lbs. stone-ground yellow cornmeal

50 lbs. stone-ground whole wheat flour

12 lbs. coarsely ground sprouted wheat

1 large pail of simmering water

10 lbs. brown sugar

5 lbs. raisins

1 basketful of corn husks

Preparation:

1. Mix both 50 lbs. of stone-ground yellow cornmeal and ground whole wheat flour, and pour in handfuls into one large pail of simmering water, stirring constantly.
2. Stir the cornmeal with stirring sticks ('Adistsiin), removing any lumps.
3. Add sugar sparingly until the entire cornmeal is used.
4. Add wheat sprouts and raisins.
5. Dig a pit in the ground about one yard across and 10 inches deep. Then build a fire in the pit. When the pit is thoroughly heated, take the hot coals out.
6. Line the pit with several layers of corn husks pre-soaked in water.
7. Pour the mush onto the layers of corn husks and cover the mush with more corn husks.
8. Cover with moist dirt, and then cover with coals.
9. Build a fire over the pit. Keep the fire going for 8 hours until the cake is cooked.

'Adistsiin (stirring sticks) are made from thin sticks of sage or greasewood tied in the middle. They are used by Navajo women to stir mush. They are also used as strainers to catch pieces of ash as the water in which the ash has been soaking is poured into the cornmeal.

cake? Why would people take the trouble to bake a cake in the traditional manner?

Serving: The cakes should be baked and served with appropriate respect for the ceremony. A storyteller who could relate one or more of the traditional stories about both boys and girls (Bruchac, 1993, 1994) would help time pass while the cakes are baking. Consider writing invitations to members of the Indian community and asking someone from that community to say an appropriate blessing before the cakes are eaten.

EXTENSIONS: Research (1) puberty ceremonies of other tribes, (2) other rites of passage (e.g., naming ceremonies, weddings, or funerals) in either Indian or other cultures, or (3) the change in traditions over time. The Apache puberty ceremony is similar to the Navajo Kinaalda. Why?

NAVAJO CAKE

The recipes for Navajo cake and ground cake are identical, only this is baked in an oven and could be easily cooked in the classroom.

Ingredients:

6 cups of water

4 cups blue cornmeal

2 cups yellow cornmeal

1/2 cup raisins

1/2 cup wheat sprouts

1/2 cup brown sugar

Preparation:

1. Put 6 cups of water in a saucepan.
2. Add 4 cups of precooked blue cornmeal.
3. Add 2 cups of precooked yellow cornmeal.
4. Add 1/2 cup raisins.
5. Add 1/2 cup wheat sprouts.
6. Add 1/2 cup brown sugar. Blend well and dissolve all lumps.
7. Pour in baking pan and cover with foil.
8. Bake at 250 degrees for 4 hours. Cake must cook slowly.

Lynch, R. (1986). *Cookbook.* Chinle, AZ: Rough Rock Demonstration School, p. 2.

EVALUATION: Through discussion, personal journals, or "I learned" statements, students should demonstrate an understanding of the importance of rites of passage and how traditions change over time—in all cultures.

MATERIALS/RESOURCES FOR THIS ACTIVITY:

Bruchac, J. (1993). *Flying with the eagle, racing the great bear*. Mahwah, NJ: Troll. Stories are related to the passage from boyhood to manhood.

Bruchac, J., & G. Ross. (1994). *The girl who married the moon*. Mahwah, NJ: Troll. Sixteen stories celebrate the passage from girlhood to womanhood.

Goseyun, A. E. (1991, Summer). Carla's sunrise. *Native Peoples* 4 (4), pp. 8–16. A poignant description of an Apache girl's puberty ceremony.

Hirschfelder, A., & P. Molin. (1992). *The encyclopedia of Native American religions*. New York: Facts on File, pp. 100–101. A brief description of the Lakota, Navajo, and Western Apache girl's puberty rites.

Roessel, M. (1993). *Kinaalda*. Minneapolis, MN: Lerner. A contemporary book that describes a Navajo girl's Kinaalda.

Seymour, T. V. N. (1993). *The gift of Changing Woman*. New York: Henry Holt. A contemporary book that describes an Apache girl's Sunrise ceremony.

REFERENCES AND RESOURCES

Armstrong, V. I. (1989). *I have spoken* (6th printing). Athens, OH: Swallow.

Bierhorst, J. (1992). *A cry from the earth* (reprint). Santa Fe, NM: Ancient City Press.

Brown, J. E. (1992). *The spiritual legacy of the American Indian*. New York: Crossroad.

Bruchac, J. (1993). *Flying with the eagle, racing the great bear*. Mahwah, NJ: Troll.

Bruchac, J., & G. Ross. (1994). *The girl who married the moon*. Mahwah, NJ: Troll.

Burton, B. (1993). *Moving within the circle*. Danbury, CT: World Music Press.

Carter, F. (1989). *The education of Little Tree* (7th printing). Albuquerque: University of New Mexico.

Eastman, C. A. (1971). *Indian boyhood* (reprint). New York: Dover.

Erdoes, R., & A. Ortiz. (1984). *American Indian myths and legends*. New York: Pantheon.

Furst, P. T., & J. L. Furst. (1982). *North American Indian art*. New York: Rizzoli.

Kopper, P. (Ed.). (1986). *The Smithsonian book of North American Indians*. Washington, DC: Smithsonian.

Lynch, R. (1986). *Cookbook*. Chinle, AZ: Rough Rock Demonstration School.

McAllester, D., & S. McAllester. (1980). *Hogans*. Middletown, CT: Wesleyan.

Ortiz, S. J. (1983). *Earth power coming*. Tsaile, AZ: Navajo Community College.

Pelto, P. J., & R. H. Muessig. (1980). *Anthropology*. Columbus, OH: Charles E. Merrill.

Roles of the School Library Media Specialist

Resource to Teachers and Students

Encourage students and teachers to extend their knowledge of Indian cultures from the past to the present, from rigid stereotypes and caricatures to realistic people, and from one part of the country to other geographic regions.

Curriculum Developer and Coordinator

Use the model that introduces the study of culture as the intersection of time (history), place (geography), and people.

Develop the study of Indian cultures in ever-increasing complexity from grades K-12 so that students develop a understanding of Indian cultures and the concept of culture.

Advocate in-depth, interdisciplinary study of Indian cultures, instead of fragmented efforts.

Ensure that students understand cultural universals - the things that are common to all cultures.

Collection Manager

Provide a rich variety of print and non-print materials about Indian cultures and lifeways at varying levels of complexity.

Develop a collection that presents Indian cultures in poems, pictures, stories, visual art, and other non-written forms.

Exhibit instructional and cultural materials in enticing thematic or interdisciplinary groups or displays.

Provide contemporary source material which provides current information regarding Indian people including newspapers and journals.

Teacher

Help teachers and students be aware of their own culture and the cultural lens through which they learn about the cultures of others.

Roessel, M. (1993). *Kinaalda*. Minneapolis, MN: Lerner.

Roessel, M. (1993, June). A Navajo couple unites with tradition. *New Mexico* 71 (6), pp. 38–45.

Standing Bear, L. (1988). *My Indian boyhood* (reprint). Lincoln: University of Nebraska.

Vecsey, C. (Ed.). (1991). *Handbook of American Indian religious freedom*. New York: Crossroad.

Waldman, C. (1985). *Atlas of the North American Indian*. New York: Facts on File.

Williamson, D., & L. Railsback. (1987). *Cooking with spirit: North American Indian food and fact*. Bend, OR: Maverick.

Teaching about Religion and Spiritual Practices

8

You have noticed that everything an Indian does is in a circle, and that is because the Power of the World always works in circles, and everything tries to be round. In the old days when we were a strong and happy people, all our power came to us from the sacred hoop of the nation, and so long as the hoop was unbroken, the people flourished. The flowering tree was the living center of the hoop, and the circle of the four quarters nourished it. The east gave peace and light, the south gave warmth, the west gave rain, and the north with its cold and mighty wind gave strength and endurance. This knowledge came to us from the outer world with our religion. Everything the Power of the World does is done in a circle. The sky is round, and I have heard that the earth is round like a ball, and so are all the stars. The wind, in its greatest power, whirls. Birds make their nests in circles, for theirs is the same religion as ours. The moon does the same, and both are round. Even the seasons form a great circle in their changing, and always come back again to where they were. The life of a man is a circle from childhood to child-hood, and so it is in everything where power moves. Our teepees were round like the nests of birds, and these were always set in a circle, the nation's hoop, a nest of many nests, where the Great Spirit meant for us to hatch our children. (Black Elk, quoted in Neihardt, 1988, pp. 198–200)

HISTORICAL OVERVIEW

The religions of the Indians of North America have their roots in traditions and beliefs that have guided them for more than 30,000 years and that are reaffirmed today. Native religions are based on a worldview that is the very foundation for their way of life. This worldview provides a structure

that helps the people understand, interpret, and order events, places, and experiences. It gives them values, identity, a feeling of rootedness, and a sense of belonging. The sacred way of life for Indian people includes their social structures; their sense of right and wrong; their ceremonies, daily roles, and responsibilities; and their deeply held beliefs that guide them from the past into the present.

American Indians believe that all creations of the earth and the relationships between them are sacred and have importance in their daily lives. Black Elk, an Oglala Sioux, spoke of the natural world and the power of the circle, and he explained Indian beliefs and ways of life. These are the Indian religions, as diverse as the tribes themselves. Although certain fundamental elements are common, the religions have evolved over time and in different geographic locations to manifest great diversity in practice and ceremony.

The ancient religions of Indian people guided their lives for thousands of years. The sacred oral tradition—including story, prayer, song, and instruction—was kept by the elders of each tribe to be passed on to future generations. The oral traditions held the wisdom of the years and the accumulated personal and tribal experiences. Their truths guided the people to flourish and have endured to this day. Many believe that the wisdom of the ancient traditions can help the contemporary world with environmental issues that threaten our planet and its inhabitants.

When the European explorers encountered the multitude of tribes that existed in 1492, they found them praying to animals and natural things in the environment such as mountains, rivers, and trees. Thus, the Europeans assumed the Indians had no belief in a supreme being. This assumption allowed them to take lands and other possessions from the Indians without guilt. In reality, however, this assumption is contrary to Indian religions and spiritual beliefs and practices. The renowned Navajo artist Carl Gorman wrote:

It has been said by some researchers into Navajo religion, that we have no Supreme God, because He is not named. That is not so. The Supreme Being is not named because He is unknowable. He is simply the Unknown Power. We worship him through His Creation. . . . We believe that this great unknown power is everywhere in His creation. The various forms of creation have some of this spirit within them. . . . As every form has some of the intelligent spirit of the creator, we cannot but reverence all parts of the creation. (Gorman, quoted in Brown, 1992, p. 70)

It should be noted that the *male* concept of a supreme being is not a part of Indian thought or language. In many Indian languages, the same word is used for "he" and "she." The belief in a supreme being is evident in the religions of tribes such as the Sioux, who use the term *Wakan-Tanka* ("Great Mystery"). Other tribes use the term *Great Spirit, Grandfather,* or *Giver of*

Breath. Although the terminology differs, there is no question that American Indians believe in a supreme being or life force.

For thousands of years, American Indians were free to practice their religions and live in harmony with their environment. Their way of life, or religion, contributed to maintaining the balance and harmony of nature; and the sacred oral traditions prepared the people for the challenges and experiences of life. There was respect for everything in the world.

This freedom began to disappear when Europeans first stepped on North American soil. From the beginning, Europeans killed Indians and attempted to obliterate their cultures and religions in the name of Christianity. The changes in Indian cultures and religious practices that were imposed by the Europeans have been immeasurable. The forced assimilation into European, then American, cultural practices; the violent suppression and attempted destruction of Indian religions and spiritual customs; and the imposition of Christianity on Indian people crippled traditional Indian religions but did not destroy them. The religions and spiritual practices were continued underground and practiced in secret.

During this time of obliteration of Indian religion, Christian missionaries became a force in Indian Country that would impact the course of history. When the first Indian reservations were established in the East, Christian missionaries became the first Indian agents, or official representatives of the federal government. They handed out food rations, regulated the Indians' lives, taught Christian doctrine, and meted out punishment for practicing Indian religions. In fact, the U.S. government discovered that it was possible to regulate Indians' activities through denial of their traditional religious practices. By the late 1800s there were laws banning the Sun Dance and other religious ceremonies of various tribes. Governmental regulations specified fines (e.g., withholding of rations for periods not exceeding ten days) for those found guilty of participating in any Native religious ceremony. Subsequent infraction of the regulations called for withholding of rations for over fifteen days—and incarceration.

The regulations remained in effect until the Indian Reorganization Act of 1934 restored tribal government. By the time the laws were stricken, countless—and often nameless—Indian people had died in the name of religion.

Christianity developed strength in Indian Country during the time that Indian religions and spiritual practices were officially prohibited by governmental policies. Indeed, Indians' lives on reservations were saturated with Christianity. Once boarding schools were established, Christianity also became a major force in the plan to take Indian children away from their families and assimilate them. They were given Christian names, their traditional clothing was taken from them, their hair was cut, and their Indian languages were banned along with Indian religions. Moreover, the

boarding schools often included Christian religious teachings in the daily instruction.

In order to survive, traditional Indian religions and spiritual practices took several paths. In some cases the medicine men who held the keys to the ancient way of life became silent and practiced their religions in secret. In other cases the Indians mixed their traditional ways with Christianity. In an effort to retain traditional ways, some elders were known to protect sacred knowledge by changing or omitting major parts of a particular ceremony when discussing traditional practices with missionaries, anthropologists, or historians. In these ways the religions were preserved.

By the early part of this century, there were several different religious groups within most tribes. Some were traditional people who believed in and lived the historical religious teachings of their people within a modern context. Others had given up the traditional religions and accepted Christianity as their way of life. Still others did not believe in a supreme being; they could be described as agnostics or atheists. Finally, some combined traditional beliefs and practices with Christianity. However, there was yet another group, which is hard to explain, of older people who actively participated in traditional religions and also attended Christian churches and believed in Christian practices. They did not mix the two religions but believed in both at the same time.

During this time, further encroachment on Indian religions occurred when land was taken for white settlers. This land often included sacred sites, which are central in the practice of Indian religions because of their intimate relationship with the natural world. Pilgrimages to sacred sites and special prayers and ceremonies were discontinued because the people did not have access to these religious sites. The natural balance of the world was injured.

The use of Indian religious sacraments was also prohibited. The most well known religious sacrament, peyote, was banned along with the accompanying religious ceremonies. Indian agents were told to find and destroy peyote. Peyotism, although unfamiliar to many Americans, is among the oldest, largest, most continuously practiced religious practices in the Western Hemisphere. Indian people in Oklahoma who practiced peyotism tried to work within the system in the early 1900s by establishing the Native American Church of Oklahoma in 1918. Their efforts helped to legitimize the practice, but the use of peyote remained outlawed.

The First Amendment to the Constitution of the United States stipulates that the religious freedom of its citizens is protected. Although this right was not extended to American Indians before 1924 when citizenship was established for them, all according rights should have followed. But this was not so. Recently, the American Indian Freedom of Religion Act (1978); H.R. 4230 (1994), an amendment to the American Indian Freedom of Religion Act to protect the religious use of peyote; and S. 2269, the Native

American Cultural Protection and Free Exercise of Religion Act (1994), are recent major legislative acts that ensure the fundamental right of freedom of religion to American Indian people.

When President Clinton met with Indian tribal leaders in April 1994, he presented a directive that stated his support for the use of eagle feathers for religious purposes by Indian people. He also directed various agencies to cooperate with the Indian people in collecting and distributing the feathers for traditional religious use. This recognition by the president of the United States of the validity of American Indian religions should allow American Indian people to practice their ancient religions without fear of retribution or punishment. However, the issue of freedom of religion remains a problem for many American Indian people (see Chapter 13).

BASIC SPIRITUAL BELIEFS OF AMERICAN INDIANS

When analyzing the religious beliefs of any cultural group and the significance of these beliefs to the group's worldview and history, it is important to understand the values that form the foundation for the beliefs, how the beliefs are transmitted to the young and perpetuated in the culture, and the role that the religion plays in daily life. It is difficult to avoid an emphasis on various American Indian religious ceremonies, yet they alone do not constitute the religion. With American Indians, the issue is complicated by the great diversity of tribes and their geographic location.

American Indian religions do have some beliefs in common. These beliefs are part of the way of life that has been maintained since ancient times, and they are the keys to Indian survival. Religion was and is the same; it is needed for life. Among the central values of Indian religions is a sense of connectedness to the rest of the natural world. The interdependence demands respect and care from and for all creations. The relatedness provides for the survival of all. Further, American Indians believe in a supreme being, or creator, who is included in their mythology, creation stories, way-of-life stories, prayers, ceremonies, and songs. Even though the natural world is honored and respected for its vital role in the existence and well-being of all things, the Creator is revered for ultimate power and compassion.

American Indian religion is not separable from the acts of living. Although there are identifiable ceremonies or rites of passage, daily life is a continuing demonstration of spirituality and religion. Therefore, the clothing, homes, cooking pots, and baskets are made in a religious fashion with spiritual meaning in their decoration and design. The shape and construction of a tipi, as described by Black Elk at the beginning of this chapter, is for sacred purposes. It gives a blessing on the people who live within and is in harmony with the natural world.

The spirit, or unseen, world plays an important role in the religions of American Indians. All tribes acknowledge the presence of unseen powers

or spirits, a world beyond the physical world. One world is not without the other, and both are real.

In ancient times, American Indian religions were perpetuated along with the other essential knowledge of the people. Stories and legends were told by the elders in the appropriate season or place. Ceremonies marking the change of seasons and the rites of passage, and other religious events, were held without fail. Elders and medicine men were held in high esteem. The people participated in their special way of life, and the children lived and learned. This is how religious beliefs and ways were shared with each new generation.

INDIAN RELIGIONS AND SPIRITUAL PRACTICES IN THE CLASSROOM

Indian country in North America is still home to hundreds of religious traditions that have endured, despite a long history of persecution and suppression by government and missionaries. These traditions are intrinsically interesting and are important as religious expressions. [It is important] to accord these native sacred traditions the respect, status and rightful place they so richly deserve among other great spiritual traditions. . . . Native American sacred beliefs are as dignified, profound, viable and richly facetted as other religions practiced throughout the world. (Hirschfelder & Molin, 1992, pp. ix–x)

It is clear that the study of traditional American Indian religions and spiritual practices is complex. Is it possible to *teach about religion* rather than *teach a religion*? Recently this issue has become even more controversial and politically sensitive. According to American tradition, it is appropriate to teach *about* religion. But *how* to teach about Native spirituality and religious practices and *what* to teach are very difficult for non-Indian teachers and are appropriately sensitive for American Indian people. The following guidelines should be useful for the school library media specialist. In teaching about American Indian religions and spiritual practices, educators should:

1. become as informed as possible about the fundamental beliefs of American Indians that form their worldview and essence of spirituality,
2. teach about American Indian religions and spiritual practices in an interdisciplinary manner and as an integral part of Indian ways of life,
3. honor the wishes of American Indians regarding their sacred ceremonies and spiritual practices,
4. avoid representatives of American Indian sacred objects, songs, or ceremonies in classroom activities, and
5. model respect for the diversity of religious expression.

Teachers should understand the beliefs that form the foundation of American Indian religions so they can integrate them with other content about Indian history and cultures. It is important that teachers read and study, for they can only teach what they know and understand. Moreover, it is not appropriate to use non-Indian structures to explain Indian religions and spiritual practices. For example, it is all too easy to teach sacred ceremonies or special events modeling the Christian emphasis on Christmas or on weekly worship services. This paradigm is not accurate and can distort students' understanding. Native American religion manifests itself in the whole of life; in food, shelter, relationships with people and the environment; in art, music, and dance.

Information about American Indian religions and spiritual practices should be integrated into all instruction about American Indians; it is impossible to separate religion from the way Indian people live their lives. For Indian people, all life and all action are sacred. Therefore, to teach about American Indians *in any subject area* is to teach about their spirituality. Teachers can emphasize that traditional Indian people believe their lives and all creations of the universe are interdependent and that this relationship is sacred.

Religious practices may be abstract for many students; but in learning about traditional daily Indian life, they can become real and meaningful. Teachers and students can learn about pottery, baskets, designs, clothing, shelters, some music and dance, and ways of hunting and cooking. All are influenced by religious belief and demonstrate how the essence of Indian religions and spiritual practices exist in all things and are continually present in people's lives. By learning about religious beliefs through everyday life and experiences, a general understanding about American Indian religious thought and belief is developed without treading on sacred toes.

It is important to remember that American Indian people themselves prefer that Indian religions be kept out of the classroom. Their spiritual beliefs define their cultures, their identity, and their roots; and they do not want to weaken, cheapen, or "sell" these beliefs and practices. Most American Indian people are offended by the casual use of "rain dances," sweat lodges, "chants," and strange "Indian" songs, dances, and ceremonies invented in the classroom by non-Indian schoolchildren. This means that there is no place for Navajo sand paintings, Pueblo kachinas, totem poles, and Iroquois masks in the classroom (see Chapter 4). *These religious items are not meant for the classroom.*

The "truth" about Indian religion cannot readily be found in books or films or videos. Therefore, the most appropriate resources for instruction about Indian religion and spirituality are Indian people themselves. There are over 500 federally recognized tribes in the United States whose members all speak different languages and have different religious beliefs. Within each tribe and religion, there are individuals with varying degrees

of traditional and Christian beliefs. When they are invited into the classroom, they can share their perspective and demonstrate for students the unique role that Indian religion and spirituality play in the modern world.

To complete the circle, the words of Black Elk seem a proper way to end this chapter:

Then, I was standing on the highest mountain of them all, and round about beneath me was the whole hoop of the world. And while I stood there I saw more than I can tell and I understood more than I saw; for I was seeing in a sacred manner the shapes of all things in the spirit, and the shape of all shapes as they must live together like one being. And I saw that the sacred hoop of my people was one of many hoops that made one circle, wide as daylight and as starlight, and in the center grew one mighty flowering tree to shelter all the children of one mother and one father. And I saw that it was holy. (quoted in Neihardt, 1988, p. 43)

REFERENCES AND RESOURCES

Allen, P. G. (1991). *Grandmothers of the light: A medicine woman's source book.* Boston: Beacon.

Beck, P. V., A. L. Walters, & N. Francisco. (1977). *The sacred.* Tsaile, AZ: Navajo Community College.

Black Elk, W., & W. S. Lyon. (1990). *Black Elk: The sacred ways of a Lakota.* San Francisco: Harper.

Bopp, J., M. Bopp, L. Brown, & P. Lane. (1989). *The sacred tree* (3rd ed.). Wilmot, WI: Lotus Light.

Brown, J. E. (Ed.). (1983). *Black Elk: The sacred pipe* (reprint). New York: Penguin.

Brown, J. E. (1992). *The spiritual legacy of the American Indian.* New York: Crossroad.

Bruchac, J. (1993). *The Native American sweat lodge: History and legends.* Freedom, CA: Crossing Press.

Deloria, V., Jr. (1992). *God is red* (2nd ed.). Golden, CO: North American Press.

DeMallie, R. J. (Ed.). (1984). *The sixth grandfather.* Lincoln: University of Nebraska.

Hirschfelder, A., & P. Molin. (1992). *The encyclopedia of Native American religions.* New York: Facts on File.

Lame Deer, J., & R. Erdoes. (1972). *Lame Deer, seeker of visions.* New York: Simon & Schuster.

McGaa, E. (1990). *Mother earth spirituality.* San Francisco: Harper.

NARF Legal Review 19 (2). (1994, Summer/Fall). Boulder, CO: Native American Rights Fund.

Neihardt, J. G. (1988). *Black Elk speaks* (7th printing). Lincoln: University of Nebraska.

Ross, A. C. (1989). *Miakuye oyasin.* Fort Yates, ND: Bear Publishing.

Underhill, R. M. (1989). *Red man's religion* (reprint). Chicago: University of Chicago.

Roles of the School Library Media Specialist

Resource to Teachers and Students

Be well-informed about the subject of the American Indian religion and spirituality.

Help teachers and students understand that the best resources on American Indian religions and spiritual practices may not be in print.

Help teachers and students critically analyze existing print resources for accuracy, perspective, and authenticity.

Develop a community resource directory that enables teachers to utilize local Indian people and Native institutions to enrich the curriculum.

Curriculum Developer and Coordinator

Be aware of activities that teach religion as opposed to teaching about religion.

Promote interdisciplinary study of Indian religion as it relates to all subjects.

Guard against the disrespectful use of sacred objects in the school curriculum.

Collection Manager

Develop a professional collection that presents the diversity of Indian voice on religion and spiritual practices.

Collect contemporary journals and newspapers that record current legal decisions as they relate to Indian freedom of religion.

Develop a rich collection that includes works by tribes and individual American Indians that share their ways of life, including their religious beliefs and spiritual practices.

Teacher

Create a learning/resource center that promotes appropriate instruction related to the sacred and that maintains accurate and authentic resources.

Guide teachers to avoid stereotypical information or inaccurate information about American Indian religions.

Create a learning environment that respects differences in religious beliefs and spiritual practices.

Vecsey, C. (1991). *Handbook of American Indian religious freedom.* New York: Cross-road.

Walker, P. R. (1994). *Spiritual leaders.* New York: Facts on File.

Wall, S., & H. Arden. (1990). *Wisdom keepers.* Hillsboro, OR: Beyond Words.

Waters, F. (1984). *The book of the Hopi* (reprint). New York: Penguin.

9

Teaching about Holidays

The early morning light enters the window, creating a golden glow in the hogan. Celinda herself is glowing with pride. Her aunts tease her, but their words aren't as sharp as they were yesterday. She is one of them now. She has finished the race.

"I can't believe that I've done it," Celinda says. "I kept telling myself, you can't quit. I know I don't look any different, but I feel different. I feel like a Navajo. Just like my mom and my aunts and my grandmother." (Roessel, 1993, p. 46)

Celinda has just completed her Kinaalda, the Navajo puberty ceremony that brings her into the world of women. The Navajo Kinaalda is a cultural celebration, not a holiday; in fact, the word *holiday* has little meaning in the Navajo world. The definition of *holiday* doesn't fit in traditional Indian life, except for national holidays that are celebrated by all Americans such as Independence Day, the birthday of Martin Luther King, Labor Day, and Memorial Day. Christmas and Easter are also holidays for those Indian people who have adopted non-Indian religious beliefs.

In this chapter we will (1) consider how certain national holidays— Columbus Day and Thanksgiving—can be recognized with respect for American Indian people, and (2) examine how the word *holiday* might relate to some of the ceremonies and celebrations that are such a vital force in Indian cultures. It is these religious and secular ceremonies and celebrations that sustain Indian identity and perpetuate Indian lifeways.

In most cases it is helpful to organize how we think of holidays or celebrations as either religious or secular. Religious holidays commemorate individuals, events, and values that are significant to a particular group.

However, they differ in regard to the individuals, events, and values a religious group chooses to revere. Secular holidays reflect the political, ethnic or racial, and social experiences of a society. They, too, honor particular individuals, events, and values (Naylor & Smith, 1993, p. 4). For American Indian cultures, the classification that separates religion from political, cultural, and social life is not appropriate. Although some Indian people participate in non-Indian religions and most honor American holidays, their political, cultural, and social events are directly related to their spiritual beliefs (see Figure 9.1).

Figure 9.1
Holiday Typology including Indian Ceremonies and Celebrations*

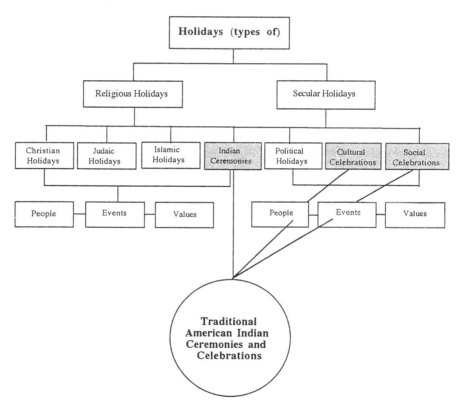

*American Indian people do not separate religion or spirituality from the wholeness or circle of their lives. The most sacred of their traditional rituals and ceremonies are not known or understood by non-Indian people; the People hold them sacred and secret from outsiders. Nonetheless, the spirituality of Native people is an integral part of their history and their everyday political, cultural, and social lives.

Adapted from: Naylor, D. T. & Smith, B. D. (1993, November/December). Teaching about holidays (pull-out feature). *Social Studies and the Young Learner* 6 (2), p. 4.

For Indian and non-Indian people alike, holidays and cultural celebrations serve three important functions: (1) *to endorse*—sanctioning which people, events, and values merit special attention; (2) *to preserve*—ensuring that certain people and events are honored and particular values perpetuated; and (3) *to unify*—bringing people together through shared participation in commonly practiced rituals and celebrations and affirmation of their shared heritage and traditions (Naylor & Smith, 1993). Indeed, Indian ceremonies and celebrations endorse the Indian people, events, and values that merit commemoration; honor those people and events and preserve Indian values; and bring the people together in their Indian identity, building and reinforcing a sense of who they are and where they come from.

AMERICAN HOLIDAYS

Both Columbus Day and Thanksgiving raise questions related to the people, events, and values that are honored and perpetuated. For American Indian people, the disease and destruction that Columbus and the Europeans brought to the so-called New World are not to be honored. For them the Columbian encounter (not the "discovery") was the beginning of the end of traditional lifeways, the loss of homelands, and in many cases the death of families and cultures. For them there is much to be mourned, not celebrated.

Thanksgiving, too, is not acknowledged by many Indian people as a historical event to be honored. From all accounts, the original feast of Thanksgiving was given by the early European settlers in thanksgiving for a harvest that would sustain them from the harsh winter soon to come. The Indian people of the area participated in the way that most Indian people first greeted and worked with the newcomers—in a spirit of helpfulness, sharing, and goodwill. Only in subsequent years did they begin to realize that colonization and conquest would follow the first Thanksgiving. It is very difficult for American Indians to be thankful for colonization and conquest.

Teaching about Columbus Day

During the Columbian Quincentennial in 1992, many excellent position statements and instructional materials were produced and new books published. Teachers were provided with an abundance of materials to present the story of the Columbian encounter; these materials supplied an alternative perspective, a more accurate historical record, and new teaching strategies. To ignore this new way of teaching about Columbus Day is not only insensitive and ethnocentric but also fails to encourage students to recognize that history often involved cruelty, that new information can alter our most cherished beliefs and traditions, and that the concept of historical perspective is important to explore.

In an alternative approach, some schools modify Columbus Day to celebrate *all* the cultural heritages that are now a part of America. In any case, teachers today must teach children about Columbus Day differently than many of us were taught. It is a professional responsibility.

In the following sections, each source listed is followed by one or more capital letters in parentheses. These designations indicate general reading level:

P   Primary
I   Intermediate
H   High school
A   Adult

Of course, the designations are approximate: adults can gain a great deal from reading books for children, and young readers can "stretch" to more difficult levels.

Sources

Bigelow, B., B. Miner, & B. Peterson. (1992). *Rethinking Columbus* (4th printing). Milwaukee, WI: Rethinking Schools, Ltd. (A)

Dorris, M. (1992). *Morning girl*. New York: Hyperion Books. (I)

Weatherford, J. (1988). *Indian givers*. New York: Fawcett Columbine. (H/I)

Yolen, J. (1992). *Encounter*. San Diego: Harcourt Brace Jovanovich (P)

Teaching about Thanksgiving

Thanksgiving is different in some respects from Columbus Day. To teach about the original Thanksgiving has some merit in that the Pilgrim settlers gathered to celebrate the bounty provided by Mother Earth; they did so with respect for and acceptance of the skills and knowledge of the Indian people of the area, and they were probably unaware of the events that were to follow. That is a generous and possibly naive position; nonetheless, it has some merit as an approach to teaching about Thanksgiving in the early grades. There are some points to remember:

- Present the Thanksgiving story accurately, not romantically.
- Stress the multicultural aspects of the feast, acknowledging the strengths and contributions of both cultures.
- Eliminate classroom/school decorations that present Indian people in stereotypical dress (Plains Indian headdresses, loincloths in New England winter weather, tomahawks, peacepipes, and warpaint) and the use of demeaning, grunting, whooping, and simplistic language ("Ugh!" "How!")

- Help older students understand why Squanto spoke English, why Indian people fought for their land, why some settlers thought Indians were "inferior" and "uncivilized," and why many Indian people do not celebrate Thanksgiving today.

Sources

Penner, L. R. (1991). *Eating the plates: A pilgrim book of food and manners.* New York: Macmillan. (P/I)

Penner, L. R. (1994). *A Native American feast.* New York: Macmillan. (P/I)

Sewall, M. (1986). *The pilgrims of Plimoth.* New York: Atheneum. (P/I)

Sewall, M. (1990). *People of the breaking day.* New York: Atheneum. (P/I)

American Indian Day

In some communities and states there is a move to designate one day in September as American Indian Day. It is not a holiday in the usual sense, but the concept has multiple possibilities for focused instruction at all grade levels. Because Columbus Day and Thanksgiving are fall holidays and are usually given considerable emphasis in the primary grades, it seems reasonable to introduce a day to celebrate the beauty and wisdom of the cultures of America's indigenous peoples.

In reservation schools or schools with many Indian students, often the day is celebrated with appropriate general activities such as rodeos, parades, and powwows or other tribal or cultural events such as conducting fry bread contests, preparing traditional foods, and creating a general atmosphere of celebration. For example, in one Navajo school the day is designated as "Navajo Culture Day" and the day is devoted to the celebration of Navajo history, government, literature, language, arts, and culture. In reality, Navajo culture is part of every day in this school; however, this is a day to celebrate as well as study.

In non-Indian classrooms, particularly elementary classrooms, it could be celebrated with typical traditional American Indian foods, stories, games, music, art and craft exhibits, field trips to museums, local historical sites, or urban Indian centers. It would be an ideal time to invite American Indian speakers to the classroom.

INDIAN CEREMONIES AND CELEBRATIONS

The following are brief examples and explanations of Indian ceremonies and celebrations that are not generally well known, for which good teaching materials are available, and that have great potential to teach about Native history, cultures, and values. The sources mentioned bring detail and the richness of language and pictures to these summaries.

Kinaalda (religious/Navajo/values)

Puberty or coming-of-age ceremonies are common in most cultures. Although certainly not the same as the Kinaalda, First Communions, Bar/Bas Mitzvahs, and Sweet Sixteen parties are coming-of-age rituals and celebrations. The Navajo Kinaalda ceremony, which is similar to the puberty ceremony for Apache girls, is deeply rooted in religious belief and has been a part of Navajo life for many generations. The first Kinaalda was performed for Changing Woman, the most revered of all Navajo Holy People. Throughout the ceremony the girl wears a red and black handwoven dress like the one worn by Changing Woman in her Kinaalda.

Supported by family and friends, the Navajo girl, soon after her first menses, is given a Kinaalda ceremony during which she learns to become a Navajo woman. During the two-day ceremony (frequently reduced from four days to accommodate contemporary school schedules), the girl runs a race by herself (a race that was begun as a child), grinds corn and prepares a traditional corncake, and stays awake during the night while traditional prayers are sung. The Navajo people believe the ceremony is a way for young girls to understand what life will be like as an adult. The Kinaalda is a test of strength, endurance, and responsibility; when the girl completes the race, she has become a woman.

The corncake is a significant part of the ceremony. It is made of corn that the girl and the women of her family have ground; it is baked in a large hole in the earth that has been prepared by the men. Today some of the corn for the cake is ground at a mill, but the girl must still grind some of the corn on a traditional grinding stone. The "paddles" used for stirring the batter are made of 8 to 12 greasewood sticks tied together. These are sacred to the women; in fact, a woman's Kinaalda sticks are kept and cherished throughout her life.

In a traditional hogan, a medicine man sings prayers during the night and the girl must remain awake. Inside the hogan, the people help the medicine man pray through the night as someone tends the fire over the cake. Shortly before dawn the girl makes her final run. She then returns to the hogan, where the prayers are finished and her childhood is almost over. The cake is cut; the center, the most sacred part, is given to parents and grandparents at the ceremony. As people eat the cake and the light dawns, the girl becomes a woman.

Sources

Begay, S. (1984). *Kinaalda*. Rough Rock, AZ: Rough Rock Press. (H/A)

Roessel, M. (1993). *Kinaalda*. Minneapolis, MN: Lerner. (I)

Ryan, D. B. (1988, Winter). Kinaalda. *Native Peoples*, pp. 2–6. (I/H/A)

Strawberry Thanksgiving (religious/social/values)

Strawberry Thanksgiving is one of thirteen yearly Narraganset and Niantic (a subgroup of the Narraganset) celebrations. It is a cultural and social event deeply rooted in spiritual beliefs. Like many Indian nations, these tribes traditionally celebrate each of the thirteen moons of the year. Each moon honors a seasonal event, and traditional legends are a part of each moon.

Held in June, Strawberry Thanksgiving is a celebration in which people come together to eat strawberries, participate in traditional dances, exhibit their crafts, and enjoy their friends and traditions. They give thanks for the abundance of the strawberry harvest and for all the gifts of Mother Earth. Traditional festival foods include succotash, rabbit or venison, fry bread, quahaug chowder, strawberry shortcakes, sassafras tea, strawberry corn bread (see recipe), and johnny cake.

At the Strawberry Thanksgiving celebration, drummers play softly while a storyteller recounts the legend. A young boy and girl are chosen to dance the roles of the characters in the legend. The girl carries a basket of fresh berries to share with her brother. Then the brother and sister perform

---

STRAWBERRY CORN BREAD

Strawberry corn bread is one of the traditional foods eaten at Strawberry Thanksgiving celebrations.

Ingredients:

1 cup cornmeal

1 egg

1 cup flour

1/4 cup milk

4 tsp. baking powder

1 pint thawed frozen strawberries

1/2 tsp. salt

1/8 cup corn oil

Directions:

Sift dry ingredients together. In a separate bowl, beat together the egg, milk, and oil. Stir the liquid mixture into the dry ingredients. Add the strawberries and mix well. Pour into greased shallow baking dish. Bake at 375 degrees for 20–25 minutes.

Source: Jennings, P. (1992). *Strawberry Thanksgiving: Teacher's guide*. Cleveland, OH: Modern Curriculum Press, p. 15.

---

a joyful dance, and the ceremony concludes with a friendship dance in which everyone is invited to participate.

Source

Jennings, P. (1992). *Strawberry Thanksgiving*. Cleveland, OH: Modern Curriculum Press. (P) A teacher's guide, posters, and audiocassettes are available for this book, which was produced by the Boston Children's Museum.

Big Foot Memorial Ride
(secular/political or historical/event)

A people's dream died there. It was a beautiful dream. . . . The nations' hoop is broken and scattered. There is no center any longer, and the sacred tree is dead. (Black Elk, quoted in Neihardt, 1979, p. 270)

The powerful words of Black Elk signaled the end of the Indian wars: the hoop was broken, the sacred tree was dead, and the Indians were defeated. Chief Big Foot and nearly 350 of his people were killed, buried in mass graves or scattered across the prairie. But students need to know that the tree is beginning to flower again and that Indian nations are mending the hoop. The massacre at Wounded Knee, although a human tragedy of enormous and far-reaching importance, was not the end of the Indian people.

In 1986 an Indian group, the Big Foot Memorial Riders, was formed to commemorate the massacre and to initiate a time of healing. The fifteen initial riders rode through South Dakota in the bitter winter to experience the hardship of the forced march that ended in the massacre; to remember what happened to Chief Big Foot and the women, children, and men at Wounded Knee; to pray for the sick, the elders, the children, and the imprisoned; and to pray for peace throughout the world. In 1990, the hundredth anniversary of the massacre at Wounded Knee, approximately 350 riders again followed the 150-mile path of Chief Big Foot to heal the wound. On December 23, in bitter weather reaching 30 degrees below zero, they began. A ceremony was held at the grave site on December 29, with the sacred pipe of the Lakota, purifying sage smoke, and prayers. It is believed this ride of courage and commemoration mended the sacred hoop.

The white flag of truce raised by Chief Big Foot in December 1890 before the U.S. soldiers surrounded the Indian camp has come to symbolize the treachery of the U.S. government that was experienced by Indian people. Today a white flag, placed by the Big Foot Memorial Riders, continues to fly in the cemetery at Wounded Knee.

To Indian people of every nation, December 29, 1890—the date of the slaughter of babies, children, women, elders, and warriors—is established as a day of infamy. In honor and remembrance of those who died, in recog-

nition of the prejudice and discrimination that has led to other massacres in other places and other times, and for the Indian people of the present and the future, it is important to acknowledge the Big Foot Memorial Riders who have commemorated the event in the name of peace.

Sources

Josephy, A. M., Jr., T. Thomas, & J. Eder. (1990). *Wounded Knee: Lest we forget.* Cody, WY: Buffalo Bill Historical Center. (H/A)

Neihardt, J. G. (1988). *Black Elk speaks* (7th printing). Lincoln: University of Nebraska. (H/A)

Stein, R. C. (1983). *The story of Wounded Knee.* Chicago: Children's Press. (I)

Wisecarver, C. W. F. (1990, Spring). Wounded Knee: Mending the sacred hoop. *Native Peoples* 3 (3), pp. 8–16. (I/H/A)

Wood, T., with W. W. Afraid of Hawk. (1992). *A boy becomes a man at Wounded Knee.* New York: Walker. (I)

Stomp Dance (religious/Cherokee/social)

During the last part of the 1800s, the Keetoowah Society of the Cherokee Nation of Oklahoma began to restore and strengthen Cherokee traditions that had been weakened after the tortuous Trail of Tears, which took them from their ancestral homelands in the East. Originally some of the members of the Keetoowah Society advocated violence against whites. Later the members endeavored to bring stability and cohesiveness to the Cherokee by reviving old ceremonies such as the Stomp Dance. Now, as keepers of the sacred fire, they keep the stompgrounds.

Religious and social in nature, Stomp Dances are held throughout Oklahoma by several of the tribes that originated in the Southeast—including the Choctaw and Seminole. During the warm summer months, many of those who live off the reservation bring their families "home" to Oklahoma for the dances. The people who belong to the stompgrounds congregate in seven brush arbors; when they have gathered, they form a large circle. Speeches are given, games are played, friends share food and visit, and the people dance the night through. After the Stomp Dance the story of the seven sacred wampum belts is told in a ceremony. These belts were created in the 1700s from bits of shell strung onto twine; religious messages are encoded in their designs.

Rayna Green (1993) speaks of tradition, change, and cohesion when she describes a Stomp Dance in Oklahoma. The Stomp Dance is traditional; the dance regalia is a mixture of the old and the new; the songs are rich, varied, and cherished; and the friends, foods, and feelings are those of being Cherokee and belonging.

Sources

Green, R. (1993). Cherokee stomp dance: Laughter rising up. In C. Heth (Ed.), *Native American dance: Ceremonies and social traditions* (2nd printing), p. 177. New York: National Museum of the American Indian, Smithsonian Institution, with Fulcrum Publishing. (H/A)

Woodhead, H. (1994). *Tribes of the southern woodlands*, pp. 150–53. Alexandria, VA: Time-Life Books. (H/A)

Powwows (secular/Pan-Indian/social)

Powwows today are far more than a salute to the past. They're not shows. They're not entertainment. Most Indians call them celebrations. . . . They're trying to carry a long heritage right into the future. This is not how it *was*. This is how it *is*. (Parfit, 1994, p. 94)

It is believed the word *powwow* came from the French, who misunderstood an Indian word; or perhaps its roots are in the phrase *pau wau*, which once meant "medicine man" or "spiritual leader." It now refers to the uniquely pan-Indian celebration that occurs throughout the United States wherever American Indian people gather. Over 930 large powwows were scheduled for 1994, and this figure does not include the multitude of small powwows that are held regularly.

One of the largest powwows is the Crow Fair held on the Crow reservation in Montana. People from all over the world travel to Montana to participate and celebrate their Indian heritage. Although the event's focus is dancing, it is a celebration that includes singing, drumming, praying, the erecting of traditional tipis, cooking and sharing traditional foods, children playing, young people courting, elders visiting, artisans displaying their works, honoring of family members, and demonstrating the generosity of the culture.

The powwow begins with the Grand Entry—an unforgettable sight! The Grand Entry, which follows a certain order, is a sort of parade into the dance arena. Those who are identified and honored as the Head Man, Head Woman, Head Girl, and Head Boy follow along with the Princesses. (A large powwow usually honors a young woman who is named "Princess," and she wears a sash naming her as the Princess of the powwow—a position she will hold for a year. Princesses from other groups accompany her with their sashes identifying the groups they represent.) Then the dancers follow in each of the competition categories: Traditional (men and women), Fancy (men and women), Grass (men), Jingle-Dress (women), and Tiny Tots (young children). The dancers in their regalia have been accurately described as a kaleidoscope of feathers, beadwork, fringe, jingles, and paint.

The Grand Entry begins in a clockwise manner to form a circle. When the arena is full and the participants have all entered, the powwow begins with prayer (as do all Indian events). Next there is intertribal dancing, and everyone dances. Then the dance contests begin, with contestants vying for prize money. In large powwows, the competition can last for days.

In large powwows held out of doors, tipis and tents are erected, brush arbors are built, and a small community is formed as old friends greet each other. There are booths with arts, crafts, clothing, materials for making dance regalia, and all types of traditional and nontraditional food.

An interesting new national powwow, Schemitzun, was held recently by the Mashantucket Pequot people of Connecticut. The purpose of this richest powwow in history is to revive tribal traditions in the small but wealthy Pequot tribe. Previously, warfare and European diseases nearly eliminated the tribe. Today there are approximately 250 peoples on its tribal rolls. Now the tribe is wealthy; it owns the Foxwoods Casino, New England's only casino and one of the largest in the Western Hemisphere. In the Indian way, the Pequots gave generously in the organization and staging of the powwow, which is similar to the Crow Fair. Although Schemitzun is held indoors with air conditioning and caterers, and the Crow Fair is held outside in the summer sun with food prepared by participants, the spirit of celebration and cohesion is the same.

To be truly understood and appreciated, a powwow must be experienced either directly, through film or video, or at least with photographs and music. Without the smell of sage and fry bread; the drums and songs; the people; the movement, color, warmth, and excitement of the powwow, it is difficult to bring its power to life. Fortunately, non-Indians are welcome at powwows and new materials help bridge the gap between the printed word and the real experience.

Sources

Ancona, G. (1993). *Powwow*. San Diego: Harcourt Brace Jovanovich. (P/I)

Combs, L. (1992). *Powwow*. Cleveland, OH: Modern Curriculum Press. (P/I)

Horse Capture, G. (1989). *Powwow*. Cody, WY: Buffalo Bill Historical Society. (H/A)

Parfit, M. (1994, June). Powwow. *National Geographic* 185 (6), pp. 88–113. (I/H/A)

Roberts, C. (1988, Summer). Rocky Boy. *Native Peoples*, pp. 2–7. (I/H/A)

Roberts, C. (1994, Summer). Schemitzun. *Native Peoples*, pp. 66–70. (I/H/A)

REFERENCES AND RESOURCES

Green, R. (1993). Cherokee stomp dance: Laughter rising up. In C. Heth (Ed.), *Native American dance: Ceremonies and social traditions* (2nd printing). New York: Na-

Roles of the School Library Media Specialist

Resource to Teachers and Students

Help teachers understand that Indian spirituality is present in the wholeness of everyday Indian life and it is impossible to separate the sacred and the secular. There are no Indian "holidays."

Develop a community resource directory that enables teachers to utilize local Indian people in learning about American Indian ceremonies, celebrations, and traditions.

Make the position statement of the National Council for the Social Studies on Columbus Day available to teachers and students, as appropriate.

Assist teachers and students in creating Thanksgiving decorations, menus, plays and pageants, and costumes that are accurate and authentic.

Curriculum Developer and Coordinator

Encourage the adoption of an American Indian Day in your school.

Review existing curriculum about Thanksgiving and Columbus day and assist teachers in making appropriate revisions.

Include, when appropriate, examples of American Indian ceremonies and celebrations in the curriculum.

Collection Manager

Search for print and non-print instructional materials that provide a balanced perspective on holidays, including Thanksgiving and Columbus Day.

Search for culturally authentic instructional materials about Indian ceremonies and celebrations from small, tribal presses and Indian authors.

Teacher

Develop awareness in teachers and students that many Indian people do not want others to know about their ceremonies and celebrations. While they are often not secret in nature, it is nonetheless believed by some traditional Indian people that too much has been taken from them already and they don't want to share these special events.

tional Museum of the American Indians, Smithsonian Institution, with Fulcrum Publishing.

Naylor, D. T., & B. D. Smith. (1993, November/December). Rethinking the holidays. *Social Studies and the Young Learner* 6 (2), pp. 4–5, 17.

Naylor, D. T., & B. D. Smith. (1993, November/December). Teaching about holidays (pull-out feature). *Social Studies and the Young Learner* 6 (2), p. 4.

Neihardt, J. (1979). *Black Elk speaks* (7th printing). Lincoln: University of Nebraska.

Parfit, M. (1994, June). Powwow. *National Geographic* 185 (6), pp. 88–113.

Roessel, M. (1993). *Kinaalda*. Minneapolis, MN: Carolrhoda.

Teaching about and Using Literature

10

> The stories of American Indian cultures are not just artifacts of "ethnic" or "minority" literature to be studied for the sociological or anthropological data they offer. They are stories that belong to the land on which we live and as such they are a truly native American literature. They can teach us about our own history and culture—why we travelled and what we have done since we "discovered" this land. They can tell us about our own literature and they can show us the harmony that exists within and without the self. (McTaggart, 1975, p. 9)

Literature for young people meets many personal and literary needs and provides a window into a world of people and experiences they may never encounter. American Indian literature can take students to other times, other places, and other cultures; it allows them to experience the world in a different way, to hear the voices of others, and to walk in another's moccasins. Used appropriately and well, literature can teach life's most important lessons in ways that are enduring, engage the heart as well as the head, and nurture and build a love for the written word that will last a lifetime.

Too often literature has been seen not as a window to an expanded world but as a mirror reflecting a white, middle-class lifestyle and worldview. Students learn that people or cultures different from the dominant Eurocentric culture are exotic or quaint at best, and deviant or inferior at worst. This attitude reinforces and perpetuates discrimination and racism (Bishop, 1994).

In this chapter we will present ways in which the school library media specialist can (1) assist teachers in using American Indian literature in ele-

mentary and secondary classrooms, (2) provide a rich collection for students' personal or recreational reading, and (3) enhance the curriculum through the understanding and use of American Indian oral traditions. We will also present a brief listing of prominent American Indian authors whose works should be available in every school.

PERSONAL OR RECREATIONAL READING

The following books about and by American Indians are recommended for students and fit the fundamental human needs identified by Maslow. At the school library students often find the reading that interests them—their recreational reading. Sometimes this reading is directly related to the curriculum, or students are led to particular authors or subjects by what they are studying; but most students are looking for information on something that interests them or for a book to read for enjoyment.

Students read and make sense of the printed word primarily in relationship to their individual needs; reading is a personal experience. One interesting approach to literature in this personal manner is through the work of Abraham Maslow (Sutherland et al., 1991). Maslow identified basic human needs as the following: physiological needs, safety needs, belongingness and love needs, esteem needs, self-actualization needs, the need to know and understand, and aesthetic needs (cited in Goble, 1976, pp. 37–53). Literature that helps students understand how others deal with these needs expands their own way of thinking about their lives, problems, and concerns. Good literature connects them in meaningful ways to the human experience.

In the following sections, each source listed is followed by one or more capital letters in parentheses. These designations indicate general reading level:

P   Primary
I   Intermediate
H   High school
A   Adult

Of course, the designations are approximate: adults can gain a great deal from reading books for children, and young readers can "stretch" to more difficult levels.

The need for physical well-being and safety. The child's need for physical security, the reassuring presence of parents, and the routines of eating and sleeping are often addressed in children's literature, in both positive and negative ways. Examples are as follows:

Joosse, B. M. (1991). *Mama, do you love me?* San Francisco: Chronicle. (P)

Maher, R. (1977). *Alice Yazzie's year.* New York: Coward. (I)

Te Ata. (1989). *Baby rattlesnake.* Emeryville, CA: Children's Book Press. (P)

The need to love and be loved. Much of children's literature, particularly picture books, has themes of family affection, friendship, and a love of pets. Examples are as follows:

Awiakta, M. (1983). *Rising Fawn and the fire mystery.* Memphis, TN: St. Luke's Press. (I)

Blood, C., & M. Link. (1980). *The goat in the rug.* New York: Four Winds. (P)

Hoyt-Goldsmith, D. (1991). *Pueblo storyteller.* New York: Holiday. (P/I)

Other books for older readers speak about the need to love and be loved in many ways. For example, the novels by Louise Erdrich address aspects of love ranging from sexual attraction to the love of an extended family (see lesson plan later in this chapter). Adolescents would enjoy Erdrich's novels with their many aspects of love and loving.

The need to belong. This has to do with being an important part of or belonging to a family, a tribe, a culture, and a nation. School library media specialists need to seek books that extend the concept of belonging in this greater sense. Examples are as follows:

Dorris, M. (1987). *A yellow raft in blue water.* New York: Holt. (H/A)

Hoyt-Goldsmith, D. (1990). *Totem pole.* New York: Holiday. (P/I)

Momaday, N. S. (1969). *The way to Rainy Mountain.* Albuquerque: University of New Mexico. (H/A)

Silko, L. M. (1977). *Ceremony.* New York: Viking. (H/A)

Sneve, V. (1989). *Dancing teepees.* New York: Holiday. (I)

Wood, T., with W. N. Afraid of Hawk. (1992). *A boy becomes a man at Wounded Knee.* New York: Walker. (I)

The need to achieve competence (self-respect and self-actualization). There is a universal need among young people to know that they are capable and competent. This is where biographies play an important role as examples and models for students. Books in the school library media center must include Indian contributions to agriculture, architecture, education, medicine, science, and other areas. Examples are as follows:

Anderson, P. (1992). *Maria Martinez: Pueblo potter.* Chicago: Children's Press. (P/I)

Henry, C. (1994). *Ben Nighthorse Campbell.* New York: Chelsea. (I)

Lipsyte, R. (1993). *Jim Thorpe: 20th century jock.* New York: HarperCollins. (I)

Mankiller, W., & M. Wallis. (1993). *Mankiller: A chief and her people*. New York: St. Martin's Press. (H/A)

Simon, C. (1991). *Wilma P. Mankiller: Chief of the Cherokee*. Chicago: Children's Press. (I)

Swentzell, R. (1992). *Children of clay*. Minneapolis, MN: Lerner. (P/I)

Viola, H. J. (1993). *Ben Nighthorse Campbell: An American warrior*. New York: Orion. (H/A)

The need to know and understand. American Indian people teach each generation that they need to know and understand how the world was created; where the first people of each tribe came from; how the sun, moon, stars, clouds, and rain came to be. Their stories, myths, and legends teach what is important to know and understand, and how to live well in beauty and harmony. Students' urgent questions about "how" and "why" are addressed in the wide-ranging body of American Indian myths and legends as well as in informational books.

Examples of myths and legends are as follows:

Begay, S. (1992). *Ma'ii and cousin Horned Toad*. New York: Scholastic. (P)

Bierhorst, J. (Ed.). (1976). *The red swan: Myths and tales of the American Indians*. New York: Farrar, Straus and Giroux.

Bierhorst, J. (1993). *The woman who fell from the sky*. New York: William Morrow. (P/I)

Browne, V. (1991). *Monster slayer*. Flagstaff, AZ: Northland. (P/I)

Goble, P. (1994). *Iktomi and the buzzard*. New York: Orchard. (P/I)

Martin, R. (1992). *The rough face girl*. New York: G. P. Putnam. (P/I)

Murphy, C. R. (1993). *The prince and the salmon people*. New York: Rizzoli. (P/I)

Spencer, P. (1983). *Who speaks for wolf*. Austin, TX: Tribe of Two Press. (P/I)

Examples of informational books are as follows:

Aliki. (1976). *Corn is maize*. New York: Thomas Crowell. (P)

Dorris, M. (1989). *The broken cord*. New York: Harper & Row. (H/A)

Echo-Hawk, R. C., & W. R. Echo-Hawk. (1994). *Battlefields and burial grounds*. Minneapolis, MN: Lerner. (I/H)

Fixico, D. L. (1991). *Urban Indians*. New York: Chelsea. (I)

Freedman, R. (1992). *An Indian winter*. New York: Holiday. (I)

Goble, P. (1992). *Red Hawk's account of Custer's last battle* (reprint). Lincoln: University of Nebraska. (I)

Klausner, J. (1993). *Sequoyah's gift*. New York: HarperCollins. (I)

Trimble, S. (1990). *The village of Blue Stone*. New York: Macmillan. (I)

The need for beauty, order, and justice. Beauty, order, harmony, and the compelling need for fairness and justice are common themes in Native American traditions, stories, and ceremonies. Examples are as follows:

Brown, D. (1970). *Bury my heart at Wounded Knee*. New York: Pocket. (H/A)

Bruchac, J. (1993). *The first strawberries*. New York: Dial. (I)

Deloria, V., Jr. (1988). *Custer died for your sins* (reprint). Norman: University of Oklahoma. (H/I)

Littlechild, G. (1993). *This land is my land*. Emeryville, CA: Children's Book Press. (P/I)

Ortiz, S. (1988). *The people shall continue*. San Francisco: Children's Book Press. (P)

Welch, J. (1986). *Fools Crow*. New York: Viking. (H/I)

AMERICAN INDIAN LITERATURE IN THE ELEMENTARY CLASSROOM

With the prevalence of whole language, the emphasis on the processes of reading and writing, and the use of trade books in content areas, the school library media specialist can be an invaluable resource in locating, making accessible, and recommending the best American Indian literature. Through collaboration between the library media specialist and the classroom teacher, American Indian literature can become an integral part of the learning process—learning to read, appreciate literature, and understand American Indians.

There are at least four reasons to include American Indian literature in the classroom, each contributing to the education of the whole child:

1. *Literary knowledge*: Through the literature about American Indians, children increase their knowledge about and develop appreciation for the traditional literary genres: traditional literature (folktales, fables, myths, and legends), poetry, historical fiction, contemporary fiction, biography, and informational books.

2. *Content knowledge*: Through time, students surrounded by the American Indian folktales, myths, legends, poetry, historical fiction, contemporary fiction, and informational books will develop a comprehensive understanding of the diversity and beauty of Indian cultures and a more realistic understanding of Indian people in American history. They will also develop an understanding of the historical roots of contemporary American Indian political and social problems.

3. *Self-esteem and self-understanding*: American Indian children gain pride and a sense of the value of their cultural ways through reading about their cultures and learning about American Indian authors. Non-Indian

children learn about themselves through learning about others—how they are similar to and different from people of other cultures.

4. *Respect for American Indian people and their contributions*: Through literature students can develop a respect for Indian contributions to literature and to the general society. Indian authors do indeed make a unique contribution to the literature of America; Indian artists bring beautiful works to American art. Further, we are increasingly aware of the lessons American Indian cultures have for our national culture in the areas of ecology, government, and spirituality.

The majority of time in the elementary classroom is spent on developing reading skills and encouraging a love of reading. Children should be surrounded by printed materials. The following sequence is recommended in developing an appreciation of American Indian literature:

Traditional Literature (myths, legends, folktales)

1. Identify distinctions among folktales, myths, and legends.
2. When age-appropriate, include oratory and ceremony as part of the oral tradition of American Indians.
3. Identify the common features and types of stories found in the stories of many tribes.
4. Summarize the importance of oral tradition, the roles of storytellers and audience, and "rules" that often apply to the telling of stories.

Traditional Literature of a Specific Tribe or Cultural Area

1. Analyze traditional stories of the tribe(s) and compare them with the knowledge gained in the introduction to the genre. For example, what rules apply to the telling of Navajo stories? What are some of the Navajo trickster stories?
2. Identify values, beliefs, and themes in the traditional tales of one tribe or region.

Historical Nonfiction

1. Analyze nonfiction for the values, beliefs, and themes identified in traditional literature.
2. Compare autobiographies and biographies. Consider the issues raised in "as told to" biographies and the problems of translation of Indian languages.
3. Compare information in historical documents with autobiographies and biographies.
4. Discuss the perspectives presented by Indian and non-Indian authors.

Historical Fiction

1. Evaluate historical fiction according to authenticity and accuracy of the conflicts, characterizations, settings, themes, language, and traditional beliefs and values.
2. Identify the author's qualifications and perspectives.
3. Compare historical fiction with autobiographies, biographies, and historical information.

Contemporary Literature

1. Analyze the inclusion of beliefs and values in traditional literature and nonfictional literature.
2. Analyze themes that are present in contemporary literature.
3. Analyze contemporary characterizations and conflicts in terms of the history of Indian people and current social problems and issues.

Children should also have an abundance of informational books. In fact, a diligent library media specialist should always be aware of unique opportunities that provoke curiosity and invite reading. For example, occasionally a current event relates to a story or legend within a culture. The recent birth of a rare white buffalo calf, which is a sacred and apocalyptic symbol in Indian culture, provided an opportunity to engage children in American Indian literature in a unique way. The calf, named Miracle, was born on August 20, 1994, on the Heider farm in Janesville, Wisconsin (Wronski, 1994). According to Lakota Sioux legend, "One summer so long ago that nobody knows how long," a beautiful young woman appeared among the Indians at a time when there was no game and people were starving. The woman gave the people a sacred pipe, taught them how to use it to pray, and told the Sioux about the value of the buffalo. Before she left them, the woman said one day she would return. The birth of Miracle is considered a miracle by many Indian people.

This story could be used in conjunction with the audiocassette "The White Buffalo Calf Woman" told by Martin High Bear, a Lakota spiritual leader (Greenfield Review Press, 1994); *White Buffalo Woman* by Christine Crowe (Tipi Press, 1991); or *Po Pai Mo: The search for White Buffalo Woman* by Robert Boissiere (Sunstone Press, 1983). The story of White Buffalo Calf Woman may also be included in anthologies. The tale could be incorporated into an interdisciplinary unit by using some of the environmental activities associated with the legend of White Buffalo Calf Woman presented in Michael Caduto and Joseph Bruchac, *Keepers of the Earth* (Fulcrum, 1988).

Perhaps the greatest contribution the school library media specialist can make to the elementary classroom is to be an informed and generous re-

source. When he or she is knowledgeable about the elementary curriculum, the library media specialist can help teachers provide a print-rich environment that includes American Indian literature in all its variety.

AMERICAN INDIAN LITERATURE IN THE MIDDLE AND HIGH SCHOOL CLASSROOM

In the middle school and high school, the emphasis shifts from the development of reading skills to academic content. Consequently, it becomes important to reflect on how American Indian literature can contribute to the mastery of social science concepts and generalizations, and how teachers can integrate American Indian literary traditions into the study of other American literature.

State and national standards for the teaching of social studies always include a strong emphasis on literature—historical fiction, contemporary fiction, poetry, biography, oratory, and informational books. For social studies teachers, particularly those who have relied solely on textbooks in the past, the role of school library media specialists is especially critical. They must be an active resource for social studies teachers, keeping them informed of American Indian literature appropriate to specific areas of social studies instruction.

Historical and contemporary fiction can be vital instructional tools to encourage students in developing alternative perspectives as well as to take history to personal and more interesting levels. In fact, many high school students rely on fiction to enliven history and make it meaningful. Books such as *Lakota Woman* by Mary Crow Dog with Richard Erdoes (Grove Weidenfeld, 1990) not only provide another point of view on a historical event (in this case, the occupation of Wounded Knee) but help students develop a more comprehensive understanding. Through such reading students can readily understand that any historical event can be interpreted in different ways, depending on the person who experienced it.

Teachers are blessed with an increased representation of American Indian literature in anthologies for classroom use. However, they also should consider Indian literature as a field of study apart from the excerpts presented in anthologies. Paula Gunn Allen (1983) stresses that the teachers of American Indian literature must place a literary work within a context that allows students to understand it in terms that do not distort it. Teachers should use historical and cultural information to prepare students to work with American Indian materials. For example, for a given work students might need the context provided by a fundamental knowledge of the oral tradition, history, contemporary life, or the religious beliefs and spiritual practices of a particular tribe. Or students may need to know more about a given historical event, or the life and times of the au-

thor. According to Allen, explanation only "without seeking to understand the context from which the materials derive, removes the book and its author from the living web of the people and tradition from which they both arose" (p. xi).

Another caution is to always guard against romanticism. Romanticism is an easy trap when you are caught up in the beauty of Indian language and culture!

When Americans cannot view American Indians as a people with histories, cultures, customs, and understandings worthy of study and dispassionate observation, they ignore the real plight of too many Indian people who must go without jobs, food, decent housing or, far too often, the simple human right to survive. (Allen, 1983, xii)

The average English teachers will likely need to extend their knowledge to provide the appropriate context and to avoid the pitfall of romanticism when teaching American Indian literature. Often they have not had this kind of professional education and are understandably unaware that they cannot teach without context. For teachers who lack this preparation or basic knowledge base, the school library media specialist can offer support as an informed resource, providing appropriate materials and background information.

TEACHING *LOVE MEDICINE* BY LOUISE ERDRICH: A LESSON PLAN

GRADE LEVEL: High School

BASIC CONCEPTS: Family, change, identity, survival, continuity

CULTURE AREA: Plains—Turtle Mountain Chippewa

TIME PERIOD: Present

BACKGROUND: *Love Medicine* has won numerous critical awards, including the National Book Critics Circle Award for Fiction in 1984, and is one in a series of books including *The Beet Queen, Tracks,* and *The Bingo Palace.* It is both a novel and a series of short stories, so it is very adaptable to the classroom. Initially the book may be challenging; some readers may find "the characters confusing, their family trees impossibly contorted, and the plot disconnected" (Beidler, 1992, p. 168). Figure 10.1 will help to clarify relationships among families and characters. The study guides for *Love Medicine* were developed by Beidler to help first-time readers and their teachers. Obviously the book has merit as a novel. However, it is also a fascinating look at Indian America today and could well be used as part of a multidisciplinary unit on American Indians.

Figure 10.1
Families and Characters in *Love Medicine*

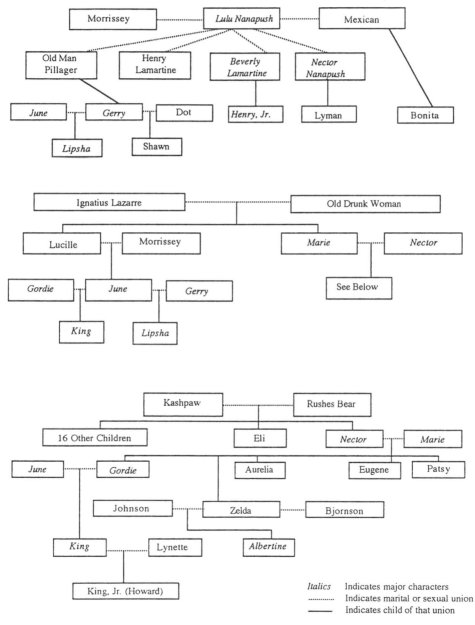

PREPARATION: Teachers should:

1. tell students about the history of novels written by American Indians,
2. discuss prominent American Indian authors (most are highly educated and are mixedbloods, including Louise Erdrich),
3. discuss Louise Erdrich: her family, her background, and her work,
4. provide some information about (a) the location of the Turtle Mountain Chippewa reservation in North Dakota and its characteristics, and (b) the status of American Indian people today (population, per capita income, health, social problems, etc.), and
5. include, if possible, an exploration of Indian values and worldview.

OBJECTIVES: Students should:

1. find the novel enjoyable,
2. increase their understanding of the problems faced by Indian authors,
3. gain insight into the strengths and problems of contemporary Indian people and cultures, and
4. be interested in continuing to read other works by Indian authors.

ACTIVITIES: "Literature and composition are both essential parts of the secondary language arts and English curricula." An excellent guide to structuring effective writing assignments is *Writing about Literature* (Kahn, Walter, & Johannessen, 1984). The teacher is urged to integrate writing assignments with reading in *Love Medicine* to promote deeper understanding and interpretation.

EVALUATION: Student understanding of *Love Medicine* will be assessed through discussion and individual writing assignments.

Key Dates and Events in *Love Medicine*

1910 (?)	Eli and Nector Nanapush born.
1913	Lulu born.
1920	Marie Lazarre born; Lulu finds body of dead man in woods.
1934	Marie scorched and stabbed in hand in the convent by Sister Leopolda, then accosted on her way home by Nector, who has just killed two geese.
1935	Gordie born to Marie and Nector.
1941	Zelda born to Marie and Nector.
1945	Gerry born to Pillager and Lulu.
1948	Lucille dies; Morrissey and his mother-in-law leave June for Marie to raise; Gordie and Aurelia try to hang June; June goes to live with Eli.

1950	Henry, Sr., killed by train; Lulu and Beverly make love in shack after the funeral (Henry, Jr., born to Lulu 9 months later).
1952	Lulu and Nector start buttery affair.
1957	The Lulu-Nector affair ends when Nector burns Lulu's house; Lulu marries Beverly, who has come to take Henry, Jr., home with him; Marie takes Zelda to visit Sister Leopolda and receive her blessing.
1958	Albertine born to Zelda and Swede Johnson.
1963	Gerry kicks cowboy and starts first of many jail terms; Bonita born to Lulu.
1965	Lipsha born to Gerry and June.
1972(?)	Lipsha fights with 10-year-old King.
1973	Henry, Jr., returns from Vietnam; he and Albertine come together in Fargo.
1974	Henry, Jr., drowns himself in river (witnessed by Lyman).
1980	Shawn born to Gerry and Dot; Gerry kills (?) trooper.
1981	June dies; King buys car with the insurance money and nearly drowns Lynette; Albertine comes home from college; Gordie gets drunk, kills deer, visits convent.
1983	Nector chokes to death on turkey heart brought by Lipsha as love medicine; Marie helps Lulu after eye operation.
1984	Lipsha discovers from Lulu that Gerry and June are his parents and that Lulu is his grandmother; visits his "brother" King; helps Gerry escape in the red convertible; then brings "her" home.

Discussion Guide: *Love Medicine*

These discussion areas are designed not to limit your thinking about *Love Medicine* but to stimulate it. If you had to add one additional topic to the list, what would it be and what would you want to say about it?

1. *Love.* The theme of love is important in this novel, from the title to bringing "her" home in the last line. How is that love shown? Does it differ in kind or intensity from the love shown in non-Indian families? Are there any anti-love characters? What is "love medicine"?

2. *Religion.* What are we to make of the Catholic presence in the novel? Is it a positive, negative, or neutral presence? Is it poison or medicine to the people? In what ways does it intersect with or conflict with a more native or "natural" religion? Does the novel offer a Native alternative to Catholicism?

3. *Family.* Assuming that the Kashpaw and Lulu/Lamartine families are "typical," how would you characterize the typical family structure, dependency patterns, communication style, and authority relationships among modern Indians? Does the family seem to be, in general, a positive or negative force in Indian culture?

4. *Marie.* How do you account for Marie's strangeness—her desire to be a nun one minute and to capture Nector in the next? Her uncertain parentage? Her strange relationship with Sister Leopolda at the Sacred Heart Mission? Her reaction to Nector's letter and Lulu's eye operation?

5. *Lulu.* Lulu might qualify as a kind of "earth mother"; she loves many different men, gives birth to many different children, and seems both kind and amoral. Are we supposed to like her better than we like Marie? Does her character help us understand June?

6. *Alcohol.* Assess the importance of alcohol in this novel. Do many of the important events take place while the characters are drinking? Think of the various deaths—June's, Henry's, Henry, Jr.'s, for example. What about Marie's efforts to control Nector's drinking? Is this an anti-drinking novel?

7. *Time and Unity.* Is this a novel or merely a collection of short stories? Why does Erdrich tell the story in what appears to be such a confused or disjointed way? After all, she could have arranged all the chapters in chronological order. Would it have been better if she had? Would the novel be more effective if it covered a narrower scope of time?

8. *Theme.* What is the main idea of the novel? Do you leave the novel feeling encouraged or discouraged about these Indians and their way of life? Is it an anti-white novel? An anti-Indian novel? Does it make a political point? An emotional point? Is Erdrich trying to "show us the way"? What way, and for whom? What alternative medicines are there to the love medicine of the title? Are they effective?

9. *Home.* Note how often "home" is mentioned in the novel and what it seems to mean. At the end of the first subchapter, for example, June "walked over it like water and came home." At the end of the final subchapter, Lipsha decides to "cross the water, and bring her home." Are they both going to the same place, or has the notion of "home" somehow changed over the course of the novel?

Materials/Resources

Beidler, P. G. (1992). Three student guides to Louise Erdrich's *Love Medicine. American Indian Culture and Research Journal* 16 (4), pp. 167–73.

Bruchac, J. (1987). *Survival this way.* Tucson: Sun Tracks/University of Arizona. Interview with the author.

Erdrich, L. (1993). *Love medicine* (rev. ed.). New York: Henry Holt.

Kahn, E. A., C. C. Walter, & L. R. Johannessen. (1984). *Writing about literature.* Urbana, IL: ERIC/National Council of Teachers of English.

Owens, L. (1992). *Other destinies: Understanding the American Indian novel.* Norman: University of Oklahoma. (See Chapter 7, "Erdrich and Dorris's Mixedbloods and Multiple Narratives".)

Towery, M. (1992). Continuity and connection: Characters in Louise Erdrich's fiction. *American Indian Culture and Research Journal* 16 (4), pp. 99–122.

THE ORAL TRADITION

Storytelling

The oral tradition of American Indian people is not part of the past; it is alive today, moving and changing, but alive. Furthermore, no one is too old or too busy to listen and learn from these simple, profound, and always enjoyable stories.

Stories require a performance, an audience of listeners as well as a storyteller. The school library media specialist should try to engage Indian storytellers, for only through them can the real power of any story be evoked. However, that is not always possible. Non-Indian storytellers thus have special responsibilities. It is very important that non-Indian storytellers clearly understand the message the story is meant to convey. They also must be aware of what is sacred and what should not be told in a story. After all, stories do not exist in isolation of the culture and life of the Indian people. Storytellers must accept certain responsibilities that encompass understanding, respect, and responsibility (Hirschfelder, 1993).

Joseph Bruchac (1989) offers some directions for non-Indian storytellers. (1) Rather than relying solely on books, learn Native American tales from the life of the people. Visit with American Indian people to find out more about their ways of life and their stories. (2) When talking with Native American people, remember not to interrupt—listening is a prime virtue. (3) If a written text is used, all versions of the story should be researched. (4) Know the type of story being learned. Find out if there were certain times when it was to be told, and be aware of how the story fits into the culture of that particular American Indian tribe. (5) If you are not certain of a story's use or origin, do not tell it. (6) If you wish to use a story heard from an American Indian storyteller, remember to obtain permission to tell the story yourself.

The school library media center can develop a collection of recorded stories that can bring an authentic experience to students because they are told by American Indian people. Joseph Bruchac and others have recorded stories on audiocassettes. Examples (on cassette) include the following:

Bruchac, J. (1991). *Keepers of the earth: Native American stories.* Golden, CO: Fulcrum. (P/I)

Hayes, J. (1983). *Coyote and Native American folktales.* Santa Fe, NM: Trails West. (P/I/H)

Momaday, N. S. (n.d.). *N. S. Momaday: Storyteller.* Santa Fe, NM: Lotus Press. (I/H/A)

For Indian people, stories offer lessons to be learned. These lessons can be valued in non-Indian cultures and make an interesting contribution to the classroom.

Oratory

Indian oratory is rich and powerful. The old speeches were first recorded by the white men who came to this continent. Later they were recorded and interpreted by the Indian people themselves. We are fortunate to have several volumes of these recorded speeches, which are hauntingly powerful; these authentic voices need to be heard in the classroom. They provide another perspective to historical events; but more important, they convey the beliefs and values of the American Indian people with great beauty and simplicity.

Armstrong, V. I. (1984). *I have spoken* (5th printing). Athens, OH: Swallow. (I/H/A)

Jeffers, S. (1991). *Brother Eagle, Sister Sky: A message from Chief Seattle.* New York: Dial. Although these are probably not the words of Chief Seattle, this book for children has beauty and captures the spirit of the great chief. (P)

McLuhan, T. C. (1971). *Touch the earth.* New York: Simon & Schuster. (I/H/A)

Vanderwerth, W. C. (Comp.). (1989). *Indian oratory* (6th printing). Norman: University of Oklahoma. (H/A)

As a final word, the beauty and reality of American Indian culture is brought to the non-Indian world through literature. A school library media center is the repository of this wealth, which should be treasured and shared.

RESOURCES FOR THE TEACHER

*Anthologies

Allen, P. G. (1983). *Studies in American Indian literature.* New York: Modern Language Association.

Allen, P. G. (1994). *Voice of the turtle: American Indian literature.* New York: Ballantine.*

Bierhorst, J. (1985). *The mythology of North America.* New York: William Morrow.*

Bruchac, J. (Ed.). (1983). *Songs from this earth on turtle's back.* Greenfield Center, NY: Greenfield Review Press.*

Bruchac, J. (1987). *Survival this way.* Tucson: University of Arizona/Sun Tracks.*

Caldwell-Wood, N. (1992, May). Native American images in children's books. *School Library Journal,* pp. 47–48.

Coltelli, L. (1990). *Winged words: American Indian writers speak.* Lincoln: University of Nebraska.

Cronyn, G. W. (Ed.). (1991). *American Indian poetry.* New York: Fawcett Columbine.*

Dowd, F. (1992, Summer). Evaluating children's books portraying Native American and Asian cultures. *Childhood Education,* pp. 219–24.

Dyson, A. H., & C. Genishi. (1994). *The need for story: Cultural diversity in classroom and community*. Urbana, IL: National Council of Teachers of English.

Erdoes, R., & A. Ortiz. (Eds.). (1984). *American Indian myths and legends*. New York: Pantheon.*

Gill, S. D., & I. F. Sullivan. (1992). *Dictionary of Native American mythology*. New York: Oxford University Press.

Greenfield Review Press. (1994). *North American Native authors catalog*. Greenfield Center, NY: Greenfield Review Press.

Harris, V. J. (Ed.). (1993). *Teaching multicultural literature in grades K–8*. Norwood, MA: Christopher Gordon.

Harvey, K. D. (1995). *American Indian voices*. Brookfield, CT: Millbrook.*

Helbig, A. K., & A. R. Perkins. (1994). *This land is our land: A guide to multicultural literature for children and young adults*. Westport, CT: Greenwood.

Hirschfelder, A. (1993, Winter). Native American literature for children and young adults. *Library Trends* 41 (3), pp. 414–36.

Hobson, G. (Ed.). (1981). *The remembered earth*. Albuquerque: University of New Mexico.*

Kruse, G. M., & K. T. Horning. (1991). *Multicultural literature for children and young adults* (3rd ed.). Madison: Wisconsin Department of Public Instruction.

Lachmann, L. M. (1992). *Our family, our friends, our world: An annotated guide to significant multicultural books for children and teenagers*. New Providence, NJ: Bowker.

Lincoln, K. (1985). *Native American renaissance* (2nd ed.). Berkeley: University of California.

Nilsen, A. P., & K. L. Donelson. (1993). *Literature for today's young adults* (4th ed.). New York: HarperCollins.

Norton, D. E., with S. E. Norton. (1995). *Through the eyes of a child: An introduction to children's literature* (4th ed.). Englewood, NJ: Merrill/Prentice-Hall.

Ortiz, S. J. (Ed.). (1983). *Earth power coming*. Tsaile, AZ: Navajo Community College. *

Owens, L. (1992). *Other destinies: Understanding the American Indian novel*. Norman: University of Oklahoma.

Ruoff, A. L. B. (1991). *Literatures of the American Indian*. New York: Chelsea.

Slapin, B., & D. Seale. (1992). *Through Indian eyes: The Native experience in books for children*. Philadelphia, PA: New Society.

Stensland, A. (1973). *Literature by and about the American Indian: An annotated bibliography for junior and senior high school students*. Urbana, IL: National Council of Teachers of English.

Stensland, A. (1979). *Literature by and about the American Indian: An annotated bibliography* (2nd ed.). Urbana, IL: National Council of Teachers of English.

Velie, A. R. (1991). *American Indian literature: An anthology* (rev. ed.). Norman: University of Oklahoma.*

Velie, A. R. (1991). *The lightning within*. Norman: University of Oklahoma.*

AMERICAN INDIAN AUTHORS: A PARTIAL LISTING

The following list includes some of the most prominent Indian writers whose works should be included in every secondary school library media center. Teachers as well as students can expand their knowledge by reading fiction, poetry, and nonfiction written by Native people. For readers of any age, literature provides a pleasurable and safe way to walk in the moccasins of another.

Sherman Alexie (Spokane/Coeur d'Alene)

(1992). *The business of fancydancing.* Brooklyn, NY: Hanging Loose.

(1993). *First Indian on the moon.* Brooklyn, NY: Hanging Loose.

(1994). *The Lone Ranger and Tonto fistfight in heaven.* New York: HarperCollins.

(1995). *Reservation blues.* New York: Grove/Atlantic.

Paula Gunn Allen (Laguna /Sioux)

(1986). *The sacred hoop.* Boston: Beacon.

(1988). *Skin and bones.* Albuquerque, NM: West End Press.

(Ed.). (1989). *Spider Woman's granddaughters.* New York: Fawcett Columbine.

(1991). *Grandmothers of the light: A medicine woman's story.* Boston: Beacon.

(Ed.). (1994). *Voice of the turtle: American Indian literature.* New York: Ballantine.

Marilou Awiakta (Cherokee/Appalachian)

(1983). *Rising Fawn and the fire mystery.* Memphis, TN: St. Luke's Press.*

(1993). *Selu.* Golden, CO: Fulcrum.

Joseph Bruchac (Abnaki)

A prolific writer and storyteller, Bruchac has written several additional volumes of stories and recorded them as well.

(Ed.). (1983). *Songs from this earth on turtle's back.* Greenfield Center, NY: Greenfield Review Press.

(1991). *Keepers of the earth: Native American stories.* Golden, CO: Fulcrum.

(1992). *Native American animal stories.* Golden, CO: Fulcrum.

(1993). *Dawn land.* Golden, CO: Fulcrum.

(1993). *Flying with the eagle, racing the great bear. Stories of Native North Americans.* Mahwah, NJ: Bridgewater.*

(1993). *The first strawberries.* New York: Dial.*

(1993). *The Native American sweat lodge: History and legends.* Freedom, CA: Crossing.

(1994). *A boy called Slow: The true story of Sitting Bull.* New York: Philomel.*

& G. Ross. (1994). *The girl who married the moon.* New York: Bridgewater/Troll.*

Vine Deloria, Jr. (Standing Rock Sioux)

(1988). *Custer died for your sins* (reprint). Norman: University of Oklahoma.

(1991). *Behind the trail of broken treaties* (4th printing). Austin: University of Texas.

(1992). *God is red* (2nd ed.). Golden, CO: North American Press.

Michael Dorris (Modoc)

(1988). *A yellow raft in blue water*. New York: Warner.

(1989). *The broken cord*. New York: Harper & Row.

& L. Erdrich. (1991). *The crown of Columbus*. New York: HarperCollins.

(1992). *Morning girl*. New York: Hyperion.*

(1995). *Paper trail*. New York: HarperCollins.

(1995). *Working men*. New York: Henry Holt.

Louise Erdrich (Turtle Mountain Chippewa)

(1984). *Jacklight*. London: Sphere Books.

(1984). *Love Medicine*. New York: Holt, Rinehart & Winston.

(1986). *The Beet Queen*. New York: Henry Holt.

(1988). *Tracks*. New York: Henry Holt.

(1994). *The Bingo Palace*. New York: HarperCollins.

(1995). *The blue jay's dance: A writer's year with baby*. New York: HarperCollins.

Rayna Green (not an enrolled tribal member)

(Ed.). (1984). *That's what she said*. Bloomington: Indiana University.

(1992). *Women in American Indian society*. New York: Chelsea.*

Janet Campbell Hale (Coeur d'Alene)

(1985). *Jailing of Cecelia Capture*. New York: Random House.

(1993). *Bloodline: Odyssey of a Native daughter*. New York: Random House.

Joy Harjo (Creek)

(1989). *Secrets for the center of the world*. Tucson: University of Arizona / Sun Tracks.

(1990). *In mad love and war*. Middletown, CT: Wesleyan.

Linda Hogan (Chickasaw)

(1990). *Mean spirit*. New York: Atheneum.

(1991). *Red clay: Poems and Stories*. Greenfield Center, NY: Greenfield Review Press.

(1993). *The book of medicines*. Minneapolis, MN: Coffee House Press.

N. Scott Momaday (Kiowa)

(1968). *House made of dawn*. New York: Harper & Row.

(1969). *The way to Rainy Mountain*. Albuquerque: University of New Mexico.

(1976). *The names*. New York: Harper & Row.

(1989). *The ancient child*. New York: Doubleday.

(1992). *In the presence of the sun*. New York: St. Martin's Press.

(1993). *Circle of wonder: A Native American Christmas story*. Santa Fe, NM: Clear Light.*

Simon J. Ortiz (Acoma Pueblo)

(Ed.). (1983). *Earth power coming*. Tsaile, AZ: Navajo Community College.

(1988). *The people shall continue* (rev. ed.). San Francisco: Children's Book Press.*

Greg Sarris (Pomo)

(1992). *Keeping Slug Woman alive: A holistic approach to American Indian texts*. Berkeley: University of California.

(1994). *Grand Avenue*. New York: Hyperion.

(1994). *Mabel McKay: Weaving the dream*. Berkeley: University of California.

Leslie Marmon Silko (Laguna / mixed)

(1977). *Ceremony*. New York: Viking.

(1981). *Storyteller*. New York: Seaver Books.

(1991). *Almanac of the dead*. New York: Penguin.

Virginia Driving Hawk Sneve (Sioux)

(1989). *Dancing teepees*. New York: Holiday.*

(1993). *The chichi hoo bogeyman*. Lincoln: University of Nebraska.*

(1993). *When thunders spoke*. Lincoln: University of Nebraska.*

Luci Tapahonso (Navajo)

(1989). *A breeze swept through* (2nd ed.). Albuquerque, NM: West End Press.

(1993). *Saanii Dahataal: The women are singing*. Tucson: University of Arizona.

Gerald Vizenor (Anishinabe)

(1990). *Interior landscapes*. Minneapolis: University of Minnesota.

(1991). *Landfill meditation*. Hanover, NH: University Press of New England.

(1991). *The heirs of Columbus*. Hanover, NH: University Press of New England.

(1992). *Dead voices: Natural agonies in the new world*. Norman: University of Oklahoma.

James Welch (Blackfeet / Gros Ventre)

(1974). *Winter in the blood*. New York: Harper & Row.

(1976). *Riding the earthboy 40*. New York: Harper.

(1986). *Fools Crow*. New York: Viking.

(1987). *The death of Jim Loney*. (reprint). New York: Penguin.

(1990). *The Indian lawyer*. New York; W. W. Norton.

(1994). *Killing Custer: The battle of Little Bighorn and the fate of the Plains Indians*. New York: W. W. Norton.

*These books were written for children.

Roles of the School Library Media Specialist

Resource to Teachers and Students

Use knowledge of school-wide and classroom curriculum to provide American Indian literature, of all genre and at differing reading levels, for teachers and students.

Ensure that teachers and students have sufficient accurate information about any given American Indian culture(s) to provide meaningful context for any selection of American Indian literature that is used in the curriculum.

Use knowledge of stages of literary development and of students' current interests to help them select books for personal reading.

Provide book reviews and study guides that have been written by American Indians for teachers (American Indian Culture and Research Journal is an excellent resource).

Encourage teachers to read American Indian literature to gain a deeper understanding of Indian history, values, beliefs, and lifeways.

Curriculum Developer and Coordinator

Include literature by and about American Indians in all areas of the curriculum.

Integrate various genre into the curriculum. For example, information, biography, historical and contemporary fiction, myth, legend, and poetry should be included in social studies curriculum. This integration helps students learn the ways of another culture more effectively.

Include American Indian oral and written literature as an integral and important part of all American literature courses.

Collection Manager

Analyze existing collections for accuracy, authenticity, and use of stereotypes, eliminating books which are not suitable for teaching about traditional and contemporary American Indian people and cultures.

Review new publications according to appropriate criteria before acquiring them. It is not advisable to purchase books of questionable quality or that do not present Indian people and cultures accurately.

Solicit catalogs from small publishers, particularly tribal presses, which specialize in books by and about American Indians.

Teacher

Bring American Indian storytellers into the library/media center, taking care to prepare students to appreciate the contributions of oral literatures.

Help teachers to develop criteria for selection of books by and about American Indians.

REFERENCES AND RESOURCES

Allen, P. G. (1983). *Studies in American Indian literature.* New York: Modern Language Association.

Beidler, P. G. (1992). Three student guides to Louise Erdrich's *Love Medicine. American Indian Culture and Research Journal* 16 (4), pp. 167–173.

Bishop, R. S. (1994). *Kaleidoscope: A multicultural booklist for grades K–8.* Urbana, IL: National Council of Teachers of English.

Bruchac, J. (1989). Storytelling and the sacred: On the uses of Native American stories. In B. Slapin & D. Seale (Eds.)., *Books without bias: Through Indian eyes* (pp. 103–16). Berkeley, CA: Oyate.

Gill, S. D., & I. F. Sullivan. (1992). *Dictionary of Native American mythology.* New York: Oxford University Press.

Goble, F. G. (1976). *The third force: The psychology of Abraham Maslow* (8th printing). New York: Pocket.

Hirschfelder, A. B. (1993, Winter). Native American literature for children and young adults. *Library Trends* 41 (3), 414–36.

Kahn, E. A., C. C. Walter, & L. R. Johannessen. (1984). *Writing about literature.* Urbana, IL: ERIC/National Council of Teachers of English.

McTaggart, F. (1975). American Indian literature and the American land. *Illinois Schools Journal* 75, pp. 9–14.

Sutherland, Z., D. Monson, & M. H. Arbuthnot. (1991). *Children and books* (8th edition). New York: HarperCollins.

Wronski, R. (1994, September 14). White buffalo born, fulfilling tribal prophecy. *Montreal Gazette.* Montreal: Southam Business Communications.

Teaching about History

History is more than dates and numbers. History is an act of remembrance. Each of us remembers our personal history in an episodic, pictorial calendar of the mind. We gauge time in terms of events—the year we moved across the country, the winter of the big freeze, the summer that the baby died, or the spring we won the high school championships. History is this kind of collective remembrance. Such Indian artifacts as the Kiowa calendar, a Comanche buffalo-hide robe, the Delaware Walum Olum sticks, the Kee-Too-Wah Cherokee wampum belts, or the Creek plates with their varied pictures, patterns, and symbols do for an Indian tribe what we do for ourselves when we measure and remember our lives. . . .

History is, in this Indian view, primarily the story of people recorded and remembered by people. Emotion and impression count in Indian remembrance in a way that dates and data never can. Indian history is thus the telling of the story of Indian people. The telling of that story involves more than recitation of the terms of the Atoka Agreement or the counting of the people massacred at the Washita. The Indians' stories, poems, pictures, and associated experiences speak volumes about life. (Strickland, 1980, pp. xi–xii)

This is Indian history—the story of Indian people recorded and remembered by Indian people. Note the importance given to stories, poems, pictures, and the many other ways of remembering. The model (Figure 11.1) we suggest to guide school library media specialists includes (1) traditional American history and the role American Indians have played in that story, *and* (2) Indian history, tribal history, and the prehistory that is central to core Indian values and beliefs.

Figure 11.1
Teaching Indian and American History

	Tribal History	American History
Pre-History	Origin stories Myths and legends Wampum, pictographs, petroglyphs, calendars etc.	Archeology Anthropology
Historical Periods	After contact, tribal history was shaped largely by European invaders or explorers and subsequent U.S. Indian policies. ← → Indian history is American history.	Contact and The First Years Separation Coercive Assimilation Tribal Restoration, Phase One Termination Tribal Restoration, Phase Two

Contemporary Life and Issues	Health and education
	
	Economic self-sufficiency
	
	Treaty rights and trust
	   responsibilities
	
	Repatriation of artifacts
	   and return of tribal lands
	
	Preservation of language and
	   cultures
	
	Sovereignty
		Health and education
		
		Gaming/resource development
		
		Treaty rights and trust
		   responsibilities
		
		Repatriation of artifacts and
		   return of tribal lands
		
		State/federal/reservation
		   jurisdiction

History encompasses the traditional disciplines of anthropology, sociology, economics, philosophy, and political science as well as technology. These disciplines cannot be separated except for scholarly analysis; in reality, they are inextricably interwoven in the real lives of all individuals and societies. Because they constitute the fabric of our individual and collective lives, change in one area will cause change in another. And change, continuity, and resistance to change are some of the most important concepts in history (National Center for History in the Schools, 1994, p. 27).

TRIBAL HISTORY

Let's begin with tribal history, the remembrances of a particular group of Indian people. Why should tribal history be taught? Where should it be included in the curriculum? How can the study of Indian and American

history meet the new standards for the teaching of history? What resources should be available?

There are some obvious places in the K–12 curriculum where the study of general Indian history is not only appropriate but necessary. For example, it is common practice to teach about American Indians as an introduction to American history. As the first inhabitants of the American continents, Indian people form the beginnings of the story of the American people. This is actually prehistory, before written records, from the beginning when "where we came from" was remembered in story, song, and ancient ceremonies and when remembrances were also recorded in clay, rock, pictures, calendars, and wampum. Prehistory, by definition, explores tribal cultures whose stories were not recorded in writing. It is also a story that is developing as new discoveries are made and as technology improves.

Interestingly, if we follow the model for teaching about the prehistory of American Indian people, we must acknowledge and respectfully teach two strands of thought. Scientists and contemporary scholars teach about Beringia, the land bridge that allowed people from Asia to follow the big game herds across the tundra bridge into the Americas. They teach about archeological discoveries; early and later migrations; and tentative theories of how, in time, American Indian people moved into warmer climates and spread throughout this continent.

However, traditional Indian nations have origin stories that tell about the beginnings of each tribe and how they came *from* this land. Tribal histories begin with these origin stories. Teachers should be encouraged to understand two major points in terms of the origins of the first Americans. First, Indian values, spiritual beliefs, and religious practices are embedded in the origin stories. Alfonso Ortiz, a well-known Tewa writer, explains:

A Tewa is not so interested in the work of archaeologist. A Tewa is interested in our own story of our origin, for it holds all that we need to know about our people, and how one should live as a human. The story defines our society. (1991, p. 7)

Second, traditional Indian people do not believe they were the first immigrants to this land, as the Beringia theory maintains. Although scholars state that the peoples whom the Europeans first encountered were descendants of these early immigrants, many Indian people believe they are *from the earth* and have always been here. As history evolves, the fact that Indian people are not immigrants becomes increasingly important. They are not immigrants who chose to relocate to become Americans, nor were they were transported to this land in slavery. The earth is their mother, and what we know as America is their homeland.

In the study of ancient civilizations, tribal histories should be taught because the ancient Indian cultures are an integral part of both American and

world history and their contributions are significant. Although attention is often given to the ancient Aztec, Mayan, and Inca cultures of Central and South America, the well-developed cultures of North America are equally intriguing. The earliest known Clovis, Folsom, and Plano cultures and the Hohokam, Anasazi, and Mogollon cultures of the Southwest—and the Adena, Hopewell, and Mississippian cultures of the eastern woodlands— should be included in the curriculum.

It is also common for Indian history, particularly specific tribal history, to be incorporated in the teaching of state history—often in the fourth grade and middle school. Every state has a rich history of Indian people. Thus, in every state there is an opportunity, if not a requirement, to teach about the particular tribe(s) that constitutes a vital part of the state's history. Each state has unique resources in its museums, historical societies, universities, and Indian communities. Teachers may want to take the opportunity to study a particular tribe of another state in order to develop greater understanding of the diversity of Indian nations and make thoughtful comparisons between Indian tribes and geographical regions.

Finally, elementary teachers have special opportunities to teach about Indian history during the study of holidays and the study of cultures. Thanksgiving and Columbus Day are certainly part of a collective heritage for all Americans. However, in teaching about them teachers should include an appropriate emphasis on historical bias. After all, from an Indian perspective both Columbus Day and Thanksgiving have different stories from what is habitually taught. We addressed this issue in Chapter 9.

HISTORICAL PERIODS

After 1492, life changed for American Indians; their lives were forever influenced by and intertwined with the European newcomers/invaders. Imagine what Indian people must have thought as they watched the strange bearded men in enormous vessels sailing into their harbors. Or how they struggled to understand and cope with the diseases that swept through their homes and villages. Would they celebrate this "discovery" of America? Although Indian history is American history, historical events were experienced and understood differently.

Beginning in 1763, the United States began to deal with the "Indian problem" through official governmental policies. These policies have changed profoundly through the years. For analysis, historians organize the history of Indian people in America according to the differing periods of U.S. Indian policy. With this chronological organization, the history of Indian people in America can be integrated into the standard American history curriculum quite easily. The following sections briefly explain these periods of American Indian policy.

Contact (1492–1620) and the First Years (1621–1763)

This period covers the years in which European explorers, beginning with Christopher Columbus, first encountered and conquered the "Indians" of the Western Hemisphere. Over 600 independent Indian nations, with their own languages, cultures, and governments, inhabited this land in 1492.

During these first years, waves of European explorers, conquistadors, trappers, missionaries, investors, and adventurers fought for land, Christianity, economic power, and political control. At this time the political destiny of what is now the United States of America was unclear; the English, Spanish, French, Dutch, and Russians were all staking claims on the land and fighting Indians and each other for dominance. Also during this time, it was not evident that Indian people would be conquered and their cultures threatened or destroyed. There were many who believed that Indian people could live peacefully in a cooperative, side-by-side relationship with the European newcomers.

Separation (1763–1887)

In time, the struggle for dominance was settled and the British and then the Americans were in control. This land was no longer "Indian Country" where the people believed they had been put here by their creator. Now the American Indians were forced from their ancestral homes as governmental policies were established to separate Indian people from the American settlers. "Indian Country" took on a new political meaning.

The period of separation began with the *Proclamation of 1763*, which established a line along the crest of the Appalachian Mountains that no English settlers could cross until representatives of the government negotiated treaties and land cessions with the Indians who lived there. Two principles in the proclamation became the policies that were to guide U.S. actions toward Indian people for some time. First, Indian nations were to be considered much like European nations; they would be dealt with through diplomacy, warfare, and treaty, and their lands would not be taken without their permission or without compensation. Second, conflict would be prevented if there were established, centrally controlled boundaries between colonists and the Indians.

The *Indian Removal Act* of 1830 created an "Indian territory" that was inaccessible to all whites. This policy enabled the U.S. government to remove the Five Civilized Tribes of the Southeast from their lands, making it possible for white settlers to "establish" their homes in rich, abundant, and desirable lands, free from the resistance of the Indians who were protecting their own homes and lifeways there. The infamous Cherokee Trail of Tears is perhaps the most well known of the forced migrations to what is now Oklahoma.

During this time, Congress passed a number of laws to promote the assimilation of the Indians into white society. Schools were used to achieve
this goal; by 1887 more than 200 Indian schools serving over 14,000 Indian
students had been established under the supervision of the federal government.

In 1871 Congress eliminated the practice of making treaties with Indian
tribes because they were no longer considered independent nations. Congress would deal with them through statutes, which, unlike treaties, do
not require tribal consent.

Coercive Assimilation (1887–1934)

During this period, whites sought to replace traditional Indian lifeways
with their own and to force them to become self-sufficient farmers and artisans, under conditions dictated by whites. This was the time of allotment
and assimilation. (See lesson plan following.)

In 1887 the *General Allotment Act* (Dawes Severalty Act) was passed by
Congress. This legislation was intended to destroy tribal governments,
abolish Indian reservations, and force Indians to give up their traditional
ways and assimilate into the dominant society. The act was based on the
belief that Indians should become farmers. To attain this goal, their com-
munal tribal lands were divided into separate parcels and each tribal
member was allotted a parcel. "Surplus" parcels were made available to
white farmers. It was thought that if whites settled on Indian reservations, Indians would naturally learn and adopt white ways. However,
much of the land was not suitable for agriculture, and impoverished Indians either lost or were forced to sell their land to whites. Only 50 of 140
million acres of Indian land remained in 1934 when the allotment system
was abolished. Clearly, allotment was devastating to Indian tribes. The
Dawes Commission (Commission to the Five Civilized Tribes) was in-
strumental in the dissolution of the Five Civilized Tribes through the allotment process.

Tribal Restoration, Phase One (1934–1953)

It became increasingly clear that the policies of allotment and assimilation were detrimental to Indian people. In 1933 President Franklin Roo-
sevelt appointed John Collier as Commissioner of Indian Affairs. Collier
soon announced that "The cultural history of Indians is in all respects to be
considered equal to that of any non-Indian group" (Pevar, 1992, p. 6).

Under Collier's influence, Congress passed the *Indian Reorganization Act*
in 1934. This prohibited further allotment of tribal land to individual In-

dians, authorized the addition of lands to existing reservations, created new reservations for landless tribes, and restored to the tribes any land that had been removed as "surplus" and that had not yet been sold. Indian tribes were encouraged to adopt their own constitutions, and funds were made available for loans to incorporated tribes.

Between 1935 and 1953, federal funds were allocated for health care facilities, public work projects (e.g., roads and irrigation projects), homes, and schools. Two million acres were added to tribal lands. But this period of restoration began to end when national attention was turned to World War II.

Termination (1953–1968)

The policy of termination was intended to terminate federal benefits and support services to certain tribes, thereby disbanding their governments and eliminating their reservations. From 1953 to 1963 Congress terminated federal assistance to over one hundred tribes. The tribes were required to distribute their land and property to their members and to dissolve their governments. Two of the larger tribes that were seriously affected and nearly destroyed were the Klamath and the Menominee.

By transferring power and responsibility for all criminal and some civil jurisdiction over Indian reservations to some states, federal responsibility was further reduced. Other states could choose to accept this responsibility as well. The action weakened tribal sovereignty by giving to states the power over Indian people.

Tribal Restoration, Phase Two (1968–Present)

In 1968 President Lyndon Johnson stated: "We must affirm the rights of the first Americans to remain Indians while exercising their rights as Americans. We must affirm their rights to freedom of choice and self-determination" (Pevar, 1992, p. 8). Later, President Richard Nixon denounced the termination policy, declaring: "This, then, must be the goal of any new national policy toward the Indian people; to strengthen the Indian sense of autonomy without threatening his sense of community" (Pevar, 1992, p. 8). Thus, the policy of termination ended and tribal restoration became policy.

Perhaps the most significant legislative action was the *Indian Self-Determination and Education Assistance Act* of 1975, which allowed Indian tribes to administer the federal government's Indian programs on their reservations. Other important legislative acts also began to allow Indian people to become self-determining.

HOW DOES IT FEEL?
A LESSON PLAN ABOUT COERCIVE ASSIMILATION

GRADE LEVEL: Grades 5–8 (can be adapted for other grades)

BASIC CONCEPTS: Tradition, change, coercive assimilation

ORGANIZING GENERALIZATION: During the period of coercive assimilation, the U.S. government attempted to (1) change the traditions of Native people in order to dissolve their unique identity and cohesiveness, and (2) force them to assimilate into the dominant American culture.

CULTURE AREA: Plains (can be generalized to other groups)

TIME PERIOD: Period of coercive assimilation—1923

BACKGROUND: Many methods were used to force Indian people to give up their traditional ways and assimilate into the dominant culture. Missionaries forced Christianity; children were taken from their homes and placed in boarding schools where their long hair was cut, their traditional clothing removed, and their languages forbidden; their traditional ceremonies prohibited; and their ways of providing for their needs modified by treaty. These actions were presented in terms that were paternal, patronizing, and insensitive to ancient lifeways. Primary and secondary source materials provide good examples of governmental policies, disdain of Indian people, and of paternalism. Library media specialists may have to search for accurate materials for this period of history and, in some cases, excerpt, summarize, or rewrite pertinent information.

OBJECTIVES:

Knowledge (Content)
Students will:

1. describe how Indian people were required to relinquish traditional ways of supporting themselves in an effort for them to become farmers and to change their traditional religious practices, and

2. demonstrate an understanding of the intent of these federal policies.

Skills
Students will:

1. use primary and secondary source materials,

2. analyze the attitudes and values revealed in governmental directives, and

3. hypothesize how Indian people might have reacted to the letter by Commissioner Burke (see p. 159).

Values (Organic)

Students will:

1. empathize with Indian people who were forced to give up their traditional ways, and

2. explore their own values related to ethnocentrism.

ACTIVITIES:

1. Introduce the term *coercive assimilation* (*coercive* = forced, *assimilation* = absorption into another cultural tradition). Give as many concrete examples and non-examples of *assimilation* as possible. Encourage students to brainstorm ways of forcing a person or group of people to give up one culture and assimilate into another. Guide students in discussing the functions of religion, education, and traditions in helping groups form a cohesive identity.

2. Form work groups of two or three students. Give each group a copy of Commissioner Burke's letter. Ask them (1) what Indians were to do, and (2) what they were to give up. Ask them also to write several paragraphs describing what, in their opinion, were the beliefs held by Commissioner Burke regarding Native people and what he intended to accomplish through the letter.

3. Discuss whether Indian people were likely to follow Commissioner Burke's directives and how they would react to his letter. What are the possible positive and negative effects of the letter?

4. Read "Pleasant Porter on the Effects of the Allotment" (see p. 160). Older students may be able to relate the "want of hope" to Commissioner Burke's letter and the assimilation policies.

EXTENSIONS:

1. Research other methods of coercive assimilation used by the government against American Indian people. The Massacre at Wounded Knee is directly related to suppression of the Ghost Dance, and abundant material is available on this topic. Allotment policies and the removal of Indian children from their homes to be "civilized" in boarding schools are other examples.

2. Investigate the traditional customs, religious ceremonies, and social dances of the Native people in your own locale. These could include the potlatch (Northwest tribes), Sun Dance (Plains tribes), Green Corn Dance (Southeast tribes), Snake Dance (Southwest tribes), and naming and puberty ceremonies (all tribes). Are these customs, festivals, and ceremonies controlled by the government? How important are they to contemporary Indian people?

3. As part of this research, students would enjoy speaking with local Native American people about ancient ceremonies that are still practiced today.

4. Investigate how people who immigrate to this country retain their culture and/or assimilate into the dominant culture.

EVALUATION: Students will be able to use Commissioner Burke's letter to give several examples of coercive assimilation

MATERIALS/RESOURCES:

1. Letter, "To All Indians" (see page 159).

2. Any print or nonprint materials that illustrate how people from other cultures have both relinquished and retained their own cultures would be appropriate for students to understand how all Americans have faced this challenge *voluntarily*. Indians were not allowed this measure of respect.

3. Teachers will need to locate books about the Ghost Dance, Wounded Knee massacre, and boarding schools. While some are available in reading levels suitable for middle school students, many will require the teacher to rewrite passages to make them appropriate for immature readers.

4. Other source materials can be readily found in books that present American Indian voices and perspective such as:

Armstrong, V. I. (1984). *I have spoken* (5th pr.). Athens, OH: Swallow Press.

Carter, F. (1976). *The education of Little Tree.* Albuquerque: University of New Mexico.

DeJong, D. H. (1993). *Promises of the past: A history of Indian education.* Golden, CO: North American Press.

McLuhan, T. C. (1971). *Touch the earth.* New York: Touchstone.

Spicer, E. H. (1983). *A short history of the Indians of the United States* (reprint). Malabar, FL: Robert E. Kreiger.

Standing Bear, L. (1978). *Land of the spotted eagle* (reprint). Lincoln: University of Nebraska.

CONTEMPORARY LIFE AND ISSUES

The study of Indian people is all too frequently relegated to study of the past, subtly inferring that Indian people are not a part of America's present or future. But the story of Indian people is being created and written today, and what is today's news is tomorrow's history. Chapter 13 will deal directly with contemporary life in Indian country; in this chapter it is reasonable to briefly sketch the contemporary issues that are creating both

To All Indians (A letter written in 1923)

To All Indians:

Not long ago I held a meeting of Superintendents, Missionaries and Indians, at which the feeling of those present was strong against Indian dances, as they are usually given, and against so much time as is often spent by the Indians in a display of their old customs at public gatherings held by the whites. From the views of this meeting and from other information I feel that something must be done to stop the neglect of stock, crops, gardens, and home interests caused by these dances or by celebrations, powwows, and gatherings of any kind that take the time of the Indians for many days.

Now, what I want you to think about very seriously is that you must first of all try to make your own living, which you cannot do unless you work faithfully and take care of what comes from your labor and go to dances or other meetings only when your home work will not suffer by it. I do not want to deprive you of decent amusements or occasional feast days, but you should not do evil or foolish things or take so much time for these occasions. No good comes from your "giveaway" custom at dances and it should be stopped. It is not right to torture your bodies or to handle poisonous snakes in your ceremonies. All such extreme things are wrong and should be put aside and forgotten. You do yourselves and your families great injustice when at dances you give away money or other property, perhaps clothing, a cow, a horse or a team and wagon, and then after an absence of several days go home to find everything going to waste and yourselves with less to work with than you had before.

I could issue an order against these useless and harmful performances, but I would much rather have you give them up of your own free will and, therefore, I ask you now in this letter to do so. I urge you to come to an understanding and an agreement with your Superintendent to hold no gatherings in the months when the seedtime, cultivation and the harvest need your attention, and at other times to meet for only a short period and to have no drugs, intoxicants, or gambling, and no dancing that the Superintendent does not approve.

If at the end of one year the reports which I receive show that you are doing as requested, I shall be very glad for I will know that you are making progress in other and more important ways, but if the reports show that you reject this plea, then some other course will have to be taken.

With best wishes for your happiness and success, I am,

Sincerely yours,
Charles H. Burke,
Commissioner

Burke, C. H. (1923). "To All Indians" (letter). Washington, DC: U.S. National Archives (File: 10429–22–063 Part I).

Pleasant Porter on the Effects of the Allotment

Pleasant Porter (Creek) described to an investigating committee in 1897 what he saw as the effects of the work of the Dawes Commission on the Five Civilized Tribes.

It was a mistake to have changed these people's relations with the government. . . . The Indians . . . haven't had time to grow up to that individuality which is necessary to merge them with the American citizen. The change came too soon for them. . . . There will be a remnant that will survive, but the balance is bound to perish, do what you may for them. There is that sense of right and wrong which will bind men together and preserve the peace and maintain virtue and provide for offense without. That is the institution out of which a nation grows. Each of these groups (The Five Tribes) must have had that; but you rub that out, you transplant them into what they have no knowledge of. . . . [T]here is no life in the people that have lost their institutions. Evolving a thing out of itself is natural, transplanting it is a matter of dissolution, not growth. There may be a few that will grow . . . but the growth will not be natural; and I don't see anything now that it has gone this far but to come to it heroically and pay no regard now to our prejudices or sentiment; do the matter up in a business-like way, for every delay changes conditions. . . .

If we had our own way we would be living with lands in common, and we would have these prairies all open, and our little bunches of cattle, and would have bands of deer that would jump up from the head of every hollow, and flocks of turkeys running up every hillside, and every stream would be full of sun perch. Those things are what we were used to in our early life. That is what we would have; and not so much corn and wheat growing, and things of that kind. But we came up against it; this civilization came up against us and we had no place to go.

Q. You told us a moment ago they were dying off pretty fast?

A. Yes, sir, the older people are.

Q. Is there any special cause for that?

A. Nothing; there is no new disease; I don't see anything other than the want of hope.

Cited in Debo, A. (1989). *And still the waters run* (5th printing), Norman: University of Oklahoma, pp. 131–32.

---

tribal and national history. These issues appear in the national and Indian media—they have their roots in history, and their solutions frequently rest on the recovery of values and strengths of the past. Further, students can understand the issues facing Indian people and nations today only when they are framed in a historical context.

Health and Education

Statistics on Indian health are appalling: diabetes, cancer, heart disease, tuberculosis, suicide, and alcoholism are major killers and in each category exceed the rates reported for all Americans. Moreover, access to health care and reasonable preventive measures (e.g., decent sanitation, adequate nutrition, and prenatal care) continues to be a problem for both reservation and urban Indian populations. Even recent healthcare reform efforts have been threatening to Indian people, because their health care has been based on treaty obligations—they gave up land in return for health care and education.

Economic Self-Sufficiency

Crippling dependence and grinding poverty have weakened strong Indian cultures. As a group, Indian people are among the nation's poorest, with extraordinarily high unemployment rates and all the domestic and social problems associated with poverty and discouragement. Reservations are often dismal centers of abject poverty, and those people who have relocated to urban areas frequently do not have the basic skills required for employment.

Recent economic ventures (e.g., gaming; use of natural resources including coal, uranium, and oil; recreational areas and tourism; and some Indian small businesses) are beginning to make an impact. However, many of these ventures are associated with difficult value choices. Do Indian people need to destroy their sacred sites through mining, lumbering, storage of nuclear waste, or tourism in order to become economically stable? Is the gaming that is bringing badly needed resources to tribes a social threat to the people? Will it entice addiction, introduce prostitution, and attract graft, corruption, and exploitation? These questions are hotly debated.

Treaty Rights and Trust Responsibilities

A treaty is a contract between *sovereign* nations, and nearly every tribe has a treaty with the United States. The treaties made with Indian tribes usually contain two provisions: (1) the Indians relinquished land to the United States, and (2) the United States created a federally protected reservation for the Indians. Interestingly, treaties do not guarantee rights to Indians, but take rights away from them. Thus, any right not taken from them by treaty or federal statute is reserved to the tribe. The United States has broken nearly every one of its Indian treaties.

In the hundreds of treaties made with Indian tribes, the Indians gave up land in exchange for promises. These promises guaranteed that the United

States would create permanent reservations for the tribes and would protect the safety and well-being of tribal members. The promises made in treaty commitments are known as the government's trust responsibility.

The U.S. government can terminate its trust relationship with an Indian tribe at any time, with or without the tribe's consent, and has done so in the past by terminating the tribe itself. Because this trust is so important to Indian people, the Supreme Court has held that only an act of Congress can terminate a trust relationship. Tribes continue to fight for the promises which were guaranteed in the treaties that they made with the U.S. government.

Return of Tribal Lands and Repatriation of Artifacts

Enduring battles continue for the return of tribal lands to the Indian people. Indians continue to fight for the lands that were guaranteed to them in the treaties made with the U.S. government. Their lifeways, their "Indianness," their religions, and their sovereignty remain intimately connected to the land. Indeed, as A. M. Josephy has written,

Without a land base, there is no cohesive people, there is no tribe, there are no longer Indians. . . . [F]or Indians and Indianness to continue, there must be a recognized, protected, and revered tribal home. (Josephy, 1986, p. 130)

Repatriation means returning an object to the place from which it came, to its point of origin. Many pieces that currently are displayed or stored in museums and private collections are central to tribal religious beliefs. American Indian people do not regard these objects as artifacts of a vanished past but as reflections of a people's spirit, binding them together as members of a particular tribe.

The disturbance and misuse of human remains is another issue. For example, the Smithsonian Institution holds the remains of approximately 19,000 Native bodies. The *Native American Graves Protection and Repatriation Act* was passed by Congress in 1990. Among its provisions, it stipulates that federal agencies and private museums that receive federal funding must inventory their collections of Native American human remains and funerary objects. The relevant tribe must be notified; and on request of the tribe, the ancestral remains and funerary objects must be returned for reburial or other disposition by the tribe.

Preservation of Languages and Cultures

Indian people strive to retain their fundamental identity as Indians. The long-term effects of warfare, forced relocation, missionary zeal, boarding schools, and urban relocation have weakened Indian cultures and de-

stroyed pride, values, and traditional ways. In addition, intermarriage, modern technology (particularly television), and the wish for the "good life" have had similar effects.

Now, through tribally controlled and culturally appropriate schools, young people are learning the traditional values and ways of being Indian. Nearly lost tribal histories and languages are being learned from the few remaining elders and are taught to young and old alike. Even schools that are funded by the Bureau of Indian Affairs and that once served to weaken tribal ways are now controlled by local Indian school boards.

Although some elders object, believing they are "giving away" that which is sacred, modern technology is being used to teach languages. Books are being written in languages that have never before appeared in written form.

Traditional spiritual ways are integral to the maintenance of culture. In this regard, religious freedom of American Indians is a battle that has not yet been won. What is meant by religious freedom can best be understood if one understands that Indians find their religious practices threatened when:

- geographical areas deemed sacred sites are degraded;
- Indian burials, particularly bodily remains, are treated in a manner Indians believe is sacrilegious;
- the capture, kill, and use of endangered or protected species (e.g., eagles) are prohibited;
- the collection, transport, and use of peyote (used in the Native American Church) are regulated;
- religious artifacts are misused or displayed;
- Indian rituals and behavior, particularly in authoritarian institutions (e.g., prisons or schools) are prohibited. (Vecsey, 1991, pp. 8–9)

Sovereignty

Chapter 12 addresses government and Indian policy. In fact, there is no topic of greater importance to Indian tribes than that of sovereignty. Briefly stated, Indian nations have a unique relationship unlike that of any other "minority" group in America: they are sovereign nations. In 1832 Supreme Court justice John Marshall defined Indian nations as domestic dependent nations, subject to the guardianship protection and superior political power of the federal government. As such, they did not fall within the category of "foreign nations" that possessed full sovereignty; they were legitimate legal and political entities that could manage their own affairs, govern themselves, and engage in legal and political relations

with the federal government and its subdivisions. This historical relationship—which so clearly defines the unique status of Indian nations and will, in part, determine their future and survival—is rarely addressed in history classes. The omission must be rectified, and appropriate and accurate information must be available to students and teachers.

Finally, in a time of increased pressures for more content and more accountability, school library media specialists must be knowledgeable about how the historical content, of both tribal and American history, meets standards set by professional organizations, state education departments, and local curriculum committees. For example, one of the content standards identified by the National History Standards Project relates to critical thinking in the analysis of historical documents, narratives, and arguments—just what we want students to do in their study of American Indian history:

To demonstrate critical thinking in their analysis and interpretation of historical documents, narratives, and arguments, students should be able to:

1. *Identify the author or source of the historical document or narrative and assess its credibility.*

2. *Compare and contrast* differing sets of ideas, values, personalities, behaviors, and institutions by identifying likenesses and differences.

3. *Differentiate between historical facts and historical interpretations,* but acknowledge also that the two are related; that the facts the historian reports are selected and reflect therefore the historian's judgment of what is most significant about the past.

4. *Consider multiple perspectives* in the records of human experience by demonstrating how differing motives, beliefs, interests, hopes, and fears influenced individual and group behaviors.

5. *Incorporate multiple causes in analyses and explanations of historical action,* including: (a) the importance of the individual in history, of human will, intellect, and character; (b) the influence of ideas, human interests, and beliefs; and (c) the role of chance, the accidental, and the irrational.

6. *Challenge arguments of historical inevitability* by formulating examples of historical contingency, of how different choices could have led to different consequences.

7. *Compare competing historical narratives* by contrasting different historians' choice of questions, their use of sources reflecting different experiences, perspectives, beliefs, and points of view, and demonstrating how their different weighting of causes contribute to different interpretations.

8. *Hold interpretations of history as tentative,* subject to changes as new information is uncovered, new voices heard, and new interpretations broached.

9. *Evaluate major debates among historians* concerning alternative interpretations of the past.

10. *Hypothesize the influence of the past on the present,* including both the limitations and the opportunities made possible by decisions in the past. (National Center for History in the Schools, 1994, pp. 50–51)

One of the problems cited in developing students' skills in historical analysis and interpretation is the conventional way in which most textbooks have presented history. It is suggested that (1) well-written historical narratives, (2) history books other than textbooks, and (3) a rich variety of historical documents and other records of the past that present alternative voices and accounts of events will enable students to confront their tendency to look for the "right" history and will allow them to struggle with more than one interpretation or perspective on the past. This kind of historical instruction points clearly to the importance of the multiple roles of the school library media specialist in providing access to a well-developed collection about the history of American Indians in the United States.

Without history, a society shares no common memory of where it has been, of what its core values are, or of what decisions of the past account for present circumstances. Without history, one cannot undertake any sensible inquiry into the political, social, or moral issues in society. And without historical knowledge and the inquiry it supports, one cannot move to the informed, discriminating citizenship essential to effective participation in the democratic processes of governance and the fulfillment for all our citizens of the nation's democratic ideals. (National Center for History in the Schools, 1994, p. 27)

REFERENCES AND RESOURCES

Armstrong, V. I. (1984). *I have spoken* (5th printing). Athens, OH: Swallow Press.

Berger, J. C. (Executive Producer). (1993). *How the West was lost* (videos). Bethesda, MD: Discovery Enterprises.

1. A Clash of Cultures; I Will Fight No More Forever
2. Always the Money; The Only Good Indian Is a Dead Indian
3. A Good Day to Die; Kill the Indian, Save the Man.

Berger, J. C. (Executive Producer). (1994). *How the West was lost* (videos). Bethesda, MD: Discovery Enterprises.

1. The Iroquois
2. The Cherokee

Roles of the School Library Media Specialist

Resource to Teachers and Students
Be cognizant of current organizing frameworks for instruction, including appropriate national, state, and local standards.

Curriculum Developer and Coordinator
Insure that tribal history is taught along with Indians place in and contribtions to American history.

Build the teaching of the concept of historical bias into the curriculum.

Guard against superficial coverage of content, emphasizing instead the development of rich, significant knowledge.

Collection Manager
Provide instructional materials that present Indian perspectives.

Seek tribal histories from tribal sources.

Provide biographies of Indian people that portray them as having positive qualities of bravery, honor, and leadership.

Provide materials that build understanding of how historical events, policies, and practices have influenced the present.

Develop a collection that presents Indian history in poems, pictures, stories, visual art, and other non-written forms.

Provide contemporary source material which provides current information regarding Indian people and issues including newspapers, government documents, atlases, and reference materials.

Teacher
Teach students and teachers to seek alternative perspectives, particularly in primary source materials.

Help students learn to distinguish between the important and the inconsequential, to develop the "discriminating memory" needed for a discerning judgment in public and personal life. *

Stress the often tentative nature of judgments about the past, and thereby avoid the temptation to seize upon particular "lessons" of history as cures for present ills.*

Help students prepare to live with uncertainties and exasperating, even perilous, unfinished business, realizing that not all problems have clear or easily discerned solutions.*

Assist students in developing an understanding of the significance of the past to their own lives, both private and public, and to their society.*

* Parker, W. C. (1991). *Renewing the Social Studies Curriculum*. Alexandria, VA: Association for Supervision and Curriculum Development.

3. The Navajo Nation
4. The Seminoles
5. The Dakotas
6. The Cheyenne-Arapaho Tribes

Brown, D. (1970). *Bury my heart at Wounded Knee.* New York: Pocket.

Debo, A. (1989). *A history of the Indians of the United States* (11th printing). Norman: University of Oklahoma.

Josephy, A. M., Jr. (1986). *Now that the buffalo's gone.* Norman: University of Oklahoma.

National Center for History in the Schools. (1994, March). *National history standards project* (progress report and abridged draft standards). Los Angeles: Author.

National Council for the Social Studies. (1994). *Curriculum standards for social studies: Expectations of excellence.* Washington, DC: Author.

Ortiz, A. (1991, October). Origins. *National Geographic* 180 (4), pp. 4–14.

Pevar, S. L. (1992). *The rights of Indians and tribes: The basic ACLU guide to Indian and tribal rights* (2nd ed.). Carbondale: Southern Illinois University.

Prucha, F. P. (1990). *Documents of United States Indian policy* (2nd ed.). Lincoln: University of Nebraska.

Spicer, E. H. (1983). *A short history of the Indians of the United States* (reprint). Malabar, FL: Robert E. Kreiger.

Strickland, R. (1980). *The Indians in Oklahoma.* Norman: University of Oklahoma.

Vecsey, C. (Ed.). (1991). *Handbook of American Indian religious freedom.* New York: Crossroad.

Waldman, C. (1994). *Timelines of Native American history.* New York: Prentice-Hall.

Woodhead, H. (1992). *The first Americans.* Alexandria, VA: Time-Life Books.

Teaching about Sovereignty, Tribal Governments, and Indian Policy

12

> In every relationship between our people, our first principle must be to respect your right to remain who you are, and to live the way you wish to live. And I believe the best way to do that is to acknowledge the unique government-to-government relationship we have enjoyed over time. Today I reaffirm our commitment to self-determination for tribal governments.
>
> I pledge to fulfill the trust obligations of the federal government. I vow to honor and respect tribal sovereignty based upon our unique historic relationship. And I pledge to continue my efforts to protect your right to fully exercise your faith as you wish. ([President] Clinton, 1994, p. 5)

In this chapter we will address three topics that are central to understanding government as it relates to American Indians: sovereignty, tribal governments, and the major Indian laws related to sovereignty and self-determination. These topics are often ignored in existing curriculum, instructional materials are limited or nonexistent, and teachers are generally uninformed about them. Yet it is under these structures that Indian people and nations are governed—and they are governed differently than other American citizens. Thus, it seems reasonable for teachers and students alike to understand how the relationship between Indian nations and the U.S. government differs from that of other racial, ethnic, or cultural groups (see Figure 12.1).

Because the tribal–state relationships and tribal–federal relationships are established political relationships with tribes, not individuals, it is necessary to clarify the political meaning of tribe. Today, the federal govern-

Figure 12.1
Indian Nations and the American Political System

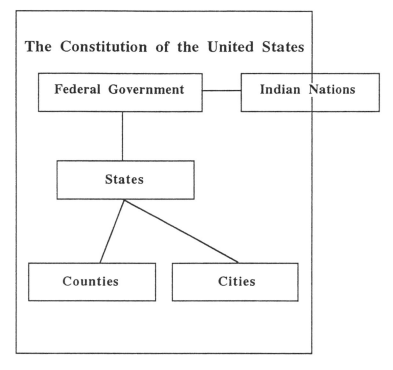

Note: Indian nations, because of their sovereign status, are only partially under the authority of the U.S. Constitution.

Source: From *American Indian Tribal Governments*, by Sharon O'Brien. Copyright © 1989 by the University of Oklahoma Press. (p. 277).

ment classifies tribes into the following four categories: (1) federally recognized tribes, (2) state-recognized tribes, (3) terminated tribes, and (4) unrecognized tribes. Although there are approximately 600 tribes in the United States today, only 502 are federally recognized. This special relationship, established by treaty or legislation, obligates the federal government to protect tribal lands and resources and provide the tribes with health care, education, and assistance in economic development. There are 26 state-recognized tribes living primarily on state reservations in the East and receiving some state funding. The remaining tribes, the terminated and unrecognized, are not eligible for special services and benefits because

they have no political relationship with the federal government. Many are seeking federal recognition in order to provide these beneficial services to their people.

SOVEREIGNTY, SELF-DETERMINATION, AND SELF-GOVERNMENT

You are quite likely, on entering an Indian reservation, to see a sign welcoming you to an Indian "nation." In addition, if you know Indian people or read about Indian issues you may encounter the terms *sovereignty*, *self-determination*, and *self-government*. These are complex legal terms with not only sophisticated legal meanings but also intense personal loyalties and tribal commitments. They are usually misunderstood by non-Indians.

This brief chapter cannot address these terms' complexity and related issues nor explain how they have evolved over time. However, we can begin to clarify how Indian nations are governed differently and how their relationships with the states and the federal government are unique. The terms *nation*, *tribe*, and *band* have been used interchangeably in Indian laws and treaties. According to Stephen Pevar (1992, p. 15), *nation* refers to a government independent from any other government, possessing the power of absolute dominion over its territory and people. Because the authority of Indian tribes has been restricted by the U.S. government, they are not, in this sense, *nations*. However, some tribal governments call themselves nations, still believing that the United States has no right to exercise any power or authority over them.

Sharon O'Brien (1989, p. 14) defines *sovereignty* as the force that binds a community together and represents the will of people to act together as a single entity. A sovereign community possesses certain rights, including the right to structure its government as it desires, to conduct foreign relations and trade with other nations, to define its own membership, to make and enforce its own laws, and to regulate its resources and property.

In reality, Indian nations have a quasi-sovereign status. For many reasons, Congress presumes it has the right to govern Indians. And it is highly unlikely that the federal government will permit Indians to be totally self-governing, nor will it return their lands. Because of the loss of their lands, Indian nations are dependent on the federal government, lacking the economic basis to truly be self-governing. The quasi-sovereign status acknowledges that the federal government has certain powers (e.g., postage, taxation) and responsibilities, but the relationship is a government–government one. Indian nations have the right to operate their own governments, control their own resources, and protect their cultures (Pevar, 1992).

Tribal-Federal Relationships

Through the years the tribal–federal relationship has changed from an equal, government–government relationship to a guardianship relationship with tribes as "wards" of the federal government, to termination of tribal special status, to a government–government trust relationship (see Figure 12.2). The doctrine of trust responsibility obligates the federal government to remain loyal to Indians and tribes, to act in their best interests,

Figure 12.2
Development of the Federal–Tribal Relationship

Dates	Policy	Major Laws	Relationship	Tribes' status
1770s–1820s	International sovereign to international sovereign	1783 Northwest Ordinance 1790 Trade & Intercourse Acts Treaties	Protectorate	International sovereigns
1830s–1850s	Removal	1830 Indian Removal Act Treaties	Government–government and trust relationship	Domestic dependent nations
1850s–1890s	Reservation	Reservation treaties	Guardianship	Wards in need of protection
1870s–1930s	Assimilation	1871 End of treaty making 1885 Major Crimes Act 1887 Allotment Act (Dawes Act)	Guardianship	Wards in need of protection
1930s–1950s	Indian self-government	1934 Indian Reorganization Act (Wheeler-Howard Act)	Renewal of government–government and trust relationship	Quasi-sovereigns
1950s–1960s	Termination	1953 Resolution 108 1953 Public Law 280 Urban Relocation Program	Termination of relationship	Termination of status
1960s–present	Self-determination	1968 Indian Civil Rights Act 1975 Indian Self-Determination Act 1978 Indian Child Welfare Act 1978 Indian Religious Freedom Act	Renewal of government–government and trust relationship	Domestic dependent nation/quasi-sovereigns

Source: From *American Indian Tribal Governments*, by Sharon O'Brien. Copyright © 1989 by the University of Oklahoma Press (p. 258).

and to fulfill the promises made to them in treaties. The current relationship is an evolving trust relationship based on international law, treaties, legislation, and judicial decisions. The federal government is responsible for protecting Indian lands and resources, providing certain services, and preserving tribal autonomy.

Protecting Indian lands and resources. In return for the promise of protection for their remaining lands and resources, Indian tribes ceded large areas of their land to the federal government. The protection they receive extends to lands, resources, tribal funds, and water, hunting, and fishing rights. Tribes are also protected from state taxation of tribal lands and resources.

Providing beneficial services. Again, for ceding much of their ancestral lands, Indian tribes were promised special services including medical and dental care, educational and employment assistance, and emergency food and housing. The eligibility of the tribes for particular services varies according to the specific treaties they negotiated. It is important for students to learn that these services are *not* charity or welfare assistance; they are rights accorded by treaty.

Preserving tribal autonomy. In the past, governmental policies were intended to destroy tribal autonomy, not preserve it. For example, the Major Crimes Act, the Dawes Allotment Act, and the Indian Civil Rights Act violated tribal autonomy. However, two recent acts of Congress, the Indian Child Welfare Act and Indian Self-Determination and Education Assistance Act, are designed to enhance self-determination and protect tribal cultures.

In the following statement, Indian leaders affirm their commitment to tribal sovereignty and autonomy:

Our highest priority as Tribal leaders has always been the protection and preservation of our tribal way of life. This sacred duty has been passed on from generation to generation for thousands of years and will continue into the future for as long as human societies exist on this earth. The most fundamental right which we consider essential to preserving our way of life has come to be known under U.S. law of the right of Tribal Sovereignty. This is the basis of Indian treaties which reserve part of our aboriginal lands to serve, in the language of the treaties, as a "permanent tribal homeland." Tribal sovereignty means that tribes are recognized, under the supreme law of the land, as the primary governments on our tribal homelands. (National Congress of American Indians, 1994)

Tribal–State Relationships

Because of the relationship between the tribes and the federal government, in some ways states have become the enemy of the tribes. Treaties are federal laws and, as such, are superior to state legislation.

Consequently, any state law that is in conflict with a federal law or treaty is illegal and states must recognize the tribes within their boundaries as self-governing political entities. Recent difficulties with taxation on reservations (states are not able to tax tribes) and the introduction of very profitable, income-producing tribal gaming on Indian lands has created even more animosity.

Public Law 280 was the first legislation that transferred some criminal and civil jurisdiction over tribes to the states. This law violated the government–government relationship between the tribes and the federal government. Some states have subsequently relinquished this jurisdiction. Other areas that continue to be of concern and that have seen battles fought and agreements made include water rights, taxation, fishing and hunting rights, and eligibility for state services. Passage of the Indian Citizenship Act of 1924 granted to Indians all the rights granted to other state citizens, including the right to vote, the right to an education, and the right to state welfare benefits and all other state services. But states have not always complied with this act; when they have, the outcome has not always been positive. For example, Indian children have not always been as successful in public schools as in culturally sensitive educational environments.

Recently, tribes and states have been acknowledging that agreements must be made regarding issues such as (1) law enforcement, for which emergency services are hampered by lack of cooperation, and (2) education, which must support the academic achievement of Indian students.

TRIBAL GOVERNMENTS

Traditional Tribal Governments

When Columbus "discovered" America, approximately 600 tribes inhabited what is now called the United States. The tribes governed themselves in different ways, but they shared certain values, concepts of leadership, and ways of making decisions.

Traditional Indian people did not distinguish between the political and the religious. Political wisdom and religious power were one. The spiritual force that lived within every being guided traditional religious and political values; the primary goal of religion and politics was to achieve harmony between all elements—the land, plant, and animal life—and the human community. Individuals had a responsibility toward all aspects of life.

Unlike the Europeans' systems of government, responsibility and harmony were the Indians' guiding values. Also unlike European systems, the community and the individual's responsibility to the community were more important than the individual and his or her rights within society.

Power resided with the people and the community, not with the leaders (O'Brien, 1989, pp. 14–15).

The following brief explanation of the traditional government of the Haudenosaunee is particularly important, not only as an example of traditional tribal government but also because it influenced early American leaders as they sought to create the Constitution of the United States of America. This gift of the Iroquois—democratic principles of governance with a system of checks and balances—is embodied in the values expressed in the Constitution that forms the foundation of all Americans' way of life.

The largest of the northeastern tribes, the Onondagas, Mohawks, Oneidas, Senecas, and Cayugas, lived in constant conflict. Sometime between A.D. 1000 and A.D. 1500 a great leader, Deganwidah (Mohawk), and his friend, Hiawatha (Onondaga), persuaded the warring tribes to form a political confederacy known as the Great Peace. The five nations came to be called the Haudenosaunee, or "People of the Longhouse." A sixth nation, the Tuscarora, was later admitted as a member. The Great Peace is also known as the League of the Iroquois, or the Iroquois Confederacy.

The Great Peace was organized into three units: the Older Brothers, the Younger Brothers, and the Keepers of the Fire. In addition, others had important roles in how the government functioned—the Council of Fifty, the clan mothers, and the Solitary Pine Trees. The Council of Fifty was composed of fifty civil chiefs, with each seat in the Council named, ranked, and given a particular responsibility. The Onondagas held fourteen seats, the Cayugas held ten seats, the Mohawk and Senecas held nine seats each, and the Oneidas held eight seats. The Onondaga, as Keepers of the Fire and moderators of the group, assumed the role of head of the Council. Two more Onondagas served as councillors and another was designated Keeper of the Council.

Each year the Council of Fifty was called by the Onondagas to consider issues and resolve differences. When an issue was brought before the Council, the Older Brothers (Seneca and Mohawk) discussed it first, then informed the Younger Brothers (Cayugas and Oneidas) of their conclusions. When the Older Brothers and the Younger Brothers disagreed, the Keepers of the Fire (Onondagas) renewed the discussion in an effort to find a compromise and then returned the issue to the Older Brothers and Younger Brothers for further discussion. Ideally, the final result of the discussions would be unanimity. The majority did not rule; decisions were made by consensus.

Although they did not hold seats on the Council of Fifty, the Solitary Pine Trees had a unique and valuable role. Having earned this role through merit and bravery, they were allowed to address the council as representatives of their communities. Women did not hold seats on the Council of Fifty, but they did exert power over the decision-making

process. In certain clans the oldest woman, the clan mother, was responsible for nominating the chiefs of the group. Women could also dismiss leaders who did not conduct themselves with honor.

Students should understand how this system with its representative government, its checks and balances, its concern for placing power over a wide base rather than in a single individual, and its commitment to peaceful decisions, not coercive power, influenced the Constitution of the United States.

Contemporary Tribal Governments

Through the years, the U.S. government's Indian policies dramatically changed traditional tribal governments. By 1930 when the Indian Reorganization Act was passed, tribal governments had nearly ceased to exist in more than half the reservations. Today most tribes have governments, although they differ in their titles, organizational structures, and powers. After years of governmental effort to make Indian nations dependent instead of independent, tribes are now gaining control of their own governments, exercising their sovereignty through self-determination. Although the political structures have changed, their purpose has not. Tribal governments still endeavor to serve the community in harmony and with respect for the people and their social and economic needs, their land, and their cultures.

Tribal governments have the following powers:

1. *Jurisdiction*—the power to make and enforce their own laws.
2. *Membership*—the power to define membership or citizenship.
3. *Administration of justice*—the power to regulate behavior according to tribal laws and ways.
4. *Regulation of domestic and family relations*—the power to regulate such matters as marriage, divorce, inheritance, and the welfare of children, including adoption, foster care, and juvenile counseling.
5. *Property rights*—the power to use and occupy their land (50.4 million acres in the continental United States) in the best interests of the tribe.
6. *Tribal control of land*—the power to assign or lease land to tribal members or nonmembers, to purchase and/or exchange land, and to control who may enter or leave the territory (extradition).
7. *Conservation and environmental protection*—the power to create conservation programs and enforce environmental protection programs.
8. *Regulating hunting and fishing rights*—the power to regulate hunting and fishing by all individuals on tribal land if there is no federal law to the contrary, and on lands and waters outside their reservations "at usual and accustomed places" in accordance with established environmental regulations.

9. *Business regulation*—the power to regulate economic activity on their reservations, including the authority to license, tax, zone, establish businesses, and develop resources.

10. *Taxation*—the power to levy taxes, including income, business, property, severance, sales, excise, and other taxes.

11. *Relations with other governments*—the power to form relationships with other Indian nations as well as other international organizations.

12. *Providing social services*—the power to operate many federal services provided to reservations, including assistance to the needy, law enforcement programs, court systems, housing programs, health clinics, and schools.

MAJOR INDIAN LAWS

Students cannot understand the unique relationship between American Indian tribes and federal and state governments unless they trace the historical path of major Indian laws. Acknowledging that this material is rarely provided in standard textbooks and that teachers themselves have limited knowledge in this area, library media specialists can be of particular support as resources to teachers, as curriculum consultants, and as collection managers. The list that follows is a brief summary of the major laws:

1787 *Northwest Ordinance*—declared that good faith shall always be observed toward Indians and their land, and that property shall never be taken from them without their consent.

1790 *Trade and Intercourse Acts*—required that those who wished to trade with Indians must obtain a federal license, authorized the prosecution of non-Indians who committed certain crimes against Indians, and prohibited non-Indians from obtaining Indian land without the consent of the U.S. government.

1830 *Indian Removal Act*—authorized the president to "negotiate" with eastern tribes for their relocation west of the Mississippi River. The removals were forced removals.

1871 *Title 25, U.S. Code, Section 71* (End of treaty making)—eliminated the practice of making treaties with Indian tribes.

1885 *Major Crimes Act*—gave the federal government jurisdiction over Indians who committed any of seven major crimes while in Indian country. This list has since been expanded to cover fourteen major crimes.

1887 *Allotment Act (Dawes Act)*—intended to break up tribal governments, abolish Indian reservations, and force Indians to assimilate into white society.

1934 *Indian Reorganization Act (Wheeler-Howard Act)*—designated to restore Indian economic life and enable Indians to recover the initiative destroyed by a century of oppression and paternalism. The act prohibited the further allotment of tribal land to individual Indians and authorized the govern-

ment to add lands to existing reservations, to create new reservations for landless tribes, and to restore to tribal ownership "surplus" lands that had not been sold to non-Indians. The act also encouraged Indian tribes to adopt their own constitutions and govern themselves, established a credit fund for the tribes' use, and gave Indians a preference in employment within the Bureau of Indian Affairs.

1953 *Resolution 108*—called for an end to the special federal relationship with certain tribes in certain states. Also known as the Termination Resolution.

1953 *Public Law 280*—conferred on certain states full criminal and some civil jurisdiction over Indian reservations and consented to the assumption of such jurisdiction by any additional states that chose to accept it. The act gave powers and responsibilities to the states that had previously been assumed by the federal government.

1968 *Indian Civil Rights Act*—conferred certain rights on all persons subject to the jurisdiction of a tribal government and authorized federal courts to enforce many of these rights. This is the only law passed by Congress that expressly limits the power of tribes to regulate their own internal affairs.

1975 *Indian Self-Determination Education and Assistance Act*—allowed Indian tribes to administer the federal government's Indian programs on their reservations.

1978 *Indian Child Welfare Act*—designed to protect the best interests of Indian children and to promote the stability and security of Indian tribes and families by limiting the powers of the states regarding placement and adoption of Indian youth.

1978 *Indian Religious Freedom Act*—pledged Congress to protect and preserve for Indian peoples their right of freedom of belief, expression, and exercise of traditional religions including but not limited to access to sites, use and possession of sacred objects, and freedom to worship through ceremonials and traditional sites.

1982 *Indian Tribal Government Tax Status Act*—extended to Indian tribes many of the tax advantages enjoyed by the states.

1988 *Indian Gaming Regulatory Act*—authorized Indian tribes to engage in gaming to raise revenue and promote economic development.

1990 *Native American Graves Protection and Repatriation Act*—provided for the return, upon request, to the tribes of the human remains and cultural objects in the collections of federal agencies and private museums that receive federal funds, and designated tribes as the owners of human remains and cultural items that are uncovered on federal or tribal land.

In conclusion, we offer one caveat. Vine Deloria and C. Lytle (1984) remind non-Indians that to understand the importance of treaties, we must recognize that there are both psychological and political dimensions that "enable us to understand why American Indians view the world as they do today." We must understand the people—their beliefs and traditions.

Roles of the School Library Media Specialist

Resource to Teachers and Students

Be cognizant of current organizing frameworks for instruction, including those which include the study of federal and state government as part of required curriculum standards.

Curriculum Developer and Coordinator

Ensure that tribal relationships with federal and state governments are taught as part of American history.

Build the teaching of the concept of the unique status of Indian nations and their sovereignty into the curriculum.

In the study of state government, include the relationships with tribal governments within the state.

Collection Manager

Provide materials such as Sharon O'Brien's American Indian Tribal Governments and Steven Pevar's The Rights of Indians and Tribes, and Vine Deloria's The Nations Within.

Compile newspaper and magazine articles that provide the most current information regarding tribal governments and tribal issues with the federal government and the states.

Provide biographies of contemporary Indian people in leadership roles within tribal governments.

Provide materials that build understanding of how historical events, policies, and practices have influenced present tribal governments.

Seek popular films television documentaries, and fiction that help students understand historical and current events.

Teacher

Lead students and teachers to explore historical events, international law, legislative acts, and judicial decisons that have formed tribal, federal, and state relationships.

Ensure that the study of the people, their values, beliefs, and lifeways, is intertwined with the study of their current political and governmental relationships and their passionate desire to regain their land and restore and maintain their sovereignty.

Although this chapter focuses on political dimensions, the teaching of these political concepts and events should be linked with the study of cultures and Indian ways of knowing and believing.

REFERENCES AND RESOURCES

Clinton, W. J. (1994, Summer). Guest essay. *Native Peoples* 7 (4), pp. 5–6.

Deloria, V., Jr. (1991). *Behind the trail of broken treaties* (4th printing). Austin: University of Texas.

Deloria, V., Jr., & C. Lytle. (1983). *American Indians, American justice*. Austin: University of Texas.

Deloria, V., Jr., & C. Lytle. (1984). *The nations within*. New York: Pantheon.

Lyons, O., J. Mohawk, V. Deloria, Jr., et al. (1992). *Exiled in the land of the free*. Santa Fe, NM: Clear Light.

National Congress of American Indians. (1994, April 14). Letter to President William J. Clinton.

O'Brien, S. (1989). *American Indian tribal governments*. Norman: University of Oklahoma.

Pevar, S. (1992). *The rights of Indians and tribes* (2nd ed.). Carbondale: University of Southern Illinois.

Teaching about Contemporary Life

> For Native Peoples in America, this is a great time to be alive. We are
> the children of cultural magnificence; the parents of the visions and
> dreams of our ancestors. We are the modern evidence of our ancient
> continuums.
>
> In these extraordinary times, even the most ordinary among us have
> exceptional opportunities within our reach. The best of us hold the key
> to healing our quarter of Mother Earth. The worst of us have the com-
> fort of traditions and values that hold the key to personal healing. . . .
> We are so fortunate to be the ones here at this place and moment.
>
> This is a good day to live. (Susan Shown Harjo, 1994, p. 5)

The primary responsibility of the school library media specialist in regard
to teaching and learning about contemporary life in Indian country is to
ensure that the curriculum, instructional strategies, and supporting resources and materials reflect the lives and realities of American Indian
people and cultures of today. In Indian country, it is a good day to live—
and each day brings greater hope and promise for tomorrow.

American Indian people today face the same challenges of yesterday in
an ever-changing, fast-paced, interdependent modern world. Colonization, Christianity, and technology have all impacted the nature of the challenges, yet the basic issues—self-sufficiency, freedom to live one's life as
one chooses, health, and survival and perpetuation of the Indian people
and cultures—remain the same. In the past, the people looked to the wisdom of the elders to guide them in daily survival. Years of colonization
forced many American Indian people to abandon traditional ways and
adapt to the outside world. Policies of cultural assimilation also forced

them to change. However, American Indian people have maintained their traditions in times of adversity; and their languages, religions, and spiritual practices are alive today and continue to shape their ways of life. Indian cultures are indeed living cultures.

THE PEOPLE

The family has always been the center of American Indian life. At one time in history, the family saw to it that children learned about the world and how to survive, cook, hunt, sew, make tools and weapons, and practice a good way of life. The family was large and included generations of parents, children, aunts, uncles, cousins, grandparents, and others. Family members depended on each other to provide the necessities of life.

Today, families still maintain many traditional roles and are central in "teaching" culture. The family provides for the material needs of its children and nurtures and supports all family members. However, like all families today, some Indian families have single parents with only one generation of family members, whereas others have three generations including grandparents, children, and grandchildren under the same roof. Moreover, Indian families are subjected to the same stresses and outside influences as contemporary families of all cultures. The difference is in how they practice their particular cultural beliefs and in how they address those stresses and outside influences.

More American Indian people today live off reservations than on reservations. The 1990 U.S. Census lists 1,959,234 American Indians residing in the United States. The ten states with the largest Indian populations are Oklahoma, California, Arizona, New Mexico, Alaska, Washington, North Carolina, Texas, New York, and Michigan. The largest ten tribes with the greatest reservation population are Navajo, Pine Ridge (Lakota), Fort Apache, Gila River, Papago, Rosebud (Lakota), San Carlos Apache, Zuni Pueblo, Hopi Pueblo, and Blackfeet. There are larger tribes such as the Cherokee and Choctaw of Oklahoma, but they do not have a reservation and are not considered in these statistics (see Table 13.1).

Almost 63 percent of all American Indians reside off the reservations. Difficult economic times along with world wars and governmental policies of relocation initiated the movement of Indian people from their reservations or rural homes for a better life, education, and employment in the city. However, the dream of economic success was realized by only a few American Indian people because they were not adequately prepared for urban life or trained for jobs. Table 13.2 indicates median family income for the ten largest tribes as of 1990.

New extended families and other support systems had to be created in the city. An interesting and new facet of this urban life was the opportunity

Table 13.1
The Ten Largest American Indian Tribes—Reservation and Nonreservation (identified through self-reporting)

Cherokee	308,132
Navajo	219,198
Chippewa	103,826
Sioux	103,255
Choctaw	82,299
Pueblo	52,939
Apache	50,051
Iroquois	49,038
Lumbee	48,444
Creek	43,550

Source: Utter, J. (1993). *American Indians: Answers to today's questions*. Lake Ann, MI: National Woodlands.

Table 13.2
Median Family Income for the Ten Largest American Indian Tribes, 1990

Iroquois	$27,025
Creek	$25,388
Cherokee	$24,907
Choctaw	$24,467
Lumbee	$23,934
Chippewa	$20,249
Pueblo	$19,845
Apache	$19,690
Sioux	$16,525
Navajo	$13,940
Highest Per Capita Income	
Iroquois	$10,568
Lowest Per Capita Income	
Navajo	$ 4,788

Source: *News from Indian Country* (Late December 1994), p. 5.

to interact with people from other tribes. Naturally, the interaction brought intermarriage. But intermarriage (which initially seemed harmless), combined with the effects of boarding schools and other pressures, caused Indian people to stop speaking their languages and practicing their tribal traditions. After several generations of intermarriage, children would be descended from four tribes, perhaps not knowing the language, customs, or religion of any tribe.

Table 13.3 offers statistics on a range of attributes of American Indians as of 1990.

Table 13.3
American Indian Statistics, 1990

U.S. Population: 2 million (1.96 million in 1990 census), up 37.9 percent since 1980

U.S. Distribution: 62.3 percent off reservation, 37.7 percent on Indian lands

U.S. Tribes: 510 including 200 village groups in Alaska

U.S. Lands: 56.2 million acres of reservations and trust lands

Languages: Approximately 250 tribal languages spoken within the United States

Median Age: 23.5 years for Indians, compared with 30 years for the entire nation

Births: 27.5 per 1,000, compared with 15.7 nationally

Deaths: 571.7 per 100,000, compared with 435.5 nationally

Median Household Income: $20,025, compared with $30,056 nationally

Poverty Rate: 23.7 percent of Indian families, compared with 10.3 percent nationally

Unemployment: 14.4 percent, but 45 percent (estimated) among Indians on or adjacent to reservations

Suicides: 15 per 100,000 (down from peak of 29 in 1975), compared with 11.7 nationally

Dropout Rate: 35.5 percent, compared with 28.8 percent nationally

Higher Education: 89,000 now enrolled

Citizenship: Granted in 1924

Other Rights: New Mexico Indians didn't win right to vote until 1962; federal permission granted Indians to drink alcohol in 1950s

Top 10 States by Indian Population: Oklahoma, California, Arizona, New Mexico, Alaska, Washington, North Carolina, Texas, New York, Michigan

Top 10 Reservations by Indian Population: Navajo (Arizona/New Mexico/Utah), Pine Ridge (South Dakota), Fort Apache, Gila River, Papago (Arizona), Rosebud (South Dakota), San Carlos (Arizona), Zuni Pueblo (Arizona/New Mexico), Hopi (Arizona), Blackfeet (Montana)

Sources: United States Bureau of Indian Affairs, United States Bureau of Census (1990).

Education

Because the majority of Indian people live off reservation, most Indian children attend public schools. Unless the schools are located near a reservation, Indian students generally account for less than 1 percent of any school population. Education of the American Indian has been the business of the U.S. government for many years; the provision of education for members of a tribe is included in all treaties with Indian tribes after 1778, when education was seen to be an effective way to assimilate Indians into the dominant culture.

Today, education of Indians has changed. Very few boarding schools of the mid-century that were so destructive to American Indians' way of life still are in existence. Schools once operated by the Bureau of Indian Affairs are now operated by Indian school boards in local districts. These schools concentrate part of their instructional day on Indian language, culture, and history, encouraging positive development of the Indian students' self-confidence and self-image. They also perpetuate the tribe, culture, and language.

Tribally controlled colleges are symbols of self-sufficiency and self-determination in Indian country. Beginning in 1968 with the Navajo Community College in Arizona, tribally controlled colleges are now located in Montana, North Dakota, South Dakota, Washington, California, Arizona, New Mexico, Michigan, Wisconsin, Minnesota, Nebraska, Kansas, and Saskatchewan. The colleges are nationally accredited and governed by local American Indian directors.

The colleges complement the Indian-controlled secondary schools by continuing the students' cultural education and enhancing their knowledge of tribal organization, national politics, and legal relationships between the tribes and federal government. The tribal colleges also offer programs that train tribal members to work in industries on the reservation and take leadership roles in the governance and guidance of the tribe. Their role is increasingly important as they contribute to the development of human resources of American Indian people.

Although American Indian people have begun to define self-determination for themselves through education, they still value traditional knowledge. They seek a balance between the two to help them live happily and healthfully. Vine Deloria, a prominent Indian scholar, expresses this well:

You are an Indian first, last, and always. You may have a degree in anthropology, law or nuclear engineering, but that is your profession, and how you make your living, it is not you! . . . Your first responsibility is to be a human being, an Indian. Once you accept that fact and use it as a positive factor, you can do whatever professional tasks are required of you but you will know when to draw the line between professional responsibilities and the much greater responsibility to be a person. You can earn money but you cannot be happy or satisfied unless you become yourself first. (1991, p. 15)

Indian Tribes

Indian tribes and nations in the United States today have the sovereign right to determine who their members are, how the tribe will be governed, and how the leaders will be chosen. As a consequence, there is great diversity in types of government and qualifications for membership. Since the time of treaties, Indian people who are members of recognized tribes have been recorded by name and number. Each member today can trace his or her ancestry through these rolls and determine the quantum of blood from each tribe that he or she represents. Some tribes require a person to be at least one-quarter Indian for membership; others grant membership to anyone who can establish a direct link to the original allottees.

No one can be a member of more than one tribe. No Indian person is just "Indian." All Indians are members of a tribe. This is true even if they have blood from several tribes. In fact, Indians are members of their tribes, citizens of a state, and citizens of a nation. This triple citizenship is unique. Indians can vote in, participate in, and receive benefits from these three levels of government, and they must abide by the laws of all three.

American Indians today do not receive money from the federal government because they are Indian. Members of some tribes receive payments from those tribes for land leases; natural resources such as gas, oil, coal, and timber; land claims settlements; and income from certain economic development ventures. The tribes with the most wealth have either lost valuable land for which they received restitution or have gaming, tourism, and other industries that earn money for the tribe.

Not all the income earned by a tribe through gaming can be paid out to members. As a condition of national gaming legislation, at least 60 percent must be reinvested in the tribe and other economic ventures. Most tribes have an eye on the future and are investing their money to prepare for future generations. Schools, health clinics, water systems, housing improvements, job training, day care, services for the elderly, and new business ventures benefit from the new income.

This economic growth and self-sufficiency are great changes from the last one hundred years, when Indian people struggled to meet the basic necessities of life. However, contemporary life on reservations is still very difficult for many Indian people. Those who have moved off reservation have similar problems. Decades of poverty, poor schools, inadequate services, and cultural genocide take a long time to overcome; and it will be years before American Indian people and nations can be fully independent and self-sufficient.

Indian Organizations

American Indians in the modern world are faced with challenges that demand new and creative solutions. As a result, several national and local

Indian organizations, modeled after traditional institutions and modern organizations, have evolved to assist Indian people. These organizations advocate for Indian people on national issues such as religious rights, gaming, and health. Other national organizations comprise groups of professionals such as educators, physicians, or writers who share a common bond and join together to share knowledge and experience. Local organizations include community centers, health centers, or cultural groups that provide a structure for American Indian individuals to work together for common goals. Many American Indians living in the city have formed Indian centers as a gathering place for cultural activities and to help each other successfully adapt to urban life.

Preservation of Culture

American Indians today believe it is very important to maintain the Native languages of their people. Most tribally controlled schools teach the tribal language; and dictionaries, language tapes, and other instructional materials are being developed. Some tribes are not so fortunate, because the elders who speak the language are already gone and there is no living link to tribal languages. This is tragic, for language is the connection that tribal members have to their religion, songs, and prayers.

The modern revival of Native languages has nurtured the growth of tribal craftsmen and artisans, and recognition from the non-Indian world of the value of the Indian way of life. It has also established an environment in which the young are seeking the wisdom of the elders; and there is increased participation in cultural activities such as tribal dances, ceremonies, and rites of passage. An example is provided by the Arapaho Nation of Wyoming, who have joined with the Walt Disney Corporation to record the Disney classic "Bambi" in the Arapaho language. The first children's animated film to be dubbed into an Indian language is being distributed on the Wind River Reservation. It is an innovative effort to preserve a Native language through contemporary technology and content.

American Indians are writing, producing, filming, and acting in their own films; writing their own books; and expressing their cultural and historical roots for the world to share. These materials are authentic and appropriate for classroom use. In addition, there are national Indian newspapers and magazines, as well as tribal newspapers. They should be used in context with other materials that provide a contemporary view of cultures and people.

Religion

Religious freedom will continue to be an issue for American Indians until they have the right to practice their religion in the way they were

taught. Recent legislation (see Chapter 8) has established greater freedom of religion for American Indians. H.R. 4230 is intended to protect Indian religious use of peyote by codifying the existing regulations of the Drug Enforcement Administration that protect such use. Currently only 28 states protect the religious use of peyote by Native Americans, and in 22 states it is a crime. Another statute refines and supersedes the American Indian Freedom of Religion Act by offering protection for Native American cultural and religious sites, Indians' use of peyote, the cultural and religious rights of Native American prisoners, and Native American cultural or religious use of eagle feathers and other animals and plants.

Health

The health and well-being of Indian people today is jeopardized by short life expectancy, increasing incidence of heart disease and diabetes, and alcohol and drug abuse. As descendants of people who once utilized the natural foods and herbs of their native homes to meet their nutritional and medicinal needs, modern American Indians face serious health problems. Once removed from their homes, the people were left without traditional foods and medicines that had maintained their health for thousands of years. Lifestyles also changed; a once physically strong people became sedentary and dependent on governmental rations and handouts. Many foods considered "Indian" such as white-flour fry bread and Indian tacos, or contemporary processed foods such as refined sugar, as well as the current sedentary way of life of many Indian people, are adaptations to colonization and reservation life; they are not compatible with Indian beliefs, values, and traditional lifeways.

Responsibility for the health and well-being of Indian people is a binding commitment of most treaties signed between the United States and Indian nations. Today, the Indian Health Service (IHS) provides a national network of clinics, health centers, and hospitals that serve Indian people. The clinics and hospitals are located on or near Indian reservations, and tribal membership is necessary for treatment. Urban and other off-reservation Indian people receive very few health benefits as a result of their tribal membership unless they travel to their reservation tribal homes. IHS services nationwide are dependent on congressional funding. Because the IHS is rarely funded in full, off-reservation services, which are usually last in priority, often take the greatest cuts in budget and the services provided to urban or off-reservation residents are subsequently reduced.

Historically plagued with problems such as inexperienced doctors, lack of resources, and practices including forced procedures such as sterilization, the IHS has often failed to provide the services needed in Indian country. This is changing today. Many IHS staff are Indian, including the physicians, and the clinics and hospitals are often operated by the tribes

themselves. This helps to increase the quality of care and supervision of staff. A unique addition is the acknowledgment of the value of traditional medicine and its usefulness in treating some patients.

One example of the treatment for disease that combines traditional knowledge and modern medicine is the practice currently employed by the Tohono O'odham, known as the Papago of the southwestern United States. At least one out of every thousand Tohono O'odham will die of diabetes. The Tohono O'odham have found that the high incidence of diabetes is a result of the dramatic change in diet and lifestyle from past times. Today they are treating the rampant diabetes with diet and exercise and have controlled the incidence of and damage caused by the disease.

Alcoholism is another modern disease that affects thousands of Indian people. Often abused in times of depression and loss, poverty, and disillusionment, alcohol seems at first to pacify the restless and hurting, and ease the pain of living. But over a period of years alcohol destroys the person, the family, and the community. Current studies indicate that American Indians may suffer from an intolerance to alcohol in the modern form. Although in ancient times there were alcoholic drinks in North America made from fermented cactus, persimmons, and other fruit, there was no use of corn or potatoes—which are the basis of many contemporary alcoholic drinks. It is theorized that Native people have not genetically adapted to alcohol processed in the new ways; their bodies overreact and addiction occurs more easily.

Alcoholism affects Indian people in a variety of ways that have long-term impact. When a mother drinks during pregnancy, the fetus can be harmed. The result is irreversible fetal alcohol syndrome (FAS) in the infant. FAS reduces the child's ability to make reasoned decisions and solve problems. Children with FAS often suffer poor eyesight and hearing, seizures, mental retardation, and a host of other physical disabilities. This is alarming to a people who have a high rate of alcoholism and over the last fifty years did not know the effects of drinking while pregnant.

Alcoholism also raises another health issue for Indians: accidental deaths. According to the Indian Health Service, accidents are the leading cause of death for Indian people living on reservations and in rural areas. Many accidents are vehicular and are related to alcohol.

Indian communities across the country are undertaking educational initiatives to address the problem of alcoholism and change the course of the future. Relying on traditional values and beliefs, tribes have renewed practices that enhance and support the development of strong, proud individuals and that work for the common good of the people. Turning away from alcohol and to Native beliefs and traditions affirms the identity of the people and their belief in tomorrow.

The study of Indian people today should recognize the tension between the traditional way of life and the demands of the modern world. Ameri-

can Indian people across the country face this challenge daily as they live and work in both worlds. The history and legal status of American Indians has been put aside and given very little attention in the past. It is apparent today that the destinies of all Americans are closely linked, and all students should learn to understand the unique status of American Indians and how it relates to them. In addition, and perhaps most important, the wisdom of the people who roamed this continent in ancient times is still here and available to guide us into the twenty-first century. It must be tapped before it disappears. John Collier, a former director of the Bureau of Indian Affairs and a student of the American Indian, wrote the following words as a reminder:

They had and have this power for living which our modern world has lost—as world-view and self-view, as tradition and institution, as practical philosophy dominating their societies and as an art supreme among all of the arts.
   They had what the world has lost. They have it now. What the world has lost, the world must have again, lest it die. Not many years are left to have or have not, to recapture the lost ingredient. (Collier, 1948, p. 7)

For Indian people, it is indeed a good day to live. There is much to live for and much to share with the non-Indian world.

REFERENCES AND RESOURCES

Books

Benton-Banaise, E. (1991). *Generation to generation.* Hayward, WI: Indian Country Communications.

Brown, J. E. (1982). *The spiritual legacy of the American Indian.* New York: Crossroad.

Collier, J. (1948). *Indians of the Americas.* New York: Mentor Books.

Deloria, V., Jr. (1991, Winter). Higher education and self-determination. *Winds of Change* 6 (1), p. 15.

Harjo, S. S. (1994, Winter). Guest Essay. *Native Peoples* 7 (2), p. 5.

Hirschfelder, A,. & M. K. De Montano. (1993). *The Native American almanac.* New York: Prentice Hall.

Pevar, S. (1992). *The rights of Indians and tribes: The basic ACLU guide to Indian and tribal rights* (2nd ed.). Carbondale: University of Illinois Press.

Utter, J. (1993). *American Indians: Answers to today's questions.* Lake Ann, MI: National Woodlands.

Vecsey, C. (Ed.). (1991). *Handbook of American Indian religious freedom.* New York: Crossroad.

Wall, S., & H. Arden. (1990). *Wisdomkeepers.* Hillsboro, OR: Beyond Words Publishing.

Roles of the School Library Media Specialist

Resources to Teachers and Students

Maintain a resource list, database, or file of newspaper clippings that relate to the contemporary news and issues of American Indian people and tribes for classroom or research use.

Maintain current listing of tribal officials and their offices with addresses and phone numbers as a resource for students and teachers.

Develop a community/state resources directory that enables teachers to utilize local Indian people and Native institutions to enrich the curriculum.

Provide a current listing of radio and television programs which address American Indian issues.

Guide teachers to American Indian authors and producers in contemporary media; keep them apprised of new authors and new resources.

Curriculum Developer and Coordinator

Work collaboratively with teachers and curriculum committees to include the study of contemporary American Indians in the entire curriculum.

Encourage the study of the "whole people" not just the curious tidbits.

Collection Manager

Gather resources that are related by tribe or geographic area to help teachers and students explore all aspects of a tribe or nation.

Maintain a strong collection of material written or produced by American Indian people including books, video, audio, and other media.

Subscribe to national Indian newspapers and magazines.

Gather resource materials from tribes and Indian schools.

Teacher

Provide instruction and support for students doing research on contemporary American Indian people and/or issues.

Host authors-in-residence or artists-in-residence, or other thematic, hands-on experiences to support a study of a particular contemporary tribe or nation.

Magazines/Journals

Daybreak Star Reader
United Indians of all Tribes
Daybreak Star Arts Center—Discovery Park
P.O. Box 99100
Seattle, WA
98199
(206) 285–4425

Native Monthly Reader
P.O. Box 217
Crestone, CO
81131
(719) 256–4848
Fax (719–256–4849)

Native Peoples
P.O. Box 3620
Phoenix, AZ
85067–6820
(602) 277–7852

Newspapers

Indian Country Today
Northern Plains Edition
P.O. Box 2180
Rapid City, SD
57709
(605) 341–0011
Fax (605) 341–6940

Indian Country Today
Southwest Edition
10415 N. Scottsdale Rd.
Scottsdale, AZ
85253
(602) 443–9100
Fax (602) 443–4002

Navajo Times

P.O. Box 310
Window Rock, AZ
86515

News from Indian Country
Rt. 2, Box 2900–A
Hayward, WI
54843

United Tribes News
3315 University Drive
Bismarck, ND
58504
(701) 255–3285

Films and Videos

Native American Public Broadcasting Consortium
P.O. Box 83111
Lincoln, NE
68501–3111
(402) 472–3522

Computer Program

American Indian Resource Services
P.O. Box 1624
Dallas, TX
75354–1624

IBM (DOS) and MAC
$89.95 plus $1.50 shipping

Includes such information as: complete listing of all BIA area offices, agencies, and BIA-supervised schools; complete address, telephone, and Fax listings of all federally recognized tribes; address listings of American Indian newspapers, magazines, and organizations that serve the Indian community; and address listings of museums and arts and crafts organizations with Indian ownership of collections.

Biography/Fiction/Informational

Ashabranner, B. (1984). *To live in two worlds: American Indian youth today*. New York: Dodd. (I)

Harlan, J. (1987). *American Indians today.* New York: Franklin Watts. (I)

Hirschfelder, A. (1986). *Happily may I walk.* New York: Charles Scribner's Sons. (I)

Hirschfelder, A. (1994). *Artists and craftspeople.* New York: Facts on File. (I)

Hirschfelder, A., & B. Singer. (1992). *Rising voices: Writings of young Native Americans.* New York: Charles Scribner's Sons. (I)

Hoyt-Goldsmith, D. (1990). *Totem pole.* New York: Holiday House. (P)

Hoyt-Goldsmith, D. (1991). *Pueblo storyteller.* New York: Holiday House. (P)

Hoyt-Goldsmith, D. (1992). *Arctic hunter.* New York: Holiday House. (P)

Hoyt-Goldsmith, D. (1993). *Cherokee summer.* New York: Holiday House. (P)

Keegan, M. (1991). *Pueblo boy: Growing up in two worlds.* New York: Cobblehill/Dutton. (P)

King, S. (1993). *Shannon: An Ojibway dancer.* Minneapolis, MN: Lerner. (P)

Maher, R. (1977). *Alice Yazzie's year.* New York: Coward, McCann & Geohegan. (P)

Peters, R. H. (1992). *Clambake: A Wampanoag tradition.* Minneapolis, MN: Lerner. (P)

Regguiniti, G. (1992). *The sacred harvest: Ojibway wild rice gathering.* Minneapolis, MN: Lerner. (P)

Sherrow, V. (1993). *The Hopis.* Brookfield, CT: Millbrook. (P/I) This book is one of a series on Native Americans that, although devoted primarily to the People of the past, nonetheless concludes with a final chapter demonstrating how the history and traditional cultures are alive in the present.

Sherrow, V. (1994). *Political leaders and peacemakers.* New York: Facts on File. (I)

Swentzell, R. (1992). *Children of clay.* Minneapolis, MN: Lerner. (P)

Walker, P. R. (1994). *Spiritual leaders.* New York: Facts on File. (I)

(P) = primary
(I) = intermediate

Using Community Resources

We've given our vision at least a dozen different names that I can think of. Living museum. International cultural institution. Museum without walls. The museum different.

I could list more, but it isn't necessary. For the National Museum of the American Indian is only days away from opening its doors in New York City, and our vision is about to become a reality.

. . . I understand fully that the accomplishments of our goals, in many ways, will challenge traditional practices within the museum community. It is not my intention to upset the proverbial apple cart for its own sake, but it is very much my goal to create not just a new museum, but a new type of museum—one that serves more fully and directly the educational needs of our country.

. . . Ours is the work of keeping our vision—the vision for which we waited so long and worked so hard to accomplish but may never know quite what to name—alive. (West [Founding director, National Museum of the American Indian], 1994, pp. 26–27)

Do you remember when *community* meant your own neighborhood, your school, your church, or your town—the places where you knew the people, they knew you, and you had much in common? Now such terms as *global community, virtual community*, and *cultural community* bring new meaning to the word. Technology has made it possible to travel beyond the immediate environment and to communicate easily and inexpensively with people throughout the world. Community indeed has a new meaning. We can seek and create community. We can become friends and colleagues with people beyond our own personal world and use a wide variety of resources in ways we could only dream of a few years

ago. The school library media specialist is the one person in the school who can create communities and expand the possibilities of new and exciting resources for learning about American Indians beyond the local community.

In this chapter we will explore how school library media specialists can utilize local, state, and Indian communities to effectively teach about American Indians. By exploring resources beyond the school, they can show students and teachers how to venture into unknown environments to expand their own sense of community and their power to access information and learn from many sources and situations.

There is no learning experience as powerful as direct experience—for children as well as adults. Further, the most powerful learning experiences connect the cognitive and the affective: the engagement of head and heart. For example, many books explain Navajo weaving and others add a personal component through illustrations, biography, or fiction. However, the significance of Navajo weaving assumes richer meaning when reading is enhanced by a trip to a museum, a well-produced video, or Navajo rugs to touch, admire, and compare. Expanded meaning is likely to result when a traditional Navajo weaver sets up a loom in the school library media center and begins to weave. Even further meaning accrues when students take a field trip to the Hubbell Trading Post in Ganado, Arizona, or Navajo Community College in Tsaile, Arizona, where displays and weaving classes are in progress. But the ultimate learning experience occurs if you are inside a traditional Navajo hogan, sitting beside a woman who is creating a rug of beauty, precision, and timeless art on her handmade loom.

How can we make everyday learning experiences more concrete, more authentic, and more enduring for students? How can we extend knowing to understanding and appreciating? Part of the answer is through the provision of direct experience—beyond reading books and listening to lectures to exploring and experiencing people, places, and things.

Using the community to teach about American Indian people and cultures fits well into a sound model that uses active learning strategies and real people and experiences to teach particular skills and dispositions as well as content (see Figure 14.1). Again, the school library media specialist can fulfill his/her particular professional mission to teach information skills meaningfully in a broad and content-rich context.

Before identifying specific resources, both Indian and non-Indian, that are generally available in small cities and large urban centers, it is important to acknowledge that some communities and schools are isolated from major cultural institutions, historical sites, and significant Indian popula-

Figure 14.1
**Using the Community to Enhance the Study of American Indian People
and Cultures**

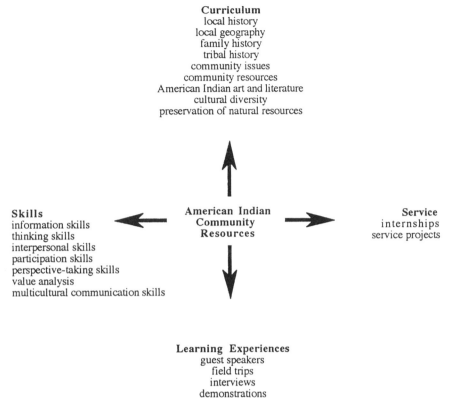

Curriculum
local history
local geography
family history
tribal history
community issues
community resources
American Indian art and literature
cultural diversity
preservation of natural resources

Skills
information skills
thinking skills
interpersonal skills
participation skills
perspective-taking skills
value analysis
multicultural communication skills

American Indian
Community
Resources

Service
internships
service projects

Learning Experiences
guest speakers
field trips
interviews
demonstrations

Adapted from: Schug, M. C. & R. Beery (Eds.). *Community study: Applications and opportunities*
(Bulletin no. 75). Washington, DC: National Council for the Social Studies, p. 6.

tions. But *no* state is lacking in Indian history; *every* state has outstanding
colleges, universities, and museums; nearly *all* communities have libraries
with interlibrary loan capabilities; *most* schools and many teachers have
computers and modems; and in *almost every* community there is a local
history buff, an avid traveler, an amateur archaeologist, or a collector of
American Indian art or artifacts. Undoubtedly, there are resources that
need to be discovered and perhaps developed. Table 14.1 suggests some
common national, state, local, and virtual resources that can be used cre-
atively and effectively to extend and enhance significant learning about
American Indians.

Table 14.1
Community Resources

State and Local Community Resources

American Indian Community
> Individuals
> Community Activities
> Urban Indian Centers
> Tribal Controlled Colleges
> Tribal Museums and Culture Centers
> Indian Schools
> Healthcare/Social Service Organizations
> Cultural/Professional Organizations
> Businesses

Cultural Institutions
> Museums
>> Art
>> History
>> Natural History
> Historical Societies
> State and Local Libraries
> Theaters
> Historical Sites

Academic Community
> Scholars
> University Libraries
> Research Centers

"Virtual" Community Resources

"Sister" Schools

National Cultural Institutions

National Political and Professional Organizations

Local and National Radio/Television

Electronic Communities

Tribal Councils

USING AMERICAN INDIAN COMMUNITY RESOURCES

Individuals

American Indian individuals have personal histories, talents, opinions, and stories to tell; and their contributions are indeed authentic and valued. From Indian people, students can learn about (1) diversity among Indian people, (2) historical perspective, (3) traditional and/or special skills and talents, (4) traditional knowledge, values, and lifeways, and (5) community resources.

When Indian people visit the classroom, most of the customary practices for effectively utilizing guest speakers hold true. However, take note of the following basic cautions:

1. Do not expect all Indian people to look "Indian." Young children usually expect contemporary Indian people to wear buckskin, face paint, and feathers. To ask a guest speaker to come "in costume" is inappropriate. The word *costume* is an insult, implying to dress up as. . . . Better words are *traditional dress* or, in the case of the powwow, *regalia*. (Would you ask a Jewish speaker to look "Jewish" when talking about the Holocaust?) In any case, Indian people today wear jeans, dresses, and business suits. Don't expect them to reinforce stereotypes. On the other hand, if you want students to see the beauty of traditional dress, ask how an Indian person can address that need in a way that is comfortable.

2. Recognize that many traditional Indian people are not comfortable in non-Indian schools. Help them prepare in advance by giving them questions or topics to discuss, describing the students, telling them what would be of particular value or interest, and specifying the amount of time appropriate for the students' age group.

3. Many traditional Indian people, especially women, speak softly. If the group is large, provide a microphone; a lavaliere microphone is particularly useful.

4. Invite contemporary Indian people such as parents, teachers, writers, artists, physicians, attorneys, and business owners to ensure that students learn about living cultures and diversity in contemporary Indian lifestyles.

5. Consider reimbursing speakers for their time. Another way to do this is to make a contribution to the community. One class that recently invited Indian preschoolers to demonstrate traditional Indian dance invited the dancers to join them for lunch at school afterwards. A high school class prepared Thanksgiving baskets for the local Indian center in appreciation for the time the director of the center had given them. Giving and sharing is part of the generosity of Indian people.

6. Prepare students adequately so they are respectful of different viewpoints and perhaps different ways of speaking.

Community Activities

Some community activities are wonderful opportunities for learning. Powwows are often the most impressive and spectacular. Rodeos are common throughout the Plains; in the Southwest, Indian markets are interesting (but commercial) events that provide a glimpse into Indian life and values. In areas with large numbers of Indian people there are unique activities, such as the rug auction in Crownpoint, New Mexico; Anishinabe sugar mapling in Minnesota; dances and ceremonies such as the Corn Dance at Santa Domingo Pueblo; Shalako ceremonies at Zuni Pueblo; and cultural events such as the Red Earth Festival in Oklahoma. All these activities, and a multitude of others like them throughout the country, are public events or are partially open to the public. Newspapers and community bulletin boards inform the general and Indian community of these events.

Urban Indian Centers

In metropolitan areas with large Indian populations, Indian centers serve the community in multiple ways. Typically they sponsor educational and recreational programs for children, teens, and elders; house social service programs, counselors, and referral offices; and serve as a vital social, political, and educational gathering place for Indian people. The Indian center can be an invaluable resource regarding activities within the Indian community and people who might be willing to work with teachers and students.

Tribal Colleges

Tribal colleges—their faculty, administrators, students, libraries, and instructional materials—are rich resources that can be utilized by educators; their focus is on education and Indian cultures. These colleges serve Indian people by offering a curriculum that combines traditional college courses such as English, math, and science with culturally oriented classes including tribal languages, religion, and the arts.

The 29 tribal colleges successfully fight the drop-out rate (which is high for Indians in non-Indian colleges and universities) by creating a sense of family and providing educational, social, and emotional support to Indian students. A tribal college administrator commented, "It strengthens them in their hearts and in their minds and makes them believe in all the things their ancestors died for" (Ambler, 1991, p. 21).

Tribal Museums and Culture Centers

Increasingly, American Indian people are recapturing their cultural history and artifacts in the creation of museums and cultural centers. "There is fundamental new thinking about issues of cultural rights and responsibilities—about who, if anyone, can speak for the carvers and basket makers, weavers and beadworkers, potters and painters whose work has been collected and studied for the past 150 years" (*Creation's Journey*, 1994, p. 30). Recent repatriation laws have intensified the importance of housing items of beauty, interest, and historical value; and Native Americans are asserting their right to control and manage their cultural legacies. Because Indian people have different understandings of the artifacts of their culture, tribal museums offer unparalleled opportunities for students to learn.

Indian Schools

Most reservations have public and private schools that serve only Indian students. While the purpose, governance, and curriculum differ, the schools usually are rich in American Indian traditions as well as generally representative of most American public schools. Many have significant numbers of American Indian teachers. In addition, large urban centers often have special schools created for American Indian students and families within or separate from public school systems as well as public schools with large Indian populations. These schools are often willing to establish pen pal relationships and other similar "exchange"-type relationships with non-Indian schools.

Healthcare/Social Service Organizations

In communities with a significant Indian population, numerous healthcare agencies and social service organizations serve the people—not only established residents, but frequently those who have recently moved from reservations. Skilled physicians and healthcare, social, and mental health workers have informed perspectives on some of the challenges and issues facing American Indian people today.

Cultural/Professional Organizations

In larger communities can be found powwow organizations, churches, veterans groups, professional organizations such as the Indian Education Association, drum groups, and so on. Through networking, these resources can become known and can enable the school to develop relationships within the Indian community. Again, students need to know Indian people; and Indian people want to speak for themselves. Because the In-

dian population is generally small, these organizations are not always visible, but they do exist.

Businesses

Depending on the part of the country and size of your community, you may find Indian-owned businesses including (1) chambers of commerce, or (2) other businesses such as art galleries or bookstores that specialize in Indian goods. Through these businesses you are likely to be able to contact American Indian artists or craftspeople.

Local Radio

On a recent Sunday morning a local radio program, which informs its audience about activities of the American Indian community in the Denver metropolitan area, provided an in-depth interview with Wilma Mankiller, principle chief of the Cherokee Nation; offered traditional and contemporary Indian music; and presented a remarkable piece about Susan Billy, a Pomo basket weaver from California who selected a number of baskets for the opening exhibit at the National Museum of the American Indian. This is an example of how radio sustains communication within the Indian community and provides informational programming via technology that has been previously unavailable. Local public radio, which is available in most communities, provides regular programming of this type that can be taped for school use.

USING "VIRTUAL" COMMUNITY RESOURCES

It is a new and smaller world, and we can create community and reach out to the larger community with technology and effort. In this brief section we would like to suggest that school library media specialists have the unique perspective and skill to encourage teachers and students to enlarge their sense of community through reaching out personally and with the aid of technology.

"Sister" Schools

An example explains this idea best. The students of Westridge Elementary School in Jefferson County, Colorado, explore, read, write, and publish books about the unique cultural heritages of America. Recently, in cooperation with Indian students, teachers, and other adults throughout the country, they have written a book about American Indians. *Kids Explore the Heritage of Western Native American Families* was written during one school year with the participation of 300 American Indian and non-

Indian students and teachers from six western states (Arizona, Washington, Wyoming, Oklahoma, South Dakota, and Colorado). Some of the Indian students live on reservations and others live in metropolitan areas or small towns. Students and teachers visited each other, spoke on the telephone, used fax messages, and communicated electronically via computer. The book is soon to be published by John Muir Publications (P.O. Box 613, Santa Fe, NM 87504; (505) 982–4078, (800) 888–7504). Not only is it a source of authentic information, but the Indian and non-Indian students who worked on it have formed multicultural friendships and enlarged their community in the process.

National Cultural Institutions and Organizations

Although it is more convenient to access state and local cultural institutions, certain unique institutions at the national level provide resources that are unavailable locally. Two prominent examples are the National Museum of the American Indian and the Smithsonian Institution. Moreover, the Library of Congress has precious resources, many of which are available for use. Extending that idea to the nationally recognized museums throughout the country is reasonable. For example, the Heard Museum of Anthropology and Primitive Art in Phoenix, Arizona; the Anchorage Historical and Fine Arts Museum in Alaska; the Denver Art Museum; the Buffalo Bill Museum in Cody, Wyoming; the Field Museum of Natural History in Chicago; and the Gilcrease Museum in Tulsa, Oklahoma, have major collections and printed resources that can be tapped.

Other groups that are less well known are potential resources and certainly extend students' understanding of Indian people and cultures. For example, the American Indian Dance Theatre presents traditional dances from many regions, including ceremonial and seasonal dances, and spiritual and social dances. The songs are sung in tribal languages, and the outfits worn by the dancers are made by each person or by members of their families. Each outfit is designed to express the individuality of the dancer while following the tradition of each dance and incorporating tribal patterns and colors.

In 1992 a group of American Indian writers convened a major conference, "Returning the Gift: A Festival of North American Native Writers," to celebrate and recognize the diverse contributions of contemporary Indian authors. Although these writers have not yet created a formal organization, they attest to the commitment of American Indian people to both the oral traditions of their cultures and contemporary print literature that give them individual, tribal, and cultural voice. The successful conference was held at the University of Oklahoma, and smaller meetings have been convened since. The University of Oklahoma, College of Arts and Sciences, is a potential resource for information about continuing meetings of this kind.

The American Indian Film Institute publishes a potentially valuable resource, *Indian Cinema Entertainment,* which (1) offers insight and opinion relating to new Indian film and media works, and (2) provides Indian personality profiles and interviews with established and emerging Indian talent.

National Organizations

In the study of contemporary Indian issues, secondary school students should utilize national Indian organizations to obtain American Indian positions and viewpoints; not to do so limits their academic inquiry and their own perspective. Organizations such as the National Congress of American Indians, Native American Rights Fund, National Indian Education Association, and American Indian Library Association all are potential sources of authentic information and instructional materials.

The Bureau of Indian Affairs, the federal agency with major responsibility for Indian affairs, is a rich resource for statistics, programs, names and addresses of tribal offices, leaders, and so on. In addition to its central office in Washington, DC, the BIA maintains regional offices in twelve states, mostly in the West, with agencies on particular reservations as well. In accordance with federal policy, many employees are now Indian people with varying professional interests and talents.

National Radio/Television

We have discussed the use of radio for up-to-date information and strongly encourage school library media specialists to avail themselves of this resource as well as television programming. Because of the recent resurgence in interest in American Indians, some of the most authentic and current information is being produced by radio and television. Impressive series such as *How the West Was Lost* and *The Native Americans,* news programs, and even commercial movies should be obtained for classroom use; the information is simply not available in print yet, nor is it as vivid or engaging. It is truly "just-in-time" technology that provides a way for students to hear American Indians speak on issues of importance to them. Radio and television, although not direct experiences, at least present Indian people as living and enduring people.

Of particular interest is the new American Indian radio network linking 25 tribal radio stations that began regular programming in 1994. Based in the Native American Public Broadcasting Consortium offices in Lincoln, Nebraska, AIROS (American Indian Radio on Satellite) will offer a storytelling series, interviews with Native Americans, historical specials, and

other public service programming. The 25 stations linked through the network are located in 10 states, and many are on reservations. Eventually the network hopes to link radio stations on the 250 Indian reservations in the United States.

For the first time, a new daily call-in program, Native America Calling, will link American Indian radio stations and listeners in a nationwide forum for Native people to discuss issues relevant to Indian country. The call-in phone number is currently listed as (907) 277–2776.

Alaska Public Radio Network
810 East Ninth Avenue
Anchorage, AK 99501
(907) 277–2776

Native American Public Broadcasting Consortium
P.O. Box 8311
Lincoln, NE 68501
(402) 472–3522

Electronic Communities

Fax machines, e-mail, Internet, and other electronic bulletin boards allow people to talk easily and inexpensively as well as to tap undiscovered resources as they explore the virtual community. Even the most remote schools on Indian reservations or in the smallest towns usually have access to computers, faxes, and Internet. The exploration of electronic communities again extends the concept of community.

Tribal Councils

Tribal councils are reservoirs of information about their own tribal history, forms of government, contemporary lifeways, and current issues. Some of the larger tribes such as the Cherokee have public relations offices and publishing centers.

Joe Medicine Crow (Crow), in speaking of the National Museum of the American Indian, said: "We want to give the public a better understanding of Indians. We want the white man to understand the Indian life, Indian priests, Indian early history, and contemporary Indian life. That way we will have better relationships among the white men, red men, black men, and all other ethnic groups. Understanding. That's important" (quoted in Agent, 1994, p. 48). This statement illustrates our belief that using resources within the Indian community will build understanding, and that's important.

Roles of the School Library Media Specialist

Resource to Teachers and Students

Identify American Indian people, community activities, urban Indian Centers, tribally controlled colleges, tribal museums and culture centers, Indian schools, healthcare and social service organizations, cultural and professional organizations, businesses, and local radio stations or programs that can be accessed to enrich student learning about American Indian people and cultures.

Help teachers and students utilize these people and resources effectively and respectfully.

Provide teachers and students with schedule of radio and television programs which present topics about American Indians, offering to tape these programs whenever appropriate.

Curriculum Developer and Coordinator

Ensure that direct experience with Indian people, events, and institutions are an integral part of the curriculum at all grade levels.

Encourage community service projects with American Indian groups when appropriate for students.

Collection Manager

Be informed about existing databases and on-line services that help to connect students to the Indian community.

Provide models of "sister city" projects including for example, the Kids Explore series from John Muir Press.

Teacher

Create a learning/resource center for exhibitions, demonstrations, presentations, and activities that enhance and extend the efforts of teachers and the entire school to interact with the American Indian community.

Help teachers prepare to work effectively with Indian people in the classroom.

Through technology, teach students how to expand their own community and to create new communities.

REFERENCES AND RESOURCES

Agent, D. (1994, October/November/December). All roads are good. *Native Peoples* 8 (1), p. 48.

Ambler, M. (1991, Winter). Tribal colleges change lives. *Native Peoples* 4 (2), pp. 18–24.

Bruchac, J. (1994, October). For Native peoples, a homecoming in Manhattan. *Smithsonian* 25 (7), pp. 40–49.

Creation's journey: Excerpts from the inaugural exhibition and book edited by Tom Hill and Richard W. Hill, Sr. (1994, Fall). *Native Peoples* 8 (1), p. 30.

Eagle/Walking Turtle. (1989). *Indian America: A traveler's companion.* Santa Fe, NM: John Muir Publications. This book is fairly old but nonetheless offers valuable resources that could be updated fairly easily.

Hirschfelder, A. B., & M. K. de Montano. (1993). *The Native American almanac.* New York: Prentice-Hall.

The National Museum of the American Indian opens in N.Y. [special edition]. (1994, October/November/December). *Native Peoples* 8 (1).

Schug, M. C., & R. Beery. (Eds.). *Community study: Applications and opportunities,* Bulletin no. 75. Washington, DC: National Council for the Social Studies.

Smithsonian Institution. (1994). *All roads are good.* Washington, DC: National Museum of the American Indian.

Waldman, C. (1985). *Atlas of the North American Indian.* New York: Facts on File, pp. 260–265. This particular section, *Museums, Historical Societies, Reconstructed Villages, and Archaeological Sites pertaining to Indians in the United States and Canada,* although somewhat dated, is an excellent resource.

West, R. W., Jr. (1994). Overview. *Native Peoples* 8 (1), pp. 26–27.

Yellowhawk, R. (1994, Winter). National Native news: The camp crier comes full circle. *Native Peoples* 7 (2), pp. 54–59.

Epilogue

A NEW GHOST DANCE

This is an excerpt from a report written by an exceptional Native educator, G. Mike Charleston, Ph.D. (Choctaw), who passed away on March 4, 1993. The entire report, originally written for the Indian Nations at Risk Task Force,* was published recently; it serves as both a vision for Native education and as a tribute to a man of great scholarship, sensitivity, compassion, and vision. The Native and non-Native world lost the physical presence of Mike as an educator and leader, but we needn't lose his vision. We believe in this vision and hope that this work in the hands of professional school library media specialists will play a small part in the achievement of Mike's dream—a new Ghost Dance.

Chief Big Foot and his band of Lakota believed in the Ghost Dance—a wave of hope that was sweeping the plains in 1890 proclaiming that the Creator would prevent the total destruction of Native people, alleviate their suffering, and return the people to the pre-war days of happiness.

There is a new Ghost Dance underway in this country today; its momentum is growing rapidly. Many people, Native and non-Native alike, are spreading the message. Like the Ghost Dance of 100 years ago, there is hope and anticipation of a revival of tribal life and the return of harmony among all relations of creation. There is unity of purpose.

---

*The Indian Nations at Risk Task Force was established by the U.S. Secretary of Education, Lauro Cavazos, to direct a national review of American Indian and Alaska Native education in the United States. This was written as a draft final report of the project in 1991, but it was not published by the U.S. Department of Education. It has now been published in its entirety by the *Journal of American Indian Education*, Arizona State University.

. . . The new Ghost Dance calls Native and non-Native people to join together to take action. It calls us to be responsible for the future of the people of our tribes. It calls us to protect, revive and restore our cultures, our
Native languages, our religions, and our values. It calls us to heal our people, our families, our tribes, and our societies. It calls for harmony and respect among all relations of creation. It promises a future of mutual
co-existence of tribal societies with other American societies. . . . It offers
our people constructive choices in education.

. . . For the thousands of Native people who are dedicated to working
for the survival and prosperity of their tribes, we must work diligently
with forgiveness and trust in the firm belief that all creation is related and
valued. We must bind our tribes together and bind our tribal societies with
non-Native societies with a treaty of mutual and honest respect for one another to co-exist in harmony. To flourish in the present, tribal identity and
tribal culture has no need to dominate life and oppress and belittle other
realities of life or other societies. Indeed, domination, oppression and big-
otry are exactly what we are overcoming in the new Ghost Dance as we
seek to establish harmony and co-existence of tribes with other societies in
the modern world.

. . . For many non-Natives working in schools, a major change in their
behaviors, attitudes and values is required. The siege against our tribes
must end. American education must teach all present and future generations of American citizens the following important topics about Native
People.

- Basic understanding, respect, and appreciation for American Indian and Alaska
  Native cultures.
- Why tribal societies of American Indians and Alaska Natives exist now and in
  the future.
- Why tribes are different from other American societies.
- How to act accordingly in matters relating to Native societies.

. . . Co-existence means that our tribes and our people participate freely
with the non-Native societies to the benefit of all.

Source: Charleston, G. M. (1994, Winter). Toward true Native education: A treaty of 1992
[entire issue]. *Journal of American Indian Education* 33 (2), pp. 28–29.

Appendix: American Indian Organizations

American Indian Dance Theatre

A unique dance troupe composed of all Indian dancers and musicians. The company presents traditional dances from many regions, including ceremonial, seasonal, spiritual, and social dances. The music includes ancient songs passed down from generation to generation as well as contemporary songs in the traditional style.

American Indian Dance Theatre
P.O. Box 2140
Tulsa, OK 74101

American Indian Film Institute

An organization concerned with the impact of Indian media and its influence on Hollywood and the media infrastructure. It promotes works that enrich the American Indian film media communities and supports established and emerging Indian talent.

American Indian Film Institute
333 Valencia Street, Suite 322
San Francisco, CA 94103
(415) 554–0525

American Indian Movement (AIM)

An organization of American Indians that began in the 1970s. AIM is the most vocal and militant coalition of Indian people. The address of each local chapter differs. Further information is available from the following:

American Indian Movement
2300 Cedar Ave. South
Minneapolis, MN 55404
(612) 724–3129

American Indian Movement
2940 16th Street, Suite 104
San Francisco, CA 94103
(415) 552–1992

American Indian Science and Engineering Association (AISES)

An association dedicated to advancing American Indians in the fields of math and science by providing mentoring, training, and support to Indian students.

AISES
1630 30th Street, Suite 301
Boulder, CO 80301
(303) 492–8658

Council of Energy Resource Tribes (CERT)

An Indian-controlled organization dedicated to developing and protecting the rights of tribes that have natural energy resources on their lands. This is accomplished through legal representation, training, mentorship, and advocacy.

CERT
1999 Broadway, Suite 2500
Denver, CO 80202
(303) 297–2378

Heart of the Earth Survival School

An Indian-controlled school in the heart of Minneapolis established in the 1970s to meet the particular needs of urban American Indian children.

(612) 331–8862

Indian Arts and Crafts Association

American Indian artists and craftspeople, retailers, wholesalers, museums, and collectors working together to preserve, protect, and promote authentic Indian arts and crafts.

Indian Arts and Crafts Association
122 LaVeta NE, Suite B
Albuquerque, NM 87108–1613
(505) 265–9149

Institute of American Indian Arts

Institute of American Indian Arts
P.O. Box 20007
Santa Fe, NM 87505–7634
(505) 988–6434

Institute of American Indian Arts Museum
108 Cathedral Place
Santa Fe, NM
(505) 988–6211

National Advisory Council on Indian Education (NACIE)

Created by the Indian Education Act of 1972, this body, appointed by the president, was charged with oversight related to the implementation of the Indian Education Act.

NACIE
330 C Street, SW
Room 4072
Switzer Building
Washington, DC 20202–7556

National Congress of American Indians (NCAI)

Founded in 1954, this organization has worked to advance the individual efforts of Indians and tribes to ensure treaty and civil rights to their descendants, to educate and enlighten the public, and to promote the common welfare of the American Indian within the United States. It is an active organization in 1995 and represents the tribes in many associations with governments and other organizations.

National Congress of American Indians
900 Pennsylvania Ave., SE
Washington, DC 20003
(202) 546–9404

National Indian Education Association (NIEA)

A national organization made up of Indians and others who are directly working toward improved educational opportunities for Indian people.

National Indian Education Association
1819 H Street, NW, Suite 800
Washington, DC 20006
(202) 835–3001

National Indian Youth Council (NIYC)

A group of young American Indians that began to meet and work together at the National Congress of American Indian national conference in 1961. They set as their goal the restoration of Indian pride. This organization remains vital in 1995.

National Indian Youth Council
318 Elm Street
Albuquerque, NM 87102
(505) 247–2251

Native American Church (NAC)

Incorporated in 1918, this religious organization is based on the traditional Indian use of peyote in the prayer service. It is based on ancient traditions and is strictly practiced. Members of many tribes belong to and worship in the Native American Church. The practices of the church have been frequently outlawed; however, the Indian Freedom of Religion Act of 1978 provides some protection today. Protection under the First Amendment is not afforded to this religion and its members. The NAC is incorporated in each state in which it operates. Individual addresses can be found at the state level.

Native American Public Broadcasting Consortium

An organization whose mission is to produce and encourage the production and successful use of quality public telecommunications programs by and about Native Americans, for both Native American and general audiences.

Native American Public Broadcasting Consortium
P.O. Box 8311
Lincoln, NE 68501
(402) 472–3522

Native American Rights Fund (NARF)

Founded in 1970, this legal defense organization takes class action suits only on behalf of tribes and Indian groups. It has become very powerful and plays a major role in many of the legal issues that impact Indian people.

Native American Rights Fund
1506 Broadway
Boulder, CO 80302
(303) 447–8760

Index

Alexie, Sherman, 143
Allen, Paula Gunn, 143
Allotment Act (Dawes Act [1887]), 177
American Indian Day, teaching about, 117
American Indian Library Association, 5–6
American Indian people, differences between, 7
American Indian students, 41, role of library media specialist, 5
Art, basic resources for, 92
Assessment: attributes of authentic benchmark assessments, 62; of interdisciplinary curriculum, 63, of performance, 22; sample lesson plan with authentic assessment, 48–50; of student achievement, 21–22
Awiakta, Marilou, 143

Basic needs: clothing, 86; food, 85–86; shelter, 85
Big Foot Memorial Ride, general description, 120–21
Black Elk, 103, 110
Black Hills of South Dakota, 48–50
Bruchac, Joseph, 143
Burton, Bryan, 81

Campbell, Ben Nighthorse, 41
Chief Seattle, 67
Child-rearing practices, basic resources for understanding, 88–89
Clinton, President William J., 169
Clothing, basic resources for understanding, 86
Collier, John, 190
Columbus Day, teaching about, 115–16
Community resources: businesses, 202; community activities, 200; cultural and professional organizations, 201–2; electronic communities, 205; guidelines for using members of the Indian community, 199; healthcare and social service organizations, 201; Indian schools, 201; list of community resources, 198; local radio, 202; model for using the community, 197; national cultural institutions and organizations, 203–4; national organizations, 204; national radio and television, 204–5; sister schools, 202–3; tribal colleges, 220; tribal councils, 205; tribal museums and cultural centers, 201; urban Indian centers, 200; virtual community, 202

About the Authors

KAREN D. HARVEY is Associate Dean for Academic Affairs at the University of Denver. She has been involved in social studies education and multicultural education for over 25 years. She is the editor of *American Indian Voices* (1995), an anthology of American Indian literature; *Plains Indians* (1993), a children's book; and is the coauthor of *Indian Country: A History of Indian People in America* (1994) and *Teaching About Native Americans* (1990).

LISA D. HARJO is program director of the Circle of Learning Early Childhood and Family Education Program of the Denver Indian Center. She is a member of the Choctaw Nation of Oklahoma. She is the coauthor of *Indian Country: A History of Indian People in America* (1994), *Teaching About Native Americans* (1990), and other publications about American Indians.

LYNDA WELBORN is senior consultant, School Library Media, Colorado State Library, where she provides technical assistance to 176 school districts. She is the coauthor of *The Impact of School Library Media Centers on Student Achievement* (1993).

.